To:

Have a good
read

Jack L Walter

A GOOD SOLDIER

A GOOD SOLDIER

A Novel of History and Adventure

JACK LURLYN WALTERS

Library of Congress Control Number:		2015918383
ISBN:	Hardcover	978-1-5144-2396-7
	Softcover	978-1-5144-2395-0
	eBook	978-1-5144-2394-3

Print information available on the last page.

Rev. date: 12/03/2015

To order additional copies of this book, contact:
Xlibris
1-888-795-4274
www.Xlibris.com
Orders@Xlibris.com
718801

CONTENTS

Introduction..xvii

Chapter 1   Rebels in the Baja 1
Chapter 2   Going to Canada 5
Chapter 3   Learning the Code 13
Chapter 4   Niagara Falls 18
Chapter 5   The Hobo in Me 24
Chapter 6   Going Underneath 31
Chapter 7   Murder in the Cafe 35
Chapter 8   The Hobo Jungle 39
Chapter 9   The Family 45
Chapter 10   The Panhandler 51
Chapter 11   From Saints to Demons.................................. 56
Chapter 12   A Big Mistake 62
Chapter 13   Moving On 72
Chapter 14   The Wrong Direction 76
Chapter 15   Back in Kansas City 82
Chapter 16   Becoming a Hero 87
Chapter 17   The Runaway 92
Chapter 18   Mason-Dixon Line 95
Chapter 19   Home in Deer Creek 98
Chapter 20   Tragedy on the Neighbor's Farm 104
Chapter 21   Reminiscing...112
Chapter 22   Turning Eighteen 117
Chapter 23   Ted's First Job 121
Chapter 24   Western Kansas 123
Chapter 25   The Roundup 126
Chapter 26   Dodge City 132
Chapter 27   Gold Mining in Colorado 138
Chapter 28   On the Mountain 142
Chapter 29   Setting up Camp 145

Chapter 30   Seeking My Fortune 152
Chapter 31   Back Down the Mountain 158
Chapter 32   The Smith Sisters' Boarding House........................162
Chapter 33   The Mountain Storm..169
Chapter 34   California-bound 174
Chapter 35   San Francisco 1906 181
Chapter 36   The Ashby House 185
Chapter 37   New Friend.. 190
Chapter 38   On the Job 194
Chapter 39   Union Indoctrination...201
Chapter 40   The Bank Robber 205
Chapter 41   The Great San Francisco Earthquake 212
Chapter 42   The Aftermath...217
Chapter 43   The Doomed City 226
Chapter 44   Leaving the Carnage Behind 230
Chapter 45   Read All about It... 236
Chapter 46   Going to Sea..241
Chapter 47   At Sea 247
Chapter 48   Man Overboard..255
Chapter 49   SOS.. 264
Chapter 50   Tokyo Harbor 269
Chapter 51   The Yakuza 281
Chapter 52   Port of Nanjing, China... 287
Chapter 53   The Lady Sharon 291
Chapter 54   The Yangtze River... 296
Chapter 55   The Village of Wang Jing..301
Chapter 56   Heading Home 311
Chapter 57   San Diego, California 316
Chapter 58   Planning The Invasion of the Baja 324
Chapter 59   The San Diego Rally 329
Chapter 60   Magonistas...335
Chapter 61   The Village of Tecate 339
Chapter 62   The Capture of Tijuana 342
Chapter 63   The Final Push 348
Chapter 64   Prison...353
Chapter 65   New Opportunities...358
Chapter 66   Railroading Again 361
Chapter 67   The Carnival...371
Chapter 68   Moving On..381

Chapter 69   A Hobo Once Again 385
Chapter 70   Traveling Companion 391
Chapter 71   Heading Home 397
Chapter 72   A New Life 403
Chapter 73   The Wedding Day...410
Chapter 74   The Blizzard..415
Chapter 75   The Army.. 424
Chapter 76   A Good Soldier..431
Chapter 77   Crossing the Sea.. 435
Chapter 78   Paris, France 440
Chapter 79   The Trenches 445
Chapter 80   Letters and Headline 451
Chapter 81   The Argonne Forest... 463
Chapter 82   Going Home 476
Chapter 83   Home 479

Acknowledgments... 485
All about Hobos.. 487

A GOOD SOLDIER

A novel of one man's life and adventures

Jack Lurlyn Walters

Famous quotes taken from
Bartlett's Familiar Quotations
John Bartlett and Justin Kaplan

Soldier rest! thy warfare o're,
Sleep the sleep that knows not breaking
Dream of battled fields no more,
Days of danger, nights of waking
                    —Sir Walter Scott,**1771-1832**

**I hold it, that a little rebellion
now and then, is a good thing.
and as necessary in the political world
as storms in the physical.
                    —Thomas Jefferson, January 1787**

**Oh, I'm a good old rebel,
That's what I am**
                    —Innes Randolph 1837-1887,
                    A Good Old Rebel (1870)

In memory of

THEODORE EDMOND WALTERS

and

VIOLA ERNESTINE WALTERS

My father and mother

To my father and mother,
my wife Shirley, and children
Linda, Sharon, Lori, and Ted

Special thanks

to

My editors Shirley Walters

and

Jessica Sloane

They kept me organized and on the right path from start
to completion of this novel.
Thanks.

INTRODUCTION

This adventure takes place in the early 1900s, one hundred years ago, and includes true historical events which occurred in my father's adventurous life as a young man. He is the principal character in this book. His name is Theodore Edmond Walters, who died at the age of sixty in 1950, and was known as Ted to his family, friends, and coworkers.

Some of the adventures in this book are based on truth, but embellished to make the story exciting, and you, the reader, can discern which part is truth or fiction. But the one event that is true took place during 1910–1911, and is a little known part of history to most Americans, especially to me who is an avowed history buff, and my father was right in the middle of it.

Several years after his death, I discovered a document when I was browsing through his memorabilia my mother gave me, and that was the moment my interest and curiosity were piqued to research this event and to find out if the document was authentic and if the event really took place. My father never talked about his early life or mentioned this event to anyone, it was a surprise to us all. After my initial research, I realized he took a secret part of his life to the grave with him, and I was motivated to find out all I could about this event in history, and I continued my research with great enthusiasm.

The document I found was a handwritten honorable discharge from the Liberal Army of the Baja, signed by General J. R. Mosby, and dated June 22, 1911. The document looked official and included these words: "honest and faithful character, skilled horseman, good scout, a good shot, and a nervy soldier under fire." He obviously was a good soldier who fought hard for this cause.

This was a different father that I had ever known, and I concluded early in my research that my dad had been a guerrilla fighter involved in a revolution in a foreign country. My dad, along with a few other American men, joined and fought in the Army of the Baja, which was called the "Insurrectos" or "Filibusterous" by the Mexican people.

This rebel army band was comprised mostly of Americans looking for an adventure, and was a ragtag army of rebels, gringos, cutthroats, even criminals and chicken thieves, and I wondered how my dad got mixed up with them. This rebel group was organized and led by a Mexican patriot Richard Flores Magon, who had fled Mexico in fear of his life. He established a newspaper in Los Angeles and wrote articles to free the Mexican people against the violent dictator Diaz, and soon got lost in his desire to free the Mexican people from slavery and subjugation and began to make his own plans to free the Baja.

His original intent was to save the Mexican people from suppression and oppression, but his cause later got hijacked by several groups with different agendas. First, by evil American politicians with substantial funding; and second, by the Workers of the World Union, known in that era as the "Wobblies." The Wobblies promoted a Socialist-Marxist agenda along with Richard Ferris of San Diego who was an ex-actor, politician, promoter, and opportunist; in other words, a popinjay.

During that period of time, the Baja of Mexico was sparsely populated and was actually considered more of a territory by the Mexican government rather than a state. The territory was primarily cattle ranches owned by wealthy Americans through land grants, and the goal of the rebel army was to seize the territory and make it a worker's utopia, a Socialist-Marxist state.

Ironically, my research of this Baja event was made easier since I was stationed with the US Customs Service at the Port of San Ysidro, in San Diego County, California. Just across the border was the city of Tijuana, where my Dad's story took place. I spent many hours in libraries and bookstores going through old newspapers and books, and even the Historical Archives in Washington D.C. Eventually, the information I gathered gave me enough understanding to put the event together.

An ironic event happened to me one day while on duty with the US Customs. I was checking a neatly dressed Mexican gentleman through the border, who often came through my line into the US. We had developed a nodding acquaintance with each other, so I asked him if he had ever heard of the Battle of the Baja and of the Wobblies. To my surprise he replied yes, and he continued to speak of the battle that took place in 1911. His grandfather, Lt. Gov. Juan Larroque from Tijuana was in the battle and was shot in the eye and killed by the rebels. He went on to tell me that there is a large placard that presently hangs in the bullring in Tijuana that commemorates this event, calling it "The Battle of Tijuana."

Needless to say, our acquaintance developed into more than just a nod. It was amazing to me that this man, who was a prominent lawyer in Tijuana, was the man I happened to ask a mere question regarding my research, and that he had such a vast personal knowledge and interest in the event, just as I did. Call it coincidence or call it providence, I prefer to call it the latter. This kind gentleman brought me a book with information written in Spanish, which I translated into English, and it added tremendously to my research. I now feel like an authority on the subject of the revolution in Mexico, and thus begin this novel.

The life of a young man, my dad, both truth and fiction, is told in an adventurous exciting way, so here we go. Read on and enjoy.

Jack Lurlyn Walters
Retired US Customs Officer

Honorable discharge document from the Liberal
Army of the Baja for Theodore E. Walters

To Whom it May Concern,

This is to Certify that this day June 22 1911 Private E Edmund E Wallace is honorably discharged from the Liberal Army of Baja Calif

Enlisted. May 28th 1911
Service. Honest and Faithful
Character Excellent
Remarks. Skilled horseman good scout, good shot, cool and nervy soldier under fire

Engagements. Battle of Tia Juana June 22nd 1911.

Signed   Signed
B Liffen   J R Mosby.
Adjt Genl. 2 Div.   Genl. Commdg 2 Div.
                                Liberal Army
                                B C

Chapter 1

REBELS IN THE BAJA

It was difficult for Ted to imagine what lay ahead of them on this foggy spring morning; he could barely see the silhouette of his fellow soldiers riding their horses in front of him. It was a haunting picture and he felt "closed in" and anxious, as if he was surrounded by ghostly figures. Everyone was quiet, and the atmosphere was eerie and tense. The heavy mist from the Pacific Ocean created a condition that was common over the Baja, but by midmorning the fog was usually burned off by the sun.

Ted was riding his newly purchased mare he bought in San Diego for seventy dollars just a few days ago. He felt certain it was stolen, but he needed a horse to ride with the Liberated Army of the Baja, and he didn't have time to look elsewhere. *The anxious seller looked and acted suspicious,* Ted thought, as he kept looking over his shoulder all the time, so he took the opportunity to bargain the price with him, bringing the asking price down from a hundred twenty-five to the seventy dollars he agreed to pay, saddle included.

That afternoon the Liberated Army rebels gathered in a field at Little Landers Colony, the last border area before crossing into the Baja, to organize Company D that will ride across into Tijuana to make their final push to take over the Baja. Ted was riding with his Winchester 30x30 strapped to his saddle, and a Colt 45 in his leather holster resting at his side, he was prepared for battle. General Jack Mosby was ready to take his rebel army into the Baja to face the Mexican federalists to further advance their cause and to finalize the takeover of the Baja once and for all.

Meanwhile, in recent days, the nervous citizens of San Diego heard increased gunfire sounding along the border of Mexico and in their generally quiet coastal town. They were aware of the Mexican revolutionists led by Francisco Madero fighting against the dictator Portfolio Diaz on the mainland of Mexico; however, this increased gunfire in the Baja was a totally new development, and the citizens looked for answers from the city commissioners.

The city commissioners were also growing anxious, especially when they became aware that the Socialist Party in Los Angeles was aiding a little known rebel group with supplies and guns who were fighting to take over the Baja. They fired off a cablegram to the War Department in Washington, D. C. asking for information, help, and advice. They worried that the increased gunfire and activity was coming from this rebel group.

In a few days, the commissioners received a reply to their inquiry, and the telegram read:

"The head of the present movement in the Baja is the Socialist Revolutionary Junta from Los Angeles. The principal leader of the junta is Richard Flores Magon who publishes a newspaper to recruit new insurgents to gain support for his cause and plans to establish a Socialist Republic in the Baja, which would include a complete takeover. They are financed and controlled purely by the socialist organization, the Independent Workers of the World Union, also known as the Wobblies.

When the rebel troops arrived in the village of Tijuana, they were greeted by a group of about seventy men made up of barefoot Indian soldiers, citizens of the village, and the mayor. The mayor greeted them and ordered them to lay down their arms and surrender, if they did not, the government of Mexico would seek them out and arrest them. One of the rebels pulled his pistol and shot the Mayor in the eye, killing him, causing the soldiers and civilians to fire upon the mounted rebels. Both sides returned fire and scattered into the buildings and behind barricades to continue the battle which lasted several hours. Finally, the Mexican soldiers and remaining civilians retreated into the hillside, and the rebels took control of the town and peace was restored.

General Mosby then ordered his rebels, Company D, to commandeer the freight train when it arrived in Tijuana from San Diego to be used as transportation to move his rebel soldiers ahead into the interior of Baja. The rebels needed to be ready to engage the forces of The Federalist Mexican Army who would be responding to the takeover of Tijuana, but their exact position was unknown. Mosby believed they were somewhere between Ensenada and Tijuana.

When the California and Arizona freight train arrived at the Tijuana freight yard, the engineer and crew was met by the armed rebels and were ordered to remain at the controls. Now the train was under the command of the army of the Baja. General Mosby then ordered his troops to board the four flat cars in preparation to move the train ahead. The mounted rebels on horseback rode beside the train on both sides as it moved out of the freight yard. When they approached a railroad bridge on the outskirts of Tijuana, the railroad bridge narrowed and the soldiers had to leave the side of the train to ride their horses across the creek with the water sloughing on their feet and the horses' bellies. But about halfway across, a burst of machine gunfire cut loose on the train, which startled the horses and riders. Now, Mosby and the rebels were keenly aware of the Federalist armies' position.

As the train moved over the bridge, the machine gunfire continued and was coming from the nearby hillside slightly ahead and above them. The soldiers on the flatcars returned fire with their rifles, but Ted knew their rifles were almost useless against the powerful machine guns. He was fully aware that they had become sitting ducks for the Federalist Army.

The rebels were becoming quite tense and anxious by this time. They blindly opened fire toward the hillside, but the machine gun blasts continued. The bullets hit the steel train engine and ricocheted into the old wooden cab sending flying splinters at the rebels. The engineer and his crew were scared out of their wits and were under intense fire when one of the rebel soldiers cried out, "We have a man hit." Ted heard him fall into the water, along with the horse, both dead from their wounds. The horses directly behind the fallen one wildly bolted, but the soldiers were soon able to get them back under control. When they approached the creek embankment, another burst of gunfire hit Ted's horse, causing it to rear up and fall backward. He managed somehow to avoid being thrown under his horse by jumping to the side as his horse fell dead. He had his rifle in his hands as he landed on to the creek bank in the mud, stunned and speechless.

He managed to crawl in the mud to reach the bridge abutment alongside the track and pull himself up. He ran alongside the coal car and reached up to grab the ladder to swing himself aboard. As Ted boarded the train, it began to slow down then finally stopped. The engineer at the controls had made the decision to throw it in reverse to avoid going headlong into the direction of the gunfire, but before he could accomplish the process, a line of gunfire pelted the engine, hitting him multiple times and he fell to the floor, his face blown apart beyond recognition. The soldiers and crew stood horrified and frozen, but not for long.

The machine gunfire intensified from both sides of the hill, hammering the train; and the rebels could now see the Mexican soldiers on the hillside.

Ted positioned himself behind the metal wall of the coal car while firing his rifle toward the hillside when he heard General Mosby shout out, "Does anyone know how to get this train into reverse so we can get out of here, for god's sake?"

Ted raised himself up from his firing position and yelled out, "Yes, sir, I do." Mosby shouted back, "Well, get yourself up here in the engine and get us out of this mess, for heaven's sake."

Ted hurriedly climbed onto the engine cab, hoping against hope he remembered what a friendly engineer had once taught him. He yelled at a soldier to start shoveling coal into the firebox, and then quickly studied the controls. He threw the lever and turned the knobs, and as luck would have it, the train began to move backward, the wheels turning and screeching, grabbing the tracks as they slowly moved. The train moved back across the bridge, and they were soon out of the range of the Mexican army's gunfire.

Once safely back at the village of Tijuana and the Mexican border crossing, General Mosby knew it was over for them, much to his sorrow. He ordered the soldiers to dismount and form a line; only about half of the rebel soldiers survived the battle. He thanked each of them for being a good soldier and ordered them to march to the United States Customs building to surrender their arms.

Nicely dressed men and women, who had gathered at the border to watch the battle, spit at them and threw rocks and eggs hitting the men as they marched through the gates to surrender themselves and their weapons to the U S military. They were humiliated and embarrassed as they were handcuffed and placed in a truck to be taken to the military camp at Fort Rosecrans in San Diego.

As he sat on his bunk in the camp, Ted was glad to be alive but could not believe what he had just been through. He wondered in his mind how and why he ended up here, here at Fort Rosecrans, no longer free to come and go as he pleased. This was not the way it was supposed to turn out; they were going to free the land of the Baja for the people. The hopes and plans sounded so good at the time, and he wanted to be a part of it.

But here, he is in a military prison and at the mercy of his country, a country that seemed very unforgiving, charging him for "insurrectionist activities." He felt confused. *How did I get here*, and he remembered his family and leaving home at the age of fifteen to go to Canada to learn to be a telegraph operator. All the events of his life suddenly flashed through his mind, and he began to question himself and wondered what was next for him.

Chapter 2

GOING TO CANADA

Just a few miles down the road after they left the farm in Deer Creek, Oklahoma, Ted knew it was going to be a long, torturous, exhausting trip. He dreaded it already. Their motorcycle sputtered along the dirt road at about twenty to twenty-five miles per hour, at the most. Ted also knew he couldn't complain to his big brother, Everett, for fear he would be labeled a "sissy" throughout the whole trip. So he just hung on for dear life, his arms wrapped tightly around his big brother's waist, which did give him some sense of security.

Everett's motorcycle was his pride and joy; he had won it in a poker game, and he had to modify it by extending a padded seat over the rear tire so Ted would have a semi-comfortable ride to Canada. He would not be pleased to hear Ted's whining this soon. His wonderful modified cycle originally cost the previous owner three hundred dollars; it was painted green. Everett was excited that his cycle was going to take him to a new life in Canada, and Ted was chosen as a recipient to share in the adventure, an adventure that had the blessings of their parents.

Their parents, Jacob and Elizabeth Walters, were hardworking farmers and had six children—four sons and two daughters. Ted was fifteen years of age and his full name was Theodore Edmond Walters. *Such a big, regal name for just a farm kid*, Ted always thought.

Their dad had become sickly of late, and Ted's sister Edith had moved back to the farm with her two children after her husband died. Money was scarce, and quite simply, Everett and Ted needed to strike out on their own to help support themselves and the family. Ted was just a few days' short of being fifteen years old. *Just old enough*, his parents thought, *to start a productive life for himself, and to go with his big brother to Canada so he didn't have to go out into the world alone.*

Auntie Mary and Uncle Charles Hopt lived in Toronto, Canada, in the Province of Ontario, and he was considered quite successful by all the family. He was a government official and was gone from home on business many days in a year; cousin Hank was a telegraph operator for the Canadian Province Railroad. They invited Everett and Ted to come live with them and apprentice as telegraph operators with Hank; Uncle Charles was glad to make all the arrangements for them. The family felt really blessed and believed it was an opportunity of a life time for them. With great gratitude, they accepted the offer; and Everett and Ted packed a few belongings and struck out on their adventure without very much knowledge of such a major trip, or what was in store for them.

The days were long and the nights seemed much too short. They camped out at night using only their tarpaulin on the ground, and their blanket they rolled up and carried on their backs by day. Ted was always hungry and was overjoyed each evening when they had the good fortune of killing a rabbit or a squirrel to cook over the campfire. And they rationed out the packet of oatmeal cookies their mom sent with them, eating only one each per day. That was the only reminder of home, and oh, how he missed the comforts and the good home-cooked farm meals his mom fixed.

Appreciation for such things is scarce until you don't have them, Ted realized. Looking up at the stars at night, however, was his way of forgetting his sore body from the day's ride. He counted the stars one by one until he drifted off to sleep.

It was a cool morning, about 6:00 a.m., and Everett was eager to get started for the day.

"Get up, little bro," he called out to Ted. "Are you going to sleep all day? Let's get going so we can get this trip over with, the sooner the better. My back-side can't take much more of this."

"It can't be morning yet," Ted said as he rolled over to see the sunrise coming up over the lake of the Ozark's countryside. He had slept soundly that night and was grateful for the rest, but he groaned loudly as he moved to get up from his bed. He was glad to hear Everett be the first to complain about the harshness of the trip; he didn't feel quite like a complete sissy anymore. He jumped up and down and ran in a stationary position to get the kinks and aches out of his body.

"Okay, let's get going, I'm ready to get this trip over with too."

"You're the driver today, little bro, I'm going to turn it over to you so I can just relax and enjoy the sights." Everett chuckled to himself as if he could relax on the back of that monster cycle he had once loved. The 'love-affair' with his beautiful cycle was becoming a big pain, literally, to him now.

"We have to buy gas for our buggy today. I think there's a small town ahead a few miles," Everett instructed. They had some trouble on the trip finding places that sold gasoline, and only a few drugstores in the towns sold it. So far they were lucky, and he hoped their luck would hold out today so they could fill up.

Ted was feeling good this morning as they headed down the road—the wind was blowing on his face, and unfortunately the dust also. He was glad he had his goggles to protect his eyes from the flying dust and rocks. His face was becoming wind- and sunburned from the elements; his old half-brimmed hat wasn't protecting him much, but it was better than none at all.

The scenery in the Ozarks was beautiful; the hills and forests made the travel slower, but the view of the lake waters gave a picture-perfect scenery to look at, hopefully it would take their minds off their sore and aching bodies for a while. The roads were winding, and Ted was feeling like "the master of the road" as he approached a steep curve. His mind told him to *slow-down, slow-down* when he heard Everett scream out.

"Look out, stop, stop, don't hit it," as they entered the curve. Everett saw the old, broken-down hay truck in the middle of the road before Ted did.

Ted swerved sharply to avoid hitting the old junk heap, throwing the cycle and its riders dangerously close to the cliff's edge. They were both stunned, could not believe what had just happened. They both jumped off to assess the situation and gasped as they saw the front wheel spinning in space over the cliff's edge. They hurriedly pulled the cycle back to keep it from rolling over into the abyss below. They were speechless for a while, but finally looked over the cliff, and to their surprise they could barely see the bottom.

Ted felt sick to his stomach, and at that moment he vowed to Everett he would never drive that cycle ever again. That green shiny monster had indeed become their adversary. Ted sat down by the side of the road to settle his jitters, and Everett quickly made a thorough check of the cycle to make sure every part was working. Everything looked good, but he would test it out before they took off down the road again.

Everett sat down beside Ted to rest and console his little brother, but Ted sat there with his face covered with his hands as if he were deep in thought. Actually, he was. Oh, how he wished he were back home, eating Mom's good cooking; beef stew was his favorite, he could almost taste it. He thought about his comfortable bed he slept in at night, and at that moment he wanted desperately what he had always taken for granted during the fifteen years of his life.

The old saying he remembered reading about one time, now had monumental meaning to him: 'We don't realize what we have until we understand what we've lost.' That kept running through his mind over and over again.

Suddenly, Ted burst into tears wondering why the world had to be so harsh. Everett tried to console him the best he could, feeling totally inadequate at the moment. But now Ted realized his big brother was all he had, he definitely understood that, and really appreciated him for the first time since he had always considered him a big pain.

"Okay, little bro, stick with me and we'll get this journey over with. We'll brave it out together and it will all be worth it, you'll see." He patted Ted's head and they both got up and prepared to get back on the cycle, understanding it was all they had to get them where they needed to go.

'Destination Detroit' were the two words that kept going through Ted's mind every morning when they took off for the day. He daydreamed about all the wonders of the world as he rode on the back of the sputtering monster. It kept him from thinking about his aching back and how tired his long legs were on his nearly six-foot frame. He felt folded up like his blanket and tarp he carried on his back. He tried hard to conquer the art of daydreaming because it really helped him keep his mind off the harshness of the new world he had entered in, and he realized he was not prepared for it.

He was feeling like an ant in a mammoth anthill, with each ant going hither and yon, working hard to make their own way. He came to the realization that growing up and being on your own without Mom and Dad was full of highs and lows; and like that ant, everyone must find his own way. He concluded the world was indeed harsh and uncertain, but it was up to him to buffer the harshness that came his way and to make his life and the world a better place.

"Destination Detroit!" Ted shouted out as they rode through the countryside of Illinois and into Indiana. He could not have imagined just a few weeks ago he would be seeing so much of the world—it definitely was big, not just big, but it seemed endless. When they passed through South Bend, he knew Detroit wasn't much farther away, and when they passed the state line into Michigan, Ted couldn't contain himself. He whooped and hollered until Everett stopped the cycle, and they both broke down in uncontrollable laughter. They decided to take a lunch break to rest and celebrate their Michigan breakthrough.

Their food supply was getting low; they only had a few crackers left. They looked along the roadside for wild berries and edible plants. They were becoming experts on what they could eat and how to search for it. They easily found blueberries and wild turnips to eat with their crackers, and they actually enjoyed their meal. They even spotted a friendly grazing cow along the roadside fence that was fully cooperative as Ted filled their tin cups with milk. Never in their wildest dreams did they imagine warm milk would taste so good.

They were speechless and in awe as they looked across Lake Erie, riding proudly into the outskirts of Detroit. Ted thought this day would never come, even though he daydreamed about it every day. They had never seen so much water in their lives; Oklahoma's little lakes and rivers never could have prepared them for what they were seeing. When they rode into the city along the bay, they stopped to take it all in. Everett gave Ted a hurried geography lesson.

"The land you see across the bay is Canada, we're almost there."

Ted was still speechless; he had never seen anything like this in his life. Everett continued his lesson.

"Lake Huron and Lake Erie come together here in Detroit and the waters narrow into what is called a strait, which is a river-like channel that connects them. The land you see across the strait is called a peninsula, which is the lower part of the province of Ontario. But the best part, little bro, is when we get across that strait, we'll be in Canada and onto Highway 401 which takes us directly into Toronto."

Everett's voice broke, tears came to their eyes and they breathed a sigh of relief; they never thought this day would come. They boarded the ferryboat to cross over into Canada, another moment they had waited for. What an adventure this had turned out to be, seeing for the first time all the action the world had to offer, many things they didn't even know existed. Ted sat back in his seat and enjoyed his first boat ride ever, oddly enough a boat that also carried their cycle, some bicycles, and he even saw a car, a Model T.

He had never seen many Model Ts up so close before, so he asked the nicely dressed gentleman if he could look inside. He happily obliged, anxious to show off his prized possession.

"Set up there in the driver's seat if you like, young man," the gentleman offered. Ted climbed in, all smiles, but felt reluctant to touch it. *It seemed like something out of a faraway place*, he thought.

"How fast will she go, mister?" Ted inquired.

"We go about fifteen to twenty miles per hour out on the road, can't go that fast in town, too many people," he replied.

"Where you from, young man?" he asked Ted when he heard his different accent.

"Oklahoma, sir," Ted proudly replied.

"How'd you get up here to the north?"

"See that green motorcycle over there, mister. My brother and I rode all the way to here. We'll trade you for your car, we're going on to Toronto," Ted challenged him with a laugh.

"Can't do that, my lad, but you both are very brave to ride that cycle all the way to Toronto—that must have been torture."

Everett rolled his cycle off the ramp of the ferry as he looked across the peninsula, relieved to be on Canadian soil. He turned around to look for Ted so they could line up to go through the Custom's house, but he was nowhere in sight. Then he heard someone shouting his name, and as he looked up he saw Ted waving his hand wildly as he rode with the nice gentleman in the Model T down the ramp from the ferry. Ted had accepted the invitation to ride, and he thought it was the most exciting thing that had ever happened to him. He thanked the gentleman profusely and shook his hand.

"Good luck, lad, enjoy your trip to Toronto."

Everett could hardly stop laughing.

"You're like a little kid on a merry-go-round. Get up here so we can get through the Custom's house and be on our way." They waved good-bye to the gentleman as they got in line to wait their turn to go through customs.

The Customs officer greeted them and asked them *really strange questions*, Ted thought.

"What are you bringing to Canada?" Everett answered all his questions to the officer's satisfaction, but Ted thought he kept looking at them strangely.

"Come on, Ted, let's go."

They climbed on the cycle, Ted on the back, ready to make the last phase of their trip.

"Why did he ask all those strange questions? Couldn't he see what we had with us?" Ted was still wondering.

"That's just what they do, little bro. They want to make sure you're not hiding something, don't worry about it."

They took off down Highway 401, which had recently been graded and had fewer ruts, and they were just a few miles away from their final destination. The scenery was beautiful and they could see the waters of Lake Erie most of the way. Ted still marveled at seeing that much water all in one place.

Ted couldn't believe it when Everett pulled up in front of Auntie Mary and Uncle Charles' house on the narrow little dirt street in Toronto. He dreamed of this moment day after day and pictured in his mind what Auntie would look like since he had never met her. He had only seen a picture of her years ago. When she came running out the door, he was overcome; she looked just like he had pictured her, just like an auntie should look like.

"Welcome, welcome," she cried out.

"You must be Theodore, you look just like your daddy." She gave him a big hug, dusty clothes and all.

Ted had heard about Auntie Mary. His dad talked about his little sister many times.

"Daddy said to tell you hello, and sends his love," he said.

"And you must be Everett," she said as she hugged his neck.

"Come on in, you must be tired and hungry. We'll get word to your folks you got here safe. They will be relieved, they have been worried about you."

Auntie Mary gave them some of Hank's clean clothes to put on after they washed up. The clothes they had with them had survived weeks of dirt and grit from travel, and she wondered if they would ever come clean.

"Tomorrow, Uncle Charles will take you down to the mercantile for a new pair of pants and shirt," she reassured them.

Ted was feeling better already, the aches and pains seemed to be going away; and as he sat down on the pretty stuffed chair in the parlor, he felt like a king. He closed his eyes for a moment and went fast asleep. It had been weeks since he felt such comfort.

"Wake up, wake up, Ted."

Ted felt embarrassed, he had fallen fast asleep and Auntie Mary let him rest, she knew he was totally exhausted.

"I want you to meet your Uncle Charles and Hank. They are home from work and we'll be having supper soon," she said. Ted was startled for a moment, she sounded just like his mom, as he remembered.

Ted and Everett took a liking to Hank and Uncle Charles right away. They made them feel welcome as they started talking about their plans to teach them telegraphy. Ted suddenly felt safe and secure again, and perhaps life wasn't as harsh as he had thought. He couldn't wait to sleep in a real bed that night; he dreamed of this day to come, and it was finally here.

Chapter 3

LEARNING THE CODE

The telegram message read:

> "Uncle Jacob Aunt Elizabeth (stop) Everett and Ted arrived safe last night (stop) tired dirty and hungry (stop) keep you posted (stop) Hank."

They were so relieved when the telegram was delivered by the station master from the Deer Creek depot. Elizabeth read it over and over again; they could finally relax now, since they had not heard a word from Everett and Ted since they left weeks ago.

Uncle Charles made sure Hank sent the message from the train station since it also doubled as the Western Union Office. *This will be a great way to keep in touch with his parents*, Ted thought. He couldn't wait to learn the code so he could send his own message. This gave him additional incentive to learn as quickly as he could, and he suddenly felt much closer to home and not so far away after all.

"Let's get to work," Hank told them after two days of rest.

"Here's your homework, learn Morse Code." He smiled as he handed them the handbook that explains and lists all the code, the ABCs of telegraphy. As Hank left for work, Everett and Ted stared at each other as they looked over their books.

"This looks hard," Ted said.

"All these dots and dashes, do we really have to memorize them?"

"We do, little bro," Everett replied with the same amazement in his own mind.

Hank had told them the experts say it sometimes takes three to five years to train the mind to think and receive the code to become really proficient. So that challenge loomed big at the back of their minds as they begin to study. Ted was determined it would not take that long for him.

Even Auntie Mary got into the act of the family training project of these two carefree boys. Although they worked hard most of the time, they took their recreation time at the local pool hall. Ted loved to play pool, but one day they got carried away spending too much time there, so Auntie Mary thought. She marched into the pool hall and quietly escorted them home after they had been there for four hours. Needless to say, that never happened again. They would avoid at all costs being embarrassed again by the discipline of their gracious host. The subject was never discussed again.

In the evening, Hank would test their progress by sending messages to them on the little portable machine he had set up at home for them to practice sending and receiving messages to each other.

"This is fun," Ted said.

"It's like a game." He spent hours playing on the machine which forced Everett to work hard also.

Hank was very pleased with their progress, so they moved on to the next step of their training: learning the system and the importance of timing and accuracy. He explained the trains had to move safely through the countryside on one track, which moved the trains going both ways. He also explained that some trains had to be directed to a side track at the station to allow another train going the opposite direction to pass through. This was why timing was so important, they had to know and coordinate the expected times of passage of each train.

They were clearly getting the message of why accuracy was so important. Ted realized it was not just about dots and dashes after all. He visualized in his mind what would happen when two trains, going on opposite directions, meet on the track and crashed into each other. It was real clear, and even made him shudder for a moment. In his young mind, he hoped he was up to the responsibility.

After a few days of intense practice, Hank was ready to take them to the station for on-the-job training. He would take them one at a time—Everett would be first. Uncle Charles also took them to the local jewelers to purchase their required time piece. Since accuracy and timing is so vital, they each had to have a certified Hamilton pocket watch, better known as a railroad watch, to synchronize their time with the whole division as the dispatcher announced the time daily. Ted thought this was unique since he had never had a watch before, he was quite proud of it.

Everett looked around the station house that first day; it was bigger than any he had seen before, having come from a small farm community. He saw the telegraph station where he would work at, a ticket window, a waiting room with benches, and as luck would have it, he saw the arrival of a passenger train, the porter stepping off and placing the step down for passengers to disembark. He watched the agent unload the baggage and mail from the baggage car, and in a few minutes, they loaded it back up with more mail and baggage to go to its final destination. As the new passengers boarded, Everett strained his ears to hear the porter call out "all aboard," and then watched the train slowly leave the station.

Actually, the first day was a bit nerve-racking when he realized there was so much to learn and remember. Hank reassured him with a pat on the back, that he would be right there with him to explain every detail. Everett sat down beside him at the telegraph desk when the machine started to send the messages, and Hank instructed him to write down the message as it came in; and if a response was necessary, to write down the return message also. They processed five departures and arrivals that day, which was their usual schedule. He loved seeing the people coming and going, and especially the children about to take their first train ride. Much to his surprise the day went well, and he began to feel he could do the job after all. Hank was very pleased with his work and even bragged about him at the supper table that evening. Ted felt really good, because he knew in his mind that he had learned to receive and send quicker than Everett had.

After three weeks Hank announced.

"This is the day, Everett, today you are going to do all the hands on, all the sending and receiving, everything that is to be done from start to finish. I'm going to be the observer."

Everett's heart almost skipped a beat, but he was anxious to get started on his own, he felt pretty confident. He knew Hank had been a great mentor to him, and he wondered how he could ever repay him.

"I'll be right here beside you, Everett. Always remember in your mind accuracy is the name of the game, and you have demonstrated that very well. Otherwise, I would not turn it over to you," Hank told him with great assurance in his voice.

Ted was excited and more than ready to start his hands-on training at the station when Hank took him that first day. Actually, Ted had taken it upon himself to soak up all he could on his own. He had always loved to read and learn new things. He thought about his parents and how often they encouraged him to learn as much as he could and prepare himself for life. He certainly didn't want to disappoint them now.

While Hank and Everett were at work, he would practice at least three hours on the portable machine, sending messages and checking his accuracy. And then, with permission from Auntie Mary, he would go to the train station and from his chosen vantage point outside by the tracks, he watched and observed all the activities, all the coming and going of the trains and the people. He was also fascinated by several people the train crew called hobos, as they maneuvered their way onto the trains for free travel. A few times he was able to engage them in conversation and learned about their lives and their hobo travels.

He loved to hear the screeching of the train wheels as the engineer put on brakes to slow down the massive engine to come to a stop, the sound of metal on metal. He loved the loud sound of the whistle announcing the train's arrival, and he loved seeing the porter step off the train to assist the passengers as they departed from their hours of riding on the bumpy tracks. He watched the excitement of the people waiting for their special passenger to step down from the train, perhaps a relative they had never seen before. He had a great imagination thinking up possible stories for each of their lives.

He loved every minute of it, and finally this was officially his first day of training and he knew he was well on his way to becoming a telegraph operator. He wanted to do the best he could for his parents, for himself, and of course, for his new family, Auntie Mary, Uncle Charles, and Hank his mentor. Now, it was all up to him.

After several weeks of successful training, Hank announced their apprenticeships were complete, and they were now certified telegraph operators. Ted was so excited he sent a telegram to his parents to tell them the good news.

'Dear Mom and Dad(stop) we did it (stop) our training is complete(stop) we are now telegraph operators(stop) hope you're proud of us (stop) Auntie Mary, Uncle Charles, and Hank send greetings (stop) we love you(stop) Ted and Everett.'

That evening Auntie Mary fixed a very special dinner to celebrate their accomplishments. Hank called it their graduation ceremony and even made up a very nice diploma, and had Auntie Mary tie it with a blue ribbon to present to them. Everett had a surprise announcement to make, only Hank knew about his good news. He had applied for a job in Kansas City, Missouri, with a brand new company, the American International

Telegraph Company. The news came through at the station just today that he had been accepted. He would be paid thirty-eight cents an hour, and was to report in three weeks. Ted was happy for him as everyone shared his good news, but also felt very sad, as he would soon be without his big brother upon whom he had secretly depended these past few months. But he wouldn't dare express any of his feelings, so he cheered along with everyone as they began to make plans for him to leave Canada.

Over the next few days, Everett made preparation to leave for Kansas City, Missouri. He sold his motorcycle; he never wanted to travel on it ever again with the harshness of their trip to Canada still very fresh on his mind. He divided up the money he received, some for Auntie Mary for room and board, some for Ted since he would stay a while longer, and kept some for himself for travel.

Hank helped Everett to make his arrangements to travel by train to Kansas City. He looked forward to the trip, actually his very first train trip, and he felt very blessed to go to his first real job. They gathered at the station to give Everett a special send-off; however, Ted could hardly hold back the tears. Everett gave him a big hug, a very sincere hug, because he squeezed him so tightly. *If only he could keep a part of him here*, Ted thought. They had grown so close these past few months. It was tough to say good-bye. Without any words exchanged between them, Everett boarded the train, turned, and waved good-bye. They stood there and continued waving until the train was completely out of sight.

Ted would remain a few more weeks in Canada until he could make his plans for the future, whatever those plans would turn out to be. He continued to work with Hank at the station without pay and helped Auntie Mary and Uncle Charles with odd jobs around the house to earn his room and board. What would be his future? he wondered every day. He felt positive about himself, almost sixteen years old, six feet tall, strong and handsome, self-assured, and everyone seemed to like his friendly manner. He knew the story of his life was just beginning if he could only be patient enough to allow it to unfold.

Chapter 4

NIAGARA FALLS

Ted headed for the train station. He was excited to go but it was tough saying good-bye to Auntie Mary and Uncle Charles, they had become like parents to him. Auntie Mary tucked a package of oatmeal cookies and other goodies into his backpack as tears flowed down her cheeks. Ted knew he could never repay them or thank them enough for all they did for him. "Just go and have a successful life," they said, that was their hope for him.

He was hoping to catch the first freight out of Toronto to Niagara Falls. The thoughts of returning to the states, especially Oklahoma, and see the family and farm again crowded his mind. He quickened his pace when he realized how much he had really missed his family and the old farm place after all.

When he arrived at the station, he was glad to see Hank, he was counting on him to help him through the ropes of getting on that freight.

"It's time for me to get out of here and go back to the farm," Ted told him.

Hank smiled at him teasingly.

"Thought you never wanted to go back to the farm after seeing the world, that's what you said when you got here."

"Never mind that," Ted replied, a bit embarrassed.

"I owe this to my parents, you know. They are anxious to see the world traveler return." Ted was glad that he had made friends with all the crew at the station. They liked this energetic young kid, and they all helped Hank make the arrangements with the conductor and crew for Ted to catch his train, which was due to arrive in one hour. They also made arrangements for him to have a choice seat in the caboose riding along with the crew.

Ted couldn't believe how helpful they were. At this moment he felt very grateful. He didn't have very much in the way of material things, but it suddenly dawned on him, material things were not the most important thing in life, it was family and friends that made it all worthwhile. Hank and Ted had grown very close, like brothers, and it was just as hard to leave him as it was when Everett left.

The crew gave Ted a rousing send-off, and he was so impressed that he felt a sense of pride he never had before. He had been accepted as one of them, one of the crew, and fully accepted as a brother in the Canadian Province Railroad brotherhood. That acceptance gave him a sense of belonging, knowing that he could count on his railroad brothers to help him get to Niagara Falls, the first lap of his journey.

As he walked toward the caboose, the station crew waved and shouted to him, and his sense of accomplishment and pride was alive and well. He couldn't help himself, tears filled his eyes but he smiled through it all and returned shouts of thanks and good wishes to them all. The ride was spectacular, the winter scenery, the snow occasionally falling, and he enjoyed getting acquainted and chatting with the train crew. However, the happiest moment of the day was when they arrived at the Niagara Falls station which meant he was almost back on American soil, just a few steps away.

Ted walked across the bridge that connected the two countries and was elated to see the sign, "Welcome to the United States of America." He passed through US Customs, and the officer passed him directly through without hardly any questions. Finally, he was back home on American soil.

He had read stories about Niagara Falls and had seen pictures of both the Horse Shoe Falls and the Bridal Falls, so he was anxious to see everything he could before boarding the next train. It was in the dead of winter, bitter cold, and the wind was blustery. He pulled the hood of his old Mackinaw jacket over his head and walked out to the observation platform to see everything.

Ted was speechless as he caught the first panoramic view of the falls, *it was so powerful and mighty*, he thought. The grandeur of it all took his breath away, and he realized that all the pictures he had seen and all that he had read about it could never fully describe the beauty and majesty of all he was seeing. There was a light snow falling, and the sight of the large icicles hanging all around the observation platform gave the appearance of a winter wonderland. He stood there like a frozen statue as he watched large chunks of ice tumble over the falls into the rolling waters below.

Ted suddenly felt very cold, and he realized his teeth were chattering; neither his long johns nor his hooded jacket gave him enough warmth. He was grateful for the knitted wool sweater and gloves his Auntie had made him for his seventeenth birthday; he knew he would be much colder without them. He began to think that no coats or apparel would ever keep him warm in such bitter cold weather.

Ted always thought that being young and tough would be all he needed to handle and conquer anything that came his way, but that was before he saw Mother Nature's spectacular power he was presently looking at. Now he knew better, nature has a way of humbling the most confident; it was much more powerful and tougher than he was. He stood there in awe, teeth chattering and nose running, with all the products of a chilled body, as he gazed down below to the bottom of the falls. He noticed a heavy mist cloud that rose up as the water hit the river below, and it was then that he realized his clothes were soaking up the mist in the air. *No wonder he was so cold*, he thought. He knew his clothes would soon be frozen stiff just like the icicles that were forming all around him. He stepped back inside the observatory to get some relief from the cold and to dry out his coat by the fireplace.

The snow was beginning to let up, and he still had some time before he had to catch the next train, so he sat there soaking up all of the beauty that was around him. His thoughts were interrupted by what sounded like increased chatter from the people out on the platform. He dismissed it for a moment, but soon heard the voices growing louder, so he went back out to investigate what was happening.

He looked down toward the bottom of the falls and saw people waving their arms and pointing to the rolling water. The sounds were muffled because of the roar, and everyone at the railing was trying their best to see what was going on. The great fear was that someone slipped on the ice and fell from the platform, but they kept their eyes glued on the crowd that had gathered far below at the bottom of the falls. The mist cleared slightly, and what they saw was astounding—three people with their arms flailing in the water, struggling to save themselves. The crowd stood speechless as they watched this unbelievable, eerie spectacle below them.

Ted saw several panic-stricken "would-be" rescuers running along the edge of the river bank below, knowing they couldn't rescue them from the ice cold water. He felt very sorry for them, knowing they were helpless and unable to do anything to change the course of events.

Everyone knew it was a helpless situation. Ted knew it, the crowd knew it, and much to their angst, the would-be rescuers knew it also. He struggled with his emotions as his eyes followed the three people fight for their lives, and then suddenly disappear beneath the rolling water. He shuddered as his thoughts overtook him, but he wasn't alone. Everyone else was struggling because of what they were witnessing. He thought about the beauty and magic he was enjoying and how it suddenly turned into a cruel, devastating time for everybody. He felt helpless and stunned.

Murmurs of what happened were beginning to filter up to the platform, and Ted listened intently trying to figure it all out. The great range of happiness he had been enjoying suddenly turned into tragedy and unfolding before his eyes; it was like watching a tragic Greek play. He saw people crying and wringing their hands, demonstrating their anguish that was in their hearts. He wanted to join them to show his despair, but he remained quiet.

He looked about him and saw the mini-icebergs continually flowing toward the precipice of the falls, only to plunge toward the bottom. *It was a demonstration of the great power that nature has over us,* Ted thought, his self-projected toughness he so confidently thought he had was just wishful thinking, and he was greatly humbled as he accepted the fact: there is indeed a "greater power" that exists.

The news of what happened finally came together and filtered throughout the crowd. A honeymoon couple and a teenage boy thought they could walk across the ice-bridge that had formed, and of course they were wrong, and all three plunged into the icy waters below. They had only been married one day, and it was not known whether or not they knew the teenage boy. *Why would they do such a foolish thing?* Ted thought. Warning signs were posted all around the grounds. What a terrible gamble. Was it a dare? Or was it a case of indestructibility, Ted could relate to that. He overheard a man say the searchers would still be looking for their bodies downstream in the springtime, and when they were finally found they would all read about it in the newspapers.

Ted knew it was time to leave the falls to get back to the train station. His visit had been bittersweet, the beauty and the magic he would always remember, but the event that surrounded it would be a lesson about life that would remain with him forever. He pulled his Mackinaw parka securely over his head and turned to have one last look at the majesty of the falls.

He saw the crowds of people down below walking up to the giant wall of ice that forms beside the falls, which extends clear to the top. He hoped in his heart that no one would have the delusion they could climb that ice wall—it would end up in disaster. He heard rumors in the crowd that there had been people who tried.

The snow seemed to get heavier as he walked down the street to the train station, and the wind hit his face with a cutting force. *Oklahoma gets cold in the winter, but never cold like this*, he thought to himself. He passed store window after store window and all the tourist shops, where people could buy their souvenirs to take home to show their friends. He came to a window of a drugstore and paused to look in; it looked inviting and warm. It had a soda fountain and coffee shop, so he decided to step inside in to have a cup of coffee and get warm.

He must have looked like a snowman as he stepped inside the entry foyer. He brushed off the snow and sat down on the bench to take off his galoshes. When he went inside, he saw a long marble soda fountain counter, and in the back corner was a man in a white coat, who must have been the pharmacist waiting on a customer. What Ted loved most about the store was the homey, warm atmosphere, and on the wall was a big Coca Cola sign. Above the soda fountain was a large picture of a very famous character in history, Daniel Boone, standing next to a large oak tree with the carving, "I killed a Bear" and it was signed "D. B."

A young couple was sitting on the fancy metal chairs at one of the small tables, eating a delicious-looking banana split. *It sure looked good*, Ted thought, but he shivered thinking about eating it, and how cold it would taste. The clerk was fixing sodas for two young boys sitting at the counter, both rotating back and forth on the swivel seats, having the time of their lives. Ted looked around the store and saw all the shelves that contained everything one could possibly imagine, cosmetics, pills of all kinds, knick-knacks, souvenirs, magazines, and other books. But the one thing that caught his eye the most was the comic book section. It reminded him of how he used to go to their little drugstore in Deer Creek just a few years back, reading the comics and placing them back in the rack when he was finished. He smiled to himself. He was standing next to the counter when he spied a glass case that displayed all kinds of pies. He couldn't resist, he sat down at the counter and ordered a piece of lemon pie and a cup of coffee.

"Did you hear about the three people who broke through the ice bridge and drowned?" the clerk asked Ted. "People just don't pay any attention to the signs anymore, they are posted all over the place," he added.

"Yes," Ted replied.

"I was there, saw the whole thing, it was awful. I don't understand why people take such chances with their lives."

"It happens a lot up here," the clerk said. "They won't read the signs, they are just too daring."

Ted got up to pay for his pie, but saw a rack of picture postcards, mostly of the falls. He made a selection of one of the cards, a picture of the falls in the winter that looked just like what he had seen. He wanted to send it to his mom and dad. He knew his mom would tape it to the ice chest and he would see it hanging there when he got home. He paid for his pie and coffee, and an extra two cents for the postcard.

"Who are you going to send that to?" the clerk asked.

"My mom and dad in Oklahoma, where can I mail it?"

"Sit right down there at the counter, young man, and write a note to your parents, I'll make sure it gets mailed for you. The postman comes right into our store."

Ted was so glad and thanked him as he sat down to write:

> 'Dear Mom and Dad, I'm in Niagara Falls, coming home soon. I will catch the train and head for home. Don't worry about me, I'm doing fine. Wish you could have seen Niagara Falls with me, tell all the family hello, can't wait to see everyone.
>
> Love, Ted

Ted paid a penny for the stamp and handed the card to the clerk who said,

"This will be special delivery, young man, just for your folks. Have a good trip home."

"Thanks." Ted smiled. The stop at the drugstore was just what he needed to settle him down from the day's event. He felt relaxed as he put on his galoshes and headed back down the street toward the train station. He decided to go on down to Buffalo, New York, just a short trip from Niagara Falls, to catch the next train toward home.

Chapter 5

THE HOBO IN ME

With a renewed sense of adventure on his mind, Ted made his way to the Buffalo Station yard to board the next freight to Pittsburgh heading south. When he arrived in the yard, his train was already in and the crew was busy switching out the cars, adding and replacing them to make up the train for the next haul. He stepped into an inconspicuous place beside the yard and watched all the activities; it was so good to see it all again, he felt right at home.

The combination of his new adventurous spirit and lack of money gave Ted the courage to make a very important decision for himself. He had decided to travel the rails on his own, rather than using his money to buy a ticket. He knew he didn't have enough to get all the way home to Oklahoma, and he would need to save what little he had for food. Besides that, he didn't want to ask his folks for money.

Since he understood all the workings of the train crew, he thought it would be fairly easy to climb aboard an empty boxcar without being seen. He remembered watching the men that called themselves hobos back in Toronto, sneaking onto the train every day, and the fascinating stories that they told. He decided to try it; he was going to travel as a hobo back to Oklahoma.

Ted saw the conductor signal the engineer as they made their final inspection of the cars. The brakeman checked every car up and down the length of the train, and when he finished and climbed aboard, the conductor stood on the steps of the caboose and waved his lantern back and forth to signal the engineer they were ready to go. The train started to crawl very slowly out of the yard, and Ted knew it was time to make his move.

With his heart pounding, he ran through the fog and smoke from the steam of the engine, slid the boxcar door open and leaped on. He was relieved he had made it, his heart still pumping fast and furious, and he felt a sudden rush of excitement that he hadn't expected. Before he could slide the door shut he heard someone shout.

"Hold up, we're coming aboard to join you!"

Ted jumped back to give them room to get on board. The first hobo jumped inside making a perfect landing as he reached out to help his friend climb aboard. Ted knew immediately that they were experienced hobos, and he was glad to have company. Slowly the train moved through the yard, entered the main line, and began to gather speed; in a short time, they were flying down the tracks. Ted breathed a sigh of relief, he was on his way, and his first attempt had been successful.

The older looking hobo reached out to shake hands with Ted.

"Hi, my name is Boxer John, and this is my friend, Willy Nilly."

"Glad to meet you fellows, my name is Ted Walters. Where are you headed?" Ted was fascinated with their seemingly carefree attitude and friendliness.

"We're heading south right now, goin' to Florida, goin' down to warmer weather to pick fruit and to make a few bucks as fruit pickers," Boxer said.

"Where you goin', fella?"

"I'm headin' home to Oklahoma, guess I'll go south to Atlanta, then west to Oklahoma," Ted replied, although he hadn't given much thought to the routes he would take.

"I've never been to Oklahoma, I hear there's lots of dust storms and Indians there, hope they all are tame, wouldn't want to get scalped. You still have your scalp, don't you, fella," Willy Nilly teased.

"Most of them are real tame. I grew up with several Indian friends and none of them ever tried to scalp me," Ted said as they all laughed together.

The train was moving along at a good speed, and Ted slid the door open to peek outside, curious to see the countryside. The fog was lifting, it had been quite heavy earlier, and he could barely see his hand in front of his face. He couldn't see very much yet, *but it must be beautiful country*, he thought, all he could see was lots of trees through the mist.

"How long you guys been hobos?" Ted turned and asked them as he slid the door shut.

"About three years now," Boxer said.

"Followed the harvest and we done a little lumbering up north, but that's too dangerous, lost a good friend a few weeks ago. A tree fell on him, so from now on we're sticking to vegetables and fruits, they can't hurt us, and besides, they taste good." He laughed.

"Where did you get the name Boxer?" Ted inquired.

Willy jumped into the conversation and came up with the answer. "He boxed three times and got beat three times. I was his manager and ring second, it wasn't workin'. He couldn't fight for sour apples." He snickered and laughed.

"We tried fighting in a couple of carnivals to pick up a few bucks, that's where he got the name 'Boxer John.' That became his moniker," Willy added. "I got my name because I like to joke and tease people. A guy up north called me Silly Willy Nilly, and Willy Nilly stuck."

"What in the world is a moniker?" Ted asked.

"You don't know? Hobos choose a name to call themselves instead of using their real name. If we are picked up by cops, they have a harder time checking up on us to see if we have a record, and unfortunately, I do have a record," Boxer told Ted.

"What did you do?" Ted asked curiously.

"Accidently killed a man, got into a fight, spent two years in prison for an accident, can you believe that?" Boxer answered.

Ted didn't know what to say, so he didn't say anything. He had never seen a killer before, let along ride the rails with one, *but he seems nice enough*, Ted thought. Boxer sensed Ted's hesitation to respond and asked.

"Tell us about yourself, how long you been ridin' the rails?"

Glad for the change of subject, Ted replied, "Well, to be honest this is my first time. I was living in Toronto, Canada, with my aunt and her family. My cousin, Hank, who is a telegraph operator, trained me to be one also. When I finished my apprenticeship, I decided to go back home to help my dad with the spring planting. I'm only sixteen and can't get a job yet. I have a couple of months before he needs me on the farm, so I decided to see a little of the country before I go home."

"What ya' know, an educated young fella riding the rails." Willy seemed impressed.

"I watched the hobos in Toronto when I was training, and they seemed to have an exciting time, so I thought I would try it to get back home to Oklahoma, since I have very little money," Ted added.

"Sounds like a right smart plan, but it's not all that excitin', fella. Ya have to learn to travel smart and learn the ropes. We might as well sit back and relax, we got a lot more miles to go to get to Pittsburgh," Willy said, as he plopped down to rest.

Ted's thoughts drifted back to Toronto, and he tried to remember why watching the hobos were so fascinating to him. He thought about what Willy said about traveling smart, and lots of questions came into his mind.

"Tell me about the life of a hobo. Why do you do it?" he asked his newfound friends.

Sitting back against the side of the boxcar with his head cushioned with his bedroll, Boxer began a short lesson on hobo-in'.

"It's the adventure of the open road, or tracks in this case. The freedom we have to travel, and it's usually because of the lack of money and jobs. We make friendships and seek opportunities together, ya' never know what the next stop will bring." He stopped to take a drink of water out of his canteen, and then continued.

"The best part for me, young fella, is the friendships we make, just like me and my good friend, Willy. When we're not travelin', we camp in the woods in a hobo camp, they are usually close to the railroad yards, and we share information and stories together and anything else we have with each other." Ted listened with great interest. He had no idea about the real life of a hobo. Boxer continued.

"When we break up camp to travel, we leave messages for each other on stopovers, letting our friends know which divisions are tough and which ones are not, and which yard bulls are mean and which ones are not. And in different towns, we leave information on which ones have tough laws and which ones don't. For instance, which town is okay to panhandle and which restaurants are charitable and let's wash dishes or clean up in exchange for a meal. When we leave our messages, we always use our moniker names.

"Dippy Dan, Chicago Ralph, L.A, Bob, Plumber Joe, White Wash Earl, are some of my hobo friends. We scratch messages and warnings to each other, usually on the water towers, so we always check the towers to see if any of our friends have been there. We always use codes, that's what we live by."

Ted was captivated by everything Boxer was saying; he had no idea the hobo life was so full of details. He thought it would be more boring and lonely; however, he was well aware there were dangers.

He remembered reading in the obituary section of the Toronto newspaper of an unidentified man who was found dead near the railroad tracks about ten miles out of town, age about twenty-five, dark hair, six feet tall, one hundred and seventy pounds, and he was buried in a potter's field, lot number three. Ted always wondered if his family ever found out what happened to him.

"Tell me about some of the dangers," he asked Boxer.

"Accidents happen, young fella. Just getting off and on a train can be dangerous, but the greatest danger comes from goin' underneath. Danger and accidents happen everywhere to all people, it's about stayin' alert and smart about what we do," Boxer told him.

They settled in for a rest since it was nighttime. Ted unfolded his bedroll and took a moment to look outside through the cracks. It was black as night, couldn't see a thing except a quick glimpse of the moon and the moonlight shining through the trees as they passed by. *The world was still intact*, he thought, as he lay down to rest. It wasn't a soft bed like Auntie Mary's, but he was tired and had no trouble falling asleep.

Early in the morning hours, their sleep came to an abrupt end when they were awakened by the train's loud whistle. Ted knew it was almost morning; he could see the daylight beginning to come through the cracks of the boxcar. The whistle blew again, and the train was slowing down and coming to a stop. *It felt like they were going into a siding*, he thought. Before long, they heard another whistle, different than the first two; and through the cracks they saw the flashing of another train passing by so fast, one car after another. It was like watching a movie screen flashing picture after picture, and then suddenly the movie was over, the train had passed.

They quickly picked up their bedrolls when they heard voices outside their boxcar. Ted tiptoed to the right side of the car to listen, and he heard a man say, "George, you check that next car, I'll get this one, and I think I heard something inside."

Boxer slid the door open on the left side of the car, and they made their jump to run for safety into the woods. It all happened so fast, and Ted followed the best he could, but fell and did a belly-flop when he jumped from the car. Boxer and Willy disappeared from Ted's sight into the woods. He jumped up quickly to catch up with them, hoping to avoid the embarrassment of being caught on his first attempt of hobo'n. When he caught up with them, Boxer and Willy were bent over laughing, but they were glad to see that their young protégé didn't get caught.

"Look at him," Willy said to Boxer.

"He's all banged up," Boxer added with a more sympathetic tone.

"Sit down here on this log, and we'll look ya' over to see how badly you're hurt." Slightly embarrassed, Ted sat down and rolled up his sleeve and pant legs for inspection, hoping he didn't have any bad injuries. They concluded he was just scratched up.

"Your clothes protected your skin, good thing it isn't summertime," Willy told him.

"That was exciting., Ted said with a smirk, not really meaning it, of course.

"Not really, talking about danger, that could have been a disaster, but we got through it this time. You were lucky you didn't break your silly neck. Ya' got a lot to learn, ya' know, young fella. Can't waste any more time, let's get ready to get back on board. It's still stopped, so we got to be ready to make our jump," he announced like the experienced hobo that he was.

They crept closer in to the train so they could get a better view. The train was a long one, *must be eighty cars or more*, Boxer thought.

"Let's get a car closer to the engine this time and stay farther away from the caboose. That's the one, right there. Let's get on the seventh car back, lucky seven you know, the one marked C&O. That's the one, that's our car."

They watched the conductor and brakeman as they finished the inspection of the cars, occasionally looking inside some of the boxcars, and finally, they boarded the caboose and signaled the engineer they were ready to go. The train jerked as it began to crawl very slowly back to the main track.

"Let's go, follow close behind, Ted, and be quick about it and make no mistakes," Boxer whispered as they started their run.

Boxer led the way, then Willy, then Ted close on their heels. He knew he had to do it right or be left in the woods all alone. Boxer slid open the door and jumped on and he quickly gave Willy a hand. They both then reached out to Ted as he made his jump, actually they pulled him inside. Just as he landed the train jerked, throwing him back against the side of the car.

"This is really dangerous, isn't it," Ted said, and they all laughed it off.

Happy to have made their jump, they settled in for the rest of the trip to Pittsburgh. The click- click of the wheels going over the track separations began to lure them back to sleep; they were totally exhausted. Ted drifted in and out of sleep, thinking about his family, thinking about the world around him, and what was ahead of him in his life, wondering if he could avoid all the dangers and pitfalls about him.

They all woke up when they heard the blast of the whistle, and they noticed the train was beginning to slow down. Pittsburgh was just ahead, the big city of steel that Ted had heard about. It must have a big station yard that will be busy and crawling with activities. The train pulled into the yard to a full stop.

"What you guy's goin' to do now?" Ted asked.

"I have a sister here that's goin' to let us stay over a few days," Willy said, "so we have a place to go."

"It's been good to meet ya'," Boxer told Ted.

"Hope ya' get to Oklahoma in one piece," he teased.

"Thanks, thanks for everything you taught me," Ted told them sincerely. He had secretly hoped he could travel with them all the way to Atlanta. He would feel much safer with them.

They watched for the right moment to "throw their feet," the hobo lingo meaning to jump off. This time Ted landed on his feet, and they praised his efforts.

"You're getting it, young fella, you're goin' to be okay," they told him.

"Maybe we'll run into you again someday. We'll leave a message on the towers for you, Farmer Ted, that's going to be your moniker. Watch for it," they called out as they walked away and disappeared in the crowd.

Even with the crowd of people around him, Ted suddenly felt alone in the world, but he knew he had to go on, alone now. He told himself, *Just buck up and do what you have to do*, as he mingled among the crowd.

Chapter 6

GOING UNDERNEATH

Ted walked into the Pittsburgh depot hoping to use the facilities to wash up and clean his scrapes and scratches from his fall the day before. He was amazed how much better he felt when he finished. He went back into the waiting room to look around, and as he strolled by the telegrapher's office, he heard the key clicking away and a message coming in. He listened carefully and caught most of it. "No. 33, arrival time 2:45 p.m." He was proud of himself that he remembered Hank's admonishment, "Keep your ear sharp."

He looked at the train schedules posted on the chalkboard on the wall above the ticket window. It listed the various train numbers, destinations, and time of arrival or the estimated time of departure. The train conductor walked up beside him, glanced through the schedule, and reached in his pocket to check the time on his watch. He turned to a man who was dressed in overalls and an engineer's cap and said, "Well, it looks like we have plenty of time to get a bite to eat across the street at Emmy's Café, are you game?"

"Why not," the engineer answered, and they both walked out of the depot lobby and headed across the street.

Ted decided it must be a good place to eat, so he followed them and waited a few moments until they sat down before he went in. He sat at the opposite end of the counter. He didn't want to be recognized by these guys just in case he ended up on their train.

He looked over the menu and was glad they had everything he liked to eat for breakfast. He was famished; it had been a whole day since he had eaten anything.

"What can I get for you, mister?" the young waitress asked.

"Bacon and eggs, over easy, hash browns, pancakes, and coffee," he quickly replied. He knew exactly what he wanted to eat, just like the farm breakfast his mom used to fix.

In no time at all, the pretty young waitress brought his order along with the steaming coffee. He quickly devoured it, and then ordered a hamburger with all the trimmings to take along with him. He was going to be sure he had something to eat later that day. When he stepped over to pay his bill, he couldn't resist the candy bars he saw on display by the cash register. He picked up one and paid what he owed to the cashier lady.

He crossed the street and went back into the depot waiting room to pick up his bedroll that he had hidden under one of the seats; thank goodness it was still there. When he glanced out of the window, he saw the conductor and engineer leave the café, so he quickly left the depot to walk down to the yard to see what train they were on. It was No. 9 going to Cincinnati, with a few stops in between. *That's perfect*, Ted thought. It's going south toward Atlanta, just the one he needed to board, it would give him plenty of options.

"Beware of the bulls" was always the message in the hobo mind. They sometimes took great glee in knocking hobos around, giving them a hard time, and sometimes arresting them and turning them over to the local police. Ted remembered a story about a really tough one who murdered a hobo without any hesitation, but not every station yard had them, usually just the division points. What he does know right now is that this station has them, and they are thorough in their inspection, and he has to deal with it; he had a crucial decision to make.

After the bulls inspected each car, they placed a seal on the door, and if the seal was broken, it would be a dead giveaway and a guarantee that the hobo would be caught. Ted's heart began to pound as he realized what he had to do. He had to do something that he knew in his mind and body he was not really prepared for. He had to go underneath; it was the only way out of Pittsburgh.

Going underneath was the ultimate ride for the hobo. It meant riding on the undercarriage, the underneath frame of the boxcar. Between the wheels of each car, running from front to back, are three or four steel rods several inches apart which serve as the support for the boxcar, and lie about a foot and one-half above the tracks.

The hobo rides lying down on the rods with his head resting on the axle frame, and his hips resting on a board that the hobo brings with him. Ted knew it would not be a very comfortable ride, but neither was the boxcar.

He left the blind to search for a board to take with him, and found just the right one in a trash barrel behind Emmy's Café. That was really all he needed, now it was all up to him.

He returned to the blind to select the car he would use, and also to build up his courage. He remembered watching a few hobos in Toronto as they hopped underneath onto the frame, and how he thought that they were really crazy. Never in his wildest dreams did he picture himself doing such a stupid thing. He never discussed this with the hobos in Toronto about what they were doing or even with Hank, he just observed and kept it to himself. Why? He wasn't sure.

Ted took out his pocket watch. He always tried to protect it, it was his prized procession, and actually it was his only possession that was worth anything. He had about twenty minutes before No. 9 was scheduled to leave. He chose his car, the rusty red one with peeling paint and marked with two faded letters—RR—on the side. It was the thirteenth one back from the coal car, and far enough away from the caboose that he probably wouldn't be spotted as he ran to catch it.

The only thing he worried about was what he heard from one hobo in Toronto about a few cruel-hearted crewmen who would try to knock an undercarriage rider off with an iron coupling pin. They would tie a rope line to the pin and drop it down to bounce off the railroad ties, and as it bounced back and forth hitting the bottom of the car, it could hit the rider and knock him off the rods, causing instant death if they were struck by the train wheels as they fell. Ted quickly dismissed that possibility from his mind, and focused totally on a safe jump onto the support rods of the undercarriage.

It was time the crew made their final inspection and signaled the engineer. Ted put his bedroll securely on his back, spotted his car, and waited for the train to start. He saw the steam increase and heard the whistle blow; it was almost surreal to him. The train made a few jerks and started crawling through the yard, which was Ted's cue to run; he never took his eyes off his car and ran as hard as he could. He grabbed the lower wrung of the boxcar ladder and swung himself underneath. He placed his bedroll under his head for a head rest and put the board over the rods and underneath his hips. He opened his belt buckle and placed his belt around an upper rod to secure himself. *Not bad*, he thought, but he knew the noise of wheels was going to be a challenge.

The click, click, click, of the wheels actually lulled him into a trance, and he dozed off on occasions, trying desperately to stay awake. He must have traveled about one hundred miles out of Pittsburgh when the train made its first stop. Ted quickly slipped off the rods, he felt exhausted but exhilarated that he had made it without incident. He wasn't sure what town they were in, he would have to go check it out. He hardly saw any crew members, only two who were uncoupling and trading out a boxcar. He faded into the evening darkness and headed toward the lights of the town directly ahead.

Chapter 7

MURDER IN THE CAFE

On the edge of town, Ted came upon a café. The lights were still on, and the door sign read, "Open 6 a.m. till midnight." He looked inside and saw the clock on the wall: it was 11:15, forty-five minutes till closing time, *just enough time to get something to eat*, he thought. Once inside, Ted saw a middle-aged lady behind the counter cleaning up the place, wiping down the countertops and the work area. "Hello ma'am," he greeted her, feeling very friendly and glad to have someone to talk to.

"What can I get you, sonny? The menu is on the wall right above me," she said as she continued cleaning. He glanced at it for a moment and ordered a cup of coffee and a hamburger.

"With or without fries?" she asked.

"Yes, please, with fries. Can I use your washroom to wash up before I eat?" he asked.

"Sure go ahead, it's out back, but don't take too long. I'm supposed to close up promptly at midnight, the town marshal checks up on me. He don't like it when I'm late, it means he don't get off on time." She laughed, but meant every word of it; she wanted to get off on time too.

"Yes, ma'am," Ted assured her. "I usually meet him halfway. He walks two blocks from the marshal's office to check on me."

She turned to fix his hamburger and fries, and Ted hurriedly went out back. He filled the old, stained sink with water from the hand pump and washed his face and hands. He had to scrub hard to get the coal soot off, it was difficult to clean with cold water and no soap. He was drying his hands when he heard a woman's loud scream followed by a gunshot. It scared him so much he froze and could hardly move. He heard the door slam and people running away; he knew it was more than one person because of the sound of feet hitting the ground. He didn't want to be seen so he waited a moment and then peeked around the corner. In the darkness he saw the outline of two men rushing down the dirt road like they were anxious to get away from something. He faintly heard one say, "Come on, we gotta get out of here."

He stepped inside the café and was stunned by what he saw. At the far end of the counter, the nice lady waitress that had waited on him was lying lifeless in a pool of her own blood. The drawer of the cash register was wide open and totally empty. Ted readily knew that those two men he saw were the killers. It was very quiet, no one else was around, and she had been all alone in the café. He reluctantly went over to her and kneeled down to feel her pulse, that's what his momma always did when he was sick or hurt. He couldn't find a pulse, so he thought she must be dead, she wasn't breathing either. He listened for a heartbeat and there was none.

He stepped carefully around her and the pool of blood, but his shoe caught the edge of the blood and it left marks on the floor as he backed away from her in horror. *This is so eerie and unreal*, he thought, *what should he do?* Scenarios of possibilities rushed through his head. He was a stranger in town, and the police would naturally think it was him, they would use the shoe prints in the blood to prove it. He quickly figured out he had to get out of there, and quickly, just like he saw the real killers running away.

He heard the whistle of the train as he rushed out of the door, and he hit the road running toward the train yard as fast as his feet could carry him. When he reached the train yard, he saw the train crew moving the freight cars off the side track to make up the train for the next phase of the trip; they were almost finished. He stood in the background in the darkness so he wouldn't be seen, and he realized he was trembling, his whole body was shaking. He was so scared he couldn't control himself. That was the most frightening thing that he had ever gone through. It didn't even seem real to him, he hoped he would wake up and it was all just a dream.

His thoughts were going wild, and his mind was uncontrollable. He started going through the whole telegraph manual, all the things he had learned and studied about trains and telegraphy were running through his head. He started quoting out loud all the rules from the rule book that he would need to know to pass the exam for a job.

"What is the definition of a train?" he muttered out loud.

"The train is a unit of one or more units, displaying markers for which markers are displayed."

He kept repeating those words over and over again as fast as he could. Where did all that come from, he really felt out of control. Finally, his eyes welled up with tears, and he broke down and sobbed. He noticed his body was relaxing, and he stopped trembling so much. He was thinking more clearly now, and he felt like he was getting himself back in control. He was also feeling remorseful for not facing up to the event like a man and a good citizen should have, like his parents had taught him. But he knew he couldn't trust the situation and the town people enough; he didn't even know them or what town he was in. He was terrified with fear, mainly the fear from the unknown.

Although he wasn't happy with himself that he didn't respect the dead woman enough to go get the town marshal and report the crime, he was consoled by the fact that he did not commit the crime or could have prevented it. He thought about Boxer John and how he spent time in jail because of an accident. He could have ended up in jail like Boxer, for someone else's crime.

The freight train was ready to move out. Ted tried to focus his mind on getting back on the train and out of town. He looked around to see if there were any more hobos coming out of the darkness to catch the train, that wouldn't be unusual, however, but this time there were none. That was probably a good thing, it was good not to be recognized or seen by anyone. He chose a car in the middle of the train, slid open the door, and climbed aboard. He went to the far end into a corner of the car, hoping not to be seen by anyone who might be making a last minute boxcar check. The one thought he harbored in his mind was that the side door would suddenly open up, and it would be the town marshal looking for the killer. He was actually more fearful of that than he was of being caught by the train crew.

Then the train jerked which brought Ted out of his deep thought. It was the train crew making a last minute switch of a car. He was so nervous, he began to realize how guilty he felt about not helping the police find the killers of the nice lady, and besides that, he had never seen a dead person before or experienced such a traumatic event ever in his life. Suddenly, the sliding door of the boxcar opened, it felt like his heart stopped beating and he couldn't breathe. The brakeman stuck his head in and shone his lantern down toward the end of the car. Ted felt sick, he took his bandanna and stuck it in his mouth to silence any gasps or utterances that might come out automatically. He lay flat against the far end of the car, and thankfully the light from the lantern missed him, the brakeman didn't see him. The door closed and Ted breathed a sigh of relief.

Finally, the train whistle blew, and it moved slowly on to the main track. The train picked up speed, and Ted began to relax again. The click, click, click of the train began its rhythm, which Ted had become so accustomed to, it seemed to give him a sense of security, especially tonight, it meant that everything was hopefully moving along smoothly.

He was exhausted, and he felt his body relax even more as he lay down to rest. His body became in tune with the rhythm and the movements of the train, and the usual sounds gave him a feeling of belonging. The train had become his friend, maybe his only friend he had right now; but at this moment he felt secure and that everything would be all right. As he listened to the rhythm, he surrendered his mind and body over to a peaceful sleep.

Chapter 8

THE HOBO JUNGLE

As the train moved farther south, Ted started to feel a little safer as he distanced himself from that nightmare town. He wasn't even sure of its name, it may have been Brighton, and he remembered catching a quick glimpse of a sign as the train passed the depot. His night's rest was frequently interrupted by the haunting wail of the train's whistle as it blew at every crossing they passed. That was usual for every ride, but on this night he found it even more haunting, probably intensified by the event that occurred the night before that left him totally traumatized. He almost felt like the train was expressing its remorse and fear along with him. But it was morning now, and Ted tried desperately to put everything in perspective.

The biggest worry he had on his mind was that the marshal of Brighton would put out an all-points bulletin, and all trains would be checked up and down the line. He reasoned with himself, however, that if that was going to happen, they probably would have already done it.

He began to concentrate on having much better days ahead. The day seemed to pass by quickly, *must be afternoon by now*, he thought. He was beginning to feel hungry and he remembered the hamburger and fries he didn't get to eat the night before. But he quickly wiped that out of his mind. It made him feel guilty all over again and reminded him of that awful event. Feeling hungry was very usual for Ted, so he felt comforted by the fact that he must be returning to normal.

He opened the boxcar door wide enough to look out and saw what looked like the outskirts of a town off in the distance. It would be sundown soon, and he thought they must have traveled at least eighty to a hundred miles since he boarded the train at Brighton. The train began to slow down. He must have been right, they were coming into a town. He decided to "throw his feet" and walk the distance into town, rather than being spotted as a hobo getting off at the train yard.

He prepared to make his jump and gathered up his bedroll. Actually, he was looking forward to walking; he wanted to walk out the kinks and cramps in his leg muscles, and look for a place to eat. *No, I mustn't think of the other café and what happened*, went through his mind. He spotted a grassy knoll just ahead that looked like a soft place to land. He made his leap, rolled down a small hill, turned a somersault, and got back up on his feet. He was amazed to see that he was standing directly on the grassy knoll that he had seen, and he told himself, *I'm getting pretty good at this*, and smiled. He had misjudged how far they were from town. He was probably about four miles out but it was okay, he needed the exercise. He crossed over the track to an adjacent dirt road to walk and spotted a small lake with a heavily wooded area behind it. It looked so restful and peaceful that he decided to stop to wash up to get all the coal dust off. It was in his hair, and actually he felt like it was in every cavity of his body; he even felt like he could taste it. He wondered how long it had been since he had taken a real bath, but couldn't even remember—it had been so long.

He looked all around him. It was so quiet he didn't see anyone or anything along the side of the road. He wondered just how far south he was, hoping there were no gators around. But he was willing to chance it and slipped off all his clothes and walked carefully to the edge of the water to avoid the sharp rocks and sticks. He paused for just a moment to listen, he had read somewhere that gators lie on the bank and slide into the water to seek their prey. He didn't hear anything, just an occasional croaking frog was all, and he saw a small fish jump out of the water which made ringlets and ripples as it fell back in.

He ventured into the lake. It felt so good—the water was cold, but very invigorating. He looked up at the sky, the beautiful sky at evening time as he bathed his whole body, scrubbing off all the coal dust to get clean. By the time he had finished his bath, the moon had come up and cast a beautiful pathway across the water. He laid on his back and watched the beauty of the moonlight ripple across the lake and suddenly felt at peace. This was just what he needed so he could forget the recklessness of life that some people perpetrate on others. He felt free, free to be spontaneous, knowing there would be a myriad of incidences along the way. Every day is like living a different story, and some of them may not be very good, he decided. But at this moment he felt close to heaven's beauty.

It was time to get back on the road, and he was really feeling hungry. He stood up to get out of the water and felt really refreshed, and even spiritually cleansed. He spotted a deer on the opposite bank standing in the ripple of the moonlight, drinking from the lake. What a beautiful sight! The deer lifted her head and looked across the lake for a few seconds, then turned and bounded away. That picture would stay in Ted's mind a long time, he knew that for certain.

The stopover had been the best decision he had made in a long time, he decided. He got dressed and gathered up all his things, and as he turned to walk back to the road, he stumbled and fell into a briar patch. He jumped up, feeling all the sharp needles that stuck in his hands. This little mishap quickly brought him out of his tranquility and back to reality. He laughed at himself as he picked the stickers out of his hands. This is just one of those incidents of everyday life that he was thinking about earlier in the day.

Ted knew he was getting closer to town, maybe about a mile and a half away, judging by the lights. He came upon a wooded area on the left side of the road and thought he heard the sound of voices. He crouched down and proceeded cautiously to have a look, and he heard the voices again. Through the trees he saw three men sitting around a camp fire, relaxing and talking, and he could smell the aroma of coffee from the gallon tin can that was sitting in the hot embers on the fire.

He knew at once he had found a hobo camp. He had learned about them from other hobos. He heard the men laugh and their voices got louder as they watched their fellow hobo bring two chickens into camp. The chickens were trying desperately to escape his clutches, squawking and flapping, but the hobo held fast. He suddenly put one on the ground, stepped on its head and pulled until the head came completely off. He threw it on the ground and it started to flop around, then he proceeded to do the same with the second one. They all watched the chickens flip and flop around on the ground until they bled out, each man thinking how good they were going to taste.

Ted watched this whole scene and hoped they would allow him to be a part of their upcoming feast; he felt so hungry. He saw them pick the chickens up and dip them into a tub of boiling water they had on the fire. They all jumped in to help pluck off the feathers to prepare them for roasting, Ted's mouth was watering already just imagining how good they would taste. He finally felt brave enough to make his presence known to them. He yelled out.

"Permission to enter camp," he said in a friendly tone.

"Permission granted," was the response.

Ted walked into camp, the men stood up in a cautious manner to greet him, all except the one that was gutting and preparing the chickens. Ted broke the silence and asked.

"Can you spare anything for me to eat, I'm awful hungry?"

"Got any money?" one of the hobos asked him.

"Well, I have some change," Ted replied.

"If you want to share our chicken dinner, ya gotta pay up."

"Okay," then Ted handed the man the thirty-three cents he had in his pocket.

"Is that's all ya' got?"

Ted nodded his head, yes.

"Okay, my friend, you're in," the hobo told him.

Ted actually had several dollars in his shoes that he failed to mention to them; he kept them strictly for emergencies. He was told by other hobos that if you have at least three dollars on you, most police wouldn't arrest you for vagrancy because that would pay for a night's lodging.

"Welcome to camp, young fella,' my name is Joe," said the friendliest one who stepped over to shake his hand.

"We're gonna' have roast chicken in about an hour or so, hope you can wait that long."

"I sure can," Ted wasn't about to leave until he got his thirty three cents worth at least.

"You have any makins'?" one of the hobos asked Ted.

"Sure do," as he pulled a sack of Bull Durham and papers out of his pocket and handed them over to him. The man only had one arm, and Ted watched with amazement as he rolled his cigarette with one hand.

"I could never do that," Ted told him.

"Necessity is the mother of invention, my young friend," he laughed as he passed the sack and papers on to the other guys. Ted sat back and rolled one for himself. He usually didn't smoke much but decided to join them to feel a part of the crowd. He stuck a small stick into the fire and lit up his smoke.

They all shared the roasted chicken from the spit, and needless to say, it was delicious. Joe took a small salt shaker out of his pocket and salted his chicken as he ate, and offered it to the others. Ted was surprised that a hobo would carry a salt shaker around in his pocket; he really must like his food well seasoned. They also had a loaf of bread, and he wondered who they had *borrowed* it from. When they finished eating and picking the bones clean, Joe got up from the camp fire to brew a fresh can of coffee. Then he walked over to the brook and pulled out a watermelon that he had cooled.

"Surprise, surprise," he yelled, and Ted was truly surprised, where in the world did he get that, he thought, it had to be an eight-pound one at least.

They all ate like they were at a gourmet restaurant in the big city. Ted felt like he had really lucked out on this night.

Joe began to tell them in a rather boastful tone, "We generally have hobo stew in camp, but tonight we are lucky, and we even have a guest who has joined us. Would you believe we *found* these two lost chickens and a watermelon, and we eat like kings tonight. The gods are looking down on us."

They sat around the campfire relaxing and having coffee when the older hobo pulled a harmonica out of his overall pocket and began to play some of the well-known old tunes that they had all heard before. Ted was so glad for the company, he couldn't help thinking about how much more pleasant this night was, rather than the horrible night he had spent before. Between the tunes, they all told their favorite "tall tales" and their favorite jokes to each other.

"Where are we?" Ted asked them.

"Where you headed, young fella?" one said.

"I am headed south, and then to Oklahoma," Ted informed them.

"Son, you're in Pennsylvania now."

"I thought I was much farther south than that. I'm going home to see my folks and to help my dad with the spring planting," Ted told them.

"Never been to Oklahoma before," one hobo said.

"I'm headed for Florida."

"How far does this line go?" Ted inquired, thinking they really must be experienced travelers.

"If I was you, young fella, I would travel as far south as this line goes, actually it goes to Atlanta, and then find a line that goes west. Are you gonna ride the rails all the way home?" Joe asked Ted.

"Yep, don't have any money to do it any other way. Sure do appreciate you feeding me. I was near starving, didn't get to eat at all yesterday," Ted said to them.

"We don't always know where we're going or where we're headed," Joe said wearily.

"We're all on our way to some place, or somewhere. We just don't know where that somewhere is. Wish it wasn't so, but the truth is the open road is our home right now."

"This is my first time in a hobo camp," Ted said appreciatively. "You've been very good to me."

"We all knew you were a tenderfoot, you didn't have to tell us. We had you pegged right from the start," Joe said.

"But we're out of here tomorrow."

They settled in for the night, Ted's first night to sleep in a hobo jungle. He was tired, very tired. He settled in around the camp fire to watch a few sparks fly in the air and listen to the crackling fire, the very last thing he heard before he went sound asleep.

Chapter 9

THE FAMILY

Morning came and Ted helped his new found friends clean up the camp. He couldn't help but think how short the bond of friendships is between hobos, and how they are able to trust and rely on each other for such a short time. He was truly grateful for the time he had spent with these guys, realizing short-lived friendships were better than none at all. This is the life that surrounds the hobo, he reasoned.

They headed for the railroad yard to catch the next freight south. They bade each other farewell, and Ted thanked them profusely as they departed to make their plans. He decided to catch the B&O line heading south. He crawled upon the roof of the boxcar, opened the trap door, and looked down into the interior. *It was quiet and empty*, he thought, but it was dark inside and he couldn't tell for sure.

From the top of the car he looked around and saw a bunch of hobos running toward the cars scrambling to get aboard. He knew he would have lots of company today. He crawled through the trap door and dropped into the car, thinking he was all alone. He heard a short gasp and a voice out of the darkness.

"Mommy, Mommy, who is that man?"

"Shush, son," she said.

"It'll be all right. Mommy is here with you." The child's voice really startled Ted; he felt like he was invading someone's home.

"Oh, excuse me, ma'am. I didn't know you were here, I didn't mean to frighten you. I can go get into another car. I'm so sorry I frightened you and the children," he said apologetically.

"Ah, such drivel, young man," she replied. "No need for you to leave, there's plenty of room down at the other end. Please stay. It will give us company and comfort knowing you're here. You look like an honest good man, we're stronger in numbers, you know. You're welcome to stay."

"Thank you, ma'am," he told her. "I'll try not to be any trouble to you."

"My husband, Donald, is sound asleep and so are the kids. My little son, Howard, is the only one who can't get to sleep. I think he's cutting teeth. My name is Eva, what's yours?" she asked.

"My name is Ted, and I'm traveling south to Atlanta, and then on to Oklahoma where my family lives. Where are you going?" he inquired, wondering why this family was so desperate they had to travel the rails.

"We're trying to get to South Carolina, back home to my mother's place. My husband is sick with lung disease. The company doctor told him he has the miner's disease. It's called black lung, and he can't work anymore."

She continued her story for Ted. "We were living in a small coal mining town near Pittsburgh. Daddy got sick and couldn't work, and now we have no money. So we have to go back and live with my mother in the Appalachian mountains of South Carolina. I'm so sorry, young man, to burden you with our problems."

"It's no burden, ma'am. I'm sorry you're having such a difficult time," Ted said sympathetically. It reminded him of his sister Edith, who had to come home to live with his parents when her husband died.

"How long have you been on the road, ma'am?"

"Only since yesterday. This is all new for us, but it's the only way we can go home," she said tearfully.

"We had an old car, but it broke down and we couldn't afford to fix it. So we sold it and got a little money to travel on. Sure hope it lasts until we get there, the kids have got to eat."

"How many kids do you have, ma'am?" He couldn't quite see how many there were because of the dim light.

"We have six, there are eight of us all together," she said.

"When did you eat last?" Ted inquired.

"Yesterday at dinner. I fixed a plate of beans for each of us before we left. We had some bread and shared a couple of apples too, but the kids don't eat beans very much."

"Ma'am, I sure hope you can make it to South Carolina soon, it's going to be tough going for the next few days," Ted sympathized with her.

"Don't I know it, but we have to get back home to my mom. We have no other place to go. Besides that, we are used to a tough life. We've never known any other way," she told Ted, with great weariness in her voice.

"I'll camp out at the other end of the car. If I can help with the kids just let me know," Ted offered.

He threw his bedroll down on a bunch of old newspapers, and found himself feeling very sad, not so much for himself but for this nice lady and her little family. Why do people have to suffer so much? Why are they in such a predicament? He was so much better off than they were, all those kids to care for and a sick husband. Ted's mind was swirling with so many questions and dilemmas. Why do people have to suffer so?

He sat in the corner of the car thinking of this poor lady. She was skinny as a bed rail; they probably don't have enough food to eat. She was trying to hold this family together with a sick husband. She can't be much older than forty, but she has graying hair already, and her dress is so faded and ragged.

He knew there wasn't much he could do at the moment, but couldn't get his mind around why everything was so depressed, so many people virtually in the same condition. It was just bad times for everyone. Night came and they settled in, hoping to get a good night's rest. They heard the usual wailing sound of the whistle when they went through the crossings, and the click, click, of the wheels which finally lulled them all to sleep.

Ted was suddenly awakened when he heard a struggle at the other end of the car.

"Please, oh, God, don't," Eva was yelling.

"Stop, stop, leave him alone! Stop, stop, and please don't hurt him! I beg you, don't hurt him. He's a very sick man!"

Ted sat straight up. It was dark, and he could vaguely see the silhouette of two men, one bending down over Donald and the other standing over the family. He noticed the trap door was open on the roof of the car, and he knew at once they had been invaded by these men. They were up to no good, probably trying to steal anything they could find.

The children began to cry.

"Leave my daddy alone."

That brought Ted quickly to his feet. The bums began to yank and throw Donald around as he held on to his billfold for dear life. The bum began hitting him, swinging back and forth.

"Let go, you old fool, or I'll beat you to death."

Ted sprang into action. He took an old packing board he found on the floor and crept up behind the bums and hit the one as hard as he could across the back of the head, knocking him down to the floor. Then he hit the other bum across the arm, and he fell to his knees crying.

"You broke my arm, don't hit me anymore, you hurt me bad."

Ted stood tall and strong over the two bums, and Eva was stunned by his strength, but she was so grateful for his presence. He told her to slide open the boxcar door as he grabbed the first bum by the shirt, pulled him up and yelled, "Get up, you bum, I'm going to throw you off this car."

The bum staggered around, still dazed with blood dripping down his face and neck. Ted checked his pockets and pulled out a dollar and a few coins, and handed it to Eva. He reached up and grabbed the bum's shirt collar and literally pushed him out the open door. He flew out head first, and with his arms flailing he flew through the air just as the train let out a wailing sound of the whistle.

Ted quickly turned to the other bum and grabbed him by the arm, he was so angry at them by now that his instinct was to hurt them even more. He knew he had to protect this little family. He patted him down but didn't find any money on him.

"You are the lowest specimen of a human being that I have ever dealt with, deliberately trying to hurt a sick man and a woman with children. You are going to jump out of this train or I'll help you out, which I will gladly do if I have to."

Ted's six foot frame towered over him—he was at least a head taller which totally intimidated the bum. He melted into a defeated old man muttering to himself.

"I will jump, just to get away from you." He was resigned to his fate and disappeared in the darkness of the night, as he jumped out to join his partner.

"Good riddance," Ted said as he turned to Eva.

"Are you all right, ma'am?"

She rushed over to her husband to comfort him, and the kids all rushed to hug their mother and daddy. Eva began to sob uncontrollably; it was like the tension suddenly burst through and she let it all out. Donald held her close, and Ted spread his arms around them both to comfort them. He knew all the problems in their lives had finally caught up with them.

Donald, who was very weak from the struggle, hugged his kids and could no longer hold back his emotions.

"Thank you, young man. I don't know what we would have done without you. I only have seven dollars in my billfold, but it's all we have and I had to hold on to it."

Eva held his head, wiped off his face and told him.

"You're still quite a man and you fought hard for us."

The baby started crying and she got up to attend to him. When she returned with the baby in her arms, she had totally regained her composure as mothers do when their children need them. It was a complete shift from the emotional upheaval from a few moments ago. It reminded Ted of his own mother.

"We are forever grateful to you, Ted. Don't know what we would have done without you. I guess there was a reason we asked you to stay, you became our protector. Perhaps God sent you for a special reason, I think so," she said.

"Well, ma'am, those men won't be bothering you anymore. You're a real fighter and one tough lady. I am so sorry that the times are so bad for you, glad I could help you," Ted told her, not wanting to sound too much like the hero she was making him out to be.

"Do you mind if we say a prayer together before we settle back into the night? I feel awful thankful and grateful to God right now. We are safe and I want to thank our Lord," Eva said, with her head already bowed in submission to the Creator.

"Don't mind at all, ma'am. In fact I would like that a lot," he said in a very humbling voice.

Ted bowed his head and listened to this little family pray together; he was also thankful he was able to help. His heart was heavy for them. When they finished, he added "Amen" also, just as his mother had taught him to do when a prayer was finished. He told her how beautiful the prayer was and turned to go to the end of the boxcar. He whispered goodnight, and he hoped everybody could go back to sleep.

The kids settled back to rest as the little family huddled together for the remainder of the night. Ted struggled to go back to sleep; he knew it would soon be morning, but he was exhausted and it wasn't very long before he fell back to sleep.

Daybreak came and the train began to slow down. Ted opened his eyes and saw the light of day come peeking through the cracks of the car. He slid the door open to see if they were coming into a town. Eva was also awake and came to look out the door.

"Looks like we'll get off here," she said.

"Yes, this looks like a changeover station, and they'll be checking all the boxcars," he told her.

"I'll get Donald and the kids ready to get off. We will need to look for some family assistance before we move on," she said with a hopeful tone in her voice.

The train came to a stop in the yard.

"I'll help you and the kids get off, but first let me check around to see if it's safe. I'll check to see if there are any railroad bulls out there that might give us trouble," Ted instructed.

"I'll get our things all together," she said.

"Thank you so much. Don't know what we would do without you."

"Here, I want you to have this," Ted said as he handed her some money he had taken out of his shoe. "It isn't much but it will help buy food for the kids."

The tears flowed down her cheeks as she managed to whisper, "Thank you. God truly sent you to us!"

It was quiet in the yard except for the changing of the boxcars. After he looked around outside, he returned to help her with each child as she lifted them out of the door one by one. She threw out all of their belongings and Ted lined the children up beside the tracks along with their baggage. She jumped and Ted caught her just in time to prevent a fall. *She is really weak*, he thought.

They both helped Donald as he slid out of the car and lifted him to the ground. They hugged each other tightly, and Ted knew that this was one more bond of friendship that he would have to walk away from.

He told them, "They usually have a soup kitchen in a town of this size. So let's go find it, and then I'll be on my way." He helped them carry the kids into town.

Chapter 10

THE PANHANDLER

There were usually other hobos around town, but in this particular southern town it was peculiarly quiet; there were none in sight. Ted had already searched outside of town for a camp, but didn't find one. *Maybe that was a sign*, he thought to himself. Perhaps this town is not hobo-friendly and the experienced hobos avoid it. He walked around to check out the people and the businesses to see if Southerners lived up to what they are best known for, their southern hospitality. He had rehearsed over and over again what he would say if he ever had to resort to panhandling: *'Hello sir, my name is Ted. Do you have some work for me to do so I can earn a meal? I'm very hungry.'* He knew that would work on his mom. In fact, at their farm home in Oklahoma, it did happen.

As a small kid, he remembered hobos coming to their back door requesting for work and food. His mom never turned them down. She believed in what the Bible taught, "feed those who hunger and give water to those who thirst." They would sit in the backyard and eat their meal they had earned before returning to the nearby tracks that ran through their farmland. The people in town seemed friendly enough as he walked through, so he was ready to try his luck. As he went door to door, he began to see the different reactions of people, and also their hearts. He tried to put himself in their place. They probably saw people like him every day needing a handout. Times were tough everywhere; the depression was affecting the entire country. They were probably scraping together just enough for themselves to get by. He was seeing the best in people, and also the worst.

Each stop was a great challenge and very different. When he approached a door and knocked, he was greeted in many different and diverse ways. Some would have a look of disdain on their face and slam the door. "Beat it, kid, we've got our own problems," and often hearing swear words he had never heard before. He would see looks of fear and suspicion, anger, and on rare occasions a smile of sympathy and a small hand out. "I'm sorry that's all I have,'" they would say. Ted began to see the depth of human sufferings and the behaviors that occur when a country lives under such difficult times.

The task of getting something to eat was proving to be very tough in this town. Finally, when he was about ready to give up, he knocked on one more door. A very nice gentleman and his wife answered, and Ted recited his carefully rehearsed speech, using a very sympathetic tone in his voice.

The man smiled and said, "I sure would like to have some wood split and stacked up in the wood box at my back door. I'm getting to old to do that anymore. While you're working, we will be glad to fix you a meal and share our food with you."

Ted was stunned for a minute. Did he really hear what he thought he heard? He gladly accepted and worked for about two hours, filling the wood box until it overflowed. When he finished, he knocked on the door and the old gentleman answered quickly,

"I watched you from my window and you did a very good job, young man. Thank you so much, your supper is ready."

Ted was amazed how nice these old people were. They were like grandparents in fact, and Ted thought they probably were. He ate heartily; three pieces of fried chicken, a slice of homebaked bread, fried potatoes, beans, two apples (one to eat now and the other to take with him), and for dessert, a slice of cake and a cup of coffee. As he ate his supper, he began to recall the stories the hobos told him while he was still in Toronto, never realizing at the time that he would have similar tales to tell others someday.

One story he vividly remembered was told by a hobo who called himself Chicago Johnny. He and a friend had some buckshot "thrown" at them, peppering their backsides. They were visiting a nearby farm to "borrow" a couple of chickens to take to camp. As they were leaving, the irate farmer became indignant and began peppering them with buckshot. However, they got away and delivered the goods to the hobo camp. They ate heartily, but the rest of the evening wasn't as pleasant. They spent the rest of the evening picking the buckshot from each other's backside.

Ted remembered asking him. "Was the chicken you borrowed worth it?" The hobo chuckled as he finished his story. The good news was, they all got to eat, and the wounds weren't fatal.

While he enjoyed his slice of cake and cup of coffee, he remembered another story a hobo once told him, which still amuses him to this day. He entered a restaurant and offered to work for food, and the man behind the counter told him to wait a moment. When he returned from the back, he handed him a large box and told him, with a sneer in his voice, "Now, get off my property and never come back, or I'll call the police."

Expecting a sandwich with lots of extras, he took his box to a quiet place to sit down and eat. But when he opened it, much to his surprise, the box contained thirty colorfully decorated cupcakes. He didn't know what to think, and tears began to well up in his eyes, who and where did this guy think he was, in the French Revolution? Who would give a hungry man just cupcakes to eat? He ate three or four of them, but had no one else to share them with. So he left the box on the ground for the birds to feed on. He left feeling both angry and grateful at the same time. From then on he was known to all his friends as Cupcake Charlie. The hobos loved to hear his story, it made everyone laugh. And now after all this time he was able to laugh with them.

Ted enjoyed his supper and his time to relax and reminisce so much that he didn't want to leave. He thanked the nice old couple for their hospitality, using every word of praise he could think of, and even asked them if he could help with any other chores. They graciously sent him on his way, wishing him well. And as grandmothers do, she slipped an extra piece of chicken into his hand.

"Go home to your mama and daddy," she advised him with a very nurturing tone in her voice.

"Thank you, ma'am, I will," he said as his eyes began to fill with tears.

Thinking about his own mother and grandmother, he turned to walk away, but took one last look back. They were still standing there waving their arms good-bye to him. He smiled and returned the wave before he picked up his pace to return to the real world that he had made for himself.

He knew it was best not to linger in any town very long, according to the stories other hobos told. Word soon gets around that a stranger is in town. If the townspeople are stirred up enough or feel threatened, they report it to the police.

And of course, they respond without hesitation by making an arrest and holding "the big lawbreaker' for thirty days in the town jail, courtesy of the city. Little do the police know that some hobos, who generally have no particular place to go at the time, really don't mind going to jail. In fact, it could be a real treat. It means they have thirty days with a roof over their head, a place to sleep and three meals a day. They always treated their "host" with respect so they wouldn't get thrown out early. They wanted their full thirty days of reward. However, Ted didn't feel that way. He was always ready to move on, looking for the next adventure. Only the hardcore hobo's had that attitude.

Actually, most town authorities considered hobos bums, but the hobos took great exception to that idea. They did not think of themselves as bums in anyway shape or fashion. In fact, they considered the comparison an insult. Ted remembered the passionate response from one of the hobos he had befriended in Toronto when he asked him what the difference was between a hobo and a bum. Just asking the question raised his "hackles," and he answered with a little anger in his voice. "When times are bad and man finds himself in circumstances usually not of his own making, he becomes a traveling worker only wanting to earn his way in life. He is willing to work for anything he gets. He is not a freeloader or a panhandler. He is just asking for work.

"On the other hand, a bum is a lazy man who will not work for his food and is willing to steal if necessary, without any guilt or regard for the other person. They, in fact, panhandle for a living, and ultimately become a person feared by society. Unfortunately, hobos and bums are seen by most people as the same, but their attitudes are very different."

Ted could readily see the difference, recalling the experience with the two bums who tried to steal from the little family he rode with. They had no regard for those little children and the lady. They would have hurt them if they had to, and he knew that for sure; he saw them in action.

Actually, Ted liked riding the rails. He liked the massive power of the big iron engine that a mere man could manage by just a touch of his hand, yet it remained the iron master. He didn't really consider himself a hobo. To him, it was an adventure, a lifestyle he was living until he got home. He wasn't homeless; he had a loving family to go to who would welcome him with open arms. No, he wasn't a hobo at heart. He was just learning the ways of the world.

It was the strong bond of friendships and camaraderie between hobos that fascinated Ted most of all. They were family and community to each other, even though they rarely saw one another again after sharing a small segment of their life together. It is the sharing of information and the support of each other that get them through. It even means their survival at times.

In the well-established hobo camps, they even had a big metal washtub so they could heat water over the campfire to wash their clothes. Nothing felt better than clean clothes to wear as they continued their journey. It brought to Ted's mind what his mom told him as he was growing up, "Cleanliness is next to Godliness," which always translated to, "Go put on clean clothes and change your underwear."

One touching story that a hobo told Ted, as they rode along the rails one night, illustrates the spirit and the bond of friendship they have in their hearts for each other. One of their comrades became very sick with a high fever, as he expressed it, "He was bad sick." They knew they could not leave him alone. He was delirious, "out of his head" as he called it, and he was "hot as a firecracker." They took turns sitting up with him all night, keeping the fire going and putting water on his tongue.

After two days, he had recovered enough to move on. They all left the camp together to go to the train yard to make sure he got in the boxcar safely, and one hobo even volunteered to ride with him. They bade him good-bye, shook his hand and wished him well. *Just like family indeed,* Ted thought.

Ted arrived at the rail yard just as evening was setting in. He found a blind where he could wait until it was time to board. It had been a good day. He was thinking how amazing the mind really is, the ability to recall the memories of the wonderful old couple that was so good to him, and he hardly thought about the people who rejected him. The mind seems to weed out the unpleasant thoughts.

He was soon aboard the boxcar headed south. He spread out his bedroll and settled in, and as the train picked up speed, he felt at ease with the familiar click click of the wheels. Just for a moment, he felt like he really was a hobo, but no, he was just a traveler finding his way home.

Chapter 11

FROM SAINTS TO DEMONS

The train pulled into a siding in the quiet little southern town of Pickle. *Strange name*, Ted thought, as he decided to "throw his feet" and check it out. Maybe they were famous for making pickles, who knows, but it reminded him of food and he was getting hungry again.

After he was rejected at several houses, he walked into the backyard of a neighboring house and knocked on the door. It was a little white cottage, neat as a pin, and it looked like a picture postcard. He waited a minute, and when no one answered he knocked again. He was about to walk away, thinking no one was at home, when the door opened and an elderly lady who was carrying a Bible, said apologetically.

"I'm so sorry it took me so long to answer. I was reading and I must have dozed off for a time. How may I help you, young man?"

"So sorry to disturb you, ma'am. I would like to do some work for food if you have something for me to do. It's been a while since I ate," he made his plea.

"Yes, my yard needs to be raked, and when you finish you can gather up all the rakings and put them in the trash and put it out by the alley for pickup. That would help me so much, and while you're doing your work I'll fix you a nice supper. Would that be all right?" she asked.

"Oh, yes ma'am, it sure would."

When he finished his work and after he found a couple more odd jobs he could do for her, she served him on a picnic table in the backyard. She fixed a pork steak, beans with ham, potato salad, corn bread, and a big piece of coconut pie for dessert. He enjoyed it so much he thought he must be close to heaven and she must be a saint.

She sat down on the outdoor swing and talked to him while he ate. She was so nice. *Guess she just liked to fuss over people*, he was thinking to himself. She definitely liked to visit, and talk she did. She told him all about her late husband, who died three years ago, and how she lost her oldest son in an accident. She also had two other children that died during a bad flu epidemic. Her husband was a farmer, and they had been married for sixty-three years.

Ted was fascinated with her story and listened intently. She has had such a sad life, but she seems so happy and at peace with herself, she really must be a saint. She turned her attention to him.

"Where are you from, young man, and tell me your name, you can call me Mrs. Jewell."

"My name is Ted and I'm from Oklahoma. My father is a farmer, and I'm on my way home to help him in the fields. I've been up north going to railroad telegraph operator's school, so when I'm old enough I can get a job with the railroad."

"Just how old are you, Ted? You look so young," she said.

"I'm sixteen, and I've been gone from home just over a year. With times so bad, I have no money to get back home, so I'm riding the rails and sometimes I get help from nice people like you, Mrs. Jewell. The food is delicious, thank you so much, you are so kind," he told her with great sincerity in his voice.

Then Mrs. Jewell took him by surprise by asking him.

"Do you know God?"

"Uh, oh, yes ma'am, my mother taught me about God."

"I hope you walk with God wherever you go, Ted, and study His word. Do you have a Bible?"

"Yes, ma'am," he could barely utter the words, knowing he didn't give much credit to God in his life.

That night she allowed him to sleep in the barn, even gave him a blanket and pillow to make him comfortable. The next morning she fed him a nice breakfast, packed him a lunch to take with him, and even slipped a half-dollar into his hand before he left.

She stood out by the white picket fence waving good-bye as he walked away. He suddenly felt like one of her children who she was sending off to school, and he could hardly contain his emotion. He was overwhelmed by her kindness. He knew he had just met a wonderful Christian woman, who loved people and lived what she believed in. He felt like he had been in the presence of God and was truly blessed.

When he reached the end of the driveway he didn't stop to put a mark on the gate post, as hobos usually do, to leave a sign that this place was friendly toward them. He didn't want to take the chance that someone might take advantage of her generosity and harm her. He knew in his heart that was the right thing to do, and he wanted to protect her.

When he arrived at the yard, the freight going south was ready to leave. He waited before the train started to move before he jumped aboard. He knew the procedure well, when the train moves out, the conductor and brakeman were already in the "shack," the term hobos called the caboose.

He took off running and jumped aboard, and as the train picked up speed, he dangled his legs out of the car to watch as the train left town. When he moved back into the car, he was surprised to see he was not alone. He counted five men who were not saying a word, but he didn't see the man lying on the floor in the corner. This may not be good, Ted was thinking. One finally spoke up.

"Welcome aboard, how are things with you?"

"Good," Ted replied.

"Where you headed? We're all headed south, nowhere in particular, just lookin' for work."

"I'm headed to Oklahoma," Ted said. "Going to help my dad on the farm."

"We have a problem here. My friend is bad sick, he is burning up," the man said as he walked over to the sick man lying in the corner.

"Do you know anything about doctoring?"

"No, not much," Ted told him.

"Do you have any water for him?"

"Yes, I have a container full of water. He's my traveling buddy, we've been together two days. Hope he don't have nothing catching."

"Let's try to cool him down with the water, do you have a towel?" Ted asked.

"I tried to cool him with a wet cloth on the head. I just have a coffee can full and I don't want to waste any. We're going to need it all. We brought it to make coffee, but he needs it worse."

"Put water on his tongue," Ted told him.

"Anyone have any whisky?" Ted asked turning to the other men.

"You can mix it with water, some people do that when they're sick." No one volunteered any, so his friend began to put drops of water on his tongue.

"That's about all I know about doctoring. That's what my mom did when we were sick. She gave us water and put a wet towel on our head." Ted walked over to the other end of the car to lie down and rest. He laid out some newspapers and his bedroll, hopefully to settle in for a while.

He hadn't been asleep very long when he was awakened by someone shaking him.

"Mister, mister, wake up. I think my friend is dead."

Ted jumped up to take a look at him. "Did you try to find a pulse?" he asked.

"No, I don't know how to do that," he was so distressed he could hardly speak. He wasn't moving, he was very still and lifeless. Ted reached down to try to find a pulse, but could not find one. He put his ear down to his chest to see if he could hear a heartbeat. Nothing!

"I think you're right, your friend is dead. How well did you know him?" Ted asked.

The hysterical young man went down to his knees and burst into tears.

"That's the first dead person I have ever seen. I didn't know him very well but he was the only friend I had," he managed to say through his broken words. The rest of the men in the boxcar were silent, they didn't seem to want to be involved so they kept their distance, never offering any sympathy or support to the tearful young man. Ted understood the feeling, but couldn't understand how they could not assist a fellow hobo in time of need. The demon of death is a "bitter pill to swallow" for most folks. It was for him, but he couldn't just ignore it.

"Do you know where he is from?" Ted asked trying to console him.

"We only met about a week ago. He was going West to find work so we teamed up. I decided to go with him," he told Ted.

"What was his name? By the way, my name is Ted, what's yours?"

"Hubert," he said.

"I think I'm about your age, I'm seventeen. His name was Tom, but I'm sorry, I didn't know his last name," he said as he began to cry, feeling guilty that he didn't know more about him.

"When was the last time he spoke to you?" Ted inquired.

"Just after we got on the car, he mumbled something about his mother. But I couldn't understand what he said, he was out of his head."

"What about these other men, do you know them?"

"No, I don't know them, they were onboard when we got on. They're afraid he has something catching."

Ted leaned down over Tom.

"Let's look in his pockets to see if he has any information on him, we need to notify his folks if we can."

The only thing they found in his overall pockets was a folded letter from his mother. Ted unfolded it and asked Hubert if he wanted to read it.

"I can't read very well, can you?" he said quietly as if he was a bit ashamed of himself.

"Sure, I will read it." Ted began to read:

Dear Son,

I sure do hope this letter finds you well, Pa and me, we been worried some about you, so we decided to write you. You were at Aunt Agnes place last time we heard from you. So I'm writing this an we sure hopes, you gets this here letter, before you head on out to that there Cal i forn ia.

Marge your sister got married yesterday, she sure is pregnant seven months along and they decided to go ahead and just get married. Her new husband is out on parole now and was working at the saw mill. He had a wife once, and they had three kids all ready. But he don't know nothing at all about her and the kids, what happened to them, they must have all died, but he is not sure, he was in prison for eight years, and she was supposed to have divorced him and remarried while he was in prison, so they just up and lost contact with one another.

Don't know what our little Marge saw in the man, but he is real nice to her, he has only hit her twice since they got married, last month, so She says. but she has this here brand new black eye, she won't talk about it to me, for some reason.

Well son Pa is down in his back again, and the rheumatism all the time bothers him some, He had to quit the saw mill, the work was slow anyhow, the mill has almost shut down, it hadn't worked regular for four months or so, and he said he just couldn't do it no longer.

Sure do hope you find work out there in Cali forn, if'in you do and can help us out with your wages from time to time. Your other three brothers and all five sisters, all say hello, Oh yes, Tommy, your youngest brother, got hit in the head the other day, by a horse, he hasn't acted right ever since. The doctor didn't say how long it would take to get right. He always did act funny but this is even more peculiar. He howls a lot, he thinks he is wolf or something, I guess. We'ins Love you son. Mother.

"This letter doesn't give us much of a clue as to who he is. Let's check again to see if he has the envelope," Ted said hopefully.

They checked his pockets again and found nothing, except an old pocket knife.

"Reckon it's all right if I keep this here pocket knife, just for memory sake," Hubert reluctantly asked Ted.

"I'm sure he would want you to have it since you are his only friend. I doubt if he would mind," Ted reassured him.

The train was slowing down, getting ready for the next stop. Ted knew they needed to make a decision as to what to do. They couldn't take the chance of being caught with a dead man.

Hubert was getting very distraught on what to do, he couldn't give any information about his friend, didn't even know his last name. He just stood there wringing his hands, so Ted stepped in to help him.

"Here, put the letter back into his pants pocket. Let the police find it and try to figure it out. They have ways of getting information that we don't have. But first, let's write his name on it so they will at least know his first name."

"Don't got no pencil," he said.

Ted ask the other men as they looked on. "Hey, any you guys got a pencil or anything to write with?" They all shook their heads no and busied themselves gathering their belongings to *throw their feet* as soon as they could, to get off this demon train.

Ted found a small lump of coal on the floor and took it over to Hubert, and wrote the name "Tom" on the letter.

"Here, put it in his pocket. It's all that we can do."

The train slowed to a crawl. The men hovered around the open boxcar door ready to escape from the demon's shadow that had encompassed them. One by one they jumped and disappeared into the woods, never looking back.

Ted and Hubert pulled Tom close to the boxcar door so the train crew could easily find him. They didn't speak to each other again. What could they say, it had been a part of this journey that each of them would like to forget.

Ted hoped the crew would find his body soon, and the police could locate his family. Otherwise, they would never know what happened to him and that would be very sad.

Ted and Hubert gathered their backpacks, shook hands, and jumped from the train. Ted hoped to free himself and his mind of this day which was so filled with mixed emotions, yet he thought of Mrs. Jewell and how she lifted his spirit from the goodness in her life. The sun was about to come up over the horizon. A new day was coming and suddenly he knew he would be all right. He had the opportunity to continue his journey home.

He didn't look back. He had separated himself from the experience of this train ride, leaving Tom and his eternal journey in the hands of God.

CHAPTER 12

A BIG MISTAKE

Ted was excited when he finally arrived in Atlanta. He had heard it was the big southern city of hospitality. He was more than ready to head out to St. Louis, however, to start the last leg of his journey home to see his mom and dad again. That was all he could think of.

He quickly jumped aboard the freight hoping the rest of his journey would be free of the misfortunes he had experienced recently. He was ready for some peace and quiet for a change. He settled in, spread his bedroll on the floor, and breathed a sigh of relief. In a short while, he noticed it was unusually quiet, and he began to feel uneasy. There were no other hobos around and he remembered it was a very short train, only twenty boxcars.

They were about an hour out when the train began to slow down, then they came to a stop at a water tower to take on water. Ted knew that something was very wrong, he must have really messed up in all his excitement of getting to Atlanta. Suddenly, he heard feet crunching the gravel, and he knew the train crew was checking each boxcar as they walked the whole length of the train, checking the hot boxes on each car.

The door of Ted's car flew open and there stood looking at him face to face were two angry crewmen.

"Hit the grinder, boy. If you know what's good for you, no freebies on this local run."

When he heard the word *local*, he knew he had made a big mistake. The local runs don't take you where you want to go, it was only a branch line. Without a word to the crewmen, Ted jumped off the car and disappeared into the woods. He hid in a blind to watch, hoping he could get back on board to ride to the next town; otherwise, he would have to walk.

But it was not to be, the crew was not going to be outsmarted by this young freeloader; they knew he was out there somewhere. They didn't walk back to the caboose, which they normally do. They waited until the train started up and the caboose moved to where they were standing, and then they climbed aboard. Ted had no chance to get back on the train, he was left stranded.

He started walking down the tracks. The next town ahead was probably closer than walking back the other way. It was starting to get dark, just about suppertime, his stomach was telling him. He saw some lights flickering through the trees ahead. If he were lucky this could mean his supper. He stepped off the track and walked a short distance farther into the woods, and as he got closer in, he could see a wide clearing with a huge bonfire in the center with sparks flying upward dancing high into the dark night sky.

Ted knew it wasn't a hobo camp, not with that big of a fire, but he couldn't figure out just what it was. He moved in closer and saw something he had never seen before. The bonfire turned out to be a huge cross burning in the center of the clearing with a large number of men dressed in white robes, with pointed head pieces that covered their faces. He thought it must be some kind of a celebration or an initiation into a special club, or something like that.

His curiosity was running wild so he crept in a little closer to have a better look. He couldn't see very well through the limbs and foliage of the trees. So he climbed upon a branch for a better vantage point, being very careful to remain quiet so he would not be discovered. *This could be some kind of a secret society*, he thought. The mystery of it all was very fascinating, and he wanted to see more.

From his new vantage point he could clearly see that what he was looking at was the most frightening scene he could ever imagine. The huge burning cross lit up the night sky, and it was then that Ted saw four black people, three men and one woman, hanging by their necks, their feet just inches from the ground. They were struggling and trying desperately to reach their feet to the ground to relieve the pain and tension.

He was confused and thunderstruck. He wanted to do something about this, he thought, but what! These white robed men are murderers. He had seen some really harsh things in his life, especially during the last few months as he had journeyed through the country, but never anything like this. "Why?" kept running through his mind. He felt helpless, but he knew these four people were even more helpless.

Ted swore the black men's eyes were looking straight at him as if they were asking for help. The woman was fighting for her life, throwing her arms and legs back and forth. Her dress was torn down to her waist, exposing her breasts. One of the robed men was taunting her, trying to fondle her as she kicked at him. He then stepped back and laughed at her, and all the other men joined in the laughter.

He walked up to her and she tried to place her feet on his shoulders, probably hoping to take the pressure off the rope around her neck. The monster in white would let her take a step or two as she tried to climb up his torso, then he stepped back quickly and watched her swing back and forth as they all laughed at her again.

What kind of hooded monsters are they? Ted kept asking himself over and over again. One of the black men, the only one now still alive, began throwing his body around, jerking on his rope and swaying back and forth, trying to hasten his death. Finally, he lost his struggle for life, his head slumped forward and his body went totally still. Blood was flowing from his mouth; he must have bit off his tongue in his final struggle for life.

Their deaths were not quick. It was not a drop hanging to break their necks instantly; it was a slow strangulation which made them suffer. Ted began to question in his mind, *Was this thing done purposely by these white robed monsters so they could watch them suffer as they died?* It certainly wasn't justice for something they had done. It had to be purposely done; he couldn't think of another reason that they would do such a thing. He just didn't understand what kind of hatred could make men do these things.

He felt sick at his stomach and wasn't hungry anymore. He just witnessed the worst kind of torture: these robed monsters watching the poor souls swing in the night breeze, and they seemed to enjoy it. Such beasts—laughing and drinking in the midst of such hideous acts, like they were celebrating.

Ted thought the ritual was over, but no, there was more to come. They all gathered around the burning cross and held what sounded like a revival meeting. They shouted and yelled, quoting Bible verses, and chanting "mumble jumble" which he could not understand. Tears welled up in his eyes; he couldn't contain his emotions any longer. He knew God would not sanction such things. He felt so confused and bewildered. This couldn't be the real world, or was it just a big horrible dream? How could anyone be so cruel and have so much hate in them? No, it was not a dream; it was real, but he couldn't make any sense of it.

He turned away and slipped off the limb to the ground and headed back to the tracks as fast as he could run. He didn't have the slightest idea where he was, the only thing he knew for sure, the tracks headed westward. When he reached the tracks, he slowed to a walk. He had never felt so scared and so alone ever before, and he started sobbing uncontrollably. Ted sometimes forgot he was only sixteen, even though he was six feet tall, a hundred and eighty pounds, handsome and strong, and most people thought of him as an adult, even he did, until now.

But on this night he was just a scared boy, drained of emotions and alone in the dark. What he didn't realize, however, was that most mature adults would have the same emotional response from what he had just witnessed. He hoped he would never see anything like that ever again. He found a comfortable spot surrounded by a small grove of trees and sat down to console himself. He felt exhausted. He thought of Mrs. Jewell and her kind words, "Walk with God" kept running through his mind. He began to pray and exhaustion took over and he fell asleep.

After a short rest, he felt stronger, strong enough to continue walking. He walked about five or six miles before the sun began to peek over the horizon. In a few minutes, he came upon a field where workers were busy preparing the ground, some were plowing, some were picking up rocks and carrying them to the side of the field, while others were planting and throwing handfuls of seeds into the plowed furrows.

Ted thought this might be an opportunity to get some work. So he walked up to one of the workers who was closest to the fence and asked, "Do you know if I could get any work here in the field?"

"I don't rightly know, boss," the black man answered.

"Oh, I'm not the boss, mister, I just want to work."

"We'ans call all you white folks boss," he replied.

"Where can I find the boss of this field? I just want to work."

"Don't rightly know where he is, they just bring us here in the mornin' and we work till suppertime, then they pick's us up and we gets to go home to our wives and chillins, then we eats our grits, turnips greens, and cornbread. The boss, he doesn't tell us where he be."

Ted noticed that all the workers were black. *This must be a plantation in the south like he had read about*, he thought.

"Thank you, mister. I'll just mosey on and maybe I'll see the boss down the road somewhere."

"Yes'um, boss," he said as he continued working, never missing a beat in his rhythmic work movements.

Ted walked on down the tracks a few more miles. He finally came to a water tower and saw a railroad depot just straight ahead. Now maybe he could figure out where he was. The sign on the depot read "Alma." He had never heard of it before, but at least he knew he was in Alma, Georgia. He walked up to the chalk board to read the schedule and there was a freight train due in at 9:00 a.m. headed west. He had time to knock on a few doors to see if he could find something to eat, but was turned away at most of them. Finally, a nice-looking lady came to the screen door.

"Yes, what can I do for you?"

"I'm really hungry, ma'am. Do you have some work for me, so I can earn something to eat?"

The lady whispered quietly, "You better leave, young man. My husband is really mean to folks like you."

But it was too late, the man came to the door.

"What do we have here, Helen?"

"He is looking for work to get a meal," she said as she stepped back into the house.

"We'en's got no work for your kind here," he said with his mouth full of food with slobbers dripping off his chin, and still holding tightly to the chicken leg he was eating.

"I had to work for my supper and I ain't' sharing it with no tramp."

Ted looked at this disgusting, overweight, and shirtless man and said, "Mister, I want to work, I don't want a hand out."

"All right then, you come down to my store in the morning and sweep it out and wash some windows, and we'll just see how bad you want to work, bet you don't show up. If I feed you tonight, I'll never see you again," he grunted an evil sound and gave him directions to the store before he slammed the door in his face.

At the next house, he saw a lady hanging clothes on the line to dry. He approached her and said, "Howdy, ma'am. I wonder if you have any work for me to do, so I can earn something to eat?"

"Give me a minute and I'll ask my husband if he has some work for you," she said as she scurried into the house.

She didn't seem very friendly, Ted thought, and he began to feel a bit uneasy, but maybe he was just over cautious. Suddenly, the back door opened, slamming against the house, and a big burly man carrying a shot gun appeared on the back steps. He had a deputy badge pinned to his bib overalls on his chest.

"What do you want, boy," he said in a very gruff, commanding voice.

Ted was very startled by such an overpowering figure and thought about running out of there as fast as he could, but he felt cornered like a deer caught in a bramble bush.

"I know what you're thinkin', boy, you don't want to do that. You stand still, right where you are, and don't move, ya' hear me?"

"Yes, sir," Ted could barely whisper.

Within an hour, Ted was standing in front of a "Judge," in the judge's own living room, asking him, "You got any money, son?"

Ted couldn't speak, the words wouldn't come. So he shook his head no.

"Speak up, boy," the judge growled at him in a loud voice.

"No, sir," Ted was able to manage. He actually did have a few dollars in his shoe but he knew it wouldn't be enough to get him out of this mess.

"Well, now, a vagrant in this county gets thirty days on the chain gang. That's automatic, boy," the judge said in his authoritative ugly voice.

"We don't cotton much to bums and vagrants hereabouts, ya' understand, and may I suggest to you boy, when your thirty days are up you get yourself out of my county as quick as you can."

Two haughty acting deputies took him by the arms and escorted him to a prison truck that was conveniently waiting outside the front door. They put him in the back and chained him to the floor, leaving him without any water and with the sun bearing down on him. Finally, in about an hour, the truck started moving and they began their trip to "who knows where."

Ted's head was swimming, wondering how and why all this was happening. He was beginning to realize the impact of the biggest mistake he had ever made, getting on that local run; it looked like he was really going to pay dearly for it. In about an hour, the truck pulled up to the prison and stopped at a big wooden gate. The driver jumped out and rang a bell announcing their arrival.

A big heavyset guard opened the gate for them to enter, and after a short drive to the front of the prison, the guard took off the chain and ordered him to jump to the ground.

"Welcome, good to see you, son," he said. "And don't try to run or I'll blow your silly head plum off."

When Ted jumped from the truck, he saw the old rundown prison that looked like a bunch of old warehouse buildings on stilts, all unpainted and totally surrounded by high-barbed fencing. In the center was a watch tower with a guard holding a rifle.

Ted was feeling very overwhelmed and very angry at himself for messing up so badly, but even angrier at this heavy-handed prison system that has denied him a hearing, just an automatic sentence. It didn't make him feel any better when they shaved his head and gave him an ill-fitting striped uniform to wear. As he waited for the next guard to shout out an order to him, he thought to himself, "Is this what they call the justice system in the South?"

He was officially checked in as a prisoner by the warden, given all his instructions, and then asked if he had any questions.

"I'm really hungry, sir. I haven't eaten in at least two days," he managed to say to the warden.

"Then you'll really enjoy our feast tonight when the rest of the prisoners come in from their day's work in the field in about five hours from now. We're having' turnip greens and cornbread and all the water you can drink. How does that sound?" the warden asked him.

"Come with us," the deputy said. "We'll take you to the barracks."

Ted took one step with the deputy and fainted, falling face down onto the floor. It had been too much, he was overwhelmed by all that was happening, and he was weak from the lack of food. When he woke up, he was lying on a cot in a long room that looked like it had a hundred or more cots lined up side by side. Still in a daze, he looked all around him. The windows were propped open by a stick, no screens, and the flies and insects were freely flying in and out taking ownership of the place.

He heard a commotion outside which sounded like chains rattling. He was right, the door of the barracks opened and all of the men from the chain gang came in from their day's work, walking in single file, in lockstep to the orders of the guard. The guards released the chains from their ankles one by one, each prisoner going to their cot collapsing in exhaustion. Ted noticed that most of the men say seventy percent were black and about a thirty percent were white.

Their rest period was cut short by an order from the warden.

"You are all due for a shower, so strip down now. It's a good rain, so step on it, you'll get your shower while there's rain coming down." Then he motioned for Ted to join them.

"March," was the order. They all marched out one by one, naked as jay birds and stood in the rain, no soap and no wash cloths, just a good rinsing. The rain lasted about thirty minutes, time enough for a good cleansing, and then they were allowed to go back into the barracks.

Ted dressed and lay back on his cot, admitting that the "shower" did make him feel revived. He couldn't stop chastising himself for the *stupid* mistake he had made. He brought all this on himself by catching a local. But one thing he was learning, the local country folks were not known for their hospitality.

In the mess hall, the hungry men ate, slurping down their food while fighting the flying insects coming in to get their share. Ted was grateful for the food, rather tasteless he thought, but it was food. He didn't feel as hungry as he had before; he had lost most of his appetite. The warden was right, they had turnip greens and cornbread, not all they could eat, of course, but enough to sustain them.

Later that evening they heard the order, "Lights out," so they blew out their coal-oil lamps and lay back on their cots. Ted was exhausted, and he wondered what it would be like sleeping in a room with over a hundred other men. However, tired men could generally sleep through most anything, like the thunder and lightning and heavy downpour that came about three o'clock in the morning. He woke up with water dripping on his face from the leaky roof, so he jumped up and moved his cot to avoid the constant drips. By this time the whole room was awake moving their cots all around trying to find a dry spot.

He was not finding it easy to get a good night's sleep through all the groans, grunts, and snoring. During one night, a totally unexpected thing happened to him. About two in the morning, he was suddenly attacked by two men, overwhelming him as he lay defenseless on his cot. He desperately tried to fight them off; he knew some boxing skills he had learned with his brothers, but fighting off two men was very different.

In the process of the struggle, the cot overturned and caused so much commotion it woke up the other men around them. An older man, the one right next to Ted's cot, was so irritated he jumped up and grabbed one of the attackers by the back of his neck and threw him several feet across the floor. The other attacker knew it was time to "bug off" and quietly sneaked back to his cot. Ted was very shaken and didn't quite know what to say, so he muttered a "thank you."

"You can call me Gregg," he said gruffly, still irritated by the sleep interruption.

"Thank you," Ted said still shaking from the struggle.

"I'll put the word out in the morning. Those guys are real creeps. They won't dare bother you again. Okay now, let's shut up and go back to sleep."

In the morning they went to breakfast, they had two slices of bread, a spoonful of jam and a hardboiled egg, and a cup of what they called coffee. After they ate, Gregg came over and sat by Ted.

"I see you have a sack of Bull Durham tobacco. I'm all out and I sure could use a smoke, would you mind?"

"No, sir, don't mind at all, you can have it. I don't smoke much, my mother doesn't like it at all," he said as he handed over the tobacco and the papers. Now Ted was beginning to understand what "putting the word out" meant. Favor for favor, it was a prison thing. If you have a protector, no one bothers you from then on; his protection payment was now paid in full.

The guards lined them all up and chained them together to take them out to the fields. The old prison truck was stuck in the mud from all the heavy rains, so they all had to push it to the gravel road before they loaded up to go. The mud spattered men arrived in the muddy fields and heard their assignments for the day, "clear the fields of all rocks." They were unchained to do their work as the guards stood by shouting their orders. Ted was experiencing his first day of working on a chain gang, with only two breaks the entire day, one for lunch and the second for water or a smoke.

This was the way it was for the next thirty days for Ted. They cleared the fields, worked the roads, filling in the holes, and smoothing them out, the hardest work he had ever known, much harder than he realized even existed. The biggest challenge for him was having enough strength to complete his work assignments. The food supply was so little that he was losing all his strength. He only hoped he would last for thirty days.

The most difficult day of Ted's stay at the prison camp came just a few days before he was released. A young black man, probably in his twenties, went crazy and was yelling and screaming, demanding his rights.

The disruption caused the guards to take action, and brutal action it was. They dragged him from the far end of the barracks by his feet to and through the front door, into the yard. They then threw him against the building, kicked him, and each guard struck him in the head at least three or four times with their clubs until he was unconscious, and ceased to move.

Ted stood at the window watching, tears running down his cheeks. The poor man after several minutes finally became conscious he with a great deal of difficulty finally got up, staggering to his feet. He threw out his arms to the heavens and gave out the loudest scream of terror that Ted had ever heard. It made him shudder as chills went up his spine. Then the man collapsed and fell in a heap on the ground. He curled up in a fetal position and gave up his life to death.

Ted was haunted for the next several days, especially at night. The image of this nightmare and the sound of his scream went over and over in his mind. He prayed for relief from this torturous event, actually from this whole experience he was suffering from.

The final morning came. The guard came and unchained Ted and they walked to the warden's office. It all happened so quickly. The warden said, "Son, you're now free to go," as the warden and guard walked with him to the gate. The warden's final words were, "You served your time, you're free to go. My advice to you is, don't let the sun set on your rear end in this county again. Next time, it will be a year."

As Ted walked through the gate, he didn't know what to say or do, so he said nothing, just nodded to them. He had a strong urge to run as fast as he could, but he walked briskly to the road, not really knowing where he was or which way to go, but anywhere to freedom was where he wanted to go. Freedom suddenly had a new meaning for Ted, and as he continued to walk, he vowed to think through every move he made from now on. He knew he had just paid dearly for this costly mistake.

Chapter 13

MOVING ON

The words the prison warden spoke to him kept running through his head, "Don't let the sun set on you in this county ever again. Next time it will be a year."

Ted began to run down the road as fast as his feet would carry him. He had no idea where he was or where he was going, but anywhere was better than where he had just spent the last thirty days.

He slowed down to a walk and was quite relieved when an old black farmer in a hay wagon, pulled by a team of horses, came upon him and stopped. "Could we carry ya' somewhere? Where ya' goin,' fella?" he asked Ted.

"I need to get into town to catch a train goin' west, can you help me?"

"Hop on, my name's Jake, I'm headed that a way. We have a train station in our town. Never ever rid a train myself, not once," he told Ted smiling, showing his missing and broken teeth.

They rode about ten miles chatting about everything under the sun. The old farmer loved to talk, and they shared with each other everything about themselves. The old farmer even shared his lunch with Ted, knowing he was probably starved to death after eating prison food for a month, or the lack of food would better describe it.

Ted was fascinated with the farmer's outlook in life. He was somewhat of a country philosopher, calmly living in a world of trials and tribulations. But for him he lived a very simple life just one day at a time.

"Ted, don't ya' worry about things, the Lord will provide for you. But you needs to talk to him regular, not missin' a day, and never take him for granted," he advised him in his philosophic "sermonette."

Ted enjoyed having someone to talk to, and he appreciated the ride into town. It was so pleasant to hear such words of encouragement rather than the harsh words of the demands he had been hearing from the prison guards.

This old uneducated farmer, Ted thought, *explained in a very simplistic way how the mighty Creator brings mankind closer to the created. This old wise farmer worked the land that feeds the world.* Ted had never thought of it that way before, and he could easily see a profound message in the simple life that the old man lived.

They arrived at the station and Ted jumped off the wagon, deeply grateful for the company and the lift into town, but he was especially grateful for the kindness of this man.

"Thank you sir, I can't thank you enough," he said as they shook hands.

"I promise I will remember your words and not ever take God for granted."

Old Jake smiled broadly at this uniquely handsome young man. He had never met a stranger quite as respectful and friendly. Actually, he had enjoyed the company as much as Ted had, perhaps even more.

"May God be a blessing to ya," he said.

Ted waved good-bye to his benefactor as the old team of horses pulled the wagon away, and he watched them until they were out of sight. He glanced up at the water tower looking for any hobo messages, but there were none. He didn't really expect to see any since this was not a main line; not many hobos get out in this territory.

He spent the next several days traveling from one state to the next, without any significant problems, and finally arrived in St. Louis, Missouri. From now on, he would be traveling on the Missouri-Pacific railroad straight into Kansas City, one that was more familiar to him.

When he boarded the boxcar, there were several other hobos already aboard. Ted was glad for the company, he didn't have to make this trip alone. Later on, when the train pulled into a siding and stopped, they heard the crew locking the boxcar doors on both sides.

They all looked at each other wondering what's up? When the train started again, they quickly checked the doors, and indeed they were locked. It looked like they were trapped, the train crew knew they were aboard.

"This don't look good, fellas. Looks like the bulls know we're here, and they are planning a big party, and we're their guests," one of the old hobos said.

They put their heads together to figure out what to do, but really, what could they do? They were trapped. Everything was quiet for about an hour before they heard men walking and talking on top of the boxcar. The trap door slowly began to open, a lantern descended into the car, and a face peered down right behind it looking straight at them.

"Hey, ya' cherries, we know you're down thar' and we're goin' cure ya' from ridin' this line ever again, once and for all. When we stop at the next siding, we're comin' in after ya'. So get ready, it's not goin' to be a pretty scene, we promise ya' that."

He slammed the trap door shut, and as he walked away, the hobos could hear him singing over and over again, "I'm goin' to a party . . .," until his voice finally faded away.

Ted felt really scared.

"They really won't hurt us, will they?" he asked the old, seasoned hobos.

"What ya' think? They caught me one time before on another line about a year ago, and they beat the hell out of me. I spent two days flat on my back. They generally use a baseball bat to hit with, that's what they used on me."

Suddenly, at the other end of the boxcar another hobo yelled out,

"Hey, ya' fella's, come and help me over here! Gather up all the newspapers and scraps of loose hay off the floor, and anything else that ya' can find, and pile it up over here on this side of the wall, right here," he said as he pointed to the place they could make the pile.

When the pile grew as big as they could make it, he lit a match and threw it right in the middle, and it blazed up immediately.

"What do you think you're doin'? We'll all burn up," Ted yelled out, scared to death.

In a few moments the fire was raging, and the side of the wooden boxcar was ablaze with flames, roaring up the side almost to the top of the car. Ted ran to the opposite end of the boxcar to get as far away as he could, and they put their shirts and bandanas over their faces to keep out the smoke, but it really didn't help much. Ted's eyes were tearing up, and he knew they would all be trapped in this raging inferno. What was this guy thinking, the party they were promised probably would not have killed them. He shuddered at the thought of being burned up alive. Just about that time, the train began to move into the siding, and the old hobo began kicking the burning side of the car until it collapsed and fell outward. It left a big gaping hole, large enough for them to jump out to safety. He jumped first and shouted.

"Follow me," and they all frantically followed, one by one. Ted landed on the gravel and skinned himself up, his hands, elbows, and arms, but he hardly felt it, thinking this is much better than being burned alive or hit by a baseball bat.

They all ran out of sight and hid in the trees. They "proudly" watched as the crew frantically walked up and down trying to put out the fire. The brakeman uncoupled the car and they pushed the burning boxcar into the siding, away from the rest of the train. It took them about an hour to clean up the mess from the fire, leaving the old wooden burned-out carcass of a boxcar in the siding, never to be used again.

The train crew was seething with anger and were exhausted from fighting the fire as they prepared the train to move out again. The hobos watched until they spotted the brakeman jump onto the caboose, and they all quickly left the blind, one by one, and reboarded the train. It slowly left the siding to return to the main track and their trip resumed. They were now back on their way to Kansas City.

Ted sat up against the wall of the boxcar, totally exhausted and thinking about his life. The hobo life was becoming quite an experience and education for him as he realized he had just escaped from a life-threatening event, wondering what he could learn from it all.

He thought about the old farmer, Jake, and how he respected his simple life, living close to God and the land. He began to question himself why he had made the choice to seek such a precarious uncertain existence. Was it the adventure and danger of it all? Perhaps it was the challenge, outsmarting the train crew and escaping their clutches was a glorious victory, he had to admit. *There's a reason for all this*, he thought. These lessons of survival he is learning from the old hobos could one day become a vital part of his life.

CHAPTER 14

THE WRONG DIRECTION

Ted stood in the depot watching the crew make up the train for the next departure. He scoped out the schedule board and studied it for a moment. There were several trains listed, coming and going twenty-four hours a day. It looked like No. 18 was the train he needed to take to head out toward Kansas City. He was getting excited by the thought of getting closer and closer to Oklahoma and actually getting home.

He returned to the yard to locate his train and to watch the crew scurrying around, coupling and uncoupling cars, preparing the trains for departure. He found a blind where he could watch and wait, and as the time of departure came closer he began to feel uneasy for some reason, but he soon dismissed it thinking it was just the excitement of getting closer to home. When the brakeman gave the signal, the train began to move out slowly. The fireman threw the main line switch and the long train, No. 18, started to enter the main line and pick up speed, it was on its way.

Ted quickly moved out of his blind along with six other hobos, all running quickly to get aboard their car. He reached up and grabbed the ladder at the front of the boxcar just as the train gave a violent jerk, almost causing him to lose his grip, but he managed to hold on. When he tried to adjust his hold the train jerked again, causing his head to bounce against the side of the car, almost knocking him off again, but he held on for dear life.

Using all his strength, he secured his hold as the train began to pick up speed. As he climbed up the ladder, out of the corner of his eye he saw a young *novice hobo* grab the ladder at the back end of the car, only to lose his grip when the train jerked once more, seemingly timed just right to bounce him into space.

Ted let out a gasp, but was totally helpless to do anything. It looked like he fell into the coupling between the two cars, and if so, it meant instant death. He hoped by some miracle he might have been thrown clear of the train. And as he looked back once more, he saw the poor kid lying lifeless at the side of the track; however, the fate of this young hobo, Ted would never know for sure. So far, he thought, everything on this trip was not going so well. He started to feel uneasy again but hoped it would all come together for him very soon.

With the event of this young hobo on his mind, he recalled one of the "rules of boarding" he once heard from an old, experienced hobo: always climb aboard the ladder at the front of the car, never the back. The old hobo made it very clear, if you lose your grip and fall from the front, you'll always fall and bounce against the side of the car and away from the tracks. But from the back, the ladder is so close to the end of the boxcar the danger is you'll bounce between the cars, meaning grave injury or death. Ted wished that somehow there could have been a way of telling this young novice that rule, it might have saved his life.

Ted made his way to the top of the car and rested for a few minutes before opening the hatch. The train was moving steadily along with the usual click-clack of the wheels, and soon the rhythm of the ride was in total stride. It began to rain so he opened the hatch and dropped down inside, and to his surprise it was a refrigerator car. He suddenly felt cold, but then he realized it wasn't refrigerating anything, the car was empty.

The "reefer" car, as hobos dubbed the refrigerator cars, were totally insulated inside, and when not in use, the car was cozy and warm. Ted was tired and exhausted so he prepared his bedroll to get some rest. He removed the bundle of newspapers he was carrying inside his shirt. He learned to do this from an old experienced hobo, and newspapers often come in handy for many uses, such as insulation to keep the body warm.

Ted smiled as he remembered a hobo once telling him the difference between a hobo and a bum. They both stuff newspapers in their shirts, but the difference between them, the hobo reads them first. The strange thing was, he had read them being curious about the world around him. He prepared his bedroll and made himself comfortable and readily fell asleep.

By early morning, the train began to slow down, waking Ted from his rest. It stopped with a jerk and it sounded like the car he was riding was being uncoupled. He slid the door open wondering what was going on, and sure enough, his car was sitting on a side track, and the train was continuing down the track to its final destination without him.

He climbed down from the car totally perplexed as to why his car was abandoned in the middle of nowhere. It was a bright clear sunny day, and he was surrounded by pastures and prairies, with only a few cows grazing nearby, and on the opposite side of the track he saw in the distance a farmer plowing in the field with his team of horses.

He started walking, what else could he do, and about a mile down the track he saw a water tower and a depot. As he got closer he saw a sign which read, "Bush, Nebraska, population 54." Ted immediately felt really stupid, what in the world was he doing in Nebraska? He was going to Kansas City.

He wanted to kick himself; he just made another major goof. He chose a train going in the wrong direction, it was going north instead of south. He really questioned himself as to why he was making all these mistakes. Then he remembered the uneasy feeling he had before he boarded the car. He knew the first thing he must change was to pay attention to his intuition. He had made two major mistakes and was very disappointed in himself, and he thought he was smarter than that.

"Okay! Get on with the day and make a decision," he was talking to himself as he sat down on the bench at the depot. He looked around the town and there was very little activity. The town consisted of about five buildings, all located around the town square, a combined grocery store and post office, the marshal's office, a feed store, a few boarded up buildings, several homes, and a little white church building with a steeple.

A few people began to gather around the depot and the town square, and he realized they came to watch the passenger train roar through their little town, probably the only excitement of the day. In a few minutes, they heard the whistle and the train came barreling down the track toward them, going about sixty miles per hour, he guessed, obviously not making a stop in Bush, Nebraska. In just seconds the train flew through town, causing a rush of air and a thrill for the townspeople.

The blast of the train whistle was deafening, and it sent a chill through Ted's body. As he watched it fly down the track a cinder flew into his eye, almost blinding him. He grabbed his face and began rubbing his eye, but he continued watching this "flying zephyr" hurl toward the crossing about a quarter mile ahead.

Suddenly, Ted and all the townspeople were watching a horrifying scene. They witnessed a horse-drawn wagon with three passengers approach the train crossing, and apparently they didn't see or hear the speeding train. They saw the wagon and horses fly in the air up over the top of the engine, with dust and debris falling everywhere like rain.

Ted held his breath. He couldn't believe what he was seeing, was it real or was it the cinder causing imaginary illusions? He ran down the track toward the crash and heard the deafening screeching of the train wheels, metal on metal, as the engineer tried to stop the speeding train, but a sudden stop was not possible.

When he arrived at the crossing he saw two dead horses lying several feet apart, their necks twisted underneath their lifeless bodies. The wagon was torn apart, pieces scattered everywhere, but the passengers that Ted saw in the wagon were nowhere around the scene of the crash. It was likely, he thought, that the bodies may have been dragged down the track by the engine catcher.

He started running back toward the depot so he could give a firsthand report to the station master, and at the same time he saw a farmer in a nearby field ahead jump off his plow seat, abandon his horses and run toward the station. They arrived at the station, the farmer just ahead of Ted, and as he stepped in the door he heard the terrified farmer blurt out his report to the station master. Ted added to the report that he had been at the scene and saw firsthand the dead horses and the wagon scattered in pieces all around the area. But, he told him, he did not see any of the passengers who were in the wagon when the crash occurred.

The station master sent word to the marshal's office and summoned help, and then telegraphed the Chief Dispatcher at the division headquarters to report the crash. A few minutes later the conductor of the train came running through the door, totally out of breath and in a panic, and could barely speak. He sat down on the bench and told them how the three men in the wagon had been caught up in the catcher, and their bodies dragged along the tracks. One was found about a quarter of a mile from the crossing, and the other two about a half mile down.

The rest of the day seemed quite long, Ted saw the wagon bringing the bodies of the men back into town and delivered them to one of the buildings across from the depot. The man who ran the feed store was also the coroner and conducted the funerals in town. He sadly received the bodies and began his work, it would be difficult because the bodies were mangled so badly. The saddest part of the day was when the townspeople began to gather at the square to mourn the loss of these men, they were their neighbors and friends, all from the same little town. Ted could see that it was going to be a sad week for them all.

The engineer backed the train all the way to the station, with all the stunned and bewildered passengers still aboard. He was still quite shaken as he sat down to write his report for the station master, in fact, he began to cry. Ted felt really sorry for this man, all that he had just been through. He probably felt like it was his fault that the crash occurred, but of course it wasn't. The station master helped him write the report, and Ted also volunteered to help as an eyewitness to the event, but he was told, 'no, thank you, young man.'

Ted slipped out of the door to join the townspeople who were gathered in the square. They were crying, mourning with one another, and shocked by such a grievous event. The driver of the wagon was an elderly farmer that they all knew and loved. He name was Lester Easley, a longtime resident of Bush, he was deaf and everyone felt he just didn't see or hear the danger coming. The other two men were farmhands and probably didn't have time to warn him; it all happened so fast.

The engineer finished his report and returned to the train to wait for the word to move out. He met with all the passengers whose trip was so grievously interrupted to give them information and consolation. In about an hour the word came in, the train could now move on to continue its journey, the train that the townspeople had gathered to watch for entertainment but soon evolved into the town's most hideous nightmare.

Along toward evening another train came through town, the first one since the accident. Traffic along the track was affected all up and down the line, and all the townspeople stared at it as it passed through, watching it move toward the crossing, no one uttering a word. The train didn't even slow down at the crossing, which seemed disrespectful to everyone, but the train had a time schedule to keep. For the people of Bush, however, on this day time was standing still.

Ted returned to the station after going to the store for a loaf of bread and sliced bologna to make himself a sandwich. The station master was sitting at the desk receiving and sending messages. The telegraph key was ticking rapidly with all the communications coming in from division headquarters. Ted couldn't make out all the messages, he was sitting too far away, but he knew they were mostly updating all the time schedules.

It seemed odd, he thought, *how quickly things return to normal after such a terrible accident.* Most of the people who gathered in the square were quietly returning to their homes and back to their lives, until finally the town seemed deserted, just himself and the station master. He remembered what a lonely job the station master had as he reflected on his apprenticeship back in Toronto.

He finished his sandwich and went out back to the restroom. He saw a sign on the door that said "Whites only," and he thought it was strange since Nebraska was not a southern state. He washed his face and hands at the pump and returned to the waiting room. He asked the station master where Bush, Nebraska, was located within the state and which train deposited the refrigerator car to the siding.

"Bush is very close to the South Dakota state line, it's just eight miles away," he informed Ted. "The freight that dropped the car off last night was No. 17 out of Kansas City, going to Omaha."

"Well, that explains what happened. Thank you, sir." Ted could have kicked himself right then and there. He had boarded No. 17 rather than No. 18.

"Is there another train going back to Kansas City today?" he inquired.

"Nope, not today, but tomorrow at twelve noon the passenger train comes through, but doesn't usually stop, it drops off the mail as it goes by." Then he added.

"As a matter of fact, I do have an engine deadheading back to Kansas City that's coming through due in a few minutes. It's supposed to pick up a work crew and a few work cars sitting on our side track and deliver them down the road a ways."

Just then a bunch of railroad hands came into the station. They were all dressed in their work clothes, blue shirts and denim overalls, and they were carrying their picks, shovels, and lanterns. They flopped down on the benches to wait for the engine to arrive to take them down the track for tomorrow's work.

As Ted listened to them talk, he learned they had been the cleanup crew from the accident. The track had not been damaged, but they described the scene as really gruesome, some of them were reluctant to even talk about it. They were all tired and exhausted, and as they waited for the engine to arrive, some were getting a few winks of sleep.

Ted thought this could be an opportunity for him to change his direction and to go back south toward Kansas City. He was secretly hoping the station master would have a compassionate heart after a day of such horrible events, and help him hitch a ride on the deadhead engine that was due any minute.

CHAPTER 15

BACK IN KANSAS CITY

It was a quiet afternoon, only an occasional message coming in to the station master. Ted offered him a bologna sandwich in exchange for a cup of coffee, which he gladly accepted. The telegraph key began, its dot da, dot, da with an incoming message, and the station master quickly jotted down the latest news from the dispatcher.

"Engine No. 19 will arrive on time." Ted read the message aloud as he heard it come in, and he was pleased with himself that he could still read the code.

The station master looked up with surprise at Ted.

"How did you know that?"

"I finished my telegraph apprenticeship as an operator in Toronto, Canada, just a few weeks ago, and I'm working my way back home to Oklahoma. What's my chances of getting a ride back south with this dead head engine crew?"

"When they arrive, the engineer and fireman usually come in for a cup of coffee, I can inform them you are a brother operator and that you want a ride," he said. "But that is strictly their decision. I have nothing to do with approving such favors."

"I understand," Ted said. "Just thought you could put in a good word for me, and I appreciate anything you can do.'

They looked down the track and the station master began to explain the standard operating procedure, which Ted already knew.

"Down the track about a quarter of a mile, you will see the green light on, and when the train approaches the station the light will turn red."

Very soon after he finished his words the light turned red, and they saw the engine approaching, puffing its black smoke across the countryside as the wind pushed it high into the air, and it floated off to dissipate or settle on the land. The engine pulled into the siding and slowly approached the station; and when it fully stopped, the engineer bled off the steam and it sent a temporary "smoke screen," almost covering the entire depot.

The engineer and fireman crawled down from the engine and came to get their "free cup" of coffee and shoot the "breeze" with the station master. In the conversation, the station master mentioned Ted's predicament and his request to get a ride back South. He looked down at the floor, shook his head "no," and then glanced over at Ted and winked. Ted understood, rules were rules, he had to say no in front of witnesses, which was the smart thing to do, and he had to protect his job.

In about twenty minutes, they prepared to leave. The *deadhead* engine consisted only of the coal car, two boxcars, and the work car and crew who were hitching a ride to the next work area. The engineer and fireman climbed aboard the engine and prepared to leave. Ted climbed up onto the engine and called out to the engineer to make his request.

"Sir, I sure would like to get a ride to Kansas City. I have just finished my apprenticeship as telegraph operator, and I am going to see my brother in Kansas City. If I can get a ride I would gladly shovel all the coal just to show my appreciation."

The engineer took his hand off the lever and shouted, "What did you say? I couldn't hear you, son" Ted repeated his request and the engineer said,

"Oh, you would, would you?"

"Yes, sir, I surely would." The engineer and the fireman looked at each other and looked down at him, and the engineer replied.

"My fireman is not feeling well today and he said he would appreciate the relief. So climb aboard and start shoveling, you got the job."

Ted waved back at the station master and climbed aboard, the first opportunity to ever be in an engine cab, and he was extremely excited. Barney, the engineer, introduced himself and told Ted that he was under the watchful eye of Tom, the fireman, and to do everything he was told.

"Yes, sir," Ted said.

Ted took off his jacket and started shoveling. He could feel the warmth of the fire in the cab, making it nice and cozy. But after a while, he was wringing wet with sweat; the work was really hard, and it took a great deal of strength to keep up with a fire-thirsty engine.

The train was moving right along at a good speed when the fireman told Ted to take a break and to go up into the coal car to break up the larger chunks of coal with the sledge hammer. He thought to himself how these guys really earned their pay. He was out of shape and struggling, and his clothes and face were turning as black as the coal.

They would make a short stop at the next station for the work crew to get off, and Ted welcomed the short break. He found a little corner in the cab where he could curl up and get some rest, but it also felt good to do some work for a change and it felt even better to get some rest from such a strenuous job.

When they approached the stopover for the work crew, the engineer asked him if he would like to pull the cord to sound the whistle which means, "Clear the tracks, we're coming through."

After the work crew departed, they were soon back on their way traveling about fifty miles per hour, the engineer informed Ted. Ted thoroughly enjoyed seeing the other side of the telegraphers' work, how important the accuracy of the time schedules really are, and how all the information work together. The engineer explained they would stay at their speed of fifty miles per hour and would arrive right on schedule in thirty minutes to go into a siding, to allow a passenger train to pass bound for Omaha.

They pulled into the siding to allow the train to pass, and Ted was surprised how the power and speed of the passenger train literally shook the massive engine cab, he thought nothing could be so powerful to shake this big iron monster.

As their engine re-entered the main line, the engineer said, "If all goes well, we'll be right on time arriving in Kansas City, about nine o'clock tonight."

He looked over at Ted and asked him if he would like to "drive the engine." With a big smile, Ted eagerly agreed. Barney called back to Tom.

"Hey, Tom, shovel for a while. I'm going to give this kid the thrill of his life. I'm going to let him run the engine."

Tom called back, "Okay, but tell him to keep it on the tracks," they all had a good laugh.

"Get on that seat on the left hand side and hang on for the ride of your life, Ted," Barney said to the excited novice engineer.

Ted crawled up into the seat as he was instructed, and Barney pulled open the throttle. The iron monster began to pick up speed, puffing and huffing the task of pulling its load, and it began to make a deafening noise as it groaned to get underway. Ted watched the engineer pull the lever that dropped sand on the track to give them more tractions. At the same time, Tom opened the doors of the firebox and tossed in several shovel loads of coal before closing the door to inspect the water and steam gauges. It all had to work together, it seemed overpowering to Ted as he watched how everything was so synchronized to make it all move so smoothly. He had a new perspective and appreciation for the train crew. They made it all work.

As they increased their speed, the engine noise began to quiet, but a new discomfort took its place. The engine began to shake and sway so much that Ted was forced to grab onto the window sill to keep from bouncing off his seat. Barney looked over at Ted and smiled, as if to say, Are you having fun yet?

Ted adapted himself readily to the engine motion and was soon able to sit without feeling he had to hold on.

Barney crossed over to Ted's seat and whispered, "Would you like to take over the engine for a while?"

"Would I," was all Ted could manage to say.

"Put your left hand on that lever, it's called the throttle. When you pull it toward you, it increases the speed, and to slow down, push it away from you. Get it?"

Ted was feeling real proud as his hand clasped the throttle, never in his life had he expected to run a real snorting locomotive, dragging its coal car behind. He was actually controlling the speed of this mighty engine it was indeed a thrill of a lifetime.

Barney crowded in behind Ted, keeping a watchful eye on everything, but not so close that he couldn't observe and enjoy the pleasure Ted was having. After a few moments Ted asked.

"Can I pull on the throttle to get the feel of it?"

"Sure, open her up to the next notch we've got plenty of steam." Barney said with a careful watchful eye.

Ted found it wasn't as easy as it looked to move the throttle into the next notch, but he held firm and pulled forward with all his strength and finally the lever moved where it should be. Barney allowed him to hold the throttle open for the next several minutes, and after going about ten miles, he patted him on the shoulder.

"Better let me have it now, Ted, you did a great job, you will make a fine engineer one day. Now it's time for you to earn your passage and start shoveling."

They pulled into the Kansas City freight yard right on time. Barney said.

"When Tom drops down from the engine to open the switch for us to enter the siding, you must get off. We don't need any problems from your ride with us, and by the way, we enjoyed your company."

"Thank you, sir, I can't thank you enough," Ted expressed rather emotionally. He truly was grateful for the help of correcting his big mistake.

They dropped off to the ground, and Tom threw the switch to allow the engine to enter into the siding.

Tom shook Ted's hand and said, "You did a good job. Take it easy and good luck to you." Tom ran to jump back onto the engine, and as they proceeded into the yard, they looked back at Ted and waved, both with big smiles on their faces, leaving him standing in the dark alone.

Ted gathered his pack, threw it on his back, and started walking to the depot. The big question on his mind, "Would Everett be there waiting for him?" He hoped he got the telegram that he had the station master send. He walked through the door, his clothes soiled with coal dust, his face smudged with soot, and he had high hopes that Everett would be standing there. And there he was, laughing out loud at what he saw.

"Hey, little bro, I hardly knew you under all that dirt. Welcome to Kansas City."

Ted ran to greet him, tears running down his cheeks, smudging the coal dust even more. Everett's white shirt soon became as smudged as Ted's face, but they didn't care, the reunion was much more important.

Ted couldn't wait to get to Everett's place to get cleaned up and actually sleep in a real bed that night. As he lay his head on a soft pillow, he thought about the day, how grateful he was for Barney and Tom, and how glad he was to see Everett. He drifted off to sleep with a very peaceful mind.

CHAPTER 16

BECOMING A HERO

The two days Ted spent with Everett were the best days he had since they departed Toronto, but now it was time to move on to Oklahoma. Everett and one of his work friends delivered him to the train station in style, in a horse and buggy.

He was grateful for Everett's generosity, a few new clothes to wear, good food, and family conversation to take with him as memories that would last a long time. After an emotional good-bye, Ted entered the depot to check the schedule, he was anxious to get home to see more family, his mom and dad.

He decided to catch a freight train rather than spend the ticket money Everett had given him. He would save it for food and other things he might need. The freight he decided to ride was on the Missouri Pacific, the line that ran right pass his dad's farm, the same trains he watched with excitement as a small boy.

From the blinds where he was watching, he saw the conductor swing the lantern back and forth and the train began to slowly pull out of the siding. He ran to jump aboard, and as usual the cars jerked in repetitive movement, the shock from one car to another throughout the entire train.

Ted was ready this time. He planted his feet firmly on the bottom rung. No, not again, his feet gave way and he was left hanging in mid-air, the bolt that held the rung had come loose from the wood, he was swinging in the wind as he struggled to find the next rung on the ladder. Finally, with his youthful upper body strength, he swung himself around to face the boxcar and was able to place his feet solidly in the next rung.

He climbed to the top of the car, his arms sore from the strain. It felt like they had been pulled right out of the socket. It seemed to him he was having a series of bad luck recently. He hoped that was all it amounted to, and it would end with that episode. He was grateful, however, that he made it as he realized how close he had come to being thrown from the train; it was a narrow escape.

The train was moving right along now, completely out of the yard and on to the main track. He slipped the bolt on the hatch and slowly opened it. As he was about to climb down into the car he heard voices, so he stopped to listen closely. He was startled to hear a gruff voice exclaim.

"I'll get even with that mealy mouthed little 'con' for throwing me off the baggage car the other day. It's him, it's the same guy. I saw him when we got aboard, I'll never forget that dirty bastard, if I live to be a hundred. I won't, I promise I'll find a way to get even. He practically ruined my left arm, couldn't hardly use it for several days afterward."

The tone in which the words were uttered were so venomous that Ted realized the speaker was extremely agitated, and was not just venting to work off his anger. He heard him use the word "con," the one he was going to get even with, and Ted took it to mean the conductor, since hobos called them cons.

The hobos inside the boxcar hadn't noticed the above hatch was open, so Ted continued to listen to them talk.

He overheard another voice asking, "How ya' goin' get even, Curt, have ya' made up your mind yet?"

Some of the words were difficult for Ted to hear. He thought the speakers must be crouched against the opposite end of the boxcar. But he heard the reply very clearly from the same agitated voice, the same voice that made the threat.

"That's easy, we're goin' put all sorts of crimps in their 'so called' perfect little schedules by holdin' up the night passenger express!"

There was total silence for a moment, and then he continued, "The officials of this railroad, those stingy little men who don't allow a fella to ride on the blind baggage car are boasting that they haven't had a hold up in years, I read that recently in the newspaper. The railroad president said, 'Hold-ups are yesterday's problems.' Well, I have news for him: it's not."

The silence among the rest of the hobos either meant they went along with the plan or they were afraid to speak up, Ted thought to himself. He had read about such things happening, and how dangerous it could be; how the passengers were terrorized and robbed of their money and jewelry. He started to think about what he should do with this information when he was interrupted by another questioning voice.

"That sure would set you even all right, but where and how would you do it?"

Another voice added, "And what about us, can we get away safely?"

"There is only one place," responded the plotter.

"Where!" came a chorus of voices.

"At the long bridge that crosses the river, that's where. It's the perfect place to pull it off tomorrow and to make our escape. We'll use the river bank to escape. We will get us a row boat to make our escape. I know where we can steal one."

"Will there be enough money aboard to make it worthwhile?" inquired one of the schemers?

"Sure, you bet there will be, No. 4 always carries a bunch of payrolls for local towns along the route."

"But how will we get aboard the train?" asked still another.

"I'll get a lantern and wave it, it works every time, they will think the bridge is out or there is trouble ahead."

"You really think they will stop?" someone questioned.

"Why do you suppose I chose that approach?" snapped the man who had proposed the scheme in the first place. Then without giving his fellow cohorts the need to ask, he answered his own question.

"If they think there is something wrong with the bridge, they'll stop, they can't risk the lives of the passengers. It'll be dead easy."

Ted's eyes were about to pop out of his head, he couldn't believe what he had just heard. He slowly closed the hatch and slid the bolt back to lock it. He sat on top of the boxcar for several moments deciding what he should do, if anything. He began to question himself, is it really his concern, is it real, or are they just expressing frustration?

Ted felt he had a real dilemma as to what course of action he should take. Finally, he decided he could not ignore what he had overheard, he knew he couldn't live with himself if he did and it turned out to be true.

Ted walked the top of the boxcars all the way back to the caboose, and he slowly dropped down and entered it. The conductor was busy going over the manifest paper work of the train makeup, and the brakeman was sound asleep in his seat. Ted broke the silence.

"Excuse me, sir! I have some information you might be interested in hearing."

The conductor stood up and grabbed his chest, he was so surprised and shocked hearing a strange voice, seemingly coming out of nowhere. He dropped his pencil and it rolled across the floor, and Ted stooped over and picked it up and handed it back to him. The conductor almost stumbled over his chair in the excitement of trying to reach out to grab the ax hanging on the wall.

"Who in the hell are you, and where in the world did you come from?"

Ted said, "I am a hobo, sir. I'm real sorry I scared you. I didn't mean to, but I have to tell you about something I just overheard, and sir, you must listen."

"Oh, I must, who says I must." By this time the brakeman woke up and grabbed Ted's arm.

"Laddie, you're ours, now."

"Just a minute, John," the conductor said.

"I want to hear what he has to say before you throw him off. Okay, young fella, tell me what you came down here to say and it better be important."

"Well, sir, a bunch of hobos want to get even with the conductor. I believe that is you, sir, for throwing them off No. 4 passenger train a few days ago and not allowing them to ride on the baggage car blind. He spotted you when he got on this freight and their intention is to get even.

"Their plan is to hold up and rob the same passenger train tomorrow. They will flag it down at the bridge, climb aboard, and rob the passenger and the baggage car of its payrolls."

"Well, lad," the conductor said, "that's a very interesting story, if it's true. I did recently throw a couple of hobos off the passenger train recently. Are they on this train presently?"

"Yes, sir, that's what I'm trying to tell you!"

"Where are they?"

"About ten cars up from the caboose," Ted answered.

"Well, we will just have to check that out," he said to the brakeman.

"John, when we get into the yards in about ten minutes from now, I want you to throw the siding switch, and then run over and throw the iron bolt on that boxcar door. I'll get on the other side, and we will call the yard bulls to take care of our would-be robbers."

"Now, young man, you sit down in that chair and stay put. I will deal with you later and you better not move, or I'll tie you to the chair, you understand me?"

"Yes, sir, I do, but is that the thanks I get for informing you?"

"Well, we will see just how grateful we need to be later. So far, all I have is your sorry story, and we will just have to check it out."

"What other evidence of my sincerity do you need from me. I freely came down to tell you these things, and I haven't committed any crime except riding on your train," Ted replied with disappointment in his voice.

As the train approached the siding and slowed down, the brakeman stepped down and ran over to close the switch and proceeded to the boxcar to slide the bolt shut. The conductor summoned the yard bulls to inform them of the situation.

"Come on out, you tramps," a yard bull called out to them. They waited for a moment but there was complete silence. They slid the boxcar door open and to their surprise, the car was empty. The potential robbers, if they ever existed, were not inside, they apparently had jumped off the car before the bolt was locked. This gave the conductor and brakeman reason to question Ted's story.

Inside the station depot, they called the police to question Ted, and he repeated the entire story to them again. They roughed him up a little, but he was adamant that his story was true, so they decided to hold him under guard at the police station until the next day. Most of the railroad people and police thought Ted was lying, but they couldn't take the chance—they had to check it out.

The next evening, the police and railroad authorities were ready just in case the story was true. To their surprise, it all happened just as Ted had told them it would. They caught the thieves red-handed, right in the act of committing the robbery, and prevented them from completing their evil deed.

Ted was greatly relieved when he heard the news. The police and railroad authorities began to congratulate him and thanked him for the information. He felt very proud of himself for this great crime had been prevented. They treated him like a hero and put him up in a small hotel for the night.

The police chief asked him to hang around town the next morning so the city fathers could meet him, and he could give his testimony for the trial. He rested in great comfort that night, but when he got up in the morning he didn't feel much like hanging around town. He didn't feel much like a hero, he just wanted to be on his way home.

He ate a big breakfast and went to the railroad yard to catch a freight out of town. He didn't want to hang around any longer to give his testimony again, he had told the story many times already. He knew the police had caught them in the act and that was enough testimony for him.

CHAPTER 17

THE RUNAWAY

Ted watched the train crew walk the entire length of the train finishing their inspection. He noticed they left several boxcar doors wide open, so he decided to jump aboard a car early, before it pulled out.

He was tired so he laid out some newspapers to fix his bedroll to get some rest. The train gave a jerk and slowly started to move out of the siding. He took a deep breath and lay down to get some well-deserved rest after his latest excitement of being a hero. The thoughts of that whole incident made him chuckle to himself.

He had just closed his eyes, when he heard a small voice call out. "Can you help me, mister?"

He quickly sat up and saw a young boy with his arms reaching out, struggling desperately to climb aboard. He was about halfway in the car on his stomach, his feet kicking in space.

Ted reached out and pulled him inside the car, and when he got a good look at him he realized he was just a kid, probably about ten or eleven years old. *What in the world is this kid doing here?* Ted thought.

"What do you think you're doing, boy?" he blurted out.

The boy began to cry.

"I'm running away, they can't do this to me."

"Running away from where?" Ted asked as he tried to console him.

"From the Hutchinson Home for Boys. They are puttin' me up for adoption. My daddy and mommy are both dead." He sobbed. "I couldn't let them do that to me, so I left."

"But where are you going? It's a big tough world out there. Maybe if you stayed you would end up with a nice family with a nice home," Ted tried to convince him.

"Nope, that's not for me. Most families only want babies, not many people want us ten-year-olds. They were goin' to put me in a foster home anyway, and besides, I have a big sister who lives in Atlanta. I'm goin' to go find her." He broke down again in tears.

Ted was surprised.

"You're planning to go all the way to Atlanta all by yourself to find your sister, are you? How come the agency didn't try to find your sister?"

"Maybe it's because they didn't know I had a sister 'cause I didn't tell them about her," he said trying to be tough and brave.

Ted asked, "Why not?"

"I haven't seen my sister since I was five, she got married when she was in school and left home. My folks told me she got divorced and then got married again. After my folks died, I didn't hear from her again. I didn't even know what her last name was."

"I'm sorry that all these bad things happened to you," Ted said sympathetically.

"But you need someone who can help you, and maybe if you go back to the boys' home and tell them everything, they will help you. I can't help you. In fact, I could get in real big trouble if you stay with me. If they catch you here with me they would arrest me and take me off to jail, and would take you back to the home. Is that what you want?"

"I didn't ask for your help, mister. You can just leave me alone if you want," he said, trying to sound tough. Then he started to cry again.

"Oh, I'm sorry, mister, I did ask for help and I just got to find my sister."

Ted knew he was just a desperate, confused kid, not knowing what to do. He was only reaching out for help, help from anyone, anyone who would try to understand his dilemma.

"By the way, what's your name, kid? My name is Ted."

"Thomas, they call me Tom."

"Okay, Tom, I'll try to help you, but you must understand that we will have to ask the authorities to help us, but you must tell them everything and try not to be so tough. You need real help and not just help to escape from the boys' home."

The train jerked and started to move faster down the track. They were well on their way to Wichita, much too late to get off to seek help.

"Well, Tom, we're on our way. I don't want trouble for you or me, so we'll think about what to do when we get into the station, okay?"

"I'm really hungry. I haven't had anything to eat since yesterday. I left the home right after lunch," he looked up at Ted with his sad and tired eyes.

"Here, I'll share my hamburger and candy bar with you that I brought with me." Ted tore the hamburger in half and broke the candy bar in two, and handed them to him.

Tom's eyes lit up, grabbed them, and started eating like a starved little animal.

"Thank you, mister, thank you! I'm so hungry." Ted smiled as he watched him eat.

Ted laid out his bedroll to rest.

"If you want to rest until we get to Wichita, you can join me." In just moments they were both sound asleep.

The train began to slow down, and the sound of the whistle woke them up. The train was moving into the siding at the Wichita station yard, and Ted knew he couldn't just turn Tom loose, he had to find help for him. He began to wonder in his mind what would happen to him and what his future would be.

"We're in Wichita, Tom, and I'm getting off the train here. I suggest you stay aboard and let the yard bull find you. They will turn you over to the police, but they will all treat you very nice, they are the ones that can really help you. They may even help you find your sister. That's what you want, isn't it?"

Tom looked sadly at Ted.

"I'm sorry, sir, and thank you for helping me."

"I'm sorry too, kid, but promise me you'll do as I say. That's the only thing we can do now. Tell them all about your mom and dad and your sister, and good luck, Tom, good luck. I hope you have a good life." Ted patted him on the back and jumped off the train as it pulled into the yard.

He stood and watched the yard bulls start their inspection of the cars. He watched the yard bull when he found Tom sitting at the boxcar door, his feet dangling, swinging in space. He watched when he lifted Tom down from the car, kneeling down beside him and patting his head.

Tom took the yard bull's hand and walked with him toward the railroad station, and he helped him get into the police car. He shook hands with Tom before he closed the door.

Ted breathed a sigh of relief and muttered to himself, "Good luck, little kid, good luck." He was quite relieved to be in Wichita. He walked into the station to check the schedules to Oklahoma.

CHAPTER 18

MASON-DIXON LINE

The passenger train headed out toward Oklahoma. Ted was rather proud riding the train legally. He had saved enough of his money to buy a ticket, and he wanted to ride into Oklahoma in style.

He noticed that there were quite a few black passengers on the train and most of them were riding in the same car he was on. The car was full and there were about an equal number of black passengers as there were white. When the conductor walked through to the back of the car he turned and made an announcement. He said, "We are about to enter the state of Oklahoma in approximately ten minutes." That was all he said. Ted was glad to hear the announcement, it meant he was closer to home.

But then when the conductor finished the announcement and left the car, it was like magic. All the black passengers stood up and gathered their packages and bags out of the carrier above them and exited the car into the car in front of them.

Puzzled by their sudden exit, Ted asked the older gentleman sitting beside him.

"What's going on, why did they all leave?"

"Son, this is the Mason-Dixon line," he informed Ted.

"What does that mean?" Ted responded, he didn't have a clue what that meant.

"Where have you been, son? When we enter Oklahoma, we are inside the Mason-Dixon Line and there are different laws for whites and blacks. You should already know that blacks and whites don't mingle together in the south." The old gentleman acted surprised.

"I guess I didn't know that," Ted said thoughtfully.

"I have lived in Oklahoma all my life on a farm in Deer Creek, but we didn't have any black folks living in our community." He had never ventured far from home until he went to Canada with Everett, and they never really noticed any difference or dealt with that apparent situation before. He remembered the old black farmer, Jake, in his travels who gave him a ride in his wagon to the train station, and how friendly and kind he was. *I guess this is another one of those prejudicial things that gets into people's head*, he was thinking.

"I guess I just don't rightly understand all I should about such things, but I personally don't think it's right," Ted said with indignation in his voice.

"Well, boy," the man said. "Maybe not, but that's the way it is, so you better get used to it, and most folks down here don't much seem to care what you think about it, but that's the way it is."

Ted settled back in his seat thinking about how much more comfortable this ride was compared to the hard floor of the boxcar. It occurred to him how it might be possible to ride a passenger train, when and if he ever went back to bumming rides.

At the back of the passenger car was a small platform where the people get on and off the car. He could jump on that platform after the train slowly pulled out of the station and wait there until the conductor passed through to collect the tickets, and the porters were all busy inside. Then that would be the opportune moment to quietly enter the car and take a seat.

It was a plan he might try one day. He had never heard of any other hobo talk about such a scheme. But of course, it was always possible he could be caught, but they couldn't throw you off a speeding train. What they would probably do is, at the next stop the conductor would either hold you and have you arrested, or, which is what most of them would do, escort you off the train and give you a tongue lashing.

As the train proceeded ahead, he stared out the window, watching the scenery and the houses, and he wondered what kind of people and families lived in them. He noticed that all the houses had the back door facing the tracks, and most had gardens, clotheslines, and outdoor toilets.

He thought about the families who might live in the houses and how many kids they had. He could see people through the windows sitting in their kitchens, and even saw a girl combing her hair from an upstairs window. At one house, he saw a dog jumping up and down and scratching at the back door, apparently wanting attention.

Ted wondered to himself what these families would say if they knew he was watching them, and he felt a little guilty for peering at them, but he wanted to see families together and couldn't wait until he was back together with his. It would be soon.

They arrived in Blackwell, and as he stepped into the waiting room at the depot, he noticed that what the old gentleman said was starkly true. It had marked sections, a section for whites and a section for blacks, and it was the same for the outdoor facilities. On the outside was a drinking barrel that had a sign which read, "Whites drink only from the right side, blacks only from the left." Ted thought that was the strangest thing he had ever seen, he muttered to himself, *That's ridiculous.*

CHAPTER 19

HOME IN DEER CREEK

Ted felt lucky, there was a freight leaving soon for Deer Creek. He thought it might be a long wait since the little town of Deer Creek is on a side line, not on a mainline that goes into the big cities. The wait would be forty minutes, but it seemed like hours. He tried hard to settle himself down and be patient; he was so anxious to get home.

Finally, the freight was ready to pull out, and it slowly moved off the mainline onto the track to Deer Creek. Ted hopped aboard and wondered if this would be his last hobo experience. Flashbacks of all his journeys flooded his mind. It really had been a great experience in many ways, but he also knew it could be a life of many unexpected treacherous things.

Watching through the slightly open door, Ted saw a familiar sign along the tracks; they were approaching Deer Creek. He jumped off the freight just outside the depot and walked into town. It all looked the same and he could hardly hold back the tears as he stopped to take it all in. He was finally home. Memories took over his mind as he saw the old drugstore, the blacksmith shop, and he wondered if the same old blacksmith still ran it. The same old feed store was still standing, and so was the grocery store where he bought penny candy on rare occasions. He glanced over at the post office and started walking to the door. His sister Edith was the town-appointed postmistress, and he was about ready to make his grand entrance to see her.

When Edith first came back to Deer Creek, after her husband died of pneumonia, she became the town's only school teacher, teaching the children out of her parent's home. The county had no schoolhouse and very little money to spend on teaching the children. She often received her pay in the form of chickens or a sack of wheat, and if there was money available, one dollar a week for each student. It helped with the family expenses and in raising and feeding her children. Actually, she taught Everett and Ted and many of their farm friends that first year, and her own two children, Clifford Jr. and Margaret. Then she was lucky enough to get the postmistress position that she has held ever since.

When Ted walked in the doors she called out a cheery "Good afternoon," not looking up from sorting the mail.

"Hi, sis," he said walking toward her.

"Oh, my heavens," she screamed.

"It's really you. Mom and Dad have been so worried about you. They will be so happy to see you." She ran over to meet him, and they hugged each other tightly, just what he had been waiting for.

When it was time to close up for the day, they climbed into the old Model-T Ford to go home, out to their farm several miles away. As she drove she caught Ted up on all the news, all about Dad's arthritis, and how Clifford Jr. was a big help to him; how the recent dust storms were so dreadful, and how the winds were blowing the top soil away. Most of the crops on the farms have been ruined.

Just about that time, a large dust cloud came blowing across the field, blackening the sky. It made breathing difficult so she wrapped her face with a scarf, and Ted tied his handkerchief across his nose and mouth. Edith could hardly see the old dirt road, for once she was grateful for the deep ruts; they helped her keep the car on the road.

The storm soon abetted and the sky began to clear, but the car was filled with dust, and they could even taste the dust in their mouths. Edith stopped at the small creek close to the farmhouse to wash their faces and the dust off the car. Ted bent down and drank from the stream to rinse his mouth. He took his shoes and socks off, rolled up his pant legs, and waded out to the cool water. He gave the car a quick rinse and cleaned the windshield so they could continue home.

They drove into the yard, and Ted breathed a sigh of relief—he was finally home. He jumped out of the car and ran through the front door into the living room and then into the kitchen. It all looked the same, *but where was everyone?* he thought? He opened the icebox door and grabbed a leftover fried chicken leg to eat and went to look out the back door.

There she was, his Mom with Margaret as her helper, hanging clothes on the clothesline. How good it was to see her, dressed in her old faded dress, bending down to pick up one piece at a time, with two or three clothespins hanging from her mouth. He smiled when he saw her, a scene he had seen many times before. She always washed on Mondays, it was washday, and she would always wipe the line down with a wet cloth, and tell us to never hang clothes on a dirty line. Even on coldest, windiest days, she would wash every Monday, never on the weekend or Sunday. Sunday was the day for the Lord.

He remembered on the coldest winter days she would hang the clothes on the line, and before she could get the clothespins out of her mouth and fastened on the line, the shirt would already be frozen stiff. She always hung things in order, the white things first, and she never hung shirts by the shoulders, always by the tails. Ted laughed as he watched her hang the sheets and towels on the outside line. They hid the "unmentionables"—she hung behind them from any onlooker's eyes. She had the system down to a science, always using one clothespin to hold two items.

He walked out and stood at the end of the line where the sheets were flopping in the breeze to surprise his Mom and Margaret. She bent down to pick up the next piece to hang and when she rose up she saw him standing there. Margaret screamed, and the clothespins dropped from his mom's mouth as she cried out.

"Oh, my dear God, Margaret, look who's here," and she ran over to embrace him.

The three of them hugged and kissed.

They laughed and cried, and finally Ted said, "Mom, I was almost afraid to speak sooner to you. I was afraid you would swallow a clothespin."

She looked at him and laughed and gently hit his shoulder.

"You smarty, the same old jokes."

"I'll finish hanging the rest of the clothes," Edith said to her mom. "You go in the house and hear all about Ted's adventures."

"That would be nice. Just don't leave any clothespins on the line, it would look really tacky to the neighbors."

Ted laughed at her again.

"Really, Mom, we don't have any close neighbors. The nearest ones is three miles away."

She put her finger up to Ted's mouth.

"Shush, son," and she giggled at him as they walked arm and arm into the house.

"We have to watch carefully for dust storms these days. They come up so fast I can't hang out the wash until they subside. I don't know what we will do if this keeps up, at least we are better off than most. Our farm is sheltered by the hillside and the woods around the creek bed, but we still get a lot of the dust."

Dad and Clifford Jr. came in from the field at suppertime, and stopped at the pump to wash up. When they walked in the back door, they saw Ted sitting at the kitchen table drinking a glass of buttermilk. They all started crying again, as they hugged and greeted the traveler.

"Welcome home, son, welcome home," Dad said with a tear in his eye, and gave him a tighter hug.

Dad looked the same, Ted thought. Weary and tired, he was dressed in his bib-overalls, the same old blue denim shirt, and the same old sweat stained straw hat. Ted saw another familiar sight, a string with a round white tag hanging from his shirt pocket, the string was attached to his Bull Durham bag of tobacco, which he was never without.

Mom was so overjoyed to have family back together that she couldn't stop crying.

Finally, Dad said, "Now, Mother, stop that. Son, we are all so happy to have you home. We really missed you."

"Yeah," Clifford Jr. interjected.

"I'm glad you're home too. We really need another hand on the farm, don't we, Grandpa!"

"We sure do, Cliff," he responded.

"We've had a rough year, son. We do need help with the plowing, that is, if we have any land left after these dust storms let up. It looks like all the Oklahoma land has decided to move into Kansas, no one can really farm right now. When we do plow, the loose soil just blows into the air and adds to the dust. Times have been really bad, son, really bad. Lots of people gettin' sick with dust pneumonia."

"Anyhow, my old arthritis is gettin' me down, goin' to have to give up this heavy farm work, son." He sighed.

After supper, Ted and Dad set on the front porch with a glass of iced tea, one of Dad's favorite places to relax, Ted remembered.

"Look, Dad, someone just drove up in the driveway."

Two priests, dressed in their black suits and snow white collars, stepped out of the shiny black Ford sedan and walked toward them.

"What do you think they want, Dad?" he questioned.

"Let me go see," he said as he got out of his chair to go greet them.

Ted watched as they shook hands and exchanged friendly hellos.

They talked a few minutes and suddenly Ted could hear his dad yelling.

"Get off my property and don't ever come back. Ya' hear me."

He was so angered that he yanked a horse strap off the wagon bed near him and went after one priest who was quickly backing away.

Ted bounded out to stop him and yanked the strap out of his hand. He saw his dad's face was flushed and red, and he couldn't believe that his dad was ready to do harm to them. Ted turned to the priests and said, "Sirs, I don't know what this is all about, but I suggest you get in your car and leave right now." They walked swiftly to the car and drove away.

He took his father's arm and led him back to the porch. He was afraid he was having a stroke.

"Settle down, Dad, and sit down in the chair." He rushed out into the yard and pumped a ladle full of cool water for him to drink, and soon he began to settle down.

Mom came out onto the porch to see what was going on.

"What happened, Jake. I saw those two priests with you. Tell us what happened," she said.

He took a deep breath and started to speak.

"Those two priest fellows told me I was in arrears in my pledges and tithes." he stuttered for a moment and then continued.

"They said I have an accumulated obligation to the church of a hundred and six dollars."

"A hundred and six dollars!" Mom sighed as she put her hand over her mouth and begin to cry.

"I told them I don't have that kind of money and not a penny to my name with this here dust storm and drought, and not likely to have it soon. I told them I could barely feed my family."

He told them the priest explained to him that the church needs the money, and they couldn't take no for an answer.

"I told them if the crops came in next year, I would try to pay."

He stopped talking for a while, and held back the tears.

Then he said, "I can't believe it, they said to get the money now or they will excommunicate me."

He stopped talking and just shook his head back and forth.

"They told me they couldn't wait for the crop, that's when I got mad at them and told them, you can't get blood out of a turnip. One of the priests got really smart-mouthed with me and that's when I ordered them off my property and told them never to come back. I told them to go ahead and excommunicate me. I was so angry I was going to whip them, and I would have if Ted hadn't stopped me. I'm glad you stopped me, son, and thank you."

"It's okay, Dad, it's okay," Ted said as he patted him on the shoulder. They all sat together very quietly for a while, thinking about what had happened. Ted knew that the visit from the priests was the "straw that broke the camel's back." There was just too much suffering and loss from the dust storms and the depressed condition of the country. Ted thought the priests should have known that they showed no compassion at all for the farmers in the community, but life must go on and they will deal with the good and the bad.

Dad finally spoke up again. "I've been a Catholic all my life, never went to church very much, but that's what my folks taught me. I don't want to be a Catholic anymore. I think I'll just read the Bible more for myself and see what God wants me to do."

"That's a good idea, Dad," Mom said. "I'll read it with you, and we'll see what we need to do."

Chapter 20

TRAGEDY ON THE NEIGHBOR'S FARM

They sat on the porch a while longer talking about the day's events. Mom couldn't get very far from Ted's side, holding his hand off and on as they sat there. He was so glad to be home, but felt very helpless and sad about how his folks and all the farmers were suffering.

He knew things were bad as he journeyed across the country, but hadn't given much thought about how people were suffering, especially his parents. He had always seen them as "incorruptible"; they could fix anything. After all, they were his parents. He felt a bit guilty, but knew there was little he could do to change the conditions they were facing.

"Let's go in the house, Mom and Dad, it's getting dark," Ted broke the silence.

"By the way, where is Margaret and Clifford Jr.?"

"He went to Deer Creek to see some girl and Margaret went with him. You know these young kids. They got no worries."

They settled in the parlor, Mom sitting right next to Ted on the fabric worn sofa.

"Dad, what can we do to make the crops come in this year?" Ted asked, really hating to bring the subject up again, but he was worried.

"Don't rightly know, son, but we will make it. Got a barn full of hay and corn stored up for the hogs and the chickens. We're better off than some. Several nearby farmers are talking about leaving the farm, like George and Mary White. I'm really worried about them. In fact, we need to go see them tomorrow to see if we can give them a hand in some way."

"Good idea. I'm really exhausted, I think I'll turn in. Can't wait to sleep in my own bed for a change, it's been a long time." Ted smiled.

Mom laughed at him and said, "Me too, it's getting late, really past my bed time. I'll get up early and fix you a really big breakfast."

"Can't wait," Ted said as he kissed them goodnight. He climbed the stairs to the little cramped up bedroom, the place he called his own all these years growing up. But tonight, it looked like a castle to him. It was his own little castle.

After a wonderful breakfast, pancakes, eggs, bacon, and coffee, Ted could hardly get up from the table. He ate like a pig his Mom had said.

"You outdid yourself, Mom. That's the best breakfast I've had since I left for Canada."

"Let's go over and see the Whites," Dad said. "I haven't seen them in the last few days, last time I saw them was at the store in town and George told me his wife was really depressed and worried. He was afraid she was losing her mind."

As they drove the horsedrawn wagon over the familiar farm roads, Dad pointed out to Ted. "Lucky thing we have that tree line over there. It protects our house and barn and most of the forty acres near our house. That's the only hope we have for the possibility of a crop and a garden this year,"

He still has hope, Ted thought to himself, which made him feel much better.

"We'll get by, your sister helps us a lot with her wages from the post office, and your Brother Elwood in California sends a few dollars now and then, he works for the government there. Besides that, we heard from one of them oil well fellows a month or so ago. They would like to drill a couple of wells on our land. Who knows where that could go? The only problem I see, son, can you believe this, if you don't agree with what they offer you, they will set up a well next to your property line and drill the oil right out from under you. They are a bunch of charlatans and I hate doing business with that kind. I guess we'll just wait to see what happens."

They drove up the lane to the Whites' house which was set upon the hill. It stood out on the bald prairie land, as Dad called it, with no tree line to protect it or the land. Mr. White had lost his crops, and what the wind left behind, the grasshoppers ate up, Dad had said.

"Don't know why he built his house there, no trees to protect it," Dad said as they passed the field with a few dead cornstalks sticking up from the ground.

Dad reminded Ted again, "This drought is of biblical proportions. The land has turned against us, kinda' reminds me of the poor Jews having to leave Egypt to find food. I read that in the Bible."

They stopped the wagon in front of the house, and there was no one in sight. They knocked on the front door several times, and Dad finally called out to them.

"George, are you in there?"

Ted turned the knob on the door and it was unlocked. They opened it to call out again.

"George, are you there? This is Jake!"

"I'm worried, Ted, let's go in."

When they stepped inside, Dad gasped as he saw George lying face down on the floor in a pool of blood, his shotgun by his side.

"Oh, my God, what has happened here. This is awful—it looks like he shot himself…"

Ted walked into the kitchen and saw Mary lying on the bloody floor with a butcher knife by her side. Evidently, it had fallen from her limp hand.

They were both stunned and couldn't speak, but that wasn't all they found. In the back bedroom was their son lying in a blood-soaked bed, and their baby girl in the crib motionless, her little throat slit from ear to ear.

Dad turned white as a ghost, couldn't say a word, but just shook his head back and forth in disbelief.

"There's a note here on the kitchen cabinet, Dad."

Ted began to read it out loud. "Dust, dust, dust everywhere, I just can't take it anymore. Can't stop it, it seeps into the house, nothing will stop it, I'm losing my mind and the baby is always sick. Can't keep the dust out of the cupboard, and all the food is covered with dust. May God forgive me." It was signed, Mary White.

"It looks like her husband found them all dead, so he decided to kill himself," Ted said to his dad.

"Looks that way. I only wish I had known how desperate they were, maybe we could have done something," he sighed through his tears. He went on to say,

"We better go into town and notify the sheriff. I guess I knew they were having a tough time, everybody is, but never suspected anything like this. Why, why? Oh, my God." Dad sobbed.

"I hate to go home and tell Mother all these things."

"Let's go, Dad. There's nothing more we can do here," Ted said as he took his Dad by the arm and walked through the front door.

"Wait a minute," Dad said. "We ought to check out the barnyard and the barn before we leave."

They opened the barn door and immediately sensed death. They saw all the animals dead, two horses, the milk cow, and all the chickens lying dead in the small chicken house. The throats of all the animals were cut.

"Can you believe this, Dad?" Ted said.

"This is absolutely the worst thing I have ever seen in my entire life," Dad stuttered.

"I don't understand, they had chickens and eggs to eat, and milk from the cow. This just doesn't make any sense to me."

"Don't try to make sense of it, Dad. She just wasn't right in the head."

They rode into town to report the happening to the sheriff. The news soon spread throughout the community. Everyone was shocked but no one was completely surprised at the feeling of despair they must have had. Many felt the same way—the same desperation—but perhaps not to the degree the Whites apparently had. No one knew what to do except to pray. The churches in the whole area were filled on Sunday, full of desperate people coming to pray.

The entire town turned out for the family funeral. Many tears were shed and some were still in shock unable to speak or cry. The family was laid to rest. The preacher delivered a solemn message and prayed solemn prayers for each of their souls. He quoted Genesis 3:19 from the Bible:

"In the sweat of thy face shalt thou eat bread, till thou return unto the ground; for out of it was thou taken; for dust thou art, and unto dust shall thou return."

One by one the people turned away to return to their homes. Slowly they walked, some arm in arm, back to their lives, back to the difficulties that the dust storms had brought upon them, back to the sadness of the times.

"Hey, Ted, is that you?" It was a voice out of the past that Ted recognized.

"Well I'll be, if it isn't Billie Mills—how in the world are you?"

"Where have you been, haven't seen you since we graduated from grade school!"

"Went up to Canada with Everett. We were there for about a year. My cousin taught us to be telegraph operators, but I can't get a job until I'm eighteen, so I came back to help Dad on the farm."

"Oh, hello, Mr. Walters. Didn't mean to overlook you, but I was so excited to see Ted," he said apologetically.

"That's okay, Billie. How's your brother John? Haven't seen him in town lately. So sorry about your folks, they were good people, I loved your old man, he was a good friend."

"They had a good life, but we miss them. It was hard on John and me. Got to get home. Ted, come over and see us and come for supper. Can't promise fancy cooking like my mom used to fix," Billie said with a smile.

"I remember your mom's coconut cake, I'll never forget how good it was. I'll come soon, in fact, I'll come tomorrow if Dad will lend me his team. Maybe we can get in some fishing, like we used to do."

"That's great, see you tomorrow. I'll tell John you're coming, he will be excited. He's the cook in our house and he will fix up something good." On the road home, Ted chattered on and on about seeing Billie and the good times they had in school and playing together as kids.

"Can't wait to see Billie and Johnny tomorrow and talk about old times," he told his dad.

"You be careful, son. Been hearing rumors about those boys, the folks in town say the sheriff is watching them. We don't need any trouble with the law, now do we, son?"

"No, no, of course not, Dad. I'm sure they're okay."

The next day Ted harnessed the team and hooked up the wagon for his trip to Billie and Johnny's farm about six miles away. All the good times with them ran through his mind as the horse's plodded along the hilly part of the country. He wondered in his mind what was going on with them and questioned whether the law was really watching them. He knew how rumors ran rampant in this town, and how distorted the story often became.

The old wagon bumped along over the ruts and finally came to the lane that led to the Mills' house. As he turned onto the lane, he saw Billie and Johnny walking up from the creek which ran through their property. They waved their arms wildly and started walking toward the wagon to meet him.

Ted pulled up and stopped. "You guys need a ride?"

They hopped into the wagon.

"It's good to see you. Billie told me he saw you in town and said you were coming today," Johnny said as he slapped Ted across the back.

"We don't get many visitors lately."

"Why not, what happened? You two used to be the life of the party," Ted replied.

"Times are rough, you know, after the folks died, Billie and I decided to quit farming. Can't raise much anyhow, with this here drought and all. The rabbits and grasshoppers eat everything in the fields and countryside."

"So how do you make a living?" Ted inquired.

"We have a nice patch of land close to the creek, so we plant corn and raise a fairly decent crop. We have become, how to you say that word, entrepreneurs, and we have our own enterprise, so to speak," John said laughing.

"We make the best corn liquor in the area."

"So that's what the rumors are all about. You know Oklahoma is a dry state, don't you?"

"That's the reason we can make a living doing that," Billie said. "If it were legal we wouldn't make any money."

Johnny continued. "We sell it to a couple of guys who take it into the city, usually Oklahoma City and Wichita, in their soup u Model-T, and they always outrun the cops. They're the ones always getting into trouble, that's the dangerous part. So far, they only got caught one time. The darn revenuers chased them, took the liquor and disappeared, and we didn't get paid that time."

"We had our place searched a couple of times by the sheriff, but he didn't find anything. Years ago, my dad dug into the side of the hill to make us a storm shelter, but never finished it. It got grown over with brush and forest, and it's the ideal place for our enterprise, and the sheriff just can't find it," Billy added to the story.

"This is the only thing we have going for us right now. The folks in town don't cotton much to our enterprise, so our reputation has gotten tarnished, at least in certain circles. Folks don't hanker to be around us much lately, but so far, I don't think the sheriff really think it's true. He knows our folks were good upstanding people," Billie said as he hung his head, probably feeling a bit guilty as he mentioned his parents.

"I'm surprised your dad let you come out here, but he was always a fair man, but it could be dangerous to be around us these days. Hope you don't get into trouble over this. Come on, we'll walk back and show you our place, if you want to," Johnny invited.

"Sure, I'm just dying to see it and taste your stuff," Ted replied, mostly out of curiosity, but a bit reluctant to believe their story entirely.

"Most folks don't talk much about us, which is good. You know we have lived here a long time, and my folks were really respected in the community. We have helped out some of our neighbors with our ill-gotten gains, and some raise corn for us. For some, we are kinda' like Robin Hood," Johnny added.

When they got to the area, Ted was surprised. He didn't see a thing until they got to the opening of the cave. The area was just like a gulley, and as they walked into the area, the entrance just suddenly appeared. Ted knew he would never have found it in a million years. *No wonder the authorities had not been able to locate it*, he thought.

They stepped inside the cave and Billie lit a kerosene lantern.

They sat down at the table, and Johnny pulled out a quart jar of their homemade "white lightening."

"This stuff is pretty heavy loaded," Billy said, as he poured three glasses for a taste test.

"Don't drink it myself, but I have to taste each batch to test it out, you know."

Ted raised his glass and took a sip.

"Not bad, it's real smooth, I think, best I have tasted." Actually, it was the first time in a long time since he found his dad's stash in the barn years ago when he was just a little kid. He remembered how he gagged and threw up after he tasted it.

After they checked out the secret enterprise, Ted suggested they go fishing for a couple of hours, that's what he remembered mostly about Billy and Johnny. How they used to go fishing since they were just boys, and when they caught a fish they were so excited they whooped and hollered over their catch.

They caught a few fish and cleaned them after supper. Johnny insisted that he take them home for his folks. They walked to the wagon and reminisced over old times; they had been such great friends. Ted enjoyed the day so much, but as he rode home, he couldn't help but feel a little sad about his friend's endeavor. *Hope they don't get caught, but eventually they probably will*, Ted kept thinking over and over again. He also kept hoping when he got home, his mom wouldn't smell the stuff on his breath. He knew she would want to "whoop" him.

Nothing was said when he got home. His dad probably knew what he had been doing, but didn't say a word; and Ted didn't volunteer anything. He told his folks goodnight and went to bed.

One evening as they sat around the dinner table, Ted couldn't wait to start eating. Mom had fixed his favorite beef stew.

Dad finished saying the prayer and absent-mindedly crossed himself, something he had done since he was a child.

When the family saw him they all burst out laughing, and he said, "Oh, I forgot, years of habit, I guess. I don't have to do that anymore." He started laughing with them.

"I'm so proud of all of you, everyone is doing just fine in spite of the drought and dust storms," Mom said.

"We are really blessed."

"I have a story to tell you," she continued.

"When your Dad and I decided to come out here from Illinois, I was expecting my first baby. Dad was developing a lung problem and I must admit, I was scared to death. But we sold our team and wagon and everything. We had to raise some money to move on. Oklahoma land was open for folks to stake a claim, and Dad wanted to take advantage of such an offer."

"I remember so well, that was thirty one years ago. We were riding the train and I got terribly sick and lost the baby. We lost our first little baby. They stopped the train somewhere in Illinois and we buried your little brother Jacob alongside the railroad tracks. The conductor found a passenger who was a preacher of sort, and he conducted a short memorial service for us." She paused a moment and wiped away the tears.

"Little Jacob would have understood. I know we were on our way to a new life, to a better place. He could watch from his resting place under two big oak trees by the track the passing parade of people traveling to their new places to settle and change the West." She paused and noticed everyone around the table was also wiping away the tears, even Dad along with Edith, Margaret, Clifford, and Ted.

"Oh, my, I didn't mean to upset everyone, but it is a part of our lives and we have never talked about it. Our first year here was tough, and I cried a lot, but I never let Dad see me. We've come through hard times before, and we are all better for it, and we will get through these hard times too. We have a good life and we will trust God to see us through."

Chapter 21

REMINISCING

Mom loved to reminisce and share her stories with the family, especially lately since so much has happened; the drought and dust storms, the crop failures, the White family tragedy, and all the events since they came to Oklahoma from Illinois. But she always pointed out the good in everything they went through.

This evening at the dinner table was no exception. She began.

"I remember one Christmas when you kids were still small and that scrawny little Christmas tree we cut down from the woods." She laughed as she thought of it.

"At the time, we thought it was the most beautiful tree in the world. You kids were so excited. We put the tree in an old bucket full of sand and set it in the parlor. You couldn't wait to decorate it."

Edith spoke up. "I remember that tree, I thought it was the best one in the world, and we all made the decorations to put on it. Everybody else wanted to make Santa Claus ornaments, but I wanted to make stars."

"Yes, you did, and you all finally wound up making Christmas trees and round balls out of paper. You tied them together with a string. . . I remember, and Ted and Everett colored theirs red, and you colored yours green, Edith."

"Well, the closer Christmas day got, the more worried I was that there would be nothing to put under the tree. No presents at all because there was just no money to spare. I remember telling you not to get your hopes up for a lot of presents. We would just celebrate the birth of baby Jesus."

Mom began to cry, and Dad cut in to finish the story.

"We just had to save the money that we had for seeds to plant. There was nothing we could do, we just couldn't do Christmas presents. I remember telling you that hopefully the next year would be better. Our pantry was pretty bare, and we were catching rabbits and fish to eat most every day."

Mom took over the story again, regaining her composure.

"Your Dad and you boys hunted rabbits or we might have starved. But that didn't stop you kids from pestering us, even after Dad told you not to expect presents. That's when I told you all to pray about it, and Dad kept telling me to quit getting the kids all excited or to lift their hopes for getting presents. I just didn't listen to him. I kept telling you not to give up," she said as she took Dad by the hand.

"On Christmas Eve, we all went to the little country church, the Church of Christ. They always had a singing to celebrate Jesus' birth . . . Do you kids remember that?"

"Yes, I do," Ted said.

"I remember telling one of the men we wouldn't get any presents that year."

"Good, I'm glad you remember that nice man. He was Mr. Floyd Garner and he took a liking to you kids. You were so excited, he kept telling you, 'don't know about Santa Claus, he just might show up.'"

Ted laughed as he thought about the special Christmas surprise.

"I remember he patted me on the head and told me to keep praying, but to remember that times are tough for everyone and there will always be another Christmas."

On that Christmas Eve, Ted and the rest of the kids watched out the window, still secretly hoping that there was a real Santa Claus to bring them some presents. Then they heard Dad tell them to blow out the lamp and get to bed.

Begrudgingly, they went to bed. Ted felt confused. Mom kept telling them to pray, but Dad kept telling them not get their hopes up, there would be no presents. Then the question came to Ted, does God answer prayers? Mom always told him that He did. But then it dawned on him, maybe God doesn't always say yes to prayers. Maybe, sometimes He says no. But on Christmas Eve, surely he won't say no. Was it not Christmas, had they not asked God to send them some presents? All these questions kept running through his head, and finally he drifted off to sleep, tossing and turning all night long.

The early morning light came through the windows. A noise outside woke Ted, and he jumped up and looked out the window. It was snowing, everything was all white and beautiful. A team of horses was pulling a wagon coming up the driveway. Ted watched intently as the man unloaded big sacks from the wagon and carried them to the front porch. It definitely wasn't Santa Claus, he wasn't wearing a red suit, but he thought he recognized the man. It looked like Mr. Garner from the church.

Ted quickly woke up the rest of the kids so they could go explore what was going on. They all peered out the window and saw the wagon pull out of the driveway just as Mr. Garner looked back and saw them. He waved good-bye to them, calling out "Merry Christmas!"

"Remember how we all gathered around our special tree, and looked at all the special groceries and presents that Mr. Garner brought?" Mom said through her tears.

By now, these memories were so very dear to her. Now, all her kids were grown and she had grandkids to build and share new memories with.

"Oh, yes, those years were difficult. But that Christmas was a bright spot for us all. There are always bright spots in the darkest times. I just wish the Whites could have found a bright spot in their lives." She sobbed openly as she remembered her neighbors' plight.

"I remember that Christmas!" Ted and Edith said together. They both laughed.

"It was the best," Edith said.

"You kept telling us to pray…did you know Mr. Garner was coming that morning, Mom?" Ted asked.

"No, I didn't, that's the reason I believe in prayer. God uses people to do His work sometimes, and that's exactly what happened. Mr. Garner was our Santa Claus that year as well as many of the other town folks. They all chipped in and made our Christmas a great one. Always remember; the most special gift that year didn't come out those bags—it was the love of God and our neighbors and friends. That was the best gift of all."

Several weeks later, they saw Mr. Garner in town and Mom thanked him profusely. He laughed and said it was his pleasure. He had always wanted to repay his Santa Claus obligation since he had a similar experience when he was a boy.

"Ever since then I have wanted to give someone else that experience. You might want to pass that along some day to some other family, someone else in need," he told her.

"That was all very special, Mom," Ted added.

"But I remember the next day, another special thing happened to us. We saw this dog chasing a rabbit in the pasture. We had no idea where he came from, but we knew he was hungry. When the rabbit got away he came up on our back porch and just hung around."

"Yes," Mom said with a smile.

"He looked at you with begging eyes and you wouldn't have it any other way, you had to feed him. He looked starved."

"Yep." Ted laughed.

"I knew he would stick around once I fed him, he was just a pup. I named him Otis, and he started following me everywhere I went."

"You even went to the library in town to try to find out what kind of dog he was and how to take care of him."

"I found out he was a golden retriever, he was such a beautiful dog. I remember grooming him to keep his coat pretty because he got so dirty chasing the rabbits in the field."

"Boy, was Otis smart. He would go with me and Everret to bring the cows in when it was time to milk. All I had to do was tell him 'Let's go gather up the cows.' He would jump and run and do all the work for us."

"Yes, you loved that dog." Mom smiled as she remembered all the good times they had with him.

"He would do anything for you to protect you and the family."

"I know what you're thinking, Mom. If it weren't for Otis, I might not be here."

"Remember when the old bull got out of the pen and out into the pasture? He was really mean at times and this was one of those times. He was coming at me with serious intent to do bodily harm and if it hadn't been for Otis running in front of him and distracting him, he would have attacked me for sure."

"Remember how Otis grabbed him by the nose and wouldn't let go until I was safe behind the fence? I yelled for him to 'break off' and he came running back to me. Otis saved my old back side that day. He was a great dog and I miss him to this day."

"He was good for all of us," Dad added to the conversation.

"Remember when he saved Edith's life?"

Now that story was on everyone's mind; it had been so scary. Dad had everyone's attention. It was a Sunday afternoon during a picnic down at the creek. Edith was sitting in shallow water, gathering little pebbles to throw in the water to watch the splash, when a water moccasin slithered up beside her. Otis saw it immediately and thrust himself between her and the snake. He fought with the struggling snake as it desperately tried to get free from Otis's mouth.

Otis shook that old snake back and forth and finally its head tore from its body. The snake fell back into the water. Mother ran to Edith and picked her up to protect her, and everyone was so grateful to Otis for saving her from a snake bite. They all hugged Otis and petted him for what seemed like an hour.

After that incident Otis disappeared for the next few days. The whole family was broken-hearted. They feared he had been bitten by the snake and was poisoned. Ted looked for him everywhere, and on the fifth day he found him down by the creek, buried in the mud. He remembered reading once that dogs would bury themselves in mud and stay for several days to rid their body of any poison. Ted brought him back to the house, gave him a bath, fed him, and everyone petted and hugged him for a long time. Otis was just fine. He was one smart dog and the family knew it.

That story always brought tears to Mom's eyes because not long after that incident, Otis got caught in a hunter's trap and had to chew off his foot to free himself. He didn't live long after that incident. He just couldn't fight off the infection.

"It was like losing a member of our family," Mom said sadly.

"Now stop crying, Mother," Dad said. "That was several years ago."

"I know, but I loved that old dog so much."

Chapter 22

TURNING EIGHTEEN

Everyone sang "Happy Birthday" as Mom carried the cake with eighteen burning candles and set it in front of Ted.

"Bet you can't do it in one fell swoop!" Cliff Jr. challenged him. "Bet I can."

Ted took a deep breath and blew as hard as he could, leaving one candle still lit. Cliff Jr. giggled. "Told ya."

It was a happy day but also a sad day for Mom. She knew Ted would be going to look for a job. Her youngest child was all grown up. They enjoyed the coconut cake, Teds' favorite.

"I hate to break up the happiness of the moment, but since I'm eighteen, I must move on and get a job. I sure hope I can get a job as a telegraph operator to put my training to work. I sure don't want to get rusty."

"You do what you need to do, son. We're awful proud of you and we sure will miss you." Dad glanced at Mom. She was on the verge of tears. He continued, "Not much farming going on here, anyway. Don't look like this drought will ever end. At least the dust storms seem to have stopped. The world likes to run in weather cycles, and one day it'll come back to normal rainfall. I just hope it's soon."

"I heard some news in town today," Edith said. "It was about the Mills' boys. Bad news for them, but it turned out to be good news too."

"They got caught, didn't they?" Ted broke in.

"Yes, the sheriff and the officers from the Federal Alcohol and Tobacco Unit raided the farm and caught them red-handed. They were loading the bootlegger's truck, but they couldn't locate the still. They arrested the bootleggers and the Mills boys and took them to the federal prison in Oklahoma City. Sheriff Harold Smith went to the city and talked to the judge, a friend of his. He told the court that they were basically good boys and had never been in any trouble before."

"What happened?" Ted asked.

"The judge sentenced them to three years. But here's the good news: he told them he would suspend the sentence if they volunteered to join the army."

"I bet they jumped at that offer," Ted guessed.

"They're in the army now." Edith laughed.

"And I bet they're saluting everyone in sight!"

Dad felt good about the outcome.

"That's awful good. I'm really glad they didn't have to go to jail. This is a better way, they can make something of their lives now."

"Well, I guess it was inevitable that they would get caught. The army will be a much better place for them." Ted added, "Those boys were my good friends growing up. I'm sure glad it turned out all right. The army will shape them up."

"Everyone grows up and leaves the nest sooner or later," Dad said. "What do you have in mind for yourself, son?"

"Yeah, it's time you consider me gone too. I sent a telegram to Everett from the train station in town the other day, and he sent word to me that it would be easier to get a job in California with AT&T. They're getting ready to open up an office in San Francisco. So if it's okay with you, I think I'll head out Monday morning. Okay, Mom?"

"If you have to go, we sure will miss you. But all you boys left the farm at a young age to go out on your own, and everyone seems to be doing well. We just wish a good life for you," Mom said sadly.

Monday morning came and it was very emotional for her. She was crying and Dad got choked up too.

"I know you love the Lord, son. Always love Him and fear His wrath. If you do, you'll have an angel looking over your shoulder all your days," Mom said.

Ted walked over and kissed her on the cheek.

"Thank you, Mom. I'll try to keep Him first in my life, just as I keep you there too. You're the best Mom, and I'm going to miss your good cooking."

"I know you pretty well, it's my cooking you're gonna miss," she tried her best to smile.

Dad gave him a hug and a pat on the back.

"Have a good life, son. Let us hear from you."

Dad gave him four dollars for the ticket, and Edith gave him two for pocket money. The six dollars and the old ragged suitcase with a few clothes in it was all he had to his name. He was ready to strike out on his own. He even felt a little rich with six whole dollars in his pocket.

Edith and Ted climbed into the car to drive to the station in Blackwell to catch the train to Wichita. After all the good-byes, Mom, Dad, Margaret, and Cliff Jr. huddled around the car to give him a special send off. They waved good-bye and threw kisses to him until they drove completely out of sight.

Edith let him out at the station door and kissed him good-bye.

"Have a good life, Teddy," she said. "Keep in touch with Mom and Dad so they won't worry about you. Love ya', bye."

He watched her drive off and a tear formed in his eye. He realized he was really going to miss them. He stepped inside the depot to buy his ticket, and to his surprise, the agent was an old school friend, Tom Markham.

"Ted Walters, is that you? It's been ages since I saw you. How's your pretty cousin Margaret doing?"

"Yeah, it's been a while. She's doing great, pretty as ever. How's your sister Sondra doing? Ya' know, I was kinda stuck on her when we were in school."

"She's doing fine. Married now and has twin girls."

"That's amazing! A set of twins."

Tom laughed. "Her husband said that same thing when they were born."

"I didn't know you were a railroader," Ted said.

"We moved to Blackwell right after school, so I've been an operator for just over two years now. I'm on the extra board so this isn't my permanent station. I work up and down the division. I'm filling in for the operator here in Blackwell for a few days while he's sick. Where ya' goin', Ted?"

"I'm a telegraph operator too. I apprenticed up in Canada, now I'm heading to California to find a job."

They shared old times for a while, and Tom told him there was a freight coming in for a stop in about fifteen minutes.

"I know the conductor and he won't mind if you ride along, so you can ride into Wichita, free."

When the freight arrived, Tom introduced him to the conductor.

"Ted is an old school friend of mine and a fellow telegraph operator. Is there room in the caboose for a free loader?"

"Sure is, Tom." He shook hands with Ted.

"Glad to have someone to talk to. Go ahead and get onboard, Ted. My name is Gene Riley."

"Thanks, Gene. I appreciate it so much."

Ted climbed aboard. It had been a while. He realized how much he missed the trains, and he was excited to get back on the road again.

Chapter 23

TED'S FIRST JOB

Ted went directly to the AT&T office when he arrived in Wichita. He entered the busy waiting room, and it was filled with noise and clatter, the continuous sounds of telegraph machines and voices. A sign on the receptionist's desk instructed the applicants to fill out a form and wait to be called for an interview. Ted filled out his form and sat down to wait with seven or eight others; some very quiet, others very nervous. He sat there for several minutes and finally struck up a conversation with the gentleman sitting next to him.

"Have you ever noticed how difficult it is to just sit and do nothing? Whether we're at home, in a waiting room, or on a train, it's nearly impossible not to search for something to do or to look at. It's funny how a person needs to be constantly stimulated."

The man just looked at him and gave him an annoyed look like "Don't bother me." The thought ran through Ted's mind, *Maybe I'm wrong. Here's one person who doesn't mind doing nothing, even casual conversation annoys him.*

Ted sat quietly and listened to the telegraph clicking away. He decided to decipher the message coming through to brush up on his skills. He was surprised at the message he heard. It was like a light bulb going on in his head. He stood up and walked over to the office door and a gentleman asked him to come in.

The other applicants waited and wondered what was going on. Ted was the last one to arrive and the first to be called. They muttered amongst themselves, hoping this interloper would be tossed out the door. It was about an hour later when Ted walked out of the office with the manager who announced, "Thank you all for coming. The position has been filled. You are dismissed at this time."

One by one the applicants stood up and expressed their anger and dissatisfaction. They had been waiting for about two hours. A man wearing a brown hat spoke up and said, "You gave the job to this one who just brazenly walked into your office out of turn. This is not fair," they all chimed in, a chorus of voices. The manager just smiled and asked them to take a seat and he would explain everything.

"Did you not hear the telegraph sending you a message?"

"Yes, we heard the telegraph," said the man. "We just didn't know it was a message for us."

The manager continued.

"The message was for all of the applicants to stand and one by one you would be given a test and an interview in the office. If you heard the message then why didn't you respond? That was your first test. This man was the only one who responded."

They all looked at each other with dumbfounded expressions.

"What do you mean, sir?" The man held the brown hat in his hands.

"If you had heard the message and responded, you would have been interviewed. It was a simple message. This young man did exactly what the message said. The job is his."

Everyone left the office still muttering under their breath. They knew they really missed the chance for the job; if only they had been more alert.

Ted got the job, his very first one, but it was in San Francisco and it didn't start till August. He had some time to kill before he had to report. He was given a free ticket to travel on the railroad to California. He began wondering what he would do in the meantime.

He had a bright idea. Ted decided to sell his ticket to a passenger going to California. Ted could use the extra money, and he didn't want to ask his family for help. He decided he was going to consider the next few weeks as vacation time so he could take his time to see the country on his way to California.

CHAPTER 24

WESTERN KANSAS

Ted had a beat to his step. Still feeling pretty proud of himself and how he outsmarted everyone in the waiting room and got the job. He was feeling pretty pumped up, and was wondering if things could get any better for him as he arrived at the train station in Wichita.

He looked over the time schedule and decided to catch the freight headed for Pueblo, Colorado. *That's the one*, he told himself. Ted had always wanted to travel through mountain country and see the majestic sights.

He slipped out of the depot to wait in the train yard. The train was scheduled to leave in twenty minutes, so he didn't have much time. Ted waited behind a gondola car, and it looked like they were ready to go. The engine was coupled to the train, and the bulls were doing their final check.

When the train began to move, Ted ran and jumped aboard an open cattle car. He was excited to be back on the road. However, he wanted to kick himself when he realized he forgot his bedroll. But it was too late to go back; the train was on its way.

There was loose hay on the floor, probably left from the last load. He swept up a big pile in the corner of the car using his hands and feet and made a bed so he could rest for the night.

He began to wonder why he chose an open cattle car. They were used to ship livestock across country. The thought had been that the freshness of the open air would be the best, but instead he smelled the tainted remains of cattle urine and manure. It was about four hundred miles to Pueblo with stops in between, so he hoped he would get used to it.

The countryside in western Kansas was no different than Oklahoma. He watched the wind blowing across the plains, whipping tumble weeds into the air, landing wherever the wind took them to wait for the next puff of wind to move them on.

Rabbits were running through the fields, stopping occasionally to feast on the buffalo grass. Little whirlwinds of dust painted the landscape. He took out his big red handkerchief from his pocket and tied it across his face to filter the dust. Ted began to wish he had used his ticket to ride in comfort rather than suffer the elements of the western plains.

The next morning, the train slowed down and pulled into a side track to clear the track for the eastbound freight. The train came to a full stop and the brakeman closed the switch to allow the train to pass. It passed them going about fifty miles an hour, Ted estimated. The cars were loaded with cattle, probably going to the market in the east. The ranchers and farmers were selling off their stock, perhaps due to the drought and the lack of water and feeds to sustain them.

Flying sprinkles of cattle urine splattered against the train and into Ted's open boxcar giving him a strong whiff that would linger on in his clothes and in his bed of hay. *Oh, great,* he thought, *this open car was the ultimate dumb decision.* In about fifteen minutes a passenger train passed them, shaking the whole train as it went by.

He lay back on his hay mattress to wait for the train to start back up, but as soon as he relaxed, he heard the sound of footsteps on the gravel. He knew right away who it was: the train crew checking out the cars. He slipped off the car on the opposite side and jumped, not knowing how far it was to the ground. To his surprise he slipped and fell backward, his arms flailing like a bird, desperately trying to regain his balance.

He landed on the slippery, muddy shoulder of a lake bank. He tried to stand up but his feet slipped out from under him again. This caused him to completely lose control and fall several feet into the lake. He sputtered and flapped his arms, but he went all the way to the bottom. He bounced back up pushing off the bottom and emerged from the depth, back to the surface. He looked around him. Except for a few stars flickering in the sky, it was total darkness. The night was silent; only the musical notes from the crickets and frogs performing their nightly symphony.

He began to tread the water and realized he was several feet from the lake bank. The moon's rays shone across the lake, giving him some direction and perspective of where he was and what he must do.

The sound of the train whistle broke the silence. Ted turned his head toward the sound. The lights of an eastbound train came whizzing by over the trestle bridge that crossed the lake. He knew the freight that he had been on was still on the side tracks, so there was hope that he could get back aboard, but he must hurry.

Then he heard the chug, chug of the freight, the wheels slipping and screeching on the metal track, 'Oh, no!' Ted yelled out as he swam faster to the bank. But it was too late. As he reached the edge of the lake he grabbed on to an overhanging tree limb. He climbed up to the bank just as he heard the long haunted whistle in the dead of the night. He knew the meaning of that whistle, the train was returning to the main track. He watched the lights of the caboose as they slowly faded into the night toward Pueblo.

The night became silent again and it seemed even darker. He stood there totally soaked to the skin. Ted could hardly see anything around him except what the moonlight revealed. The moon suddenly disappeared behind a cloud and the wind began to whip up. He started walking west using the train track as his guide. It was then he realized he was all alone. All alone in the night.

Chapter 25

THE ROUNDUP

His clothes began to dry as he followed the tracks walking past the trestle bridge into the darkness of the night. The tumble weeds came tumbling across the track as the wind picked up, and he felt tired, very tired without some rest. But he kept on walking. He was without anything, a change of clothes, nothing, not even a match to light a fire. He had thrown his matches away; they were ruined in the water. He was thinking to himself, *I'm some hobo, allowing this to happen to me,'* as he walked on farther. The moon returned from the clouds giving him some light, but there was not much to see, just the prairie which went on for miles and a few trees scattered here and there.

To keep his mind busy, he walked on the narrow rail to see how many steps he could take before losing his balance and stepping off. Fifteen was the most he could do, it seemed. He began to wonder how many railroad ties there were on the railroads throughout the country. He stepped from tie to tie counting them. One, two, three, then he realized it would be impossible to know how many there were, hundreds of thousands. But he counted on, *ninety-eight, ninety-nine, one hundred,* as he kept on walking.

The morning light began to peek over the horizon. His clothes were dry by now, and he was glad when he saw the sun show itself for a new day.

There was a hazy look in the sky, however, caused by the dust in the air, giving the morning an eerie look which gave him a strange feeling.

Off in the distance about a quarter mile away, he saw a farmhouse with a light flickering in the window. He felt really encouraged that signs of life was close by; maybe they would share some breakfast with a stranger, he was hoping. At least he would give it a try.

He left the track and crossed the ditch to crawl under a barbed wire fence. One of the barbs caught his shirt and tore a hole in it. He slipped out of it to keep it from tearing more and held up the fence with a stick so he could crawl completely to the other side.

The fence was loaded with tumbleweeds that became entwined in the wires, and there were row after row of dust dunes which had been formed by the wind. *This is like Oklahoma*, Ted thought. Just like home.

He crossed the pasture toward the farmhouse, and as he got closer he heard dogs barking, apparently announcing his arrival. Ted saw a man stick his head out the door and heard him call out to his dogs.

"What's up, boys. come on Carl, Ben, and Onyx, is someone out there?"

"Yes, sir," Ted spoke up.

"The dogs have me cornered against the chicken house, and I am afraid to move for fear they will attack. Could you call them off?"

"That all depends, what is your business here? They are mighty ferocious animals, they're my watch dogs here on the ranch. He walked over to the chicken house and took a close look at Ted as the dogs growled and bared their teeth, ready to charge if given the order.

Carl had a hold on Ted's pant leg and wouldn't let go until the rancher called him off.

"Back off, Carl, come here, Ben, Onyx, stay," the man ordered.

"Now, young man, who are you and what is your business here. What are you doing on my property?" he asked Ted as he held his shotgun at his side. He saw Ted's clothes were all wrinkled and muddy, and he looked totally disheveled. "What happened to you, young man?"

"Sir, I fell into a lake several miles down the tracks and I have walked all night, I'm cold, and when I finally saw your place I walked over here and got cornered by your dogs. I am hungry, and I would appreciate anything you can do for me. My name is Ted Walters and I am from Oklahoma."

"Now that is a pitiful story, but I guess we can help you, come on up to the back porch and I'll give you a change of clothes. I have some old overalls you can wear. My missus is fixin' breakfast and I'm sure she wouldn't mind fixin' some for you too. Come on, let's get you fixed up."

"Yes, sir, thank you." Ted followed him upon the porch where he left Ted and went into the house. In just minutes he returned with a shirt and a pair of overalls for him to change into.

"When you finish, come on in and we'll have some breakfast," he said.

"Oh, by the way, my name is William Kizer," and he reached over and shook Ted's hand.

Ted washed up at the water pump, changed his clothes as all three dogs watched every move he made. At least they weren't growling at him and showing their teeth.

He followed the dogs into the kitchen and very shortly they were sitting at the kitchen table having a nice hot breakfast and a hot cup of coffee, which tasted so good. He felt a bit uncomfortable with all the dogs, sitting and watching him.

Mrs. Kizer laughed and said, "I think they like you, but please don't feed them anything from the table. That's what they really want, they are such beggars. My name is Laurie, what's yours?"

"My name is Ted Walters, ma'am, and I'm from Deer Creek, Oklahoma, on my way to California to take a job as a telegraph operator."

She replied, "I think most of Oklahoma has slowly found its way to Kansas, with this drought and the dust storms."

"Now, Mother, don't bother this young man with our troubles," Mr. William interrupted.

"Sir, I'm well aware of what this drought has caused. I just left my folks' farm in Oklahoma, and there are no crops to speak of, and what does grow the grasshoppers seem to devour," Ted sympathetically shared with them.

"Yep, we know, we're on the same boat. The cattle ranchers have trouble growing enough feed for their stock. We are losing livestock every day. My hay is almost used up. Sure hope we get some rain soon or we stand to lose everything."

"Yeah, I'm fortunate to have a job, but it doesn't start for six months, so I'm bumming my way on the railroad like the hobos do 'cause I have very little money. I was given a ticket to get there, but I sold it so I could have a little cash to travel."

The old rancher sighed.

"I have a little work here if you would like to stay and help out. My ranch hand just got sick and died, and its roundup time for branding the cattle. I got about three hundred head to round up. Ever done any branding before?"

"No, but I sure can learn. My folks are crop farmers, and we never had more than a couple cows at a time, and they didn't need any branding."

"I'll give you a dollar a day plus board and room. Of course, the room's in the hay loft, if that's okay with you. It's fixed up with a bed and dresser." The rancher smiled, hoping he would say yes. He was beginning to like this young man, thought they would get along just fine.

About that time they were interrupted by a loud clap of thunder. They jumped up from the table and looked out the door.

"Is that thunder I just heard? I don't believe it," Laurie cried out.

They saw dark clouds on the horizon with lightning flashing across the sky. Sure enough it looked like rain, maybe a good one, they hoped.

"Lord be praised," Laurie said as it began to rain. "Here it comes!" She ran out in the yard to feel the raindrops against her face, and Mr. William and Ted followed close behind. They couldn't help themselves; they were so excited they danced back and forth in the rain and praised the Lord, giving thanks to Him.

It seemed like ages since they saw rain and they celebrated, not caring that they were soaked and wet and acting like kids at play. They jumped up and down, singing and enjoying the raindrops on their faces.

It rained all day, and they watched it with utter happiness. Mr. William asked Ted once more if he wanted to stay and work for a while.

"I sure do, sir, sounds real good, but I can't stay very long, I'll have to be on my way to my job."

For the next few days, Ted was doing all manner of farm work and ranching, riding the horses on the vast open prairie, getting ready for the roundup. It rained off and on for the next few days; the rain was always a welcome sight for everyone.

The rain had settled the dust, and Ted saw green shoots of grass popping up on the prairie. It looked like the land was revitalized, and nature was bringing life back to normal.

Ted loved roundup time; he sat on his horse feeling the careless grace of youth, his dark eyes looking and searching for the cattle. Every movement of a twig or tree branch turned his eyes to search for them. They could be hidden by low hanging trees and branches or in the brush.

Suddenly, a bunch of quail exploded in flight just a few feet from him. It startled his horse and it reared up, throwing him to the ground where he landed on a thorny bush, ripping his pant leg.

Ted got up and brushed the dirt from his clothes. He was glad that no one was with him to witness what he thought would be an embarrassment. But he was mostly grateful that the horse didn't run off and leave him stranded. It was just a few feet away, grazing on the grass as if nothing happened.

He patted the horse's nose for a moment and remounted, ready to go about his business of rounding up the cattle. Finally, he spotted the last of the herd and rounded them up, joining the rest of the ranchers and merging his cattle into the sea of moving animals. Each animal was fighting its way through the crowd, back to back, obviously objecting to what was happening to them. They made their guttural moo-like sounds as they pushed forward into the corral.

Ted jumped off his horse to help Mr. William close the gate when all the cattle were inside the fence. They all breathed a sigh of relief when the herd was finally secure behind the corral fences. They were now ready to separate the calves from the herd to start the branding.

On the last day of the roundup, Mrs. Kizer and the neighbor ladies fixed the noon meal to feed the crew. They had cooked all morning to feed the hungry men, and Ted had never seen so much food in one place before. He couldn't believe his eyes. There were platters of fried chicken, corn bread, and all sorts of vegetables, buttermilk, fresh baked bread, salads, and a whole row of apple pies for dessert.

All the men ate heartily like they had never eaten before. Ted ate so much he thought he might be sick, but they all needed the energy to tackle the next step, the big task of branding that was ahead of them. They took the rest of the day off to rest. The next several days would be busy from sun up to sun down, wrestling the calves, holding them down and branding them. It would take every bit of energy that they could muster.

Mr. William loved to tell his story when the cattle rustlers came to his ranch about a year ago and how he and his dogs broke up their intended "party." He began:

"In the darkness of the night, the rustlers cut a hole in the fence and had about a dozen of my herd out in the road, ready to lead away, when I rode up on them close enough to observe what they were doing. I slipped off my horse with my rifle at my side and my dogs following close behind. We knew they were up to no good, so we quietly snuck up from behind a thicket. Fortunately, the rustlers had not seen or heard us.

"When I got close enough, I called out, 'Raise your hands, now!' just as I pumped the rifle back and forth so they knew it was loaded and ready to fire. One of them pulled out his six-shooter and shot it in the dark. I returned a shot and hit him in the leg, but I was aiming at his gut and missed. He fell to the ground and the other two threw up their hands and surrendered immediately.

"I told them to lie down on their bellies alongside their wounded buddy, which they did. The dogs kept watch over them, snarling and showing their teeth. Then I told the dogs, 'If they move, feel free to eat them.' I fired my rifle two times in the air to signal the neighbors, and they came as fast as they could. That's when I wrote a note to my pretty Mrs. for Carl to carry back to the house. It read, 'Rustlers, get the sheriff.' One of the neighbors rode up and said he saw Carl running as fast as he could to the house and he was almost there. A while later, I fired two more shots into the air so the sheriff could locate us, and it wasn't long until help came and the sheriff's posse arrested those three no good rustlers and hauled them off to jail. It turned out to be three town boys thinking they could make some easy money by rustling cows for a crooked rancher in the next county."

"That's a great story, Mr. William. You tackled all three of them all alone. Ending up shooting one," Ted expressed.

"Thanks, I take no pleasure in it, but we have to protect our property if we want to survive in this old world."

It took about a week for them to finish the branding, and they were glad to finish such a hard and tiring job, but Ted enjoyed every minute of it. He felt like he had worked on a real ranch, just like he had read about in books. But it was getting time for him to move on. His work for Mr. William was finished. It was going to be hard to leave them; they had become like family.

He felt a great warmth for them, and he loved to watch Mrs. Kizer's pet goose that followed her around every time she stepped out of the house. When she did her outside chores, it was comical to watch Elvira, the goose, run beside her; and when the dogs got too close, the goose chased them away. That goose demanded all the attention and definitely ruled the barnyard when she was out in the yard.

Mr. William gave Ted his wages for each day, even for Sunday when they didn't work.

"Thank you, sir," Ted said gratefully.

"But you don't need to include Sundays. You were nice enough to take me to church with you."

"Oh, yes, I do," Mr. William replied. "You earned it all, you were a big help when I needed it the most."

"I appreciate the opportunity for the work. You and the Mrs. did a lot for me, thank you."

Mr. William took him to the train station the next day.

"Come back any time, Ted, I'll find some work for you to do."

Ted watched him turn the wagon around to leave and he waved good-bye as they left, the dogs sitting in the back of the wagon watching him. He swore all three of them were still snarling and growling at him and showing their teeth. Maybe this time it was because they didn't want him to leave, he hoped.

He was going to miss them all, he thought, as he watched the wagon pull out of sight. A tear came to his eye and he felt a wave of sadness, just like he did when he left Deer Creek.

CHAPTER 26

DODGE CITY

Ted bought a ticket to Pueblo, Colorado, that cost him three dollars and twenty cents. He had some time to kill so he mulled over in his mind what he had read and heard about the infamous Dodge City. He remembered reading about Wild Bill Cody, Wyatt Earp, Bat Masterson, the Dalton gang, and the shootout at the OK corral and wondered if that story was really true.

He looked around town and could no longer see the historic western heroes of the past, shooting up the streets, although he imagined in his mind they would soon appear around the corner and he would have to run for cover. He even caught himself looking around for a place to hide if that happened.

He didn't see the old gambling houses or saloons, or the places of ill repute with painted ladies walking around the street. There was nothing that he saw that reflected the stories he had read about or anywhere he would want to spend time or his hard earned money, if he were so inclined to do so.

Dodge looked just like any other town, just a sleepy little place. What he did see was a drugstore, a mercantile, a barber shop, and a little white church building with a steeple on top, a few other merchants, a land office, and a real estate office, and not much else. It sure didn't look like the rip roaring, rough, dangerous town that was so often portrayed in the books.

He had heard that Wyatt Earp was still alive and living in California. Maybe he would run into him when he got there, he laughed to himself. The only law officer he saw was the one that looked him over as he walked back to the station to wait for the train, and he didn't bother him at all or give him another glance.

The westbound Missouri-Pacific passenger train arrived on time; and when it was time to board, Ted found a nice comfortable seat, put his feet up on the seat across from him, and settled in. He pulled his hat down over his eyes and was ready for a comfortable ride and sleep, quite different from the hobo style of travel he had become used to.

The conductor walked through the car and took up the tickets as the train proceeded out of the station yard. They were no more than outside the city limits when the train stopped and pulled into a side track, which confused him and the rest of the passengers. In a few moments, the conductor came back into the car and announced a delay.

"Sorry folks, we will be delayed for a while. There is a very serious storm reported ahead, and it's headed this way. According to our telegraph message that just came in, it is headed this way. It is reported to be a big storm, houses, lines, poles, and trees have already been up-ended. We will have to make sure the track is clear ahead before we can proceed.

"This is a very serious storm, folks. The train is all buttoned down for a heavy hit. We want you all to get down between the seats and stay on the floor. Please do not panic, try to remain calm, we'll get through this together."

While everyone was positioning themselves, Ted decided to go to the rear of the car and step out onto the platform to get a better look. He tried to roll a cigarette but the strong wind just whipped it right out of his hand. He grabbed hold of the rail and held on tight, but he felt the suctioning of the wind trying to pull him loose from the car. He tried desperately to open the door to return back inside the car, but he realized the pressure of the wind was so intense. He was trapped outside the car. He knelt down on his knees and held on for dear life.

The winds were getting stronger and stronger, blowing dust and debris which swirled around him in the air, almost blinding him. He felt a great force was trying to suck him away from the platform to include him in the twisting and violent wind that was circling around the train.

He could barely see the outline of the buildings in town, but he knew they were in the direct path of the storm. He glanced toward the open spaces of the prairie and saw the blackest cloud he had ever seen, twisting and spinning, roaring toward the town. He saw the most unbelievable sight he could ever imagine, a horse attached to a wagon flying through the air, crashing to the ground just a few feet away from the train. The horse lay lifeless on the ground, but was still attached to the shattered wagon.

The sound of the storm rattled the windows of the train, some breaking allowing the wind to whip into the car, causing the passengers to scream out in fear. He saw a large uprooted tree flying in the air and with its tangled roots it looked like a huge flying umbrella, which looked extremely bizarre. The train began to rock back and forth from side to side, and Ted heard the cries of the women and children; he wanted to join them, but didn't. A barn door flew past the train, chickens were flying at the will of the wind, some hitting the side of the train cars. Rocks and other small debris pelted the side of the passenger cars, but for some reason, the train cars did not tip over from the force of the wind, they just rocked back and forth.

Ted had never seen a tornado before, but it was everything people described it to be and even more; it was real to him now. The winds picked up to extreme speed as the storm consumed them, and the velocity had to be over a hundred fifty miles per hour, he guessed.

A sudden blast, like a giant thunder, sounded, and he cowered close to the floor of the platform and covered his head with his arms. He closed his eyes for a moment and held on tight. A giant vacuum was trying to pry him loose. It seemed like it would never end, although it only lasted a few seconds. It was suddenly quiet, a deadly silence, which frightened him even more than the noise. Had the storm destroyed his hearing, he questioned?

Then it happened, the brightest flash of light, which looked like a streak of fire, came down on them just a few feet from the train, followed by an earthshaking clap of thunder he could ever imagine. It made his whole head hurt, even his ears and teeth, and he smelled something burning, like hot metal.

He tried to look back and forth to see if the car was on fire. He could see nothing, but he noticed a second of quietness before the rain started pouring from the sky. The lightning and thunder continued, not quite as intense, but he found himself bracing for the next blast, still holding onto the train rail, his hands feeling paralyzed.

The lightning, thunder, and rain continued, and he tried to straighten his fingers, but he couldn't move them. He tried to open and close his fist, but his hands were so stiff they would hardly move. The train was within a few yards of trees that were uprooted and lying across the tracks and many more were down back toward the station yard. He managed to move toward the door to get back into the car.

Along with the other passengers, he saw the black twirling cloud move out toward the open prairie and away from the town. They all huddled together and peered out the windows. Things were quieting down some, but the wind still blew the rain into the broken window panes, but they were all just glad to be alive.

They saw what looked like a two-car work train just lying over on its side in a gulley just a few yards away from the track. A work train usually houses the work crews, using the cars as living quarters, and it appeared the storm had lifted them into the air, carrying them a few yards from the rails like they were mere egg crates. They hoped none of the crew was hurt, but knew that was probably too much to hope for; the passengers all looked around them in horror.

The train crew ran out into the rain, rushing down toward the overturned boxcars. The cars were torn apart and mangled together with pieces of debris and tree limbs, and there were broken boards scattered all around the area. Ted and the other men jumped off the train and followed them; they wanted to help.

When they arrived at the scene, they saw forty or fifty rail workers, mostly Mexican, who had taken shelter in the cars when the tornado hit. Some were dead and some were injured and couldn't get up.

People from town were coming from all around, riding horses, some running, some in buggy and wagons, but all were coming to render aid to the injured. It was still raining, but that didn't stop them. They dug into the rubble to help those who were trapped. Ted helped two injured workers walk to more solid ground—one who was bleeding profusely looked like a wheat straw was driven into his eye. Ted couldn't believe what he was seeing. The power of such a storm that could drive a straw, hammered into a man's eye like a nail.

He lay the man down and told a doctor who had arrived on the scene to attend to him while he went on to help others. Everyone was totally drenched by the rain, when all of a sudden the rain turned to hail the size of golf balls; when they hit it stung the skin like fire. It lasted only a few minutes, thank goodness, but it still continued to rain. They loaded the injured into the buggies and wagons, and they put a couple who were not severely injured, on the back of a horse.

Some of the horses were rebelling, bucking, and kicking up their feet. A couple of mules broke loose and ran full steam, pulling their wagon which bounced and flew over the track and ruts in the road. They headed straight for the barn; they wanted no part of what was happening. Other men were having trouble controlling their horses, but they soon settled down after a few minutes, especially after the hail subsided.

The town volunteers began the sad task of loading the dead into the wagons, to take them to the coroner's office. They took the injured to a makeshift hospital to be treated by the volunteer women of the community. Many of the injured and dead were their friends, people they saw every day and attended worship together on Sundays. It was heart breaking for everyone, but they rose to the need and helped each other when they needed it the most.

Other volunteers set up a water and food station to assist those who lost their homes. The rescuers were silently sobbing as they worked, sobbing for their friends and neighbors, but grateful for their own lives and the lives of others who lived through the ordeal.

When things began to settle down, the conductor of the train and the train crew worked with the volunteers to hand out towels for the passengers to dry themselves. He went through the passenger cars, thanking the people for their help and making sure they were not injured. They would have to wait to proceed to their destination while the tracks were cleared of debris and it was safe to move the train ahead. The passengers sat numb, most were unable to speak.

Ted wondered in his mind about the Kizer family, if they were all right and had escaped the ravages of the tornado; he sure hoped so. Many of the townspeople had been affected, if not directly, they were feeling the effect of their friends and neighbors. He saw the community come together and how the people cared for each other. *Maybe things happen for a reason*, he thought, just like his mother always told him.

The next day the conductor received word that the train could proceed. He walked slowly through the passenger cars, thanking them again for their help and they were so sorry for the delay. He walked out of the car, stood on the platform, and waved his lantern, signaling to the engineer they were ready to go. The engineer sounded the whistle in acknowledgment and slowly the train left the side track and began to move out onto the main line. All the townspeople gathered by the tracks, waving good-bye, grateful for the passengers' help during the storm.

The passengers, especially the women, had tears flowing down their cheeks, still traumatized by the storm, but glad to be on their way. They all felt a bit guilty, however, thinking there was much more they could have done to help the people through such a difficult time. They all knew time would heal most of them, but the hurt they suffered from the loss of loved ones would take much longer.

Ted fell asleep, just as most the passengers did from shear mental and physical exhaustion. Around seven o'clock the next morning the train pulled into the Pueblo, Colorado station. Ted disembarked and walked around the town for a short while, his clothes still very wrinkled and damp from the rain. He saw a café and decided to have some breakfast. He ordered the usual, pancakes, ham, eggs and coffee, he was hungry.

As he looked around town he saw a barber shop which looked like a place to clean up. He took a hot bath, dried out his damp clothes next to the coal stove, which made him feel so much better. He had more time to kill before he caught the next train, the Denver and Rio Grande to Salt Lake City, Utah. He needed clothes and supplies desperately, he knew just the place to go, and the mercantile he saw close to the café.

He bought a blanket, and rain slicker, a warm jacket, he knew it would be cold in the mountains, and some clothes and a sleeping bag. His best purchase, he thought, was a new pair of boots. All together he spent about ten dollars, which took a large amount out of his pay he had received, but he needed all the items he got and they would last a long time.

He went to the station and asked what it would cost to go to Salt Lake City, and was told fifteen dollars. So he asked what the next town was and how much the ticket would be. The clerk told him the next town was Buena Vista and the ticket would be three dollars. He bought a ticket to Buena Vista, leaving him two dollars for eating until he found work.

He sat down and waited for the train and all the events of Dodge City flooded his mind. He smiled to himself as he remembered when he got there he was looking for the Wild West that the town was noted for, but the wildness that he experienced was not what he imagined, but it was indeed wild.

The train arrived and Ted boarded, ready to move on to the next chapter of his life. They passed through Canyon City and what a magnificent sight. The majesty of the mountains with snow on the peaks was a sight to behold, sights he had never seen before. It took about five hours to get to Buena Vista, but he wasn't in a hurry, he took every moment to enjoy the spectacle of the mountains.

CHAPTER 27

GOLD MINING IN COLORADO

Ted stepped down from the train and the first thing he saw on the typical looking wooden station building was a sign, BUENA VISTA, COLORADO, ELEVATION 7,965 FT. As he crossed over the tracks to walk down the street, he saw an old three-story hotel with a small building attached, a restaurant with "Emily's Café" written in big letters over the door.

On the other side of the street was another building with "The Wild Horse Saloon" above the door, and on each side of it was a mercantile store, Ed's Barber Shop, an Assayer's Office, and the Constable's Office, and jail. Down the street were a few houses, and he could see a church steeple off in the distance at the end of the dirt street. *So this is Buena Vista*, Ted thought to himself.

He entered the saloon and walked up to the bar and ordered a beer. The bartender didn't ask him his age, which disappointed him since he had just turned eighteen; he just served him without question. He sat down on a bar stool to relax and drink his beer, and about halfway through his beer, he noticed his head was feeling quite dizzy. This had never happened to him before.

"Whoa," he said aloud as his head was swimming.

"What is making me so dizzy?"

The bartender heard him talking to himself, more or less, and said, "You haven't been in town very long, have you young man."

"No, sir," he replied.

"I just arrived on the passenger train a couple of hours ago."

"That's the reason you're so dizzy—you're not drunk, you are undergoing altitude sickness. May I suggest you wait a day or two before you have anything more to drink until you get acclimatized to the altitude." He chuckled. "That happens to all you lowlanders when you arrive in town."

Ted didn't finish his drink. He told the bartender thanks as he stood up to leave. He started weaving and was very unsteady on his feet as he left the saloon to walk across the street.

He went into the café and sat down on a stool at the counter, and it wasn't long until he started to feel a little better. His head wasn't spinning as much, but he still had a slight headache. He looked over the menu and ordered his old favorite, apple pie and coffee.

As he sat there enjoying his pie, a tall lanky handsome blond-headed young man took the seat next to him.

"Howdy, man," he said. "I just saw you get off the train. Are you by any chance headed upon the mountain to do some gold prospecting?"

"Well, now, I hadn't given that any thought, I'm just passing through on my way to California," Ted told him.

"Yeah," the young fella said, sounding skeptical. "I'm goin' up the mountain to do some prospecting tomorrow. By the way, my name is Chris Schmitt, and I thought maybe you might be here to do some prospecting and we could form a partnership."

Ted, surprised at such an offer, stuttered a few words.

"My name is Ted Walters, I'm from Oklahoma, and I haven't the slightest thought or interest in gold mining. I'm only traveling through. I'm planning to take the next freight train out of town."

He continued, "I didn't know they even mined gold here. All I ever heard about gold was up in California, the Sutter Creek strike in 1840, and the one in Alaska, I think they called it the Klondike. I read about it in a book written by a fella called Jack London, it is called *Call of the Wild*. You ever read that book?"

Chris smiled.

"Like I said, I'm looking for a partner. I have a grub stake for you already. I bought supplies for two. I'm not going up on the mountain alone. I'm looking for a partner, if you're interested."

Ted asked, "Why are you asking me? You don't even know me."

Chris answered, "You are about my age and look trustworthy, healthy-looking, and strong, and quite frankly I can't find anyone else to go, and I don't want to go alone, it can be dangerous. And another thing, I saw you get off the train and most people who stop off here are gold prospectors. I just thought you were the same."

"I'll offer you a grub stake if you will go up with me, and I'll give you twenty percent of all our findings. Are you interested?"

"What does grub stake mean?"

Chris told him. "Well, it means I'll furnish all the grub and equipment, including a rifle and a mule and twenty percent of our findings."

Ted was surprised.

"You mean I don't have to put in anything except my time and effort, is that what you're saying?"

"That's exactly right." Chris replied.

"How long would we be gone hunting for this here gold?" Ted inquired.

"I have supplies for three months, no longer. And if we don't find anything by then, we have to come out because winter will set in and we gotta get off the mountain or be snowbound. If you stick with me that long, you can then finish your journey."

"Do you have some kind of information or a map or something that shows you where to look for gold?" Ted was still a bit skeptical.

"Look here," Chris took out a map to show him.

"I bought it from an old prospector who came down out of the mountain last week. We sat around and talked and he told me he had made a strike and he thought it could be a good rich pocket. He was goin' to work it himself, but he got sick and had to come down, thought he was having heart problems and got scared. He was at an elevation of 13,000 feet or better. When he got well, I was goin' back with him, to partner up.

"We never got to go. That night he went across the street to the saloon to do some drinking and card playing. He got terribly drunk and got into a fight and ended up dead. No sir, we never got to go, but I have the map. I bought it from him before he went to the saloon."

"How did he die?" Ted asked.

"He got so drunk at the Wild Horse Saloon and got into a knife fight with another drunk. He ended up the worse. Before he died, he came staggering back and banged on my hotel room door, holding his guts in with his hands. When I opened the door he yelled, 'Help me!' but there was nothing I could do for him.

"The hotel manager tried to help, but he was too far gone, lost too much blood, and he died in my room a while after that. We had already called the city marshal and he arrived before he died."

"Who killed him?" Ted looked at Chris, perhaps suspiciously.

"The killer is in jail. If you want to verify my story, check it out with the sheriff. But now that he is dead, I don't have to split it with anyone, that's' why I'm asking you. He had told me not to go alone, it was too dangerous."

"Tell you what, Chris," Ted said. "I need a stake going out to California to my new job, it's in San Francisco and I'll need some money. My brother was going to finance me and my trip but he up and got married and couldn't help me. So I think I'll take you up on your offer. I want you to know that I don't know a thing about gold mining, I wouldn't know gold if I saw it. The only gold I ever saw is my mom's wedding ring, so you'll have to teach me."

"Let's shake hands on it, partner," Chris said as he held out his hand for a handshake.

"I went over to the county seat and did some checking on the different gold claims, and it's near the head water of the Cottonwood Creek. Several claims have been made around that place and a good percent of the mines have been fruitful while in operation. So you see, I'm not traveling blind. I've been doing my homework and have a pretty good idea where we can find the gold. I have talked to several old prospectors who have been there."

"What do we do next," Ted asked.

"I have my ex-partner's map, and if you're willing to join up with me, that will make me awfully glad. To repeat myself, you look like an honest and strong fella and what you'll need is a strong back, and hopefully some good luck to boot."

'Well," Ted said. "I'll need a few personal things. I would imagine I will need a good rifle, a hunting knife, a blanket, some gloves, and a winter hat. I suppose it's pretty cold up on the mountain."

"Let's go over to the mercantile store and get all the things you will need, like long underwear, it would be fitting to wear," he said.

They ate supper together and made their plans to leave the next morning after a good night's rest at the hotel. Early the next morning, they loaded up two mules with their provisions, which included shovels, an axe, and several cooking utensils, also a tent and plenty of ammunition. The mules were pretty well loaded down. Ted was amazed; Chris paid for everything, and he must have spent at least three hundred dollars for all this stuff.

Ted thought to himself, *I really don't have anything to lose.* He had nothing invested but his time, and he had plenty of that. He could practice his telegraphing when he had the opportunity, and anyhow this ought to be fun.

He quickly wrote a letter to his mom and dad to tell them what he was going to do, so they wouldn't worry about him. He dropped it in the mail box before they left for the mountain.

CHAPTER 28

ON THE MOUNTAIN

Ted followed Chris up the rocky slope as they each led their pack mule burdened down with their three months of supplies, and the higher they got on the mountain the more difficult it became. The air was getting thinner as they entered the higher tree line and the trail became rougher.

"We need to stop and rest. I can hardly breathe and I'm getting sick to my stomach," Ted called out as he sat down on a huge rock beside the trail to catch his breath.

"They call that altitude sickness. We do need to stop until we get acclimatized to this thin air, I'm getting tired myself," Chris admitted. They still had a lot more climbing to do, above the tree line and onto the upper rough slopes of the mountain.

They found a clearing and Chris made a campfire. "We'll camp out here for the night and take it easy this first day. I'm ready for a rest too. I was feeling a little weak myself, but it doesn't bother my appetite a bit." Chris laughed.

"I'm not hungry, you can have my share." Ted was still feeling a little sick and was having cold sweats.

"You'll feel much better tomorrow. It takes a few hours, but you'll be all right. I remember my first trip up the mountain, and you're doing much better than I did," Chris told him sympathetically. He opened a can of beans and ate some hard tack. Ted couldn't eat at all. In fact, he fell asleep and slept for several hours.

In a couple of days, they were moving up the mountain trail and crossed over a beautiful mountain stream, just above the tree line. They looked down on the entire valley, and it was a sight to behold. Ted was in awe of the spectacle and had to look away as he began to feel a bit squeamish looking so far down into the valley below.

Clouds were gathering so they decided to make camp near the stream; it was the Cottonwood Creek, Chris thought according to the map. They built a nice cozy fire and set up their tent.

It began to rain and the lightning bolted across the sky, followed by roars of thunder. Ted began to feel he was encompassed in the rain rather than it falling on them. He had a bird's eye view of the storm with the lightning flashing all around him.

Within an hour, the stream was full and running rampant, forming waterfalls over the rocks. They knew that higher up on the mountain the stream was probably a raging torrent, and they were glad they had crossed it and made camp before the rains came.

After a few hours, the rain stopped and the sun broke through the clouds. They came out of their tent to build a fire, and they looked down at the panorama of beautiful mountain scenery all around them. The mountains looked freshly renewed by the rain and showed their splendor as the sun lit up the slopes and the valley.

They watched from their vantage point on the side of the slope a phenomenal saga of animal behavior. A large elk herd was grazing below, and Chris and Ted watched a display of instinctive patience and love the animals had for each other and their young.

The herd crossed over a raging stream, swimming without difficulty, except for one young fawn that was swept downstream; the current was too strong for the fawn. The force of the water pushed the young elk against a sand bar, where it managed to get its weak legs back under her, and crawled back onto the bank. She stood there and shook off the water, and walked back up stream where the rest of the herd crossed.

The herd waited patiently on the other side and watched as the young fawn made another try, only to be swept downstream again. Finally, after three attempts, the mother swam back over the stream to help her young one. She led her fawn upstream and nudging her along helped her successfully reach the other bank. They shook off the water and joined the rest of the herd.

Ted and Chris watched this wonderful spectacle from an elevated vantage point and cheered them on, and celebrated with them when they finally made it. The herd had patiently watched and waited, and afterward when they were all together again, several walked over to the fawn and rubbed their noses together, as if to say "Well done."

Ted was so fascinated with them that he continued to watch them as they grazed and moved up the valley. A mother elk with twins took time out to feed her young, and as they tried to feed they were so full of energy they knocked their mother off balance causing them all to fall to the ground. She hurriedly stood up and came over to them, nudging them with her head, and Ted swore she was scolding them. They came to her again, but this time they approached her more carefully, and this time they successfully fed from their mother's milk. They settled in for the evening around the fire, and Ted told Chris.

"I wouldn't have missed those sights that we saw today for anything in the world."

"Me neither," Chris replied.

Chapter 29

SETTING UP CAMP

It was early morning and they were on the move again, their fifth day of climbing the slopes to seek their fortune. They recognized the landmarks that were on the map, and as they went up the slope Ted noticed a few abandoned mining holes that had been dug by other prospectors.

He had learned from some old prospectors he had talked to in town that the code of miners was to fill in the hole when they were finished digging to heal the mountain. It was obvious to him that some folks just ignore the rules of the game, not only in mining but in many other aspects of life.

They proceeded to climb and came to a bend in the trail that looked like an old animal trail or Indian path. Chris led the way, they were at approximately thirteen thousand feet and the air was beginning to get very thin, but the trail opened up and they were looking out into open space.

They could see the snowcapped peaks in all their glory; they rose above them like magic. They were so impressed by the vastness of the earth around them, the rise and majesty of the giant mountain peaks, and at the same time they could look down into the canyon depth, so far into a deep ravine that never ended.

Around the curve of the trail, they were suddenly on the side of a cliff causing them to feel precariously on the edge of the world. Ted held tightly to his mule when suddenly they heard a rustling sound and flutter of wings beating in the air. They both looked up and saw a giant golden eagle, almost close enough for them to reach out and touch. It swooped down and barely cleared the top of their heads, squawking as if it had been disturbed from its nest. It flew out over the canyon rim and up the side of the opposite canyon wall, squawking all the way. What a sight, they watched the eagle intently and were amazed with its majestic beauty and freedom of flight. But then, just ahead of them, they saw the reason for the eagle's sudden flight: a giant grizzly bear standing on his hind legs, looking straight at them.

The ten foot tall grizzly caused heart stopping moments for Ted and Chris; they couldn't take flight like that golden eagle, they had no place to run. Over the cliff and into the ravine was the only place to go, but of course they couldn't do that, that would be plain suicide.

They made sure Chris's pack mule was between them and the bear, but the old mule began bucking and protesting such an encounter and tried to break loose from Chris' grip. They slowly started to back down the trail, and Ted got close enough to his mule to quickly pull his rifle from the pack. The mule was becoming a bigger problem for them than the bear. The crazed mule was in a real state of panic, bawling and kicking and was completely out of control, but Chris managed to hold his rein.

Chris and Ted remained as quiet as possible and stayed behind the raging mule when suddenly for some unknown reason, the grizzly dropped down on all fours, turned around and ran off around the cliff and disappeared. When they could no longer see or hear the bear and got the mule under control, they began to move forward. They stopped in a small clearing away from the side of the cliff and discussed the grizzly bear event.

"I think I need to change my underwear," Chris said to Ted.

"Me too, that was a close call," Ted said as they both laughed a nervous laugh.

"I was paralyzed with fear, I couldn't move, we really didn't have any options, and jumping off the cliff would have meant absolute death. We had to stay and take our chances with the bear," Chris related to Ted.

"That ornery mule was trying to break loose from me. I was so scared, I'm afraid I wet my pants."

"Yeah, that bear gave me the fright of my life too. I think I lost ten years off my life. But I do think the mule probably saved our lives. That grizzly didn't look too anxious to tangle with a bucking and kicking out-of-control mule. It just gave up and left. He wasn't in a fighting mood, thank goodness," Ted expressed.

After resting a while and settling their nerves, they were ready to get back on the trail. They studied the map and followed it closely. They figured they were getting close to their destination. They came upon a small magical-looking valley, surrounded by pines and cottonwoods and followed a small stream bed for about a quarter of a mile.

Proceeding up a rather steep incline, Chris kept close track of their whereabouts on the map, they came upon a cliff that looked like solid rock, and close by was a little brook. A few feet from the brook was a small pool which had an odd appearance and a sulfur smell with steam rising from it. They followed the little brook and found that it emptied into a waterfall which fell into a lake far below. *What a beautiful sight*, they thought.

Chris studied the map.

"You know what, I think we're right here at the hot springs that is listed here on the map," Chris said as he showed the map to Ted.

"This is Chalk Creek, the beginning of the head waters, and we're close to the continental divide."

"It sure is majestic," Ted said as he looked all around him.

"This is the place we're supposed to be. I'm pretty sure it's right here on the map, everything matches. My old prospector friend said he was right here, but he didn't tell me how picturesque it was. It takes my breath away. Look, there is no dust, it's just beautiful and pristine."

"I bet this place looks beautiful in the autumn when the cottonwoods and aspens turn a golden yellow. Things look so clean and fertile," Ted described as he looked all around him.

"Well," Chris laughed.

"You sound like a poet. Hopefully, we'll have three months to make our strike before we are forced out of here by the weather."

Chris continued.

"The old prospector thought this was the spot, he felt that if we could find a small vein it would lead to a larger one. I sure hope he was right."

They walked over to the pool and dipped their finger in the water, it was warm and steamy. The sulfuric smell really smelled awful, but they both thought a warm bubbly bath would feel good.

"This is an ideal place to camp, a warm place to take a bath and a cool running stream close by to give us our drinking water. I'm sure that this is the place he marked on the map, everything checks out. Well partner, we're here," Chris said.

"Let's unpack and set up camp and get to work."

"You mean this is where I'll find my fortune," Ted commented with a smile and a hopeful sound in his voice.

"I sure hope so, Ted, I sure hope so."

Ted laid down at the rim of the spring and took a long cool drink, it was cold and refreshing and was the sweetest tasting water he had ever had.

When he stood up, he wiped his mouth with his sleeve, feeling just like a mountaineer, however they felt, they must have felt the same way.

He looked all around him still in awe of the beauty. He commented to Chris. "Isn't this the most enchanting valley you have ever seen. It smells so fresh, with fresh spring water on one side and a bubbly hot spring on the other. I can smell the meadow flowers, I swear. We couldn't ask for much more from mother nature than this. It seems almost like heaven."

They found the right spot, a little clearing away from the hot pool and near the fresh spring water to set up camp. They unloaded the equipment from the mules and set up their tent, anxious to get started looking for their fortune. Ted cut down two young trees to use them as poles to hold up each end of the tent. He whittled the ends into sharp spears and drove them into the ground. While they were working, Ted looked up across the meadow.

"Shh," he said to Chris as he pointed his finger, "look, it's a herd of deer."

A big buck, with a huge rack of antlers, pranced out into the open meadow from a wooded area and looked all around as other deer followed to graze and drink from the spring. They quietly pulled their rifles from their packs and poised themselves to watch. The buck lifted his head and tensed up, his ears pointed upward to listen to his surroundings. *Did he hear something*, Ted was thinking, *or was he just being the protector of the herd?* Finally, he settled down and started grazing with the rest of the herd.

Chris lifted his rifle and aimed it at the buck, and when he had it squarely in his sights, he fired. The buck jerked his head into the air and fell to the ground. The herd bounded at the sound of the gun and ran back into the woods.

They had to do it, both of them knowing they had to prepare food for the camp, but that didn't make it any easier. That buck was a real beauty. It lay still on the ground, and they knew it was dead. They walked toward the buck and dozens of butterflies rose up from the disturbed meadow and flew to a new location, only to disappear again in the grass.

"That was a good shot, Chris," Ted told him hoping to make him feel a little better.

"I'll go get the mule to help us get him back to camp."

"We need to gut him right away and then we can take our time to skin him out. I'll scrape out the hide and dry it," Ted told Chris.

"You know how to do all that!" Chris was surprised by his response.

"Sure, remember I'm a farm boy. We butchered hogs and cattle to put food on our table. I helped my dad do a lot of different things like that on the farm. But this will be the first deer I have ever butchered."

"This is great news," Chris said with relief in his voice. "I have never done this on my own before. I helped an old prospector once when we were out on the mountain, but he did most of the work. This is my first kill, and to tell you the truth, I don't like to do it. I'm basically a city boy, but I know we have to survive up here."

Ted took out his knife, leaned down, and gutted the deer. When he finished, they tied it to the mule and dragged it back to camp. Their work had just begun.

They hung the deer from a tree limb to quarter it and cut up the meat to smoke and dry.

"So you're just a city boy," Ted said, "you sure learned how to shoot somewhere."

"Yeah, I always lived in the city. My dad owned and ran a penny arcade. He taught me to shoot the clay ducks to knock them over. He used me as a shill at the carnivals, and when the folks saw a kid shoot like that, they wanted to try it to see what they could do. This was the first time I ever shot to kill, and to tell you the truth, I didn't like it very much," he told Ted, acting a bit ashamed.

"Don't feel that way, if you had lived on the farm like I did, that was just a part of providing food for our family. How in the world did you ever decide to be a gold miner, being such a city boy?" Chris laughed.

"Well, I was in my third year of college and I got kicked out for getting in a fight. It was over a girl I flirted with, she was a real beauty, but her boyfriend didn't like it. He got the best of me and had political pull, so he got to stay in school and I got kicked out. My dad was furious with me when I got home," he continued.

"He gave me five hundred dollars and told me to go make my own living and not to come home until I doubled the money. I think he was telling me to go find out for myself how hard money is to come by since I had thrown away my education chances. So here we are. I had heard that gold mining was a quick way to get rich, so I went up with some old prospectors to learn all about it. Now, I'm going to use my money to strike it rich, and hopefully, I can go home to see my folks with double my money."

Chris unloaded the pans they used for sluicing for gold.

"After supper, I'll teach you how to pan for gold in the stream."

"Sounds like a deal to me," Ted said as he finished up his butchering job. They laid the meat out to smoke and dry, a process Ted learned from his dad to cure the meat against early spoilage.

Ted cooked supper that night over the campfire. They ate to their fill, and afterward he said to Chris, "Okay, it's your turn to teach me something, let's go pan for gold."

They rolled up their pant legs and waded out into the stream. Chris pushed the pan into the sediment of the stream bottom, racking up the pebbles and gravel.

"This is how you do it," Chris instructed as he moved the pan in circles to splash the water and mud from the pan allowing only small pebbles to remain. They inspected the pebbles and sediments to determine if it held any gold, not really expecting to find any but to instruct Ted on how it's done.

"This is fun," Ted said.

Ted practiced the process and after several times Chris showed Ted some little flakes of gold in the bottom of the pan so he could get a good look at what to watch for.

"You have to look carefully, Ted. They are sometimes small and it takes a little time to know just what to look for. At first, we'll always look together when we pan, so we don't miss anything. Sometimes, four eyes are better than two."

It was getting dusk and time to hang up the pans to settle in for the evening around the campfire. They were feeling good about the day. They were all set up for their quest to find their fortune. They looked at the snow-covered mountain peaks and their silhouette in the night sky not far off in the distance. What a sight. Ted was still enthralled with the beauty of the mountains all around him.

Exhausted from the trip and the harrowing grizzly bear experience, they were ready for rest and a quiet night. *It was exhilarating*, Ted decided. He felt like he could reach out and touch the moon, it looked so close. He couldn't believe how the heavens displayed its magnificent pageant of stars, sparkling like diamonds across the vast sky. He lay there and absorbed the sights, but after a few minutes turned over in his bedroll and drifted into a sound sleep.

For breakfast the next morning, they enjoyed a deer steak, hot cakes, and coffee, but they were anxious to get out and explore the mountain. They packed their spades and picks and other equipment on their backs, and started out their first day of prospecting for gold.

They walked a short way into the heart of the canyon bed to get closer to the cliff and came upon another canyon, which appeared to be about a quarter of a mile in depth. It all checked out on the map so far. They ventured ahead and spotted a large boulder, which at first glance looked like a round Buddha-like figure with no nose. It sat upon a column of rocks with two smaller columns on each side. Again, everything checked out on the map.

"This is it," Chris said. "It's supposed to be about twenty feet up from that boulder."

They were so excited they started running, and Ted thought he could see evidence of yellow where the vein or pocket was supposed to be. He ran ahead to get a better look, but suddenly gasped and screamed out. Lying on the ground just in front of him was the decayed body of a dead man, and amazingly, his boney fingers were pointing toward the cliff.

"Chris!" he screamed. "Come here, quick!"

They both stared down at the dead man, not knowing what to think.

"I don't know what to make of this. I don't know any more than what I already told you."

"Did you know anything more about that old prospector that found this claim?" Ted asked.

"He told me he knew where the claim was, but then he got sick and had to come down from the mountain. He's the man that got into an argument and ended up in a knife fight, the one that died in my room," Chris said.

"It all sounds very suspicious to me," Ted continued. "Do you think that old prospector had anything to do with this?"

Chris thought for a moment.

"Looks like maybe I might have come here with a murderer if he hadn't gotten killed." He shook his head in disbelief, not sure of what to make of it all.

"I wonder if the map is legal. What do you think, Chris?"

"They must have been real serious about this claim, or they wouldn't have gone to this extent. Do you think we are in any danger by having the map?"

"I sure hope not. You know more about prospecting and staking claims than I do. We'll have to notify the sheriff when we go down. What do you think, should we give him a burial?" Ted asked.

They buried him in a shallow grave and put a marker on the ground so the sheriff could find it later when he investigates. That's all they could do, they decided.

Chapter 30

SEEKING MY FORTUNE

Back at camp, still shaken by the incident earlier that day, Ted began to wonder what in the world he was doing here. He began to have reservations about this game of mining. It just might be a cut-throat proposition, even more dangerous than riding the rails in the hobo world.

'It's too late now, I'm here. This is where I am so I'll make the best of it,' he chuckled to himself.

"Oh, my God," Chris screamed, bringing Ted out of his self-pity thoughts. He jumped up.

"What's wrong," as he looked around at Chris. He not only saw Chris running with a scared look on his face, he also saw a giant grizzly at the edge of camp, standing on his hind legs baring his teeth and growling at them. He looked like the same grizzly they had seen days before, but who knows for sure, they all look fiercely wild and menacing.

The bear moved from side to side rocking on his hind legs, slobbers dripping from his mouth, grunting and growling as he came forward toward them. Chris and Ted froze on the spot, wondering how they could reach their rifles. Chris sputtered out, "I was out looking for firewood back in the bushes when I first saw him," he shouted hysterically.

The bear dropped down and rambled over to their food stock, tearing off the canvas and raking his huge paws through the canned foods, totally tearing it all apart. He rose up again, smelled the air, and strolled over to the deer meat Chris and Ted had hung so carefully between two tree limbs. He raised up high enough to tear it down from the tree, and began dragging the carcass with him, and soon disappeared back into the depth of the forest.

They breathed a sigh of relief and ran to get their rifles. They hurried over to the rock cliff and squatted down behind a boulder to watch.

"I ought to have my head examined. I've heard bears can smell meat from fifteen miles away," Ted said.

"Really, you've got to be kidding," Chris retorted.

"No, really, I think I read that somewhere. I'm sure there's something to it," Ted told him.

"Sure hope that old grizzly is pacified for now with all that meat he stole from us. We must be close to his den and in his territory."

"Yeah, sure hope he is pacified," Chris sighed, becoming quite tired of all the trouble they were encountering.

"You know, if we are in his territory, he will be back for more. He needs all the fat he can get to store up in his body for winter when he goes into hibernation. They live off their fat until spring when they come out of hibernation," Ted continued.

"You sure know a lot about bears."

"I read a lot growing up on the farm, not much else to do at night," Ted replied.

Still hunkered down behind the boulder, watching for the bear to reappear, Ted looked back into a little gulley behind them.

"What's that, I wonder," Ted said as he looked at a box partially covered with weeds.

"What do you mean?" Chris said. "Where?"

"Behind me, down in the gulley," Ted turned and pointed to it.

"Looks like a box with red letters on it. I don't think the bear is coming out of the woods, so let's go check it out," They got up to go look.

They pulled the box out of the gulley, and written on the side of it in red letters was "Dynamite."

"Talk about luck, our dear dead benefactor must have left it there," Ted said. "I wonder if it's any good, we could use it to blast out the rocks in the cliff."

"When I got my stuff at the store, the clerk didn't mention anything about dynamite when he outfitted my supplies," Chris told Ted.

"I didn't even think about using it. Wonder if it's any good. Let's check it out."

He lit one and threw it into the stream, the blast surprising both of them, throwing rocks and water and several trout into the air. One of the fish hit Chris in the back of the head as they ran for cover.

Ted said, "It sure works all right." They both laughed as they stooped over and picked up several fish from off the ground. "Looks like we got our supper for tonight."

Chris rubbed the back of his head and they both started laughing. "Sure looks like it," he said. They were surprised at the outcome and couldn't quit laughing at their inexperience with explosives.

"I'll clean them if you'll cook them."

"Sounds like a deal to me. You know, that dynamite looks like good stuff. I bet it will help us out a lot, it should save us a lot of digging, you think?" Ted said as he built the fire for the evening meal.

For the next several days, with the grizzly experience behind them, they put their complete focus on finding their fortune. They studied the map carefully before they started digging in the spot they thought was the right area. They found some evidence it was the right pocket, and they worked enthusiastically at the rock wall until they found the vein.

They dug carefully for several more days; the vein was beginning to get wider just as they had hoped. They began to wonder if it was really the mother lode they were looking for or just a small pocket like most of the other mines.

"I know this is the right place," Chris said. "I wonder if the old prospector overestimated his prediction for this pocket."

"He may have," Ted retorted. "Seems like they had all kinds of problems predicting this vein with the dead man and all! There's gold here all right, but the question is, how much?"

"Let's try the dynamite. We don't have anything to lose here, maybe we found that stuff for a reason," Chris suggested.

"I'm all for that, let's call it a day and do it the first thing tomorrow. I'm totally wiped out!" Ted said as they packed up their picks and equipment to return to camp.

The next morning bright and early they woke up wondering if this would be the day. They ate a big breakfast and packed up their gear and made their way to the cliff. Chris prepared the sticks of dynamite, not sure how much to use, their experience with such things was totally nil. They finally agreed on how much and where to place the sticks. They dug out a hole in the wall with their pick axes and drove an iron stake into the vein, making a hole to place the dynamite. They used a long fuse so they could hunker down far enough away to keep themselves safe.

"Here goes," said Chris as he lit the fuse. They both ran like crazy and hid behind some large boulders.

They waited, what seemed like a long time, but of course it was only a few seconds until the explosive blast threw flying rocks and gravel into the air, and falling like hailstones everywhere around them. The earth opened up and blew away a great portion of the cliff, they weren't quite ready for that big of a reaction, but they didn't really know what to expect. A rock flew down and hit Ted in the head, he fell backward to the ground and was dazed for a few moments. Chris was motionless, not knowing what to do. He thought, *I killed my partner!* Hoping it wasn't so.

Ted sat up, blood running down his head onto his face. Chris jumped up to get some water to clean his head.

"Are you, okay," Chris stuttered. "I'm so sorry . . ."

"What hit me?" Ted asked. "Must have been a flying rock."

"It was, let me help you up. You scared me to death," Chris said as he helped Ted to his feet, still a little wobbly at first.

They were both grateful that it wasn't worse. When Ted felt better they went to check out the results of the explosion. What they found looked very encouraging. A large pile of rocks had fallen from the cliff and they saw evidence of large gold flakes imbedded in the rocks, larger than they had seen before.

They immediately picked up some rocks and examined them closely, it looked like they may have hit pay dirt, but it was hard to say how good the vein really is. With great excitement, they began to build a sluice wash box over the next several days, using a diagram Chris brought with him, cut from a prospector's magazine. They knew hard work was ahead of them, crushing the rocks, washing it through water to separate the gold from the rock debris, but it was going to be worth it, they knew that for certain.

For the next few weeks, they crushed up the rocks with back-breaking labor, swinging the sledge hammer to brake each rock until it was almost dust. They washed the crushed rocks through the sluice box, each time rewarding them with a few ounces of gold. Over the next three weeks, the vein of gold they were working narrowed off into just a small line. Both of them decided further efforts would not gain them enough to continue the hard work they were putting in day after day.

They had worked the mine for almost two months now and was satisfied with their take, but each day their take became less and less. Their several sacks of gold dust began to accumulate into what they guessed was a couple of hundred ounces of gold, not a fortune, but more than they had expected.

"Time to hang it up," Chris said one morning. They were exhausted from the hard work, and they knew the vein they were working was also exhausted.

The one thing they both loved to do after a hard day's work was to strip and jump into the hot bubbling pool. It seemed to revitalize them, plus it cleaned their sweating bodies. After that, they would go lie down in the cool brook, which regenerated them, bringing them back to life. Splashing in the water made them feel like kids again. They felt like it was a reward for all the hard work they had done that day. But the real reward for all their hard work would come from the assayer's office, when they get back to Buena Vista.

Fall was beginning to show, the leaves looked like they were beginning to turn, and it was getting colder at night. They had to remember they were in the mountains, frost and cold could set in any time now. They worked diligently to put the mountain back together, filling in the holes to heal the mountain as a way of saying thanks for all its bounty. They both felt very strong about the cleanup; it was very important to them.

They packed up everything they could, leaving the tent as the last thing to take down and pack on the mules. He folded the tent and pulled out the two poles he had sharpened to hold the tent up and threw them into a small little gulley just behind him. By the afternoon, they were packed and ready to go, getting anxious to be on their way.

Ted checked his pack mule, making sure everything was tied down and secure, when Chris came running out of the thicket yelling and screaming "Bear! Bear!" trying desperately to pull up his overalls from around his knees.

Just a few feet behind him was their old grizzly adversary, coming to terrorize them one last time. Chris stumbled into camp and fell, tripping on a rock.

Ted dropped everything when he saw the bear—slobbering and growling and shuffling from side to side on his large paws, heading directly toward them. He quickly helped Chris up and they slowly moved backward to where their rifles were leaning against a rock, but there was no way to reach them. The bear stood watching them, his head swaying from side to side, *it wasn't looking good for them*, Ted thought, their last day in camp, *why hadn't they left yesterday?*

As they moved backward, they stumbled into the gulley and fell on top of the sharpened poles Ted had just discarded. They each picked up a pole and thrust it out in front of them just as the bear jumped in the gulley a few feet from them, so close they could smell his hot, ugly breath. They jabbed the poles toward his angry face, and the bear knocked Chris's pole away with his giant paw, striking Chris across the face throwing him to the ground.

The bear threw his weight toward Ted and took a swipe at him with his paw, but when the grizzly lunged forward he impaled himself in the rib cage on the sharp pole Ted was holding, causing him to retreat backward. He began flinging his body from side to side, dislodging the pole from his side.

Ted picked up Chris's pole and jabbed it into the bear's neck, breaking the pole and leaving the end of it embedded in the base of his throat. The bear dropped down on all fours and moved backward, obviously injured. He turned and rumbled off into the thicket and disappeared, and they could hear him thrashing and growling as he went deeper into the woods. His growling sounded more like he was suffering from pain, rather than the roar of attack.

They didn't know how badly the bear was injured, but they knew he was very dangerous at this point. They decided not to track and shoot him, just let him go off to recover from his injuries.

"Let's get out of his territory," Chris said.

"I don't know," Ted questioned. "Should we track him and put him out of his misery, isn't that the sporting thing to do? If you injure a mad beast you should kill it, that's what I always heard."

They went into the woods with their rifles until they came to an area of boulders where they saw spots of blood scattered over the rocks.

"We gave it a try," Ted said.

"There's no way we're going to find that bear out here. We made an honest attempt, so let's get out of here and get off this mountain."

"You're right, we're not hunters or trackers. This is too dangerous."

They went back to camp and couldn't wait to leave. The mules were packed up and on edge because of all the commotion, and off in the distance they heard the roaring of the bear once again that soon faded away. They finally began to relax and the mules settled down. They led the mules out of the camp with their rifles in hand, and they were soon back on the trail, relieved to be going home.

Ted looked at Chris.

"That bear really got you and left his mark on your face. Does it hurt?"

"I was so scared I never really felt it until now," Chris admitted.

They stopped at the stream and Chris bathed his face.

"Here, I have a bar of soap in my backpack, wash it good," Ted said with concern in his voice. "I've got some salve I always carry with me. It's from my mom, we'll put some on your face. The last thing we need is an infection."

CHAPTER 31

BACK DOWN THE MOUNTAIN

Fall was in the air, it was getting much cooler at night. They just hoped they had left the mountain soon enough to avoid the winter storms. Chris led the way along the trail, and as they made their way down, they guessed and speculated on the worth of the gold they had found.

On the third day of their downward trek, the clouds began to move in, and they were soon encompassed with fog and cold winds. An early winter storm was moving in, much to their dismay. The sleet came down, stinging their faces, but it soon turned to snow. In just a couple of hours, several feet accumulated and they knew they could be in a dangerous situation.

They could no longer see the trail and plodding through the snow exhausted them as they fought to breathe in the thin air; walking became almost impossible. The mules suddenly refused to move. They were so burdened down with the packs of supplies on their backs.

The wind increased in velocity and blew down through the canyon with such ferocity they could no longer move. One of the mules slipped and almost fell over the canyon edge, but by some miracle was able to stop. Ted and Chris unloaded them and let them loose. They were no longer able to hold them by their reins. The old mules floundered around in the snow and soon disappeared from sight. The visibility was very limited.

They dug into their packs and retrieved the canvas tent; they huddled down behind a large boulder, covering themselves with the canvas. They used their blankets and sleeping bags to keep them warm, there was no way they could build a fire. They found themselves on the side of the mountain, totally at the mercy of mother nature's elements.

The blizzard continued its wrath upon them throughout the rest of the day. Ted began to question his survival, and the thought rushed through his mind, imagining a rescue team finding their dead bodies in the spring after the snow melted.

He tried desperately to rid his mind of such thoughts. He knew he had to think of survival and fight for it. He began to pray, in fact they prayed together until they both fell asleep, exhausted but hopeful.

In the morning, they were greeted by the sun when they woke up. That was what they had hoped and prayed for, and it gave them incentive to dig themselves out of their igloo-like cave. When they finally freed themselves from under the snow, the whole mountain sparkled from the radiance of the sun's reflection—what a beautiful sight—but at the same time it could be lethal to the frail human beings that they were. They knew they were totally at the mercy of a power far beyond them, blankets of snow everywhere was all that they could see, they tied a rope around them in case they got separated or fell. "I think it will be safer this way," Ted said.

"That's a good idea. Let's leave everything but our gold and get moving," Chris said as he rescued some rope from the pack.

"I'm taking my rifle," Ted said. "I'm not taking any chances of meeting another grizzly or any other animal. I just want to get off this mountain. Hopefully, those old bears have gone into hibernation by now. They are probably warm and cozy, and here we are freezing our rear ends clear to the bone."

They battled the snow for another two hours when they heard a roaring sound behind them.

"Oh, my God!" Ted cried out. They hugged the cliff wall and prepared for the worse, they knew it was an avalanche rolling right toward them, coming from higher up in the mountains. The snow came cascading over the cliff, falling into the depth of the canyon below, sounding like the roar of a train that Ted was quite familiar with.

They dug themselves out again, thankful they were protected by the cliff, and thankful they were not on the valley floor below where the avalanche finally came to a rest. Their unpredictable situation motivated them to proceed on down the mountain, and they continued until the evening sun went down on the horizon.

They felt encouraged when they came closer to town, they guessed about eight miles out. Luckily, they stumbled on an old, abandoned log cabin where they took refuge to get a long needed rest. As they approached the door, they saw one of their mules, Old Buck, lying frozen in the snow, and again they felt grateful, that could have been them.

They broke into the door and went inside. It looked very inviting, and finally, they had shelter from the cold. Chris built a fire and after they had rested for a while, Ted went outside and butchered Old Buck; that's all they had to eat. They roasted the meat in the fireplace so they could feed their famished bodies. They even gave thanks to Old Buck for his sacrifice. They were so grateful for the food that they also gave thanks to the Lord for saving them from the blizzard and providing them with something to eat.

It snowed for the next two days, but they felt rested and had regained their strength by the time the snow stopped, and so they were anxious to get started again.

The cabin door was stuck, it wouldn't open, and they were snowed in. Chris pushed on it with all his strength, and finally it opened just enough for him to squeeze through, causing the snow to fall from the roof blocking the door and burying Chris under the snow.

He dug himself out and crawled back to the door, sputtering and shivering from the cold snow that had fallen down into his clothes and on to his bare back. He was totally out of breath but was able to dig the snow from the door, so Ted could get out. They were ready to struggle on down the mountain, and on the ninth day after they had left camp, they saw a beautiful sight: smoke rising from the chimneys in the town of Buena Vista, welcoming them home. They were ecstatic. They finally felt like they were going to get home safe from the pending peril that they had faced. The snow-covered town was very picturesque, and the smell of the Pinion wood burning in the fireplaces penetrated the air. Ted and Chris took deep breathes to enjoy the pleasant smell, and Ted thought it looked like a Christmas postcard, he couldn't remember seeing such a beautiful sight ever before. They registered at the hotel and couldn't wait to go to the assayer's office to weigh their gold and find out how much it was worth.

"Eighty nine ounces," they heard the assayer say.

"The gold today is at $20.63 an ounce."

They made a total of $1,836. 07. That was more than Ted had ever heard of before. They were happy with their investment of time and money, and began to feel the payoff made it all worthwhile. Mining wasn't as easy and glamorous as it sounded, it had great peril attached, they decided.

Ted's portion as they had agreed upon was $280, more than he had ever had at any one time in his life. Chris was happy too, he had more than doubled his money and could finally go home.

"Would you do it again, Chris?" Ted asked as they ate supper together at the hotel.

Chris laughed.

"I think I got mining out of my system," he replied.

"Would you?"

"No, let's just chalk it up as one more learning experience and stay on flat ground."

"What's your plans now, Chris?"

"I'm going straight to Denver to my father's place, and then go back to college to finish my education. I hope my girlfriend, Erin, is still available. I want to date her and someday get married. She is in school, training to be a nurse."

"Good luck to you, Chris. I hope all of your plans work out. I'm going on to California. I have my job waiting for me there." Ted shared with him.

At the train station the next morning, they shook hands.

"It's been great, partner, thanks for trusting me," Chris said.

Ted stepped aboard the passenger train, and as it moved out he looked back and waved and yelled good-bye. Chris smiled and nodded as he waved back.

CHAPTER 32

THE SMITH SISTERS' BOARDING HOUSE

The train arrived in Salida, Colorado, the first stop after it left Buena Vista. Ted slept most of the way, so the time went fast and he woke up very hungry. He found a diner close by to grab a bite to eat, and of course, he ordered his favorites: fried chicken, potatoes and gravy, pecan pie, and coffee. He savored every bite, and before he left he had drank his third cup of coffee, he had time to kill before he had to go back to the depot. When he arrived back at the station, he decided to travel "hobo style" to save his hard-earned money. He was reluctant to do it, but saving money was more important. In about an hour, he jumped aboard the first freight headed west.

Unfortunately, the boxcar was an empty cattle car. He had mistaken it for a regular car so now he had to put up with the smell. He thought about changing cars, but it was too late. The train was gaining speed and moving on down the track.

The weather was cold and it started to snow. He huddled in the corner of the car trying to get warm. He listened to the rhythm of the click, click of the wheels trying to ignore the cold, but he just couldn't get warm; he just sat there shivering.

He gathered up as much straw as he could from the floor to make a bed to cover himself. It made him a little warmer, but it was not perfect; he would just have to make the best of it. He remembered how the old hobos advised him to stay off cattle cars, the lingering smell of urine and manure was always there, so between the two he couldn't decide which was worse, the cold or the smell.

After about an hour of dozing and waking, the train stopped, evidently picking up others cars. Several stops later, the freight pulled off onto a siding and he wondered why so many stops and what was going on.

The sign on the depot read, Rifle, Colorado, and the train made a complete stop about a quarter of mile from the station and dropped off about fifteen cars on to the siding, which made Ted wonder what was going on. The train remained on the siding the rest of the night, and as far as Ted was concerned, they were in the middle of nowhere.

He tried to get some sleep and slept off and on until morning, but when daylight came he got off to see what all the activity was around the train. *This must be at a sheep farm*, he thought. They were unloading hundreds of sheep from the boxcars and herding them into sheep pens. He was close enough to hear them counting the sheep, and when the last car was empty, he heard the man call out from the stockyard gate.

"That's all eleven hundred of them."

Ted was puzzled why they were moving sheep this time of year, which seemed unusual to him. He walked over to the depot to check the schedule for the next train out, and saw that he had enough time to get some breakfast at the café across the street. He sat down, but the waitress wouldn't come to take his order. The café owner approached him.

"Sir, my waitress doesn't want to wait on you. Hope you don't take offense to this, but frankly, I want you to leave, you smell awful. Why don't you go across the street to the barber shop and get a hot bath, it costs only fifteen cents. Then you can come back, it will make us all feel better."

Ted felt a little insulted and embarrassed, but knew the man was right. He quietly got up, nodded and left the cafe. He had gotten so used to the smell that he didn't realize how it penetrated his clothes and had stuck to him, making him smell just like the cattle car.

He took the café owner's advice and went across the street to clean up. The barber told him he could get his clothes washed and dried while he took a bath and shaved. He paid for the complete service. It wasn't pleasant being rejected like that, maybe he needed to think a little more about going hobo style the next time, if it was really worth it.

He went back to the café when he finished and ordered the blue plate special, pork steak, fried potatoes and beans, it all tasted so good, he was famished. The waitress asked him, "Is there anything else I can get you, honey." She smiled at him in a flirtatious manner.

"What's your name, my lovely lady," Ted responded.

"Alice," she told him, still acting very flirtatious.

"Well, Alice, I sure have my heart set on that last piece of pie I see in the glass case, that and another cup of coffee."

She looked a bit disappointed at his request but served him the pie and coffee. He wolfed it down, enjoying every bite. He did love his pie, it reminded him of his mother, and she loved to bake pies for him. Before he left, he had finished his fourth cup of coffee, just killing time before he had to be back at the station.

"Here's your bill, honey. Are you sure there isn't anything else you need," she said as she handed the ticket to him.

"There just might be if I didn't have a train to catch," Ted nodded and paid his bill of forty-five cents, leaving her a quarter tip.

Alice didn't look real happy when he left, but he thought to himself, *She looks like trouble, I could have caught a later train but I better keep moving, she looked a little old for me anyway.* He went out of the door and kicked a rock down the street. He had never had a lady be so forward with him before. He sighed, "Oh, well," and kept walking.

At the depot, he overheard some men talking about the sheep that had been unloaded earlier. The state of Colorado's agricultural department had ordered the sheep destroyed because they were infected with hoof-and-mouth disease. Ted had never heard of that before, but it must be bad if they had to destroy them, but it did answer his earlier question of why they were moving all those sheep this time of the year. That had to be a big loss for the sheep rancher, the thought ran through his mind.

Ted settled in the station's waiting room to watch the earth graders dig huge holes in the ground in the empty field across from the tracks. They must need to bury the sheep pretty deep, and he wondered if they would burn them also, to prevent the disease from spreading to other ranches in the area.

He watched the process until the passenger train pulled into the Rifle, Colorado station with a fifteen-minute stopover before moving on to Montrose, the next town west. He bought a ticket, glad to be leaving this sheep town. He felt spooky about them having to kill all those animals.

It took an hour to arrive in Montrose and he gladly got off the car to stretch his legs and walk around before they proceeded on their way to the next town.

The baggage handler was pushing the baggage and mail wagon, which was fully loaded, and unfortunately he didn't see Ted as he moved his wagon directly in front of him, throwing him off balance. Ted fell, hitting his head against a concrete step, knocking him unconscious.

After a few moments he woke up and tried to stand, but he fell back down, he couldn't remember what hit him. He felt terrible, his head hurt, he was nauseous, his ankle hurt like it might be broken or sprained, his shoulder hurt and he felt very stiff all over. He must have fallen very hard, he thought, whatever it was really packed a wallop.

"What happened, what happened?" he kept repeating.

The baggage clerk anxiously ran into the station to get the station master and called the company doctor. They carried Ted into the waiting room and explained to him what had happened. They knew his mind was still "fuzzy" and couldn't remember anything.

"The company doctor will be here soon," the station master reassured him.

Very shortly the doctor came in carrying his black bag.

"I'm Dr. Don Slocum. Tell me where you hurt, young man."

"My shoulder is hurting bad, and my arm feels numb. My leg hurts all the way down to my ankle," Ted told the doctor.

The doctor bent down and examined him.

"I think your ankle is just sprained, but that shoulder might be fractured. I'll put it in a sling and take you over to my office to get a better look at it."

Ted sat up, his head was feeling better, not quite so dizzy.

"We have some papers to fill out regarding the accident before you go with the doctor. Do you feel like answering a few questions?" the clerk asked.

"I sure do," he replied.

"Do you still have your ticket stub, we'll need the number on it," the clerk informed him. He managed to pull it out of his pocket and gave it to him.

They finished the paper work and the doctor helped him hobble over to his office just a couple blocks away. After examining him further, the doctor put a "figure eight" sling on his shoulders.

"You may have a slight fracture, but it's not dislocated. This sling will make it feel better. You'll be all right in a few days. Here's a cane you can use to keep you steady and support you when you walk. I wrapped your ankle with an elastic bandage to give you support, it will help."

"Thanks, doc, for fixin' me up. I don't have any place to stay What do you suggest?"

"The railroad will pay your expenses. We suggest the Smith sisters' boarding house just around the corner. They will take good care of you for the next three days, then I'll check you again and probably let you go on your way."

He called for a horse and buggy rig to take Ted to the boarding house and went with him to get him settled in. He was feeling much better by now. Ted couldn't believe how nice everyone was to him; they were all so nice and friendly.

The boarding house was a three-story white building, much bigger than Ted imagined for such a small town. The doctor helped Ted up the steps to the front door, and he took a seat while Doc Slocum went to get the sisters.

Two gray-headed ladies, both heavyset and smiling big smiles, emerged into the foyer with a friendly "Welcome to the Smith House," as they held out their hands for Ted to shake.

The doctor placed his hand on Ted's shoulder to put pressure on him to remain seated. He wanted to stand up to greet them, but just shook their hands instead.

"Mr. Walters is a guest of the Denver Rio Grande Railroad. He had an unfortunate accident on railroad property and will be staying with you for the next three days. He has a sprained ankle and a possible fractured shoulder, so he needs a comfortable place to rest and get better," the doctor told them.

"We are the Smith sisters," one said.

"Welcome to our establishment. We have one room on the ground floor which is available. That will be the best place for you, that way you won't have to climb any stairs."

Ted nodded as she continued, "The washrooms are out back, the men's room is on the right, and the women's is on the left. Each room is provided with a wash basin and a pitcher of fresh water every morning. If you need help getting to the washroom, just let us know."

"Sounds fine, ma'am. I'm sure I'll be very comfortable and I'll do fine," Ted reassured them.

"We serve two meals a day, breakfast and supper, but since you're recovering, we will serve you lunch also. You see, we also serve walk-in customers from the town, all you can eat for forty cents."

"Make yourself at home now. You may feel free to smoke in your room and in the living room, and we hope you enjoy your stay. Now come with us and we'll show you your room."

Ted and the doctor followed them down the hallway. The room was large and had a nice comfortable bed, a rocking chair, a chest of drawers, and hanging on the wall was the picture of a wolf sitting on the top of a snow-covered hill, howling at the moon. Ted smiled when he saw it; he had seen that picture so many times, and in fact they had one at home hanging in their living room, his mom's favorite picture; it made him feel at home.

"We'll leave you now. We're preparing dinner for the evening. We serve at six o'clock, and breakfast is at seven in the morning, all in the main dining room."

Ted thanked them for being so kind, he knew they would take good care of his needs.

"I'll be going too," the doctor said. "I'll notify the railroad that you're all settled in and comfortable. I think you will be just fine, but if anything comes up just send for me."

"Thank you so much, doc, you have been so helpful," as he bid the doctor good-bye.

"I'll see you in three days."

Ted hobbled over to the rocking chair and sat down, feeling much better. He smiled to himself. *I can rest here for a few days and have some wonderful meals, and it won't cost me a thing, maybe I fell into a pretty nice situation.*

He hobbled into the living room to relax and have a smoke. Other guests had the same idea, several who were already there greeted him with a friendly hello.

"Come on in and join us. My name is Leroy Dedmon. I board here during the winter and use this place as my headquarters to run for governor on the Vegetarian Party ticket, perhaps you have heard of me."

Ted tried hard not to laugh, but he thought his pitch sounded rather strange. He was a big talker and went on to tell Ted that in the summer months, he bought up junk metal to sell to big companies. He made enough profit to provide funding to run for governor. So far he had not made many inroads on getting elected, but he had big plans, he told Ted.

Another guest, Richard Bohannon, introduced himself. He was an author from New York and came to Colorado to write another novel. He said he could write better away from the big city. The book was coming along well, but during the last few days he was stuck, he was having writer's block. Ted noticed that he coughed a lot and carried a handkerchief in his hand, *Maybe he has tuberculosis*, Ted thought, but hoped that he didn't.

One more guest, a rather quiet man named Ken Kalender, stood up and shook Ted's hand. He was a sheep rancher and told his story how he just lost a large herd of sheep to hoof-and-mouth disease and had to put them all down. Ted felt great distress for him, and didn't have the heart to tell him he had just witnessed that event just a few days ago.

Ted told them all about his accident at the train station and they all offered their assistance if he needed it.

At dinner that evening, he enjoyed the conversation with all the guests he had met, but he did notice one thing, Mr. Dedmon, the Vegetarian Party ticket candidate, ate meat for dinner, Ted thought that was a little strange. Also at dinner, an attractive middle-aged lady, Rita Austin, introduced herself. She owned the town's hardware store that her husband had operated before he passed away. She has lived at the boarding house ever since her husband died because she didn't want to live alone in a big house, this way she was never lonely. She invited Ted to join them after dinner in the music room. She loved to play the piano and sing, and they could all have an enjoyable evening together.

"Do you like to sing, Ted?" she asked.

"I never thought of myself as a singer. I did sing in a church choir when I was a boy," he said smiling at her.

Another interesting man he met that evening was Matthew Amos, who was a clothing salesman, and he loved to play the clarinet as a hobby. He played along while they all sang songs around the piano. He sold women's apparel to all the stores in Colorado and traveled throughout the year, filling orders. He liked to travel, but he needed a place to stay in the off season, so he stayed at the boarding house to take his two months off and to relax and rest from his travels.

Ted enjoyed the evening gatherings at the piano, and he truly enjoyed all their meals together. Those Smith sisters really knew how to cook, but what he enjoyed the most was playing cards with the guys practically every evening.

Learning to play bridge was great entertainment. He had never played it before. Mr. Dedmon was a great instructor and made the game fun. Ted knew it was going to be hard to leave the boarding house; it was a great place to be and he had met many new friends.

When his three days were up and his doctor dismissed him because he was "doing well and healing," he decided to stay an extra three days using his card playing winnings of nine dollars and ninety five cents to pay for it.

Despite his injuries, he had a great stopover, but it was time to move on. He bid his good-byes to all his new friends, and sadly told them he had to be on his way. His boarding house experience and memories of the wonderful people he had met would always remain with him as a very enjoyable and special time.

CHAPTER 33

THE MOUNTAIN STORM

The freight train pulled in just as Ted arrived at the station. The crew immediately added several cars from the side tracks to make up the train before it pulled out again. He walked down to about the middle of the train to wait and watch until it was prepared to move out.

They coupled up all the added cars, and the train began to move down the track to the main line, ready to go. To Ted's surprise, a group of about a dozen hobos emerged from their hidden camp in the woods and ran to jump aboard. He hadn't seen that many together in a long time. He followed them and jumped aboard a boxcar; it seemed like old times.

The train moved slowly along and seemed to be constantly climbing up an incline, in fact the crew had added an extra snow plow engine to give the train the extra power it needed to climb and to clear the tracks of snow as it moved up the steep divide to the pass. Ted knew this trip might be a little different; he had never traveled in the high mountains before. Of all the times Ted rode the rails, he never once felt for his personal safety. He felt like a free spirit, met lots of nice people, but this time he had an uneasy feeling. He couldn't understand why he felt so uneasy, he even had a premonition of danger; he just felt something wasn't right.

Riding the rails for him usually gave him a real sense of independence and a panorama view of the beautiful countryside. He loved it when crossing the Kansas plains and seeing the golden wheat fields, and when he got to soak up the beauty of the patches of wildflowers and yellow sunflowers in the vast open spaces. And now here he is up in the Colorado mountains, watching the snowcapped mountain peaks off in the distance. *This is awesome*, he thought.

He loved to daydream as the train moved along the track. It gave him the feeling of freedom—freedom to make his own choices—but the freedom was often interrupted by random events that seemed to pop up every day, forcing him to quickly evaluate his situation and act upon it if necessary, but that's life.

Just like this very moment, he thought to himself, *not a living soul of his family or friends know where he is right now.* That's total freedom and independence. Yet he didn't want to be totally independent of them, just able to spread his wings, yearning to grow up and be his own person.

He was fully aware they were in the high mountain country. Maybe that was why he had this pending feeling of danger. It was cold, the ground was totally white with snow, he had never traveled in such high country before, and it was just different. But at the same time, he felt that independence and excitement as the train chugged along, climbing and moving cautiously up the divide.

The train slowly moved into a siding to allow a passenger train to pass, and then proceeded back to the main track through the heavy snowdrifts, the engines groaning and moaning all the way. It seemed to Ted they were getting nowhere fast.

The train finally came to a complete stop. Ted slid the door open and looked back at the long line of cars. What he saw took his breath away. The last half of the train was sitting on a very high trestle, high above a canyon so deep he had difficulty seeing the bottom; he felt like he was suspended in air. He looked to the front and saw the crew disconnecting the big snow plow engine from the train. They were approaching the entrance of a tunnel which was blocked by a huge pile of snow from an avalanche. He knew they weren't going anywhere until they could break down the snow pile so they could enter the tunnel.

Ted thought they would be there for a while and it was cold, so he lay back on to his sleeping bag and tried to get warm, and maybe get some sleep. This was a whole different experience than he ever had before. He wondered if this might be the impending danger he was feeling. They could even freeze to death if they were stuck here for a long time. The thought came to him as he remembered his journey down the mountain with Chris, and how cold and uneasy they were. This is even more harrowing—they are stuck here, high over a canyon with nowhere to go.

He tried to relax, but the cold and the feeling of impending danger wouldn't allow his mind to slow down. *He could possibly freeze to death*, he kept thinking. His mind was racing head-on, it wouldn't stop, and he kept thinking, *What will happen to us?* He remembered reading one time that when people freeze to death, they just go to sleep, it wasn't a painful end.

He began to hope that was true. He thought of his family, how dear they were to him, and finally he remembered to pray. He prayed harder than he had ever before. It was in God's hands, he kept saying.

The snow plow kept stalling out, the wheels kept slipping as the engineer tried to clear the track for the train to move ahead, but it began to seem hopeless. Ted lay there in his bedroll and his thoughts were suddenly interrupted by a rumble that soon erupted into an earthshaking roar, not like the sound of thunder, but more ominous than that. "Is this it," Ted questioned as he braced himself for whatever was to come.

The entire train began to shudder and vibrate. Ted's car was located directly over the canyon. He jumped up, slid open the door, and jumped down to the track. He felt a great sense of peril and ran toward the tunnel entrance, hoping somehow to find safety. Something told him to move quickly, perhaps it was a whisper from God.

He ran toward the tunnel entrance and the engineer and fireman jumped down from the engine and followed him just a few steps behind. The snow was high and deep; they all lost their footing and fell, but frantically got up and finally made it to the tunnel entrance.

Ted looked back and saw two men, probably hobos, running and falling, struggling to escape the peril. The rumble and the loud resounding roar returned even louder than the first, bringing a cascading avalanche of snow and rocks plummeting into the canyon, virtually rocking the mountain side. The lower half of the train began to sway, throwing the men from the trestle, sending them into the canyon below.

Ted felt paralyzed. Everything seemed to move into slow motion as he watched the train being pulled backward. One by one the cars, still attached, plummeted downward as the trestle gave way, finally pulling the engine downward with its headlight shining through the snow. It was difficult to watch the mighty engine falling into space; its light pointed upward like a beacon through the falling snow, as it tumbled and crashed into the gorge far below.

The echo of the crash reverberated through the mountains, seemingly forever. All that remained was the snow plow engine, which had been detached, the engineer, the fireman, and Ted, all unharmed. They couldn't utter a word to each other, just stood motionless and stunned by what they had just witnessed.

For a moment Ted's mind played the "what if" game with his thoughts— what if I hadn't jumped off that boxcar. No, he just wouldn't allow his mind to play that game.

The blizzard continued for most of the day, and they continually heard the trees and rocks falling into the canyon, creating muffled explosive sounds which echoed through the canyon.

Ted helped the engineer and fireman dig their way through the pile of snow and rocks, which was about six feet high, to open up the tunnel entrance to get out of the storm. But when they entered the tunnel, the wind was so strong and cold it was too miserable to stay, it offered no protection for them. They decided to stay in the engine cab to see if they could fire up the boiler, hoping to get the track cleared so they could get off this mountain.

Ted helped the fireman shovel coal into the engine furnace to fire up the boiler again. It worked, they got the boiler going, and after a while they had a much warmer cab to spend the night in.

The next morning, the engineer and fireman put their plan into action to clear the tunnel entrance for the engine to pass though. The snow plow engine moved back and forth pushing and throwing the snow off to the side, and inch by inch they slowly chiseled their way, clearing the track to open the tunnel entrance.

They inspected the track and felt it was clear enough for them to move the engine through. Fortunately, they found the opposite end of the tunnel passable, nothing that the snow plow couldn't handle. Finally, they were on their way off the snowy mountain that had totally interrupted their journey and lives. They began to relax and took a deep breath as the engine moved slowly down the mountain.

After several hours, they pulled into the Leadville, Colorado freight yard, just the three of them and the crippled engine and coal car. They were greeted by anxious railroad officials and relieved passengers who were waiting for the news of what was happening down the line, they had lost all communications. There were freight trains and passenger trains backed up and waiting for clearance to proceed.

They were devastated when they heard the news of the loss of the freight train and trestle bridge, and also the loss of lives. The news was much more troubling than they had expected. They were only expecting delays from the storm, not the terrible news that they received.

For the waiting passengers, the disappointment of delay soon turned to sorrow, just as it did for the railroad officials. This news also meant it would cut off traffic on this route through the mountains for several months, maybe even years. The cost of rebuilding the bridge and tracks would be tremendous for the Denver Rio Grande Western Railroad, and for all the people who lived on this side of the mountain. They would be isolated from the rest of the world.

The people walked away from the station with their heads lowered in despair. Ted asked the engineer what the trains heading east would do.

"This station has a turntable, we are fortunate, we can turn the engine around to go back west and connect with another line," he told Ted.

"That's what we will do here in Leadville."

Ted went to the closest restaurant and ate the biggest meal he had ever had. He was starved, it had been about two days since he had eaten. When he returned to the station yard, he watched the crew make up their trains, all having to change their plans because of the devastation of the day.

After a long wait, he jumped aboard a freight going west. He was exhausted, both physically and mentally, but he was moving on and would soon be in Salt Lake City.

Chapter 34

CALIFORNIA-BOUND

They arrived in Salt Lake City without incident. He had slept most of the way so he didn't remember much about the trip. He went outside to the men's room and washed up as best he could before going to the diner to get some lunch. He was hungry as always.

After ordering his favorites, except this time it was chicken fried steak, he counted his money and was glad he still had most of his gold prospecting money left. He needed to get some clothes before he arrived in San Francisco. His traveling clothes were getting totally tattered and worn through all the events of the past few days.

After he gobbled down his lunch, he went across the street to the men's haberdashery to get some new clothes. He was surprised at the fancy styles; all he wanted was plain old clothes to travel the rest of the way, and perhaps a suit to wear to report to his new job.

The helpful salesman complimented everything he tried on for size with comments like "That makes you look very handsome," and "That was made just for you." He liked everything, but he didn't want to look like a dandy. So he decided on a very conservative handmade suit, sixteen dollars; an overcoat, nine dollars; three shirts and a tie, a new pair of shoes, two pairs of trousers, a brown derby hat, and a suitcase to carry all his new stuff, forty-five dollars in all. Now he was outfitted for his new job in California.

Ted went to the barber shop and took a hot bath, got a haircut and changed into one of his new shirts and trousers, and put on his new overcoat. He threw all his old dirty clothes into the trash can behind the barber shop and went back to the train station.

He purchased a ticket to San Francisco for twenty-two dollars, which would leave that evening on the Southwest Pacific line. He wanted to arrive in California in style and comfort, not in a cold boxcar looking at the countryside through a crack in the car. This way, he could look out the window and take in all of the beauty of the land.

After eating sirloin steak for supper, he returned to the depot to board the train. He looked at the clock as he got on the train. It was seven o'clock in the evening. He saw an empty seat.

"Excuse me, sir. Is this seat taken?" he asked the fellow sitting next to it.

"No sir, it isn't," he replied. Ted sat down and leaned back into his comfortable seat thinking he could easily get a good night's sleep.

The conductor came through the car and asked for their tickets. Ted handed it to him.

"You'll need to change trains in Los Angeles to go on to San Francisco, should arrive in the morning about six o'clock."

"Thank you, sir," Ted said smiling at the conductor as he moved on down the aisle to collect the rest of the tickets.

"Howdy, mister," a little girl said to Ted from across the aisle.

"My name is Sondra Alley, what's yours?"

"Sondra, leave the gentleman alone. He is trying to rest," her mother tried to quiet her.

"Yes, Momma. I'm sorry, mister. I didn't mean to be a bother to you," she reacted.

"That's all right, Sondra, I'm not sleepy right now. Where are you going?" he asked her.

"We're going to Los Angeles. My daddy lives there and I'm going to see him," she said as her eyes lit up in excitement.

"Your daddy will be awful glad to see you, I'm sure. You're such a pretty little girl. How old are you, Sondra?"

Sondra blushed.

"I'm four years old," she said as she held up four fingers. "Where are you going, mister?" she inquired.

"I'm going to San Francisco," he said as the man next to him broke in and said he was going there also.

"I'm glad to hear that." Ted held out his hand to greet him with a handshake.

"My name is Ted Walters."

"Harold Smith, here, I'm from Georgia. I'm traveling to San Francisco on business. Maybe I'll run into you while we're there."

"I'm travelling on business, sort of. I'm going there for my new job. I'll be a telegraph operator for the American International Telegraph Company."

"Sounds like a great job, I wish you lots of success," Harold told him.

"Thanks," Ted said as the conversation began to quiet down for a while, everyone settled in for the trip. Sondra colored in her color book, Harold went back to reading in the faded lamp light, and Ted pulled his hat down over his eyes to take a nap.

The train traveled on down the track. The only interruption in the quietness was a loud snorer a few seats back and a cigar smoker permeating the entire coach with his smelly cigar as he puffed away.

A lady spoke up.

"There ought to be a special place for smokers, maybe a smoking car," she spoke loud enough for everyone to hear. Others agreed, one saying, "It's rude and disgusting," and others were shaking their heads in support.

The smoker then remarked, "Someday they probably will make a law against it." But he continued smoking and puffing on his cigar and smiling an ugly grin, showing his yellow teeth.

Everyone settled in for the night, and most everyone went sound asleep. After a couple of hours, Ted felt someone shaking his arm.

"Mister, mister, wake up," little Sondra said crying and shaking him.

He quickly sat up.

"What's the matter, sweetie?"

"My mommy is hurt and just fell off her seat to the floor, please help her."

"Can you tell me what's wrong with her?" He reached out to help them. "Did you see her fall?"

"No, I was asleep," she was crying and sobbing.

Ted knelt down and felt her pulse, but couldn't find one.

He quickly sat Sondra in his seat.

"I'm going to ask you to be very brave for a while. We'll get the conductor to help us."

Harold went to find the conductor and in a just a few moments they rushed back in. The conductor knelt down and placed a small mirror glass over her mouth to see if she was breathing. Nothing, no sign of breath.

He looked at Ted.

"I think she's gone," Ted agreed.

"Mommy, Mommy," Sondra cried. "She can't be gone. Mommy, Mommy."

Ted picked her up.

"I'm really sorry, honey, was your mother sick?"

"She has cancer. We were going to California for me to be with my daddy while she got better," she said through her sobs.

The conductor got help to carry her to the baggage car.

"That's my mommy, please don't take her away," she screamed out. Everyone in the car was stunned and many, especially the ladies, began to sob.

"I'm sorry, Sondra," Ted tried to console her.

"They are going to take your mommy back to another car where they can let her lie down on a nice warm blanket and be comfortable. Remember, your mommy loves you so much and wants you to be very brave for her."

She put her hand on Ted's shoulder and sobbed loudly. Almost everyone joined her, even Ted.

The conductor came back to the car.

"Your mommy is resting in heaven, sweetheart. She loved you a lot, I'm sure. Do you know someone in Los Angeles? Are they meeting you there?"

"My daddy is meeting us, I'm going to see my daddy."

"Why don't you come with me. I have a special seat for you up in the next car so we can sit down and talk some more."

"Yes, sir, can he come with me?" she said as she snuggled up in Ted's arms.

"Of course he can," the conductor said as they walked up the aisle, Sondra sobbing all the way.

"We know you feel very sad, but we will take good care of you and help you to find your daddy when we get to Los Angeles," the conductor told her.

Ted held Sondra as she drifted off to sleep. He slept off and on as the train ran on through the night.

In the morning, he took Sondra to the dining car to have some breakfast. She wasn't very talkative, just ate some toast and sipped on her chocolate milk, and Ted had his usual, bacon and eggs, toast and coffee. He enjoyed watching the landscape while he had his coffee, passing by the acres of lemon and orange groves that California was famous for.

The steward asked if he could bring anything else and Ted replied, "No thanks. How long have you been with the railroad, sir?"

The old steward smiled.

"Well, sir, since you asked, right on twenty-three years, or so, I believes."

"Bet you have some interesting stories to tell," Ted commented, which brought a broad smile to the steward's face.

"It's been a good twenty-three years, and yes, sir, I have more stories than a man can tell. One can't do this very long without having lots of stories. When ya' find something you like to do, ya' should stick to it, and I guess that's what I've done," he remarked.

Ted smiled as he continued, obviously enjoying hearing every word he was saying.

"Saw a man shoot his wife one time, in fact, happened right there where you're sittin'. It made a terrible mess.

"I helped deliver a baby, that was a sweet moment, lots of things happening at once, glad when it was over though and the baby cried, yes, sir. That was a nice moment, the times I remember the most."

He went on to say all the getting off and on the train, which was his life.

"When folks get on my train, mostly they are perfect strangers, then they sits down by one another and become neighbors, and before they get where they're goin,' they have a new friend.

"It's kinda like a family," he said.

"What do you mean?" Ted questioned.

"We rides the train of life, we get off, we get back on and rides some more, but there are accidents and there are delays along the way. At certain places there are surprises, some has joy, some has sorrow, and some has great sorrow like the lady who just died."

"Life is like a train ride, is that what you're saying?" Ted asked him.

"Yes, sir, when we are born we gets on the train of life, we meet people we think we'll be with for the entire journey. Those folks are you parents, the parents travel with their children as long as they are absolutely needed, then they get off the train. Isn't that like life? Folks grow old then they die, they get off and leave you to travel on your own journey, they have a new journey to another place."

"Whoa!" Ted said. "That is so true, that's the way life is, all right.

"Yes, sir, they lives on in the memory of those they left behind, those they love. Farther down the track, perfect strangers get on and sit down with folks and the first thing you know, they become very important to one another, sometimes for a lifetime.

"Brothers and sisters, wives and husbands, friends and acquaintances who we learn to love and cherish, and the first thing you knows they gets off one at a time, but eventually they all get off the train when it gets to the end of the line.

"Yes, sir, I have lots of stories to tell, all the perfect strangers moving through life, getting off and on, all of them make an interesting story, many who have made a lasting impression on my life, some make me sad, when they leave. I have too many stories to recall, sir."

"I've enjoyed talking with you and hearing your story. You've had an interesting life," Ted told the steward as he reached in his pocket to give him a nice tip.

"Thank you, sir. Hopes to see again, it's been a pleasure talking to you, have a good day. I has to close up this dining car now to clean up before we gets to the next station. Thank you, sir. I hope you come this way again."

Ted took Sondra back to their seats.

"That man that gave us our breakfast was nice, wasn't he," she said.

"Yes, he was, he was a very wise man." Ted smiled, thinking about the great memories of all his train rides, the people he had met, and how philosophical the old steward was.

The train rolled along, Ted looking out the window just watching the world go by. Much of the country looked the same in every state that he had passed through. Eventually he drifted off to sleep.

When he woke up he watched a young woman across the aisle nursing her baby, covering herself with a linen towel. Her feet rested on her travel bag, and next to it was the baby's bag with all the required things, such as diapers, water, and a pink hand-knitted baby blanket, showing someone's beautiful handcrafting skills.

When she finished feeding the baby she pulled the blanket out of the bag and gently covered the baby as it nestled against her breast sound asleep. Ted watched the blissful scene, its fat little cheeks and triple chin, and her little fists doubled up together.

The baby opened her eyes and looked over at Ted and made a cooing noise, then burped up a small portion of milk which dribbled out onto the beautiful pink blanket, and then closed her eyes and went back to sleep. Her sleeping mother didn't stir during the whole episode.

The gentleman sitting behind the lady was eating a sandwich and drinking a bottle of beer. Ted was fascinated by the way he was eating, like it was a ritual. He would take a bite and then take a drink, until all of it was gone. In the seat beside this gentleman was another good-looking, tall man with rumpled blond hair, and what looked like several days of light hair growth on his unshaven face, as if he was trying to grow a beard. Ted smiled to himself, remembering he had tried that too.

Tired of observing his fellow passengers, he turned his eyes away and smiled, thinking about what the old steward had said about passengers coming and going. He leaned back in his seat and closed his eyes and smiled, completely satisfied with his life at the moment.

The train arrived in Los Angeles, and the conductor came by and took Sondra by the hand to go find her father. She said good-bye to Ted with very sad-looking eyes. He got off the train and walked with Harold to their connecting train to San Francisco.

Ted thought about the old steward again. How true it was, life is like a train ride, all the folks who come in and out your life during the ride. He looked at his ticket, his assigned car took him to a different car than Harold; they nodded to each other and parted to board their cars.

Life's passing parade, people coming and going, little girls crying, mothers dying, babies nursing, the continual life cycle. He turned his head and saw the old steward. He waved good-bye and got back on the train for the next ride.

Chapter 35

SAN FRANCISCO 1906

The train pulled into San Francisco at seven o'clock in the morning. Ted was so excited he couldn't believe he was actually there. He left the train station and looked down the busy boulevard called Market Street, which ran downhill all the way to the bay.

He had never seen such a big, bustling city, and more traffic and people than he had ever seen before. Cars and pedestrians, horses and carts and buggies in abundance, and the most fascinating thing that caught his eye was the famous transportation system they called the cable cars.

There didn't seem to be any rules of the road for any of the traffic, just the open air passenger cars and buggies going up and down the streets, carrying beautiful ladies with big hats and fancy long dresses. But the men were peddling their wares, trying desperately to make a sale.

Most interesting of all, Ted thought, *were the people getting on and off the cable cars while it was moving.*

He remembered when he had his first car ride from the gentleman who gave him a ride while up in Canada. Things sure have changed since he was a boy in Deer Creek. The only person who had a car then was the banker, and he was an older gentleman who most folks said was half blind because he drove on the wrong side of the old dirt main street that ran through town. But what difference did it make—no one else had a car, and besides, what constable would dare give the banker a ticket. It was kind of a town joke, they would say, "Here comes the banker, look out, and for goodness' sake get out of his way."

Here in San Francisco, the streets were very different. They were paved and filled with people walking every which way, crossing streets in front of the cars, the cable cars, and the wagons. He noticed many horse-drawn delivery wagons, some pulling large barrels of beer to be delivered to different bars around the city, and bread wagons taking freshly baked bread to the stores to stock the shelves, and added to all the activities, the street vendors peddling their wares, trying desperately to make a sale. The streets were never quiet and serene with all the activity and the clanging of the cable car bells. There was always lots of movement.

With all the horse traffic, Ted noticed the cleanup crew hard at work: two men walked alongside the wagon, shoveling manure off the street into the wagon. The horse didn't need a driver, and it seemed to move automatically down the avenue.

Ted was fascinated with all the sights and sounds of the city. He looked up at the tall buildings until his neck got sore. He looked out across the bay, what a beautiful sight, an island with a picturesque light house with its light beaming out to sea to warn the weary seaman. He could be entertained for hours just looking at all the sights that surrounded him.

The streets were becoming really crowded and busy—folks coming and going; all the men dressed in their Sunday clothes and derby hats, most of them sporting well-trimmed beards or mustaches; and the women in their long bustling dresses with fluffy trim over their shoulders, and wearing trim-fitting long coats. Their wide-brimmed hats with frilly ribbons hid their faces, but he knew they were pretty because they had to be, dressed in such finery.

Even the children dressed similar to their mothers and fathers, except that the young boys wore knickers down to their knees with longs socks that covered their legs, and little beanie hats on the back of their heads.

As a countryboy, Ted couldn't believe the grandeur of people's lives in the city. It suddenly began to rain, and like magic, the umbrellas appeared, all at the same moment in unison it seemed. The street became a solid mass of umbrellas everywhere, some people ducking into a store or business, but mostly, everyone went about their business.

Ted stood under an awning out of the rain, and he noticed the wind started to blow, making it more difficult for people to hold on to their umbrellas. One gentleman he watched seemed to have more difficulty than most, his umbrella completely inverted when it was caught in a strong gust of wind, causing him to abruptly stop to fix it, and getting all wet.

The rain soon let up. He stepped out from the protection of the awning to go purchase his own umbrella that apparently was a must because everyone had one.

He asked the store clerk if the cable car on this street would take him to the bay. "It sure does," he was told, so he joined the crowd of people who were waiting. He jumped aboard the car as it was still moving, and he was so excited it was hard for him to contain his exuberance. He smiled at everyone, and they returned the smile. As they got closer to the bay, he could hear the roar of the waves splashing against the wharf, and he saw hundreds of birds flying and landing, apparently looking for food.

He stepped off the cable car and suddenly felt overwhelmed by the immenseness of the San Francisco Bay, and how often he had wanted to see the mighty Pacific Ocean, and there it was right before his eyes.

When the passengers were off the cable car, they all gathered to help turn it around on the turnstile to head back up the hill. It was the routine, everyone was expected to jump in and help, and it was just a part of the ride.

Ted walked along the wharf; there were a few ships coming in and some leaving the harbor, heading out to sea. It was magical to him; he saw things he had always read about, funny-looking sea animals lying on the rocks, they were seals he was told, and they were making sounds like barking dogs.

He went in an open air restaurant to get a sandwich and a cup of hot chocolate. As he ate, he watched and admired the wonders of the sea as the waves methodically hit against the rocks. Men sat on the wooden wharf, hurling their fishing lines out to sea, and he knew they were enjoying themselves. He had another cup of hot chocolate and opened up his newspaper, turning to the ads to see what was available for lodging. There were several boarding houses with three meals a day available. The cost was twelve dollars a week.

A boarding house was the best way to live, he decided, as he remembered his boarding house experience in Colorado. He marked two prospective ads in the paper and later returned to the cable car to go back up the hill to the city. He sat down by a pretty young lady.

"Miss, if you don't mind, could you tell me which car I should catch to go to this address," he pointed to his two marked locations in the newspaper ad.

"Don't mind at all, sir. You can catch the Powell-Mason line when you get up the hill to California Street. You need to get off where they turn the car around and get on the 'L' car, it will be along shortly. Remember to look for the letter L on the front of the car. It will take you right to that area," she told him with a pleasant smile.

"Thank you, miss."

He boarded the cable car marked L. It stopped this time so an elderly gentleman could get aboard. Ted dropped his coin into the box and took a seat. He sat next to an older lady and unfolded his newspaper to show her the address he was looking for.

She told him in a friendly voice, "I get off on that very street. You just follow me when I get off, and the boarding house is right near that street corner."

A few minutes later, she got up from her seat, pulled the cord, and waited for the car to stop. Ted followed her. She walked to the corner and pointed down the opposite street.

"It's right there, young man," she instructed.

He nodded to her and walked toward the boarding house. He was anxious to get settled and have a place to stay.

CHAPTER 36

THE ASHBY HOUSE

Ted was impressed when he saw the stately three-story white boarding house with the sign on the front, "The Ashby House."

It was freshly painted with beautiful large colonnades and a wide front porch that looked inviting and comfortable with the porch swing and wooden deck chairs. He pulled the rope bell at the front door and as he stood there. He heard it ringing inside. Through the beautiful cut glass panes, he saw the outline of a woman coming to answer the door.

A middle-aged lady in a long black dress with a white lace-trimmed apron opened the door.

"How may I help you, sir."

"I read your ad in the paper this morning, ma'am, and I'm looking for a room," Ted spoke to her, nodding very politely.

"Won't you step inside," she replied.

Ted stepped in and she directed him to the parlor.

"Please have a seat and the mistress of the house will be right with you."

"Thank you, ma'am," he said as he sat down in a high-backed leather chair to wait.

Very soon, a tall lady with graying hair, fixed in a German-style circle braid on the back of her head, entered the parlor looking crisp and clean in her long, black flowing dress and white apron.

"My name is Mrs. Rose Ashby, I am the proprietor of this house. What is your name, young man?" she asked.

Ted rose from his chair and cleared his throat.

"I am Theodore Walters, and I want to inquire about a room I saw advertised in the newspaper. Do you still have the room available?"

"Yes, I do, Mr. Walters.

"We have a single room, which is four dollars a week and eight dollars total if you include two meals, breakfast, and dinner. A double room is also available with your own sitting room, if you're interested."

"The single room will be just fine," Ted told her.

"We have laundry service available for one dollar a week, and also lunch in the dining room, or we will pack it for you for an extra thirty cents a day," she told him.

"May I see the room," Ted asked.

"Of course. I'll have Mary show you, and if you wish to accept our offer, we require two weeks in advance, and you can tell Mary if you want lunches and laundry service. It was a pleasure meeting you, Mr. Walters. We surely will welcome you as our guest and you will enjoy our other residents. They are all very sociable."

Mary took Ted up the stairs to the second floor.

"This is a very nice place," Ted told her.

"Yes, it is. We hope you will enjoy your stay with us. There is no smoking allowed, except in your room and the game room, and there is no drinking or entertainment in the rooms allowed. This is a respectable boarding house," she announced emphatically.

She unlocked the door to the room, and Ted stepped inside. It was nicely furnished, not elaborate, but comfortable, especially the easy chair and bed. He smiled as he saw the picture on the wall, the same one that is in their living room back home: the lone wolf in the snow howling in the moonlight on top of a hill.

"We change sheets every Monday, and the towels are in the closet next door to the bath facility just outside the back-door, just follow the gravel path to the shower and wash-up room," Mary instructed.

"After your shower, just leave the wet towel and wash cloth in the basket in the shower room. "If you wish to bathe in your room, just notify the maid and she will have a tub brought up to your room with two buckets of warm water. That service is ten cents extra, payable to the attendant at the time you use it."

Ted nodded and smiled as Mary continued. "Would you require a packed lunch?"

"That would be nice," Ted responded.

"I have a job at the International Telegraph Company, starting Monday morning. Yes, a packed lunch would be nice," Ted responded.

"That's thirty cents extra each day, so have you decided on the room, Mr. Walters?"

Ted nodded his head as if to say yes.

"Very well, sir. I will give you a key and as you know we require two weeks in advance. I'll give you a receipt for your payment," she said.

"I will pay for a whole month," Ted announced.

She smiled and began to write the receipt when she turned to him and said, "I should warn you, Mr. Walters, there is a gentleman living next door, Mr. Perkins. He is a fine man and a retired sea captain, but he has a serious fault. He is a loud snorer, sometimes loud enough to wake the dead."

"I snore pretty good myself at times," Ted responded with a smile.

"Mr. Perkins is a very friendly man. In fact, he probably will knock on your door shortly to meet you and to warn you of his snoring, hope it doesn't create a problem for you. We hope you enjoy your stay with us. Dinner will be served at six o'clock in the dining room. Welcome to Mrs. Ashby boarding house and have a grand day," she handed Ted a receipt and promptly left, closing the door.

She had no more than walked away from the door when Ted heard a knock. He knew who it was if Mary's warning was right.

"Hello, my name is Robert Perkins, I live next door. Thought you wouldn't mind if I offered you a welcome drink. I brought a bottle of my best brandy for the occasion."

"Come in," Ted invited. "I was told there is no drinking in the rooms."

Mr. Perkins laughed as he stepped inside.

"It's only what the devil sees."

"My name is Ted Walters. I'll see if I can find a couple of clean glasses."

"There are two glasses on top of the dresser," he said as he pointed to them. "They come with the room."

Ted took the glasses off the dresser.

"Please grab a seat. Have you lived here very long?"

"I've been here four years. I'm a retired sea captain and don't have any family. I found this place and it's a very good place for me to dock."

"Where are you from?" Ted said, noticing his accent.

"I was born a wee lad in Manchester, England, then moved to Glasgow, Scotland, where I spent my childhood. I returned to England to attend Eden University until I decided to go to sea."

He raised his glass to Ted.

"Welcome to San Francisco, lad, I hope you enjoy your life here. Here's looking at you, my friend." They tipped their glasses and took a drink. He went on to say he was seventy-two years old and still in good health, but he couldn't go back to sea. He retired because he was beginning to suffer from sea-sickness, he laughed a hearty laugh.

"Now, what about you, young man, where are you from?"

"I just got into town this morning Sure is a big city, isn't it? I went down to the wharf and saw the ocean for the first time in my life. It's really big!"

"Yep, I sailed most of it over the years," Perkins laughed.

"I'm just a country boy from Deer Creek, Oklahoma, and I came here to work for the International Telegraph Company. They're opening a new branch office here, and I start tomorrow morning."

Perkins poured another brandy for them.

"Let's toast your new life here. Welcome to our humble abode and good luck on your new job," he said holding up his glass. They tapped their glasses together.

"I'm not a big drinker, but thanks for the toast," Ted responded as he sat down on the edge of the bed. He took a sip and had just swallowed it when all of a sudden the room began to shake, the hanging coal oil light fixture started swinging from the ceiling, and the framed picture fell from the wall and broke.

"Whoa, that was some drink," Ted managed to say, still a bit unnerved.

Perkins laughed.

"You'll get used to those tremors. We feel them here in San Francisco pretty often, that one was a little stronger than most."

Ted answered the knock on the door. It was the maid.

"We wanted to check to see if you're all right. As you know, we just had an earthquake tremor. Was there anything damaged in your room?"

"Yes, the picture fell off the wall and broke, but I think that is all the damage," he told her.

"I'll send someone up to your room to clean up and repair your picture."

Mary peaked around Ted and saw Mr. Perkins.

"Oh, hi, Mr. Perkins. I see you have met our new guest."

"Yeah, Mary, me lass, I'll check my room and if I have any problems I'll let you know. It was a pretty strong shake."

"Yes, well, I guess, I better go check on the other guests. Thank you," she curtsied and left.

"I better go check on my room. It was good to meet you, Mr. Walters. Hope we can have a long conversation soon, glad you're with us. I'll see you at dinner," he said as he walked to the door.

"Here, Mr. Perkins, don't forget your brandy, and thank you for greeting me in such a grand style. I'm looking forward to having a conversation with you and hear about your many journeys at sea."

"Thanks, I'll see you soon."

Ted unpacked his suitcase and put his clothes away in the dresser and closet. He then lay down on the bed to try it out; it was so comfortable he fell asleep.

CHAPTER 37

NEW FRIEND

He must have been exhausted. It was almost dinnertime when he woke up, and the bed was so comfortable. He walked down to the end of the hall and down the stairs to the washroom.

After he had taken a shower and shaved, he went back upstairs carrying his shaving cup and razor in his hand. He saw Mr. Perkins down the hall, all nattily attired in a jacket and tie. He thought, *Oh my, I'm glad I saw him, now I know how everyone is expected to dress for dinner.*

He put on a new shirt and trousers, and hoped he remembered how to tie his necktie as he rarely wore one. He slipped on his jacket and combed his hair. He looked in the mirror as he was ready to leave and felt rather stylish and handsome. When he arrived at the dining room, he admired the two long dining tables, each covered with a beautiful table cloth. There were fancy dishes and stemware glasses, and a beautiful centerpiece of flowers. But best of all, the table was covered with delicious-looking food.

A maid attended each table and helped the guests with the different dishes. There were two choices of meats, Ted took the beef, and when the mashed potatoes were passed around, he took an extra big helping. He loved them. He covered his meat and potatoes with gravy and barely had enough room on his plate for a helping of greens.

His mouth was watering. It was just like Mom's cooking, and he couldn't wait to start eating.

"Tea or coffee," the maid asked.

He chose the tea. The food was so good, no one bothered to talk very much, especially Ted, who was savoring every bite. Then the dessert was passed around, "Apple or peach cobbler," the maid announced.

He was so caught up in the pleasure of such elaborate dining he was startled when the lady next to him said, "You looked like you really enjoyed your dinner, young man."

"Yes, this is my first day. I know I will enjoy living here. My name is Ted Walters, what's yours?"

"Welcome, Ted, I'm Lois Clinger." By this time all the residents were leaving the dining room, so Ted got up and helped Miss Lois from her chair. He followed every one into the large game room, it was filled with card tables and comfortable divans and easy chairs for those who were not playing cards. Some rolled their cigarettes for an after dinner smoke, and a few men lit up their cigars. An older gentleman invited Ted to play cards with them.

"I would be delighted to join you, what are you playing?"

"Tonight is pinochle, tomorrow is poker night, and we also have bridge for bridge players, a penny a point. It all depends on what you like to play, just no gambling is allowed on Sundays," he continued.

"I have played some poker, but I don't know the game of pinochle I would like to learn," Ted replied.

"I'll teach you the game if you like, we don't play for money until you have learned the game, that wouldn't be fair. Come on over to this table and I'll introduce you to the folks."

"Ladies and gentlemen, I would like to introduce our new guest who has graciously agreed to play cards with us, Mr. Ted Walters. At our table are Kenneth and Martha Turner, Martha is a senior at the University, and Kenneth is a published writer presently working on a new novel about Mexico, I believe he calls it 'Barbarous Mexico.' They have just recently married and have been here with us for the past two months. We have certainly enjoyed the pleasure of their company."

They rose from their chairs and greeted Ted.

"It's our pleasure." Ted nodded and greeted them.

"Now," the gentleman continued.

"My name is Bill Hayworth, most of my friends just call me 'Big Bill,' as you can see it's an apt description, and I like it, so if you please just call me 'Big Bill,' I like to answer to that name.

"By the way, Ted, would you like a good cigar instead of that cigarette you are about to light up."

"No, thank you, sir, I have never been able to handle a cigar, they're too strong for me."

Big Bill continued, and Ted knew he was also a big talker but a likeable fellow.

"I am one of those much despised and often brow-beaten troublemakers, I am a union organizer."

"Glad to meet you, Big Bill," Ted was thinking to himself, *What does a union organizer do,* obviously they talk a lot.

Ted's thoughts was interrupted when Big Bill asked.

"What line of work are you in and may I call you Ted?"

"Of course, I'm going to my new job, starting tomorrow as a telegraph operator for the American Telegraph and Telephone Company. They have opened a new office in San Francisco. I'm pretty excited to get started."

"And you should be," Big Bill broke in.

"We won't play late tonight so you can get a good night's rest to be bright and shiny for tomorrow."

Ted purposely didn't mention to Big Bill that he and his brother Everett worked after school in the pool hall in Deer Creek and literally grew up playing cards. The truth of the matter is, he was considered a young pool and card shark in his hometown, but they never played for money, except with few strangers who just happened to pass through town.

In fact, he never told his mom and dad if he made a buck or two playing with a stranger. Some men even heard about Ted and came into town just to test him and his reputation around the country side, he was known as a teenage pool hustler. Many found it to be a great challenge to try to beat him at his game.

Ted recalled how the manager of the pool hall in Deer Creek would bank roll him and give him a cut of his winnings whenever certain challengers came into town. The manager considered him a child prodigy at pool and cards, but Ted never pursued that as a course for future earnings, knowing his parents did not approve of gambling.

As the cards were dealt, Ted wondered if maybe he wasn't just a bit rusty at playing, but he would take it in one hand at a time.

"Mr. Turner," Ted asked.

"What is your book about that you are writing about Mexico?"

"It's about the down trodden Mexican peasants and the torturous life they live under the present dictator, Porfirio Diaz. He is an evil man and they live a terrible, depressive, ugly life under his despicable regime."

"Well, I guess I have never heard of him," Ted replied as Big Bill cut into the conversation.

"Let's just play cards, that is just too deep a subject to discuss during a card game, particularly when we have such a novice player. He needs to apply all his thinking to learn the game, so we won't skin him out of all his money later," he chuckled.

Ted smiled to himself.

"Yes, let's play cards. I want to learn."

CHAPTER 38

ON THE JOB

Ted woke up bright and early at 6:00 a.m., the house was very quiet as he went to the washhouse to shave and shower. He dressed in his new suit, he wanted to look his best, and was setting at the breakfast table eating breakfast at seven.

He was so anxious this morning he could barely eat.

"You're up bright and early this morning and you look very handsome," Mary told him as she served his breakfast of eggs, bacon, and toast. He ate a portion of it and slurped down a cup of coffee, and just a few minutes later he was on the "E" trolley headed for work.

As he entered the big glass doors of the tall building, his stomach was churning.

"Can you direct me to the American Telegraph office, please, ma'am?" he asked the receptionist.

"Yes, of course, sir," she said.

"That's on the third floor. The elevator is at your right."

He had never ridden on an elevator before, so he debated in his mind whether to take the stairs or ride. He pressed the up button and when the door opened the operator announced, "Going up."

He stepped inside and the operator closed the inner doors which looked like a gate, and made Ted feel like he was in jail. The elevator jerked and started to move up, which almost took his breath away; and when it stopped, he gladly stepped off, not sure he trusted such a contraption.

When he saw the glass doors to the office, which had "American Telegraph and Telephone" painted across them, he was impressed. He walked in and right away heard the telegraph keys rattling away as he approached the reception desk.

"May I help you?" the receptionist asked. He handed her his letter of introduction that he had received when he was tested for the job back in Wichita.

"We have been expecting you, Mr. Walters. I'll tell Mr. Moody you are here. Please have a seat. I'll see if he is in his office or back in the shop."

In a few minutes, she returned with a bald-headed heavyset man who had a very pleasant smile. He reached out and shook Ted's hand.

"Hello, Mr. Walters. We have been anxiously waiting for you to get here, we just opened our new office last Thursday, and we are still in the process of setting up to get all our lines working. Welcome to California. I see you have met Mrs. Elliott. She transferred from our eastern office recently herself."

"How do you do, Mrs. Elliott. Happy to meet you," Ted told her, thinking how formal everyone was here in California.

"Likewise, Mr. Walters, I think you will enjoy working here."

She took her seat at the reception desk, and Mr. Moody pulled his glasses off his forehead and placed them on this face.

"If you will follow me, Mr. Walters, I will show you around our facility and you can meet the rest of our staff."

Ted followed him through the door, and he saw several telegraph operators working at their assigned desk, their fingers moving quickly over the telegraph keys sending the mounds of messages they had before them. He couldn't wait to join them; he loved doing the work.

"This is where we receive and send the news to the opposite side of the world, and this desk receives mostly incoming messages. I'm going to set you here for a while, I understand it's been a few months since you worked on the code. You will have some time to re-acquaint your skills, but with the trained ear, it all comes back rather quickly."

"Yes, sir, I'm confident it will," Ted said.

"In this office the messages come and go mostly to and from Europe, some from the Far East but mostly Europe. We will be connecting to many more areas, but we are still fairly new and haven't reached our tentacles all over the world yet. It's just a matter of time. As you know, it's basically news going out and news coming in to and from different countries. It's amazing what we can do in this modern world, isn't it?"

"Yes, sir, it is amazing," Ted said as he was taking it all in, a bit overwhelmed, but confident he could do the job.

"Your desk is the British desk, most of that news will go through you. I'll let you work with Mr. Druzba for a few days until you get the swing of our routine, hope you don't mind," he instructed.

"No, not at all. Thank you, sir. I appreciate the opportunity to get my feet wet, so to speak. I want to do the best I can," Ted told him, speaking in a grateful tone.

"I'll leave you here then with Mr. Druzba, and I'll return to my office. We are pleased to have you. May I call you Ted?"

"Oh, yes, of course. I prefer that, sir."

"Good luck, Ted. Any other questions you might have, Mr. Druzba will be able to answer them. Good having you in our company," he said as he turned and left.

"Please call me Perry," the pleasant white curly-headed Druzba said as he shook hands with Ted.

"Welcome, you will enjoy your work here. It's a big responsibility, that's why we are paid twelve dollars a day to do our very best. You'll have to work on a Saturday and Sunday once a month, and when we grow and expand we will go to a twenty-four-hour operation, that means the night shift. But right now it's only a daytime operation.

By the end of the day, Ted was exhausted. Mr. Moody was right, it is stressful receiving and sending all the latest news coming in minute by minute, some good and some bad. But Perry made it easier as he was a very pleasant work mate, who never got over excited about much of anything—news was just news to him. But Ted got excited about receiving hot news items from different parts of the world, and he soon became adept at his work and at the same time cognizant of the world's problems.

There were floods, famines, uprising of wars, countries being overthrown by the assassination of its leaders, and all kinds of political and financial troubles all over the world. The Russians and the uprising of the Bolsheviks were causing riots and agitations in the country, and there seemed to be a global socialist movement spreading over most of Europe. Ted was learning all about the world, things he had never thought about before, but he recognized there was turmoil everywhere, even in America.

The twelve-hour days were very long and tiring, but he loved the job and Mr. Moody would proudly say, "that's why we pay you so good." The job was challenging and rewarding, and Ted knew that most people worked this kind of hours for a lot less money.

He acquainted himself with many of his co-workers and found it interesting how they differed in their thinking, especially in social and political views. He was often invited to go to meetings and lectures, which he usually declined, but one gentleman, Don Williams, who he enjoyed working with invited him to go to an opera starring Enrico Caruso. He had never been to an opera before, but he had heard they were very high brow and thought it would be interesting.

He could hardly refuse to go, after all, it was a free ticket, but he didn't have a tuxedo to wear, and you just didn't go to the opera unless you wore a tuxedo. A gentleman at the boarding house had one, hardly worn it, he declared, and he wanted to loan it to Ted.

At the opera, Ted felt completely out of place and wearing a tuxedo made him feel funny. but he was really impressed with the beauty of the production and the stage, all the beautiful costumes, and the voices of the people who were singing such high notes that he had never heard before. *How could people sing like that*, he thought, *their voices going up and down the scale with rapid speed, and then other singers would cut into the song and take over the music.* But strangely enough he enjoyed every minute of it; however, he had no idea what anyone was singing about. After the opera, he thanked Mr. Williams profusely.

"Thank you so much, I enjoyed it, but I'm afraid I'm just an old country bumpkin. I just didn't understand what it was all about, but for some reason I enjoyed it a lot."

"You're not a country bumpkin. Opera is a story told in music and songs, and the human emotion of the story is expressed through the voices of the singers. Most operas are presented in the language of the composer and most composers are Italian. Opera singers study for many years to train their voices to tell the story in music and songs. It helps to read about the story before you go. That's about the best I can do to explain opera to you."

When Ted went to dinner the next evening, much to his surprise Big Bill was introducing Enrico Caruso, who was a friend of his, to everyone in the dining room. Mr. Caruso was staying at the Palace Hotel, the finest in the city, but when he was in town he often ate at the Ashby House. The hotel food was no equal to Mrs. Ashby's home cooking, and of course she enjoyed the notoriety. Mr. Caruso lifted his glass and everyone joined him in a toast to the cook.

After dinner, they went to the game room, but this evening they didn't play cards. Ted had heard that Mr. Caruso was the finest opera singer in the world and here they were, sitting in the same room enjoying the conversation, some enjoying a sherry and a cigar, but all had their eyes and ears focused on every word Mr. Caruso spoke in his wonderful, clear, and strong accented voice. Everyone at the Ashby House thoroughly enjoyed the evening, hearing about his world travels and experiences.

The next few days were busy. Big Bill went to Chicago on business, Mr. Turner spent his time on his book, and Mrs. Turner was getting ready to graduate from college. And of course, Ted spent his long twelve hours at work, busy as usual and hearing about the news from around the world, which was beginning to intrigue him.

One evening after dinner, the conversation turned to politics, which Ted had little interest on. It was often confusing to him with all the different views. As a child growing up, his folks never expressed any such views; they were just hard-working farm people. This was all new to him, one view he was hearing about was how Carl Marx was the hope for all mankind. Only a few agreed with that view, while the majority of others vehemently disagreed.

Ted's curiosity began to peak as the news from around the world came across the wires. Such news as Lenin's rise to power in Russia and the Socialist movement in Spain and throughout Europe. He was also hearing more and more about a group called the Wobblies, the Workers of the World Union, who were creating unrest in our country and in other parts of the world.

As his curiosity built up in his mind, Ted asked Big Bill one evening after dinner why the International Workers of the World Union was called the "Wobblies"; it just didn't make sense to him.

Big Bill laughed and began his explanation.

"Now, I'm glad you asked me. It's really kind of funny how that all came about. It was almost three years ago that we had a big railroad strike going on in British Columbia, Canada, and it was there that the term Wobbly became a nickname for the IWW members. Previously, they had been called many things, from "International Wonder Workers" to "I Won't Work."

Legend has it that a Chinese restaurant innkeeper, with whom arrangements were made during the strike to feed the IWW members passing through town, began the term because of his language. He would say in broken English, 'A soo Wobbly?' and that's how it happened. Since then, they were called Wobblies," he chuckled as he took a big puff on his cigar.

"That's pretty funny, but that makes sense. That's usually the way things get started." Ted laughed.

As they were discussing the political world and dealing a poker hand, they were interrupted by Mrs. Ashby, who entered the room with two guests.

"Excuse me, ladies and gentlemen, I would like to introduce to you our new guests who have just arrived from New York. This is Mr. and Mrs. Ferris. They are staying with us for a few weeks. They are actors and will be in a new play at the People's Theater starting next month. I would like each of you to introduce yourselves to them, if you would," she told them as she excused herself and left the room.

They all stood up and one by one introduced themselves, shaking their hands and giving them a grand welcome. Ted couldn't believe all these famous people he was meeting at the same boarding house where he was living. It was turning out to be a very interesting place. Mrs. Ferris was a beautiful, well-dressed woman, and Ted was impressed by her charm as he met her. He felt like she was flirting with each one as she met them, flitting her eyelids as she smiled and spoke to everyone.

Days later at the dinner table, Mr. Ferris announced the play would be opening at the Peoples' Theater next Friday, and free tickets were available for them if they wished to go to the grand opening. He gave each of them a publication which read:

Peoples' Theater a Dick Ferris Production "Life in Chicago"
—Starring—
The Grace Hayward Company
—Featuring—
Dick and Debra Ferris

"With Mrs. Ferris starring in it, I must go see it," Big Bill said as he readily accepted the invitation along with everyone else.

"I have never been to a real play in a theater before," Ted said.

One of the men at the table spoke up, "Where have you been living all your life, young man? Under a rock?"

Some of the guests laughed, but some were a little embarrassed by the remark.

"No, sir," Ted said rather nonchalantly. "I have been to barn dances and fiddle hoedowns in Oklahoma when I was growing up, but we didn't have fancy theaters and plays like in the big cities."

Big Bill broke in, noticing that Ted was a bit embarrassed by the remark.

"We all have to be educated in the arts. This young man went to the opera the other evening. Now just how many of you have gone to the opera?" Only a few raised their hands.

Mr. Ferris was impressed with Ted, he loved his country style. And Mrs. Ferris thought he was charming as she didn't know many people from the country. They finished the evening together playing cards and visiting for another couple of hours before they broke up and returned to their rooms.

Ted thought to himself as he walked back to his room, "Some of them may think I'm a country bumpkin, but who always walks away from the game with most of the table winnings, tonight it was three dollars and twenty cents in all." He felt vindicated.

Several weeks passed and Big Bill came and went on two or three trips, and Ted was becoming more knowledgeable about the world around him. He became increasingly troubled with some of the news coming in. It seemed to him that the downtrodden always gets the short end of the stick.

Chapter 39

UNION INDOCTRINATION

An evening walk after dinner was always a pleasant experience for Ted. He enjoyed the city, seeing the people come and go, the children playing and the clanging of the trolley down the street. When he returned one evening, Big Bill was standing on the porch, just returning from one of his many trips.

"It's good to see you back, Big Bill. I missed you at dinner and I especially missed taking the ante from you at the table. Where have you been this time?" Ted joked with him.

"Sure, you did," Big Bill laughed.

"We had a big union strike up in the mining fields, both in Nevada and Colorado, and we've been busy trying to organize the miners. I've been a very busy fellow lately," he chuckled.

"How's your job coming along, Ted?" he asked.

"Just getting settled in and enjoying it a lot. I'm supposed to get a raise in the next month or so if I keep up the good work. They just recently told me they liked my work and someday I will most likely be a supervisor. The company is expected to grow in the next few months, I sure hope so. I can make more money as a supervisor."

"That's good news," Big Bill said.

"I've been meaning to talk to you about your job and your company. I have something in mind to present to you, but that can wait. Right now, I'm hungry. I missed my dinner. You reckon Mrs. Ashby will have the cook fix me a sandwich or something, I'm starved."

"I'm sure she will. You're a very good tenant here, she'll be good to you."

"I'll be traveling more from now on since I'm now the vice-president of the union, the one they call the Wobblies." He laughed as he looked at Ted.

"We will be working harder all over California for the next few weeks and months."

"Oh, here comes Mary now. Hi, Mary, my love. I'm back and I'm starved to death. Do you think you could rustle me up a nice sandwich or two, I would be forever in your debt."

"I think we can alleviate your hunger, Mr. Bill," she replied rather shyly.

"Thanks, Mary, I'll be up in my room. I'll take my suitcase up and unpack. I am exhausted! See you tomorrow, Ted. Perhaps after dinner we can continue our talk."

"That's a deal, Big Bill. See you tomorrow."

The next day after twelve long hours of work, Ted enjoyed a nice dinner in the dining room with Big Bill and the rest of the folks.

"Let's go out for a drink, Ted, there's a place down the block. Are you free, or did you promise someone a big card game?" Big Bill said teasingly.

"Sure, I'm free. It would be good to go out for a breath of fresh air."

As they sat down and ordered, Big Bill's expression turned serious.

"Is your office unionized yet, Ted?"

"No, we are not unionized," Ted answered.

"As you know that's the kind of work I do with the I.W.W. We work hard to organize the workplace for the working man. California is a new open field for us, and I have been very busy reaching out to the different areas of workers. Such as the miner in the coal mines, the field hands on the large farms and orchards, and the railroad workers, we're ready to break into other fields of work. You know, Ted, we stand for the working man and we can represent them for better working conditions and salaries."

"My workplace is very good, sir," Ted said.

"I'm not sure what to think about the union. It's all very new to me."

"We have been working hard to get the railroad employees into our union, but the resistance has been tough. I hear they're planning a separate union, but we almost have the CPR railroad in Canada convinced. Would you be interested in being a union representative to help me organize the telegraph operators, Ted?" Big Bill said looking straight into Ted's eyes.

"Well, sir," Ted spoke clearing his throat, quite surprised by the question. I'm not certain that would work for us, you see we only have ten operators so far here in San Francisco. I have heard rumors that the company will expand into Los Angeles and then later into San Diego. The company is in its infancy, but growing rapidly, and they have great plans here and elsewhere, even in foreign countries."

"I was thinking I would sign up for a foreign position if that happens, and I don't believe I want to jeopardize my position with the company at this time. My working conditions are good and my pay is among the highest for the working man. My future sounds really good with the growth of the company, and I want to grow with it. To press for a union might slow down the intended growth, and I just don't believe I want to get involved in any union right now," Ted explained.

"I would like for you to think some more about it. You could be our point man and start talking it up with your fellow employees, on the quiet, of course, just to plant the seed and see how they feel about it. We would give you twenty-five dollars for everyone you could sign up, or if you think it's too soon to push it, just start talking it up," Big Bill insisted.

"I don't know, Big Bill, my co-workers are very satisfied, I think," Ted shook his head in confusion.

"Don't push it too hard, but like I say, go slow. It's easy to get discouraged in this work. Just mention it in confidence and ask them if they think a union is needed, and focus on higher wages which are possible with unionization, that makes them think more about it," Big Bill was pushing hard.

"The union is going to be a big force in the land, there is a big movement for change. The barons of wealth in the land need to stop starving the working man and pay them what they're worth and stop amassing a fortune for themselves. Oh my, excuse me, Ted, I could rant and rave all day. I'm sorry, but I take this very seriously," he raved on and on.

"I'd like to see you get on the ground floor of this opportunity, Ted."

"I don't feel like I can do that, but thanks just the same," Ted said as they left the restaurant to walk back to the Ashby House.

"We have a great speaker coming in a few weeks and I want you to hear him. Please go with me, he's a brilliant man. He is Leon Lane Wilson, the US Ambassador to Mexico, and he will be here with a stopover before returning home to Mexico. He will board a ship out of San Francisco harbor to Mexico. He's a good friend of mine," he pleaded with Ted. "You would love to hear him, he also knows the Turners who live at the Ashby House. Remember, he's writing a book on the barbarous Mexican leadership. Turner is in Mexico right now doing more research, and I hope you will read his book when it's finished, I'll get you a copy."

"Thanks, I'd like to read it. Well, good-night Bill, enjoyed the evening. See you tomorrow."

Ted was glad to return to his room to think about all Big Bill had to say. He was tired and really didn't want to think about the union anymore tonight. All the rants and rave from Big Bill gave him a lot to think about, like the injustices of society around the world, which sounds like an impending revolution, if Big Bill is right.

For the next few days, Ted thought about what the union was doing around the world. He watched the news carefully; it was being reported that there were indeed people being oppressed and starving, and in his young mind it bothered him a great deal.

Big Bill was out of the city for the next three months and the end of year was almost here. It will soon be 1906 and he had been employed in his job for eighteen months, and there was talk of him becoming a supervisor in the company's expansion. The promotion would be to manage the department of the Eastern European Theater and that was of great interest to him. There will be three operators working with him, and the news coming in from those areas is already very heavy.

He remembered when he got his job back in Wichita. He didn't imagine at that time he would be making twelve dollars a day and have the opportunity to receive the news "hot off the press" before the others were able to know about it. He was the one who disseminated it to the rest of the country. It truly was a job with great responsibility and he loved it.

He felt like he was on top of the world when he received his promotion and a pay raise so soon after his employment. The office crew surprised him with a big party to celebrate his promotion the day before the New Year's holiday. He felt very pleased and blessed.

Chapter 40

THE BANK ROBBER

Quite by accident and under very unusual circumstances, Ted met a beautiful lady he had previously noticed at the Wells Fargo Bank. He first saw her at the cashier window as he stood at the counter, filling out a deposit slip.

She was dressed very fashionably with a long flowing skirt, and she looked very sophisticated in a large brimmed hat that made it difficult to see her face. He couldn't take his eyes off her, and he felt enchanted as she turned her face away from the window and looked directly at him as she left the bank. He had never felt like that before, and he wondered if he would ever see her again.

Three weeks later, Ted was in the bank feeling good about himself. He was about to open his first savings account. As he stood in line to wait for the cashier, the beautiful lady he had previously seen came into the bank and stood in line directly behind him. They exchanged smiles and he felt like his heart skipped a beat, and he wondered what he could say to her that would make sense. But his thoughts were suddenly interrupted by a loud booming voice that echoed throughout the large marble lobby.

"This is a hold up. Everyone lie down on the floor, NOW, or we will shoot you. Do exactly as we tell you."

The customers froze in motionless panic. Everyone gasped and were in shock, they couldn't move. Some of the ladies began to scream, and one began to cry hysterically. It created havoc for a few seconds when one of the robbers, all three of them wearing black masks over their faces, raised his gun and pointed it to the lady.

"Lie down on the floor, all of you, or I'll shoot each one of you, one at a time, until you do exactly as I tell you."

She fell to the floor along with the rest of the customers, about twenty in all. The other two robbers proceeded to order the bank president to the back of the bank to open the big vault door. Ted was lying next to the beautiful lady and they stared helplessly at each other. He saw tears of fear in her beautiful eyes.

He whispered, "We'll be all right," as he wrapped his arms over her in a protective cover.

Just then an elderly man entered the front door of the bank, startling the robber, and he immediately shouted for him to get on the floor. The man was crippled and walking with crutches and had a difficult time getting down to the floor, and the irritated robber walked over and kicked the crutches out from under him and pushed him down. Someone cried out, "Oh, no, don't do that!"

The robber looked around trying to identify who shouted, and it was during this moment one of the brave bank employees reached out and hit the alarm button causing the panicked customers to cry out again in fear.

The bank robber became extremely nervous by the sound of the alarm, and all the customers on the floor became totally unnerved by the piercing loud ringing. Some ladies began sobbing loudly again, no longer able to suppress their emotions and fear. Some held their hands over their mouths to quiet their sobs, and the atmosphere became very tense as they heard the police cars pull up to the bank. They began to feel a glimmer of hope when they knew the police had arrived.

The robber stepped directly over Ted's head as he rushed to the front of the lobby to try to ward off the police, and figure out what to do next. At that moment, when the robber was distracted, Ted saw an opportunity to pick up a porcelain umbrella stand next to him, and as the robber stepped to another window to check out the police action, Ted hit him across the head, knocking him to the floor and shattering the umbrella holder into pieces.

The dazed robber dropped his gun to the floor and another man who was close to Ted on the floor, a bank clerk, pulled the gun to him and hid it under his body. When one of the robbers in the back heard all the commotion, he ran to the lobby and stepped out from behind the counter and pointed his gun at the customers. The bank clerk fired the gun at the robber hitting him in the shoulder, causing his gun to fire and the bullet hitting a picture hanging on the wall, just inches above the customer's heads. The shattered glass from the picture fell to the floor on all those who were close by, including the beautiful young lady.

The robber fell to the floor, his arm bleeding profusely as he dropped his gun. Ted scrambled to pick it up just as the third robber came running out of the back with the money bag in hand. He jumped over the counter and stared right into the gun that Ted was holding on him. He immediately dropped the bag to the floor and raised his hands, realizing his fellow robbers were already down.

Ted and the bank clerk had literally broken up the entire robbery in just a few moments, even before the police had time to enter the bank. The head teller, who had also been on the floor, went to the door to let the police know what the situation was and that everything was under control. He called out to them.

"Come on in and arrest these ugly robbers and take them away."

A sea of blue uniformed police entered the bank, all armed and ready for trouble if it came, and ready to help the victims who had been affected by such an unexpected event. All the customers got up off the floor, grateful the ordeal was almost over. Ted took the hand of the beautiful young lady and helped her up.

"I'm Ted Walters," he said in a soft tone. "Are you all right?"

"Yes, thank you," she said through her sobs. "I'll be fine. My name is Audrey Oswald."

The bank president explained to the police what had happened and identified the robbers for them. A few newspaper reporters started showing up with their big flashing cameras and began firing questions fast and furious to all the customers. Within a few minutes, the "heroes" of the hour were identified as the customers told their stories.

A reporter rushed up to Ted and wanted a picture of him and John Fielding, the bank clerk, so he could write his story for the headline news for the evening edition of the newspaper. Another reporter and many of the townspeople started rushing in, trying to shake hands with Ted and John, asking them about their courageous act. Ted just shook his head; he didn't feel like he did anything so brave, they had just acted to save themselves and the others around them.

"It all happened so fast and I was so scared. We just did what we had to do. I really didn't know what to do, it just happened. The real hero in all this is this gentleman, John Fielding, and the great shot he made downing the robber." Ted laughed nervously as he finished his report to the newsman.

The police escorted the robbers out of the bank and put them in the paddy wagon to take them to jail, and the wounded one to the doctor to get his arm patched up. The bells clanged as the paddy wagon drove off, and all the people were so relieved it was over. Some were laughing and cheering through their tears, while others were still stunned, unable to talk. *The San Francisco Chronicle* newspaper continued taking pictures and getting statements from the customers and bank employees. They also interviewed Audrey as she stood next to Ted, holding on to his arm, as the photographer took their picture.

The edition of the paper that evening and the next morning displayed very interesting headlines. One read, "Young handsome telegraph operator saves beautiful damsel in a foiled bank robbery." Another read, "Young man's quick thinking saves customers and the banks money."

As everyone read their newspaper, Ted became the hero of the Ashby House and at the office. Everyone wanted to congratulate him and came up with their own version of the story, and he felt a bit embarrassed by it all.

"All I did was break an expensive container over the robbers head. It was John Fielding who disarmed him, and he is the real hero." During all the newspaper stories and hype, Ted found out a lot of information about the beautiful Audrey, where she lived and all the details about her family, who is a very prominent, successful family in San Francisco.

Three weeks after the attempted robbery, the city and the bank held a party in honor of the "Heroes of the Day," John Fielding, Ted, and the chief of police. Mayor Schmitz, the president of the bank, and the city council members, and their wives sat at the head table along with them, and they seated Audrey next to Ted. It was a very special occasion; a lot of flowery speeches were made and awards were given.

Ted's head was swelling and he felt a bit embarrassed by all the attention. He didn't feel he had done anything different that anyone else would do. It all just happened that way and they acted to save themselves and the others around them. Each received a "Key to the City," a cash award of $100 dollars, and a plaque with their name and a statement, "for your outstanding act of bravery as one of San Francisco's outstanding citizens."

The mayor honored them by saying, "The city of San Francisco honors you as our heroes of the hour and adds you to our list of outstanding citizens of our fair city."

Ted was happy and life was good here in San Francisco. After the ceremony, he asked Audrey out for a date and she accepted. He was feeling quite smitten with her. She was a beautiful demure girl from a well-known family, who were longtime residents of the area. She lived in a big three-story mansion in the Nob Hill district, and her father was in the shipping business, a very successful longtime, family business.

Ted sent his reward money home to his family. He had regularly helped them through winter months on the farm. He also sent all the newspaper clippings of the event. He knew his mother would cry as she read all about it, and they would be as proud as they told the story to all the neighbors.

The headlines even made the paper in Sacramento where Ted's cousin, Elwood, lived with his family. He made a weekend visit to see them. It had been years since he had seen his cousin and had never met his wife and children. Elwood greeted his "hero" cousin with open arms and introduced his family, Marie his wife, Mike his son, who never took off his cowboy hat and boots without protest, and his sweet little girl, Beth Ann. They all enjoyed the three-day weekend visit, mainly reminiscing about home and their growing up years.

They especially remembered the times when they were supposed to be working around the farm, and how they would sneak away to the pool hall to play billiards by the hour instead. And the times when the owner, Uncle Fred they called him, gave them odd jobs to do around the building and how over the years they became expert pool sharks and card players themselves just like Uncle Fred, and everyone wanted to challenge them in a game, mostly pool. Uncle Fred was no fool; it brought lots of business into the pool hall.

Their parents were dead set against the boys spending so much time at the pool hall, and many times they would sneak off and go, or claimed they were 'working' if they got caught. 'Nice families just didn't hang around such places,' their mom would say. During all those years their parents forbade them to go, except for work, and Ted always felt guilty every time they went, he didn't really like to disobey his parents, but as a kid he went anyway, the draw of the excitement always won out.

Ted and Elwood laughed over the stories of another Deer Creek card shark they called Uncle Joseph. He was another one that also taught them the game. Ted recalled one story of how a card shark from a neighboring town came into the pool hall to challenge Uncle Joseph to a game, and they played for higher stakes, much higher than usual.

Uncle Joseph shook the stranger's hand before they sat down, and he noticed a ring on his right hand, the kind of ring that hid a sharp needle that cheaters use to mark the cards. When Joseph shook hands he felt a light prick on his hand, and he knew immediately what this guy was up to. But he didn't say a word, he just let on like nothing happened. Uncle Joseph watched the cards as they played, and when it was his turn to deal, he could feel the marked cards, and knew what the player had in his hand. Uncle

Joseph kept raising him every time and finally the guy threw in his entire stack of chips on the table, smiling and chewing on his cigar, knowing he had the winning hand for sure with his three aces.

But Uncle Joseph had dealt himself four nines, he knew all the tricks. He never cheated anybody in a game, except, of course, when someone was trying to cheat him. He waited for the right time and then he cheerfully took the hand with his four nines. The guy was so sure he had won he reached out to rake in his winnings.

"Excuse me, sir," Uncle Joseph said. "I believe that's my pot, if you don't mind," as he laid down the four nines.

The old card shark stood up, shocked by what just happened.

"My friend," Uncle Joseph said, "that sure is a nice ring you have. Would you like to sell it? I've been admiring it a lot while we played, what do you want for it?"

He knew he had been caught in the act, and had been outmaneuvered by his own game. He didn't say a word, just walked to the door and left.

Uncle Joseph handed back the winnings to the rest of the players at the table and said, "Friends don't cheat friends."

Ted remembered asking Uncle Joseph, how he had won, knowing somehow those four nines were marked also.

"Well, boys," Uncle Joseph said to them. "I just stacked the deck until I knew the time was right, and then he showed them his sharp finger nail and how he had marked the cards.

Elwood and Ted had a great time together as they reminisced about their growing up years and the days with Uncle Fred and Uncle Joseph at the pool hall. On the way back to San Francisco, he was so glad he decided to go visit his cousin. It was a very good time, but now it was time to go back to work.

The next morning at work, Ted picked up a newspaper from a co-worker's desk. The headlines were all about the big art theft from the Museum of Fine Arts in Los Angeles. A Rembrandt painting on loan from Paris, valued at $800,000, had been stolen. The picture was a portrait called the "Lady in Black."

"I sure hope they catch the culprit who did this soon," Ted said. "Do you have the sports section?"

"No, George took it. He wanted to read all about the upcoming games," his co-worker said.

It was 1906 and the year was well underway. His fondness for Audrey was growing, and he was feeling a bit uncomfortable with her family's wealth and status in the city, but they enjoyed each other's company. He knew after a few dates they shouldn't rush into a serious relationship. He recognized the lifestyle her family lived was far above what he could ever provide, and wondered if she would be happy with him and could adapt to a less opulent style of living.

He felt like he was too young to get married anyway, and he needed to save some money and grow in his job. They had never discussed anything like that, so why was he even thinking about it. He really knew why. He was feeling himself getting more serious, and so was she.

Chapter 41

THE GREAT SAN FRANCISCO EARTHQUAKE

It was 5:15 a.m. on a Wednesday morning of April 18, and the sky was showing a hint of light. The bells of old Saint Mary's church chimed on the hour and the gas lights that had illuminated the dark night streets were snuffed out, as they were every morning. The sun would soon peek out over the horizon. All these were the usual signs that the night was slipping away and the city was ready to greet and celebrate a new day.

The cable cars that were idle through the night began to move out of the station, clanging down the track, ready to move the passengers and workers to their various destinations. The early morning risers began to quickly arrive, filling the lonely night streets and in just moments, the city was bustling with activity. It was fully awake and alive.

Ted lay in his bed sound asleep, but was suddenly awakened, not by his alarm, but by something unusual—his bed was shaking back and forth. He swung his feet over the side, but he felt dizzy and strange, and he wondered if he was dreaming and not yet fully awake. But very soon he knew it was real; his bed was shaking violently in all directions.

As he dangled his feet over the side, he was bouncing up and down; and when he tried to stand up, he could feel the floor moving beneath his feet. He quickly reached over to the bouncing chair to grab his pants, when the chair toppled over and bounced to the middle of the room. He managed to slip on his pants, almost losing his balance as the unsteady floor jerked, causing everything to slide to the other side of the room. He got down on his hands and knees and crawled to retrieve his shoes which had been tossed across the room from where he had left them.

He managed to get dressed just as the entire house began to shake so intensely that the plaster began to fall from the walls and ceiling. A ceiling beam fell across his bed barely missing his head, and his door flew wide open and fell off its hinges. He could see his friend, Mr. Perkins, out in the hall, barefoot and dressed only in his robe, desperately holding on to the unsteady wall. Ted quickly followed him, knowing he needed to get out of the building as soon as possible. He could hear the crashing of pictures falling from the walls, the dishes and crockery falling and braking into hundreds of pieces, and the roaring sound from outside was deafening, and it seemed like it would never stop.

When they reached the stairs, the entire stairwell and banisters were shaking violently, but they managed to reach the bottom of the stairs stepping over household articles that were rolling and tumbling across the floor. In the dining room, the large hutch had tipped over, spilling all the beautiful dishes and stemware onto the floor, crashing and breaking into thousands of pieces.

Suddenly the shaking stopped, and the stark silence was frightening, just as frightening as the violent shaking, not knowing what would happen next. All the Ashby House guests and workers, including Mrs. Ashby, huddled in the front yard still in their nightclothes, they were stunned and in shock, hardly able to speak. One of the cooks, who was fixing breakfast at the time, was holding on tightly to a plate of pancakes she had fixed for one of the guests, not realizing that she still had them in her hand. They huddled closely together, frightened and chilled from the damp cool air as most mornings are in northern California springtime.

How long did the earthquake last, was the question on every one's mind, it seemed like an eternity while it was happening, but actually it was only a few minutes. Off in the distance, they could see fire and smoke rising over the entire city with sudden bursts of flames shooting like geysers into the sky from the broken gas lines. Ted imagined it looked like Dante's furnace that he had once read about. They could see buildings collapse and fall, some very close by, just down the street. They could hear faint shouts from people crying out for help, but felt so helpless themselves, not knowing what to do or how to do it.

Robert Perkins, feeling quite humbled by this horrific event, said he was thrown out of his bed and could hardly reach his bathrobe from the back of the bouncing chair to cover his nude body so he could escape from his room.

"The place was shaking so much it made me think I was on a ship riding the rough seas. It was a dreadful nightmare and reminded me of the typhoons and earthquakes I was in when I was a sea captain plying the seas. Once, when I was over in Indonesia, an earthquake tore up the whole village we were in, but this one was the worst," he muttered shaking his head.

Rose Ashby, trying to remain calm from all the destruction, was standing next to Mr. Perkins in disbelief.

"All of a sudden, I was staggering and reeling, the earth was slipping from under my feet. I staggered to the street, and then came the sickening sway of the earth that threw me flat on my face. I struggled along with Mr. Perkins and Ted to finally reach the street. I couldn't have made it by myself. They helped me. Buildings continued to crumble and crash with a roaring sound that crushed my ears," she related as they stood and watched a large building crumble, as one might crush a biscuit in their hand.

Across the street, a large cornice of a building came crashing down on a man, crushing him in the rubble. There was nothing anyone could do for him. He was a man wearing overalls and carrying his lunch pail, probably on his way to work at the Iron Works.

Three people came running out of a house just seconds before the roof collapsed, and they were shocked to see such a sight as they realized most of the area had been demolished. The foundations of the houses were lifted from the ground, causing them to fall completely over, only to crash into the house next to them, resembling dominos falling into each other. Most of the houses broke out into a blaze of fire, with flames jumping from one to another, just like trees in a forest fire.

Strangely enough, the Ashby House survived the quake with less structural damage than most of the others; however, the water lines were broken and water was gushing everywhere. The smell of natural gas from the broken lines encompassed them, and fires were breaking out all around them, but so far the Ashby House had escaped the fires.

"I think it's probably safe enough for us to go back into the house to get some clothes and our belongings. We will need blankets and some of us need to get properly dressed." Ted continued, "Like Mr. Perkins, he has only his robe and no shoes. We can go a few at a time, but only stay a few minutes to get what you can salvage, and then come right back for others to go. Don't linger in the building very long. Get your things quickly so others can go. The house could collapse or catch fire at any time, so if you're willing to take the risk we will stand by for you," Ted instructed.

They went five at a time and returned to their rooms to retrieve the things they could, and hurriedly left for the next group to go until all had successfully returned with their belongings they wished to salvage. They were all able to get fully dressed and had a blanket draped around their shoulders, and bags of precious treasures they held close to them.

Ted and Perkins looked down from the top of the hill, where the houses once stood, down into the main part of the city, and the scene they saw could not be described by any words they could utter that would make any sense to anyone. It was a ghastly nightmare.

Ted muttered, "This has to be like the destruction of Sodom and Gomorrah that the Bible tells about. I remember my Sunday school teacher reading that story to us."

A policeman ran up to them.

"I need some able-bodied men to help me search for people trapped in the houses, the whole city is in distress and on fire," he said as he looked directly at Ted. He felt compelled to go with him to help, but it seemed like such an insurmountable task. He had no excuse not to go, he was young and strong and the people were desperate.

Ted followed the officer and motioned for the other men to join him which they did. What they saw was heartbreaking: people were standing among the rubble crying, stunned, confused, and dazed.

Ted saw a little boy standing on the sidewalk, crying for his mother and father. He immediately took the little boy's hand, and he latched on and clung to Ted.

"My mommy and daddy and little brother are in the house and it's on fire."

A man came stumbling out of the house, and just as the police officer and Ted ran to him, he fell at their feet. The man cried out.

"My wife and baby son are on the second floor. Please go help them."

Without hesitation the officer and Ted ran into the burning house, fear seemed to have left them. Ted wrapped his handkerchief around his nose and mouth and bounded up the stairs, at least the steps were still intact. He heard a choking cough and a child's cry, so he followed the sound. He kicked in the door and lifted the baby from the crib, barely able to see him from the smoke that had permeated the entire house.

He handed the baby boy to the officer.

"Here, take the kid outside. I'll go look for the mother." The officer grabbed hold of the boy and bounded down the stairs only to fall as they reached the landing, he was an older man and was overcome by the smoke.

Ted saw them fall and ran down the stairs to help them out of the door to safety. He handed over the baby to a grateful father who was lying on the ground still coughing and fighting for his breath.

The officer and one of the men from the Ashby House covered the father and two little boys with a blanket. The older boy, clinging desperately to his father, looked up at Ted with tears falling from his cheeks.

"Did you find my mommy?"

"I'm going now," Ted said to the boy.

"Stay here," he told the exhausted officer.

"I'll go back and look for her."

Ted adjusted his handkerchief on his face as he ran back into the burning smoky house. He called out, "Anyone here?" as he ran from room to room with burning pieces of ceiling falling all around him. He kicked in a closed bedroom door and saw a woman lying across the bed, smoke had overtaken the room. As he entered the room, a burning piece of wood fell from the ceiling, and as he reached the bed he saw the large beam that had fallen, crushing her head and killing her instantly as she slept.

He hurriedly ran out of the house back to the waiting family, dreading the thought of telling them the news, especially the young boy who was crying for his mommy. He stumbled out of the door, grateful to get some fresh air to breathe, and knelt down beside the father and his two little boys and broke the news to them. The sobs of grief broke his heart as the father clung to his little boys. They were all he had now, and he didn't want to let them go as he drew them close to his chest. All he could manage to say was, "Thank you for saving my baby."

The officer had recovered enough to organize rescue teams to go up and down the block to help whoever needed help. Ted joined with them and they began their rescue efforts, which they knew was going to be a huge undertaking. Each crumbling and burning place had its own story to reveal. Ted was not anxious to know the stories they would tell, but anxious to help wherever he could.

Chapter 42

THE AFTERMATH

The old man walked aimlessly down the street, stepping over broken tree limbs, stumbling over the cracks and crevices in the earth and the scattered wood, which had once been a part of a beautiful home. Ted caught up with him to see if he needed help. He was obviously dazed as he told Ted his haunting story and his experience of the quake that shook him to the depth of his heart.

"Off in the distance I saw the hills roll like great billows, and I saw the earth crack open and explode. The crevices looked over eight feet deep in places. Houses were swallowed up in the earth, and I saw a big boarding house collapse with all the people in it. They are all gone," the old man said with a quivering voice, barely able to speak.

"Stay with us," Ted took his arm. "We'll see that you have a place to go."

Across the street, the officer and his team entered a damaged burning house and found a man pinned under the burning wreckage. The helpless man, still conscious, watched in total terror as the fire began to burn his feet and legs, and he screamed the loudest blood-curdling scream anyone had ever heard and then begged for the officer to shoot him. The officer knew they couldn't get to him because of the wall of fire between them.

"What's your name?" shouted the officer.

"Jonathan M. Miller," he screamed, "please, a bullet is better than burning to death."

The officer raised his gun and shot the man through the head. None of them could bear the thought of him burning alive in the fire, but it was almost more than they could bear. A few moments ago they were going about their lives, comfortable in their daily routine. But now, their world was turned upside down and in total disarray, and no one could have ever prevented that. It was an act of unimaginable nature.

How could everything change so suddenly? Ted thought, but he began to realize he and the Ashby House residents were very lucky; they were able to escape without injury. It was one of the few houses that didn't burn or sink into the depths of the earth's crevices. The flames began to spread like fury all around them, jumping from block to block as far as they could see. The water mains were all broken, rendering them useless to fight the fires. But even if they did have the water available to fight the fires, it would have been an exercise in futility, like pouring a glass of water into a lake of flames.

They approached the Nob Hill area and it was going up in flames, just like the rest of the area. Even the very wealthy could not escape such fury. As he got closer to Audrey's house, he could see it was ablaze like all the others. He saw a lady standing in the middle of the street.

"Lady, have you seen the Oswald family?" She just shook her head and cried, unable to speak. He had to know if Audrey was all right; he had to see for himself. He ran toward her house, jumping and stumbling over all the debris, only to be stopped by an armed soldier.

"What are you doing here, mate. You cannot go into this area, it's being marked off for the firefighters to dynamite, hoping to build a fire break."

"I have to get to that third house over there. That's where my girl lives. I have to see if she got out or if she is trapped inside. I have to go see!" he shouted as he ran toward the house.

"I suggest you forget it if you want to live. Stop! I order you to stop! STOP, you bloody fool!" he yelled out.

Ted ran upon the porch and could see the whole house was in flames. He looked through the window and saw that the stairway had collapsed. Audrey and her father were lying on the broken stair steps, flames looming all around them.

He tried desperately to open the door, but it wouldn't budge. He pounded the door with his shoulder, only to bounce back from the force. He went back to the window to break it out so he could climb inside to bring them to safety, but it was too late. The entire ceiling fell onto the stairs covering them, and he could no longer see them. He knew they were gone. He just hoped they were already dead before the ceiling caved in on them.

Grief stricken and stunned, he started pounding his fist against the porch. Blind with tears he fell into a mental collapse, but flames began roaring all around him. The heat became so intense that his self-preservation mentality clicked in and commanded him to jump from the porch just seconds before it collapsed and fell.

He rolled across the front lawn to escape the heat and fire. It almost scorched his back. He got up and ran away, back to where the soldier was. He walked past him, crying bitterly and hating himself for not getting there sooner to rescue his beautiful Audrey.

"I'm sorry, son. I'm sorry you had to witness that. Move along, now. Don't linger here, they will start the dynamite soon."

Ted walked away, staying in the middle of the street to avoid the intense heat from the burning ruins of what was left of the city. He was desperately trying to make some sense of it all, but his thoughts were interrupted by the screams of two women running from a burning building.

He quickly ran to help them, one had covered herself with a blanket and the other was enveloped in flames. Ted whipped the blanket off the lady to smother the fire and she fell to the ground, fighting desperately to breathe. She lay motionless, no longer fighting to stay alive, and as difficult as it was for her, Ted knew she could not have survived the horrible burns on her body. *It was probably the best*, he thought.

He tried to find a police officer, but saw none, so he put his ear to her chest to listen for a heartbeat, but nothing was there. He turned to the other lady who was in complete shock and unable to speak, he took her hand and said,

"I'm so sorry . . . she's gone."

With a blank stare in her tearful eyes, she screamed, "Oh, no!" and fell to the ground in total disbelief. She grasped the hand of her friend and muttered over and over, "Please don't leave me."

Ted covered the lady with the blanket, knowing there was nothing more he could do for them. He stood up and walked away to help the others, wishing in his troubled mind it would suddenly all go away and things would return to the way it was before all these happened. It seemed like nothing was real anymore, just a bad dream. He kept repeating to himself, "*Wake up, wake up.*"

People were milling around aimlessly, many were crying, not knowing what to do and where to go, and off in the distance he could hear screams. He could hear children crying for "Mommy and Daddy," and he wondered if he could keep going. The scene all around him was the same, it was heartbreaking and he couldn't escape it. People were on their knees praying, some were crying hysterically feeling lost, and others were just wondering around in circles. He wanted to reach out to help but inside he himself felt so lost.

He walked through what was once the vibrant beautiful heart of the city. Ashes were falling from the sky like black snow, covering everything two or three inches thick. The pride of San Francisco, the Palace and Grand Hotel, was ablaze and beginning to crumble to the ground. People were watching in disbelief. A few yards away from it was the Hall of Justice and it was a blazing inferno with no way to save it.

Ted gasped for air and began to cry. It was too much to absorb. But then, he felt someone jerking his hand.

"Mister, mister," a small boy said, "will you come help my daddy? He has a big wooden board on him and he can't get away. It's too big for me to move, and I can't get him out."

He hurriedly followed the boy, who wouldn't let go of his hand. They ran around the corner, but the building that his father was in was now only a pile of burning rubble. The boy looked up at Ted very bewildered.

"My daddy was there and now it's all gone. Where's my daddy?" he cried and held Ted's hand tightly.

The boy stared at the spot and was only able to mutter, "Daddy, Daddy."

"What's your name?" Ted asked him as he picked him up in his arms.

"Joey, my name's Joey."

"Joey, your daddy is gone. You can be proud of him, he was a brave man and he wants you to be brave too. Can you be brave for him?"

"Yes, sir, mister," he answered through his sobs as he lay his head on Ted's shoulder, crying softly.

Ted carried Joey to a first aid station that had been set up by the army and turned him over to the attendants. Joey held on to him tightly, not wanting him to leave. One soldier placed his army cap on Joey's head and told him he could be a soldier too, and they would make him a "sergeant."

"Okay, Joey, let's get to work."

Ted slowly walked away, he felt so lost and so helpless, just like Joey and hundreds of others people who were just milling around, all in the same state of mind as he was; it was a pure nightmare.

The army was out in full force now, blowing up buildings to create fire breaks. They had no water to put out the fires, which caused great frustrations for the firemen. It was hard to watch the city administration buildings that stood so tall and proud yesterday, and the other bustling places that generated the city's daily newspapers, *The Examiner* and *The Chronicle*, all going up in flames and being destroyed right before their eyes.

Ted jumped in to help the firemen for a while until he could move no longer—he was exhausted and he had had no rest or food for hours.

The army set up some makeshift tents and shelters for people to come and register their names and to provide a place for people to come in and rest. The tents were made of sheets, blankets, rugs, anything that could shelter the people from the cool air and mist that usually covers the city at evening time.

At the shelter, a sweet little old lady walked about as if she were in a trance, holding a bird cage in her hand. Her pet bird chirping happily with no concern of the devastating horrors that were all around them. She had no shoes and the evening was becoming very cool. Ted tried to speak to her, but she was unfazed by her surroundings; she just kept talking to her bird. "It will be all right, Daisy,' she kept saying as she disappeared into the foggy mist that was slowly engulfing the entire wounded and battered city.

Ted got a blanket and went to look for a vacant spot to make his bed.

It was on the ground, of course, but at this point he didn't care, just a place to lay his head was all he wanted.

He heard a couple of men talking that Chinatown had been completely destroyed and burned to the ground. One of the men had a white preacher's collar around his neck, and he was discussing the destruction. Ted heard him say, "It's no great loss, in fact it may be a blessing. That place was a blight on the face of the earth, nothing but sin, sin, sin," he kept repeating.

Ted picked up his blanket and moved farther away. He didn't want to listen to that kind of talk during a time that everyone was suffering from a great tragedy such as the earthquake. He knew the people who lived in Chinatown were suffering just like everyone else. This was no time for such talk about our fellow human beings, he decided. His eyes filled with tears and he couldn't stop thinking about the day, his dear sweet Audrey, the children, and Joey who lost his father. But his exhaustion soon overcame him and he fell into a much needed sleep.

Three hours later he woke up, cold and shivering in the night air. Through the fog, he could see the city still burning, which lit up the sky with an eerie red, smoky, and misty covering. Thoughts of the day over took him again as he stared into the night sky. In a way it was a strangely beautiful sight, but to think of it as beautiful made him feel guilty, the suffering of all the people was so horrific. He gazed down the hill and could no longer see the portrait of the skyline of the city that he had always taken for granted.

In the morning light, the men, women, and children started moving through the ruins of the city toward the outskirts of the city to look for a place to camp. Many were carrying their overloaded suitcases and trunks, struggling to keep what little possessions they had left.

Ted heard from one of the soldiers say that the death toll was beyond guessing, how could anyone know? Of all the many downtown buildings, the business buildings and houses, how could anyone know how many people were inside, possibly thousands were consumed by the quake and fires, and what chance did they have? It was indeed a ghastly nightmare, the answer would not be known for months, maybe years, or perhaps not at all.

Ted volunteered to help the army and was assigned to accompany a corporal who carried a rifle, to guard against looting on Third Avenue. They saw a man about a quarter of a block away who appeared to be looting. The corporal shouted for him to halt, but instead he jumped and ran. He fired at him bit missed, but then they heard another shot from another direction, and the man fell to the ground. They ran to the fallen man and arrived at the same time as the shooter, who was a member of a citizens group called Regulars, who protect their property from scavengers during a crisis. It was common practice for them to help the army, although they had no legal authority.

The man who was shot was a black man. The corporal helped the regular throw the body into a fire to avoid any repercussions that might come later. The dead man may have been a looter, but who was to know for sure. This made Ted very uncomfortable, and he decided he couldn't do this type of work. He would much rather rescue and save lives, not to take them away.

He told the corporal he was leaving to volunteer for rescue work, and walked down the street toward a big building that was aflame and crumbling to the ground. He saw three men on a rooftop, fire blazing all around them. An army officer close by ordered his men to shoot them, which they did, killing all three just as the roof gave way under their feet. Ted knew they had to do it, at least they would not suffer being burned alive, but it was almost too much for him. He realized not all people could be rescued; it was so ugly to see, but he knew it was the merciful way out.

He walked away from that crisis only to face another. In the park area, he saw a woman run from a burning building carrying a baby in a basket. She put the basket down on the sidewalk and returned to enter the burning building. Ted couldn't believe his eyes, what was she doing? Was there another child in the building? Or was she just out of her mind with fear. He watched for a few seconds to see if she returned, but she didn't reappear before the building collapsed. He picked up the baby and took it to the nearest aid station and turned it over to a lady with a Red Cross band on her arm. At least he knew the baby was safe.

Three days passed and the fire raged on, and Ted helped where he could. At night he was utterly exhausted, he camped at Union Square where the army set up tents for people to receive food and rest. They handed out hot coffee and sandwiches, Ted's first food and drink since this all began.

The next morning the army posted two bulletins on the board. The first one read:

Proclamation as of April 18th, 1906

City of San Francisco declares Martial law, All Federal troops, members of the regular police force, and all special police officers have been authorized to shoot any and all persons found engaged in looting or the commission of any other crimes.

Signed.
Mayor Schmit

The second bulletin read:

Notice: From The General of the Army Adolphus Greel, Commanding Office Pacific Division U. S. Army. As of this date, April 18th, 1906, I have ordered and dispatched 4000 troops around the city. They will control all aspects of the law at this time.

The San Francisco Police and the Fire Department will assist us in fulfilling our task. All citizens will comply with this order and will assist in maintaining law and order. I have given orders to all officers to shoot any and all looters. The Army is setting up refugee camps in and around the city for all people in need to receive food and comfort. Thank you for your cooperation.

Signed: Commander General of the U. S. Army Adolphus Greely

People gathered around the bulletin board to get the latest news, and Ted heard a man speaking loudly, as if preaching to the crowd.

"It's Jesus's fault, it's all Jesus's fault, he did this."

"Jesus didn't do this, the earthquake did," Ted said in a calming voice.

A woman ran up to Ted and grabbed him around the neck.

"Save me, save me," she cried.

Ted pushed her away in shock, and the crowd of about a hundred people began to panic. With nerves already on edge, they started to run and get restless, but they didn't really have any place to go.

A nearby policeman saw the commotion and approached the "preacher man" who continued to proclaim the Lord's message of despair. After asking him to calm down, which he would not, he tackled him and threw him to the ground still shouting and yelling. He took out his night stick and clubbed the man, knocking him unconscious. He soon became conscious and started to get up. The policeman helped him to stand.

"Did you have a nice rest, you darlin' man?" he said in his lilting Irish voice.

"We'll have no more of that, so off with you. We can't have that kind of rabble rousing here."

Then he addressed the crowd.

"Now, that will be enough. So go on with your business, work together, we're all in this together, so let's pray together. Remember, what happened here is the will of God, and we won't stand for any rowdiness. Move along, find someone to help and God's blessing on each one of you, you lovely people," he said.

Ted smiled to himself, thinking how quickly and easily he handled a possible explosive situation. A man next to Ted said, "So glad the officer stopped that man, we have enough in our hands to get through all this. The last thing we need is a panic situation, but tomorrow will be a new day."

"You're not from around here, are you?" the man asked Ted, wanting someone to talk to. Ted sensed that he was tense and needed to talk to make things seem like they were normal and relaxed.

"I was born and raised in Oklahoma. I am here for a job as a telegraph operator," Ted told him.

Then the man went on to say, "You know, I was at the San Francisco zoo late in the afternoon of the seventeenth. I was with my daughter and three grandchildren, and we noticed the animals were restless and not acting normal. I go to the zoo a lot with my grandkids, and the animals that day just didn't act right. The big elephant was trumpeting and pacing back and forth, throwing his trunk around, and the trainer was having difficulty with him. In fact, the elephant chased him, and he had to get out of the pen. The other animals were restless too. The lion roared excessively, even the carriage horses were acting different as we traveled home that day."

Ted listened intently as the man continued.

"When we left the restaurant that evening, we were celebrating my grandson's eighth birthday. The horse was acting skittish and as we passed the livery barn, I noticed the horses were restless also, and you could hear their whinnies all the way down the street."

He continued.

"I guess we should listen and observe the animals more closely. They seem to sense nature's occurrence, even before they happen."

"That's really interesting. I have never heard of that before. But I recall growing up on the farm, one time our cow got out of the barn and ran toward the creek. We found her standing in the middle of the water when the tornado hit the ground. We thought that was really strange."

A police officer who was standing nearby joined the conversation.

"I was on duty at 5:12 in the morning, and I heard a deep rumble that caused me to look down the hill. I saw a shocking sight: the ocean was spilling immense waves which rolled down Washington Street, and the earth seemed to rise up and buckle and crack open. Several of my fellow officers saw the same thing.

"Most of us stayed on duty, but after several hours I had to slip away to go check on my dear crippled wife. When I got there, my house was not standing. I know she didn't suffer, it all happened so quickly." Tears came to his eyes.

"Forty-six lovely years we were together. I had nothing else to do so I came back to work on the streets. Oh, God!" he cried out, and everyone came to comfort him.

The people tried desperately to comfort him, but it was so sad the tears flowed from the crowd also as he told his story. They wanted to comfort him but needed comfort for themselves. They all had similar stories to tell. Ted walked away sad and lonely, his eyes filled with tears.

Chapter 43

THE DOOMED CITY

Ted walked through the heart of the city and in his mind it was a beautiful evening. He imagined the magnificent buildings towering upward, and there were no fires, all was in perfect order. Every building had its doorman standing to greet everyone who entered, and for a moment he felt everything was all just a bad dream. The city was orderly and he would soon wake up.

But he couldn't wish it away. It was real; reality came back full force to him when two US Calvary rode up on their horses asking him to abandon the area. There was not another person in sight, and the wall of fire was still burning in the distance, with ashes falling down on them like rain.

"Move on, young man, they will dynamite this area soon, many buildings are ready to fall in and it isn't safe here. Now move along."

Ted surrendered to the reality of it all and began to walk back up the hill, out of the heart of the city he loved. He stood at the corner of Kearney and Market, the innermost heart of the city, and took one last look. He wanted to remember how it used to be, but reality was much too harsh; he knew he couldn't change a thing.

On all sides of him he saw and felt the devastation. The tottering walls of *The Examiner* and *The Chronicle* buildings, where the city's newspapers were published daily, were now shut down. Ted wondered what they would have written about the earthquake to tell their readers, but he knew it would be a long time until they could print the story, if ever.

He saw the burned out Call building and the smoldering ruins of the Palace Hotel and Grand Hotel, both hotels were the pride of the city of San Francisco.

Ted came upon Union Square and it was packed with homeless families, men, women, and children. Some were setting up tents, supper was cooking over open fires, and children were crying and clinging to their parents in fear.

The Red Cross and church organizations were handing out blankets and food to lines of people who had formed around the square, having nowhere else to go. On all sides, the picture was the same, destruction was everywhere.

At three o'clock in the morning, the great San Francisco Hotel ignited in flames and shot heavenward, lighting up the sky and waking all the Union Square campsite residents. They hurriedly packed their belongings and within a few minutes the square was completely deserted.

The Calvary, the Red Cross, and all who took refuge at the square were gone, but where would they go? They didn't really know, safety and relief was their only hope, but they didn't know where to find it. By morning people were milling around the city looking for a safe area to stay, an area where there were no fires or tumbling buildings, and many were trying to escape out of the city.

Ted came upon a man standing on Market Street, not far from Union Square. He was a chubby fellow dressed in a black tuxedo and a fur coat. He recognized him immediately. It was Enrico Caruso who had performed in the opera, Carmen, at the Mission Opera House just the night before. Ted remembered how Big Bill introduced him to all the guests just a few days ago.

The billboards advertising his special appearance had been plastered all over town, but now they were just a part of the ruins scattered beneath the rubble. Ted overheard Mr. Caruso bargaining with the driver of a horse-drawn cart, to either buy or rent his cart to haul his luggage to the Oakland Ferry landing.

"Sorry, Mr. Caruso, I can't sell my team and wagon to you, but I'll take you where you need to go."

"That's a deal, my friend," Caruso replied.

Ted walked over to help them load the luggage into the cart.

"I wondered what happened to you, Ted," Mr. Caruso said. Glad you are alright."

"Glad to meet you again, Mr. Caruso, a lot has happened since we first met. Sorry this earthquake has interrupted your visit," Ted said to him sympathetically.

"Indeed, glad to see you again, Ted, and thanks for your help. This visit will be a memorable one, from the kindness of all my friends here, to the dreadful nightmare we all went through together," he said as his valet helped him climb into the cart to start the first lap of his travel back to Italy.

Ted waved good-bye to him as the horses started up jerking the wagon, causing Caruso to hold on to the side to prevent him from falling. Ted also saw another famous actor while standing there near the ruins of the Palace Hotel, it was John Barrymore. He had just seen his latest movie just a few days ago, and the thought ran through his mind, *No one is immune from nature's wrath, not just the poor and the unknown, it also includes the rich and famous.* Flames were encompassing the area near Union Square. He left and went to help a man he saw using crutches to walk.

"Today is my birthday," the man said, "Last night I was worth thirty thousand dollars and I bought five bottles of fine wine, some fresh delicate fish filets and other food for my birthday celebration, but tonight I have no food to eat and nothing to celebrate. All I own are these crutches to cripple through the rest of my life."

They walked to a place of safety and sat down to rest on the steps of a house, which no longer stood in the beautiful Nob Hill district. The owner of the house where they were sitting spoke in a cool and hospitable voice.

"Yesterday morning, I was worth six hundred thousand dollars, and this morning, my house is completely destroyed, and will soon be totally gone. My wife's china cabinet, where she kept her prize china pieces, is now all gone, and the rug in our living room cost fifteen hundred dollars, and her piano which had a beautiful tone, is ruined and destroyed. There were very few like it, it was a real prize, but now everything we owned is gone."

Just down the street was the old Mark Hopkins's famous residence, another of San Francisco's palatial mansions, and it was still burning. A military trooper rode up to them.

"You must move out of this area now," he said. "This area will be detonated with dynamite very soon."

They moved out into the street, the evening sunset was breaking through the smoke-filled air, the sky was rose red in color and seemed to flutter with shades of lavender, and then fade into a yellow-orange dingy film over the sun, covering any brightness that was left.

They passed by the shattered dome of City Hall and it exhibited the great force of the quake. Only the steel frame of the dome was visible, its beauty had shown over the city but was now gone, it was peeled from its perch and now lay on the ground below. The great pillars of the Hall lay in a crosswise section on the lawn like puzzle pieces ready to be put back into place.

Over on Mission Street lay a dozen dead steer, lying in a row, stretched across the street. They were struck down by the flying debris like bullets, and the fires came through afterward and roasted them as they lay. The human dead had already been carried away to the makeshift morgue, awaiting families to claim their remains, if that was possible.

A milk wagon on Mission Street was overturned, and the milk cans lay scattered on the street, spilling their contents to run down the street. The driver lay lifeless in the driver's seat, a telegraph pole lay across him; he could not escape the sudden crash that hit him.

The flames and destruction raged on the rest of the evening, conquering the business and Telegraph Hill districts and miles of warehouse and dock areas. Ted was exhausted, but where could he go, where could he get some rest? The skies were getting dim with day fading away, and the air continued to fill with smoke. He walked with the rest of the survivors, but where could they go? It seemed like they were going into the end of the world.

Chapter 44

LEAVING THE CARNAGE BEHIND

It was a cold night, but in spite of the coolness, Ted got a couple hours of much needed sleep. He stood in the food line in the morning, waiting his turn for a cup of coffee and something to eat. *Anything would taste good*, he thought.

He was given a jelly roll and it tasted so good, a bit of sweetness in all the carnage the quake left behind. The army gathered food from wherever they could, commandeering produce from bakeries, restaurants, grocery stores, and produce warehouses to feed the growing mass of people in the camps.

While he was enjoying his cup of warm coffee, a dashing young man with a pad and pencil in his hand came up to him.

"Howdy, may I interview you for my news magazine?" he inquired of Ted.

"Who are you," Ted asked feeling a little reluctant to say much.

"My name is Jack London and I'm a special correspondent for *Colliers Magazine*," and continued talking without giving Ted the time to answer.

"And where were you when the earthquake hit?"

Ted began to tell his story, how he was thrown from his bed and everything he had done up to this very morning. He related everything he had seen, the people he had helped, the suffering and death, the children like Joey who couldn't find his father, the baby he rescued for a grateful father, and the man that was shot for looting. Everything came back to him like a bad dream, shaking him emotionally.

He took a deep breath to gain his composure and London reached out to comfort him.

"You've had a busy few days, I know. You have quite a story to tell. Sounds like you have been a hero for many people."

"I hope so, sir, but we couldn't do enough. It was all so devastating, no one could stop it. Where were you when it hit?" Ted asked.

"I was at my home about forty miles from here in Piedmont. We felt it too, but not as much as you did here. I received a telegram from my paper to get over here fast and find out about the earthquake firsthand, and I'm seeing it all right. Never in my mind could I have imagined such carnage."

"I sure appreciate your help. May I mention your name in my article?" he asked.

"Yes, of course. I'm Ted Walters. It seems like I've heard your name before somewhere, but I'm having trouble remembering where," Ted asked him.

"Well, Ted, I guess, you're entitled to know. I've achieved a small amount of fame through the books I have written, the best known one is written about Alaska, perhaps you have read it.

"*The Call of the Wild!*"

"Sure, I've heard of it, but I haven't read it, but I bet I will when I get the opportunity," Ted told him with a bit of excitement in his voice.

"I sure appreciate you letting me interview you. You have made the whole story of the earthquake easier to write about, how it has affected the lives of many and the human suffering it caused." He shook hands with Ted.

"Good luck to you, my friend," and he walked on through the crowd of people looking for more interviews and information.

After breakfast, Ted decided to walk back to the Ashby Boarding House to check out the area and possibly hope to find some of his boarding house neighbors. But to his amazement, the entire block of houses was gone, the fires had ravished the area leaving, only ashes and a few stone chimneys standing bare. It was a shock to him. For some reason he expected the house to still be standing. He wondered what happened to the people, where had they gone, where was Mrs. Ashby and Mary, the Turners and the nice lady, Mrs. Clinger, his next door neighbor, Robert Perkins, the retired sea captain and Big Bill.

He couldn't get them out of his mind. The Ashby House and the building where he worked were gone, where were the people he had worked with, whatever happened to all the friends he had made. The sad realization came to him, he might not ever know.

He joined the parade of people walking south toward the edge of the city. There were literally thousands on the move, some carrying and dragging heavy trunks, families walking together pulling loaded wagons, all trying to save the only worldly possessions they had left.

They walked several miles, he didn't have the slightest idea where they were going. He didn't even know how far it was to the next town. They walked till evening and rested for the night. He was glad he had carried his blanket the army issued to him. He lay down totally exhausted, both physically and mentally, and went fast asleep.

He joined the mass of marching people the next morning, walking next to a man and woman who were engaged in a conversation. She was telling about her friend that got up early every morning to go to the beach. That's where he was that morning, right there on the beach. He loved to swim in the ocean early each day and he told us on that morning there was something about the water that wasn't normal. The waves had a different look, and the breakwater was hitting the strand more furiously and stronger than usual.

But nevertheless, he discarded his robe, hat and shoes and hit the surf, he thought the water would relax his sore shoulder. Then an enormous wave hit him, and it scared him, and the next one lifted him up and carried him out much farther in the water than he usually went. Luckily, he was a strong swimmer and was able to get back to shore. Then he felt a strong shock and noise that sounded like a cannon blast explosion.

Stunned, he was thrown to his knees and was covered with salt water which he began to take in and swallow. He tried desperately to get out to get his robe, but suddenly felt something like an electrical shock run through his body, and he felt paralyzed for a second. Then he saw a phosphoric glow on the sand and he was so mesmerized that he couldn't move.

In a moment, he was able to get back into his robe to get out of there. He had never been so scared in his entire life. As he left the beach, he realized this was something much bigger than just the ocean. There was destruction everywhere as he made his way home, only to arrive to find it completely destroyed.

Ted walked along with the people, many dropping their trunks and baggage on the way. They had become too burdensome to carry any farther. One family was digging a hole on the side of the road to bury their belongings, probably hoping to return someday to get them. Others were just leaving them on the side of the road. They were completely exhausted, barely able to move on.

An old man trudged along the road walking with crutches, and the woman beside him had two children holding on to her hands. None of them had shoes on and their feet were bleeding. But they walked on quietly; there were no complaints or tears, just determination on their faces.

Just ahead of them the army had set up a rest stop, and Ted sat down to rest with the whole group of his fellow travelers. They all felt like refugees leaving a war-torn city and were glad to receive an apple and sandwich to eat. Some of the people related their stories of the quake and the terror they had faced.

One gentleman, with his voice still shaking from shock, told how he tried to help a man who was trapped in a burning building. A large steel beam had fallen across his body, trapping him under the rubble. He tried to lift the beam away but the fires were coming so close and the beam was too heavy, so to save himself he couldn't stay. He didn't want to abandon him but he had to. It was the most difficult thing he ever had to do. As he left, the man was yelling, "Don't leave me." He was haunted with guilt as he told his story to them.

"I'll never get that out of my head."

Everyone's eyes were tearing up when they heard his story. Even Ted felt great compassion for him, remembering those he tried to help, but couldn't. They rested for a while but began to move on. The aid station attendant told them when they got to the next town, the railroad would be available to take them free of charge anywhere they wanted to go, as far as the line went.

Ted walked with the group all night, some stopped to rest, but others kept going. He wondered how many miles they had covered, he couldn't' even guess he was so tired. But he felt a streak of energy when he saw the railroad tracks; that meant they were probably close to a town.

Tired and worn out the sign on the station was a welcome sight to him, it read Fair Oaks, California. They couldn't even get close to the station door. There must have been 800 people or more standing around the tracks and building.

The news spread through the crowd that the San Francisco/San Jose railroad lines were destroyed by the earthquake, so getting out by rail was going to be a very slow process, due to so many people and limited cars and tracks.

Ted and many others were at a loss on what do next. They heard the ferry was just a few short blocks away and it went across the San Francisco Bay to Oakland, but they would have to wait their turn. It could only hold about hundred people at a time. He had about twenty dollars in his billfold, and was relieved when he heard the ferry was taking as many as they could free, because very few people had any money with them.

When his turn came he boarded the ferry, finally feeling like they were making some progress. He napped during the ride. The water was a little rough at times, but he didn't mind, it seemed to rock him to sleep.

When they arrived, he walked through a park and saw an empty bench with a newspaper laying on it. He was anxious to see the paper, to get some news from the outside world. He wasn't really anxious to read about the earthquake, he had just lived it, but wanted to know if the world around him was still there and in order, he needed to confirm that in his mind.

He read about the Mayor of San Francisco issuing the edict, "All looters will be shot on sight." He continued to read, "On April 20, eighteen sailors supervised the evacuation of 20,000 San Francisco citizens on the *U.S.S. Chicago*, the largest evacuation by sea ever in the history of the United States.

The *U.S.S. Chicago* had received a telegram from San Diego Admiral Goodrich to proceed at full steam to San Francisco, this marked the first time that wireless telegraphy was ever used in a major disaster.

Ted put the paper down and walked away, he didn't have the heart to read the news, and he wanted to get the whole event out of his mind. He wondered what he would do next, did he still have a job? Did his co-workers survive the quake? He had so many unanswered questions. At the other end of the park he saw a familiar face, Mr. Perkins, his next door neighbor.

"Hey, stranger, it's good to see you."

Perkins looked up.

"Ted, it's very good to see you too, I was feeling all alone here in the world." They both laughed and clasp each other with a big bear hug.

"Glad you made it out of the madness, young man," Perkins said.

"Likewise, sir."

"What are you future plans, Ted?"

"I was just thinking about all of that, I'm not sure." Ted replied.

"I was going to send a telegram to my folks and let them know I'm all right, but I'll have to wait till I get to a place where the telegraph equipment hasn't been destroyed. What about you, sir?" Ted inquired.

"Well, after I get something to eat, I'm going to catch a train south to Los Angeles and get on a ship to sail off anywhere, I'm not sure where. I kept my captain's rating, so I may check to see if there is a need for me. I don't plan on being a land-lubber again, it's too dangerous out here," he said laughing.

"When I get to Los Angeles, I'll go to the Seaman's Union hiring hall and see what's available. By the way, why don't you join me, Ted. They may have radio or telegraph positions open. You could see the world with me as your travel guide," he said, and Ted knew he was sincere in his invitation.

"I just might look into that. There isn't much difference in the International Code and the Morse Code. In fact, we were using it most of the time at work. I'm just a vagabond right now, I had plans to get married to a beautiful girl, but that has all gone away with the quake. She was killed along with her family. My heart is broken and I need something new in my life right now, some new direction." Ted lowered his head in his sadness.

"There's a train leaving Oakland in three hours to Los Angeles. They're allowing earthquake folks to ride free, can't beat a deal like that. Let's get something to eat and then go to the station, are you ready, my friend?"

"Let's go," Ted smiled.

Chapter 45

READ ALL ABOUT IT

Before leaving Oakland, Ted sent a telegram to the American Telegraph Company headquarters in St. Louis, and received the disturbing news. Most of his fellow workers at the office were thought to be dead, and the office could not reopen for at least a year. So he was out of a job, but they would keep his file open for rehire at a later date.

His separation papers and pay would be sent to the Western Union office in Los Angeles, and he would receive his pay plus two weeks separation pay that would be a total of fifty-six dollars. He also sent a telegram to his parents in Oklahoma and his cousin in Sacramento. He knew they would be relieved to know he was safe. He was sure that they had heard about the earthquake by now and would be anxious to hear from him. He could just hear his mother's cry and "Praise the Lord" for the good news.

As soon as they arrived in Los Angeles, they went directly to the Seaman Union hiring hall. Perkins asked Ted to wait while he checked on the possibility of any openings for a "good sea captain." While he waited, he picked up a copy of the *Los Angeles Times*, the new edition of *Colliers Magazine*, and a chocolate bar at the newsstand. The odor of the cigars and tobacco products were overwhelming that he felt tempted to buy a cigar but walked away instead.

Ted sat down in a lounge chair to wait for Perkins and read his magazine. There it was, the article written by Jack London entitled, "The Earthquake: an Eyewitness Story." He immediately began, and it echoed his words as he told them to Jack London. The account of the personal stories of those he helped and the stressful emotional toll it took on all the people, including those who came to their rescue.

The article continued:

"The earthquake shook the entire city of San Francisco and caused immense damage to properties, leaving only a few brick chimneys spiraling from the scorched conflagration from the raging fires that followed throughout the city, burning up millions of dollars' worth or properties.

"Never in history has a modern imperial city been so completely destroyed as San Francisco. The city is gone. Nothing remains but its memories and a fringe of houses on the outskirts. Its industrial section is gone, the business section is gone, the factories and warehouses are gone, the hotels and palaces of the rich are gone, the great department stores and newspaper centers are gone, the only ones remaining are the surrounding waters and the skeletal remains of the once famous buildings.

"For three days and nights, the fires created a lurid tower of smoke over the city that was visible a hundred miles away. That lurid tower swayed in the sky, reddening the sun and darkening the day, hiding the moonlight by night, and filling the atmosphere with smoke that contaminated the sea-misted air which the suffering people depended on.

"There was no opposition to the flames, nothing to fight them. There was no organization, no communication system, no water, nothing to fight back to oppose such a monstrous act of nature. None of the cunning inventions and adjustments of the twentieth century city could intervene. The streets were humped into large ridges and depressions, or piled high with falling debris. Steel rails were twisted into perpendicular or horizontal angles, and the telephone and telegraph systems were disrupted or destroyed. The great water main systems are broken, and all the shrewd contrivances and built-in safeguards of man were thrown out in forty seconds of twisting of the earth's crust.

"Within twelve hours, half of the heart of the city was gone. I was present to watch the vast destruction from out in the bay. The bay was dead calm, not a flicker of wind stirred, yet from every side on land, the wind was pouring in over the city. East, west, north and south, strong winds were blowing and circling around the doomed city, causing heated air to rise, making an enormous sucking sound. Thus, the fire built its own colossal chimney throughout the atmosphere. This continued day and night; but on the bay, the dead calm continued.

"The next day saw the total destruction of the very heart of the city. Dynamite was lavishly used and many of San Francisco's proud structures were crumbled by man himself to build fire walls, and time after time stands were made by firefighters, but every time the flames flanked on all sides or came from the rear to defeat their attempt of a victory.

"The number of buildings destroyed would fill a directory of the city, and the count of buildings undestroyed would only be a short list and few addresses. But the enumeration of the deeds of heroism would stock a library and bankrupt the Carnegie Metal Fund, and that number will never be known. Every act of heroism happened spontaneously, and all vestiges of them cannot be traced and will be lost to history. South of Market Street, where loss of life was particularly heavy, was the earliest area to catch fire and the number of victims from the disaster will never be known.

"Remarkable as it may seem, the night seemed quiet, even while the city roared into ruin. There were no crowds of people in panic, shouting or yelling. There was no hysteria, no disorder; not one person I saw was in the slightest degree of panic. Tens of thousands were homeless; some were wrapped in blankets, while others carried bundles of bedding and their dear household treasures.

"A whole family harnessed themselves to a delivery wagon that was weighted down with their possessions, struggling together to escape the holocaust. Baby buggies, toy wagons, and carts were used while others dragged trunks of belongings down the street. Most everyone was courteous to one another, never in all San Francisco history were people so kind to each other as they were during their days and nights of terror. After all, they were all suffering from the same devastation.

"All night, tens of thousands fled the scene before the flames came upon them. Many of them were the poor from the ghetto. They left their homes burdened with possessions, but now and again lightened their burden by flinging out upon the street their clothes and treasures from home that they had dragged for miles. They held on the longest to their trunks, and the hearts of many strong men were broken that night as they climbed the steep hill of San Francisco dragging them, only to become exhausted and falling across them. Trunks were strewn upon the streets with their exhausted owners lying on them, men, women, and children.

"Picket lines of soldiers marched before the flames to keep the people moving. As the flames advanced the picket lines retreated, and the exhausted creatures were stirred on only by the menace of bayonets, they would stumble and then arise to struggle up the steep pavement, pausing every ten feet from their weakened condition.

"Most often, after climbing a heartbreaking hill, they would find another wall of flames advancing upon them, only to be compelled to change anew the line of their retreat after toiling for hours like giants.

"Thousands were compelled to abandon their trunks, and the shopkeepers and soft members of the middle class were at a disadvantage. Some of the working class of men dug holes in vacant lots and backyards to bury their possessions."

Ted realized how Mr. London's account was so real, to the point he was reliving each moment as he read. He laid the magazine aside and began to read the newspaper instead:

"The last stand of the fire fighters was made Thursday night on Van Ness Avenue. If they failed here, the few remaining houses of the city would be swept up by the fire. Some of these homes were the magnificent residents of the second generation of San Francisco's rich, but it was not to be These homes were dynamited down across the path of fire. Here and there flames leaped the fire zone, but firefighters and volunteers beat out the roaming flames principally by the use of blankets and rugs they could scrounge up from the rubble.

"San Francisco at the present time is like the crater of a volcano, around which are camped tens of thousands of refugees. At the Presidio alone were at least twenty thousand refugees. The surrounding cities and towns are jammed with the homeless ones, and are being cared for by the relief committees. Some refugees were carried free by the railroad to any point they wished to go, and it is estimated that over one hundred thousand people have left the peninsula where San Francisco stood. There is a slight possibility of a famine, but the bankers and businessmen have already set about making preparations to prevent it, and also to rebuild the city. The government is lending a hand, and thanks to the relief coming in from the entire United States."

"What are you reading so intensely, Ted?" Mr. Perkins said as he walked up to him.

"It's the newspaper and *Colliers Magazine*. I'm reading the account of the earthquake written by Jack London, he interviewed me at Union Square on that terrible day. He interviewed several others, and I must say it's an accurate account of the disaster. It's a great article and I bought it to send to my parents in Oklahoma."

"He saw the same things we all saw that day but through the eyes of a writer. They have a way of giving a better perspective of what happened. For me, I was just a scared kid, never experienced anything like that before, I was just trying to be of help and do as much as I could. I lost most of my friends and co-workers that day, and that really hurt a lot."

"It will take time to put all this behind us, Ted, but I think I have some news that will help us move on from all this," Perkins said in his usual matter of fact style.

"What did you find out?"

"Well, Ted, my lad, you're looking at Captain Perkins, who is now an employee of the American Shipping and Freight Lines, and the captain of *The Wonderer*. As soon as she returns from sea in a few weeks, we will depart on a new adventure."

"Really, that's great. Congratulations, Captain Perkins."

Ted was ready for a new adventure, and going to sea with Mr. Perkins gave him something exciting to think about to help him forget the carnage of the past few days.

CHAPTER 46

GOING TO SEA

"That will be fifty dollars, Mr. Walters," the Seaman's Union representative said as soon as Ted finished all his paper work. "That will complete all your papers and get your membership all set up."

"Yes, sir, how much is the monthly fee?" Ted asked.

"Two dollars and that amount is taken out of your pay check every month as you receive your salary," the representative replied.

Ted turned and saluted Captain Perkins with a big smile on his face.

"I'm ready to go, sir, when do we leave?"

"As soon as they give us the word and the ship is ready to go. It's sitting over there in berth nine. They're loading it up right now, and our destination is Japan," Perkins told him as they walked out of the Union Hall to the docks.

Ted felt excited, the most he had felt in the past few months since the earthquake. He saw the ship for the first time—it had the look of a large old iron scarred bucket, and the crane high above it was loading scrap metal into the hole from a large barge on the leeward side.

A small stream of smoke was escaping out of the two large smoke stacks. The boilers were being primed and prepared for the departure, and above the main deck was a white superstructure called the bridge.

"That's my area up there," Perkins said as he pointed to it.

"That's my area of responsibility where I will do most of my work running the ship."

Captain Perkins and Ted climbed up the gangway. The day had finally arrived for them to depart. Ted paused a moment to look at the large letters *THE WONDERER* on the side of the ship, and couldn't believe he was actually going out of the country, to Japan of all places. When he stepped onto the quarterdeck of the ship, a scruffy, heavyset Santa Claus-looking first officer greeted them with a pleasant smile that was almost hidden behind his well-groomed beard.

"Good afternoon, Captain, delighted to see you, sir," he said as he saluted. "I need to inform you, sir, the broker is awaiting you in your cabin, and impatiently, I might add."

"Thank you, and your name, sir?" the captain asked.

"First Officer Jack Lewis, sir, it is a pleasure to work with you, sir. I've been aboard this ship for three tours, actually since 1901. She is a steady tight ship and makes seven knots in good seas. She is about eight thousand or so gross tons, and has a 28 foot draft. She is British built, sir, and carries a first officer, that's me, six mates, an engineer, a doctor, two wireless operators, ten deck hands, twelve stokers, two greasers, a steward, a purser, and two carpenters. Oh, yes, three cooks and two cooks' helpers, we have to eat you know, and I might add, the food is pretty good."

Perkins smiled and nodded, grateful for the information.

"This is my second wireless operator, Ted Walters. Would you see to it that he reports to the radio shack, and make sure he gets a good cabin."

"Aye, aye, sir. Also, sir, we are carrying eight passengers on this trip. They will board in the morning, and we are scheduled to leave tomorrow when they give us the word, and one more thing, the purser is presently ashore making a few last minute purchases."

"The doctor, Dr. Paul Dotson, has been aboard since the ship was first commissioned in 1898. Let's hope none of us get sick at sea to keep him busy, but you must know, he's an awful good bridge player," he said with a chuckle.

"Good to meet you," Ted said. "This is my first experience at sea. I may need your advice now and then."

"I notice that you don't have your duffel bag or any belongings in tow. If I may, sir, I would suggest you get some things to wear other than the clothes you have on your back."

"We left San Francisco rather unexpectedly without any of our belongings. We were both living in San Francisco up to few days ago, and we had to leave very promptly," Ted replied.

"That was a rough one, sir, so I hear. There is an outfitter's store just on the other side of that warehouse you just walked past, I believe the ships' company will advance you a clothing allowance so you can get the things you need," First-Officer Lewis said.

"Thanks, we will take advantage of that offer as soon as I finish talking with the broker and we get our shipping orders and manifest cleared away," the captain replied.

"If that's all, sir, I'll show Mr. Walters to his quarters," Lewis nodded for Ted to follow him.

"One more thing, officer," Perkins said. "Who is in charge of the loading dock at the present?"

"That is Officer Charles L. White, sir. However, he insists we call him C. L. He is also our supply officer, and he reports the loading will be completed by midnight."

"Thank you, officer," Perkins departed to his office to meet with the broker, and Ted followed Lewis to see his quarters for the first time. They passed through the narrow companionway and Ted saw the numerous shipboard gadgets and equipment for the first time, he knew he had a lot to learn about ships and what made them function.

"This is your cabin, Mr. Walters," Lewis said.

"Thank you, officer," Ted's head was swimming. The cabin was small and was on the main deck of the ship, close to the wireless station. It had a bunk, a small desk and chair, a very small closet and a window port. He had never lived in such a small space before, but he thought he would have everything he needed. It didn't squelch his excitement; however, space wasn't really necessary. He just wanted to do the best job he could do for Captain Perkins.

"I'll leave you now, sir. Can you find your way out?" Lewis asked Ted.

"Oh, I'm sure I can, thank you, officer. I'm looking forward to this," Ted expressed in excitement.

"Welcome aboard," Lewis said.

Ted replied. "Thank you, sir," as Lewis departed.

Two hours later, Ted heard his name called over the loud speaker to meet the captain at the gangway. Ted knew it was a summon from the captain to go shopping for clothes and supplies. Ted purchased a pea coat, a warm sweater, three pairs of uniform dress trousers, one pair of pants, a hat, shirts, an officer's dress jacket, work shoes, underwear, dress shoes, shaving equipment, a tooth brush and comb, which all came to a total of forty-eight dollars.

The captain looked very classy in his new uniform. Ted was definitely impressed, and the storekeeper gave them special attention. After all, not everyone was the captain of the ship. Ted recognized early that the captain is the one they all look up to, and Captain Perkins was the man! They were all outfitted and ready for a new day and a new life.

Ted woke up the next morning in his small cabin, and he hurriedly jumped up out of bed, this was the day they would start on their new adventure. He washed up in the facility adjacent to his room, dressed in his new uniform and reported for duty. He met the number one operator.

"I'm so glad to meet you, my name is Ted Walters."

The operator stood up and shook his hand. "Glad to meet you, Ted. I'm Larry Crawford, welcome aboard."

"Thanks, sir."

"Been an operator very long, Ted?"

"Yes, for a couple of years, I worked for American Telephone and Telegraph Company in San Francisco before the earthquake, receiving and sending the news worldwide."

"You've had lots of experience then, probably a better operator than I am. I've been working on this freighter for two years, but you probably had more line work in one week than I have in my entire career," he replied sounding rather impressed.

"On ship we are known as 'Sparky,' so if someone calls you by that name they are referring to your position, and the wireless office is often referred to as the shack."

"I've had absolutely no experience aboard a ship. I don't know a fantail from a forecastle, or port from starboard, so I appreciate all the help you can give me," Ted responded feeling a bit overwhelmed.

"You'll find it all about the same, except on ship we are not as busy as the news business. But don't worry, you'll do fine. I'll show you the routine and all the gadgets we have to work with. You'll be a ship's operator in less than a week, I'm sure," he told Ted reassuringly.

"I heard about the earthquake up in Frisco. We had some small tremors down here in the Los Angeles area, knocked a few pictures off the wall and groceries fell off the shelves, that's about all I heard reported here. But it must have been quite an experience for all of you up there," he said with sympathy in his voice.

"Yeah, it was pretty bad, did a lot of damage, burned up the city, and caused the death of thousands of people. I haven't seen the exact number, maybe never will."

"We'll be leaving soon when we get the clearance, so make yourself at home, and go explore the rest of the ship. I'm going ashore to spend the rest of my time with my wife, Kathy, and the kids. By the way, we go by military time on the ship, so we will report no later than 1600, that's four o'clock to the land lubbers," he laughed as he left.

Ted walked around the ship and went up to the bridge to watch the huge crane finish loading. The galley was open for the crew to have lunch as they were aboard to prepare for departure. He met one of the engineers, Officer Tom Markham, who invited him down to the engine room to see the workings of this large iron boat. Ted was fascinated by it all, it was such a large heavy iron monster, and he wondered how it could stay afloat. He had always been so fascinated by trains, but this was even more of a puzzle to him and how it all worked.

Men were cleaning and oiling all the machinery. They carried their oil cans and rags, wiping and polishing every little piece; it was known to them as "housekeeping." Engineer Markham introduced Ted to the men.

"This is where it all happens. We are the ones that make this ship go. We shovel the coal into the furnace, and these men are known as stokers. When the ship is underway we work in relay teams taking turns shoveling coal to keep the ship moving until we reach our destination.

"We carry several hundred tons of coal in the mammoth coal bins. We need a huge supply to keep the boilers steaming day and night. It gets pretty hot down here, as you can tell, but that's the nature of the job and the men earn the two dollars a day that they are so generously paid. Any time you need a good sweat bath, come on down."

All the men laughed, and Ted joined them as he noticed the bulging biccps on their shirtless bodies. After leaving the engine room, he walked completely around the ship thinking about what a big change his life would take, from land to sea, but he thought he would enjoy it. He was eager for something different and exciting, and going to sea would definitely be different.

He walked up to the upper deck and stood at the rails watching several well-dressed men wearing suits and hats, and elegantly dressed women board the ship, walking up the gangway. Porters carried their luggage, several big trunks and suitcases; apparently they were well prepared for a long trip. It seemed odd to him that people dressed like royalty were boarding a tramp steamer that hauled scrap metal, but maybe getting passage on a luxury liner was difficult, who knows for sure.

He watched as a horse-drawn carriage rolled up to the dock, and the couple that got out appeared angry, swearing at one another. The man tossed some money onto the front seat and grabbed the bags the driver had set off and began to struggle up the gangway, followed by the lady who was carrying a large odd-shaped package. Ted watched them stagger and weave as the porter tried to help, offering to carry the package, but she refused and pushed him away. They definitely were in a foul mood, and everyone around was relieved when they stepped onto the ship and the purser quickly escorted them to their cabin. *It was odd*, Ted thought, *for them to have such a bizarre beginning to the trip*, and it crossed his mind that such behavior was not a bad omen for a difficult trip at sea.

Everything was happening quickly now. The ship up anchored and the harbor pilot came aboard to join Captain Perkins and the helmsman to direct them out of the harbor. The fog was moving in from the sea, making visibility more difficult. The fog horn sounded its continual drone as *The Wonderer* slowly moved through the harbor toward the open sea. The harbor pilot left the ship at the mouth of the harbor, back to his small pickup boat that followed them. Ted looked down and could barely see the small boat through the fog, and he wondered how boats and ships navigated the sea and kept their direction, but he would have to put himself in the hands of the captain; he was the one who knew the sea.

The captain was in full charge as the ship plowed into the open sea, slicing its way forward like a knife, deeper and deeper into the fog. Ted watched the lantern cast its eerie light into the misty air, the fog horn blasting its warning to the other ships, and in a few seconds, the eerie echo of the horn bounced back to harmonize with the continuous sound of the fog horn.

They moved farther into the depth of the foggy sea, and Ted felt excited and very strange at the same time. He stepped into the wireless room to begin his first ships watch, the lantern light was warm and cozy and he suddenly felt like he belonged to this new home at sea.

He heard the ship bell sound eight times, which gave everyone the time of day. He busied himself sending communications to the home office. He noted that *The Wonderer* left the Los Angeles Port on time, and at the present they were under full steam at seven knots an hour in heavy fog, the compass reading was according to the sailing orders destination, Tokyo, Japan, as per the ship's manifest, carrying eighty tons of scrap metal and other cargo, with eight passengers aboard. Date March 3, 1907."

Chapter 47

AT SEA

It was the third day at sea and the fog was finally beginning to lift. The water was getting choppy and Ted was feeling more and more queasy in his stomach. He sat in front of the telegraph equipment, finding it harder and harder to concentrate, and finally it happened.

He ran out of the shack to the ships rail and the contents of his stomach emptied into the dark blue water below. He opened his eyes and looked down, his head swimming. He held on to the rail and was glad when Larry came to his rescue.

"Why don't you go turn in for a while, you don't look so good. You have a case of old fashioned sea-sickness. It happens to all of us the first time at sea. You'll feel better by dinner," Larry reassured him.

The thought of dinner made Ted's stomach churn again, especially when Larry told him they were having greasy pork chops and fried potatoes, all you can eat. He ran back to the rail again and gagged and retched, but there was nothing much left to come up.

He wobbled over to his bunk, fell on it, and felt miserable the rest of the day, making frequent runs to the rail and the facility. He drifted off to sleep and woke up the next morning feeling much better. Finally, he thought, he had developed his "sea legs."

He had several messages to send that day and was relieved that he felt like working. The equipment was old and different from the instruments he was used to, but Larry was a very good and patient instructor. They studied the manuals, the ships working instructions, and the regulations together for several hours.

He ate his first real meal that evening since coming aboard. After dinner, he went to the washroom and he noticed when he washed his hands the water drained clockwise out of the basin rather that counter clockwise like it did on land as he remembered. He asked an old hand why the water drained that way, and the old fellow decided to kid around with this novice seaman.

"Well, it depends entirely on the motion of the ship. One time I remember we were in Mozambique and the water went straight down the drain, that was because we were on the equator." He walked away from Ted laughing, leaving him confused and not knowing if his question was really answered.

The next morning Ted went to the dining room for breakfast. The posted sign announced the serving times:

Serving time Crew hours: 0600 to 0700 a.m.
Guest's hours: 0600 to 0800 a.m.
Coffee available 24 hours a day

Ted noticed three ladies sitting at the guest table. They were very friendly with each other and acted like longtime friends, but he noticed the inebriated lady he saw on the gangway was not with them; maybe she was sleeping off a hangover, he thought.

The passengers and the crew did not socialize together; however, the captain would visit with them in the lounge to make sure they were enjoying the voyage and that they had everything they needed. The passengers spent most of their time in their rooms or in the lounge, which had a bar, a game table, a piano; and it was off limits to the crew when guests were using it. This was standard procedure on a tramp steamer, but the passengers did eat the same food as the crew, and ate in the same dining room, but at separate tables. The ship's steward placed deck chairs on the main deck also, for them to relax and enjoy the open air of the sea.

Ted finished his breakfast and went to the shack. The work routine was set for the next several days; it could become boring at times, but they had to be alert to receive and send the required messages to the brokers and the owners, and also other ships at sea that may be in their vicinity. He could listen in to other ships and pick up tidbits of information and any emergency situations that may occur.

He went up to the bridge on his break and the helmsman asked him to take over the helm while he took his break. He showed Ted how to keep on the assigned compass reading, and it sounded simple enough. He loved standing on the bridge and feeling the power of the ship in his hands. It made him feel a bit giddy, but at the same time gave him the strong feeling of being a man. The windows were wide open, and the fresh salt air and occasional spray of water hit his face, keeping him alert. The clean ocean wind whipped in from all four quarters of the globe; there was nothing like it.

The ship beneath him felt like a living thing as they plowed through the sea. He liked to help out the helmsman and offered to volunteer again to help out. He was enjoying learning new things, being at sea was totally different than anything he ever done before. He liked the serenity of the sea, it was pure joy. After a day's work he enjoyed watching the activity of the sea, the flying fish skipping across the waves, and especially enjoyed the sunsets in the evening as the day gave way to the night. Seeing all these things was sometimes overwhelming, and watching the luminescence of the ship's wake behind them fascinated Ted, as the moonlight shone magically down upon the water. He hadn't been at sea very long, but he understood the strong attachment that most sailors had for the mighty sea and all its moods. Most of all he liked drifting off to sleep lulled by the throbbing of the engine and the sounds of the sea, and the movement of the ship through the water.

Ted often went down to the boiler room to shovel coal for a couple of hours with the guys just for the exercise, and he also enjoyed talking and visiting with the stokers. They were rough talkers, some of them were foreigners who spoke in different languages and guttural English, but all of them had muscles beyond belief, and he enjoyed shooting the breeze with them. They had their own sleeping quarters and their own dining room and lounge on the lower deck. It was rare to see any of them top side; they were very clannish and kept to themselves.

On the six day at sea Ted saw the couple that he heard arguing with one another on the day they boarded. Ted smiled to himself hoping they were in a better mood by now, but as they stood by the rail the woman was talking very intensely to him about something, shaking her fist. As Ted came close to them she stopped talking, he tipped his hat to them as he strolled by, and he knew they would hear more from them at some point and time during the trip, their dispute was definitely not over.

Days followed days in a reeling procession of blistering sun, followed by miraculously starry night. Being at sea was a new and wonderful experience for Ted. He never imagined the sky held so many stars, and the strangely different feel of the humidity and the pure air of the atmosphere that constantly surrounded him.

On look-out duty one evening Ted saw a bright light on the sea while he stood on the flat edge of the main deck. He made the decision it was an approaching ship and immediately rang the ships bell two times to warn the crew. Two bells meant the location of the approaching ship was starboard, one bell was for port, and three bells was for straight ahead.

The second mate on look-out located on the bridge above Ted had the advantage of height and saw the light as the first rising star of the evening. He shouted down to Ted that he had sent out a false alarm, and informed him the light came from a rising star. Ted was embarrassed because of his lack of experience which caused an unnecessary response of the crew. The crew was not fond of false alarms and he knew it would take a while for him to live this mistake down. The ringing of the bell caused all hands to assemble at their assigned stations to meet any situation that arises, and he learned that being a look-out was a heavy responsibility. The crew groaned and made their derogatory remarks to him as they returned to their stations, and Ted greatly regretted his mistake.

The first-mate assigned Ted to work with others on look-out before he was assigned again, but he knew he would face many continuing remarks for the next several days. He studied the situation very closely from then on, until the first-mate received good reports from the other crew members.

The beautiful sunsets were a sight to behold—the different shades of red, orange, and pink, and the color and shades of the sea which depended on the depth of the water, from shades of blue, shades of turquoise, to dark blue which looked almost black at times, all these fascinated Ted. With the rhythmic movement of the waves and the beautiful colors, the majesty of it all inspired him every day. He wrote down his thoughts every day before he went to bed to send back home to his parents in Oklahoma, but he found it difficult to find the words to describe the true beauty of the sea.

Watching the sea animals was another past time Ted enjoyed; every time he saw them, it was like a circus performance. One afternoon, he watched a pod of whales surface and follow along the side of the ship, and in unison they would jump out of the water only to disappear back into the depth of the sea. He couldn't believe his eyes, it looked like someone had trained them, but of course he knew that wasn't true. They were spectacular to watch, but he worried that they would collide with the ship and be injured, but he was reassured by the crew they could take of themselves.

Several days later, a group of porpoise put on a show for the crew. They jumped out of the water and sank down into the sea. The crew assembled to watch the acrobatic creatures, and Ted looked up and saw Captain

Perkins watching, and even the passengers were totally fascinated. Word got around fast whenever such a spectacle occurred, the porpoises would jump high in the air and then walk backward with their tails for several feet before returning to the water, all diving in unison. Everyone cheered them on as they performed over and over, Ted swore the porpoise were smiling; it intrigued him so much it was like they were communicating to the audience saying, "look what we can do!"

"When you see the porpoise playing around, you can be sure there are no sharks around, they are the arch enemy. It's strange but the porpoise are very astute, if they have to protect themselves from a shark, they will gang up on it and attack to protect themselves, but I have heard they prefer not to fight. It's been said that on occasion a porpoise will actually save a human from drowning, that's what I have heard, maybe it's just an old wives tale, but I tend to believe it, they are an amazing creature," The old seasoned sailor told Ted.

One day on a break Ted stood next to one of the life boats watching the sea when he heard something move behind him. He turned but saw nothing, so he listened carefully. Then he saw the canvas on the life boat move slightly and saw a hand reach out and pull on the corner of the canvas. A leg began to protrude out of the life boat, and a young black man emerged from the boat.

"What in the world are you doing hiding in there?" Ted asked, startled by his appearance.

"I is a stowaway and I catch me a ride to escape from the sheriff who wanted to send me back to my momma. I just can't do that, suh', she gone and married up with the meanest man I ever seen, and he runs me off. Suh, I haven't ate for several days, and I don't feel so good. Twice I snuck down to the kitchen and got some bread and cheese, but I'm awful hungry right now, suh'. I had to get out of that boat, I couldn't stand being in their much longer, suh', I'm all cramped up."

Ted smiled in sympathy to his story but asked, "How old are you?"

"Sixteen, I think, suh."

"What's your name?"

"Nat Brown, you can call me Nat."

"Well, Nat, I'll have to take you before the captain. He will have to decide what to do with a stowaway, so come along with me," Ted told him.

"Yes, suh."

The captain was standing in the wheel house with First Officer Lewis having coffee.

"Hi, Ted. Who you got there with you?" Captain Perkins inquired, looking a bit surprised.

"Sir, this is Nat Brown, he is a stowaway. I found him hiding in one of the life boats. He is hungry and he crawled out when I was on the main deck, right in front of me. He was ready to give himself up," Ted told him.

"How old are you boy?" the captain asked.

"Sixteen, suh."

"Why did you run away lad?" Perkins asked.

"The police put me in a paddy wagon and were taking me to jail because I was a runaway, the team of horses began to run, scared by something, and the paddy wagon turned over. I was thrown out and I ran and saw the ship, ran up the gangway and hid in the life boat. My step father is a mean man, and beat me, suh', I can work for you. I sure ain't done nothing wrong," Nat said pleading for understanding.

"Well, Nat, I guess we're stuck with you. I can't very well throw you overboard, that wouldn't be Christian-like, now would it. So you really want to work?" the captain asked.

"Sure do, suh', I want to work for my keep," Nat said begging.

"Okay, lad, take him down to the purser, and have him sign up Nat as a member of the crew, and then turn him over to the chief steward, I'm sure he can use a good dish washer and kitchen helper. But first, take him down and make sure he gets bath, and be sure he gets some clean clothes to wear."

"Yes, suh', thank you, suh'."

The next day, Ted sat in the shack working, and it was particularly hot and stuffy on this day. An attractive lady walked in and asked him to send a wire for her, the same lady that was quarreling with her husband on the day they boarded. She was crying and seemed very upset. She had the message written out on paper, and watched Ted as he sent it.

The message read:

To: Switzerland National Bank Bern, Switzerland. "Please close my account and transfer the money in the form of a bank certificate made out to Florence Craig. (stop) Please send the certificate to my account at 1st Bank of Tokyo, Japan, for deposit in my account (stop) My ship is due in Japan in about four weeks. (stop) Mrs. Florence Craig."

She paid the cost of the wire and said "thank you" as she turned around and walked away, still acting very distressed. Ted knew their story wasn't over, and that they were still having very serious problems. He began to feel very sorry for her, it sounded very serious.

They were closing in on the Hawaiian Islands and the water was becoming very rough. The wires coming in from the other ships were sending warnings of a hurricane and high gale winds. Ted took the message to the captain.

"Looks like we are in for a big blow," he said.

"It's probably too late to go around it," the captain said.

"We're in for a big storm it looks like, we need to be ready. This is your first storm at sea, Ted. We'll all feel a bit squeamish before it's all over."

The winds hit the next morning, and the loud speakers sounded, "Batten down the ship, all hatches, all port holes must be closed, make sure all the small boats are secured, secure the ship, we are really in for a big one."

A strange quiet came over the ship, probably most of the crew had experienced storms at sea, but Ted really didn't know what to expect. He stepped out onto the deck and could see and feel the sea swelling as the large waves began to roll *The Wonderer* back and forth. In a few moments he returned to the wireless shack office, and when he tried to sit down in his chair, it rolled out from under him, the ship was plunging up and down, and he was thrown against the bulkhead. He knew the ship was under stress and he would have to ride it out. Crawford stumbled back to the shack to relieve Ted.

"It's going to get bigger," he said. Ted left the shack and climbed the gang ladder to go topside to deliver the latest messages to the captain. The winds swept the giant waves onto the deck, and Ted held onto the rails but he was almost washed down the main deck as the ship plunged upward and then downward. He grabbed the safety rope tightly and began to feel very scared. He knew he could be swept overboard in a second. He was soaked all the way through his clothes, and he wasn't sure he hadn't wet his pants, he was so scared. The captain called out to him, and the first-mate looked up and said,

"How ya' doing Ted, you don't look so good."

Ted could see the helmsman struggle with the wheel, and the ship went head long into giant waves. He looked down through the giant windows and could see the ship almost completely submerged as it moved upward and downward through the water. They were tossed around in the storm in spite of the weight of the ship and the heavy load; and with the violent movements of the ship, the rudder and blades would often be completely lifted out of the water. Ted couldn't believe it— they were being tossed around like a small play boat in a pond. The helmsman was the one who fought the hardest to maintain the ship and ride out the storm.

When the storm had let up some, Ted left the cabin and heard a noise outside the companionway. A crewman was lying on the deck and was unconscious. Ted felt his pulse and saw blood coming out from his ears. He must have fallen and hit his head. Ted summoned the doctor to come, and he grabbed his bag and followed the two sailors, who were carrying the injured man to the medical cabin.

"This doesn't look good," Dr. Dotson said. "He is showing signs of a fractured skull and the pupils in his eyes are uneven, it doesn't look good at all, men."

Ted fastened his slicker and left to go report to the captain. After he reported the incident to the captain, he returned to his own cabin feeling very sick, sicker than he felt earlier at the beginning of the trip. He lay on his bunk and held on as the ship rocked back and forth, feeling like he might die.

He was so glad the next day when the storm subsided and the ship returned to normal, maintaining its normal speed. He sat at his desk as the captain came into the shack and put his hand on Ted's shoulder, he had fallen fast asleep. He jumped up and was startled when the captain woke him up.

"I'm so sorry, Captain. I was just wiped out after that storm, I'm so sorry," he said.

"Don't be upset, Ted. I hope you weren't in the middle of a nice dream. I understand, all the men are wiped out today. The doctor reported on our injured sailor and told us he has a cracked skull. Not much they can do except for rest and to watch him closely."

"Hope he will be all right, sir," Ted told him.

"Anyway, Ted, I need your help, so please come with me. I just received a report that one of our passengers is missing. I need your input on what might have happened. So come along with me."

"Aye, aye, sir."

CHAPTER 48

MAN OVERBOARD

The cabin was in total disarray when the captain and Ted arrived. They were overwhelmed with the stench of the room, and felt the presence of something dark and murky which far exceeded what the captain expected when he received the message to respond to a call from a passenger.

Someone had been very sick. In fact, Ted stepped in a puddle of vomit as he entered the cabin and came face to face with a very distraught lady. The lady was Mrs. Craig, the one who sent the telegram, the one who was having angry exchanges with her husband as they boarded the ship, and again as Ted observed a few days ago when he was walking on the deck. On that particular evening, they were having another heated discussion.

"How can we help you, ma'am. Is this about your husband?" the captain asked as he tried to comfort her.

"I'm so sick. I haven't left my room since the storm hit. On that morning my husband left the room, that was two days ago, he was feeling sick and I haven't seen him since. I asked the steward to inform you that my husband is missing. I am so sick I can't go look for him," she managed to say through her sobs.

"We will immediately implement a search party to look in every nook and corner of the ship to find him. You can be sure of that," the captain reassured her.

"I'll send Dr. Dotson to attend to your medical needs, and we'll also send in the steward to clean the cabin for you and bring in some food for you to eat, perhaps some soup, something easy on the stomach," he said sympathetically. Mrs. Craig covered her face with her hands and muttered "Thank you" as she rolled over on the bed and faced the wall, sobbing bitterly.

As they left the cabin, the captain asked Ted to summon the doctor to check on Mrs. Craig and he would organize a search party to begin an immediate search of the entire ship.

"Also, talk with the crew and the stewards in the dining room to find out the last time any of them saw him. I can really use your help."

"Good luck, sir. You know they are the couple who argued continually, and she is the lady who sent the telegram to her bank to transfer her money. Something is going on with those two, sir. I hope we can find him soon," Ted said.

The captain left hurriedly to find First Officer Lewis to help organize a search party. He didn't feel good about this whole situation. He had hoped for a smooth journey at sea. They had weathered the storm with only minor repairs of the ship, and they certainly didn't need another crisis. What he really suspected in this case, but hoped he was wrong, was that Mr. Craig was washed overboard during the storm.

Ted went to his cabin and took a quick shower, changed his clothes, and cleaned his shoes. He couldn't get the stench out of his head; it seemed to linger all around him. He hurried off to the dining room to carry out the captain's orders and the strong smell of coffee penetrated the air, which was a welcome relief from the stench. He filled his mug and took a sip. *What a relief,* he thought, *coffee never smelled or tasted so good.*

He talked to the steward and filled him in on the crisis at hand, but he could not recall seeing Mr. Craig that morning. He called in another steward to question, and there was only one person that came in that morning and he didn't stay because it was too difficult to sit and eat with the ship bouncing around in the storm, and that person, he said, was not Mr. Craig. None of the kitchen staff had seen Mr. Craig since the storm. He had not been in the dining room for meals or had not been seen in the lounge or relaxing on the deck.

Ted took his report to the captain and there was nothing new that he had found from the interviews. The captain went to the loud speaker system and made an announcement:

"Attention, all crew members and passengers. We have a missing person, Mr. Floyd Craig. Please organize a complete search of your area of the ship from top to bottom. Look for anything that might be suspicious, a scrap of clothing or anything that might help us find this missing gentleman. Please report your findings to the captain in two hours. Thank you, we need everybody's help!"

"Ted, thank you for your help. I want you to go talk to Mrs. Craig again and find out as much as you can about this situation and try to find out what their problems and arguments were about, if you can. Please take notes, we need detailed information for our official report to the company and to the authorities. We will need to report to them as soon as possible," the captain instructed Ted.

"We'll have Crawford take over the shack until you get through with your interviews. You have your work cut out for you, Ted. Please report back to me as soon as you finish," the captain requested.

Ted stopped by the shack to fill Larry in on the captain's latest request.

"Sounds like the captain has made a detective out of you, you'll have your hands full for a while. I'll bunk here until you finish. Larry chuckled.

"I'm sorry, Larry, this wasn't my idea," Ted answered apologetically.

"It's really no problem for me, Ted. I'd much rather do what I'm doing than do what you've been asked to do. Good luck, Mr. Detective!"

Ted smiled. "Larry, I'll start my interview with you. When was the last time you saw Mr. Craig?" He sat down beside Larry to take notes.

"This may surprise you, Ted, but I don't think I ever saw him on this entire voyage. I don't even know what he looks like except for his passport picture. You know the captain has us keep all the passports in our custody during the trip," Larry said as he pulled out the Craig passport from a file drawer to show to him.

"I have seen most of the passengers in the dining hall, but I just speak to them and really don't pay a lot of attention to what they look like," he added.

"Let me see all the passports," Ted requested.

They looked them over and learned that six of the passengers were Italian, three men and three women, all born in Naples, Italy, all living in the United States but traveling on Italian passports. Ted made a note of this on his pad, wanting to keep accurate information for the captain.

"Thanks, Larry, my friend. I'll check back with you later. If you think of anything else that might be helpful, just let me know."

"Sure thing, Ted."

He left the shack and went to the dining room. It was 1700, dinner hour, and he hoped to catch the passengers and to speak with them. The passengers, three couples, were sitting at the table, so Ted walked over to address them.

He cleared his throat, and said, "Excuse me for interrupting your dinner, but as you know we have a missing person on our ship. I would appreciate it very much if each of you would talk with me, one at a time, to see if we can put the puzzle together of what might have happened to him, and if you have any other information that might be helpful to our investigation."

They all nodded.

"Of course," they said.

"When you finish your dinner, please come to my table, one at a time, and please don't leave the dining room until we're all finished," Ted instructed.

"I hope you will all be cooperative, we're talking to everyone on the ship to gather all the information we can—our hope is to find him. We need all the information we can gather for the insurance company and the police when we arrive in port." They all nodded as if they understood and continued with their dinner.

Ted sat down at the table to prepare for the questioning and waited patiently for them to respond. In the meantime, he observed their behaviors and their·reactions as they talked with each other over dinner, and he was somewhat amused as he watched their expressions and the prolific use of their hands as they talked. At times they looked rather heated and uncomfortable as they carried on their conversation, and Ted thought these interviews could be rather interesting.

The first gentleman came to the table and introduced himself.

"I'm Luigi Ammani," he said as he shook hands with Ted.

"Please have a seat, Mr. Ammani." Ted pulled the chair out for him to be seated.

"Did you know Mr. Craig?" Ted began his questioning.

"No, we are traveling with our friends, the others you met earlier, but we didn't know the other passengers, the Craigs. I spoke to them a few times, but they kept to themselves most of the time. I haven't seen either of them since the storm."

"Where do you live, Mr. Ammani?"

"I live in Hoboken, New Jersey. I'm from the same community as my friends. We're off on a six-month holiday together."

"Are you employed, Mr. Ammani?"

"Yes, I'm in the insurance business."

"What is the name of your company?"

"The Naples Insurance Company."

"Is that a Naples, Italy, insurance company, sir?"

"Yes, sir, it is. The others we are traveling with are my fellow associates in business."

"Do you have any idea of what might have happened to Mr. Craig?"

"No," he replied. "I sure hope he's ok and didn't get swept overboard during the storm. We stayed in our cabins the whole time during the storm, mainly to protect ourselves. We were sure relieved when it let up," he expressed.

"Thank you, sir. Would you send you wife over to talk with me?"

Mr. Ammani got up from his chair and Ted jotted down a brief note of his interview and added, "He seemed somewhat nervous, but English is not his native language and it may have been because he was uncomfortable speaking English."

Mrs. Ammani approached the table and Ted stood up and offered her a chair.

"Thank you, my name is Maria Ammani. You just finished talking with my husband."

"Yes, ma'am, tell me about your trip so far, and if you have met the Craigs or had a conversation with them."

"Only spoke to them once or twice. They kept to themselves and always seemed unhappy about something."

She answered the questions the same as her husband. She was a housewife and they were on a six-month holiday. She had been very frightened during the storm and stayed in their cabin. Ted interviewed the other couples and the stories were about the same. They were from the same community, were business associates, and they all immigrated to the United States about twelve years ago from Italy to set up their insurance business. There was one thing that Ted thought was interesting about the men—all three had a tattoo on their right hand, a small insignia, round in shape between their thumb and forefinger. He had never seen that before and thought it was strange that each of them had the same tattoo mark. It made him curious enough that he had Larry send off a wire to the Hoboken, New Jersey, police department to inquire about these men and if the tattoo had any meaning.

His final interview was with Mrs. Craig. He looked over her passport before going to her cabin and noticed it didn't show the name of Craig, but gave the name of Florence Fey instead. He knocked on the cabin door and when the door opened Mrs. Craig was standing in her long, flowing negligee which took Ted by surprise. The last time he saw her she was sick and distraught and was mourning for her husband.

. "I'm sorry, Mrs. Craig, when you get dressed would you come up to the dining room, I need to talk with you and get more information? I would really appreciate your cooperation. It might help us locate your husband."

"Yes, of course, I'll come up shortly. Won't you come in first and have a drink with me before we talk. I'm so sad and lonely without my husband. I need to spend time with others socially."

Ted cleared his throat and was embarrassed and surprised by her sudden change in behavior.

"I'll be waiting in the dining room for you." He turned and hurried away down the corridor having difficulty in his mind understanding what just happened and the sudden change in her demeanor.

He waited about thirty minutes before she came into the dining room. She was dressed elegantly in a very provocative low cut neckline dress, revealing as much as a lady dared. She sat down at the table with Ted and told him she was prepared to answer his questions regarding her dear husband.

"Thank you for coming, Mrs. Craig. When was the very last time you saw your husband?" he asked.

"He left the cabin the morning of the storm. He felt very shut in and wanted to get some fresh air. I was feeling ill so I didn't go with him. That was the last time I saw him, and then the storm got much worse."

"Were you married to Mr. Craig?" Ted asked. "I see your passport lists another name."

"Well, yes, or course we were married. We got married two days before we left for this trip. I had to use my current passport because I didn't have time to get a new one." She showed Ted her marriage certificate and it showed the date of their marriage, two days prior to the trip, as she had said. Ted smiled when he saw the marriage certificate, he had noticed her birth date, showed her to be thirty-four, which was different than her passport; she was four years older than her marriage certificate showed.

"I was a showgirl and worked under the stage name of Flo Fey in Los Angeles, that's where I met Mr. Craig. He was a dealer of rare art. He owned his own gallery in Los Angeles and was considered in the art world as quite successful. He had recently purchased a rare piece of art and we were on our way to Japan to sell it to a prospective buyer. It is a very expensive piece," she added.

"What else can you tell me about his work," Ted was very curious by now.

"I don't know much else about him. We had what is known as a whirlwind romance, you might say," she smiled.

"I only knew him less than thirty days, when he whisked me off my feet. We met at the theater after a show one night where I was the lead dancer, and he came back stage to my dressing room with a big bouquet of roses and insisted I join him for dinner."

She looked down for a moment and then said, "It was love at first sight, or so he told me."

"May I inquire why you transferred such a large sum of money from the bank of Switzerland to the bank of Japan?" Ted asked.

"Yes, of course you may. Before I agreed to marry him, we made an agreement that since he was several years older than me. We wanted to be sure I was financially secure. He was a very rich man and he agreed to give me a million dollar dowry as a wedding present, so he deposited that amount in the Switzerland bank in my name.

"When I agreed to take this trip with him, I decided to transfer the money into the Japanese account so I could have access to it when we arrive and actually hold it in my hands. I wanted to see what it felt like to have a lot of money."

She smiled as she added, "Isn't that a crazy reason, I just had to know what it felt like."

"What was the painting, did it have a name?"

"Oh, yes, it was quite famous he told me, it is a Rembrandt and is titled, the 'Lady in Black.' It is supposed to be worth a lot of money but I don't know a lot about art, just what he told me. He made me carry it aboard the ship. It was heavy and I was upset with him and I told him so. He had too much to drink and he couldn't carry such a priceless piece up the gangway. He was afraid he would damage it." She seemed agitated just talking about it.

"Thank you, you have been very cooperative, that will be all for now," Ted informed her.

"Sure, honey, I like to cooperate with good-looking young men, would you like to have that drink now," she smiled flirtatiously.

"Sorry, ma'am, it's against the rules. You know I work for the ship's company, and we are not allowed to fraternize with the passengers. Company rule you know."

She walked away acting very disappointed, and Ted took his pad and pencil and returned to the shack.

"Welcome back, have you found anything new?" Larry asked.

"No, nothing new, he must have been washed overboard during the storm, everything leads to that," Ted told him with a sigh.

"I'll report my findings to the captain, but there is one thing I want you to do for me."

"Sure," Larry said.

"I would like for you to send a wire to the police in Hoboken and inquire about the three Italian men who are all traveling together with their wives. I'm curious to see if they have any information on them. They all have the same tattoo mark on their hand like gang members." Ted gave him the information and Larry quickly prepared the message to send.

"I'll get it right off, and I'll also send a wire to the Los Angeles police to inquire about Mr. Craig."

Ted went up to the bridge to report his findings to the captain. Perkins was smoking his large mechum pipe, sitting back very relaxed in his deck chair. He jumped up when Ted approached him, he must have been half asleep.

"Whoa, you've been dreaming, haven't you!" Ted laughed, "Did I scare you?"

Perkins smiled. "I was about to get a nap in, don't think I was dreaming anything yet. Well, what did you find out, any new thoughts about what might have happened to our missing passenger?" He inquired of Ted.

"None of the interviews or the searches gave us any new information about the missing man, but I think we may have discovered something else new."

"Oh, what's that, Ted?"

"You know our passengers, the three Italian couples, I believe they may be members of some type of organization. They are really suspicious. The men all have identical tattoos on their hands and are all associated with the Naples Insurance Company, an Italian business located in New York. I just don't like the way it looks or sounds," he related to Perkins shaking his head.

"We sent a wire to the Hoboken police and also to Los Angeles requesting information."

"You sound like a real detective, young man. You're getting pretty smart. You're not the innocent young man you were when I first met you." Perkins laughed.

"Good work, Ted, I appreciate it. We'll turn over the information to the Japanese police about our missing person when we arrive in Tokyo. I agree with you, it sounds like he was washed overboard during the storm. Let me know what you find out about the other passengers when the wire comes in."

"Sure thing, Captain," Ted said as he left to go back to the shack to relieve Larry. Several hours later the message came in from the Hoboken Police Department. The telegraph key tapped away as Ted deciphered it, and he was surprised at what he learned. His suspicions were confirmed. The news was not good, he couldn't wait to tell the captain.

The message read: "All three men are known as members of a group called 'the black hand,' and it is believed they could be dangerous. Suspects in the murder of a man who was found in a barrel with his head cut off at the location of Avenue A and Elizabeth Street on February 21, 1907. They were last seen in New York on that date and are wanted for questioning. Signed: Chief of Police, New York City."

Ted couldn't wait to tell the captain about this news. It was a bombshell of information. Just as he was about to call Larry to relieve his post to go up to the bridge, another wire came in from Los Angeles. It read:

> "Mr. Floyd Craig, an art dealer in Los Angeles has no known criminal record, but is known as a wealthy successful businessman. The painting, 'Lady in Black,' was reported stolen years ago in the year 1870 from a Dutch merchant and was never recovered. According to the U. S. Customs service, the antique and arts department, it is doubtful that the painting that the Craig's have in their possession is the original. Since there is no longer a hold on this painting because the crime was committed years ago, we cannot place a hold on it. It is reported that Mr. Craig was recently married to a Florence Small, known by her stage name as Florence Fey, departed Los Angeles on March 7, 1907 for an around the world trip as a wedding present. We will report this incident to the U. S. Consulate in Japan for follow up. Signed: Chief of Police, Los Angeles, California."

Ted reported the messages to Captain Perkins, and the captain knew they hadn't heard the last of these incidents. His quiet peaceful journey that he had hoped for had now turned into an international incident. He listed Mr. Craig as missing at sea, and after a complete search and interviews with the crew and passengers, he concluded he was washed overboard during the storm causing his accidental death.

CHAPTER 49

SOS

T he next few days were relatively calm despite the recent news and activities concerning the missing man and the big art deal. Ted was enjoying the more leisurely life at sea, just as it was at the beginning of the journey.

He went about his duties and once again could notice and appreciate the sounds of the sea, which he loved. He enjoyed the ship moving through the water, the bells sounding announcing the time, the fog horn blowing, and all the other workings of the ship as it made its way through the rough sea.

He even noticed the sounds of the crew climbing up and down the ladders, and walking down the corridors and bouncing against the wall when the ship cut through a large wave in the rough waters, causing them to stagger against the bulkhead.

Later that afternoon their calm was interrupted by an SOS call which came through the wire. A ship that was in distress gave their longitude and latitude repeatedly, which indicated they were about 80 leagues away from *The Wonderer*.

The ship was in dire circumstances and was sinking. Ted notified Captain Perkins the troubled ship was a German vessel, the Von Getz, and is listed as a private charter yacht.

The captain immediately ordered their ship to change course and proceed at full speed to respond to the SOS, hoping to render assistance. He ordered Ted to keep sending out the SOS to all ships to let them know *The Wonderer* was on its way, and he added they should arrive in the area by the next morning.

When they drew close to the area, the captain alerted the crew to be on constant lookout for signs of wreckage or survivors. As they arrived at the scene in the early morning hour, the sun was up and burning off the foggy haze. They slowed to quarter speed and the captain ordered all emergency procedures in place.

A crewman shouted, "I see something floating in the water, I can't determine what it is at the point." Closer in they could readily see it was a man lying on top of a wooden pallet floating in the water, the captain ordered "all stop" and for the crew to lower a small boat. Ted climbed into the rescue boat to help, and when they reached him they found he was dead and had been dead for several hours; rigor mortis had already set in.

"Bring the body aboard," the captain ordered.

"We'll search the area further for more bodies and then we'll have a proper burial service for the deceased man."

They muscled the body into the boat using all the strength they could muster. He was a big man and twice he slipped from their arms, almost causing them to lose him back to the sea. They rowed to the ship and connected to the boatlift to raise them out of the water back onto the deck. They turned the body over to the doctor for examination to determine the cause of death, and his immediate examination revealed the man had died from exposure.

The crew continued to search from the deck using the telescope to circle the area, to look for more debris or bodies. Another boat was sighted which looked to be about a quarter of a league away. The captain quickly ordered another rescue boat launched, and again Ted and three other crewmen climbed aboard as they were lowered into the water.

They quickly rowed the boat to the location and as they came closer they could see the name written on the bow, *The Van Getz*, and they could also smell a stench coming from the boat. As they got even closer they saw a ghastly sight, the boat was filled with twelve men, all obviously dead slumped over their oars, and the stench was unbearable.

One of the crewman went aboard to visually examine the bodies and look for identification, but no names were found on any of them. He noticed a piece of paper in one of the men's hand with a scribbled message written in his own blood, 'Chinese Pirates.' He could readily see that they had been killed by machine gunfire while apparently trying to flee from their attackers, and their bodies were already beginning to decay from the hot sun which bore down on them.

The captain ordered his crew to sink the boat and to bury the people at sea. They were not equipped to handle that many bodies on board for a burial ceremony. As they watched the boat sink into the depth of the sea, the captain read the seaman's burial eulogy from the deck.

The crew rowed their small boat back to the ship and the stench began to dissipate, they could begin to breathe fresh sea air again. One of the young crewmen was so overtaken by it all that he stood up and bent over the side to throw up. But suddenly the boat rocked to the side throwing him overboard and the waves swept him several yards away. He began to struggle in the water, waving his arms and yelling for help, and it was easy to see that he couldn't swim. One of the crewmen yelled out "Sharks!" and everybody looked to where he was pointing. The sharks were swimming around the sunken boat feasting on the bodies, and they knew right away the young man could be in dire trouble.

Without even thinking, Ted jumped overboard to rescue the young sailor, and as the old story goes, most sailors can't swim, it was true for Ted also, he was a weak swimmer. Ted grabbed the boy and started pulling him toward the boat, but some of the sharks shifted their focus and came toward them. The crew pulled the boy inside and Ted managed to partially pull himself up on the side of the boat, his legs still dangling in the water. A shark lunged at the boat just as the crew pulled him inside, just a split second before the shark hit the boat. The shark then turned on his side with his mouth wide open ready to strike again, and at that moment Ted saw what his possible fate could have been as he looked into the eyes of death, only the intervention of God and the last second action of the crew saved him. The shark retreated and hit the side of the boat once again almost knocking another sailor off his feet, but luckily he landed in the bottom of the boat, it all happened so fast it didn't sink in for Ted what a close call they had.

The young sailor that Ted had saved began to cry and was shaking uncontrollably.

"Thank you, you're my blooming hero, oh, thank you, sir, you saved my life. Thank you, and me darlin' mother thanks to you, God rest her soul," he managed to say. He was so scared he rattled on and on, he couldn't stop himself.

"It's all right, my friend. I'm glad it turned out as it did for both our sakes," Ted said as he tried to comfort the young man.

One of the crewmen took a big deep breath and said, "That was as close a call you'll ever have, Ted, that was a magnificent gesture on your part to save the boy's life, but it almost cost you yours. I thought you were a goner for sure. Can you share that kind of luck to the rest of us, by chance? I swear

I saw a seaman's shirt in the shark's mouth as it made its attack. That was the most scary thing I ever saw."

It finally sank into Ted's head that he had been very fortunate. He bowed his head in reverence and said a silent prayer to the Lord for saving him and the young crewman.

After a few hours of further search, they failed to find anything more, so the captain ordered the ship to return to its original course. Ted sent a telegram, per order of the captain, to the Port authorities in Hamburg, Germany, to report the information concerning the yacht, *The Van Getz*, the location of the SOS, and their findings when they answered the call.

They also sent the information to the ship's broker in Japan and to the home office, reporting the search they had performed and their findings, and the hour they returned to their original course. All in all, they spent about twelve hours in the search and rescue process.

"Unless the port authorities in Hamburg, Germany, can identify the people aboard *The Van Getz*, it may remain a mystery to us who these unidentified people are who lost their lives at sea, and we may never know the circumstances of what happened here. We may never know who committed this piracy and murdered these people, and what their motives were," the captain announced to the crew.

"What we do know, there are apparently pirates out here at sea, so we must keep a very watchful eye from here on out."

The captain conducted a burial at sea for the unknown man they brought aboard. He read the sailor's eulogy as he slid into the sea and quickly sank beneath the waves. The crew stood quietly and reverently at the ships rail and watched the emotional scene. Ted could not help but form a tear in his eye as he watched, and he gave thanks for his own life.

After the ceremony Perkins commended Ted for his bravery.

"I saw you jump into the water, I was very afraid for you. Why would you take such a risk, your life was in danger?"

"I don't rightly know, sir, never gave it a thought. It was just instinct, I guess."

"Well, it all turned out all right this time, but please don't ever do it again," the captain admonished.

Later that week, their location was just off the main Japanese Island. The birds began to engulf the ship; they were everywhere, hundreds of them on the deck and on the rails. They literally turned the deck into the familiar saying we know as the "poop deck."

There were birds high above on the rim of the smoke stack. Ted had never seen so many various kinds of birds before. It looked like someone had left the door of a bird sanctuary open.

Most of the birds were white sea gulls, which made the deck look like it was full of snow. Ted laughed as he watched them, and the thought crossed his mind, they are all free loading, catching a free ride into the harbor. He wondered if there might be a storm nearby that drove them to *The Wonderer* as a safe haven and roost. He went up to breakfast and when he returned to the shack, the birds were all gone, that is, except the big mess they had left behind on the deck.

Chapter 50

TOKYO HARBOR

Seven weeks and three days after leaving Los Angeles, California, *The Wonderer* slowly pulled into Tokyo harbor. Ted watched from the bow of the ship and could see how large the harbor was, the largest he had ever seen.

As they made their way through the harbor, the crew watched the oddest, but most entertaining thing they had ever seen. They were literally being escorted by a group of dolphin as they playfully jumped, skipped, and dived in front of the ship as they proceeded into the depth of the harbor. It was as if they were performing a welcome ceremony for the crew, and knew they had an appreciative audience. Ted enjoyed the performing dolphins as he stood on the bow and also noticed the usual scent in the air, the typical fishy smell that penetrates every harbor, but it seemed stronger here in Tokyo.

The sky was an absolute clear blue, and as the pilot boat led them through the harbor, they passed many ships from all over the world, both big and small. There were strange-looking Japanese fishing boats, called sampans, large tramp steamers, freighters, and even several Japanese warships parked along the docks.

The Wonderer was directed to a remote side of the harbor to an industrial area used mainly for unloading scrap metal. Ted was fascinated as he watched the giant cranes reach down into the bowels of the ship to lift the scrap metal onto the large barge which lay in the harbor next to the ship. There must have been at least twenty freighters lined up waiting their turn to unload.

Ted kept busy sending messages back and forth to their company headquarters. The message included arrival time, wharf number, and the information from the captain that they were awaiting the Customs and

Immigration inspectors and the broker to board the ship to process their arrival.

During their waiting time, no one was allowed to disembark. They could only leave the ship after the Japanese officials came aboard to clear them. When they arrived, the captain invited them up to the bridge and ordered all passengers to report at 1300 to the deck for clearance, and for the crew to report at 1500. They were also to bring their passports and luggage with them for declaration.

Ted and Larry were busy returning the passports to each passenger and crew member, and they checked off each name on the list as they handed them their passport along with a declaration form to fill out to list their baggage and every article they were bringing into the country. The line formed for the officers to inspect and clear each person and their baggage before they disembark, the passengers would be processed first.

Ted took the passport and personal belongings of the missing passenger, Mr. Craig, to the Captain's office. Perkins explained to the Japanese officers they had a missing passenger who was apparently lost at sea, probably washed overboard during the storm, but there were no eyewitness to the event that may have occurred. He introduced the officers to the ship's broker who would handle all the details of the event, all the reports of the search and interviews, the death certificate prepared by the ship's doctor, his personal belongs, and the information that his wife, Florence Craig, was travelling as a passenger and would be debarking in Tokyo.

The broker finished his report to the officers and gave them the copy of the telegram the ship had received from the Los Angeles police in answer to their inquiry concerning the missing passenger, Mr. Craig, who was traveling with his wife to deliver an expensive painting, called the Lady in Black to a perspective buyer. Ted was fascinated by the detailed process and the meticulous questioning and observations of the officers. He remembered going to Canada at the age of fifteen, the only other country he had traveled, but that was a much less detailed process than this.

Captain Perkins gave the officers the information of the three Italian couples traveling under Italian passports and the information they received from the Hoboken police department, and told them about the suspicions that surrounded them. The Japanese officers took immediate note of the information since it involved a murder case, but no warrants existed or charges made, the New Jersey police only wanted them for questioning.

The officers processed the line of passengers and crew, but they held the Italian couples for further questioning. They didn't have any warrants or any reason to arrest them, but they had Italian passports and the Japanese government had received a dispatch from the international authorities in Italy concerning their suspicions. The Japanese officers were expecting them to arrive and escorted all six of them off the ship and placed them in a paddy wagon drawn by horses, to hold them for questioning by the authorities. Ted watched the whole process, maybe his suspicions of these Italians were real, maybe these men were actually guilty.

He continued watching as Mrs. Craig was escorted from the ship by the broker and a steward, helping her with her numerous pieces of baggage and her valuable painting. She apparently was of no interest to the Japanese officers. They elected not to question the grieving widow of the man who was unfortunately lost at sea.

They escorted her to a waiting mass of rickshaw boys standing by the docks, each trying to catch the eye of a prospective passenger. She climbed aboard one of the rickshaws, and the boy delighted to have a customer, helped her load her luggage and started running pulling the rickshaw as if it were as light as a feather toward her intended destination.

After the ship's crew were all cleared they could now come and go from the ship as they pleased, but they were reminded they must carry their passports and stay within one hundred miles of the city.

"How long will the ship be docked?" Ted asked the captain.

"The broker says we will be tied up in port waiting to be unloaded for probably five or six weeks," the captain answered.

"There are about twenty other ships ahead of us waiting to be unloaded."

"That long!" Ted was surprised.

"Yeah, the crew will receive half pay for the total time we're here, but that doesn't include you and Larry, you are on standby and will receive full wages. You are free to go on liberty. You and Larry can coordinate your schedules so one of you is always here to send and receive the wires,"

Larry told Ted, "I plan to stay with the ship, I've been here many times before and I'm getting to old for all the excitement, especially the *geisha* girls."

"What's a geisha girl?" Ted asked innocently.

Perkins and Larry laughed out loud.

"You need to go and find out for yourself," Perkins said and continued.

"Most of the crew will head out for the city and the geisha. You can figure that out for yourself, most of the crew won't deny themselves of their company, if you know what I mean. Just be sure you watch your money when you go into the city, Ted. Your money will go a long way here in Tokyo."

Ted seemed embarrassed when he finally realized what Perkins was talking about.

"Go see the city, Ted, you owe that to yourself. There's lots to see here in Tokyo, all their customs and traditions, you'll enjoy it," Perkins reassured him.

Later that morning, Ted stopped by the shack to coordinate his schedule with Larry.

"So you don't plan to go into the city while we're here? What do you recommend as a first time visitor to Tokyo?" Ted asked him.

"I can enjoy my time right here on the ship for the next several weeks. I've got a couple of new novels I picked up to read, and with all this free room and board and very little to do. I'll have plenty of time to finish them. Also, I'm a married man and have a family. I need all my money for when I get home. I have a daughter who wants to go to college, got to save my money for her college expenses, so I'll just stay aboard."

"But you're young, Ted, and this is your first visit here, so you need to go see the city. You'll enjoy it, it's a very interesting place. I'll hold down the fort for a few days, and if I were you I would go to some nice hotel and check in, and when you're out on the town you'll love their public baths, and go taste all the foods, it's so different. You'll have a blast, we'll be here for several weeks, you know," he said.

"I have never touched the ground of a foreign country, except Canada, and I think maybe I'm scared and excited at the same time," Ted told him.

"If I were you I would take a sightseeing tour around the countryside, that will take you out among the people so you can see all their customs and how the people live. Believe me, there's lots to see," Larry added.

Ted decided to go ashore that evening and as he walked down the gangway he noticed some of his shipmates walking down the street toward the city lights. He didn't want to be by himself, so he decided to tag along and follow them. They went into a night club about two blocks from the ship, the sign on the front of the building read "The Red Dragon Club."

Ted followed them in and when he got inside it was pretty dark, but he spotted his fellow shipmates sitting at a table. He walked up to the table and they all recognized him right away and greeted him with a friendly whoop and holler, shaking his hand and slapping him on the back, giving him a warm and welcome reception.

Someone set a glass of a clear liquid drink in front of him, and one of the men said, "Tommy is buying the first round, so drink up."

They all stood up and raised their glasses to salute Tommy, and someone yelled "Down the hatch!" and Ted followed suit.

He sputtered and spewed, coughed and choked, and finally caught his breath, and with tears in his eyes he managed to say, "What in the world was that you guys just gave me?"

They all laughed and seemed to enjoy his discomfort.

"That's *saki*," one of them said.

Someone else said, "First time, huh, well it goes down pretty smooth on the second round, so drink up," and another drink appeared in front of him.

After several rounds a bartender came to the table and asked what he could get for them. Ted said in somewhat of a slurred voice.

"Bring another round for everybody. I guess it's my turn to buy."

One pretty young Japanese girl moved in on Ted.

"You buy me drink, big guy." He wondered to himself, *Is this one of those geishas they talked about?*

Ted said, "Sure," and the bartender brought it to the table for her. It didn't look like the saki they had been drinking, it looked more like tea. Ted thought through his hazy muddled mind they were charging him the same price for her drink that looked like tea. Ted bought another round for everyone, and after a few minutes he stood up feeling very sick, like he was going to throw up. He needed some fresh air so he slowly made his way to the exit door. His shipmates didn't really notice him trying to leave because the bar girls had them all surrounded, sitting on their laps, laughing and giggling and keeping them company.

The girl who Ted bought a few drinks for followed him out, and when they stepped outside she was still hanging onto him, begging and pulling on him to go to her place, just down the street.

"Not verilly far," she kept saying in her broken English. "Come we have lots of fun, you lika me, you come with me, big boy, me lika you verilly much, you'll see, I'm verrily nice. You see!"

Ted knew he didn't want to go anywhere with her or anyone, he only wanted to get back to the ship and go to bed; he felt really sick. The girl kept pulling him to go one way and he shook her off, and finally she gave up pulling on his sleeve.

"You pay me money, big boy, pay me, or I'll scream," she said angrily. Ted reached in his pocket and took out a dollar bill and handed it to her. She let go of his arm and laughed as she walked back toward the bar, muttering to herself something that Ted didn't understand.

He felt awful, he had never been that drunk before. He hoped the fresh air would make him feel better, but he began to vomit as he staggered back toward the ship. When he finally reached the ship, he managed to stagger up the gangway, stopping to throw up once again into the harbor water below as he held on tight to the side of the railing. After a while he managed to stagger up onto the deck and made his way to his cabin. He fell onto his bunk and slowly slipped into a twirling spinning state of mindless haze, and finally into a state of drunken semi-unconsciousness. His last words as he faded into the dark pit of sleep was, "Oh, mommy, I'm so sorry," the words he spoke as a little boy when he was in trouble.

He slept until late the next day. It was almost noon when he awoke. The sun was shining bright in his eyes through the portal window, and along with that he had an ugly mouth full of cotton and the biggest headache he had ever had. After he managed to finally get up, he took a cold shower for the longest time, and after he shaved he started to feel human again. He decided to go to the galley to get something to eat, and when he arrived he ran into Larry.

"Thought you went into the city, Ted," Larry said surprisingly.

"No, I didn't go. I just went over to the nearby bar with several of the stoker crew. They are a great bunch but I can't drink like they do, they really put that stuff away. I got sick as a dog and just barely made it back to the ship."

Larry laughed. "That wasn't very smart."

"No, I guess not, I actually didn't have much fun, the fun only lasted for a little while, then I got sick. I don't know how they drink like that."

"Years of practice, my boy, evidently you weren't raised to be a rounder so don't start now, you've had your stupid fling, so let that be it. Go see the country and be a tourist, this is a very interesting place to see and enjoy. Don't waste your time in a stupid bar.

"Yeah, yeah, Larry, you're right, you sound like my dad." They both laughed and Ted interjected.

"I'll be a good boy from now on, I promise."

"That's one of the lessons of life growing up, knowing what's good for you and what hurts you. Now you know, so go have some real fun and excitement."

"You're right, Larry. I just didn't want to venture off by myself, guess I was scared to be alone in a strange country. So I teamed up with those guys, they really aren't interested in anything but the girls and getting drunk. I guess they think that is having a good time."

"I'm going to take one of those rickshaws right into the heart of the city tomorrow to see what Japan is all about," Ted told Larry.

"Good, you won't regret it. When you get back you'll have some great memories of Japan, all the memories your stoker friends will have is that they got drunk and wasted their money."

The next morning bright and early Ted hired a rickshaw to take him into the city. He arrived in front of the Grand Imperial Hotel, the beautiful, famous majestic hotel in the heart of Tokyo. He walked in and immediately felt self-conscious and out of place. He wasn't dressed appropriately for such opulence.

But there he was standing in the middle of a palatial palace with people milling around the lobby, many different nationalities, all dressed in there different traditional native dress.

He finally walked up to the desk.

"I would like a room please."

"Your passport please, sir," the clerk said with a pleasant smile.

Ted handed it to him.

"Please sign the guest registry, if you would." He rang for a bellhop to escort him to the fourth floor. The bellhop opened the door, and Ted was immediately overtaken by the elegance of the room, he had never seen such a beautiful hotel room before. The bellhop opened the curtains to the balcony for Ted to see the beautiful city, the view was breathtaking, and he could see the city for miles around. He tipped the bell hop and asked him for directions to the dining room. He graciously told him and advised him to make reservations. The dinner hour was always very busy.

Ted took his advice and called before he took his shower. He dressed up in his new suit and shirt he bought in Los Angeles before they left on their trip. Now he could wear it and he felt rather handsome in it as he admired himself in the mirror before going down to the lobby.

When he arrived at the restaurant he heard someone call out.

"Is that you, Ted? My goodness, I hardly recognized you. My, my, you're looking very elegant and handsome tonight."

He turned to look, and there stood Florence Craig.

At first he felt very strange about it but he managed to say, "Well, hello, fancy meeting you here."

"I am so glad to find someone I know. Would you mind having dinner with me?" she said.

"Why would you want to have dinner with me?" he hesitantly asked her.

"I don't know anyone else here, and besides I won't bite you. I just don't like to eat alone, and we know one another, so why not."

"In that case, I will. I'm not on duty now, and you're not a guest on our ship, so I guess it would be okay."

"I'm buying dinner, you're my guest now. So take my arm and escort me into the dining room, you handsome man," she said.

"I was so nervous being here all alone in a big foreign city. I feel better now that you're here," she giggled. The maître 'd showed them to their table; it was a window table with a beautiful view of the sparkling bright lights of the city.

"I don't know what I would have done if I hadn't spotted you. I got here last night and I was too scared to leave my room so I had dinner in, and then I slept the night away. I must have been very tired. It was good not to have the feeling of a rolling bed like the one on the ship." She laughed.

She chattered on and on during the whole evening. They ordered fish, highly recommended by the waiter. It was good but Ted felt a little squeamish, he had a hard time looking at it because it was served with the head still on and he felt like the fish kept looking up at him.

They went to the lounge after dinner and he insisted that he pay for the drinks. They sat and listened to the orchestra play for a while, and afterward chatted the rest of the evening.

"That was a very nice dinner, thank you so much. But I think I'll turn in for the night."

"It's still early, Ted, will you please escort me to my room first?" she said thinking he was trying to dismiss her. She was several years his senior, in her thirties, and she knew he didn't appear to have any romantic interest in her.

"I really have something important I'd like to talk about. It's a business proposition."

"I don't know," he said with a bit of hesitation in his voice. "Let me escort you up to your room. I want to be sure you get back safely."

"I'm on the third floor. This is a very fancy hotel, isn't it! I understand it's the premier hotel in Tokyo," she said as they entered the elevator.

He unlocked the door to her room and followed her in.

"Please have a seat," Ted sat down in a chair across from her.

She smiled.

"If you don't mind me asking, just how old are you, Ted?"

"I'm nineteen, will be twenty soon."

"I would have guessed you to be twenty-two or twenty-three, at least. You seem rather shy. Have you been around many women before?"

"No, just my mom and my sisters and my only sweetheart who was killed in the earthquake in San Francisco, but I have a girlfriend back home in Oklahoma now."

"I didn't think you were interested in me as a woman, that hurt my feelings at first. Then I realized you were so very young. What I wanted to talk to you about is I'd like to hire you to be my escort and bodyguard while we're here in Japan. I'm really afraid to go out into the city alone. I have to see the man about buying my painting. My husband had told me about him buying the picture and that he is a prominent member of a very powerful secret society called the Yakuza. This was the whole purpose of our trip to Japan, and I'm scared to go alone. I have his name and phone number, and if you're willing to help me, I'll pay you a hundred dollars a day."

Ted gulped.

"How could your husband have known about this man's history, that he was a member of a gangster sounding society?" he asked.

"I'm not sure, but he was a powerful man in the art business and knew all the societies around the world that dealt in art, both legally and illegally. He felt that this man probably was interested in buying it, if it was truly an authentic painting, which it definitely is according to my husband," she reassured Ted.

"What do I need to do to earn that kind of money," Ted said, a bit distrustful of the whole thing.

"I just want someone with me while I'm here in Japan. I've never been outside the United States before. I now have a great deal of money and will be making an art deal with this gangster person, and that really scares me. When I finish my business here I'm going back home. Nothing more is required of you, unless you decide you want to explore this man-women thing," she giggled.

"You remind me of my aunt back in Oklahoma. She is your age and besides I have a girl back home who said she would wait for me." Ted smiled at her. He knew he was lying about the girl back home, but that was the story he was going to stick to. He didn't want to encourage a relationship with an older woman.

Ted thought for a few minutes and then said, "For a hundred dollars a day you have a deal. That kind of money doesn't come around very often."

"I can easily afford it. I want to go to the bank tomorrow and check on my million dollars. Then I'll call the Japanese art dealer. I want you to go along with me, you are so wise for such a young age, and I want your protection and advice."

"I have nothing else planned for the next few days," Ted told her.

"My husband was also a bit scared of this man because he didn't know whether he could trust him. He was known for his questionable history. He had several art dealers and experts check the painting over and over and every one of them felt it was authentic".

"We're dealing with a lot of money and it scares me to know my husband had some shaky connections with this Japanese art dealer. I hope he was dealing art legally, but you know the old saying, 'birds of the same feather flock together'."

"I'll do the best job I can, call me in the morning when you're ready to go," he told her.

He got up from his chair to leave. "Good night, I'll do what I can to help and protect you."

"Thank you, Mister Ted. I feel better now, you have a good night's rest," and she escorted him to the door. She turned and threw her arms around him and gave him a big embrace and a long kiss.

"You sleep well, big boy, if you can," she giggled as he walked toward the elevator.

The next morning after breakfast, Ted met Florence in the lobby and she greeted him with a smile. They walked through the lobby to the street and stepped into two waiting rickshaws. The hotel concierge instructed the two runners to take them to the Tokyo Imperial National Bank.

It was a fascinating ride through the city streets, hundreds of people dressed in their traditional style, the women in kimonos with colorful sashes, and the men with short cotton jackets and pantaloons, and wearing strange looking hats, but there were a few wearing western style business suits.

In about fifteen or twenty minutes they arrived at the bank. The rickshaw runner stopped and let the long handles down for them to step out onto the street.

The rickshaw men bowed as Ted pushed the money into their hands. He paid them the amount the concierge advised him was the fare. Ted wasn't sure the men understood him, they spoke no English, but he asked them to wait for them. They bowed and nodded indicating they would wait.

When they entered the bank Florence asked to see the manager. A well-dressed man in a business suit approached and greeted them with the traditional bow. She showed him her bank receipts and papers of deposit and he nodded his head to follow him. He escorted them down to the vault, several feet down the stairs beneath the street level.

He opened the door, actually it was iron bars, and Florence went in. She approached the man at the desk and presented the documents and a key to him. He took her back to a large area that contained safety deposit boxes, and he took a large box out of the vault and escorted her to a private viewing room where he unlocked the box. He stepped out of the room leaving her to do whatever she wished with the box and the money it contained.

She spent several minutes looking and handling it before she began to count the money. She shook her head in excitement and after a few minutes called the banker to sign as witness of a withdrawal of a few thousand dollars. They relocked the box and put it back into the bank vault.

She cashed some of the money into Japanese yen and left the rest in American money. The banker placed it in a nice carrying case for her and when she came out to where Ted was waiting for her, she suddenly realized why she was so scared and wanted someone to be with her— she would be carrying several thousand dollars with her. Ted smiled as he watched her and saw a greedy look on her face, but also a look of uncertainty.

They walked out of the bank and the same rickshaw men were still there waiting; they had indeed understood what Ted had wanted. They climbed aboard and were on their way back to the hotel, and when they arrived Ted paid the men some extra yen because he felt like they had earned it.

They took the elevator to the third floor and Ted unlocked her room. She ran in and threw all the money onto her bed and acted like a kid with a new toy. She lay on the bed and threw the money into the air and then pulled a handful of cash into her chest. It was comical to watch, lying on her back and throwing money into the air, she was in her glory.

"Let me pay you in advance for five days," she picked up five hundred dollars from the bed and handed it to him.

"Thank you, Florence," he said.

"Please, call me Flo. I will have the concierge call the prospective buyer tomorrow and we'll go see him," she said, still giddy from her good fortune.

"If that's all for today, Flo. I'll go back to my room. Call me if you need me," he said. He was anxious to get away, she was acting rather crazy, and he felt she had a strange vexing, sensual look on her face, like she could buy his love. He thought to himself, *She needs to be alone to regain her composure. She is in a rapturous state with all that money.*

But he wondered to himself how he would act if he came into that much money, perhaps the same way. What he knew for sure was he was glad to be away from her for a while, but he was also excited. He had never had five hundred dollars at one time in his life, and he wondered what the next few days would bring.

Chapter 51

THE YAKUZA

"The concierge contacted the man who wants to buy the painting and told him we were here in Tokyo, and to contact me at the hotel if he was still interested. Guess what, I received a note a few minutes ago that he would be in his office, and to bring the painting. He was excited to see it," Florence told Ted.

"His name is Mr. Tsukasa."

They arrived at the office later that day and were met by a group of armed men standing at the door with samurai swords in their waistbands, all looking very serious and stoic. Flo and Ted removed their shoes before entering the office and Mr. Tsukasa greeted them with a very cordial bow.

His jet black hair was tied in a knot on the back of his head. He was wearing a blackrobe-like garment with pantaloons, with his long stockings meeting the pantaloons at his knees. He was wearing the typical sandals on his feet that were common for Japanese men.

The office was quite ornate with black lacquered furniture trimmed with colorful designs and beautiful decorative oriental vases placed around the room. A magnificent painting of Mount Fujiyama in winter hung on the wall, and there were strange-looking small trees with crooked limbs displayed from the table tops. There were also large pillows and a small low table with a tea set in the far corner of the room.

Mr. Tsukasa could not speak English but he instructed his translator to offer them a seat, which he did, the pillows on the floor at the tea table. They graciously took a seat and Florence handed the painting to Mr. Tsukasa to look at. He unwrapped the art work and took a few moments to look at it, both up close then backed up a few feet to view it at a distance.

After looking at it from every angle, he asked a question through his translator.

"I thought I was making this art deal through Mr. Arthur Craig, is he not here?"

Florence bowed her head in sorrow as she told of how he was lost at sea during a storm while they were making the crossing to Japan, and that she was his wife and would now be handling the sale.

He seemed shocked by the news and muttered his condolences to her. He told her he liked the painting very much but it would take several days to authenticate it. He asked if she was willing to leave it with him for authentication, he wished to have an expert art dealer exam it.

"I'm sorry, but I can't let the painting out of my control until it is sold. I suggest that payment in full be credited to my bank in the amount of eight hundred thousand dollars to be held for fifteen days until you are satisfied. Then at the same time, I will release the painting to you, that way the bank will control the sale until the deal is complete."

Ted was rather shocked that Florence was that astute and business savvy. Mr. Tsukasa agreed with the arrangements and told her it sounded fair and equitable.

"I will authorize the payment to the bank pending the agreement if it is acceptable and authenticated by my art expert."

They thanked each other and bowed. They were served tea and when they finished Mr. Tsukasa asked if they would like to see his garden before they left.

They agreed and walked with him through the beautiful, meticulously groomed garden, and it felt like they were in paradise. It was such a relaxing place they both were amazed by its beauty; they had never seen anything like it before.

They both expressed their appreciation of the tour to Mr. Tsukasa and how impressed they were by its beauty and thanked him profusely. He seemed to be extremely pleased to share it with them, and when they completed the tour they all bowed as they prepared to take their leave and to say their farewells.

The next day Flo and Ted went to the bank to finalize the agreement. She took the painting to the vault to be held and to confirm the deposit of the eight hundred thousand dollar check in her behalf, to be effective in fifteen days. Mr. Tsukasa would then have full access to the painting.

"Do you know who you are dealing with?"

The bank manager asked Florence.

"I met him only once to make our sale," she replied.

"You are dealing with one of the most powerful men in Japan, if not the most powerful man. He is head of the Yakuza, an army of very powerful and violent people who everyone in Japan fears. You are to be commended for your fortitude in appeasing him in this manner."

The bank manager continued, "This man is very dangerous. Most people are scared to death to even see him, this bank included. I tell you in the strictest confidence, be very careful in the future with this man."

"I'm sure he is everything you say, but on the day I saw him he was very kind and served us tea in his office, and afterward gave us a personal tour of his magnificent gardens. Even the powerful appreciate art and beauty, I guess," she said.

The bank manager smiled and they completed their business. As Florence and Ted walked through the bank to leave, many people watched them leave with staring questioning eyes, as if to say, "Who is this woman who makes deals with such a man?" She shivered as they walked out the door.

"I think they found someone else they fear as much as they do Mr. Tsukasa, and that someone is me."

"I don't know this man who is buying your painting, but it's my guess there's more behind this art piece than you know about," Ted told her.

"Maybe so, but I'm glad it will soon be out of my hands and I made a very good profit from it," she whispered.

For the next fifteen days they toured the entire city of Tokyo, the museums that told the history the Shogun, the powerful landowners who controlled the country until 1837. They visited the pagoda towers, the religious shrines of Shinto and Buddhism, the traditional regions of Japan, and the fantastic palaces of the Emperors and other rich and prominent men of Japan.

They went to a bathhouse where entire families and the community bathed together, the men, women, and children. To Ted's surprise they all bathed in the nude, but it all appeared rather formal and respectful. The attendants who were nude Japanese women poured warm water over each person and massaged their backs.

Ted was very embarrassed at first, but realized it was regular routine for the Japanese people. They decided to join the bathing, but Ted went to the opposite end of the pool at first and then later joined Flo. They bathed together, both feeling rather strange, but soon relaxed and enjoyed the warm water that was therapeutic to their sore feet and legs from their walking tours of the city. The Japanese girls massaged their backs, and there were never any sexual suggestions, except the Japanese girls seemed to giggle a lot. The feeling of great relaxation seemed to be paramount to everyone and it was treated very formal. Ted thought back to his Oklahoma days as a youth, here they call it group bathing, but back home they call it skinny dipping at the creek.

At the end of the fifteen days of touring and experiencing the traditions and culture of Japan, Ted was ready to go back to the ship. When they returned, Florence had a message from the bank, the check for eight hundred thousand dollars has been cleared and the painting was picked up by the new owner, Mr. Tsukasa.

Florence breathed a sigh of relief, happy the deal was done and she didn't have to meet with that questionable man anymore.

"Ted, Ted," she said. "It's all done, and I'm even richer than I was before, now I can return home."

She made arrangements for her return trip, leaving the next day. She paid her hotel bill and at the same time paid Ted's expenses at the hotel. She invited Ted for dinner that evening in the hotel dining room, her last evening in Japan, and she was ready to celebrate her success in Tokyo.

Ted was enjoying the evening, the good food and conversation, but felt very circumspect at the same time. He was so grateful for her generosity, she paid him the amount promised, plus and extra five hundred dollars bonus.

"I don't know what I would have done if you hadn't helped me. You were such a great support to me. Thank you, Ted."

"I can't thank you enough, Flo, you are very generous and I don't feel like I did very much to earn it," Ted responded.

She smiled at him as they continued eating. Ted changed the tone of the evening by saying.

"Can I ask you a serious question, Flo?"

"Of course you can, Ted."

"When I was questioning you on board the ship about your husband, I noticed you were quite nervous and you seemed very guarded when you answered my questions."

She reached out and took his hand, and smiled in a rather sad-looking way.

"Ted, my dear, that day of the storm, he was so drunk, and we had been arguing as usual. I was feeling very seasick, I just wanted to be left alone to die in my misery. He kept bugging me and I shouted at him to stop. He opened the cabin door and went out onto the deck and I called him to come back into the cabin out of the storm."

She sighed and continued.

"He was very drunk and had lost contact with reality. He climbed upon the rail and told me he was going to jump overboard. By that time I was at my wits' end and I told him to go ahead and jump! I don't think he actually jumped, a strong wind and a large wave hit the ship and swept across the deck at that very moment and I never saw him again. He was swept overboard.

"I was so sick and so troubled I went back into the cabin and stayed in bed for two days, filled with remorse and guilt. He was an alcoholic. I didn't realize that when we were married, I was so naive and yet flattered, having a very rich art dealer interested in me. He thought he could push me around and I would take his guff because he was rich, but I couldn't live like that. We argued all the time from the time we said I do." Flo continued with tears in her eyes.

"I was too scared to tell you my story when you questioned me. I thought you and the Captain would think I pushed him overboard. I didn't, but I felt very responsible at the same time. I just wanted him to come back into the cabin out of the storm."

"Thank you for your candor, Flo. I never believed you had anything to do with his death, but I felt you weren't telling the full story either," Ted told her.

"I don't think anyone, including the captain, felt you were responsible, that's what we put in the report, that he was swept overboard during the storm.

The next morning Ted accompanied her on a giant shopping spree buying many beautiful items to take home, the beautiful hand-painted oriental vases were her favorite. She bought Ted an expensive tailored suit, much to his objection, but as she said, "I owe it to you, sweet Ted."

He escorted her to the ship and helped her with her ten suitcases and large trunk filled with her prize purchases from their shopping spree. They shook hands and she kissed him on the cheek.

"I'll be forever grateful to you, Ted. When I get home, I plan to just disappear for a while." She shook her head and continued.

"I don't really know whether that painting was authentic or what the true story was behind it, but I must confess I always had a few doubts about it. I'm just going to make sure I'm not easily found."

She waved good-bye at the top of the gangway and Ted felt relieved. He shook his head in doubt as he walked away thinking, *If I were her I would also disappear.* In his heart he felt like she knew exactly what she was doing all along, it all felt like a con job to him. The question would always remain with him, if it were a true famous Rembrandt, that would easily be known by the experts, and why did the wealthy Japanese man Mr. Tsukasa want the painting so desperately. He wished he knew the true story behind it all, but he felt certain someone along the line really got scammed.

He returned to *The Wonderer* the next day, actually glad to be back aboard the ship, back into his own world. The captain informed them the ship would be in port for one more week and then they would be on their way to China. They were to pick up a load of hemp to take to China, and from China they would take a load of tea back to the States, but they would be in China for about two months.

He decided to stay aboard the ship until it pulled out of the Tokyo harbor. He had seen many wonderful things, the culture, the traditions of the people, and the different sights and sounds of the city. He was grateful for the opportunity, but he was a bit uneasy about the Rembrandt sale with Flo. He hoped the Yakuza didn't associate him as a part of the sale and a possible scandal. He was just going to lie low and relax until the ship left the port.

Chapter 52

PORT OF NANJING, CHINA

The Wonderer was finally unloaded of its scrap metal and reloaded for its next journey to the Port of Nanjing, China. The Japanese broker came aboard with new orders for the captain, and the crew readied the ship with new supplies, bunkers of coal for the engine room, and the entire crew was back onboard and all accounted for. This journey would take them across the Yellow Sea, up the Yangtze River to the Port of Nanjing.

New passengers came aboard, a group of missionaries all dressed in black, two men and three women, the women wore white starched bonnets on their heads. They were going several hundred miles up the Yangtze River to a hospital and school for their church mission, the men were listed as citizens of France and the women were all Americans.

Ted observed the passengers as they came up the gangway, the porters assisted those who struggled with their luggage, and the captain greeted each of them as they boarded. Finally, they were all aboard, twelve in all, and the stewards escorted them to their cabins which were freshly cleaned and ready for the new guests.

While they were in the Tokyo port, the ship was cleaned from top to bottom. it looked spic and span and even had a new paint job. The crew felt like they were aboard a new ship, and the captain was very pleased with the ships repair, cleaning, and refurbishing, knowing it was very presentable and clean for their new guests.

The ship pulled away from the dock when they received the word from the port authority; and as they left the harbor, they passed by several Japanese war ships, three cruisers, five destroyers, and two very large battle wagons with their large guns sticking out of the turrets.

Captain Perkins chatted with the crew as they departed, especially concerning the warships in the harbor. He kept abreast with the current times, particularly world events, and informed them that Japan and Russia were at war with one another, which could cause many problems for Korea and China. Japan had recently sunk a Russian fleet in Vladivostok in an overwhelming battle. Russia had just built the Trans-Siberian Railway through Russia to the Port of Vladivostok. Japan opposed this railway because it violated their sphere of influence with Korea and China, and gave access for the Russians to move in.

He went on to say that it was possible that Czar Nicklaus II of Russia would drag Japan into the war to obtain a warmer water port. The Russians had a much bigger navy and army than Japan and really didn't fear their wrath, which they quickly came to regret. Japan had had enough so they attacked Russia at Port Arthur and sank their fleet in February 1905, and two of the Russians' proudest and biggest battleships were sunk. They fought back and forth for several months until the Russian fleet was finally destroyed on the Tsushima Straits. Japan had virtually destroyed the Russian navy, and the Czar had no other choice but to negotiate a peace agreement. The Russian defeat was a great shock around the world; they were known for their superior army and naval forces, but to the surprise of everyone they were defeated.

"That many warships at anchor in the harbor makes you wonder what Japan has in mind now. It sure looks like they are staying well prepared," Ted commented.

"I wondered why they were buying so much scrap metal from the United States. You think they are preparing for another war, maybe?"

The captain shrugged his shoulders.

"You never know," he said.

Ted returned to the shack to relieve Larry for the morning duty, and the ship headed out of the harbor for the open sea. The beginning of the journey started out well for the first three days but then the skies began to turn dark and ugly. It was monsoon season and the winds began to whip up and the water began to get rough; the high waves banged against the sides of the ship.

The Wonderer did not have the ballast it had when they arrived in Japan since the cargo was much lighter on this lap of the journey. It caused the ship to ride higher out of the water and made it easier for the rough seas to toss the ship around, sometimes like a cork as the captain described it.

The monsoon weather made it rough for the crew, even the experienced sailors got sick at times. Most of the passengers were suffering from seasickness, and the crossing of the Yellow Sea became very difficult for everyone. But they received some relief on the fourth day, however, as they neared the Yangtze River basin and entered the mouth of the river.

The harbor pilot boarded The Wonderer and guided them slowly up the river for the next three days. As they neared the port Ted could see it was a large city, but it looked very old.

"I was here many years ago," the captain told Ted. "It's an old city and was once the capitol of China. It has a large old fortress on the hillside that I recommend you go see. You will never see anything like it again. Their commerce is strong here in China, mostly tea, and that's why we're here. Tea is a very profitable commodity and will be our cargo on our return trip home."

When they entered the harbor Ted noticed an old paddle wheeler tied up at the dock, it was quite colorful and looked freshly painted. It reminded him of the books and magazines he had read, especially the book *Tom Sawyer*, which was centered on the old Mississippi River boat days. He let his imagination run wild; he could visualize the passengers roaming the deck listening to the music as the black face singers and dancers performed. He laughed at himself allowing his imagination to get carried away, but it was good memories of a story he thoroughly enjoyed.

The Wonderer came to a stop and was berthed close to the old paddle wheeler. It was still raining that day, and Ted didn't think it would ever stop, after all it was monsoon season. All the passengers were cleared by the Chinese authorities and left the ship.

The company broker came aboard to see the captain. The ship would not be unloaded for several weeks and the cargo of tea would take a few more weeks. *It looked like we would be here for quite a while*, Ted thought. The weather had prevented the new shipments of tea from coming in to the warehouses, so they were low on stock. They would have to wait to load the ship until the next shipments arrived from the provinces.

The Chinese authorities restricted visitors from venturing into the providences without a permit, so the crew was more or less confined to the ship and limited areas of the city. Ted toured the city the next day, it was very crowded and the open street markets were busy, it seemed like a million people were milling around though the streets and the markets. *It was much different than Tokyo*, Ted thought, *but extremely interesting.*

The people were dressed in heavy-looking cotton jackets of different colors, but mostly black or brown, with loose-fitting pants and sandals on their feet. Most of the people, both men and women, wore big brimmed straw hats on their heads shaped like an upside down bowl, which was held on by a chin strap.

The markets were full of different varieties of fish and vegetables and strange-looking foods that looked like roots, and Ted saw many other things that he couldn't even guess what they were. The fish were even different, long snake-looking fish called eels, and shark fins that were famous for making soups; the Chinese considered them a luxury.

Ted enjoyed seeing all the different sights, but the only thing that bothered him was the smell of the city. The air was saturated with the strong smell of fish, and it just wouldn't go away.

Chapter 53

THE LADY SHARON

Ted returned to the ship in the afternoon after touring the streets and open markets of the city. Captain Perkins was talking with a distinguished looking gentleman wearing an officer's uniform and a captain's cap.

"Ted," he called out.

"I want you to meet someone. This is Captain Samuel Snyder, the captain of the paddle wheeler you had your eye on. He's a true Scotsman, right out of Scotland."

"Glad to meet you, laddie," he said to Ted in a heavy brogue as they shook hands.

Ted had to listen carefully to understand him, but nodded and answered, "Glad to meet you, Captain."

A lovely lady standing nearby walked closer to them.

"This is my bonnie lass, Sharon Snyder, who really is my first-mate. She knows more about our ship than I do." He laughed as he introduced her.

Ted smiled and tipped his hat. "A pleasure ma'am."

"I see my husband has been accentuating that Scottish accent on you," she laughed.

"I'm not Scottish, I'm pure English, born here in China. My parents were English and served as missionaries for years here in China. This is where I grew up."

Ted thought Sharon was a very attractive lady, all dressed in traditional Chinese clothing; even her hair was braided in a pig tail, dangling down beneath her straw hat.

In their conversation Ted learned that Captain Snyder brought his wife back to this sometimes violent part of the world for a business opportunity. Before leaving England they bought and refurbished an old paddle wheeler and had it shipped to China in sections. With her ability to speak fluent Chinese, the Mandarin dialect, their intent was to use the paddle wheeler as a work vessel to carry passengers and cargo up and down the river.

"We're here to make our fortune." She laughed.

"We had a small working barge on the Thames River in England, and that made a nice living for us. We had the chance to buy this old steamboat at a reasonable price. So here we are, hopefully to fulfill our dreams."

Ted was fascinated hearing their story.

"The fact that Sam is Scottish, and he dislikes the English as most Scots do, except for me, of course, he was willing to leave England to do something new." She continued, "I was born and raised here in this very city, that's how I learned the language. My parents died when I was fourteen, that's when I was shipped back to England. I was away from China for ten years, but this seems like home to me. I do have dual citizenship so I guess it is home. I met Sam when I was eighteen and we decided to marry."

"With her being a citizen of China we were able to get a government contract to carry the mail and haul passengers and merchandise on the river. It's really quite a feat for us to be able to get something a noncitizen can't get," Sam told Ted.

"We are ready to make our first trip on the river, but we still need a couple of crewmen. I have three Chinese coolies working for me as stokers, and a longtime friend of Sharon's family is our cook, so we are almost ready to leave. I understand according to our ships broker that we might have some passengers going up the river with us."

"Did you enjoy your visit into the city, Ted?" Sharon asked.

"At first, I was overwhelmed by the number of people and the poverty I saw," he answered.

"It is a glorious mess of humankind, the likes you have never seen before, if it's your first time to visit here," she agreed.

Captain Perkins approached Ted.

"Captain Snyder has been talking with me, wondering if anyone of our crew would like to join him for the next few days as he makes his maiden voyage up the Yangtze River in *The Lady Sharon*, which is appropriately named, of course."

"It really will be a trial run to work out all the kinks, and I need experienced men with me to help evaluate everything. I want our trips up the river to be the best, my lad, so we can offer a successful experience for our customers," Captain Snyder added.

Ted volunteered to go along. It sounded good to him and he could make some extra money. When the word got around to the rest of the crew, another one volunteered, Ray Hastings, a boiler man, who was more than willing to join them, just as Ted was. It was a good opportunity for them to see more of China, and the greatest benefit, it wouldn't cost them a cent.

Captain Snyder was elated that two experienced crewmen would be with him. "I haven't been able to train any Chinese lads yet for the job, but they are good workers. They don't understand all the 'blooming mechanics' of how a steamboat works, so they will have to be taught from the bottom up. I have a couple of trained people from England on their way to join us, but they aren't due to arrive for several weeks."

Captain Perkins released Ted and Ray from their duty temporarily to work on the steamboat, but they must return within six weeks, that's when the broker said *The Wonderer* would be loaded up and ready to return to the United States. Ted and Ray packed their belongings to leave, and they had some of their money changed into the Chinese yuan. They took their gear to the steamboat and Captain Snyder gave them a tour to orientate them to the boat. It was actually bigger than it looked, but of a rather simple design, not nearly as complicated as the large freighters were. The crew all slept on the main deck, and it had three staterooms for the passengers. The Captain's quarters was located next to the wheel house on the top deck.

The Snyders were proud of their steamboat. When they purchased it, they had it shipped to the river in sections, and reassembled under the close supervision of Captain Snyder and Sharon. Ted and Ray were shown to their cabin and they settled in to wait for further information.

When the word came, they would depart the next day. The captain explained to them the big test on this first trip was to evaluate if burning wood would be the satisfactory fuel for the boat. It is difficult to find fuel in this godforsaken country, and wood would be the most plentiful.

"If the wood is satisfactory, I will have a contract here in Nanjing to have all the wood supplied, and that's the biggest thing I want to find out. If it isn't, I may have to convert to an oil burner, but we will see what works best. My lads, are you ready to go?"

"Yes, sir, Captain," they both said in harmony.

Ray went to the engine room to oversee the loading of wood in the furnace, and within an hour they had enough steam in the boilers to leave the port. The passengers began to board and the cargo was all loaded. The time for their maiden voyage had come; it was really going to happen.

Captain Snyder and his first mate, Sharon, greeted all the passengers as they boarded and Ted directed them to their cabins.

Ted was surprised to see familiar faces: the missionary ladies from *The Wonderer* came aboard. They had received special permission from the Chinese government to proceed east to the village of Wang- jing, where they would began their work. He greeted them like old friends and escorted them to their quarters.

The ship's whistle blew three times, the signal they were ready to leave the port, and the wharf ropes were loosened. The paddle wheel was engaged and the boat began to move; smoke began to pour from the two tall smoke stacks and drifted out into the air, they were on their way. Captain Snyder proudly manned the wheel as they left the dock while First Mate Sharon was given the task of engaging the levers as instructed by the captain.

"Pull the middle lever out," the captain called out, "and let the paddle wheel fully engage."

The boat slowly moved forward to proceed up the river, and after the boat was fully positioned the captain told Ted, "Here, take the wheel for me, just keep it in the middle of the river."

"Consider yourself the official wheelman. I've got to go check on the kitchen and help the cook fix dinner. Besides, this is a good job for you," First Mate Sharon said with a smile.

Ted laughed and saluted.

"Very well, madam Captain Snyder, I will gladly take over."

She laughed.

"We only have one captain, but actually we do have two bosses." She laughed out loud as she walked away.

The ship handled well, Ted thought. He kept it in the middle of the river, travelling at the rate of six knots per hour. They were loaded with passengers and had a full load of cotton to deliver to some big merchants up the river. They were all praying and hoping for a safe and successful "maiden run." It was so important for Captain Snyder to show the Chinese government and the people he had a growing and needed service to offer their country.

The captain entered the wheel house, satisfied that they were off to a good start. He checked all the levers and controls and asked Ted how he was doing. "It's going well, sir. I was wondering, Captain, how long is this river?"

"I have heard it is about four thousand miles long, I'm not really sure. The river is called the Chang Jing by the older Chinese people, but my bonnie lass tells me, the rest of the world calls it the Yangtze. It's a language thing, I guess," he informed Ted.

"Stay in the middle of the river, that's our course, and watch out for small boat traffic. Call me if you need me, just give me two toots on the whistle. I won't be far away." He nodded and left Ted at the wheel to proceed up the river.

Chapter 54

THE YANGTZE RIVER

From the wheel house, Ted saw many interesting sights on the river as they proceeded east. The river was very wide and appeared brownish in color and was full of activity, especially in the harbors. He saw the fishermen in long canoe-looking boats, and perched on the boat rim were big black pelican-like birds, a type he had never seen before. He watched in awe the method they used to catch the fish, not the old fishing pole way he fished at home as a kid, but a unique way of fishing using the birds instead of a fishing pole. He would tie a line tightly around the bird's neck so it couldn't swallow, and attach another line to its feet. He released the bird into the water to dive for the fish, and when it resurfaced he would pull the bird back to boat with the line on its feet, and extract the fish from its mouth. The birds were actually doing the fishing but denied their catch, but Ted was sure they were rewarded for their efforts at the end of the day.

As they traveled farther up the river he was astonished by how crowded it was with so many different kinds of boats. Some looked very strange to him; he remembered pictures of boats he had seen in the World Books at his school when he studied about China back in Oklahoma, and the boats were called junks. He remembered reading about families, generation after generation, living their entire lives on the boats, traveling up and down the river.

The junks were of all sizes, some large and some small, and there were hundreds of them. They are considered the "work horse" of shipping and transportation, and they carry commerce up and down the river. Ted wondered how the people felt about seeing this large steamboat on the river which would be competing for the commercial trade.

Along the river bank Ted saw two men sitting on a board high above a waterwheel- like structure, moving the wheel as they peddled with their legs.

The waterwheel pumped water from the river into a ditch in the field to irrigate the crops, and the Chinese coolies worked the fields to make sure the entire crop was receiving the water. *This is ingenious*, Ted thought, never having seen such things before, the coolie would put a stop-board on one row so the water would channel down another. It was hard work, working in the mud fields, with mud up to their knees, planting, watering, and tilling the rice crops, but it was their livelihood and the entire family worked in the fields, men, women and children. It was quite a sight to see, the workers were bent over, doing back-breaking work, all wearing their typical straw hats to protect their heads from the sun.

Up the river they passed a small village that had mud-constructed huts with straw roofs, and the children were standing along the river bank waving at the big steamboat as it passed by. Ted smiled and waved as the steamboat plowed through the water, and he sounded the horn to recognize them. They jumped up and down with excitement, never hearing anything like that before. They kept waving until the boat disappeared from their sight.

In the village Ted could see mothers working with their infants strapped to their backs, and often he could see the little baby's bare bottoms sticking out in the open. He realized just how different the cultures really were, especially when he saw the water buffalo being used to plow the rice fields, with two of them yoked together plowing the field with a strange looking wooden plow, *It's a whole different world here in China*, Ted thought to himself.

Farther up the river as they passed a larger village he saw what looked like a giant floating building anchored at the river bank. He couldn't believe his eyes, the building was painted bright red and had two full length balconies with scantily dressed women hanging over the sides, waving and hollering to all the boats as they passed by.

"Hey, you want to have some fun with me," the ladies shouted, at least that's what the Chinese cook said they were saying.

"What in the world was that, Captain Snyder?" Ted asked with caution in his voice.

"Oh that," he laughed at Ted.

"Let me educate you on such things. That is called a 'flower boat,' it's a floating brothel, they service the men up and down the river."

Ted laughed.

"Oh, thanks for that information, sir, I can stop the boat if you wish, sir, just give the word."

The captain smiled and chuckled.

"The Lady Sharon doesn't stop for such things," and within just a few minutes they were out of sight of the flower boat, to the relief of Captain Snyder. The captain instructed Ted to pull up at the next open beach for the night.

"The river is just too busy and too dangerous to travel at night, we'll tie up and have dinner together and get a good night's rest."

Ted docked the ship into the bank, and they tied up ready to wash up and relax for the evening meal. Ted wondered what First-Mate Sharon and the cook had prepared for supper, he was really hungry.

Sharon had selected fish and fresh garden vegetables from a small boat vendor, and the cook, Chang, had brought plenty of rice. Chang was the chief cook, but Sharon supervised it all, she had to make sure it was just right for the crew and passengers. They all gathered in the dining room when the dinner bell rang, everyone was hungry and ready for a relaxing meal. The fish was grilled over an open fire, the standard fare and generally the only meat served in China, and the vegetables were very tasty. To top it off, Sharon surprised everyone with plum pudding for dessert served with tea, a perfect finish to a wonderful meal.

While in the dining room, Ted engaged in a conversation with the three missionary ladies. They were going to the village of Woo-Sung, in the province of Chang Ta, to establish and open a hospital. Two of the ladies were nurses and the other was a doctor, this was the work they said they were 'called' to do by their missionary society. They were anxious to get started, they had to wait for several months until the government accepted them to come to China, but they were finally given their permit and they were anxious and ready to go to work.

They told Ted the Mandarin of the province also had to approve and accept them to come, and that he was apparently a progressive leader who had a strong desire to do good for his people. The ladies even heard he had outlawed the binding of little girl's feet, a tradition throughout China to keep their feet from growing normally. Small feet for women was considered a sign of beauty by the Chinese, but actually it contributed to lameness in many of them. When they finished their visit, Ted bid them 'good-evening' and best wishes in their work, and left to go to his cabin for a good night's rest.

The boat proceeded up the river the next day and Captain Snyder was on the look-out for a place along the bank to cut firewood. When he saw the most promising area they tied up and all the men grabbed their axes and saws and went to work. As they were stacking the wood to load onto the boat they were surprised by a group of men on very small horses who rode up on them with their guns drawn. The leader of the band shouted to Captain Snyder.

"You pay."

The captain, being a prudent Scotchman, and wanting to avoid problems said. "How much?"

The bandits looked at him very strangely, like they didn't understand what he had said, so Chang answered for him.

"How much do you want, you bloody bandit?" Then Chang turned to the captain and said,

"I didn't really call him a bloody bandit, I didn't want to make him mad."

The captain haggled with the bandit for several minutes, with Chang as his interpreter, and when he became weary of it, the captain handed the leader four yen. The bandit smiled and nodded, and they quickly turned their ponies around and rode away.

"Where in the world did they come from?" Ted said. They hadn't seen or heard anyone around, yet they were able to quietly sneak up on them.

"Sure didn't see that coming." They hurriedly loaded their wood onto the boat and were relieved when they took off up the river again.

After two weeks on the river they were almost to their final destination, Wang jing. Ted noticed an area which looked to him like a river branch that flowed into the Yangtze. At the river's mouth he saw a small village, and a short distance up from the village, he couldn't believe what he was seeing. He grabbed the captain's binoculars to have a closer look, and what he saw sitting among the junks in the harbor was a large yacht with the name printed across the bow, *The Von Getz*. It was the German ship that *The Wonderer* had received the SOS from when they were crossing the Pacific.

Ted immediately called for Captain Snyder to come to the bridge, and he came quickly, Ted's voice sounded a bit urgent, he thought.

"See that ship, the Von Getz, we answered an S. O. S. from that ship several weeks ago as we were crossing the Pacific, and we found all the crewmen dead when we arrived at the scene. The Von Getz was stolen by pirates, and lo and behold, it's here."

"Pirates and bandits are a big problem, Ted, they usually don't raid ships here on the river, but they raid the larger ships at sea and bring them here. This area is called the pirate and bandit village, the village of Wu-Han, the pirates are a dangerous bunch of cut throats."

Captain Snyder continued.

"There are pirates all over this part of world, from China, Burma, and the Philippines. When they capture a ship at sea, they ransom the crew back to their country of origin, it's a vicious dirty business, but it's been going on for centuries."

He went on to tell how they constantly prey on settlements, raiding villages and holding prominent politicians and business men for ransom, and they also sell village women into the sex trade. Sometimes he had even heard of situations when a captain didn't surrender everything to them when first accosted, they will kill everyone on board, but if they are cooperative they will often take the ship and its merchandise and leave the crew alive.

"Now days, since the Boxer Rebellion War, you'll sometimes see American, British, and even German gun boats patrolling the river. They are protecting the people against the warlords, they say," he continued. "but actually, it's all just a blatant display of power by the European and the American governments to poke the Chinese government in the eye, to force them to negotiate and comply with their trade treaties. The Chinese don't really want the gunboats on the river, but can't do anything about it, the Chinese can't protect their own citizens against the pirates, and the pirates are more powerful than the government."

"The Western and European business men are working to advance trade with China, and China has tried to block them for years. China has kept a tight control on their country for centuries, but now have lost control, at least on the river, the gunboats are opening up this hidden country to the rest of the world."

"That's all very interesting, Captain, obviously there's lots of turmoil going on within the country," Ted said.

"When we get back aboard The Wonderer, I'll notify the German government that the Von Getz is anchored in China at the mouth of the river, located at the village of Wu-Han."

The Lady Sharon proceeded up the river to their final destination without any further incidents. The captain congratulated the crew for a job well done, they were half way finished on their maiden journey and he breathed a sigh of relief and counted his lucky stars that they made it this far.

Chapter 55

THE VILLAGE OF WANG JING

As the boat proceeded up the river for the next couple of days, the farther they went the more remote it became, it seemed.

"China is a huge country," Ted remarked to Captain Snyder. "Actually, it seems more like a whole world within itself rather than a mere country."

"I know what you mean, it sure does," the captain agreed.

"It seems so brown and dusty looking and I hardly ever see any birds," Ted observed.

"You're right, lad. I never really noticed that before. I see a few ravens now and then. Probably what happens, the Chinese people eat a lot of birds and that's why you don't see very many. They have a whole different attitude about the food they eat than we do."

"The other thing I don't see much in this area is trees, the type of trees that we can get wood. I need wood to burn in this old wheeler and this worries me," he confided in Ted.

"We may have to convert from wood to oil, if indeed wood is going to be scarce. I was so hoping we could stick to wood, but we'll see how it all turns out on the rest of the trip."

Several hundred miles up the river from their starting point of Nan Jing, they could see the village of Wang Jing on the side of the mountain. This is their stop and also the location the three missionary ladies will be staying to begin their work.

The Lady Sharon pulled up to the small wooden wharf and the crew laid the gangway onto the dock for the passengers to disembark. Ted helped the ladies with their luggage, and the crew unloaded the cargo and merchandise that had been ordered by the local merchants, along with a small bag of mail. The coolies who met the boat loaded up the cargo and the mail onto carts to take into the village just over the hill.

The three ladies said their good-byes. Ted bid them his very best wishes, and Sharon shed a few tears as they hugged each other. She had enjoyed visiting with them and hearing all about their hopes and plans for the people of Wang Jing.

The missionary ladies were met at the dock by an elderly gentleman who was dressed in a black cotton jacket which hung to his waist, black pantaloons trousers, and a black skull cap on his head. He was a dignified looking man with a long white beard, and he greeted the ladies with a deep bow, and led them up the path toward the village.

Ted watched as they walked away, and he wondered what they would find and how they would handle their new adventure. The one thing he did know was he had great admiration for them as they totally dedicated their lives for the benefit of others.

The captain asked Ted to go into the village with him to buy some fire wood, hoping it was available. They took along Chang to interpret; they knew they would be lost without him. When they reached the top of the hill and looked out onto the immense valley, they could see the smoke rising in the air from the chimneys of the quaint huts all nestled in the gentle slopes of the hill, which led down to the beautiful valley below. From their vantage point they could see the snow-capped mountain range off in the distance which towered over the hillside of this picturesque village.

In the fields of the valley below, they could see many people working—men, women, and children, all wearing large straw hats, tilling the fields, and working side by side with their hoes and rakes. They saw several water buffaloes pulling wooden plows in the flooded field, and the people were standing knee-deep in water, planting rice in the paddies. They were like ants; everyone was moving and working.

They followed the path down to the valley and it seemed like they walked several miles before they arrived. There were about fifteen hundred mud brick huts in the village, built mainly with the bricks with some wood used to frame the structures. On the main street were many people shopping and bargaining with the street merchants who were selling fish, assortments of vegetables, chickens, piglets, and many other non-food items. It was a very busy commercial area.

Chang inquired at one of the street vendors where they could buy some wood to fuel their steamboat. He was told they needed to apply for a permit from the chief of the village, who was the Mandarin, and he resides down the street in a compound called the Palace. It is the residence of the honorable one and also serves as the administrative offices.

When they arrived at the compound it was surrounded by a high wall, and the guard directed them to the wooden gate around the corner. Chang pulled the rope that rang the bell, and after a few moments they were greeted by a Chinese servant who inquired about the nature of their business.

"We need to talk with the person in charge who will grant us a permit to buy wood to fuel our steamboat. We understand it is the Mandarin who gives permission, is that correct?" Chang asked the servant.

"Oh, yes, he is very busy, you come back tomorrow." He closed the gate and quickly turned to go back into the compound.

They stood there at the gate scratching their heads.

"Well," the captain said,

"Guess we'll have to try again tomorrow. Let's go into the village to see if we can find a place to stay the night, it's a little too far to walk back."

Chang asked a merchant where they could find a place for the night.

"Oh, yes," He bowed and pointed down the street to an inn for travelers, they will feed you and entertain you with stories, he told them. They expressed their thanks and moved on down the street to look for the inn, and along the way they bought some fruit that tasted like a plum, they weren't sure what it was, but it was delicious.

When they arrived at the inn they walked inside and was approached by the same man that greeted the three ladies at the dock. He bowed.

"How may I help you gentleman?"

"We are looking for a room for the night," the captain told him.

"Yes sir, we have rooms. If you want a communal bed, it is two yen a person and includes a blanket and head block, and also a bowl of rice and hot tea for breakfast."

"Can we see the communal bed?" the captain asked.

The man turned and pointed to an area behind him, it was about forty feet long and seven foot wide at the back of the room where they standing. They could see the sleeping space was built of stone and was raised up off the floor about three feet, and underneath was a place to burn hot coals to heat the beds during cool and cold winter nights. Ted thought it looked like they would be sleeping over a large cook stove, heated by hot coals.

"When in Rome, do as the Romans do," the captain laughed.

"Or I should say, when in China do as the Chinese do." They paid the required amount and the man gave each one a pallet, a blanket, and a head pillow and reminded them that it got cool at night.

When it came time to go to bed they were surprised to see about thirty people climb upon the communal sleeping area, and among them were the three missionary ladies that were on their boat. They were all dressed in native Chinese clothing and with them were two Chinese ladies, each with two children.

Captain Snyder, Ted, and Chang followed the crowd, all thirty or thirty- five of them, to stake out their space. The people were all quiet as they laid out their mat to settle in their narrow space for the night. There was no talking or sound, but the captain whispered to Ted.

"I wonder how my bonnie lass would feel about this, spending the night with three missionary ladies."

Ted laughed and whispered back.

"Once you tell her who they are she will forgive you, I think."

They had a warm and restful sleep, and in the morning the tea and rice tasted good. Ted tried using his chop sticks to eat, but found he was a real novice and used them mainly to push the rice into his mouth. There were no bathing accommodations available for them, they had to sleep in their clothes, so they were anxious to get their wood permit and get back to the boat.

They walked down to the government house to make their request and again rang the bell at the gate. The servant arrived, bowed graciously, and said,

"How my I help you?"

"We wish to see the Mandarin to request a wood permit," the captain requested.

"He's busy with his six wives and children, he will not see anyone till afternoon," he answered.

"What time can we see him?"

The servant answered.

"After the trials, he holds court for the people in the afternoon, never know how long that will take."

They shopped and walked around the markets to kill some time. Captain Snyder bought a cotton padded jacket for Sharon, and they each decided to buy one for themselves, all choosing a black one.

That afternoon they went back to the gate once again, hoping to have better luck. When they arrived the gate was wide open and they walked into the courtyard and joined the crowd of people. They saw the Mandarin sitting in his black lacquered chair on an elevated platform.

Out of the building came two large Chinese men virtually dragging a man by both arms to what looked like an execution block. The man was forced to his knees and suddenly an executioner brought an ax down and severed the man's head from his body. Ted and the captain watched in disbelief as the man's head rolled into a basket at the base of the block, they were speechless and stunned at such an unexpected sight.

The same men dragged the body away and the crowd quietly dispersed, it was all so matter of fact, no one spoke for the man before or after the execution, and everyone left without a word spoken.

"If that was a trial, it sure was short and swift," Ted said as he held back the desire to gag, it was such a terrible thing to witness, yet the people didn't seem to blink an eye.

"That's what they call swift justice," the captain commented, "it's not pleasant to watch but necessary at times, at least it's their justice system."

The servant appeared to the Captain, bowed, and said, "The Mandarin will see you now, come with me." They followed him into the administration hall, and there the Mandarin stood before them and all the other petitioners. He was a small short man with a long stringy gray beard, dressed in his long black silk robe with a black skull cap on his head.

When their turn came to see him, the Mandarin bowed to greet them and said,

"How may I serve you?"

The captain bowed in return and made his request for the wood permit they needed for their boat.

"Wood is very scarce here, but I'm sure I can help you. I would imagine it will be expensive, however, Mr. Captain. It is a good thing to have your business and good to have your ship come to us, nice to have outside contact, such as your steamship. We will get your wood for you, see my man and he will help you. Please come back to see us soon."

The captain bowed and thanked the Mandarin and they turned away to wait for the servant. The Mandarin continued to see the people and each person bowed to their knees as they faced him, and each would ask.

"Are you well?" and he always answered.

"Yes, I am well."

"That must be the common respectful greeting, I guess," the captain observed.

As they waited, a Chinese army officer came into the courtyard to speak with the Mandarin, it appeared urgent. After they spoke the Mandarin stepped upon the raised platform to address the people, a loud bell sounded and many people came running to gather in the courtyard to hear the latest news.

"My people," he began, "bandits have raided Gang Sha, and have raped and pillaged the village. Our army is preparing to engage them in battle. Unfortunately our army is outnumbered. The bandits are expected to attack us here in Wang Jing. My people, I cannot tell you what to do, but you must prepare yourselves to save your families and properties before they get here. Our army does not have the manpower to stop them, so my advice is to leave, take your family and belongings to avoid capture and torture from these ruthless blood thirsty bandits who do not care about your lives."

"Prepare now, hide in the mountains, do whatever is necessary to save yourselves. Do not wait, you all are in danger. I don't know what more to do as your Mandarin, but we will try our best. Now go, prepare and may the one on High protect you."

The people scattered and ran to their homes, frightened and chattering to one another, the women were crying carrying their babies, and the men were angry and determined to protect their families.

Captain Snyder took Ted aside.

"When I studied the map before we left, I know the village of Gang Sha is about twenty miles up the river, I wonder if it would help the army to transport them by my steamboat to Gang Sha so they can pull a surprise attack on the bandits. The bandits will be exhausted and probably drunk after raiding and pillaging the village, and it will be a good time to attack them."

"Sounds like it might work, Captain," Ted said.

The captain instructed Chang to request an audience with the Mandarin to discuss the plan, he was hesitant, but the captain insisted. They went with Chang and stood by him as he approached the Mandarin.

Chang bowed and said to the Mandarin.

"Are you well?"

"Yes, I am well, why do you bother me now?"

"My master, Captain Snyder, has a plan to fight the bandits that he would like you to hear, Oh, great master, please here me out. I am only following my master's instructions."

The Mandarin looked over at Captain Snyder and Ted and motioned for them to approach him.

"Your servant said you have something important to say to help us with our serious problem with the bandits and warlord."

"My servant speaks the truth, we only want to be helpful. I was thinking that your officer with his men might be more effective in their battle if they were able to surprise attack them, rather than waiting for them to attack your village. If you meet them and command the high ground, your army will have the advantage, and a better chance for victory. I will transport your men up the river in my steamship to Gang Sha to prepare for the attack."

Chang smiled as he interpreted and in turn the Mandarin reached out and patted him on the shoulder, and smiled to him in return.

The Chinese officer listened intently and shook his head in agreement to the Mandarin.

"How many soldiers do you have?" the captain asked.

"Two hundred thirty men with arms here in Wang Jing," he answered.

"How many bandits do you estimate they might have?" the captain continued.

"I have heard as many as six hundred, possibly," he answered.

"How long would it take you to go up the river to Gang Sha?" The officer asked.

"Six hours," he answered.

The officer and the Mandarin talked together, they thought his idea sounded very good. They turned to the captain and told him they would be honored to do what he suggested.

"Very good, we are ready to help in any way we can. We'll need more wood for the steamboat, and then we can get your men aboard."

The Mandarin nodded and bowed in respect to the captain, and immediately called for a crew to provide the wood.

"Another thing, sir, I really don't want to tell you how to wage a war, but I have one more suggestion," Snyder said to the officer, feeling rather confident by now.

"Yes, what is that, Captain."

"You might have your buglers sound their horns continuously to make lots of noise so it will echo up the mountain. It will distract the bandits and make them think you have more soldiers than you really do. Have your men drag brush along the ground to stir up lots of dust, it will block their vision of your soldiers and give them the impression you have a very large military force and that you are attacking them from below."

"It will be done, Captain," the officer said.

Within an hour the Lady Sharon was fully loaded with wood, the Mandarin had instructed the entire village to form a line to the steamboat. They virtually passed each piece of wood, person to person, to fill the steamboats bin of the needed wood, it took less than one hour to complete and they were ready to go.

Two hundred and fifty soldiers boarded the steamboat under the direction of Major Hu, and Captain Snyder ordered the steamboat to cast-off for the area of Gang Sha, twenty miles up the river where the surprise attack will take place.

The captain placed First-Mate Sharon Snyder at the wheel, and Ted with Major Hu to organize the men aboard the steamboat to finalize their plan of attack when they reach their destination.

When they arrived in Gang Sha the Major marched his troops from the steamboat to an area just outside of the village, and they waited in formation for the appointed time.

The bugles sounded right on time, and the soldiers stood at attention to await their orders to move forward. The guerilla bandits heard the bugles and began to move down the mountain to meet the attacking Chinese army. At the same time Major Hu ordered his men to move quietly and follow the bandits downward to prepare for their surprise attack from behind, while Ted and Captain Snyder observed from a safe distance. When the army was close enough the Major ordered his men to stop and fix their bayonets, and then ordered them to fire a volley. It surprised the guerrillas so much that they became confused and did not know from what direction the shots were coming. Some of them panicked and started to run away fear stricken, dropping their weapons as they tried to escape.

The leader of the guerillas soon became aware that the attack was from behind them and turned his forces around to fight. But it was too late, the Major had advanced his troops close enough that the bandits were being mowed down from the heavy gunfire, and it became a very ugly display of mass killings.

Major Hu had the battle under control, Ted and the captain thought it was safe enough to move in closer. As they approached Major Hu, Ted stumbled over some brush right beside a group of fallen guerrilla soldiers. He picked up a rifle from one of the fallen and stepped over several others just as one of the wounded bandits raised himself up and aimed his gun at Major Hu. Ted fired the rifle at the guerrilla, the guerrilla's gunfired harmlessly into the air. Ted felt overwhelmed with emotions as he watched the guerillas that were left alive drop their guns and surrender.

The plan had worked, these guerrillas who were arrogant enough to think they had the advantage over the Chinese army, were totally caught by surprise. The remainder of the bandits were rounded up, including their warlord, Wong Do, and he offered no resistance since he was among the wounded and had been thrown from his horse.

The seriously wounded who could not walk were bayoneted on the spot, and Major Hu ordered the remainder of the guerrillas to be tied together with a rope, about a hundred-fifty of them, and they marched the prisoners back to the village of Gang Sha. They were met by the people who were happy and elated, shouting and cheering the soldiers on. They had been victims of these evil bandits just hours before, but now felt the freedom that these soldiers had brought them. They gladly gave the glory and honor to these men who freed their village.

"Congratulations, Major, that was a magnificent battle plan you put together, sir, your General will be impressed with your victory, as well as the Mandarin," Captain Snyder said as he shook his hand. The Major smiled, and bowed graciously.

"Sir, with your permission I will withdraw and take my ship back to Wang- Jing and be about my business," Snyder said to the Major.

The Major heaped many accolades on the captain and expressed his hope that they would meet again one day. As they walked back to the steamboat all that had happened finally sank in with Ted, and he began to feel very squeamish in his stomach.

"I understand how you feel, Ted, seeing all that carnage and death is not a pleasant experience, but you did save the Major's life. There is good and evil in the world, and you fought for the good, that should give you a great deal of consolation," the captain told Ted sympathetically.

Two hours later the Lady Sharon was steaming down the river back to the village of Wang Jing. When they docked at the landing, many of the townspeople were gathered, waiting to praise Captain Snyder and his crew. They were singing and chanting and sounding extremely happy and the big village bell was ringing, welcoming their arrival, the news of the victory had arrived before the Lady Sharon.

The Mandarin was standing among the people and he raised his hand to speak. He praised and thanked them for the entire village and Captain Snyder and Ted would become honorary citizens of Wang Jing, they were always welcome to do business with them.

The people cheered and the three missionary ladies shook their hands and kissed Sharon on the cheek. The ladies were extremely happy as they told them the Mandarin had approved their building permit for the hospital and placed a priority for it be built at once.

Captain Snyder and Ray prepared the steamboat to return back down the river toward home when they received the latest news from the Mandarin. All the captured bandits, including the Warlord, had been executed and they would no longer be a threat to the village or to their country.

"You mean they shot all the bandits without a trial," Ted said in disbelief.

"That's their justice system, Ted, the people demand it for the atrocities they committed. They don't have enough prisons to hold them, or a way to feed them, they are a poor and backward people," the captain explained.

The people stood on the dock and waved good-bye to the captain and the Lady Sharon. The Mandarin was in the foreground leading the way, his servants carrying him in his travel chair with all the pomp and ceremony of his rank. The people were showing their love and gratitude to their new citizens, Captain Snyder and all his crew, for all the help that they had given. They continued waving and cheering until the Lady Sharon slowly disappeared from view.

Three weeks later they arrived back in Wang Jing and Ted was glad to see The Wonderer sitting low in the water, fully loaded and ready to leave.

"You men were of great help to me on our maiden journey, I'll miss you both, lads. You have a job with me at anytime you wish, just say the word," the captain voiced in his exaggerated Scottish brogue.

"We'll miss you all," Ted said as he kissed Sharon on the cheek. "Thanks for the trip, it was quite an adventure," Ray nodded in agreement.

With tears in her eyes Sharon paid Ted and Ray forty American dollars each.

"I'm sure the Mandarin will help provide and promote our ship with lots of work, I think we have a good future here, thanks to you both."

Chang waved good-bye to them from the steamboat, he stayed aboard to prepare for its next adventure, hoping it wouldn't be quite as active as this one.

Chapter 56

HEADING HOME

The Wonderer pulled away from the docks in Nan Jing and headed back out to the China sea and the Pacific Ocean, they were headed home. Ted sent a wire to the German Consulate in Hong Kong to notify the "The Van Getz" was spotted in the Yangtze River in the harbor of Wu Han. It read:

> 'The Von Getz,' the ship captured by pirates in the Pacific was spotted in the harbor of Wu Han in China. A German gun boat is patrolling the Yangtze river and will probably assist in the recovery of your ship. If any reward is available please notify Theodore E. Walters. Union membership number W-376, Seaman's Union. Los Angles, California.'

A few days later, when they reached the open seas the ship plowed slowly along at seven knots per hour. It was quiet, the ocean was calm, and the crew was relaxed. Captain Perkins chatted with Ted about the future of shipping on the high seas, and believed the coal burner ship would soon be replaced by oil burners.

"That will be a sad day, that means fewer crew members, we won't need that 'shovel man-power,' but it will be less expensive, cleaner and easier than coal."

The next several days were rather dull, Ted thought. No interesting passengers, no ship activities, just work, eat and sleep, and an occasional card game. They only spotted one ship headed toward Japan, possibly carrying scrap metal, that was the big thing now days, it seemed, the captain commented. They were so glad to see life other than themselves, and they were close enough to wave and shout, and happy that they weren't all alone in the world after all.

The Pacific ocean remained rather quiet for several days. Nothing was happening but a few gales of wind on occasion, and the ship plowed along at the usual seven knots per hour. But during the third week at sea, the weather changed. It was so calm that there was no breeze stirring, the air was very still, and it became hot and steamy. They could actually see the heat waves bouncing off the steel deck, and the crew stripped down to their shorts and straw hats and avoided walking on the hot metal decks and stayed under the shade whenever possible.

Late one afternoon, they came upon a sailing schooner just floating on the glassy ocean water, and there were no signs of life. The sails were hanging on the broken yard arms. The mast lay broken over the side of the boat, dragging in the water.

It looked abandoned, and there was no response to *The Wonderer*'s hails of ahoy. The ship's name *The Sand Castle* was printed on the bow, and Captain Perkins blasted the fog horn several times and called out over the megaphone; but there was no response.

Finally, after many attempts to hail the ship's occupants, the captain made the decision to stop The Wonderer and lower a small boat and prepare to board the schooner to render assistance if needed. He had the feeling that their uneventful journey back home was now quickly changing.

First-Mate Jack Lewis was designated by the captain to prepare a small rescue crew to respond to the distressed boat and Ted volunteered to join him. They took a revolver and shot gun with them just in case they were ambushed, although they didn't really expect that to happen.

They rowed the boat in the devilish heat across to the schooner, and when they came along side Ted jumped over and caught the net hanging over its side and climbed aboard. He tossed a rope over to the small boat, so they could tie up to the ship's side.

Ted checked the deck and it was clear, so he gave the okay for the rest of the crew to board. First-Mate Lewis ordered them to search the ship and they found no sign of life top-side, so he gave the order to search the lower deck. As they went down the gangway they could smell a stench that increased in intensity as they got closer, the terrible gagging stench of human death, they knew it at once.

Ted tied his kerchief over his nose, it really didn't help much, but it did give him incentive to go on, they had to determine what had happened. The first cabin area was the dining room and kitchen, but they didn't see anyone, so they went to the next cabin door where the stench was much stronger, and Ted shuddered at what they would find.

It was the crew's quarters, and they found nine sailors lying dead in their bunks. Ted's eyes watered up and he began to gag, but he had a job to do. He noticed everything appeared wet, including the walls, the sailors were fully clothed, even had their shoes on, they must have all died in their bunks was his first thought. It looked like someone had placed each one in their bunk with their hands folded across their body, but they all had a look of peace on their face. It looked to Ted like it was carefully planned and staged.

Lewis walked up behind Ted and was equally shocked at what he saw. They slowly backed out to search the Captain's quarters and that's when they saw the captain slumped over in his chair at the desk, still holding his pen in his hand. He had tied himself in his chair before he died, and it looked like he had made an entry into the log book. Everything looked wet except the log book, that was really strange, they thought.

Lewis read the log book aloud to the crew, hoping it would explain what happened: 'I take pen in hand to describe the terror of the last six days. My entire crew is dead, I have killed them, yes, I have poisoned them all, and as you can see they are laid out on their bunks with their arm crossed, each one placed at rest. I poisoned them with the last meal the cook fixed, without his knowledge, of course. I placed cyanide into the soup, they did not suffer, death was immediate.

I don't want to appear a monster, so I am writing the reason this terrible decision was made by the entire crew, and I want to emphasize, we all made the decision together. We had a terrible storm that lasted three days, we battled mightily to stay afloat, the ship's rudder was broken and we floundered helplessly in the ocean, unable to control our ship.

The immense waves were so high, about the height of a five story building, and when they thundered down upon us we thought many times we would roll completely over.

You can't imagine being in the trough of the walls of water that were above us and then slamming down on top of the ship with all the power and weight that paralyzed the crew and myself with fear.

A few times our ship was pushed down into the depth of the ocean, yes, I'm telling the world we were beneath the ocean for a time, it seemed like an eternity to us. This happened three times.

Why we did not drown is a miracle, but each time we popped back up to the surface. Each time I recalled a poem that I had read years ago:

The sea is still and deep All things within its bosom sleep, a single step and all is over, a plunge, a bubble and no more.

We should have all drown, but we didn't. We were like corks being pulled under by a huge fish and then reappeared back to the top. We were under water for a minute or so, it seemed like an eternity. It was awful, I really can't say how long.

In case you are wondering why my log book is not wet it is because I kept it sealed in a container under my desk and pulled it out only to enter this message to you. I did not have the strength to return it back into the container.

The storm finally subsided and we sat in the calm unable to move, total exhaustion. Two of my crew killed themselves and another had drown. The rest did not have any strength left and lay in their bunks expecting to die. Our water supply was gone, we had no food except three cans of soup of which I prepared the poison.

The men voted to die and asked that I assist them, so had each one sign the book stating they wanted to die. I stubbornly held out for several days, but we were all dying a slow death, no one wanted that, so I prepared the soup and they didn't hesitate to drink it, death was preferable than living in the condition we were in, knowing it was an eventual death for us all.

God, forgive me for what we have done. I saved my portion for two days before I drank it. Why? I don't know, perhaps insanity by this time.

This all happened just the way I have written. May God forgive me and have mercy on us all.'

Signed: Captain Mark Walker. The ship, The Sand Castle. Owners: Three Baldwin Brothers, San Francisco, California.

Lewis returned his crew to the Wonderer, all stunned by what they had witnessed. They took the log book with them to give to Captain Perkins, and when he finished reading it he ordered Crawford to send a wire to their home office for instructions of what action to take concerning the disabled schooner and the remains of the sailors. When the home office in San Francisco replied they confirmed they would notify the Coast Guard and the United States Merchant Seaman Office of the situation and await information on a plan of action.

Orders came the next morning to bury the schooner and the crew at sea, and to forward the list of names to the company office. Captain Perkins was instructed to open the sea cocks on the Sand Castle, if possible, or chop a large hole in the hull of the ship and let it sink. They were instructed to stay and confirm that the ship had sunk, and its crew went down with the ship.

That afternoon the captain held a memorial service for the crew of The Sand Castle and they all witnessed the ship sink into the depth of the sea.

The Wonderer proceeded on after such a disturbing event and all the crew were very anxious to see their home harbor. When they finally arrived and saw it from a distance, a great feeling of relief ran through their minds, especially Ted. They were all shouting and saying. "we're home, there's no place like home."

The next morning on the tide, The Wonderer entered the Port of San Diego. They anchored in the bay and awaited their docking orders. U. S. Customs boarded the ship to clear them through the Immigration and Customs procedures, and when they were completed the crew was free to disembark and walk on U. S. soil once again.

Captain Perkins released his crew and the paymaster paid each their final pay. He told each of them they were welcome to go on The Wonderers' next assignment and to stay in touch. He asked Ted if he would like to go back to sea again.

"I had a great time, it was a great experience and you have been a truly great friend to me. But, I think I'll hang around California for a while and get a job in telegraphing, or I might decide to go back to Oklahoma to see my folks. I guess I'll just be a 'land lubber' for a while," Ted expressed with a very strong handshake that ended up in a hug between the two men, they had become very close friends.

"Thank you for the opportunity, I saw things I never thought I would ever see. What are you going to do now, Captain?" Ted asked.

'I'm 75 years old and I have to decide whether I want to go back to sea, I'll take some time to make my decision. I've been thinking about going back to San Francisco and opening a boarding house, I have the funds to do it and I love the city," the captain replied.

Perkins and Ted stood at the gangway and shook hands with the crew as they disembarked.

"Good luck," Jack Lewis said as he almost ran down the plank, and Larry Crawford bid them good-bye and was happy to be home to go see his wife and little girls.

Ted checked into a hotel near the harbor and walked over to a Western Union Telegraph Office to send a wire to his family. He was back on U. S. soil, he told them, but planned to look around Southern California for a while before making a decision to settle down, or to come back home to Oklahoma.

He sent three hundred dollars to his family to help them with their financial difficulties. He felt blessed that he could help them, and still have enough money to take care of himself, he actually felt like he was rich.

Chapter 57

SAN DIEGO, CALIFORNIA

After sleeping soundly in his room at the U. S. Grant Hotel, Ted went to the coffee shop for breakfast. He picked up a newspaper, he hadn't read a paper in weeks out at sea, and was anxious to read the latest news while he had a leisurely breakfast and coffee.

He noticed on the hotel roster of events for the day a union rally was listed that evening in the hotel convention hall, and the speaker was Bill Hayworth. Ted was surprised as he read the name, that's Big Bill he thought to himself, he had known him from the San Francisco boarding house. He had nothing else to do that evening so he decided to go and hear what his old friend had to say and perhaps renew an old acquaintance.

He spent the day looking around downtown San Diego, it is a beautiful city that sat beside the Pacific Ocean. He was rather glad to look out over the sea from land for a change, although he felt good about his experience at sea, it was quite a journey seeing the world. He got a haircut, had lunch at a little sidewalk cafe, and killed time in the bookstore and looked in the stores at the latest merchandise. It really was great being home, the thought kept running through his mind.

He dressed in his suit, white shirt and tie for the evening event and headed down to have dinner in the dining room before going to the evenings event. He knew nothing about unions, just what Big Bill had told him back in San Francisco and his short experience with the seaman's union. He had rather dismissed such thoughts from his mind, he wasn't really going to hear the message, he was going to see Big Bill and renew an old friendship.

He walked down the curved marble staircase and entered the hotel lobby. People were gathering, making their way to the convention hall. He asked the concierge for directions, and he told him to follow the crowd down the hall.

At the door the gentleman asked Ted if he was a union member. He replied that he was not, but his friend and acquaintance was the main speaker. He signed the roster, put on his name tag and entered the hall.

He was escorted to a seat, the room was filling up fast and the speakers of the program took their places on stage. There sat Big Bill, surrounded by several other rather dignified looking people, and a well dressed attractive woman sat on the stage next to Big Bill. Ted recognized her at once, it was Martha Turner who he had also met at the boarding house. Setting next to her was another much older lady, Emma Goldman, who he recognized from the newspaper pictures and articles he had read that morning.

The host of the event stood and opened the evening by welcoming all who came, and he proceeded to introduce the speakers for the evening. After several short speeches the host gave a flowery introduction of the main speaker for the evening, Mr. Bill Hayworth. He rose from his chair, and much to Ted's surprise, the audience stood up, shouting and clapping, and chanted over and over, "Go, Big Bill."

It took several minutes before calm was restored, but Ted could tell Big Bill was enjoying every moment of it.

He began to speak and told the audience how privileged he was to stand before such a fine group of strong devoted and dedicated union men and women. The crowd burst out again in cheers, but Big Bill quickly calmed them by raising his hands to quiet them. Ted knew he had the audience in his control, they seemed mesmerized by everything he said to them.

He spoke briefly of the history of the Industrial Workers of the World, the I.W.W., and when it was first organized in Chicago by two hundred concerned, dedicated Unionists who came together to put their concerns into a plan of action. This group was mainly from the Western Federation of Miners who were opposed to the mine owners' practices and policies, and were also opposed to the policies of the American Federation of Labor for their ineffective representation of all the working class. At the present time, according to the policies, only about 5% of the working class was represented, and other craftsmen, such as miners, carpenters, and plumbers were not included. These policies and principles have divided the workers of America in all crafts and the I.W.W., also known as the Wobblies, has become the strong organizational group that has risen up 'to right the wrongs, and the world must listen.'

The crowd stood and cheered, chanting, "Wobblies, Wobblies." He raised his hands to call for calm as he continued. He impressed upon them that all workers should organize together and have the same representation, which is the preamble and goals of I.W.W. constitution.

Big Bill explained the main purpose and goals of the I.W.W. was to promote worker solidarity for all the working class, and to overthrow those who continually support and aid the 'employer class,' the shop and factory owners, and such. The I.W.W. will hold to their motto, which is 'an injury to one is a concern to all.'

He continued by saying the working class and the employer class have nothing in common. There could be no peace as long as hunger and want is found among millions of the working class people. The struggle must go on between the two classes until the workers of the world organize the people and take procession of the methods of production and abolish the wage system, and live in harmony with the earth.

The crowd stood up and loud cheers erupted, which Big Bill thoroughly enjoyed, he had a way of playing the audience like a fiddle. He smiled, coughed, and took a drink of water during the pause, and like obedient children the audience sat down and prepared to hear more inspiring words from their 'guru' of the working class.

"Our movement sometimes meets with great criticism," he said.

"We are labeled as socialists, anarchists, and radicals. The press and politicians see the I.W.W. as a threat to the market system and rally great opposition against us. Large corporations hire goons to literally beat us and threaten death, and business groups arouse the city fathers to force the local police to pressure us. It is a battle we must fight, and we are making inroads, and in the end we will succeed, but it won't be easy."

"This is my dream," he told them. "Sometimes we have to use our strength by hard means to get our message out." He told them of an incident in Nevada during a strike at the Pressed Steel, a car parts company, about a Wobblies organizer that was arrested, claiming he broke a city ordinance. The arrest caused a great outcry among the union workers and they responded in numbers and descended on the jail and invited the authorities to arrest them all.

Big Bill paused for the aroused audience to quiet down, and then continued by saying five hundred people went to jail that day. The tactics of fighting free speech was very costly to that community and is still costing other communities such as Spokane, Fresno, Aberdeen, and right here in San Diego. Success for the working class does not come without a cost.

"The local officials use vigilante methods, and use the powerful business men as their counter-offensive. They ran our people out of town, have made threats to 'tar and feather' and other such means to drive us away. They have even made threats of possible hangings."

"We will not allow this to stop us," Big Bill began to wind down his speech.

"We will go forth and spread the word concerning our cause and seek the justice we deserve."

Big Bill brought the house down with huge applause and a standing ovation. When the applause and shouting subsided Big Bill introduced Emma Goldman, and the audience was silenced. They listened to her rhetoric on Women's rights in the work place, and she talked about the need for a 'worker's paradise' which included a livable wage, social justice, affirmative action, and sustainable development. She told them her studies of the communist manifesto and its ten planks led her to believe all these things were attainable through its decree and through the Workers of the World Union.

Ted listened intently, but he was confused by her speech, he didn't really understand much of what she said. The meeting finally came to a close and after several minutes of clapping, shouting and hand shaking, the crowd began to disperse into the hotel lobby.

Ted saw Big Bill talking with a couple of his friends, they were laughing, shaking hands, probably evaluating the rally and all the activates of the day, and Big Bill seemed pleased. Ted walked up and interrupted the conversation.

"Hi, Big Bill, do you remember me?"

"Well, I'll be, if it isn't my favorite bridge player, how in the world are you, Ted? What are you doing here? The last time I saw you was in San Francisco, the earthquake, remember!" Big Bill seemed glad to see his old friend.

"I'm staying here in the hotel and I saw on the roster that you were speaking tonight and I wanted to come to see you and hopefully say hello," Ted replied with a handshake.

"What have you been up to lately?" Big Bill asked.

"Just got back from a trip overseas, I've been working on a ship as their wireless operator. Had a great adventure doing that and seeing a lot of the world."

"Let me call you tomorrow, Ted, we'll get together for lunch, what room are you in?"

"Room 503, this is quite a coincidence, both of us staying here at the same time. Good to see you again, talk to you tomorrow," Ted said as he left to go back to his room.

"I'll call you in the morning, good to see you," Big Bill said as he and the other men walked away as their cigar smoke trailed behind them.

The telephone rang as Ted returned to his room after breakfast. He picked up the phone, and Big Bill was on the other end of the line.

"How about let's get together for lunch down in the hotel dining room, can you meet me around twelve thirty, say, I have a couple of appointments this morning, but I'll be free by that time."

"Sure, Bill, I'll be there, it sure was good to hear your voice again." Ted replied.

The dining room at the U. S. Grant Hotel was always busy at twelve thirty, and when Ted arrived the maitre-d asked if he had a reservation.

"I'm meeting Big Bill Hayworth for lunch," Ted replied.

"Yes, sir, he is here and he said you would be joining him, I'll have you escorted right away to his table."

Ted was greeted with great gusto, Big Bill stood up and hugged him.

"It's great to see you again, seems like you have grown up since I saw you last, you were just a kid in San Francisco. I never expected to see you and the others from our earthquake experience again, glad to see you made it through and are alive and kicking."

They sat down at their table and Big Bill said.

"If I recall correctly, the last time we talked in San Francisco I offered you a job as one of our organizers for the union. What are you doing now?"

"Just got back from over-sea's, I took a job with Captain Perkins on a freighter, we were gone over three years," Ted told him.

"If you're not working now, I sure would like for you to go to work for our cause, it's not a physical or manual labor job, but it can be very interesting work, I sure need a bright young man such as yourself. We're here in San Diego to organize the dock and agriculture workers, and hopefully the railroad workers too."

"What do you say, Ted?"

"Tell me about it," Ted requested.

"I'll pay you thirty five dollars a week, plus your expenses. You can stay right here at this fine hotel and eat your little heart out, of course, you'll have to travel some now and then, but we will furnish your transportation and a couple of body guards to see that you don't get your legs broke," Bill said with a laugh.

"Wait a minute," Ted backed off a bit. "Are you telling me this work is dangerous?

I'm not sure I'm cut out for that kind of heavy duty work. I'm just a sweet, gentle, peaceful soul, you know."

"So am I," Bill said with a chuckle. He continued to say,

"Why don't you just try it and if you don't like it you can always quit, no hard feelings, I would understand. I really think you would like it, all it amounts to is talking the union up with the people, and stirring up interest in the I.W.W. and do some recruiting. You may at times have to assist in squelching the opposition, but mainly you'll be telling how organized labor can help the working man and his family, which is a noble thing," Bill said.

"It's the squelching of the opposition I might not have the heart for," Ted smiled.

"We sometimes have to do things in life we would rather not do, but everything has its value you know," Bill told him.

"I'll have you work with one of our finest labor organizers to help get you started, and when you're ready to go it alone, you can branch out and do your thing. How does that sound?"

"That sounds a whole lot better, I'll give it a try, as long as I don't get my legs broken," Ted told him as they both laughed.

"No guarantees," Bill said.

"But we have only lost four or five organizers that way this year," he said with a hearty laugh.

"When do I start?"

"Actually, you started yesterday, I put you on the pay roll after seeing you at the meeting. We wanted you that bad, Ted, in fact we were prepared to pay you more, if we had to, just to get you," he kidded with him.

"I'll expect you in my office tomorrow morning at 8:00 a.m. My office is here in the hotel, Room 19 on the second floor."

They ordered lunch and Bill continued.

"I'll have your mentor there also to get you started with your training and show you the ropes. I like my organizers to look nice, so be sure and wear a suit and tie, and also, get a nice hat to wear."

"I'll advance you a clothing allowance, and like I said you will be on an expense account." He handed him a paper with the account number, and a list of expenses that were covered.

"Go get yourself ready to work, my friend."

Ted moved his belongings into another room on the second floor, just down the hall from Big Bills' office. *Apparently, the IWW had lots of money,*

Ted thought. They spared very little on living comfortably; they had the whole second floor of the hotel leased.

Promptly at 8:00 a.m., Ted walked next door to the office. The secretary greeted him and sent him directly into Big Bill's office.

"He is expecting you," she said.

There were two other men in the office with Bill as he entered.

"Grab a seat, Ted, everyone is here now, so we can start our meeting, let's all listen up."

"I have just recently been approached by two very interesting proposals from some very prominent Mexican political revolutionists who want us to help by financing their revolution through the Workers of the World Union."

"It's a very worthy and interesting project that they have been working on it for several years. You remember when we were together in San Francisco before the earthquake, Ted, we played bridge with a gentleman and his wife, Mr. and Mrs. John Turner, who wrote the book 'Barbarous Mexico.'"

"Yes I remember him, a really nice guy. I didn't get to read the book, I never got the chance," Ted said. Bill continued.

"I read it and it made my blood boil, it's all about the terrible treatment the Mexican Indians receive, and they are virtual slaves in Mexico perpetrated by the tyrannical President, Porfiro Diaz. He has murdered and caused the death of thousands of the Indians and the poor in Mexico. You probably know that Mexico is now in the throes of a civil war being waged."

"A fellow by the name of Francisco L Madero is involved in the battle to overthrow President Diaz, and things are getting critical and about to explode down there."

"Mexico has long been a country controlled by the dictator Diaz, and the people are without political freedom, freedom of speech, or free press. They are without the cherished guaranties of life, liberty, and the pursuit of happiness as Turner brings out in his book. The poor have no rights, especially the Indians, they are virtually slaves, in fact they are called 'Yaquis' which means slave."

"Even though the Mexican constitution prohibits slavery, they are made slaves in insidious and devious ways. Mainly through big debts to the land owners that they can never pay back, and entire families are enslaved by the land owners for life."

"Ted, I want to introduce you to two gentleman, former revolutionists, who for several years were in Mexico and tried to overthrow the dictator Diaz, but lost the battle. They fled to America to save their lives and ever since have been busy organizing and publishing revolutionist pamphlets and writing articles against the present situation in Mexico. They have been actively working against Diaz for several years now, and got into a lot of trouble with the American government, and were even imprisoned for such 'seditious' acts. Ted, please meet the gentlemen sitting beside you, Ricardo Flores Magon, and Antonio Villarreal."

Chapter 58

PLANNING THE INVASION OF THE BAJA

"These two gentlemen have come up with a plan that interests me greatly," Big Bill said sounding very enthusiastic, "and with our financial help I think they can make it work."

"You see, what they have in mind is to invade and overtake the Baja with a volunteer army while all the attention is given to the civil war being fought on the mainland in Mexico between Francisco Madero and his revolutionary troops against the Dictator Diaz and his army."

"The Baja is more or less ignored at this point and that makes it more accessible for our cause, which is to capture it and turn it into a paradise state for free workers to own and control. We will call it 'The Free State of Baja,' the very first of its kind anywhere. That's what we want for the working man."

"Now is the ideal time for us to strike, you know me, I never want to miss an opportunity to take advantage of a crisis situation!" Big Bill said laughing his deep throaty laugh.

"Bill, are you guy's communist?" Ted said in astonishment. "Sounds a lot like what I understand the communists to say and the way they think."

"No, Ted, we're not communist, but we are progressive, we want fair working conditions with fair wages for our workers, and we will fight to get those things. We are a new movement and we're growing in the country, the progressives are on the march, but we're not communist, let me assure you. I think the progressive movement in time will engulf the entire country and possibly the world."

"If you say so, Big Bill, I sure can't say I go along with what I heard that old lady talking about in your meeting about communists and all that nonsense."

"Ted, don't worry about it, that's not what our movement is about, and that lady is not a part of our movement."

"I think I agree with a strong union supporting the working man, that part I agree with," Ted said.

"Good, that's okay, Ted, you'll work out fine, that's our aim also."

"Our biggest problem right now is getting weapons into the Baja to arm our volunteer soldiers to fight and takeover the land from the rich Mexican land owners."

"At the present time President Taft has stationed the military along the U. S. and Mexico border to prevent Mexican sympathizers from smuggling weapons to the Madero army. I understand about one-third of the entire U. S. army has been detailed to patrol the border, and along with that action the U. S. Navy has stationed a fleet of warships and has completely surrounded the entire mainland of Mexico."

"This action does not include the Baja, but the patrols do hamper our ability to furnish guns and ammunition into the area. Did you know that the U. S. is even using an airplane to patrol our border from the air, the very first time in history an airplane is used in that way. That's an exciting thing, but it's not good for our cause."

"We also have good financial support from some very influential people in Southern California and also in the U. S. government who are interested in making Baja a free state. There are other sources high up in state politics who would like to confiscate and incorporate the five Mexican States along the border into the U. S., and they are very vocal about it, and I think that could come about it time. If so, it would certainly strengthen the United States and would increase our Union influence throughout the country."

"There are other countries, like Germany, who already have huge investments in Mexico and have financed a great deal of the railroad system in Mexico. They are thinking about sending military forces to protect their investments, and that's another reason why the Navy is stationing war ships around Mexico's mainland, to keep those countries from invading Mexico."

"Strange as it seems, the U. S. Military has no real interest in this war in Mexico, other than protecting our own border at this time, and that makes it ripe for our purpose. There is only a very small contingent of the Mexican army personnel in the territory of Baja at this time and they are stationed in Ensenada about a hundred miles down the coast from Tijuana."

"What will the Workers of the World Union get out of this if it all succeeds?" Ted asked.

"Well," Big Bill said, "I'm glad you asked, how about a hundred and sixty acres for each volunteer soldier of the I.W.W. to call his very own, to either keep or to sell."

"That sounds good, but isn't it against the law to invade a foreign country and confiscate property?" Ted questioned.

"Oh, yes!" Big Bill said, "If they dare to do anything about it, why would they concern themselves about the Baja right now? To their way of thinking it's hardly a part of Mexico because of its isolation from the mainland. There are just three fishing villages in the Baja, Tijuana, Mexicali, and Tecate, that's all, and hardly any population to speak of, maybe seven or eight thousand people all together, and most of them are peon's who could really care less who's in charge. If we send a small military force of four or five hundred men down there, who's to stop us? I like the prospect."

"Let me get this straight, you say the American army wouldn't stop us from taking troops into the Baja because they don't have the necessary manpower to guard the border. But wouldn't the invasion violate the treaty with Mexico that could possibly mean war between Mexico and the United States?" Ted asked.

"We're willing to take that risk, the Mexican army is all tied up fighting the civil war on the Mexican mainland, so whose left to stop us?" Bill answered.

"So you're saying, taking the Baja looks ripe for picking?"

Big Bill laughed and said, "Yes, exactly, because all the focus is on the mainland, and that war may go on for years. Right now, Ted, let's get back to the work at hand, I want you to go with me to Los Angeles in the morning to their headquarters, so we can meet with these two Mexican gentlemen to work out the details of the invasion, that is your assignment for now."

"Now that you know what we have in mind, it's time for you to at least consider if you want to be a part of this, and if you don't I will understand, and you can be just a plain union organizer and miss all the fun, that's your decision entirely. Think it over and let me know tomorrow morning what part you want to play."

The next morning after eating a big breakfast in the hotel dining room on his new expense account, Ted reported for work promptly at 8:00 a.m. "Good morning, Ted, did you have a good breakfast this morning?"

"I sure did, and thank you very much. I don't generally eat steak and eggs for breakfast, but since I'm not paying I really splurged." Ted said laughingly.

Big Bill joined in the laughter and said, "Be careful, you'll get fat if you eat too much rich food, Ted. I'm awfully glad you're with us, so let's get started and let me know what you're thinking about your work with us. Ted, I want to support Magon in his efforts, and I would like for you to be my eyes and ears in this project, I need for you to act as my observer. I think it will be exciting and a great adventure for a young man like yourself. I would do it myself, but I am not a young man anymore and the doctor has recently diagnosed me with a permanent affliction, my old ticker is wearing down. I have to start taking things easier and back away from such excitement if I want to continue living and get older. Are you still with me, Ted?"

"Tell me more about the details of what you want me to do and what part l will play in all this."

"Since we play a large part in financing this undertaking we need somebody on the ground to keep us abreast of whether our money is achieving the goal we are working for. There is a lot of money involved, some coming from very high influential and wealthy people who will be working with us, and we must be able to keep track of the expenditures and account for it, and make sure it's not misused. It will take a young man, such as yourself to do this, because things can be very fluid for a while once it starts. You will probably be on the move a lot of the time."

"I'm not a revolutionist, how can I possibly fit in? I'm wondering if I'm the man you want for this job!"

"We do think you're the right man, and we certainly don't think that you can in any way control the events that occur, or the outcome that we hope to achieve, it will either work, or it won't. Your role is to observe and relay the account of what is going on back to us. You will be my eyes and ears and send back reports to keep me abreast of what's happening on the ground in the Baja."

"We have already raised most of the money to finance this operation through various groups and organizations, but whether we continue to support this effort will be based on your reports. I understand that Magon is organizing a group of Mexicans and Indians, led by Jose Mario Leyva and Simon Berthold, to make their raid on Mexicali to capture the town in the very near future. I want someone I can trust to give me the right and correct information, whether it's good or bad. If Magons' group captures Mexicali it will be a big boon for the Workers of the World Union and its cause."

"Okay," Ted said.

"I guess I will give it a try, but I want the right to quit if I see it's not for me, I hope you understand."

"Of course, Ted. You do what you feel you need to do, don't let me talk you into anything that you're not comfortable doing, okay. If we do this we will need everyone's full commitment. We will be going to Los Angeles to meet with them in the morning, and when he is ready to make his move to Mexicali, I would like you to go with the invasion force of men to send reports back to keep me informed. We need to know the continual progress, and if all goes well, raising the remainder of the finances for this project will be much easier."

"Okay, boss," Ted said, "let's go to work!"

Chapter 59

THE SAN DIEGO RALLY

Big Bill and Ted left early the next morning for Los Angeles to meet with Magon and his men. They pulled up at 519 East 4th Street and printed on the window was 'Magon Printing and Publishing Company.' It was located in an industrial area of the city that was inhabited by the working class, Mexicans and other foreigners, and writers and artist types of people. Magon's office was the headquarters of his organization, the Baja Junta and the Insurgents, and where he published his newspaper, The Regeneration.

Magon introduced his intended Generals, Jose Leyva and Simon Berthold to Ted and Big Bill, both men were members of the I.W.W. He also introduced another gentleman who was present, Richard Ferris, who was there to attend the meeting.

"I know you, Ted," Richard spoke up, "didn't we meet in San Francisco at the boarding house where my wife and I stayed while we were performing at the playhouse?"

"Yes, you are right, good to see you again. I went with Big Bill to see your performance, 'Life in Chicago,' and enjoyed it very much," Ted responded.

"Thank you," Ferris said with a smile.

"Are you still acting?" Ted asked.

"No, I just ran as a democratic candidate for the office of Lieutenant Governor of California, but got defeated by a mere six thousand votes. I thought I was well known and popular enough to win, but it wasn't to be. We had given up our acting career to run for office, and when that didn't work out, I accepted the post as Director of the Panama-California Exposition and its yearlong fiesta in San Diego to be held in the beautiful sprawling Balbo Park.

"Now, I believe we will be able to help this cause in Mexico, and possibly promote it in our exposition endeavors. What have you been doing since I saw you last, Ted?"

"After the earthquake I went to sea and recently returned from a few months in the far-east, I went on a tramp-steamer as a telegraph wireless operator and spent time in China and Japan, and did a lot of sightseeing."

"Sounds like quite an adventure," Ferris responded.

Big Bill spoke up to get every ones attention.

"It's good to be together and get re-acquainted, it's sure interesting how our paths cross in our lives, but it's time to get down to the business at hand. We have enlisted Ted as my liaison man and representative in the field, and he will be with Magon and his company of men who will be engaging in the process of freeing the Baja.

"The Workers of the World Union is honored to be involved in this noble cause to free thousands of poor peasants in the Baja from the oppressive Dictator Diaz, and hopefully that will lead to freeing the entire country of Mexico. This is our goal, to raise up the people to be independent and free.

"Let me summarize the history of the movement so far; in August 1910, Magon, our leader, came to the U. S. from Mexico after spending three years in prison for his political activates. After arriving here he was again imprisoned for his subversive activates and has recently been released. He organized a meeting in Los Angeles, aided by the American Socialist Party, on Sept 3rd and began the publication of his newspaper, 'The Regeneration.' The publication has a circulation of over thirty thousand readers."

"Magon will tell you he is just a mere patriot, but he is much more than that. He is the catalyst for the present revolution in Mexico and because of his tireless work and efforts since 1900 against the tyrant Diaz, at great expense to him, he was forced to flee Mexico for his own safety.

"Since he has been here in the U. S. he has never stopped his tireless efforts. He has published his magazine and newspaper in several cities around the country which led to Dictator Diaz hiring secret agents to harass and pursue him, eventually causing his arrest and imprisonment here in the U. S. for violation of neutrality laws. Since then, he is back in business ready to move ahead with our present plans."

"That was quite a speech, Senor Bill," Magon said, a bit embarrassed by the praise. "I appreciate all you gentleman and with your help we will free my country from these tyrants, mainly Diaz and the new pretender, Francisco Madero. Madero has stolen my efforts for his own, and forced me to leave my own country to save my life. I will continue my work with your help. If we can capture the Baja and develop it into a free workers society it will embolden the Mexican people, and my countrymen will embrace our efforts throughout Mexico."

After the meeting with Magon ended Ted was instructed to return to San Diego. Big Bills' plan was to send several hundred union members and organizers to attend street rallies that were to take place the following week in the downtown area of the city, starting at the square. He thought Ted would see what an organizers job was all about, and Magon didn't need Teds' service, not yet for a few days.

Big Bill was sending his Union speakers to the rally, and he warned Ted that Emma Goldman, the devout communist, would also be there as a speaker to spew her communist rhetoric, and the County Sheriff and Police Chief were expecting a lot of trouble.

Ted remembered Emma Goldman, she was the one he had great reservations about with her communist philosophy. She was known as Grandma Goldman, not like any grandmother he had ever known. She was a 'dyed in the wool' anarchist, and she rallied forces to create friction among the people. In fact, her speeches and her publications had been credited as the cause of a fanatical anarchist assassinating President McKinley. Ted shuddered at the thought of having to listen to her speak.

He had read a recent article she wrote concerning the Mexican war saying; 'I call upon you as Americans to use every effort to call on the President to withdraw the American troops from the border. You who preach liberty and boast of independent freedom should not allow American interference. Let the Mexicans fight it out among themselves.' She was assisted by two members of a newly formed group called the 'Anti-Interference League,' formed by the known Socialist Kasper Bauer and the liberal lawyer, E.E. Kirk.

Ted was uneasy about the upcoming rallies and the potential street riots and violence, but he tried to keep his mind on the main purpose of the group, to free workers to become landowners and be in control of their own lives. But, the following week he readied himself to attend the rally with Big Bill, and they left the hotel to walk to the square.

The square was filled with hundreds of people and as they approached it they saw a skirmish up ahead. They watched as several men pushed and shoved some people into the back of a car, yelling and screaming. The men immediately jumped in the car and drove away.

Ted and Big Bill watched the car drive away, but they were too far away to intervene or help.

332 JACK LURLYN WALTERS

"What was that all about?" Ted wondered out loud.

"Don't know, but those are the kind of things that happen during these kinds of rallies," he told Ted.

"You'll probably see some crazy things in the next few days."

They entered the square and listened to the speeches between shouts and rants, and when it was time for the next scheduled speaker, Emma Goldman, it was announced she was cancelled for the evening.

It wasn't until the next day that Ted understood why she was cancelled when he read the San Diego Sun newspaper account of the incident that they had witnessed, it was Emma and her assistants, Bauer and Kirk, who were abducted and driven to the county line. They were stripped down to their underwear and forced to run through the gauntlet where they were beaten and knocked to the ground. They were tarred and feathered and left without their clothes, except Emma, she was allowed to keep her pantaloons on, and they were told not to come back to San Diego or they would be hung by their neck.

Ted was stunned, they had observed the abduction the night before, and had no idea what the commotion was all about and who was involved. It was beginning to sink into his head just how committed and dedicated these people were to their cause, regardless of what side they were on. But this was only the beginning of the violence and riots this rally would create. He began to wonder if he was doing the right thing, getting involved with this project.

A group of men who were San Diego citizens and vigilantes, rounded up five radicals from the I.W.W. that same evening. The vigilantes were quite drunk and they threw the captives into a cattle pen full of manure and urine filled slush after beating and torturing them. One of the captives was a seventeen year old boy who they kicked and prodded as he ran through the gauntlet which left him bloody from a head wound. No mercy was shown to him as they made him kiss the flag and sing the Star Spangled Banner, which he could barely project from his mouth.

Another captive, who they called a 'Jew,' was hit in the back of his head and his legs knocked out from under him with a bat, and they put him through the same ritual. Ted began to feel sick as he heard about such violent accounts.

It went on and on, and the frustration of the Police Chief and his officers, along with the city fathers, became very upset and angered by it all. They had lost control of their city, and they knew it, and they had finally had enough. The citizens of San Diego called for stronger measures to rid their city of these hoodlums. The entire city was in an uproar.

The police rounded up as many of the union radicals as they could and ran them out of the town, but the I.W.W. responded by sending in more union people to rally and support their cause. This caused the city fathers to mobilize their forces to stop and apprehend as many of the I.W.W. agitators at the county line and turn them back.

At the same time the citizen vigilantes became more angered and took action. They gathered as many of the I.W.W. radicals as they could, kicked and beat them, tarred and feathered them and left them wounded, bleeding and naked, and dumped them at the county line, warning them to never return. The once quiet little town of San Diego shuddered with anxiety and confusion as hordes of Wobblies streamed into the city, profanity poured from the soap boxes in the park and square, which shocked the law abiding San Diegans. Women were frightened by the seedy looking strangers which loitered on the street corners, and they knew they were losing control of their town, it had erupted into total violence and all the ordinary citizens demanded something be done.

The downtown merchants petitioned the city council to ban street assemblies in the area, but the police held back waiting for an overt act, something they could act upon. It finally came when a tire was slashed on an automobile the driver moved slowly through the crowded street which was jammed with hundreds of Wobblies and other agitators and protestors.

Police Chief Wilson called out the riot squad and ordered the mob to disperse, and when they refused the police started hauling in the dissidents, charging them with inciting riots, and the jails soon were filled with angry prisoners.

The riots lasted for several days but began to quiet down as the rioters were arrested and locked in boxcars and taken out of the city by rail. Some of the boxcars were left on railroad sidings in the hot sun for hours, the prisoners were left without food or water before they were let go out in the middle of nowhere. Many San Diegans were injured, many were distraught, confused and saddened by the destruction of their beautiful city.

A high city official told the residents : 'The actions of the I.W.W. and their radical manifesto tactics and socialist philosophy which they have imported from Europe is condemned and has also led to violence in our cities, such as Spokane, Washington and Fresno, and now in San Diego. It will menace the peace and welfare of the entire country.'

Big Bill smiled and thought to himself, '*they may do this to a few of our people, but I will just order more than they can comprehend or deal with into this scene. Let them use their tactics, it will just further our cause, they can't stop us, we're too big. We'll stay in the fight if it takes years, we will organize the working man in spite of what they try to do to us.*'

Chapter 60

MAGONISTAS

Flores Magon dispatched his small eight man force, with Ted as an observer, and made camp at Laqunda Salada, a dry desert lake bed in a neutral border area. His plans and hope for a free Baja and to eventually over throw the Dictator Diaz was about to begin.

This small force was soon joined by others who were dedicated to the cause, Mexicans, Cacopa Indians, and Anglo-Americans, most of whom were I.W.W. member sympathizers. Magon named Jose Leyva as his General, and Simon Berthold second in command. He named his rag-tag army of rebels, which now numbered 150, the Magonistas.

General Leyva and Berthold outlined their strategic plan of attack with Magon, and they wanted to move quickly since the troops were growing weary and dissensions and clashes were increasing among them. The dissensions were mainly between the Mexicans and the Anglos over political and racist views. But, Magon knew the one thing they all had in common was the takeover of the Baja, and that was where the general kept his focus with the troops as he readied them for battle.

At dawn on a cold January morning in 1911 Leyva led his troops into the sleepy little border village of Mexicali with Ted at his side. He divided his troops into three groups, the first group, led by Berthold, stormed the Mexican Customs Office and captured two officers, waking them from their nights' sleep. They raided the safe and confiscated a hundred and fifty dollars. They had hoped for a much larger amount of money and gold to help finance their project, so they were very disappointed, needless to say.

The second group headed for the home of the Police Chief. They broke into his house dragging him out of bed, with his wife and children screaming and crying as they hid in their bedrooms.

The third group, led by Leyva with Ted riding with him, went to the jail house and demanded the keys, but when they heard the jailer cock his shotgun from behind the door, Leyva fired his rifle and shot him. As it turned out, that was the only shot fired during the entire takeover of Mexicali.

After the capture of the jailhouse the takeover of Mexicali was virtually over, the Magonistas secured the village and began to celebrate their victory on main street. Many of the freed prisoners and some townspeople joined the celebration, most of them not really knowing what they were celebrating, but at the moment they felt free from the suppression of the Diaz regime. Some of the people, especially the freed prisoners signed up to join the movement, and the Magonistas quickly grew into a rebel army of over 400 men.

During the aftermath of the takeover, Ted kept very busy observing and jotting down notes to prepare his report for Big Bill. The captured Customs Officers were very cooperative, they paid $385. 00 for their release and quickly disappeared across the border into California. The Mexican police officers and the police chief, who had been stripped of their clothing when they were captured, headed for the border when they were freed and disappeared in a forest of trees, clad only in their underwear.

After the celebration of their victory was over and they returned to camp, the strife between the Mexicans and the Anglos began to increase again, and it grew to the point that a serious split in the troops occurred. The Anglo-Americans accused General Leyva of incompetence, claiming he refused to carry out orders given by Magon. As a result of the infighting General Leyva resigned and left for Texas to join forces with Madero.

Berthold also left the Magonistas, being a strong supporter of Leyva, causing Flores Magon to re-organize the troops. He placed the Magonistas under the command of General Vasquez Salinas and Lieutenant Carl Pryce, a Welch soldier of fortune, both men were strong activists for the cause and had recently joined up with the group.

But the strife continued and General Salinas soon found himself at odds with the divided troops who were siding with Pryce. The troops simply ignored Salinas' commands and his leadership became totally ineffective. Physical altercations began to occur, the Mexican troops called the Americans 'gringos', while the Americans called the Mexicans 'greasers.' As this increased the Americans and Mexicans began to fight duels among themselves, totally ignoring their original common purpose of coming together in the beginning.

Ted was very disappointed in their behavior and asked Magon what he planned to do to solve the problem, and very soon Lieutenant Pryce separated the American troops out of the force and left to prepare them to go into Tecate, which Magon commissioned him to do.

Ted returned to San Diego a few days after the victory in Mexicali to report to Big Bill. Although Big Bill was happy with the capture of Mexicali, the biggest disappointment was the failure to find any gold at the Customs House. Apparently, the report that a large stock of gold that was being held in the safe was not true.

Big Bill and Ted read the newspaper accounts of the capture of Mexicali, and much to Ted's surprise, a 'manifesto,' written by the famous and well known novelist writer, Jack London, was printed in the newspaper. Ted was eager to read it since he had met Jack London during the earthquake in San Francisco, and he read it with great interest and was shocked by what he read. London wrote the following words:

'We socialists, anarchists, hobos, chicken thieves, outlaws, and undesirable citizens of the United States are with you heart and soul. You will notice that we are not respectable, but neither are you. No revolutionary can be respectable in these days of reign for property. I for one wish there were more outlaws of the sort that formed the gallant band that took Mexicali.'

"Is this the way Jack London sees us, this man is an anarchist!" Ted said to Big Bill. He knew London was very liberal, but he was now calling himself an anarchist. Ted was confused, he didn't see the Magonistas movement and their purpose as anarchist, in his mind it was just doing the right thing for the people.

Big Bill didn't comment much about the articles, but smiled as he read them. *One article that summarized the Mexicali takeover in the San Diego Sun newspaper was really an accurate account,* Ted thought. It read:

> "The rebel soldiers presented a grotesque appearance, the majority being Mexicans. Only eight of the men were mounted astride their horses, some without saddles or bridles and using only halters to guide their steed. The white men in the company had the appearance of ranch hands, and all the men were armed with rifles and small arms and it appeared they had an abundance of ammunition. Although the capture didn't get them any gold, their force was joined by a hundred and fifty additional men, mostly

I.W.W. union renegades who crossed the border and joined the forces after the initial invasion. Their future goal is to takeover Tecate and then move on to capture the Mexican garrison at Ensenada, and later take control of the entire Baja to create a socialist state."

Ted confirmed the accuracy of the article since he was present while it all happened, and Big Bill declared success and felt the revolution had a very good beginning. The biggest concern, Ted told him, was the infighting of the troops, but Magon and his rebel leaders would have to deal with it. The next move will be Tecate and that will occur very soon, hopefully before the troops and their own little infighting war destroys them. Big Bill laughed at the thought, but knew it was a problem Magon would have to deal with.

"This is a crazy way to run a war," Ted said.

"Sometimes I wonder if I'm cut out for this, I really don't see myself as a progressive or socialist, and especially an anarchist, and I ask myself continually if this is all worth it."

"Don't worry, Ted, it will all come together. I've got your back, believe me, it will all turn out all right, I assure you."

Ted nodded, but he wasn't really sure about it all.

Chapter 61

THE VILLAGE OF TECATE

Ted joined Lieutenant Pryce and his I.W.W. Anglo-American troops as they rode their horses toward Tecate. It was early in the spring and the cool winds swept across the Baja valley floor. The dust began to fill the air and the beautiful scenery of the hills that surrounded Tecate were becoming obscured as the constant breeze blew the dust in from the desert. Ted tied his handkerchief around his head to protect his nose from filling up with dust.

He saw a lonely burro restrained by a tether braying in distress, but the sound was soon lost in the winds. Other animals were in the fields all bunched together, huddled under trees and under thatched lean-to shelters. Ted saw the small thatched roof huts, and the women and children peeking through the windows at the troops as they rode by. He knew they were probably filled with a chill of fear, not from the wind, but from the fear of the unknown. From the neighborhood saloon the men watched as they sipped their tequila, unsure of whether they faced pending danger in their little village.

The people had heard about the news of the war on the mainland between the Dictator Diaz and the Mexican peoples' defender,

Francisco Madero, and they weren't sure who these approaching men represented. They had become cautious about who they could trust, and fear constantly clutched at their hearts. Just two weeks ago, another rebel group had raided Tecate and pillaged the village, so it was no wonder the people were so fearful and why some had escaped to the protection of the U. S. army on the American side of the border.

The people had heard of the news from the north, the United States President Taft had ordered the American troops to patrol the border to prevent smuggling, and from the east came word that Mexicali had been captured by an American rebel force called the Magonistas. The people wondered who all these different fighting groups were and who they could trust, if any of them.

What Pryce, Ted, and the troops realized as they entered the dusty little village was that very few people had remained in their homes, the majority had already crossed over the American border to escape the rebels. The families that remained were huddled in improvised shelters, and Ted could see the women and children looked starved, apparently there was very little food available for them. There were crude little huts and shelters located in the hills above the town, with some families living under trees and in tents, and even under wagons. The necessity for relief for the people had been reported to the 115th Coast Artillery Company of the U. S. army, the same troops who were guarding the U. S. border against smuggling and to enforce the neutrality laws.

Ted began to give serious thought as to what he and these rebels' forces were all about and what they wanted to accomplish as they rode into the town. He was only twenty one years of age and in his careless inexperienced youth, he is involved in a military insurrection and the armed capture of Tecate, it really didn't seem real to him at times. He often felt confused as he thought about it, hoping his participation in this cause was a noble one.

At the same time they were entering Tecate, and unbeknownst to them, a Mexican force called the Regales under the command of Captain Mendieta, were setting up defenses on a hillside on the opposite side of the village, and some of the townsmen climbed the hill with their weapons to join the Regales to help protect their village. On the American side of the border hundreds of refugees who had fled Tecate, were assisted by concerned San Diego citizens who set up tents and food stations to give them protection from the cold winds and the possibility of battle. It was a tense time for everyone, not really knowing how this would all play out in the end. The people from both sides of the border were poised to watch from the hillside as Pryce's rebel army entered the village, arms in hand ready for battle.

Suddenly a shot rang out alarming everyone, and they all knew the battle for the town of Tecate had begun. Many of the people hurriedly retreated farther back into the hills for protection, the shot came from somewhere on the hillside. Pryce's troops were caught by surprise, they usually didn't face any opposition, but on this occasion it was different. The men of the village were not going to hand over their town without a fight, and the battle waged on for two days with Pryce and his rebels finally taking charge. But when he heard the Mexican army was sending re-enforcements, he knew he could not hold the village any longer, they would then be outnumbered. He ordered his troops to withdraw and return to their camp near Mexicali and he was highly disappointed with the final outcome of Tecate.

Pryce realized he had not been given accurate information before the battle began. He had depended on his scouts, headed by Jack Mosby, who was an ex-marine and a newcomer for the cause. He found out later that Mosby and his men had been involved in the looting of ranches and surrounding farms instead of gathering information to keep him informed of where and what the enemy was planning.

Ted left Mexicali and crossed over to the American side to San Diego to make his report to Big Bill. He felt anxious about the outcome of their Tecate experience and explaining it all to him. He knew Big Bill would be highly disappointed in the final outcome.

Chapter 62

THE CAPTURE OF TIJUANA

With the disappointment of Tecate behind them, Ted felt hesitant as Ricardo Flores Magon and the Workers of The World Union pushed forward with Big Bill to plan the capture of Tijuana. The rumors were flying on both sides of the border, and the residents of Tijuana were in a near state of panic and excitement, they knew their village was the next to be taken over by the rebels. But some of them welcomed the troops hoping it would free them from the suppression of the Dictator Diaz, while others were skeptical and worried.

Many Tijuana citizens were packing up and leaving their homes taking what valuables they had with them and scattering into the surrounding hills of San Diego County. Since the threat of battle loomed upon them, Tijuana had become of very little economic, political, or geographical significance other than catering to the tourist trade from the United States who crossed the border to shop for Mexican trinkets so they could tell their folks back home they had been to Mexico, and the tourist trade was diminishing quickly.

A core group of helpful Tijuana citizens came across the border to help their American neighbors assist the refugees to prepare for the days ahead by providing tents, medical supplies, food and clothing. No one was anxious for another disruption that these rebels cause, but they wanted to be prepared for whatever happened. The only ones left in Tijuana was a small band of defenders who patrolled the streets, about seventy armed citizens who were committed to defend their village by watching and waiting.

In May, 1911, the day arrived when Ted rode with General Pryce into Tijuana with the Magonistas, about two hundred men in all. They were met in the village square by the citizens group, led by a Military officer and twenty Mexican Federal Army Indian soldiers carrying ancient looking rifles. The Mayor of Tijuana, Senor Lorroque, was also present and was commonly known by several different titles, such as Sub-Prefector or Commandante, and was highly respected by the people.

The mayor bravely stepped out of the group and spoke with a tone of righteous indignation in his voice. General Pryce and his rebel soldiers, with Ted at his side, sat on their horses and faced the mayor as he spoke in his broken English pronunciation.

"We represent the President of Mexico, the Honorable Porfiro Diaz, and you are insurrectionists who are committing a heinous illegal act of invasion of our sovereign country. We will support the Mexican government and assist our army to protect the people and defend our government interests against the American filibusterous invaders. I order you to leave our country voluntarily before blood is spilled on our soil, if not, you will be hunted down and captured and shot on sight."

Ted was amazed how brave this man was, how he stood and faced a group who totally outnumbered them and were there to take over their village. The mayor was dressed in a black suit with a wide silver, green, and red banner across his shoulder which draped to the bottom of his jacket and denoted the lofty station of his office. While Ted was lost in thought a shot rang out, catching everyone by surprise.

"Oh, no, where did that come from," Pryce shouted out.

One of the rebel soldiers became over anxious and drew his gun and fired, shooting the mayor in the eye. Everyone was stunned, it all happened so fast, but it was too late, the mayor fell dead. Both the Magonistas and the Mexican defenders scattered to take cover, and the skirmish began with both sides firing.

"You fool," Pryce shouted out in anger.

"There is not much we can do now except fight." Ted jerked the reins of his horse to follow Pryce and get out of the firing range just as three of their rebel soldiers were shot out of their saddles and fell dead to the ground. The rebels hurriedly positioned themselves to fight, and Ted jumped from his horse and entered the back door of a casino with Pryce and several other rebels. They raced to the windows which faced the village square to assess the action.

In the square the Mexican soldiers engaged in battle with both sides firing wildly. The battle raged on for several hours, the Mexican army defenders moving from building to building firing at anything that moved. Several of the Magonista soldiers rode their horses up and down the street shooting up the village, creating pure chaos, but soon the Mexican defenders reached a point they had to disengage, they were running out of ammunition. The Mexican army left the village and retreated into the hills and countryside, and General Pryce ordered his troops to disengage, claiming victory.

The entire battle lasted for about sixteen hours, killing thirty two and wounding twenty four of the Mexican forces, while the rebels lost twelve of their men. The curious San Diego and Mexican citizens who lined the border on the American side to watch the drama unfold, used their telescopes and spy glasses to get a closer look. The area took on a carnival like atmosphere by the way the people were behaving, and the onlookers scrambled to get a good seat on the hillside, like it was theater play. Many of the people were dressed in their finery, some of the ladies wearing fancy hats and holding umbrellas to protect them from the sun. Actually, the onlookers outnumbered the rebel forces by several hundred. Some of the people wanted to cross the border after the battle to join in the celebration, but the U. S. Army guarding the border doubled their forces to hold the crowd back. In fact, a rather humorous event became known; two criminals escaped from the San Diego jail, stole bicycles and somehow avoided the border guards showing up in Tijuana asking to join the rebel insurrectionists.

Opportunists were coming from everywhere, especially those who had read the ads in the newspapers published back east which were written by Richard Ferris' to encourage and recruit volunteers to join the Magonistas to help fight the battle for the cause of the working man.

After the battle the rebels raised the red flag of victory over Tijuana which created the ire of many people and caused quite a stir. Most people equated a red flag as the symbol of communism and anarchy, so Ferris angrily told Pryce to 'get that flag down now. 'The flag immediately came down and was replaced by a new one designed by Ferris which indicated the annexation of Tijuana, and it flew side by side with the United States flag. People all along the border joined in the celebration and the entire area became very chaotic.

Pryce retreated into San Diego after a few days to avoid the crowd and the press and registered at the hotel under the name of Graham, bringing with him a sizeable amount of looted funds. The Los Angeles Times newspaper reported: 'Pryce, one of the leaders of the Tijuana invasion is missing along with a sizeable amount of funds. The hopes and dreams of these Utopian men, such as author John Turner, received a set back today when it became known that their leader, General Rhys Pryce and the funds were missing. E.E. Kirk, a local attorney and supporter, who represents the liberal rebel forces, declared that Pryce was called away on a mission and would return to take over the reins of this new model country in the Baja that will be formed for all those who desire to be free in this new born nation.'

Two days later U. S. authorities identified Pryce when he attempted to flee the area, he was arrested and taken to Fort Rosecrans and placed in prison. The rebels held the village of Tijuana for forty five days, but during that time Tijuana fell into utter chaos. Buildings were vandalized, the bull ring was destroyed, churches were burned to the ground and businesses were looted.

Opportunists began to exploit everything they could, the whole scene became like a side show, and the biggest opportunist turned out to be Richard Ferris himself. He drove into Tijuana in his fancy convertible car loaded with elegantly dressed ladies, and brought his newly designed flag to display over Tijuana and declared himself the governor of the Baja. Ricardo Flores Magon was so distraught over all the chaos that was occurring, he realized he had lost the battle.

Even though they had captured Tijuana they had totally lost control of the situation in the aftermath. Magon declared the 'Insurrectionist movement' doomed and announced he was withdrawing his financial support and advised the rebel group to leave the Baja. The very next day the International Workers of World Union, better known as the Wobblies, withdrew their financial support, and Big Bill, President of the Union, suddenly resigned his position for 'health reasons.' It seemed they had won the battle but somehow lost the war, it didn't bring the results they had hoped for.

Ted felt like he was left hanging in the wind. The Rebel Army to Free the Baja was out of funds and couldn't even pay the soldiers their wages, leaving them abandoned and in dire straits without any real validity of their past actions and battles. Ted felt so ashamed, especially because of Big Bill, the man who he trusted and now has left them all to fend for themselves. He suddenly felt honor bound to stay with the rebel forces, to see them through no matter what transpired. They weren't ready to give up their cause just yet.

Many of the rebels deserted and crossed back into the United States abandoning the cause, leaving a remnant of two hundred men in shambles. Those who remained were made up of rag-tag volunteers, men who had no place else to go. Most of them were military deserters, adventurers, scoundrels, criminals and others who saw themselves as 'soldiers of fortune' and wanted to stay in it for whatever they could possibly get out of it.

After the dust settled the men elected Jack Mosby, one of the rebel volunteers who the men trusted, as the new General of the Rebel Army of the Baja. He was a deserter from the U. S. Marine Corp, but a fierce fighter with a sharp mind. He immediately began raising money for the cause by charging tourists to enter Tijuana and collecting fees from the casinos and bars to pay his men. One of Mosby's first orders to the rebels was concerning Ferris. The order was; 'if Ferris ever returns to Tijuana with his fancy ladies and convertible acting like he is in charge, he will be told to leave and never return, or he will be shot on sight.'

The news came to the Baja from the mainland of Mexico that Francisco Madero had defeated Dictator Diaz who was exiled to the country of France. In a few days the government of Mexico announced Madero would be the next President of Mexico. Madero's first order to the Mexican army was to move north and recapture Tijuana, rescue its citizens and destroy the insurrectionist movement.

When General Mosby heard the news he called his men together and explained the situation to them. He advised them that from this moment on, they would conduct themselves as soldiers and assigned each man regular duties. In his arrogance, Mosby was determined to stay with the cause feeling he could still be the victor to free the Baja. Ted felt honor bound to stay, he felt the cause was a just one and he actually had no other options to chose from. By this time, he was well known by the press and in a way he felt trapped, he was also known as one of the I.W.W. spokesmen, so decided to stay with General Mosby and officially joined the rebel forces, and strangely enough, he still thought it was a great exciting adventure.

The first night of General Mosby's command, Ted was assigned guard duty. As he walked his post he responded to a noise, "Halt, who goes there, advance and be recognized and give the password." General Mosby appeared out of the dark giving the password, and Ted was so surprised by seeing him, he forgot to call out the counter password, forcing the general to pull his gun.

"I'm sorry, sir, I guess I forgot the counter password."

"Well, son, I could have blown your head off, but I knew who you were. Conduct yourself as a soldier and man your post properly."

"Yes, sir." Ted was one scared soldier and he never forgot to call the password again.

General Mosby put his men through rugged training for the next few days to prepare them for the impending battle ahead of them, the battle of the Baja.

"The outcome depends on our victory, there is no turning back, we are in this together, up to our necks in this cause and we must be ready."

Chapter 63

THE FINAL PUSH

On a foggy day in June, 1911, Ted rode his newly purchased horse along with 'Company D' as they headed toward the Baja. But this time it was different for him, he was a soldier in the I.W.W. Liberal Army of the Baja which was led by a new commander, General John Mosby. They left from a place called Little Landers Colony, the last border area before crossing into the Baja of Mexico.

Ted had his forty five pistol in his holster and a Winchester rifle strapped to his saddle, and the entire company was equally armed. They were ready to face the battle. General Mosby carefully plotted his strategy for their final victory in the Baja. He would use the California and Arizona train as conveyance to move his troops into Mexico. They would commandeer the train in Tijuana and proceed toward Ensenada to intercept and overtake the Federal Mexican Army who were located somewhere between these two villages. This would finalize the grandiose victory of the Baja that Mosby had in his mind once and for all, the victory would be theirs. Mosby was convinced and he convinced the troops this final push would lead them to victory and they would soon be celebrating the takeover of the entire Baja for the working man of America.

The rebels watched as the California and Arizona freight train chugged into the outskirts of Tijuana and waited for Mosby's signal. When the train entered the yard and came to a full stop, he signaled the rebels to ride their horses alongside the cars on both sides of the track. Ted felt nervous, hoping all would go smoothly. The engineer was met by the rebel troops, their guns pointed directly at him, and he was ordered to remain at the controls. Mosby then climbed aboard and stuck his gun into the belly of the conductor and said,

"I'll take charge of your train, and you can tell the owners of the railroad they will get their train back when I get through with it."

"Yes, sir, you go right ahead," and the conductor quickly ran from the train and disappeared into the near-by woods.

The rebel soldiers, which came to a total of 150 men in all, boarded the last four cars, two flat cars and two boxcars, as Mosby took command of the train. He ordered his rebel Calvary soldiers of forty men to line up their horses on both sides of the track to escort the train out of Tijuana, and told the engineer to prepare to move the train out of the freight yard.

So it was on this date of June 22, 1911 that General Mosby captured the train as he had planned which was to intercept the Mexican forces to carry out his plan. The train moved slowly ahead out of Tijuana loaded with the rebel soldiers with the Calvary soldiers riding their horses on both sides of the tracks. *So far, so good,* Ted thought to himself. Just outside of town the train approached a narrow railroad bridge over a creek and the Calvary rebels had to break away from the track and ride their horses through the water to meet up with the train on the other side. But halfway across bursts of gun-fire suddenly cut loose on the train, the bullets zinging past their ears into the water with some hitting the train with loud explosive sounds. Everyone panicked by the sudden blasts and the horses began to scatter with some rearing up and throwing their riders into the water.

The rebels on the flat cars of the train returned fire toward the blasts which were coming from both sides of the hills above them, and Mosby realized at that moment the exact location of the Mexican Federal Army, his rebels were surrounded and he knew they were in the fight of their lives. His outrider scouts had failed to locate the enemy's position correctly and they had ridden directly into an ambush.

The train continued to move ahead, the bullets hitting the engine and ricocheting everywhere. It became obvious to the rebels that the Mexican army was using machine guns, and Mosby's heart sank, he knew right away they were out gunned. A rebel soldier suddenly cried out, "We have a man hit!" and Ted saw the horse leap up and dump the rider, both falling over dead into the water.

As they approached the creek embankment a burst of gunfire hit Ted's horse, causing it to rear up and fall backward. He was thrown from his horse onto the muddy creek bank hitting his head which dazed him momentarily. He managed to crawl out of the mud and pull himself up onto the bank. He ran beside the train until he could finally pull himself up on the ladder of the coal-car and swing aboard. The train began to slow down and, the engineer had had enough. He made the decision to throw on the brakes and stop the train to avoid going head long into the cross fire of the Mexican forces. But before he could throw it into reverse, a line of gunfire pelted the engine splintering the wooden cab. A bullet ricocheted off the cab hitting the engineer and he fell dead at the controls, his face blown apart beyond recognition.

The rebel soldiers were horrified and frozen for a moment, but not for long, the machine gunfire began to intensify. They were firing non-stop blasting the train and riddling the wooden cars. The men on the flat cars laid flat on their bellies unable to move and return fire.

Mosby shouted out, "Does anyone know how to get this train in reverse so we can get out of here!"

"Yes, sir, I do." Ted called out.

"Get yourself up here and get us out of this mess!"

Ted climbed over into the engine cab and hoped he could recall what he once knew about running a train. He told a soldier to shovel coal into the firebox as he quickly looked over the controls. He threw the lever, hoping it was the correct one, and the wheels screeched and the train slowly began to move backward. He breathed a sigh of relief as the train moved out of the range of fire.

The train backed up all the way to the border crossing but General Mosby knew his battle for freedom was over, much to his disappointment and sorrow. His hope to become the hero and leader for the cause of the working man of America and Mexico was in great jeopardy. The activities of the noble 'Wobbles' and the Liberal Party movement was at a standstill, much to their dismay, in fact it was going backward.

Mosby ordered his men to line up in columns of four, and he marched them through the village of Tijuana, back to the border station. They passed by a red painted livery barn, and they were shocked to see one of their fellow comrades hanging from the loft door. They all knew him by the name of Tom Cagel, and Ted shuddered and looked away as they passed, he was a young man only seventeen years old.

Ted couldn't get that image out of his mind, the thought *that could have been me*, kept running through his head. He could not keep from crying, he fought back the tears. All the rebels knew the young soldier had been ill treated by the irate citizens of Tijuana, and had been severely tortured before he was hung. Ted felt very lucky knowing the same thing could have happened to anyone of them, but they had survived.

At the border they were met by hundreds of spectators, San Diegans who were tired of the battles and all the gunfire and unrest. They shouted and hooted at the rebels, throwing rocks and dried horse dung as they marched past, some hitting Ted in the neck. Even some nicely dressed ladies attempted to spit on them as they passed by, he couldn't help from feeling humiliated.

Mosby ordered his men to form a single line and lay down their weapons. He thanked each one for being a good soldier for the cause, and then ordered them to march single file into the U. S. Customs building and surrender to the U. S. Military. They marched as they were ordered and proceeded through the gates of the Customs House where they were taken into custody. The Customs officials ordered them to march to a camp about an eighth of a mile beyond the Customs House. During the march some of the rebel soldiers, mostly the Mexicans who had joined the cause, tried to escape and merge with the crowd or into the surrounding woods. Some were shot and killed, but a few made it to safety.

The insurrectionists were handcuffed as they arrived in the camp, the reporters from the San Diego newspapers waited eagerly at the scene to flash pictures and write their reports of the humiliating defeat and surrender of the event for the late editions of their papers. They wrote:

'Many San Diegans were dressed in their finery as they huddled on the hillside and at the U. S. Customs building to watch the march of the insurrectionists and their leader General Mosby as they surrendered in defeat. It all became an American side show as many onlookers took advantage of the chaos and engaged in looting, while others took photographs to sell their pictures for postcards and books.'

Ted's head was swimming, he could not believe what was happening. Everything was happening so quickly, and all they had fought for was falling apart right before them and he was facing military arrest. Looking back he realized his decision to join the rebels was probably a bad one. He had been taken in by men, mainly Big Bill Hayward, and he knew the approach to solve the working man's problems was wrong, that their plan opposed the laws of his country.

His hands were tied behind him, and they were packed into trucks so tightly he could hardly breathe. They was taken to Fort Rosecrans Military camp, a military prison where they were not even told what the charges would be, but in his heart he knew.

The military processed the prisoners and escorted them to their cells. Ted sat on his narrow bunk, his head in his hands, and at that moment he realized he was no longer free, and the cause he had fought for was gone, everything seemed so confusing. His prison number was 123 and was printed on his back, and to his dismay he had to answer to his number instead of his name. He was now at the mercy of his own government, the country he loved, and imprisoned as an insurrectionist and an anarchist, how was that even possible, he thought.

Chapter 64

PRISON

Ted's initiation into the Rosecrans prison made his morning memorable, but not good memories. He couldn't even compare it to his previous jail experience when he was incarcerated back in Georgia on the work gang for thirty days when he was only sixteen years old. This time he was in a real prison. They were all thrown together into one large room with multiple bunks, the food was like slop, Ted thought, and the prisoners carried it into the food hall in big wooden buckets and gave each man a bowl and a spoon. The food looked like rice porridge with small bits of meat and they couldn't tell what kind of meat it was.

It was tough, the Marine guards were right down mean, they pushed the inmates around, seemingly for the fun of it. They would hit them with their baton or sometimes slap their faces, just for the slightest infraction or what they deemed an infraction. Ted had only been there less than twenty-four hours and had been punched twice, knocked down once, and for what, he didn't really know. He wondered if they treated their fellow marines with the same treatment, or was it just for civilians? He wasn't a marine or a deserter, so he wondered why they put him in a military prison in the first place.

Rumors were circulating among the prisoners that they had violated U. S. laws by actively participating in a foreign war and they may possibly be turned over to the Mexican government or go to prison in the U. S. for those charges. The true facts, as Ted saw it, they had joined in a civil action against the sovereign state of Mexico, and he hoped against hope that if he had to go to prison that he would be in the states, and not in Mexico. Mexican prisons were brutal he had heard, but so far no charges had been formally lodged against them, they were in the hands of the U. S. army.

After several days of prison life he struck up a conversation with a fellow prisoner named Joe Dillon.

"I know you don't recognize me, but I saw you climb upon the train engine the other day and take charge of that train, and I personally want to thank you. I wouldn't have given you two cents that any of us would get out of there alive if you hadn't done what you did," Joe expressed.

"Thanks, Joe, it sure didn't look very good for us, I have never been so scared in all my life," Ted replied.

"I passed the General's cell, you know they put him into a separate one, but I couldn't see him, it was too dark," Joe told Ted.

"Hope he is all right."

"What do you think they will do with us?" Joe asked.

"I couldn't even guess," Ted pondered.

"I haven't the slightest idea," he sighed as he laid back on his bunk, hoping to get some sleep.

The next morning at breakfast, such as it was, General Mosby joined Ted and Joe at their table.

"Good to see you, General," they both stood and greeted him. While they ate Mosby told them about his life. He was a Marine deserter and he could be severely prosecuted by the U. S., probably sentenced to a federal prison for twenty or thirty years. He told them he was planning his escape and that he would rather die than be in prison for life.

"What do you think they will do with us?" Ted asked Mosby.

"I really don't know," he told them.

"But you and the others are not deserters from the military like I am, so they may not do much with you. They don't have much against you for anything you did in the states. I really don't think Mexico will ask for your extradition back there either, at least I hope not. If they did that, the Mexican government would probably shoot you all."

He went on to say he was very concerned about his fellow military deserters and himself, they would definitely be imprisoned in a Federal penitentiary, probably at Fort Riley, Kansas.

"I will not be taken as a prisoner, they will have to kill me first, I will try to escape," Mosby went on to say. Ted shuddered when he heard him say that, he knew the military would do just that.

A few days later as Ted sat on his bunk, Mosby came by and handed him a note. He was surprised when he read it, it was a discharge document from the Liberal Army of the Baja. and it read:

To whom it my concern:

This is to certify that on this day, June 22, 1911
Theodore E. Walters is honorably discharged from the
Liberal Army of the Baja, California.

Enlisted: May 28, 1911

Service: Honest and Truthful Character: Excellent
Remarks: Skilled horseman, a good scout, a good shot.
and cool and nervy soldier under fire.

Engagement: Battle of Tijuana June 22, 1911

Signed: T. J. Laflin J. B. Mosby Adj. Gen. 2nd Div. Gen.
Comm. 2nd Div. Liberal Army of the Baja

Ted smiled as he read it.

"Thank you, sir," Ted said as he stood up and saluted to him; he personally liked the man.

"Do you have any more thoughts on what they will do with us?" Ted asked.

"I really don't have any idea, Ted. But I doubt seriously if they will hold you very long," he said to Ted with some encouragement in his voice.

"Thank you again, sir, I really appreciate this document."

"That's the least I can do, I appreciate your service to the cause. Thank you, and I hope you have a good life after all this. But take my advice, stay out of Mexico!" He laughed as he was escorted back to his cell.

After about three weeks in prison they were called to attention by the prison guards. They all stood and one prison guard shouted out.

"Step forward as I call your name."

Ted stepped forward when his name was called along with the other rebels.

"You are free to go," the guard announced to them. The gates were opened and they walked out of Fort Rosecrans Military Prison with no explanation and no charges held against them. Ted couldn't believe it, no hearing or judgment was given, they were free to go. He walked out of the prison with nothing but the clothes he had been wearing for over three weeks and the hand written discharge document from the Liberal Army of the Baja.

As he walked into San Diego he thought about his parents and family back in Deer Creek and decided not to tell them what had happened. He thought unless he wrote and told them, they would never hear such news. Deer Creek didn't have a newspaper and his parents didn't have a radio, at least they didn't when he left there.

When he got into the city he went to the U. S. Grant Hotel. No one from the I.W.W. office was there, he was told that the office had closed down, and Big Bill had apparently left the area.

He had no job to go to and the city was settling back into a more peaceful place, only a remnant of the trouble makers were still present. He saw a newspaper in the rack with headlines that read; "Wobblie Rebels Numbering about One Hundred—Released."

This news did not set well with the San Diegans, as the article stated, 'they were turned loose on the citizens of San Diego which is a dirty trick.'

Ted decided to leave town, there was nothing left for him here. As he walked to the railroad station to catch a train out of San Diego, he tried to put some sanity in what he had just experienced. He knew the Workers of the World Union were the real culprits behind all this misguided mess with the Baja, and he realized the cause was only a pipe-dream. Its promoters had totally abandoned it, separating themselves and their names from it all, or at least they tried.

Ted crawled up into a railroad car at the yards and for the first time in days he began to relax. He was moving away from this chapter in his life, but to what and where, he wasn't sure. He picked up some newspapers in the boxcar to catch up on the worlds' news, and to his surprise the papers were full of the account of the San Diego-Tijuana invasion of the Baja and the aftermath. The account written by one reporter was very interesting, and Ted was glad to catch up on all the news, especially what was said about the battle that took place in the Baja.

He learned that Mosby had been shot and killed as he attempted to escape while he was being transported to Fort Riley, Kansas, for his sentence of life in prison. Ted remembered his words, 'I won't go to prison, I will die first!' He shivered as if he were cold when he read it, he had ridden side by side with this man. Those words kept reverberating through his head.

He also learned that Pryce, Magon and Ferris were indicted, but the charges were dropped against Pryce and Ferris. Pryce went to Hollywood and played in several cowboy movies and then joined the British Army.

Ferris had resigned from the San Diego Exposition and capitalized on his so-called notoriety by playing in stage plays, one which was called, 'Being the Man from Mexico.' Magon, the money man behind all the plans and his brother Enrique were found guilty of violating the neutrality laws and sent to prison.

Ted felt relieved that he was moving away from San Diego, and he began to question his judgment about all that occurred. He wondered why and how he allowed himself to be a part of this complicated mess he was in. He remembered reading in the papers, 'thirty rebels were left dead on the field as the Mexican soldiers pushed the invaders back north across the border.'

He felt very fortunate to be alive, he was exhausted, both mentally and physically, as he prepared his bed in the boxcar for the night. The rhythmic sound of the wheels on the track as the train moved through the night gave him the sense of comfort and peace. He was glad to be moving away from it all, and he was finally lulled to sleep.

Chapter 65

NEW OPPORTUNITIES

The freight train arrived in Los Angeles a few hours later and with some rest Ted was ready for a new start. He jumped off the boxcar, hoping no one noticed him, and walked across the tracks of the Southern Pacific railroad.

He located the dispatcher's office and walked to the information window to inquire about a telegraph operators job.

"Have a seat, sir, someone will see you in a few minutes."

Ted took a seat, thinking that sounded hopeful, and in a few minutes a gentleman came out of his office and introduced himself as the Chief Dispatcher.

"My name is Mark Alley, I understand you're looking for work as a telegraph operator."

"Yes, sir, I am," Ted replied, feeling somewhat embarrassed about his clothes and appearance.

"Tell me about your experience in the work," he said to Ted. Ted related his experience and his present situation, he had come out of some 'bad luck' and was ready for a new life and job.

"Sounds like you have had some very good experience in the field, come on in and let us test you and you can fill out a job application." He invited Ted into the office, and turned him over to one of his operators for testing.

"Good luck," he told Ted.

"Let me know how he does, John."

"Yes, sir, Mr. Alley. Come on inside, Ted. I'll send you some messages and I'll receive some from you. We'll test how well you know the code and interpret the message."

Ted finished the rigorous test hoping he remembered everything correctly. John gave him an application to fill out *and that was very encouraging*, Ted thought.

In a few minutes, Mr. Alley called him into his office.

"You're a pretty good operator," he said. Ted sighed in relief.

"I'm sorry, but I don't have anything open in a depot station that I can send you to right now."

Ted's heart sank for a moment until he heard Mr. Alley say, "but, I can sure use you in Bisbee, Arizona. I have a work-train crew in need of an operator. You'll be assigned to the work crew to keep our dispatchers informed of where the crews are working and the condition of the tracks so our trains can move safely and smoothly through the area."

Ted listened intently, it sounded interesting so far. Alley continued.

"Our beginning operators are paid forty-five cents an hour, hope that's suitable." Ted nodded in the positive.

"I hope you can climb a telegraph pole, you look strong enough. You'll need to climb them at times to connect the wires to the line at different locations when the work-train moves from one spot to another."

"I can do that," Ted reassured him.

"When we have a regular station assignment available you will be given the chance to bid on it. You know seniority is what guides our job assignments. I can also use you as a relief operator, relieving vacations and sickness's in our division. You will be travelling up and down the entire division, does all this sound appealing to you?"

"Oh, yes, sir," Ted told him.

"Sir, I'm flat broke, how can I get to Bisbee?" Ted asked.

"I will give you a pass and the railroad will advance you two dollars that will be deducted from your first pay check. You will be guaranteed forty-eight hours a week, and you will be paid once a month, no overtime pay however, straight hourly pay. Room and board is furnished on the work train, that's where you will be living. So, Ted, do you want the job?"

"Yes, sir," Ted smiled.

"Go to the cashier and get your advance pay and the train pass to Bixby. I expect you to be on the job Monday morning, that's just two days from now. Good luck!"

Ted shook his hand and thanked him for the opportunity. He crossed the street to the diner and had the "blue plate special," which cost him twenty-two cents, his first meal in two days. When he finished, he hung around the station to wait for the passenger train to Bisbee.

Around eleven o'clock at night, Ted arrived at the Bisbee station. The station agent unloaded the mail car onto a cart and locked it up in a secure room. He turned off the lights at the station and prepared to go home. Ted introduced himself to the agent and he was to wait for the work crew foreman to take him to the work train site in the morning.

"Oh, yes, we heard you were coming in, my name in John Weaver, welcome to Arizona!" He said as he shook hands with Ted.

"Pleased to meet, you, sir," Ted replied.

"I have to close the station down now, but if you're going to a hotel, the closest one is across the tracks. But let me warn you, it's a terrible flea bag of a place. I'm not sure you wouldn't be better off sleeping on the mail cart here at the station, you're welcome to do that. I'll unload the mail cart for you and pull it out here next to the building. It's a nice warm night and I don't think anyone will bother you, I'm going to camp out with my wife and kids in our back yard tonight. But, if you prefer you can go to the hotel, it will cost you thirty five cents and you may have to share the bed with another person, it's strictly up to you."

"If you don't mind I'll just sleep here on the mail cart, it sounds like the best deal, and thank you so much," Ted said.

He prepared the mail cart for Ted and parked it alongside the building.

"I'll be leaving now, good night."

"By the way," Ted asked.

"is there an all night beanery close by."

"Sure is, just a block away, I go right past it on my way home. I'll walk with you."

When they arrived at the diner, the agent wished him good luck and said, "The day agent gets in early to open up, hope you have a restful night and welcome to the job."

"Good night, and thanks for your help," Ted said as he stepped into the diner. He ordered his usual, a cheeseburger, a cup of coffee, and a piece of pie. When he finished he walked back to the station, crawled up on the mail cart, put his jacket under his head for a pillow and fell fast asleep.

Chapter 66

RAILROADING AGAIN

"**W**ake up, sir," the foreman said as he shook Ted's shoulder. "Are you Mr. Walters?"

"Yes, sir, that's me," Ted responded.

"I'm the foreman of the work crew, my name is Frank Rhodes and I have orders to take you to the work site with me. Are you awake?"

"Yes, sir, I'm ready to go," Ted said as he stood up blinking his eyes trying to get fully awake.

"Let's step into the station and get a cup of coffee, I imagine you can use one," he chuckled.

"Sounds good to me. Is there a place I can wash up?" he asked Frank.

"Out back close to the back door there's a water pump next to the outdoor facility, I'll wait for you inside."

He poured Ted a cup of coffee and introduced him to Charlie, the telegraph operator. He waved hello to Ted and kept working, he was receiving the train orders from the clicking telegraph machine.

"Guess Charlie is too busy to chew the fat with us," the foreman said. So drink up, we have about nine miles to go out to the work site. We have a hand-car to pump our way out to join the crew. Hope you have a strong back. By the way, do you have a suitcase, Ted?"

"No," Ted responded.

"What you see is what you get."

"We have some extra overalls at the work-site, you can put them on when we get there. One of our workers recently died and left his clothes and his shaving mug and razor, and I know he wouldn't mind if you used them."

"No, no, that's great. I'm thankful to have them. Right now all I have is what I'm wearing. I fell on a little bad luck recently and lost everything, so beggars can't be choosers," Ted said with a smile.

They went out to put the hand-car on the track.

Frank said, "You lift that end up and I'll get the front, and we'll set it up on the track and make our trek out to the work site."

They lifted it onto the track and Frank instructed him on how the hand car works. In the middle of the car was the hand pump, and Frank got on board and told Ted to push the car to start it to roll, and when it started rolling, he began to pump.

When it was rolling at a good pace Frank yelled, "Jump on, Ted, let's go!"

He jumped on, all out of breath and wringing wet with sweat. He rested for a moment and then helped with the pumping. They came to an incline and the car came to a complete stop. They jumped off and pushed it to the top of the crest and then jumped back on and rode it on the downhill. The pumping was easier for the next few miles, and Ted even had a break from pumping to watch the panorama of the countryside as they rolled along the track.

It took about two hours to get to the work area. There were four boxcars sitting off on the side track, and Frank explained the boxcars were their work and living quarters. One was the kitchen and dining room, one was the office, telegraph and equipment center, and the others were the living and sleeping quarters for the crew.

"You will be working in the telegraph center which is also my office and our sleeping quarters, our bunks are separate from the work crew. It's not first class, but that bunk feels really comfortable after a day's work," Frank explained to him.

"This looks fine to me," Ted told him. He was just grateful to have the job.

"We have a water tanker coming in today, we use lots of water for showers after a hard day's work, a shower always feels like a great reward. We also have a place to wash clothes, so our water supply is very important to us in this desert land."

Frank pointed out the telegraph pole.

"You'll need to climb up to connect the wires to get on the main telegraph line. The information manual on our work procedures is in the office on your work desk, it tells you all you need to know and who to contact. Are you ready to go?"

"Okay, I'm ready to get started," Ted said.

"I know it will take some time to get adjusted to everything, I'm sure."

"I'm sure. By the way, I'm not your boss. I'm responsible for the track crews only. I will depend on you to receive all the information we need to know to keep in touch with the trains coming and going so we can do our work."

"Yes, sir. I'm sure we'll get along well. I'll sure try to do my best," he reassured Frank.

"Ok, help me set the handcar off the tracks if you will, and we'll get started."

They set the car aside.

"I don't see any work crews, where are they?" Ted wondered out loud.

"Oh, they are up the line a short distance, you'll see them this evening, you can get yourself set up and I'll walk up there to check on their progress. We'll be in this area for a few more days before we finish this job and then we will move on to another location."

"The evening meal is when the men all meet at the kitchen and dining car; everybody is hungry and ready for supper. "Frank told him.

"Looks like you eat pretty good here," Ted commented.

"Yes, we got ourselves a great cook, you will die and think you're in heaven when you taste his soppapias, they are beyond belief. Jose is our cook and he makes up some of the best Mexican food you ever tasted."

"I have never heard of 'sopa,' what did you call it?" Ted laughed.

"Tacos and refried beans is my only knowledge of Mexican food."

"Jose also makes the best biscuits you ever locked your lips around, just wait, you'll see," Frank said smacking his lips.

"I do like good biscuits," Ted chimed in.

After they had a bite of lunch, Ted gathered his equipment to climb up the pole to connect the wires. He read the instructions and was ready to tackle the job, however a little reluctant, climbing poles was something he had never done before. He got the safety belt and the ankle spurs for his boots out of the equipment room, and put the spurs on his boots.

He looked up at the top of the pole to prepare his mind for the climb and he picked up the belt as he walked over to the pole. Before he started climbing he decided to take off his shirt, the temperature was getting hot and he didn't want his shirt to get sweaty, it was the only one he had with him. He placed the belt around his waist and secured it around the pole and started climbing. So far so good, he thought. But, about halfway up he made the mistake of looking down and the height gave him a wave of fear.

He kept telling himself, "Don't look down, just keep climbing." He dug the spur in the pole on the next step much too hard and had difficulty pulling it loose. He struggled to free himself, he twisted and turned and then realized he was beginning to panic. Through his struggle to free his foot, the spur was digging deeper into the pole.

He wanted to yell out for help, but he knew no one was around except the cook in the boxcar, and he wouldn't be able to hear him. He paused and took a deep breath to settle his panicked fears before he started moving his boot back and forth to loosen the spur. Then he made one giant effort, but he pulled so hard his whole body reared back and he lost his balance. He did free his boot but his body slammed against the pole bruising his knee, and leaving him dangling in the air upside down.

He was stunned for a moment but realized the safety belt had kept him from falling. He pulled on the belt to pull himself upright, and finally managed to pry his feet against the pole to help turn his body around. Thank heaven for the safety belt, that thought kept running through his mind. He was soaked with sweat and he paused again to catch his breath and calm his nerves and to decide what to do next. Should he go back down or continue to climb? The overwhelming desire was to go back down and quit the job, but he decided he had to learn how to do it, this was his job, at least he knew he could depend on the safety belt. He had just learned a big lesson, to set his spur enough to hold him, but not to hinder him.

Ted let the thin desert air fill his lungs, he took a deep breath of hot air and proceeded to climb the rest of the way up. Using his safety belt to hold him, he used his hands to clip the telegraph wires to the main line. That was easy enough, he thought, the most difficult thing was climbing the pole and conquering his fear.

He scanned the scene of the countryside from the top of the pole before climbing down. The sun was bearing down and he could see an incredible distance in all directions. The mountain ranges looked majestic as they rose from the horizon in the far distance, and he could see the dried sage brush bushes dance across the valley floor blown by the wind, the dry desert shimmering like water in the sun.

He watched a jack rabbit running hither and yon from one sage brush perch to another, squatting silently under them to keep from being seen by a predator hunting for food. He thought about how all things in nature seemed to balance, and he wondered what the rabbits ate here in the desert. He remembered how he chased the rabbits out of their garden when he was a kid. There certainly weren't any gardens in this land.

In the sky Ted saw a large beautiful American eagle swooping across the desert floor, its eyes peeled to spot food to eat. Suddenly, it made a quick turn, dipping one wing and headed downward. With one swoop it had a rabbit in its claws, all happening in a blink of an eye, or so it seemed. It flew upward, climbing over Ted's head, apparently heading to its nest to eat its reward.

He was fascinated by all the cactus varieties that grew wild in the desert. He was especially impressed by the tall majestic ones called Saguaro, some standing twelve feet tall with thorny branches like arms sticking out as if they were directing traffic throughout the desert.

He wondered why anyone wanted to live in this "godforsaken," hot country; it was like living in a furnace. Actually not many people did live here directly in the desert, except maybe some old prospector miners who came looking for gold and riches.

The wind blew one way and would suddenly change and blow the opposite direction. He could see heat waves shimmering on the desert floor and saw what people called devil dust dancers, which were caused by a sudden whirlwind of dust created by a sudden change of the wind, which twirled across the barren landscape of the desert floor from one side to the other. Suddenly, there were two dust devils dancing at the same time. Ted thought it was awesome to watch.

After taking in the bird's eye view of the surrounding desert and mountain ranges he began to carefully climb down, making sure his footing was just right. He made it down without anymore incidents and began to walk back to the office on his very shaky and weak legs. He felt sore all over his body, but he proceeded with his work to make the final connection to the telegraph line in the office.

The telegraph works from a battery system which is a large glass jar filled with a chemical solution, copper sulfate, with wires made of copper and zinc immersed in the solution. Ted placed the wires in the solution which produced the power he uses to send his messages.

To send a message the operator presses the key, a quick press is the dot and a longer press is the dash. The alphabet is turned into a code system using different dots and dashes to make up each letter of the message that is being sent. Ted could read about forty words a minute by just listening to the coded dots and dashes, so now he was anxious to try it all to see if it worked.

After he completed the hook up it was ready for the test. He sent a message to the Chief Inspector in Yuma to let him know they were now on line and fully operating, he hoped. He sat back in his chair and waited for a response. It wasn't but a few moments until a response came, the telegraph key was clicking away. It was from Chief Inspector Amos, CIA, which was his code letters, to work train operator, WTO, which was Ted's code letters. He interpreted the coded message which read; 'Good afternoon, nice to have you aboard. My name is Matt Amos, hope to meet you in person soon. Message clearly received. Welcome aboard.'

Ted was relieved the connection went well, even better than he had hoped, he still had the magic touch, he thought to himself, but his self praise was short lived. He noticed how red his arms and shoulders were, they were beginning to sting and he was sure his back looked the same. He began to wonder how he could have been so stupid to expose his skin to the unrelenting sun of the desert, he was only thinking of trying to cool himself rather than protecting himself.

He looked around for a first-aid kit, but he couldn't find anything to sooth his burning body. Frank came in from the day's work and took one look at his sunburned operator.

"Goodnight, Ted, what did you do to yourself?"

"Is there anything around here to put on my skin?" Ted begged.

"I'm afraid we don't have much to help you but some baking soda and maybe some axle grease. You need to take a soda bath to help take some of the sting out."

Frank helped him fill the old metal tub with water and poured a whole box of baking soda into it. Ted gladly crawled in, hoping to get some relief. It helped some but the blisters on his back were getting bigger and bigger and more painful. He spread some axle grease on his face, arms, and back and put on his long sleeve shirt and trousers to go with Frank to eat supper and meet the work crew.

"Attention everyone," Frank said as he stood up.

"I want you to meet our new telegraph operator, Ted Walters. He just arrived this morning while you were out on the job, so introduce yourself when you get the chance and welcome him, but please don't ask him how he got that beautiful sunburn or pat him on the back. "Frank laughed. "But we are glad he is here, he will make our work much easier with a better communication system."

"The Road Master will be here tomorrow to test him and you know how stiff the test is for the operators, so he will be studying the rule book this evening. Wish him luck, just don't forget and pat him on his back." Frank chuckled again.

After supper that evening the men all sat around, some visiting and playing cards, while others sat outside after sundown hoping to cool off, smoke, and tell tall tales to one another. Most of the men were Mexicans and their families were still in Mexico, and they would tell stories about their families and how much they missed them, and of course they would send their wages back home to care for their family.

At night most of the men camped out and slept under the stars, the boxcars were just too hot to rest well. Ted joined them and took his bedding outside, and as he laid there he was fascinated as he looked up at the vast sky. It was like looking at the large expanse of heaven, brilliant with glitter, and it felt so close to him that he could reach out and touch the stars. He saw some falling stars speed across the vastness of the sky as if it were a private extravaganza meant for him alone.

The larger planet stars rose in a straggling line to illuminate the blackness like they were an old friend. First, there was Venus followed in regal style by the sublime Saturn and Mercury, and then Jupiter and Mars.

Ted watched in awe and was beginning to feel a part of all the grandeur of the heavens as the symphony of light widened around him, and it seemed the stars bent down close to him as if fireflies and jewels were invading his space.

But his trance of rapture was soon interrupted by mosquitoes and other pesky bugs that buzzed around his head, so many he couldn't count them. They were annoying, not only did they interrupt his rapture with the stars, but he knew they would interrupt his sleep as well. He gave up, he picked up his bedding and moved back inside about midnight, the bugs and mosquitoes won the battle. He noticed that all the men who slept outside had mosquito netting and he knew he would have to get some if he wanted to sleep out under that stars.

The next morning as he drank his coffee relaxing under a shade tree he noticed a motor car coming down the track at a pretty fast clip, he couldn't believe what he was seeing. It was the Road Master, he was on a motorized hand car which surprised Ted, he had never seen one before or even knew they existed.

When it came to a stop the Road Master introduced himself.

"I'm John Weaver, are you Ted Walters?"

Ted answered in the affirmative.

"Would you help me set this car off the track, I sure would appreciate it," John asked.

"This is the first motor driven side car I've seen, I didn't know there were any," Ted told him.

"You are looking at the very first one, they had me test it out to see how it worked and if I liked it. You don't have to pump it, it sure saves a fellows back. It definitely will make me more efficient and will also cut costs, I can get over tracks faster and get more work done."

"Well, Ted, you know why I'm here, I'll give you the rule book test this morning." Ted had studied and reviewed the rule book, and knew most of it by memory, so he felt prepared to take the test. They met in the office boxcar, and the first question the Road Master asked him was 'what is the definition of a train'? Ted replied as per the rule book, 'a train is a car or a series of cars coupled together, with or without cars displaying markers or for which markers are displayed.'

Frank spent the next two hours grilling Ted, and when they finished he had Ted sign his card, telling him he 'passed with flying colors.'

He took a box out his lunch box and gave it to Ted.

"I brought your railroad watch from the company jeweler, you are required to have one, you know."

"Yes, sir," Ted answered.

"I was instructed to collect eighteen dollars from you or have you sign this contract for twenty-four dollars," he said.

Ted was a bit surprised.

"I know I need the watch, but why do I have to pay twenty-four dollars for an eighteen dollar watch?"

"There is an interest of six dollars for finance charges, the jewelry store will take out one dollar a month for the next twenty four months from your paycheck, unless you elect to pay for it in cash."

"Thanks, where do I sign," Ted said.

Frank notified the foreman and the Chief Dispatcher in Yuma that Ted was all set to receive all work orders, he was now clear and approved for the job.

He told Ted about an incident that happened on another line.

"Keep a watchful eye, Ted, when you're standing at the side of the track handing up the train orders. We had a recent incident that you need to know about where the operator agent was hit by a loose metal strap off a boxcar which struck him and decapitated him. Don't get to close to the train without making sure it is safe."

'Yes, sir, thanks for the warning, I'll keep an eye out for such things."

"I brought some local newspapers and magazines for you, please pass them around to the men, I know it's difficult to get papers and reading materials out here. I know some of the men can't read English, or read at all, but there are lots of pictures in the magazines they can look at, even some pictures of pretty girls."

"Thanks," Ted smiled.

"Ted helped Frank load his car back on the track, they shook hands and he put-putted down the track headed for his next destination.

Ted telegraphed the Chief Dispatcher in Yuma to inform him he was checked out and ready to receive any and all train orders and messages, and he was glad to be fully approved.

He received a message in return stating: 'Congratulations, your office is now open for official business. The shift dispatcher will inform you of all train orders he has for your area, but you are to notify him whenever the train passes your station regardless of whether you have a hand up for him or not.'

Ted returned a message. 'Yes, I gotcha, sir, over and out. WTO.'

He was glad to be on line and prepared the next train order to be handed up to each train that passed. The message he prepared contained the condition of the tracks, and 'the train must slow to quarter speed to receive the message, and to slow at pole number 397 to 420 to ten miles an hour.' Everything was working smoothly and Ted felt good about it all, except for his sun burned back, of course.

After work Ted picked up a newspaper to read that evening. He noticed an article about an insurrectionist group that was causing lots of problems there in Arizona and Texas areas. The headline was 'The Dogs of War.'

Ted was curious to read it, anxious to find out what it was all about. Before he left to return to his living quarters he went to the privy, an outdoor one which consisted of a large box with two holes. It had a dusty canvas hanging over a line to protect the user from the blowing dust and to provide some privacy from the passenger trains that passed by. However, the other side was wide open looking out in the far regions of the desert, only the prairie dogs and wild life could see.

It was an extremely hot day as he sat there, often times Ted had heard, when the men went to use the privy, they would have to chase the vultures away. They would grab a rock to throw at them so they would scatter. He sat there looking at the newspaper and noticed the news wasn't much different than several months ago. The local Mexicans were up in arms because of the threat by the Gringos who wanted to invade and annex the five Mexican states into the United States. It told about a Mexican bandit, named Poncho Viva, who wanted to attack the U. S. and was making threats of raiding and attacking various towns along the border.

The American Army was still on the Mexican border to protect against smuggling of arms, and another article told of the murder of the newly elected President of Mexico, Francisco Madero, who had liberated Mexico from the despised Dictator Diaz. It seems that the Chief General of the Mexican Army, who Madero had personally appointed, took matters into his own hands and had the newly elected President assassinated. Ted felt sad about Madero, a President who he felt was a real hero and was for the people. It confirmed his thoughts that not much has really changed, and brought back memories in his mind, the memories of him riding with General Mosby and the Army to Free the Baja as they tried to overthrow the Mexican Government just a few weeks ago. His conscious started bothering him as he thought about it.

The article of Madero's death also described the attitude of the people of Mexico, many citizens were fearful as innocent civilians were being shot down in the streets by the Generals of the army, who were acting against the new President and his democratic ideas.

Nothing had changed, the Insurrectionists were still attacking and the government was responding, and as Ted thought about it, all of this was what caused him to be thrown in prison.

The whole southwest was in turmoil, conflict, and war. He was glad he had escaped all that, but was sad it was still occurring. He vowed to himself never to get involved in such causes ever again.

The day came at work when the foreman announced to Ted to notify the Chief Dispatcher they were finished with the track repair in this location and were ready to move to a new assignment.

Chapter 67

THE CARNIVAL

Ted received a message from the Chief Inspector in Yuma addressed to WTO. "Disconnect and terminate your present location. An engine will be dispatched to arrive at 7:15 a.m. to move your work train and crew to your next location, Post No. 1401, for trestle repairs. Work orders will arrive later today. Thanks, over and out. CIA."

The engine arrived right on time the next morning and they were packed up and ready to go. The engineer said.

"We'll get you guys on down the line, your next location is near El Paso, Texas, right near the Rio Grande river."

After several hours they entered the out-skirts of El Paso and Ted guessed the population was probably a couple thousand people, and the town looked old with mostly dirt streets and horse traffic with very few cars. There were lots of saloons, several shops and stores, and a large Catholic Church that stood prominently in the center of town. Otherwise, nothing looked very inviting or interesting except he noticed they were setting up a carnival that would be in town for the next several days. *Good*, Ted thought, it would give them something to do during their off hours, and it reminded him of the carnival he attended as a kid in Oklahoma.

They set up their work station on the side track and waited for orders from their headquarters in Yuma, and when the orders came they were notified of a delay in their work, the trestle repair materials and equipment would not be available for several days. Frank told the men they would have a few days of rest until the materials arrived and they were free to do as they wished until the orders came in, but to check in each day until further notice.

Ted and several other men went into town to watch them set up the carnival which was scheduled to open the next day. They were setting up large tents, and even had an elephant to help pull the ropes tight to anchor the tent in place with large stakes. The merry-go-round was being assembled, as well as the Ferris-wheel and all of the other children's rides. On one tent was a large picture of a bearded lady with a sign that read, 'Come on in and see the bearded lady.' Another picture showed 'the fattest man in the world,' and another, a picture of a man swallowing a sword, Ted almost gagged as he saw it. This tent advertises all the freak shows, he thought, and other tents advertised more side shows which included 'human and animal freaks' and dancing girls.

The next morning Frank took Ted to the train depot in El Paso to notify the agent they had arrived and were waiting for work orders, and that they would coordinate their work with the station to keep them informed of their progress. The agent confirmed that they had been notified by the Yuma office that the work train and crew would be arriving, and the work site would receive their water supply from the depot water source.

Some of the Mexican crew workers decided to go into Mexico for a few days instead of hanging around the work-site or visiting the town and carnival. Frank reminded them they needed to have their immigration papers in order so they could re-enter the country to return to work, and for them to keep in touch until the work orders came in.

The next day Ted and Frank decided to go to the carnival and take in all the sights. It brought back many memories for Ted when he was a small boy, and there was one time he remembered distinctly. He had saved his money for weeks to ride the Ferris-wheel and get some cotton candy and he remembered how excited he was. A carnival man who was extremely friendly yelled out to him, 'Hey, kid, ya' got any money?' He recalled how naive he was and how proudly he showed him his dollar and a half, all in quarters, that he had saved up.

'I can help you double your money, son,' the man said to him.

'That would be great, mister,' Ted replied fully trusting him.

'All you have to do is put a quarter on the table and I'll match it, and I will put a pea under one of these three cups. I'll shuffle them all around and you must keep a sharp eye on the one I put the pea under, then all you have to do is tell me where the pea is hiding. If you guess right the two quarters are yours, but if you don't guess right, then I win. Now, if you watch very carefully you will know where the pea is.'

Ted handed the quarter up to the man and he shuffled the cups all around the table, and Ted guessed right. 'Hey, boy, you are right, you're really good, kid,' the man praised him. 'You want to try it again and double your money?' He proudly gave the man both quarters thinking he could win a whole dollar, that seemed easy enough. But this time the carnival man shuffled the cups a little faster and he lost. 'That was just a streak of bad luck, kid, put up your dollar again and this time I know you'll win two whole dollars, but remember, keep your eye on the cup with the pea.'

'I don't know, mister, I want to get some cotton candy and ride the Ferris-wheel, what if I lose?' Ted remembered asking him.

'Yeah, you could lose it, but you could also win and have two dollars. I have never seen a boy with a sharper eye than you have, you picked right the first time, didn't you? I have a hunch you will win easily this time if you just try once more.'

He was convinced and handed him the dollar. 'Now watch close, kid,' he said as he shuffled the cups much faster. Ted guessed wrong and his money was all gone, and he remembered how he cried all the way home because he didn't get to ride the Ferris-wheel or get cotton candy. He told his big brothers how he lost all his money and how they later recruited a couple of friends, jumped the con man and beat him to a pulp. At the time that really didn't matter to Ted, he just remembered how disappointed he was when he didn't get to do the things he really wanted to do, and all he did was watch the other kids having fun. Ted laughed at himself and thought it was funny how things run through your mind, maybe it was because he had no money to spend this time either, he was waiting for his first pay check.

He looked up and saw a sign which read, 'Fighters wanted, apply at ring side.' The barker shouted over a megaphone.

"Hear ye, hear ye, win ten dollars if you can stand up in a fight for three minutes with the toughest man on the planet, Tom Murphy, who is known from coast to coast. He is well known for knocking out his opponents in the first round in less than three minutes, so step right up if you are brave enough to accept the challenge."

Without thinking Ted raised his hand to volunteer and Frank was shocked.

"Are you crazy, Ted, did you see the muscles on that ape? He could kill you with one blow."

"Well, I guess I better not let him hit me then," Ted smiled.

"Why in the world are you doing this, what are you thinking?" Frank said still in shock.

"I'm flat broke and I need the money," Ted laughed.

"I'll buy your beer or whatever you need," Frank begged.

The barker nodded at Ted and said,

"Ladies and gentlemen we have a brave soul in our audience today who has accepted the challenge. If he lasts three minutes and is still standing he will win the ten dollars. Get your tickets now and let's see how strong and brave he really is."

"Step up here on the platform, young man, and allow the good folks to see a real brave man such as yourself," the barker said to him.

Ted stepped onto the stage.

"Are you sure you want to do this, son?"

Ted nodded his head.

"Under one condition, I want that deputy sheriff standing right over there to hold the ten dollars so there won't be any problem getting my money when the fight is over."

"Well, son, you sound pretty sure of yourself, that's an unusual request, but not an unfair one, so we will gladly let the sheriff hold the money." The deputy agreed.

"When does the fight begin?" Ted asked.

"The fight will start across the way in that big tent over there in about thirty minutes, we will allow the crowd time to buy their tickets. Please come with me to the ring and we'll get you suited up and give you a pair of gloves."

Then he shouted out to the crowd again through the megaphone.

"Purchase your tickets at the box office, and please take a moment to say a prayer for this poor young misguided soul who has agreed to fight Big Tom Murphy."

Ted and Frank followed the barker to the tent where they met the 'meanest man in the world,' Tom Murphy.

"Don't worry, son, I'll try not to hurt you too bad and I sincerely hope I don't inflict any permanent damage on you," he mumbled to Ted as they shook hands.

"That's awfully nice of you, sir, I appreciate your concern for my health," Ted replied.

Ted looked over his opponent to see what he was dealing with. He was middle-aged, had sagging shoulders and looked like his fighting days in the ring were over. The veins in his neck stood out, and Ted could see them stand out as they pumped blood through his body, and he thought that was unusual. He had a crooked finger, probably broken sometime during his fighting years and never properly set, and he also had cauliflower ears which were typical for professional fighters who spent years in the ring taking all those punches. There were numerous scars on his face and Ted noticed his speech was also affected. But now, he was a carnival fighter and Ted could easily see he had taken a lot of abuse during his fighting years that affected him, but Ted was certain he still had some fight left in him.

The barker gave Ted some shorts and boxing gloves and Frank reluctantly helped him put on his gloves. He agreed to be Ted's ring man, but was still in disbelief that he had agreed to fight him.

"Just in case something happens to you, where and who do I contact to let them know?" He asked Ted, partly serious and teasing at the same time.

"You shouldn't worry, I'll be all right. I've never been knocked out, and I have had several fights back in Oklahoma. My brothers taught me how to fight, one was a professional fighter for a short while, but if you're worried that something could happen, my mother is in Deer Creek, Oklahoma."

The barker called the fighters to the middle of the ring and explained the rules, 'no hitting below the belt or rubbing gloves in your opponents eyes, and if either of you run and do not fight, it will be declared a no contest.'

Ted nodded that he understood the rules, but asked one question.

"Do the same rules apply to both?" Murphy and the barker smiled and confirmed the rules did apply to both of them. They were sent to their corners to wait for the bell to ring.

When the bell sounded Ted jumped up and went to the center of the ring and touched gloves with Murphy and the barker reminded them again of the rules. He nodded for the fight to begin and Murphy led off with a round house swing which was intended to knock Ted's head off, but he was too quick and the punch whizzed over the top of his head. He stepped back and Murphy threw a second punch that glanced off Ted's gloves. Ted danced around, moved back and forth on his toes and then hit Murphy with a left which stung him. It aroused Murphy into a raging bull and he began to stalk around Ted, swinging wildly, but Ted kept jabbing with his left and Murphy kept missing. Ted knew he had to step in and get this thing over, it was obvious that Murphy could take a lot of punches, so he hit him in the gut with all the strength he could muster and followed with a hay-maker to his chin. Murphy went down to his knees, obviously stunned, and the referee counted to eight before he got back up on his feet. Murphy staggered back and realized he was up against someone who had some knowledge of the ring. Ted tried to stay away from the ropes so he didn't get trapped in the corner, he pranced back and forth, always moving to his left and counter-clock wise.

Ted wasn't sure he had enough strength to last the whole three minutes, he felt like his legs getting weak. Murphy got a solid punch on Ted's head, which caused him to reel back and bounce against the ropes. He regained enough strength to move forward just as Murphy moved in on him and made several more hits to his head. They traded blows, both jabbing at each other and the crowd roared with excitement, yelling for Ted to 'kill him.'

This inspired Ted to keep on fighting and he punched at Murphy's head as he danced in and out around him. Finally, the three minute bell rang and Ted breathed a sigh of relief, the time had seemed so much longer. The referee stepped up and raised Ted's arm into the air saying.

"You lasted the three minutes, so you win the ten dollars."

Ted took some deep breaths and looked over at Frank who was clapping and cheering in total disbelief. He got out of the ring and walked over to the sheriff and the deputy put the money in his hand.

"You really earned this money, young man, most of the fighters don't last against old Murphy."

"Thank you, sir," Ted managed to say, still out of breath. He put on his shirt and walked out into the crowd with Frank at his side. The people cheered him and patted him on the back yelling out, 'congratulations, you earned it.'

Frank was beside himself.

"My goodness, Ted, that was something to watch, you're a pretty good fighter."

"That was one tough hombre, I'm glad I didn't get a real solid blow from him because his punches on my arms and shoulders really hurt. When I hit him and he went down to his knees I'm not sure he was hurt as much as he was surprised. I was lucky this time, but I'll never do that again."

"Well," Frank laughed.

"You have your beer money now. Let's go have one and celebrate."

"Well, I don't really drink, I don't like the taste of the stuff," and both burst out laughing at each other. Ted added.

"I'll buy you one anyhow, now that I'm rich."

When they were about to leave the area, the carnival barker caught up with them.

"Would you come again tomorrow night, we will up the ante to twenty dollars if you stay for an extra round, how about it."

"No thanks, sir," Ted said shaking his head.

"I'm not interested, I just needed a few bucks to tide me over till payday."

Since they had nothing to do the next day they decided to go back to the carnival, and Ted stashed five dollars from his win the day before in his office desk so he wouldn't be tempted to spend it, he remembered his experience with the cups and the pea. They roamed around the carnival grounds taking it all the sights and Frank met a young lady that took a shine to him who kept him busy seeing the sights. Ted wondered off and went to the tent to watch the fights, and when the barker saw him, he begged him to get back in the ring again.

"Your fight was a real money maker for us, we'll put up thirty dollars if you can last three rounds."

"Thanks, I'll think about it," Ted responded.

Ted began to question himself, 'Am I willing to take that punishment, three rounds is a long time to get punched on?' But the next day, he couldn't get it off his mind so he decided to make a deal with the barker only if he would up the ante. He offered to get back in the ring for forty dollars, and if he lost he would still be paid thirty. The barker agreed and was delighted and told him they would take in enough money to pay him forty dollars, so they made the deal. They shook hands and agreed the fight would be the next evening which was Saturday, the last day the carnival would be in town and the night they would draw the biggest crowd.

Ted told Frank about the upcoming event.

"Are you crazy, Ted," was all he could say, shaking his head.

The carnival moved the fight to the main tent and advertised the big fight all day long to draw a big crowd.

"Are you sure you want to do this, Ted?" Frank asked.

"That's a lot of punishment."

"Since I already fought him once I've had time to study his moves. I watched him last evening while you were courting your new girl friend and I believe I have him figured out. He is an old ex-fighter and just a brute, much older than me, and I have age on my side, he seems to tire out quickly. He has been hit so many times I think his brain must be damaged so I think I can outsmart him."

Ted rested all day Saturday and when evening came they walked to the carnival and met up with the barker to get ready for the fight. As they climbed into the ring the crowd was roaring and cheering, and the people were making side bets, mostly on Ted. One man yelled.

"Hope you're feeling good and strong today, boy, I bet ten on you, that's mommies milk money, so don't let me down or my kid's will have to go without their milk next week."

"You feeling OK?" Frank asked.

Ted said he felt a little nervous, but he was glad Frank had given up his new love interest to be there with him, however, she was in the audience cheering them on.

"I'm feeling pretty good," he told Frank.

"so don't worry."

The barker made his pitch to build up the fight and excite the crowd. He told them how Ted challenged 'Killer Murphy' two days ago and won ten dollars.

"This upstart fighter and winner of ten dollars has agreed to a three round bout tonight," he told the crowd as they roared and cheered, while a few boos were also heard. A man from the crowd yelled out, 'I bet the fight is fixed.'

When the barker finished his remarks he called Ted and Murphy to the center of the ring and explained the rules. They touched gloves and returned to their corners to wait for the bell to sound.

The bell rang and round one began. They circled around each other a few times and after a moment Murphy stopped and stood still and dropped his arms to his side. Ted continued to circle him and jabbed him in the face with a left, leaving a stinging blow. He hit him two more times in the head and on his cauliflower ear, which was already purple in color. Ted's plan was to keep moving and dancing around him, but staying back and jabbing at every chance.

Murphy seemed to revive himself and got a blow in which grazed Ted's chin, but didn't sting him that much. Ted continued his dancing and jabbing, stinging him and wearing him down. At one point, Murphy sneered at him.

"Where did you find that punch, boy, in some alley fight with your sister?"

Then Murphy gave him a rabbit punch to the back of his neck which caused Ted to stagger back and fall. The referee started counting, but he got up on the count of seven and the crowd cheered him on. The referee signaled them to continue the fight, but he didn't penalize Murphy for the illegal punch.

This angered Ted and he knew Murphy would try anything to win. He danced around to clear his head and then threw a couple of shots to Murphy's head which stunned him. He staggered around, and Ted could tell his punches were coming slower and his body was drained of strength. Ted kept up the punches until the end of the first round and the bell rang.

He went to the corner and Frank gave him a sponge full of water for his mouth and poured water over his head.

"You nailed him good, Ted."

"I got careless, I'm really getting tired, I sure hope I can last. The referee should have called him on that rabbit punch he laid on me, but I came back, and I think I'm winning."

The bell rang and round two was underway. Ted quickly gave Murphy a couple of jabs to his gut, and he grabbed hold of Ted and whispered.

"Look out, I'm going to nail you."

"Thanks for that info, I'll be looking out for it," Ted muttered.

Ted hit Murphy with a hard gut shot and he went down. The referee started counting but Murphy jumped back up, staggered around the ring holding his chest. Ted knew something was wrong, he looked like he was having some kind of an attack. But just then, Murphy grabbed Ted in a clinch and gave him a head butt and muttered.

"I have to win this one or lose my job, this is all I have left."

Ted was stunned from the head butt and fell back to the floor. He heard the referee counting and the crowd roaring, and on the count of eight he quickly jumped up and it was at that time that he saw Murphy grab his chest and look up to the top of tent and fall backward flat on his back.

Realizing something was wrong, Ted kneeled at Murphy's side. The referee came over and lifted his head and called for the doctor to check him. Ted walked back to his corner and stood there watching for a moment, and then put his hands over his face and leaned over the ropes as he heard the referee announce to the crowd that Murphy had died.

Ted couldn't believe what he heard, he was aghast at Murphy just laying there so silent, and the crowd gasped and stared at the body laying silent in the middle of the ring. Ted began to feel guilty, what if he had caused it to happen, he questioned himself.

Frank jumped into the ring to console Ted and help him take off his gloves. The ring master announced to the crowd that they regretted the death of this great fighter. He told the crowd about Murphy and his many accomplishments over the years. He was once a contender for the light weight championship of the world, and lost his only son in the Spanish-American war, and also lost his devoted wife of many years to a serious illness.

"This was his last fight in the ring and he lost the battle of life to a heart attack, so this brave challenger is determined the winner of this fight," he said as he raised Ted's arm.

The crowd was silent and in shock, the unexpected outcome of this event was very emotional for everyone. The ladies were crying and dabbing their eyes with their handkerchief's, and even the carnival workers were in shock. Murphy had become one of their carnival family members, and they all joined in with the crowd in sorrow.

Ted looked out over the audience and saw the lady who was sitting on the front row that yelled out to him during the fight, 'kill him, kill him.' But now she was crying, her words probably coming back to haunt her. Ted looked down and shook his head at the tragedy, he thought old Murphy must have had a real bad heart problem, he didn't look very healthy to him.

The carnival barker kept his word and gave Ted his thirty dollars. He took it but felt guilty, and wondered if it might be dirty money, even though he knew Murphy had died of a heart attack. He remembered the Bible story about a fellow named Judas and the thirty pieces of silver he received because he betrayed the Lord. He was sure he didn't cause Murphy's death and tried to sooth his thoughts by telling himself Murphy had fought one too many fights. He wondered if Murphy was all alone in the world and if he had any family that would have a memorial service for him to mourn his death.

Later that evening Ted went to church and kneeled down to pray, he felt so mournful. He prayed for Murphy's family, hoping that he had one, and he prayed for forgiveness for himself in the terrible tragedy, all for just 'thirty pieces of silver.' As he left he placed the money in the contribution box and walked out.

Chapter 68

MOVING ON

The orders from the Train Master came in, and the trestle repairs would begin the next day when the materials and equipment arrive. The trestle was located over the corner of a large lake close to the Texas-Mexican border and the Rio Grande river. Apparently, the trestle had been damaged during a flood when the river roared out of control and into the lake, and they expected the repairs would take several weeks to complete. Ted completed and checked the telegraphy hook-up and notified the dispatcher they were ready to go to work.

After work hours Ted took advantage of the lake and river to do some fishing, which was one thing he truly enjoyed. He managed to scrounge up a fishing line, hooks and sinkers, and other things he might need from the equipment boxcar, and searched for the perfect tree limb for the pole. He begged the cook for some scraps to use for bait in exchange for a promise he would catch a good mess of fish for them to have for supper.

It was about a ten minute walk to the lake and he looked forward to the quiet and serenity of the lake bank to relax and day-dream, and hopefully catch some fish. He caught several fish during the first couple of hours and decided he would explore the area before going back to his boxcar home. He was on the smaller side of the cove when he found a deer path that led into the woods. He followed it for about a quarter of a mile and it immerged into another larger cove than where he was fishing.

He looked around and saw an old abandoned row boat turned upside down and decided to turn it over to inspect it. Under the boat was a big rattle snake all curled up, it's rattlers sounding and ready to strike. Ted jumped back as it struck at him and thank goodness it missed. He realized he was very lucky as he watched it crawl off into the thickets, and breathed a sigh of relief. He took it as a warning, however, not to get so careless as he strolled through mother-natures territory. 'Sorry to disturb your home, ole fellow, but thanks for the warning,' he said to himself.

He looked over the boat to see if he could repair it to use for fishing. It had several holes in the bottom and he decided it was not sea-worthy, but he thought it was worth repairing. When he got back he told Frank all about the boat and the snake, and the next time he would take him out on the lake to fish. Frank declined the invitation, he was busy in the evenings with his new girl friend, but he told Ted he loved to eat the fish but he was not a fisherman.

Ted spent the next several evenings fixing the boat to use for some good fishing out on the lake. When he finished he took the boat out on the lake to explore the opposite side, and he saw what looked like a cave entrance. His curiosity got the better of him and he had to check it out. He ducked his head at the entrance of the grotto and rowed inside, but it was pitch dark and he couldn't see a thing.

Still curious about the cave he took an old train lantern with him the next evening, the curiosity of seeing inside that grotto got the best of him. He lit the wick of the lantern and rowed inside and was surprised how large it was. On the other side he noticed day light which looked like another entrance, so he rowed over to check it out and anchored his boat against the side of the cave bank. The entrance extended several feet out onto dry land, so he stepped out and walked through the cave entrance and saw a well worn path that he followed through the brush and the trees. He heard rushing water which sounded like a waterfall, and he came upon a natural spring that flowed out onto the banks of the Rio Grande river. It was a beautiful sight and as he investigated it further, he saw horse tracks and dried horse droppings on the path, this is getting very interesting he thought, and he became even more curious.

Beyond the path he saw a horse corral hidden back in the woods and he decided not to explore the area any further. It all started to look rather suspicious to him and trouble was one thing he didn't need. He hurried back to the cave entrance and got into his boat and as he lifted the light to look around the grotto he was surprised to see a number of large crates stashed upon the sides of the cave. He rowed closer to them and saw stenciled on the side of the boxes, 'Winchester Rifle Company,' and he counted about twenty crates in all.

He opened one of the crates and it contained rifles that were lever operated, 30X30 caliber, the very latest repeating model. Ted was sure this must be a smuggling operation and were evidently smuggling guns across the river into Mexico. He decided to get himself out of there, hoping he had not been seen by the smugglers, he thought they probably did their smuggling operations at night. He hurriedly rowed back out to the other side to the shore, anchored his boat and walked back to the work train site.

He took his catch of fish to the cook to clean and he was undecided about telling anyone what he had just discovered. He certainly didn't want any trouble, he had left all that behind. If he said anything to the authorities they would definitely involve him in the investigation. With all his rebel trouble in the past he didn't want any of that to follow him into their work camp. They had been at the trestle work site for about a month and should be receiving new orders soon, and he could leave all this behind.

But after several days he couldn't shake it from his mind as he thought about it, and he wasn't sure who was receiving these guns in Mexico. If he made the wrong decision many innocent Americans could be killed.

He had read in the newspaper that the war was heating up, in fact the United States was preparing to enter the great war that was eminent. This war was a great concern for all the people and the whole world was in a state of uncertainty about an impending war. The countries of Europe, especially Germany, was concerned that the United States would enter the war against them, and was making noises and innuendos to Mexico about collaborating with them against the United States. One newspaper speculated that if Mexico opened a harassment front against the United States, Germany would help them regain California, Arizona, New Mexico, and all the states that were taken from them. The United States currently had troops all along the border which was always a threat to Mexico, and Germany suggested that Mexico's harassment front would keep the United States occupied and would help them achieve their goals.

Ted also read about the increased threat of Poncho Via and his men raiding towns and robbing banks in the United States, threatening and murdering farmers, and he even bragged about murdering people who were fifteen years old or older. That made Ted shudder, what if those weapons he found ended up in the hands of the wicked Poncho Villa and his men.

That evening he sat down and composed a letter to the United States Customs in El Paso and told them what he had found and suggested they use their mounted horse patrol to find the cave. As he wrote the letter he remembered reading about several hero's of the old west, like Wyatt Earp, who worked as a Customs agent and apprehended smugglers along the Mexican border, and the outcry it caused from the public concerning these things. He finished the letter and drew a map to show the location of the cache, and mailed the letter to the U. S. Customs authorities the next day.

Frank received orders that they would be moving from this location since they were finishing the trestle repairs within the next few days, and they would be moving into upper New Mexico. Ted was having thoughts about moving on, he was getting tired of living in a boxcar out on the prairies, both in hot and cold weather, and besides that he started thinking more about girls and settling down.

He worked for the next several weeks and resigned his job from the Southern Pacific Railroad, and gave them two week's notice. The work train had moved to the Santa Fe, New Mexico area and when his two weeks were up he said good-bye to Frank and the crew and decided to catch the next freight out. He rolled his few belongings into a bedroll and stood behind a blind to wait for the next freight train out of town, he was ready to move on.

Chapter 69

A HOBO ONCE AGAIN

The train engineer finalized the makeup of the train cars and when the hookup was completed the conductor gave the signal to proceed. The engine puffed with steam and the wheels screeched to grab hold, and when they caught hold the train started up and the line of cars crawled slowly out of the yard onto the main line. Ted spotted an open boxcar and when he saw the conductor board the caboose he ran from his blind and threw his bedroll into the open door and jumped on. He didn't notice any other hobos boarding, he seemed to be the only one. He wasn't sure where the train was headed, all he knew was he was headed north out of El Paso and he felt like a hobo once again.

He gathered up the loose hay on the floor of the car and piled it up to make a bed, and closed the boxcar door to shut out the excess rail noise and air, it was getting cooler especially at night. He laid down and put his bed-roll under his head for a pillow and wondered why he caught this freight like a hobo, he had the money to buy a ticket. It must be the thrill of it all he decided, and besides, he didn't really have a plan or destination in mind. He admitted to himself there was a streak of hobo blood still in him.

He was ready to hit the open road in vagabond style and think about what he wanted to do with his life. He enjoyed being on the move, seeing and doing different things, and there was nothing yet in his life that compelled him to settle down. He enjoyed the thrill of not knowing what was around the corner, whether it was safe or dangerous, he never gave that much of a thought.

The train ploughed along, the clickity-clack of the wheels singing its song on the rails, and every now and then the haunting train whistle sounding, warning everyone who was near the track of its presence.

On the second day and after covering many miles, the train came into a town that had a beautiful view of snow capped mountains off in the distance. It was early morning with the sun rising and the air was cool. Ted felt hungry and he hoped they would stop so he could get some food, he looked forward to a big breakfast of eggs, bacon, pancakes and the works. He wondered where in Colorado they were and opened the door enough to look out, hoping to determine their location.

He could see the spectacular mountains that encircled them, and the townspeople moving about in the early morning hours. A lady was standing in her yard feeding the chickens from the grain she held in her apron, and the feeling of hunger came back to his mind.

The train slowed and the whistle blew at the crossings and the town was becoming alive with people to greet the day. At a crossing Ted saw a milk cart pulled by a tired looking old horse out delivering the milk to all the houses on his route. At the railroad depot he saw the name of the town, La Junta, Colorado, populations 1420. The train came to a stop and he jumped off the train and walked across the tracks to the main street. He looked up and down and saw several business's just opening for the day, and spotted what he was looking for, a sign that said cafe. He walked to the door with several other people and he thought that this must be a good place to eat because so many of the town folks also come. He could smell the aroma of fresh baking and coffee which made his mouth water, he was so hungry.

The cafe had several tables and a counter that was filling up fast so he took a seat at the counter and felt lucky to get it. The waitress gave the customers her friendly good-morning greeting and placed a cup of coffee in front of each one. She handed Ted a menu and gave him a special good morning.

"What can I get for you today, sir. "

"I'll have a stack of cakes, three eggs over easy, bacon, fried potatoes and biscuits and jelly," He said without hesitation.

"You're a real eater," she laughed.

"You must really be hungry."

"Yes, I am," he said.

"Haven't had much to the eat the last few days."

"She turned in the orders she had taken while the customers had their morning coffee and chatted with each other. Ted listened in, it was obvious he was the stranger among them, all the people knew one another and were catching up on the latest news in town.

He ate his full breakfast, every bite of it, and finished up his third cup of coffee. He paid his ticket of seventy five cents and left a quarter tip for the friendly waitress, and she smiled at him as he left. He walked across the street to a hotel, he needed to get a room and a hot bath, the bed of hay in the boxcar had left him rather smelly. The hotel clerk pushed the guest registry in front of him to sign.

"That will be a dollar and a quarter for the night, sir, and check out time is eleven in the morning."

"Does the room charge include a bath?" Ted asked, hoping it did.

"No, sir, you'll need to have several buckets of hot water brought up to your room, and that will be sixty cents more," he informed Ted.

"I want the bath and three extra buckets of hot water," he informed the clerk.

"The clerk responded with surprise.

"That will be another dollar and twenty cents then, sir. We will send the tub and the water up shortly, the bellboy will show you to your room." The bellboy grabbed his bag of belongings and Ted followed him to his room on the second floor. He tipped him a quarter and looked forward to a real bath and a real bed.

From the hotel window he saw a gambling casino and saloon across the street, he smiled because he had learned a lot about gambling from his uncle who ran the pool hall and gambling tables in the town of Blackwell, Oklahoma when he was a kid. When he went to visit his uncle he and his brothers would spend a lot of time playing pool and cards, and they had all become quite skilled.

His uncle gave his parents a pool table when he closed his business due to ill health and political pressure from the local citizens in town, and Ted and his brothers spent many hours out in the barn honing their skills when they were not working and doing their chores. The pool table was located in the barn because his mother would not allow such things in her house. His uncle lived with them until he died from cancer, but while he was still alive he would often demonstrate the art of gambling and the tricks that were used to enhance the odds of winning.

Ted remembered how his mother was so opposed to card playing and pool, she was very religious and a daily Bible reader and active in the church. He never forgot her words that resounded in his mind when she found out what her ornery brother was teaching them. She made him and his brothers promise her they would never take money from people who didn't have the same skills they had, but she really hoped they would resist the temptation of gambling.

She called it the 'devils game' and his Dad would say.

"Now, Mother, the boys are really good boy's and it gets lonely out here on the farm with nothing but work to do, so give them a break, they won't misuse their skills. They are honest and it's good for them to have the knowledge so others won't take advantage of them."

Ted relaxed in his hotel room and took a much needed bath and a nap until evening. He brushed off his two dollar second hand suit that he had purchased in a used clothing store, and got dressed to go the hotel restaurant. He ordered a T- bone steak, medium rare, and it was so large it nearly covered the plate. For dessert, he ordered his favorite, apple pie and coffee.

After supper he stepped out of the hotel and crossed the street to the casino, he decided to test his rustic skills at cards and pool, it had been a while since he had touched either. He moseyed around the casino hall and watched the gambling styles of the people and the dealers. He particularly watched one dealer at the twenty-one table who was dealing from the bottom of the deck, and he had observed long enough that he felt the casino was a honest one except this one dealer. Ted smiled to himself and decided to test his skills against this dealer and bought twenty dollars worth of chips. He sat down at the table and bet conservatively and played slowly at first, and he won some hands and lost some. So far he was ahead by eight dollars and after several more hands he bet his total winnings on one play. It was then that he observed the dealer deal himself an ace from the bottom of the deck, and Ted knew it was the time for a show-down and what he had been waiting for.

The dealer won that hand, he actually was pretty slick with his moves and his trick plays, and Ted knew the ordinary unsuspecting player would never have seen it. What the dealer had done was pull a handkerchief from his coat pocket to make his diversion play to place an ace card in the palm of his hand that he took from the bottom of the deck.

With the next hand Ted placed a bet of thirty dollars and went into action, hoping to teach the dealer a lesson. He managed to palm an ace card when he diverted the dealer's attention by dropping a chip on the floor and leaning over to pick it up. Ted then waited until the other players busted out, leaving only himself and the dealer left to play the hand, and it was then that Ted replaced the nine card with the ace.

The dealer knew he had dealt Ted a nine card and thought he had Ted set up to lose. He dealt Ted a queen card up and when it came time to turn over his down card, which the dealer thought was a nine, he saw the ace starring him in the face which made a total of 21 points and Ted winning the hand.

The dealer was surprised and perplexed thinking he had handily won, he hadn't observed Ted closely enough and he slowly handed Ted his sixty dollar winnings. The dealer knew he was exposed and out-smarted, but he didn't dare complain because the manager believed all the house dealers were straight honest dealers. He was so distraught that he called for a replacement dealer.

The dealer didn't dare expose Ted for cheating because he knew he would also be exposed, so he played a few more hands until the replacement dealer arrived. All in all Ted won a total of eighty-five dollars and the dealer played straight until his replacement arrived.

Ted leaned over and whispered to him, "You're not planning to stay in this town, are you? If I were you, I wouldn't be here tomorrow or show my face around this town ever again, you're really very much an amateur."

Ted walked out and waited across the street, and after a while the dealer walked out of the casino, his suitcase in hand and headed for the train station.

Ted smiled to himself and walked to his hotel and had a very restful night's sleep.

The next morning he walked to the station and telegraphed a money order for eighty-five dollars to his mother, but didn't mention to her that he won it gambling. He went back to his hotel room and in just a few minutes he had a knock on the door, and when he opened it there stood two tall tough looking men asking if he was Mr. Ted Walters.

"Yes, I am, but how did you get my name?"

"We got it from the hotel registry," one said.

"Well, what can I do for you, gentlemen," Ted asked them.

"We work for the casino across the street and the manager would like to see you. Would you please accompany us?" he asked Ted in a rather intimidating tone.

Ted responded, "I haven't had my breakfast yet, but I guess I can."

He followed the two men and felt a little nervous, but he knew he had done nothing wrong. When they arrived at the casino, the men escorted him to the manager's office and he was sitting in his big leather office chair.

"Come on in, Mr. Walters. My name is Fred Hurst and I appreciate you coming at my request. Please have a seat."

He continued.

"First of all I want to tell you that you did the house a big favor last night exposing our crooked dealer. We have been watching him for a while, but now he is gone and we don't have to worry about him anymore, so thank you."

"Secondly, we observed your play also and we can't prove it but we believe you made a substitution and palmed a card also, very cleverly I might add. We run an honest house and don't tolerate any card slickers in our casino. We know you took the house, but once is all you will be allowed to do so.

"We are asking you to be on the next train out of town to avoid any accidents, do you get my point?" He stared at Ted, and then at the two tall gentlemen.

"Yes, sir, I'm as good as gone. I was just thinking you have a very nice town here but in a way it's much too small for me. Thank you for your suggestion, and I'll be gone just as soon as I have my breakfast, and I'll catch the first train out of town."

"That's very nice of you, Mr. Walters. You have a nice trip and I wouldn't bother about ever coming back to our town every again, so good-bye."

Ted nodded and extended his hand to shake, but the manager declined the offer. In his mind all he wanted was a showdown with the dishonest dealer and to see if he still had the magic touch of card playing.

He walked across the street to the cafe for breakfast and then checked out of his hotel. He gathered up his belongings and walked to the freight yard to wait for the next train heading north.

He waited for about an hour and when the conductor gave the signal for the train to proceed, he emerged from his blind and jumped aboard. It was good to be leaving La Junta, especially when he looked out the boxcar door and saw the two tall gentlemen standing at the station.

Chapter 70

TRAVELING COMPANION

Ted rested comfortably on his makeshift bed of hay as he lay in the boxcar listening to the resounding clickety-clack of the train wheels over and over again. It was a welcome sound to him, it was comforting and finally lulled him to sleep.

He was aroused from his sleep when he heard the sweet sound of the train whistle, and he felt something heavy on his stomach that moved each time he moved, and he also heard the sound of someone breathing. He quickly sat up realizing he wasn't alone, he had company. He looked down and saw a big beautiful dog, just lying there, all cuddled up beside him using Ted for a pillow and soft spot. He reached down and stroked the dog's head and it sat up immediately and began to lick Ted's face. He continued to pet him and he wondered how he got in the boxcar, but was really glad for the company.

"How did you get in here, fella? Did you jump up here all by yourself?"

Ted really felt like someone must have put him in the car hoping he would find a new home. He lay back hoping to get some more sleep and the dog resumed its position with his head across Ted's stomach, and they both quickly fell back to sleep and slept until daylight began to peek over the horizon.

The sun cast its rays across the land and through the slots in the boxcar. Ted sat up blinking his eyes as the sun shown across his face and in his eyes. The dog stood up, stretched and shook, and began to walk around the car with his long tongue hanging from his mouth, and he joined Ted in greeting the day.

"What kind of dog are you, fella, you look like a German Sheppard." He was black and brown with lighter brown streaks on his fur and Ted thought he was really beautiful. He wasn't normally a dog person, but this time he was glad to have the company; he didn't feel so alone.

The train passed through small towns and farm lands, and he could see mountains on the horizon as they moved down the tracks. He knew they would soon be in the mountains going through the passes that were covered with snow, and as they approached the higher altitudes snowflakes began to fall and it began to look like a winter wonder land.

The weather began to look more and more like they were moving into a winter storm, and he hoped they would come into another town soon before nightfall when the temperature starts to fall and it gets really cold in the mountains.

He had some food stashed away that he brought with him from La Junta, he was planning ahead not really knowing when he would have access to food again once he boarded the train. He had two egg sandwiches and two donuts, so he pulled out one of his sandwiches to eat and the dog readily joined him, licking his chops and ready for any crumbs that might come his way.

Ted looked at his 'begging eyes' and reached out to pet him.

"Of course, you're hungry too, fella. All right, I'll share with you."

Ted gave the dog one of his sandwiches and a donut, and his hungry companion gulped down the food in just a few bites.

"That takes care of that, hope we get to a town soon so we can replenish our stash, that's all we have for now," he said to the dog as he reached out to pet him.

In a few hours they passed some houses and it looked like they were coming into a larger town or city. As they got closer Ted could see it was a larger town, he could see taller buildings off in the distance. The train began to slow down and he could see horse and carriages and a few cars on the dirt roads of the town, and he saw some commercial buildings like factories and warehouses.

He looked down the tracks and saw the brakeman open a switch and the train entered onto a side track, and on the station above the doors were the words, Denver, Colorado.

He jumped from the boxcar when he saw a safe place to land, and right beside him was the dog standing and waiting for Ted to move. He saw a cafe and decided to get a hot cup of coffee and as he went inside the dog stayed back and found a comfortable spot to lay down and wait for his new master. It was getting close to lunch time so Ted ordered the blue plate special which was liver and onions, mashed potatoes and gravy, navy beans and cornbread, and a glass of buttermilk. When he finished he ordered two hamburgers to take with him for the dog who was waiting patiently for him outside.

The dog ate the hamburgers with great relish, and when he finished they walked on down the street. Ted didn't really have any plans for the day so he decided to see the city, he had heard about Denver and the gold rush, and how thousands of people left their homes and migrated to Colorado to get rich. In fact, he remembered going gold hunting with his friend, Chris Schmitt, who now lived in Denver, and he wondered if he could look him up and renew their acquaintance.

He went into a hotel and ask to see the telephone book, more and more people were taking advantage of this new way of communication and were getting phone service into their homes. But Chris was not listed in the book, maybe he didn't have a phone or was away at college, he didn't really know.

They walked on through the city streets looking in the shops windows and just as they passed a grocery store, a man came running out of the front door and bumped into Ted, knocking him to the ground. He was wearing a mask and carried a gun, and he turned and pointed the gun at Ted and ordered him to stay on the ground.

Just then another bandit ran out of the store carrying a gun and the bag of stolen money, and standing at the wagon post was a man holding three horses by the reins, his face partially hidden by his coat collar. Everything was happening so fast Ted tried to gather his thoughts. He started to get up and the bandit fired his pistol, grazing his shoulder and spinning him around causing him to fall back down.

Just then the dog, which the bandits had ignored, went into action and jumped into the face of the first bandit who ran from the store, causing him to fall and drop his gun. The gun fired as it fell and hit the other bandit as he ran from the store and he threw up his arms and fell backward, dropping his pistol and the bag on the sidewalk.

The store manager came running from the store and picked up the pistol. The horse handler mounted one of the horses to escape, but the manager fired the gun and hit the horse. The horse rose up on his hind legs throwing the bandit off, and then the horse fell on him pinning him to the ground.

He immediately started shouting, "Don't shoot, I surrender!"

The dog was still holding the first bandit to the ground, and the store manager stepped up to Ted.

"I had my clerk call the police and an ambulance, they should be here shortly, so just lay quietly, mister, help is on the way. I think I hear them coming now."

The police and ambulance arrived with their bells sounding, and the police arrested the bandits, and the medic helped Ted to his feet and placed him in the wagon with the dog jumping in taking his place by Ted's side. The money bag was retrieved, however, it came open and some of the bills were blown by the wind into the streets. Many of the bystanders ran to help retrieve the money and to be a part of the action, they wanted to help wherever they could.

Ted was lucky, his shoulder was just grazed and he had a flesh wound only, no bones were damaged or broken. The hospital cleaned it with antiseptic solutions and bandaged him up. They put his arm in a sling to wear a few days, telling him 'you are a mighty lucky guy.'

A police officer met Ted at the hospital and escorted him to the police station to give his account of the store robbery. He told his story as he remembered it, how he was knocked to the ground and was hit by a bullet from one of the bandit's gun and how the dog went into action and fought the bandit and held him down.

The officer thanked him and told him he was free to go.

"You were an innocent bystander, but that dog probably saved your life and helped us with the capture of the others. Where are you staying, we will need you for the hearing tomorrow morning?"

The city fathers put Ted up in a hotel for the night, and the dog in a kennel, both were treated as heroes. The story went to the press and was reported on the evening radio news, and the town was very grateful that the bandits had been caught and the money recovered. Ted had a free meal at the hotel that evening, and the dog had a nice warm kennel to sleep in and free dog food.

The bandits appeared before the judge the next morning, and Ted gave his account of the event. The courtroom was full of reporters and they made Ted the center of attention, more so than the bandits or the store manager. The bandits were held over for trial without bail, "They must not be out on the streets," the judge said. The store manager offered free hotel and meals for Ted for the next couple of days and a kennel for the dog. Ted thought about it, but knew it would soon be yesterday's news; he was ready to move on.

The next morning after breakfast, he went to the kennel to pick up the dog, and walked to the freight yards to wait for a train. He sat in a blind and watched while they added cars to make up the train. He didn't see any boxcars with the doors open, so when the train started up, he grabbed the ladder on one of the cars and bounced around for a moment holding on with one hand, but finally managed to gain his balance.

The dog ran alongside the car barking and whining, seeing his new friend about to leave. Ted was so touched, he couldn't leave him all alone in the world again; so he dropped off the train ladder the dog ran over to him and literally knocked him down, and there they lay on the cinders of the train yard with the dog licking his face and whining with relief.

After the emotional greeting, Ted had to push the dog away from him just to get up and back on his feet. He went back into his blind with the dog close behind to wait for the next train. This time he spotted an open door on one of the boxcars and when the conductor gave the signal for the train to proceed, Ted and the dog ran to catch up with the open door. He reached down and lifted the dog into the boxcar and then jumped in himself.

The dog started to growl.

"What's up?" Ted said.

In the back of the car was a group of boys, all teenagers, cowering in the corner, and one yelled out.

"Hey, mister, call off your dog, he really looks mean."

"Come here, Carl," Ted called the dog, and he immediately stopped.

"Good fella, I'm not sure why you responded to the name Carl, but that's going to be your name from now on."

Ted recognized the boys for what they were. He had heard about the hobo youth gangs who traveled around the country, stealing and terrorizing the people.

"Where's this train going?" Ted asked them.

"Colorado Springs," one answered.

"You sure?" Ted questioned.

"Yep, we rode it before," one answered who appeared to be the ring leader. Then he asked.

"Ya' got any money, mister?"

"No, I don't, but what I do have is a derringer in my pocket. Why do you ask?" Ted remarked.

"Just wondering, don't mean anything by it," and acted rather taken back by Ted's answer.

"You all just stay back in your end of the car, and you won't have any problems from me," Ted told them.

"I'm not a drunk for you to roll or rob, but I am all the trouble you can handle if you mess with me. This dog will eat you alive and I can blow your heads off, if I have to. Do we understand each other?"

"You sure are a friendly fella, aren't you," the ring leader remarked.

"As friendly as I need to be. I've been around the road a long time and I've heard about you young hoodlums who like to gang up on the helpless and drunks and steal everything they have, including their clothes and shoes, and I'm neither one of those, so do we understand each other?"

They all stayed in their corner of the car, Carl at Ted's side as his protector, and the dog didn't take his eyes off the boys during the entire trip into Colorado Springs.

When they pulled into the station, the boys jumped out and merged with the crowd into the dark, and Ted waited until they disappeared before getting off and then walked with Carl staying close to the station lights until he spotted a cafe. He ordered four cheeseburgers, two to go, fries, and a coke and sat at the counter to watch out the window while he ate. He saw the boys emerge from the dark and following an old drunk as he walked down the street. He thought to himself, *That old man is going to wake up soon cleaned out of any belongings and money he has with him, those youth gangs are merciless.* He had heard about them even killing their victims if they resisted.

Ted and Carl walked back to the station to wait for the next train going east. He watched them shuffle the cars and connect the engine and he knew when the train was about ready to move out. He had been around trains long enough that he knew all about their timing.

He would soon be on his way on a trip across Kansas, seeing mile after mile of golden wheat fields, and it made him think about his growing up years and appreciate the beauty and wonders of Mother Earth.

Chapter 71

HEADING HOME

The Missouri Pacific freight out of Colorado Springs moved along the tracks faster than most trains, but Ted concluded it was an express freight headed for Wichita with no stops in between; it could maintain a steady speed.

He climbed aboard early that morning with Carl totally unnoticed, the brakeman didn't check any of the cars before departure or during the trip.

As the train came near the town of Dodge City, Kansas, Ted watched for the Kizer farmland. He had pleasant memories of the time he worked there and how he enjoyed the family. He especially remembered Mrs. Kizer's cooking and the biscuits and homemade jelly, which was his favorite. He wished he could stop over to see them but knew it wasn't possible since the train didn't stop. He did plan to stop over in Wichita to see his Aunt Edith and Uncle Lum Mahoney before going on to Deer Creek, Oklahoma, he hadn't seen them since he was a boy still living at home and he was excited to see them and hoped it would be a great reunion.

The train arrived in Wichita right on time and they jumped off the boxcar in the freight yard and no one seemed to notice them. Carl waited obediently outside the door of the station while Ted went inside to call his Aunt Edith, he hoped the station agent would allow him use the phone. He had very little experience using a telephone or calling anyone, but the agent was friendly enough to help him find the number and make the call. Their number was 59F31, which was two long and one short rings.

He heard Aunt Edith's voice.

"Hello, who's calling?" Ted held the receiver to his ear and spoke into the phone.

"Hello, Aunt Edith, this is Ted, Ted Walters, your nephew. I just got off the train and would like to come and see you."

She was so surprised and excited to hear from him.

"You must come to see us, I'll send Uncle Lum to the station to pick you up."

"I must warn you, there's two of us, I have a friend with me, is that all right?"

"Of course, I'm so glad you have a friend. Who is he?"

"It's my dog, Carl, and he loves to eat. There will two mouths to feed."

Aunt Edith laughed.

"I hope he likes leftovers and scraps. We recently lost our dog, Mattie. She was very old and we miss her very much, so Carl is welcome. See you soon, Uncle Lum is on his way."

Ted waited on the bench outside the station door for his uncle to arrive. It wasn't long until a Ford coupe with a rumble seat pulled up and Ted recognized his uncle and waved to him. They greeted each other with a handshake and a hug, and loaded Carl into the rumble seat before they took off.

Carl loved the ride, he held his head high sniffing the air and his tongue hung out as he watched the passing parade of people and cars. Uncle Lum was all smiles.

"How in the world are you, Ted, it's been a long time since we saw you, you were just a boy, and where did you get that fine looking dog?"

"Actually, he attached himself to me a few days ago on the train and he won't leave my side, and so far we've had some exciting times together."

When they arrived home Aunt Edith was waiting in the front yard.

"Oh, my word, you're all grown up and look how tall you are!" she greeted him with plenty of hugs and kisses.

"Come in and make yourself at home."

Carl made himself at home also, and followed her around the house. She loved it, and of course she immediately made sure he had something to eat.

"We just lost our Mattie, so Carl is welcome in our house," she told Ted as she leaned down to pet him.

Uncle Lum showed Ted his greenhouse while Aunt Edith fixed supper. His favorite passion and pastime was horticulture and growing new varieties of roses.

"This one here is my prize rose," he told Ted with great pride in his voice.

"I plan to enter this new rose I grew in the Kansas State fair this year, I know it will be a winner."

"It's mighty pretty, all right, I'm sure it will win," Ted told him in agreement.

"I have never seen a dark purple rose before."

While they enjoyed their supper of delicious fried chicken and mashed potatoes and gravy, Ted asked about his cousin.

"Where is Junior these days, where does he live?"

"Well, you'll be surprised at this, he went to barber school three years ago and now has his own barber school and shop here in Wichita. He's doing really well, he's married and has two children of his own, twin girls who are the pride of our lives. He bought the barber school from the previous owner who became sick with cancer. The school and shop is located downtown on the corner of Topeka and Douglas Avenue, it's a great location and the shop keeps busy all the time."

"Glad to hear he's doing so well, hope to see him before I leave for Deer Creek."

"Oh, you will, I'll take you downtown to see him," Uncle Lum promised.

They spent the next two days catching up on all the family news, both good and bad. He learned all about the aunts and uncles and cousins and the work they were doing, and one cousin was a police officer there in Wichita.

The next day Uncle Lum took Ted downtown to visit Junior at the barber shop since he planned to leave for Deer Creek in the next couple of days. "Let's go get a free haircut and you can visit with Junior while we're there, and besides I need a haircut."

"So do I," Ted said.

Junior was standing out in front of his barber shop when they arrived, his mom had called him on the phone to let him know they were coming. He greeted them very affectionately and was surprised to see Ted all grown up, they hadn't seen each other since they were just young boys.

He proudly showed Ted the school and shop and his office where he did all his school and business paper work, the financial accounts and such.

"You have a very nice set up here, I'm very glad for you, it looks like you're doing well," Ted remarked.

They each climbed into a barber chair, and Junior introduced them to his students.

Uncle Lum said, "We'll take the works, a little off the sides and round off in back, and oh, yes, a shave."

As they received "the works" Ted ask Junior the cost of barber school and the length of the course.

"The total cost for the three month course is $250, and when you graduate you will take a test to pass the Kansas State Board requirements for your license. So far, all my students have passed and gotten their license, that's a pretty good record, I think. Only one student failed to pass the test on the first round, but with a short review course he passed the second time."

"That's an excellent record." Ted was impressed.

Uncle Lum climbed out of his chair with his graying hair all trimmed and combed, and with his aftershave lotion of rose water on his face he smelled like a rose. Ted was also very pleased with his haircut.

"Thank you so much, it looks good," he told the young barber. Both Uncle Lum and Ted gave their barber a tip of twenty five cents each, which delighted them.

"You must come and meet my wife and kids before you leave town. I'll take you home with me this evening and you can spend a day or two with us." Junior said to Ted.

"You'll love Junior's beautiful wife, she's also a great cook. But, I must say, not quite as good as your Aunt Edith, but almost as good," Uncle Lum told Ted.

"I'll go on home and you can hang around the shop until it's time to close up. You'll enjoy Junior's family, he is married to the sweetest gal in the world." He said as he waved good-bye to go to his car.

Ted's student barber was Phillip, one of the best, Junior told him.

"Where do you live while you're in school," Ted asked him.

"I'm from the farm and I stay at a boarding house over on Topeka Street, just a few blocks from here. It's close to the barber shop, the cost is reasonable and the meals are great," he informed Ted.

"Sounds interesting, do they have any rooms available?" Ted asked him.

"Well, yes, I think they do. Why, are you interested in a place?" he replied.

"I've been mulling over in my mind about going to barber school, it really looks promising and something I might like to do. I've been working the extra board as a telegraph operator for the railroad, going from place to place, and I'm ready to settle down with a more permanent job and get out of the railroad business."

He continued.

"The trouble with being a railroader, you have to move all over the division until you get enough seniority to bid on a regular location, and

I'm ready to settle down in one place. Barbering just might be the answer, it sure wouldn't hurt to try it."

"Are you ready to go?" Junior called Ted.

"It's six o'clock and time to close up. We'll catch the trolley home, it takes us within a block of our house. It goes through Riverside Park with a view of the river, you'll really enjoy it, so come on let's go." Their home was a very nice three-bedroom cottage, and Junior's wife Sue, was a warm beautiful blonde with sparkling eyes. Ted met their three year old twin daughters and the evening was wonderful with great food and chatter from the twins and also from Junior and Sue catching up on all the family news.

"You know, Junior, I've been thinking about going to barber school. I was on my way home to decide what to do with my life, railroading is becoming difficult moving around all the time and I'm ready to settle down."

"That would be wonderful, Ted, I'd be glad to have you as one of my students. It's really a great vocation and I'll only charge you half the cost of the tuition, how about that!" Junior offered Ted.

"Oh, really, you don't have to do that, I'll be glad to pay the full amount."

"I don't have to do a lot of things, but that's what I want to do. It will be good to have you around for a while, my family is very fond of you, in fact, Sue things you're really cute," he laughed and Sue blushed.

"Oh, stop it, I'm not cute, I'm down right handsome," and they all had a good laugh.

"You won't regret it, Ted, you meet a lot of nice people, and it's a business where there is always a need, every man gets a haircut on a regular basis. You can stay here with us and when you finish you can decide if you want to stay in Wichita or go back to Oklahoma."

"Okay, it's a deal, but I think I will get a room at the boarding house that one of your students was telling me about, I have a little savings and it is close enough I can walk back and forth to school."

"You're welcome to stay here, but that's your decision. You can come every Sunday and have dinner with us after church."

"Now, I'll take you up on that," Ted said.

The next day they broke the news to Uncle Lum and Aunt Edith. They were so excited, especially Aunt Edith.

"I will keep Carl here with us," she said.

"I miss Mattie so much, and I love Carl, he really takes her place."

"You know your auntie has become awful fond of Carl and since you will be staying at the boarding house we can give Carl a permanent home right here, and you can come to see him whenever you want," Uncle Lum offered.

"Now, that's a perfect deal. Carl need's a permanent home and I know he will be in good hands, so he's yours to keep."

Chapter 72

A NEW LIFE

Ted was up bright and early Monday morning to start barber school and apprenticeship at Kenny's Barber College. It was an easy walk from the boarding hour; it only took him a few minutes. A new group of ten students began their training with Ted and after a general orientation of the school and shop on their first day, they began their study. Every student was closely monitored by Junior and given the necessary tools —scissors, combs, razors, and towels—which were included in the tuition.

They were trained to greet every customer and escort them to a chair. Junior impressed the importance of welcoming each customer and to treat them as a special guest. Ted studied all about the care of the scalp and hair, the anatomy of hair growth and cleanliness, and the methods of cutting and trimming. Junior always emphasized the importance of pleasing the customer; when they are pleased with the service they become a permanent customer and will tell others. That's how to build up a good customer base.

Ted was assigned to work with Phillip, the student who cut his hair; he was due to graduate in just two weeks. He closely watched everything Phillip did. He combed the hair downward and then went underneath the hair with the comb and cut upward. He was very good at demonstrating to Ted every move and every technique and all the tricks of the trade.

Finally, it was time for Ted to do his very first haircut. Phillip carefully supervised him and offered advice when needed, and the final result was a twenty-five-cent tip and a hearty thank you. Ted was pleased with himself, but what pleased him most was a pat on the back and a "good job" message from Junior and Phillip. He felt like he was well on his way to becoming a barber.

Within a few weeks, Ted required very little supervision. He progressed rather quickly, but when he required advice he always asked for assistance. The thing that bothered him the most were the wayward cowlicks, beards, and mustaches, especially the outrageous mustaches some men sported with great pride.

At the end of the day, Ted was usually very tired being on his feet most of the day; he always looked forward to a restful evening. At dinner one evening at the boarding house, he sat next to Jim Davis, another barber student, and a young lady came into the dining room and sat in the chair next to Ted just as the food was being passed. Ted looked up and when he saw her he almost spilled the bowl of peas. He hadn't seen her before and was shaken by her beauty, a feeling he had never experienced before. She was very petite, about five foot four inches tall and very slim, and she had beautiful dark hair and a sweet smile on her face.

"May I join you." She smiled.

"Of course," Ted managed to say.

The boarding house hostess introduced her.

"Listen up everyone. I want to introduce our newest house quest, Viola Birdsell. She is my niece, my sister's daughter from Pretty Prairie, Kansas. She just arrived in Wichita and now works as a secretary at The Coleman Lamp Company, so please introduce yourselves and pass the food around before it gets cold."

As they passed the food and began to eat they introduced themselves and welcomed her.

"My name is Viola Birdsell," she responded, "and I am so happy to meet you all."

When Ted heard her voice he stood up.

"I am equally delighted to meet you," and then he felt embarrassed as no else was standing. When he sat down he almost knocked the butter dish out of Jim's hand, and his face flushed with embarrassment. She extended her hand to Ted.

"I'm delighted to meet you also, Mr. Walters."

As soon as dinner was over, the people retired to their rooms or the living room where some gathered socially. Viola walked into the living room with another lady who was a school teacher, and sat down to visit. Ted came in and sat on the opposite side of the room, and wondered in his mind what to say. He wanted to get to know her, but yet didn't want to look foolish or to look like a young, smitten teenager.

The school teacher got up to leave and said her good evening greetings. Ted got up from his chair like a gentleman and acknowledged her departure, and immediately moved closer to Viola.

"I'm new in town. What does a person do for entertainment here in Wichita?"

"That depends on what you like to do. There is a new theater over on Broadway Avenue, the Miller Theater. They show the latest movies, and there is also a sports arena where boxing and wrestling enthusiasts go. What are you interested in?" she asked.

"I have never been to very many movies, but I've heard they're great and entertaining. Could you recommend one for me to see?"

"There's a new Charlie Chaplin movie showing now at the Miller and everyone says it's really good. Other movies I've heard about is *Twenty Minutes of Love* and *Late For Work*. I saw a movie recently called *Making a Living* and it was great. My fiancé and I went to see it last Saturday."

Ted's heart sank when he heard the word "fiancé," and he blurted out without thinking.

"Would you care to take in a movie with me tomorrow evening, Miss Viola. I'm sure we would enjoy it."

"I'm sorry," she said blushing, "but I'm engaged to be married and I'm afraid my fiancé would not appreciate my going out with another man, and besides, I really don't know you, we have just met."

Ted was so flustered hearing her words.

"I am so sorry to hear you're engaged, that doesn't give me much of a chance to get acquainted with you and everyone deserves a chance," and he couldn't believe the words that came out of his mouth. She sat up straight in her chair just staring at Ted, not really knowing what to say. Everybody in the room was smiling and staring at Ted, not really knowing what he was going to say next.

"It's perfectly obvious that you're a lovely lady, and I am overcome by your beauty and charm. What if you foolishly get married and don't take the time to meet others. Are you sure he's the one for you? Do you believe in love at first sight?"

Viola couldn't believe what she was hearing. She was speechless, yet touched by his forwardness.

She stood up and managed to say, "I must go to my room."

"All right, if you must, but won't you stay and get better acquainted with me," he hastily said, sounding desperate.

Viola began to cry.

"Excuse me, please just leave me alone. You are brash and rude and I don't necessarily appreciate your attention." She quickly ran down the hall to the stairs and returned to her room.

Ted stood in the dining room feeling like the biggest stupid jerk in the world, but somehow he knew she was the one for him and he wondered how he could convince her, or if he had thoroughly messed up any chance to win her over.

The next evening after leaving the barber shop, Ted stopped at a flower shop and bought a dozen red roses. When he arrived at the boarding house, he went to her room and knocked on the door. She slowly opened it, and before she had a chance to close it in his face, he shoved the roses in her hands.

"I'm sorry I offended you by my forwardness, but I meant every word I said. I just want the opportunity to get to know you."

She slammed the door shut in his face, and he stood there for a minute, wondering how she really felt about him. He questioned whether she was playing hard to get, or whether she truly didn't like him; but he knew he wasn't ready to give up on her yet.

For the next several days, he quietly pursued her with flowers and candy he left at her door, and she would leave them and the unopened notes on the hallway table outside her room. Finally, he decided to change his tactics, perhaps she really didn't care for him at all, after all she was engaged to someone else, so he took a more casual approach.

"You look lovely this evening," he said to her at dinner. "Is this a special occasion?"

"My fiancé is in town and we're going out for the evening. He's a traveling salesman and he came in on the train this afternoon."

"I hope you have an enjoyable time," he told her with a smile.

After dinner, he told her to have a nice evening and offered an apology to her.

"I hope you will forgive me for my rash behavior. I realize I have embarrassed you and I'm terribly sorry. I guess I was just overcome by your gracious charm and I was impulsive, I'm afraid."

"I appreciate your apology, it's all right. I was so flabbergasted and taken back by your direct pursuit, and I didn't know what to do or what to say, but I must admit that down deep in my heart, I was delightfully charmed by it all." She laughed.

Several days passed by and Ted absorbed himself in barber school; the state board exams to get his license would be coming up soon. He took one evening off from his studies to join the others in the living room after dinner, and Viola came in and took the open seat next to him. He noticed she didn't have her engagement ring on her finger and he wondered why, should he ask or just let it pass.

During their conversation he felt more comfortable to ask.

"I notice you're not wearing your beautiful ring tonight. Is everything all right?"

"I've decided I'm not ready to settle down and marry just yet. I'm still very young. His traveling salesman job was very troubling for me, and he told me he was not able to give me the attention needed for a real marriage relationship and that caused me great concern."

"I'm sorry," Ted said empathetically.

"No, it's all right," she said.

"I couldn't stay engaged to him feeling the way I do. He kept telling me he would take me to meet his parents and family but he never did. I didn't know anything about them or where they lived. All he talked about was his job and how it kept him busy all the time. I think he loved his job more than he loved me. I'm just not ready to settle down yet, especially with him. I'm sorry to burden you with my problems," she said apologetically.

"No, no, it's all right. I still want you to know I care about you. When you're ready to go out with someone else, just let know," Ted said trying to open the door for him again.

"I don't see any reason why we couldn't go out this Saturday evening," she said.

"We could go to the play at Center theater and have dinner, how about it?" Ted asked her.

"That would be very nice, Ted. I will enjoy that," she said as she looked up at him with her sparkling eyes.

"Will six-thirty be a good time," he asked.

"I'll be ready, see you Saturday," she said as she got up to go to her room.

Ted sat there amazed at how lovely she looked and by what just happened. He went to his room with his head in the clouds and couldn't wait until Saturday, and wondered if this was real or if he was just dreaming. It was real all right and he wanted to shout, but he quietly walked to his room and was ready for a good night's sleep and pleasant dreams.

Saturday evening they walked arm in arm to the trolley to go into the heart of the city. The play they saw "Kid Kabaret" was delightful and starred the new stage actor and vaudevillian named Eddie Cantor, and they enjoyed it thoroughly. Eddie Cantor was made up in black face and danced his way into the hearts of the audience, and they laughed and clapped during the entire show. Another actor in the show was an older vaudevillian named Ed Wynn, and he was extremely funny in his stove-pipe hat and red nose. He carried a cane with a rubber balloon and when he squeezed the balloon it quacked like a duck, and each time it sounded, he would shout, "Do you want to buy a duck." Everyone laughed each time it happened. Ted really didn't know why, but he went along and laughed just as loud as everyone else.

On the way to dinner, they sang a song from the show, "The sun shines east, the sun shine west, but I know where the sun shines best." Ted was trying to sound like Al Jolson, and then he would make a quacking sound and say, "Ya want to buy a duck." They broke up with laughter, and Ted knew Viola was having a great time.

At the restaurant they sat at a candlelit table, and the atmosphere was very romantic. Ted felt like splurging and they ordered steak dinners and it was worth every cent; the entire dinner was delicious. A small three-man orchestra played in the background, and Ted reached in his pocket and pulled out a small box. All the people in the restaurant saw what was happening, and Viola looked at the box and knew exactly what Ted was preparing to do. She giggled nervously.

"You mean you're getting ready to propose to me on our first date!"

"Yes, I am, that's exactly what I am doing. Will you marry me? You know how I felt about you from the moment I met you and all I think about is you. I'm really in love with you, and it's making me crazy." The people in the restaurant stopped eating and all eyes turned to Ted and Viola's table.

"When I first met you I felt I couldn't listen to my heart because I had declared my love for someone else, but when you made your advancement of love for me I think I felt the same way, but I was very confused. I do love you and now I know I have loved you ever since I sat next to you at the table when we first met. Yes, I will marry you."

All the people in the room clapped and wished them the best. Ted stood to acknowledge the crowd and took a bow, while Viola blushed and wiped away the tears that flowed from her eyes.

"When can we get married," Viola asked Ted as they walked to the boarding house. "When do you finish barber college, Ted, would that be the best time?"

"I finish in five weeks, but I must ask you, where do you want to get married? If we get married here, we can have the Justice of the Peace marry us and it will cost less than a big wedding. But if you want a big wedding that's what I want too. My Aunt Edith and Uncle Lum Mahoney live here in Wichita, they are the reason I'm here. I stopped over to see them on my way home to Deer Creek and decided to stay and go to barber school. I'm sure glad I did, or I would never have met you. You see, everything happens for a reason. We could get married at their house. There are all kinds of options for us. What would your family want?"

"I don't have any relatives living here in Wichita, except my aunt here at the boarding house. My family is not a close-knit family, I almost feel like an orphan. My mother died when I was a small child, and the lady who raised me is a distant relative, but we're not very close anymore. It was my grandfather who got me the job at Coleman's. He knew Mr. Coleman real well and he agreed to help me out. My family felt disgraced by my mother who married a full-blooded Indian who was a drunk, and when he died the family, shunned her and severed all relationships. She later died of pneumonia and my brother, half-sister, and I were farmed out to relatives, and I hardly know any of them anymore."

Ted felt brokenhearted for her.

"You've had a very hard life, and I'm so sorry. I promise, you will always be loved and we will build our own family. One that will always be filled with love."

"We can get married at your parents in Deer Creek if you want," she suggested.

"What if I can't wait?" Ted questioned.

"Well, then we can get married here in Wichita by the Justice of the Peace."

"That's a deal, that's what we'll do. It's all decided."

The next Sunday they spent the afternoon with the Mahoney's and Junior and his family. Aunt Edith fixed a wonderful Sunday dinner of roast beef and they enjoyed the day visiting and getting acquainted. Aunt Edith loved Viola and they immediately took to each other, and of course, she wanted to help with the wedding plans. Carl liked her too, he crawled underneath her chair while they ate dinner and from time to time she secretly dropped a piece of meat to feed him. Besides all the love from Aunt Edith, Uncle Lum, and Junior and his family, the twins wouldn't leave her side. Viola was a big hit with everyone.

Chapter 73

THE WEDDING DAY

It was all settled, they would be married at the court house by the Justice of the Peace on August 20, rather than spending a lot of money for a big wedding. They wouldn't have to dip into Ted's small savings and instead use it to start their lives together. Junior and Sue agreed to be their witnesses, the matron of honor and best man, and stand with them at the ceremony, and Aunt Edith would plan the reception at the Mahoney home and even bake and decorate the cake. The twins were so excited because they would be the flower girls, wearing little pink dresses that will be especially made by their "Grandmommie Edith."

This was the most exciting event in Aunt Edith's life since the twins were born, and she took Viola shopping for a dress. The one she really liked was so expensive, it cost eighteen dollars, and Aunt Edith said, "We can make your dress at half the cost, dear."

They shopped for satin and lace netting and found just what they needed for her to design the pattern just like the one Viola loved at the store; after all Aunt Edith was known for her seamstress creations. They purchased the needed materials and the pink satin for the twin's dresses, and the cost was almost half the cost, as Aunt Edith pointed out. They couldn't wait to get home to get started.

When the day of the wedding came the dresses were all finished, and of course they turned out perfect. The family dressed in their Sunday best and loaded up the car and gathered at the courthouse. It was a beautiful warm sunny day, almost too warm for suits and ties, but they all looked handsome, especially Ted in his new suit and bowtie. They were escorted to the sanctuary hall to wait for the Justice of the Peace, and the crowd at the courthouse clapped and cheered when they saw the wedding party arrive. Viola looked absolutely beautiful in her long flowing gown and

Aunt Edith couldn't have been prouder. The twins danced around like little princesses, and Ted, Uncle Lum, and Junior waited in a little ante-room for the ceremony to begin. After all it was customary that the groom didn't see the bride until she walked down the aisle.

The courthouse was unusually crowded because of a trial that was being held across the hall from the sanctuary. Large crowds from the community and reporters from the newspapers had gathered in the hallways, many more than could squeeze into the small courtroom. The trial being heard was over a cult leader who was charged with polygamy and murder. The leader had a big following and promoted marriage for men to have multiple wives, and some of his wives were young underage girls.

The cult members lived on a large farm in the community of Mulvane, about thirty miles southeast of Wichita; and the newspapers were covering the trial and had articles in the daily papers, so it had the attention and curiosity of the community who were following this bizarre story. The cult leader was charged with murder of one of his followers who had disobeyed the rules which he deemed punishable by death. But of course this was totally contrary to the laws of the land, and the cult claimed they obeyed the 'laws of God,' not the laws of the land.

Uncle Lum told Ted the cult leader was arrested several weeks ago and he taught his followers that multiple marriages were legal since the Bible taught in the Old Testament that such practices were acceptable to God, starting with Abraham and on down through the prophets, and that disobedience was punishable by death. After all, the cult leader claimed to be a 'prophet' of God.

Suddenly, a scuffle broke out in the crowd and gun shots rang out in the hallway of the courthouse, and Ted, Uncle Lum and Junior rushed out into the sanctuary to protect the family. The police went into action to disarm the shooters who had brought in their guns, apparently to rescue their leader.

This caused a panic in the crowd and they began to push and shove, hoping to run to safety, but in the process an officer was shot and wounded. The courthouse went into lock-down, but the cult group busted through into the Judge's chambers and took him hostage, and took charge of the cult leader.

More shots rang out and the screaming and yelling got louder. The door of the sanctuary suddenly burst open and Ted and the men threw themselves in front of the ladies and the twins to protect them. They all ducked down to the floor and covered their heads with their hands, and the gunmen just stared at the wedding party and slowly backed out, but no shots were fired. All the ladies and the twins were sobbing and crying, and Viola reached out for Ted and he cradled her in his arms.

"What in the world is happening," Uncle Lum said. He peeked out into the hallway and saw a young man on the floor bleeding from a bullet wound in his leg. He pulled him inside and took off his necktie to tie a tourniquet around his leg to stop the bleeding.

"I don't believe it's too bad young man, you'll be all right," he told the boy to console him.

The people in the hallways were hysterical and running in all directions to try to escape. The gunshots had stopped for the moment and the attackers took the cult leader outside the courthouse to escape, but the police were in close pursuit. Ted went into the hallway and shouted to the crowd.

"Listen up, the gunmen have gone outside, so let's get control of this situation before more people get hurt. Let's calm down, the danger is gone for now, so let's wait for the police to help us to safety."

"That was good, Ted, the people are extremely scared and rightly so, we are like sheep in a pen, all trying to get out the gate at the same time, and that doesn't work. I've been following this story in the newspaper and the cult leader is a real nut case, but his followers are very dedicated to him. He had several wives and he murdered one of them because she disobeyed him."

They heard shots outside in the street; the police had cordoned off the courthouse and the surrounding area, leaving the cult group very little chance to escape. They fired at the police, but in a very short time the police had it under control and the cult leader and the gunmen were arrested and hauled off to jail.

Uncle Lum and Ted watched the scene unfold from the courthouse window and it was quite intense, the cult had getaway cars ready but they were riddled with bullets as they tried to drive away. The car hit a fire hydrant knocking it down and creating a water geyser that shot into the air and showered down on the streets. Two of the cult members were killed and wounded during the battle, some of them were women and Ted couldn't believe such a nightmare had occurred, especially over such a false premise of religion that was being promoted by such a depraved mind. Uncle Lum and Ted relayed all the information back to the family that they were safe and the gunmen had been taken away. All the wounded, including the young man Uncle Lum helped were taken by ambulance to St Francis Hospital, just down the street.

A clerk from the Justice's office came to the sanctuary.

"I'm so sorry your wedding day was so terribly interrupted, but everything is now under control. As soon as peace and order is restored and the crowds removed from the courthouse, the Justice of the Peace will come and perform your wedding. The police will soon release the Justice to resume his duties, they held him to keep him safe during the melee. Please accept our apologies. We are so sorry your very special day was so rudely interrupted."

After the police released the Justice he arrived in the sanctuary to greet the wedding party.

"Unless you have changed your minds during all this excitement, I'm here to perform your ceremony. I trust you have your marriage license with you !"

"Yes, of course," Ted said as he took it from his pocket.

They said their vows with quiet voices, still shaken from the events of the day. Viola sobbed quietly during the entire ceremony and Ted held her hand tightly as he placed the ring on her finger.

"With this ring I thee wed," he said, and Aunt Edith sobbed, she thought Viola looked so beautiful in her dress and Ted so handsome in his new suit he bought with the money his parents sent for the wedding.

The twins stood like little pixies in their pink dresses holding their little bouquets of flowers tightly in their hands, and Sue instructing them where to stand and how to act. It was all very sweet, but emotional; and Junior was the first to congratulate them after the ceremony.

The Justice of the Peace shook their hands and smiled.

"I know this was not the day you expected to have but in time you'll have exciting memories to share with your children. Congratulations, we wish you the very best."

"Thank you, sir," Ted said as they greeted the rest of the family, Aunt Edith still dabbing her eyes and Uncle Lum spouting good advice for the groom. Junior and Sue escorted them to the car and they rode in the rumble seat to the reception.

Viola planned their honeymoon, three days at the new Broadview Hotel in downtown Wichita, all paid for by her friends at Coleman's as a wedding gift. The Broadview was the prize new hotel overlooking the Arkansas River and it was so convenient, just three blocks from the courthouse.

After three glorious days together they returned to the boarding house and were greeted by all the guests with a shower of practical gifts and best wishes. It was time to resume their life, not as it was, but as Mr. and Mrs. Ted Walters.

Viola E. Walters (left) Theodore E. Walters (right)

Chapter 74

THE BLIZZARD

Life resumed back to the normal work routine, Viola was back at work bright and early Monday morning and Ted was back in school preparing for the state board exam coming up soon. He told Viola one evening.

"I don't think I'll try to work as a barber right now, it will take a while to save enough money for my own shop, so I applied for a job with the Missouri Pacific Railroad as a telegraph operator and they have accepted me. I'm not sure where I'll be working since I'll be on the extra-board, but it's an opportunity for us to get on our feet."

After a few days on the job the news came in that there was an opening for a regular operator in Benton, Kansas that would be permanent for about a year.

"Just think, I will have normal working hours without having to leave you and going out wherever they need me," Ted told her with great excitement.

"I think I would like that a lot," she responded.

"The job will last for about a year, the present operator is very ill and is expected to be out for a long time, and it's doubtful that he will ever return to work. We can get an apartment in Benton and spend a lot more time together, that's what I'm looking forward to."

He accepted the position and they picked up and moved their few belongings to Benton; and what she liked most was not having to go to work every day, she could be a real housewife. She loved to cook and make their little apartment comfortable and pretty, and she especially spent time cooking Ted's favorite meals for supper.

The winter months were approaching and they received a telegram from Ted's mother asking them to come home for the Thanksgiving holiday, and that all his brothers and sisters would be there. She also told him his father was not well and should retire from farm work. He was not able to do the hard work any longer. She added, "I need your help to convince him to sell the farm and move into town, but he won't listen to me, he's just to bullheaded."

They were excited to go and when Thanksgiving came, Ted asked for an emergency leave which was granted. They made their plans to go to Deer Creek, Oklahoma, and Viola couldn't wait to meet the family, but she was also excited about something else. She broke the news to Ted.

"I'm expecting and the baby is due in June," she said as she hugged Ted's neck tightly.

He was speechless for a moment, and tried to picture himself as a father. He held her close. *She is so young*, he thought, only seventeen. He remembered how she had told the people at the courthouse when they applied for the marriage license that she was eighteen. He felt like he needed to protect her as the tears flowed down her cheeks, mainly because she was happy and partly because she didn't know what to expect. It will be a new experience for them both. He gently wiped the tears from her face. "I'm so happy, a baby! I can hardly believe it."

They boarded the train the week before Thanksgiving for Deer Creek; it was cold as most winters are on the plains of Kansas and Oklahoma. It began to snow and snowed all the way to Oklahoma, but on arrival the weather began to turn into blizzard conditions. The Deer Creek station was deserted, only the station master was there. They were greeted by Mr. Kyle, the station master, when they got off the train.

"Hi there, Ted, it's been a while since I saw you, how ya' doing."

"I'm doing fine, Mr. Kyle, and how's your family, how's Gary, does he still live at home?"

"Yep, we can't seem to get rid of him, but he's working, thank the Lord," he replied.

"I recently got married. I want you to meet my wife, Viola. I brought her home to meet my family," Ted told him.

"Well, you sure picked a pretty one," he smiled. "Yes, sir, you sure did, but it sure don't look like you picked a good time to come visiting though, with the snow and all."

"I agree, it looks like we might get caught in a real bad blizzard," Ted said hoping the weather would let up so they could get home.

"I was sort of surprised the passenger train even made it through, from what I hear from the weather reports it's supposed to blanket the whole southwest. They predict it will be the heaviest snow seen in Oklahoma in years. It sure is the worst I've ever seen. Supposed to be five feet or more by tomorrow and they say it could be the snow storm of the century. I doubt if your folks will be able to get out of their place to come and get you, the roads are all snowed in and nobody is hardly able to get around."

Ted smiled. He had known Mr. Kyle all his life and he knew how he loved to talk.

"You're probably right, Mr. Kyle, looks like we may have to walk out to the farm," Ted said reluctantly.

"Your folks got your telegram, I delivered it myself so they know you're coming."

"Are you going to close up the station, Mr. Kyle?"

"Yep, have to, it's regulations you know. I'm sorry, Ted, but I'm going to close up now. Congratulations there, Ted, you sure got a pretty gal!"

"Thank you, I think so too. Well, honey, looks like we are going to have to walk out to the farm, luckily we wore warm clothing. Do you think you'll be warm enough, we sure don't want our baby to get cold?" he said with a smile.

"Don't be silly, that baby is nice and warm right where it is," she reassured him.

"I'm sure Dad will try to come to get us, but we can't just sit around here and wait since the station will be closed. There's no place to stay here in Deer Creek so we might as well start walking, it's seven miles out to the farm and hopefully Dad is on his way to meet us," Ted said as he took Viola's hand.

"I don't know what else to do, honey."

Ted wore his boots, and thank goodness Viola wore her goulashes, so they took off walking hand in hand through the snow carrying their bag. It was coming down really heavy, Ted guessed four or five feet by now. The wind was howling and in some places the snow was over knee deep. They plodded along for over two hours, the snow was blinding and their vision was limited as they struggled along in the deep snow. Finally, they saw a dim light in the distance and they hoped it was Dad's lantern, they were so tired they could hardly walk another step. Ted had Viola climb upon his back and he pushed on, almost falling at times, his steps were slow and laborious each time he lifted his legs out of the deep snow. The gap between them finally began to close and Dad spotted them, they were so exhausted they fell to the ground.

"Hey, Dad, is that you?" Ted called out, but with the wind howling and his Dad being 'hard of hearing,' he doubted that he heard them, but luckily, he did.

"I hear you, I can see you, I'm coming to get you." Dad had old Buck, their twelve year old mule with him, and when he rode up he saw them lying in the snow, totally covered, looking like snowmen. They hugged each other in an unlikely scene in the middle of a blizzard, and with Viola laughing and crying through her tears as she met Dad for the first time.

"I'm so glad you have old Buck with you, Viola is exhausted," Ted said so relieved.

"Old Buck was just hangin' round in the barn, didn't appear to be doing anything, so I figured he would want to come with me," Dad quipped.

"But now, I'm not sure he appreciates me draggin' him here in the middle of this blizzard."

They put Viola upon Buck's back.

"We can't make a lady walk in this snow, now can we?" Dad said.

They wrapped her in the blanket that laid across old Buck's back and started trudging their way home through the drifts. They tried to follow in the foot prints that old Buck left, but the snow was so heavy they were already covered up. Dad got so exhausted that he kept falling down.

"Get up there with Viola on old Buck, Dad, you're just plain worn out," Ted told him. He hated to give up, but he reluctantly climbed on old Buck's back, he knew he couldn't go on.

They slowly inched toward home, cold and shivering, but they finally saw the lights in the windows of the old farm house, and they couldn't have been more relieved. Old Buck had carried them home safely, but he was totally exhausted and stumbled into the nice warm barn to rest. Dad gave him a special meal of oats, but he was so tired he just laid down, the oats could wait.

They walked upon the back porch and opened the screen door, kicked off their wet shoes and boots and called out.

"We're home, Mother."

The fireplace was blazing and was a welcome sight, the warmth felt like paradise to them. The odor of freshly baked bread was like heaven and brought back childhood memories for Ted, he was so glad to be home and out of the blizzard, and to see his parents again, it had been a while.

Mother ran out to greet them with tears running down her cheeks.

"I was so worried and nervous about you out in this terrible blizzard, I'm so glad you're home, the rest of the family won't be able to come because of the storm, and that makes me so sad," she cried out as she hugged each one of them not wanting to let go. She hugged Viola and welcomed her as they both cried. Dad had been gone for over six hours and she was so glad they were finally home safe and sound.

"I keep busy the whole time baking bread, cookies, and cakes so I wouldn't worry as much, but I was really counting on old Buck to get you home safe," she admitted.

"We were lucky the road was treelined. We couldn't even see the road, it was so covered with snow, we had to use the trees as our guide. We're glad to be here, the snow was blowing so bad we had trouble seeing, and besides the cold was unbearable," Ted told her.

They each took a hot bath. Mother had a large tub of hot water on the stove she had all ready for them, she knew they would be cold and worn out. She warmed their change of clothes by the fireplace, and fixed a hot cup of coca for each of them as they settled in by the fireplace, all cozy in their nice warm clothes.

"I'm so happy I finally got to meet you, Viola, you are such a sweet pretty girl, I can see why Ted wanted so desperately to catch you," she said as she could finally relax.

"but you are so young! I got married very young myself, I was only fifteen when Dad asked me to marry up with him."

"I'm glad you're happy for us, Mom, but we have another surprise for you, we are expecting our first baby in May or June," Ted broke the good news to them.

Mother smiled and acted very pleased.

"You didn't have to tell me, I just knew it, women's intuition you know. We must celebrate, we just love all our grandchildren. Oh my, I'm so happy, congratulations."

They ate a wonderful supper and caught up on all the family news, but they were all sad that the rest of the family couldn't come, the blizzard was so bad they just couldn't venture out in it. They all went to bed early that night after such an exhausting day, and Ted and Viola slept in the guest room which was all furnished with a nice feather-bed covered with a heavy quilted blanket that was hand made by Mother. It kept them cozy-warm through the whole night, even though the logs in the fireplace and old wood stove had burned out.

Ted got up early the next morning and stepped out onto the cold bare floor. He quickly got dressed, poured himself a cup of coffee and parked in front of the fireplace which was blazing again since Dad got up early and built a fire. Mother was busy making cinnamon rolls for breakfast while Dad was out at the barn feeding the livestock and milking the cow. He left the livestock in the barn and in the fenced pen to protect them against the blizzard, it was just too bad to turn them out to the pasture.

"Please go and help your Dad, Ted, and bring in the eggs from the henhouse before they freeze. This is absolutely the worst snow storm I have ever seen here, haven't seen anything like this since we left Illinois way back when, sure hope the snow doesn't cave in the roof, wouldn't that be a awful? If this keeps up we might have to dig a tunnel out to the barn."

After the chores were done they all sat down for a breakfast of cinnamon rolls, pancakes and sausage, and plenty of hot coffee that tasted so good and warmed their insides. Viola especially enjoyed it, it was a wonderful farm breakfast, she thought.

"Let's listen to the radio, I got it for Mother for Christmas, maybe they will tell us something about the weather." Dad proudly said.

"You know, Ted, I had to string a wire up into the attic to tune into the radio station. The station we get is only on three hours a day, and I like to listen to a newsman named H. G. Kaltenborn, he has such a deep clear voice, and he gives all the news of the day, and we can tune into a station way off in Del Rio, Texas, can you imagine that?" Dad expounded on all the amazement of the radio.

It was the morning of December 2, 1917 as they listened during breakfast that morning, and much to their surprise President Woodrow Wilson came on the air to address the American people. They couldn't imagine such a thing. They were hearing the president talk in his own voice, it must be very important, Dad told them. President Wilson ask the Congress of the United States for a declaration of war against Germany. They all sat there at the table unable to speak, they couldn't believe what they just heard. They strained their ears to hear as the static on the radio made it difficult to hear clearly.

"I almost forgot, Ted, you got a letter in the mail a few days ago, it says it is from the draft board," Mother said.

"Quiet, Mother, we're trying to hear the President. If I heard him right, he just declared war on Germany."

"They've been talking about that for weeks," Mother said.

"I guess they finally decided to do it. I heard that German submarines sank some of our ships recently, but Germany denied it, but we all know they did. Many of our sailors lost their lives on that ship, I read that it in the newspaper recently. When that happened President Wilson said that we needed to declare war, and now he went and did it."

"Did you say I got a letter from the draft-board, Mother?" Ted said.

She handed it to him and he opened it knowing in his heart what it was:

> Greetings: Mr. Theodore E. Walters On receipt of this letter you are classified 1-A in the Armed Service of the United States of America. You are ordered to report to th Recruitment office in Oklahoma City within fifteen days of the receip of this letter. You may file for another rating if your circumstance have changed, such as marriage, children, illness, or death. Please understand that failure to comply with this notice well cause the law t be enforced by the U. S. Marshal's office.

> Your Local Draft Board Chairman, Mr. Guy Hydrick
> They all sat there at the table totally flabbergasted.

"Thanks, Mom, this really made my day," Ted managed to say. Viola immediately began to cry, holding her head in her hands.

"What are we going to do?" she cried.

"I'm expecting a baby and you're being drafted, what are we going to do?"

"Don't cry, honey, please don't cry, we don't know yet what will happen, maybe they won't take married men, at least I hope that's still the case. I read in the paper that if war comes they hoped there would not be a need to draft married men, only those who were single," Ted tried to console her.

"I wouldn't be surprised that when I register they will turn me around and send me right back home," he added.

Dad said.

"I hope you're right, son, but I just heard they took the Willis boy and he's married, but I'm not sure he was drafted, he may have volunteered."

"I heard he went just to get away from his responsibilities, he has always been a worthless so and so," Mother added.

"We'll just have to wait and see," Ted said.

"I'll report before we leave for Wichita next week and ask for a deferment and see if they will grant it because I'm married and expecting a child. Or maybe my job on the railroad will be considered essential, and if that's the case they will re-classify me, it's worth a try."

"As soon as this storm lets up and the roads are clear I'll take you into the city so we can quit worrying and fretting about it, so let's all just wait and see," Dad said hoping everyone would calm down.

That night as they went to bed, Viola lay in Ted's arms, sobbing again.

"Do you really think there's a big chance you won't have to go, I really hope so."

"Right now we just don't know, please don't worry, we can't really do anything about it right now so let's get a good night's sleep and things will look better in the morning after we've rested."

The next morning it was still snowing. He finished his second cup of coffee and put on his old mackinaw coat that had been hanging on a peg in the kitchen near the back porch since he was fourteen years old. He put on his gloves and old coon skin hat he made for himself from a raccoon he tracked and skinned years ago, and again the memories came pouring back into his mind.

He stepped out into the cold to help his Dad. They shoveled out pathways in the snow to the barn, the henhouse, and outdoor toilet. The snow drifts had piled up at least seven feet against the house and drifted several feet high between the house and the barn. The pump was frozen so they couldn't pump any water, but Mother had prepared ahead of time and filled the wash tubs, just in case, she had learned from past experiences over the years.

They broke the ice on the water troughs every morning so the animals had water to drink, and they fed the stock grain and hay from the 'stockpiles' in the barn.

"Thank you, son, this work is getting to much for me, you know, I'm not getting any younger. Mother wants me to retire and sell the farm and I'm beginning to think she's right. I'm not sure I could handle another winter like this."

"She's right, Dad, you need to listen to her. Go on in and have breakfast and some hot coffee, I'll finish digging the tunnel so we can get around better."

Several days passed and the snow finally let up, and Ted felt they would be able to travel back to Wichita in a few days. The warmer temperatures began to melt the snow and the water ran like a creek, which backed up into the pasture. The roads were muddy, nothing could get through except on horseback or a wagon. Ted reported to the draft board, but they referred him to the Wichita office to register when he got back home, so he still didn't have an answer to his draft status, they would have to wait until they got home.

On the day Ted and Viola left for home, Dad told them to ride the two farm horses into the railroad station.

"When you get there just release them and they will come home on their own. They know the way back to their warm barn and they are very partial to the oats that I feed them every day," he said to them as they tearfully said their good-byes.

Chapter 75

THE ARMY

The draft board in Oklahoma transferred Ted to the Wichita office where he now resides and requested he make his appeal for deferment before them. He wrote a letter to the board making his request on the basis of his marriage status and soon to be father, and he hoped his job as a telegraph operator was essential for the civilian war effort to maintain the railway system. He mailed the letter hoping the board would agree with him and would grant him a deferment, especially for Viola's sake, she would be brokenhearted if he had to leave her.

But it wasn't to be, several days later he received a letter which took them both by surprise. He was to report to Fort Riley, Kansas, on January 19, 1918, and it read:

> Greetings: Mr. Theodore Edmond Walters The local draft board composed of your neighbors for the purpose of obtaining your eligibility for training and service in the Armed force of the United States, hereby notifies you have been selected for training and service in the United States military forces. You will therefore report at the railroad station in Wichita, Kansas, at 5:00 p.m. on January 19, 1918, to be transported to your induction station at For Riley, Kansas.
>
> Guy Hydrick Chairman of the Sedgwick County Selection Board.

Viola immediately burst into tears, everything seemed to be happening at once; she couldn't imagine not having him there when the baby came. Ted tried to console her.

"Don't cry, honey, we can get through this and beside we can't do much about it, it's just providence at work."

They decided she would go back to work at Coleman's and live at the boarding house, and about a month before the baby was due she would go to Deer Creek to have the baby. They hoped by then his request for deferment would be granted and they could resume their lives as they planned.

"There's one good thing, if I go to the army my seniority with the railroad will continue, which means when I get out I won't have to worry about a job, I'll have one waiting for me," Ted reassured her.

The good-byes were agonizing for them both when Ted reported at the station, they were so in love. Viola didn't want to let go of his hand.

"I'll write as often as I can, I love you," Ted cried as he pulled away from her.

He boarded the train along with hundreds of other men who were facing the same as he was. They took their seats in the coach car and Ted was able to get a window seat to catch one last glimpse of his beautiful bride and wave good-bye. As the train moved out he began to contemplate in his mind about his life and his future, he felt so unsophisticated and uninformed about national politics and world affairs. He had left all that behind him with the Wobblies in Mexico, and wanted to forget about politics and all about that time in his life and move on. Now he wasn't sure what to expect, he didn't even know very much about the country of Germany, the country that has declared war on the U. S.

The only Germans he knew was his friend growing up on the farm, Hugh Meckler, whose family immigrated to the United States from Germany when he was just a small boy. Hugh was a good kid, so he naturally thought all Germans were like him. He felt so confused and questioned in his mind, why would we have to fight and defend our country against people like him? He read his induction notice over and over again as the train proceeded through the night until he fell asleep.

In the morning the conductor shook him on the shoulder and told him they had arrived and it was time to get off the train. He jumped up and took his bag from the rack and prepared to disembark. The draftees were met by a big, ugly looking drill sergeant with a loud deep voice who used a bull-horn to round them all up and give them instructions. Ted carried his bag as instructed and reported at the desk, and after they signed in they were immediately sent to the side of the building to form a line.

Within a few minutes the Sergeant's deep voice sounded again from the bull-horn.

"Attention, you are now in the army, so you will form two lines, and do it now." The draftees struggled to form their lines and the sergeant continued to shout.

"That's a very disorganized line-up, I see we have a lot of work to do, gentlemen, so listen to me, straighten your line," he shouted loudly.

"Now that is better, turn to your right and march to those trucks that are lined up in the street and you will be driven to Camp Funston, a few miles from here. March!"

They boarded the trucks as they tugged along their bags and rode for the next thirty minutes to the camp which was on the outskirts of Fort Riley. As they approached, Ted saw a large sign at the entrance which read, 'Camp Funston,' and he also saw row after row of newly constructed barracks, some still being painted. He could tell it was a brand new training camp out in the middle of the Kansas prairie, and it was built in a hurry to prepare for the war ahead.

The truck pulled up to the barracks and a drill sergeant stood by and waited for them to unload.

"Welcome to Fort Funston," he shouted over the bull horn.

"My name is Sergeant John Hicks, you will address me as Sergeant. Think of me as your new 'daddy' for the next few weeks, if you need anything see me first, and if you don't you will regret it. Advise me about anything and everything, and I should warn you, I don't suffer fools well. Now march into the supply building where you will be issued your uniforms, bedding, and everything you will need to be a soldier in the United States Army. Later, you will prepare your civilian clothes and suitcases to ship home to your wife or family."

They marched single file into the building where they received their clothing, boots, a belt, jacket and overcoat, a dress uniform, two pairs of trousers, shirts, dungarees, shoes, and they were also issued a mattress, a pillow, sheets, blankets for their cot, and a shaving kit. They were instructed to disrobe and dress in their uniform, and if their uniform doesn't fit they were to return it immediately for an exchange. They were given two hours to complete this process before meeting in the mess hall for dinner. Ted changed his clothing and everything fit that had been issued to him, but a few of the men who had vainly given a smaller size than they actually wore had to go back and exchange their clothing and face the embarrassment. Ted boxed up his civilian clothes to send home to Deer Creek and went outside where they were ordered to report. He asked the corporal for permission to smoke, which was granted, so he pulled out his bag of Bull Durham tobacco and rolled a cigarette to smoke while he waited.

The corporal lined them up to march to the mess hall, it seemed to Ted that what they did mostly in the army was 'form a line and wait.' When he got his food he ate ravenously, he hadn't eaten since he left Wichita and he was starved. They had twenty minutes to eat before they were to report back outside, where they were once again instructed to form a line in single file. They marched to the medical building to received their medical tests and shots of every kind, and Ted knew one of the shots was tetanus, an important one if they were injured in anyway. He finished all the tests, the physical and psychological ones, and passed them all with high marks he was told. As they marched back to their barracks several men began to fall down, they passed out after all the rigorous marching, tests and shots, and the corporal instructed the men to assist their fellow soldiers back to the barracks. He continued to shout instructions to the rest of the men and didn't miss a beat as if he was used to the reactions that occurred.

When they returned to their barracks they were instructed to locate their assigned bunk and make it up with their mattress and sheets, and when they finished they were dismissed for the day until 5:00 a.m. the next morning. The drill sergeant ended his instructions with this message: 'Good night ladies, lights out at 2200.'

The name Theodore E. Walters appeared on two bunks both the top and bottom, and Ted was confused thinking they made a mistake. He chose the bottom one just as another young soldier arrived and took the top bunk. Ted said.

"Hello, it appears we have the same name. My middle name is Edmond, what's yours?"

The young man replied.

"Mine is Eric."

"Eric, it's good to meet you, call me Edmond, and I'll call you Eric from now on so there won't be any confusion, if that's okay with you. I'm from Wichita, where are you from?"

"I'm from Yates Center, Kansas and have lived there all my life, and this is the first time I've been away from home, except when I was on vacation with my parents."

"Well, Eric, I don't think this is going to be any vacation, we can almost guarantee that," and they both laughed.

Ted made sure he had brought writing paper, envelopes, and stamps with him, so he sat down at the table in the center of the room along with several other men, and wrote to Viola. He missed her already and couldn't get her off his mind.

My Dearest Wife.

Well, my love, I'm in the army now and everything is very busy. I arrived here this morning at 9:30 a.m. and we were met by this drill sergeant who marched us out to a truck that delivered us to the base. They gave us everything we need to wear, about six or seven pairs of clothing, two pairs of shoes, and lots of other stuff like bedding and such. They then gave us a bunch of shots in our arms and one other place, which makes it hard to sit down, but its better now. Several of the men had reactions and a few fainted. But I'm all right, We're here in the barracks now and they have ordered lights out, so I'll have to write again another time: So I'll say goodnight.

P. S. Oh, yes, a funny thing happened, the fellow whose bunk is above mine has the same name of Theodore E. Walters, but his middle name is Eric. He is from Yates Center, Kansas and a very nice guy, anyway I thought it was odd that we have the same name.

That's all for tonight. my love. I'm fine, I miss you- and love you so very much. Write as soon as you can. Miss you lots!Love you, Ted.

Ted crawled into bed totally exhausted, and he laid there thinking about Viola and about the day, but after a while when he was almost asleep he heard the sound of sobbing and crying. It had to be coming from the men, or boys, since some of them were only seventeen years old. Ted thought it was probably the first time some of them have been away from home.

"You hear that, Eric, that means we're not alone in here. I guess it's all right to be a little scared, but I understand. I feel like doing the same thing, this is a brand new experience for us all and the future of war is really unknown."

Just as they were about to fall asleep the drill sergeant walked through the barracks.

"At ease, no need to get up, gentleman, this is the last and only night you are completely free of any duties. Starting in the morning you will be sworn into the army of these United States and army life will begin promptly at 5:00 a.m. Get used to it, boys, because tomorrow you will all start to be real men. Good night."

As promised, at 5:00 a.m., the bugle sounded, *and it sounded like it was right next to his bunk*, Ted thought, as he rolled out and quickly got dressed. Sergeant Hicks walked in and ordered them to stand at attention beside their bunk.

"We will march to the mess hall for breakfast and when you are finished we will gather as a unit on the parade grounds where you will be sworn in and take your oath of allegiance to the United States. Then, my fellow soldiers, we will begin to teach you what hell is like and how to survive as soldiers in the U. S. Army. Attention! We will now march in rows of two out of the barracks and to the mess hall. March !"

After a hearty breakfast they marched to the parade grounds and into the large administration building where they began the process of becoming legitimate soldiers. They were given numerous forms to fill out asking every question imaginable about their lives, their families' name, the schools attended, and on and on. Maybe this was the time they collected the information needed to grant deferments, Ted hoped. They were given an I. Q. test and personal interviews, and soon after the testing some men were dismissed to go home, especially after they finished the I. Q. test, Ted noticed.

When he was interviewed the Sergeant seemed very interested in his work as a telegraph operator, and he immediately filled out a document to submit to the Assignment Officer suggesting Ted be transferred to the Army Railroad Division if there was a vacancy to be filled, but he didn't know at the moment whether they needed more men in that department, he informed Ted.

"I'm a married man and we are expecting a baby, sir," Ted told him during the interview.

"I need to ask for a deferment."

"I can't promise you anything at this time, but it is duly noted on your form and it will be sent to the proper department for consideration. You can apply for a hardship discharge but if it's not granted, I recommend you see the chaplain, he may have some influence in that area."

Day after day of basic training started the same as the day before, the Sergeant ordered them to stand at attention, but on this morning the Sergeant walked up to a young soldier to inspect his bunk, and then ordered the nervous young soldier to take his mattress and all issued equipment to see Captain Riley in the administration office. All the men wondered what had happened to him as the young soldier hung his head and walked out of the barrack carrying his gear and bedding, but not a word was said by anyone.

"Attention, men, I see you need to hear an explanation, there are some men who have issues that are not suitable for service in the U. S. Army.

We hope this young man will be able to resolve his issues soon, but the military is not the place for him to do so. Today after chow, you will continue to learn to distinguish your left foot from your right, and we will spend most of the day on the grinder learning how to march, and as usual we will march to the shooting range with your rifles in hand where you will continue to learn the fundamentals of the Springfield rifle and how to shoot and take care of it. Now, lineup in columns of four and march." *So far*, Ted was thinking, *the army is all about lining up and marching.*

The rumors quickly passed through the barracks about the young man who was dismissed, but the true story was finally revealed, he was physiologically unfit for service in the U. S. Army and was given a medical discharge. It was also revealed that he wet the bed for three nights straight, which caused him great embarrassment and made him unfit for service.

Each day was the same, they marched the five miles to the range for shooting and bayonet practice, rope climbing, and climbing up a twenty foot high wall and dropping to the other side. *But the biggest challenge*, Ted thought, *was swinging by a rope across a large mud puddle without falling.* Only four in his unit made it the first time, and needless to say, he wasn't one of them so he didn't earn any bragging rights.

The days were long and weary and when Ted got back to the barracks each evening he sat down to write to Viola. He told her all the tiring things they had been doing, and reminded her he had been to the chaplain to plead his case. 'Keep the faith, honey, I will have a two week leave when I finish my basic training, and I can't wait to see you. Hope you and the baby are doing fine, this in month number four and I know the baby is growing. I love you.' He signed his name and quickly dozed off to sleep.

The final days of basic training finally came, drill after drill, shooting and bayonet practice, running the obstacle course, marching mile after mile, eating, sleeping and standing watches. They learned to take their rifles apart, clean them and put them back together. In one of his daily letters he wrote, "I go to chapel every day just for the peace and quiet, and especially to have some solace after a day of activities that never stop. Honey, the chaplain has written a hardship letter for me and sent it to the proper officer for a decision, but please don't set your hopes to high, I'm doing all I can. I'm so glad the training is nearly finished, but the important thing to me is I can come home soon and be with you for a few days, and another good thing that has come from all this is the friendships I am making and I hope some of them will last a life time.

Chapter 76

A GOOD SOLDIER

With boot camp finished, Ted was anxious to get home for his two-week leave. When the train arrived in Wichita, Viola was waiting at the station, and as he stepped off the train in full uniform, looking handsome and proud, she ran to him and cried on his shoulder, not about to let go of him.

"I missed you so much," they both said over and over.

The two weeks were the best days they had ever spent together, but the days passed much too quickly. Her little tummy was growing and she could feel the baby moving. They both thought that was so exciting and they couldn't wait until the time came so they could see their sweet little creation. But the day came when he had to return to camp and the good-byes were anguishing, especially for Viola, but at the same time she was so grateful for the wonderful two weeks they had together. She stood at the station, waving good-bye trying hard to be brave, and she didn't leave until the train was completely out of sight.

The next day Ted was back in the army routine. The bugle sounded at 5:00 a.m. and the Sergeant shouted the morning announcements.

"Attention, this is the day you will receive your assignment and division orders, so be prepared to assemble on the parade grounds as usual after chow."

During breakfast Ted and Eric discussed what they thought the possibilities were for their new assignment, and they agreed it could be an overseas deployment based on the rumors that were running rampant throughout the barracks. They finished eating and anxiously gathered with the rest of the men on the parade grounds to hear the news from the Sergeant. Ted really didn't want to leave the states and be so far away from Viola, but he couldn't help but think the experience ahead could also be intriguing and uncertain at the same time. What he wanted to do most was to serve his country the best he could, and be a good soldier to keep the country safe for Viola and his child.

He recalled when he was a rebel fighting in the Baja years ago, and the discharge document given to him by General Mosby calling him a good soldier. But it was different this time, now he wanted to be a rebel for his country to protect it for his wife and child from a power mad king who threaten them. He wanted to be the best he could be and be recognized again as a good soldier for the cause.

They were ordered to board the trucks to go to the supply depot to receive additional equipment and clothing needed for their new assignment. They were given a heavy overcoat, a new rifle, a large amount of personal care items, a rain poncho, gas mask, canteen, and they were also issued heavy boots with spats, the army called them puttees, that wrapped around their boot tops and pant legs. The Sergeant warned them emphatically.

"If you lose or misplace any of the equipment issued to you, you will replace it at your own cost, and I will not hear any complaining if that should happen, you are the one responsible for it all."

Back at the barracks they were given demonstrations on how to pack their canvas sea bag for deployment. and it was presented by a corporal who was a long time regular army man who had served since the Spanish-American War. He laughed as he shared with them some of his army stories. He told them how he had been busted so many times because of infractions, but the army always forgave him and let him stay. Although the stories were funny and entertaining he added a warning, 'keep your noses clean, it isn't worth going though the hassle to clean up your mess.'

The new soldiers couldn't believe how much stuff the old corporal packed in one bag, it was beyond belief. No wonder they kept him in the army, no one else could pack a bag like that, they all thought. That evening Ted wrote to Viola and told her about the day's activities and that she may not hear from him for a while, they will receive a new assignment and be moved, but he didn't know where. When the Sergeant announced lights out that night he collected all the letters to be mailed and told them they would be in transit for the next few days, but their letters would be mailed for them in due time. Ted went to bed that night and mulled over in his mind where their new assignment might be, but he felt certain they would be going into battle.

The bugle sounded at 5:00 a.m. the next morning, and the Sergeant entered the barracks.

"Gentleman, assemble your full gear and be prepared to move in ten minutes. You will load your gear and yourselves into the trucks outside to be moved to the shipping point at Fort Riley, and you will receive your breakfast when you arrive."

At Fort Riley they disembarked from the trucks as ordered and were marched to the mess hall. During breakfast everyone was rather quiet, everything seemed so uncertain. Afterward, they re-assembled to receive their orders and were issued a patch to be placed on their uniform shoulder, a red patch with the number '1' on it. The Sergeant announced.

"You are now in the First Expeditionary Regiment, the 2nd Battalion of the 16th infantry, and after lunch you will be transported to the station at Fort Riley to board the train for your new destination, so welcome to the 'Big Red 1'."

That afternoon each man was checked by the Sergeant for a complete field pack as they boarded the train. Ted and Eric loaded their packs on the overhead rack and took a seat, and after each soldier settled in the Sergeant once again walked the aisle to check each man, and after an hour of waiting the train finally pulled away from the station and they were on their way.

They travelled throughout the afternoon and evening passing through Kansas City and several smaller towns along the way, stopping only for rest stops and canteen services from the Red Cross ladies who handed out sandwiches, coffee, and cigarettes to each soldier, and to change the train and engine crews. They continued for the next three days until they arrived in New York where they were met by a large crowd of cheering people who were obviously supportive of the war effort. They offered the soldiers gifts of all kinds, sandwiches, cookies, coffee, chocolates, cigarettes, newspapers, and magazines, and welcomed them to New York. The Red Cross turned out in full force to hand out box lunches to each soldier, and the soldiers were overwhelmed by all the attention. Someone in the crowd yelled out to them, 'bring us back the head of Kaiser Wilhelm!' After a two hour stop over and a visit with the crowd, the troops were ordered to re-board the train to travel on to their next destination.

Ted anxiously read the newspaper about the war efforts, and the article he was reading called the soldiers, "doughboys," how they got that name Ted really didn't know, and it told how they were on the road to adventure. It made him think about the men who had been killed in action and those who were facing battle, and he thought if people really think of war as an adventure, they must be crazy.

That evening Ted looked out the window and saw the depot sign, Hoboken, New Jersey, and he thought this must be our destination as the train slowed and pulled into a siding. He could see they were in a very large freight yard and he could smell the salty sea air. The Sergeant came through the car and announced.

"Attention men, keep your eyes on me and listen to my instructions. Be prepared to exit the train in an orderly fashion from the rear door, gather all your equipment and on my orders we will disembark, is that clear? We will march to the harbor to an awaiting ship which will take us to our final destination. Any questions?"

"Yeah, Sergeant, what is our final destination?" one soldier yelled out.

"Can't tell you men, don't know, you will be told at the appropriate time," he replied.

The men all laughed. "Sure, sure," they said among themselves. "No one seems to know where we're going."

No other questions were asked as they all gathered their belongings and prepared to disembark and march when the Sergeant gives the order. When the order came they started marching between the rows of passenger cars in the switching yard and moved toward a large warehouse harbor building. They could see the top of a large ship on the other side, and it looked mammoth. Now, Ted knew he was going overseas and his suspicions had been correct all along, but their final destination was still unknown. He knew he was on his way to becoming a real soldier and would be going into battle which would take him farther away from his sweet Viola.

Chapter 77

CROSSING THE SEA

One by one, the Big Red 1 Division marched up the gangway to board the ship carrying their full packs on their backs, it was a difficult climb because of the steepness of the steps. Ted turned his head and looked back across the landscape to get one last look at the country he was leaving behind and wondered when he would see it again, if ever.

This wasn't the first time he had crossed the seas, but this time was very different. Before, he was in his late teens and was on an adventure to discover the world, but this time it is to defend his country and he wasn't sure he would ever return. Chills ran through him as his mind wandered into the many unanswered questions, but he quickly regained his composure as he stepped onto the main deck of the ship they had seen in the harbor, the *U.S.S. George Washing*ton.

This grand ship had once been a luxury ocean-liner built by the Germans in 1908, and they named it the *U. S. S. George Washington* after the first President of the United States. It was the third largest ship in the world and seized by the United States in April 1917, when the German captain sought refuge in the United States to escape his countries war against Europe.

When the United States entered the war, the ship was converted into a transport carrier and was commissioned in September,1917. When Ted stepped onto to the main deck he couldn't believe the grandeur and size of this mammoth floating vessel, it was beyond anything he had ever seen. They were directed to a large stairwell downward to the lower level compartments which was the living and sleeping quarters for the troops. Each compartment was huge and entirely filled with sleeping bunks that were stacked five high from the deck to the bulkhead above, with just enough room to walk between the rows of bunks. Ted looked around him and tried to visualize each man, hundreds of them, all tucked into their sleeping quarters like an item on a shelf.

After leaving their full sea packs in the designated area, they located their assigned bunks. Ted was number five in his unit so that meant his bunk was on the top, he struggled with his carry-on pack as he climbed the ladder, and once he arrived he noticed over his head was a large pipe, about twelve inches in diameter, that ran the length of the compartment. He could hear the roaring sound of the running water that constantly passed through the pipe, which supplied the water for the hundreds of men using the bathing and toilet systems of the entire ship. *Oh, this is great,* Ted thought, *I'll just have to get used to the sound I guess, and make do with what is handed me.* He looked over his bunk and his small storage space which was about two feet wide and was located between his bunk and the water pipe. He stored his clothing, personal items, and boots on the shelf and settled into his new quarters.

He read over the ships instructions that each man was handed, to learn about the ships rules, specifically to find out when they could smoke. They could not smoke at anytime unless the ships 'smoking lamp' was on and it was announced over the loud speaker, and they could only smoke on the top deck. At night the ship was under 'black out' and a no smoking ban was in effect, no lights could be shown above deck and all port holes were to be covered.

The loud speaker suddenly sounded, 'Attention, all hands on deck, report by section to the main deck wearing your life jackets and prepare for departure.' Ted's section quickly responded and joined the hundreds of other men on the deck to watch the *U.S.S. George Washington* sail from the harbor on February 29, 1918, for an unknown destination, at least unknown to the troops. Ted watched as they passed by the Statue of Liberty and the skyline of New York City as the ship slowly steamed out of the harbor toward the open sea.

The first mate announced the ships rules to the troops as they stood at attention. He told them, all soldiers must wear their life jackets when on deck; the dinner time is twenty minutes for each unit of two hundred men to allow time for the next unit; during free time they could gather on the top deck, but they must stay out of the way of the crew doing their assigned duties; smoking is allowed only when the smoking lamp is on; and life jackets must be worn at all times during rough weather.

When they were dismissed Ted looked out across the sea at its blue color and how it changed to a darker lead color as they approached the deeper water. He was continually fascinated by the sea and how the white caps sparkled and glittered as the sunlight hit the waves, and how the sea was never still, it was always moving. As he looked at the vastness of the ocean he suddenly felt home sick, thinking about Viola and his family, he knew he was going to miss them a lot, and wondered if he would ever come back. He wasn't all alone out on the sea, there were five other troop ships in their convoy with four destroyers and a tanker which accompanied them. He couldn't help but think they must be headed for a big battle front somewhere in Europe, but he didn't know where.

During their free time, which was scant, the troops liked to play cards and Ted usually suggested poker, which he normally won. He felt good that he could still outwit the other players by carefully watching their reactions and the way they bet, he could generally read his opponents pretty well. As they played he remembered how his uncle taught him to play when he was just a kid, and how his uncle had owned a pool hall that allowed illegal gambling. He also remembered how his mother fussed at him about the sinful nature of gambling, and how his father defended him. But on the first evening out at sea he won thirty dollars, and he decided to keep all his winnings to send home to Viola so she would have extra money for the baby.

They were constantly kept busy doing lifeboat drills, calisthenics, rifle care and safety drills, and they were also assigned duties to help keep the ship clean, it seemed like the drills never stopped. At night Ted was completely worn out, even the noisy water pipe above his head that he was worried about didn't keep him awake, he would always go fast asleep.

Twelve days at sea they neared the Irish coast, and it had been relatively smooth sailing without incident all the way across, but suddenly the destroyers began running full steam, circling the troop ships and laying a smoke screen around the convoy to hide them. Ted's unit was assigned to be on look-out for any possible signs of the enemy, and they were ordered to be under continuous procedural watch, they were definitely entering the war zone and the troops all knew it.

A sense of danger and quietness was in the air. The troops' composure and demeanor changed from a relaxed mood to an intense feeling of danger. A feeling of seriousness penetrated the troops and all eyes were on the water watching for any signs of enemy submarine periscopes, and Ted could feel the tension growing. But the intense quietness and tension was soon interrupted by sirens from the ship, the *U.S.S. Tuscania*, which was under attack and was hit by torpedoes from a German submarine.

Ted saw the *U.S.S. Tuscania* ride high out of the water when she was hit in the midsection by two torpedoes, creating a loud explosion and leaving a gaping hole in the side of the ship. Ted watched from his vantage point and saw the ocean water rushing into the gaping hole, raising the ship high out of the water and then crashing back down into the sea. He shuddered at the spectacle and heard a fellow soldier scream out.

"Oh, my God, my brother is on that ship, my poor brother, dear God, no."

Ted's heart sank as he heard the soldier cry out in his grief, and tears came to his eyes as the realization of war hit him, and he looked at the chaos below him and saw men scrambling to get on lifeboats to escape the exploding ship, while others jumped from the upper deck into the icy Atlantic water below. And during the chaotic situation one of the lifeboats filled with men suddenly fell while it was being lowered, throwing the men crashing into the frigid waters, apparently the mechanism broke tipping the lifeboat forward spilling its contents into the sea.

The *U.S. Destroyers* located the German submarine and moved in closer to drop their depth chargers overboard, which exploded deep beneath the water creating powerful waves that rocked the lifeboats. The boats rocked up and down and back and forth and Ted thought they were going to tip over, but he hoped that was not the way it would all end for those men being rescued.

The sirens on the destroyers sounded the warning and orders came from the loud speakers as they circled the ship, all transport ships were ordered to scatter from the area and move away as fast as they could and head for the port in France. Each ship was on their own, the destroyers would not be able to protect them any longer, they were to move away quickly and each were wished 'God's speed.'

Ted held the rail tightly as he watched below, and he saw a torpedo speeding through the water headed directly for the *U.S.S. George Washington*. There was no place for them to go or hide as they all watched in horror, but somehow a miracle seemed to occur. Ted hadn't noticed the direction the ship had turned, but the *U.S.S. George Washington* was zigzagging in the ocean as it broke away from the other ships, and it had changed directions just enough that the torpedo missed the ship, but they could hear it scrape against the hull and bounce off the side and then sink beneath the sea unexploded.

Ted took a deep breath, not realizing he had been holding his breath expecting an impact, but he felt relief that somehow God had just intervened to save them. He raised his head to the heavens and gave thanks to the Lord, he knew death had just passed him by. They were at war, it wasn't just preparing any longer, the war had arrived and they were in the midst of it.

The troop ships moved slowly away and the German submarines had disappeared, they either had been destroyed or expended their supply of torpedoes and moved from the area. Ted thought another possibility might be that they may have gone deeper into the sea to avoid another attack by the destroyers who were honing in on them. The men on the *U.S.S. George Washington* stood on deck watching the Tuscania sink into the sea. They could still see the evacuation and the life boats filled with men being lowered to safety into the sea. The explosions sounded from the fateful ship with fires burning in different areas, causing rocket like bursts into the air, and in the water below they could see men struggling to reach a lifeboat.

The *U.S.S. George Washington* moved farther away from the wreckage, and Ted looked back to watch the rockets shooting into the air, but they were moving on, hopefully to safety, but he knew there would be more war zones ahead. But for the moment they were soon relieved to see one of the destroyers who had rejoined them laying out smoke screens to protect them, and after two more anxious days their ship pulled safely into Le Havre, France.

They disembarked and assembled in their designated training area and temporary barracks, and after they were dismissed for the day, Ted sat down to write a quick note to Viola.

Chapter 78

PARIS, FRANCE

It was a cool morning in France when the troops were loaded into the transport trucks to make the ninety-six-mile journey to Paris. When they arrived, they were met by a cheering crowd of Parisians and French government officials as they lined up in formation to march into the city. A French military band led them through the streets, and it seems a parade was planned to welcome the US troops and to bolster the morale of the French people who had become demoralized by the war, and also to bolster the French troops who were totally fatigued by weeks of battle.

They proudly marched through the streets with the people cheering, and were led to the statue and tomb of Lafayette, the famous French general who assisted the US during the Revolutionary War. Ted was surprised to see General Pershing at the statue to greet the troops and give an inspirational speech to them and the French people. He was quite impressed as he heard the speech, especially when the general uttered the words, "Lafayette, we are here."

They were dismissed for the day and given liberty in the city of Paris, and Ted and a few fellow soldiers visited the famous sights and a restaurant to get a taste of French food. But when he learned they serve a lot of horse meat in the country—he wasn't crazy about eating it—it just didn't sound right to him.

The gardens in the city were beautiful; everything looked so well cultivated and cared for, he hardly saw a weed growing anywhere. The people greeted them and treated them with great respect and appreciation, and when they communicated with the troops Ted was amused how they moved their hands back and forth to express their greetings.

"This is surreal, here we are in Paris parading in the streets and in just a few hours from now we'll be in the trenches fighting the enemy," Ted said to Sergeant Hicks.

"You're right, it's quite a day, but we are here for a purpose, and we will soon see the difference," the Sergeant replied.

The next morning Ted's entire battalion was loaded into trucks and taken to their headquarters which was about a quarter mile from the front. They were met by a French officer who welcomed them and spoke in a broken English accent.

"We are glad to see you, gentlemen, our men have been on the front lines for weeks and have been waiting for relief, so welcome to our country. I noticed as you marched you appeared excited and exuberant, like you are glad to be here. Well, gentlemen, that enthusiasm may be short lived when you see the elephant, then you will understand why it may not be the place you want to be."

"What do you mean, when you say 'see the elephant,' sir?" One soldier asked.

"Young man, you will understand shortly. What it means is that war is bigger than any of us, and some of you will die fighting on the battlefield, but some of you may die by just being plain stupid," the officer replied.

"Just what does that mean, we are well trained and are not stupid," Sergeant Hicks said and was offended by the answer.

The officer went on to explain.

"Plain and simple, gentlemen, protect yourselves at all times, and even then some will die fighting for your country, especially when you are ordered to 'go over the top on the offensive.' What you want to avoid is dying because of stupid curiosity. That happens when you first get in the trenches, and out of curiosity, you stick your head up because you are curious to see what's going on and what the battlefield looks like."

He continued.

"When you do this you can kiss your life good-bye because some sharp-shooting German sniper is just waiting for you to do what comes natural and that is to stick your head up out of the trenches. And if that doesn't get you killed, when you hear someone shout 'gas', you must get that mask on immediately or it will kill you. The Bosch, a name we call the German soldiers, are constantly shelling our front lines, and we constantly fire back in return, so keep your heads down and stay alert and remember the old saying, "Curiosity killed the cat. Another thing to remember: keep your boots and socks dry. If you don't you will regret it. You don't want what we call trench foot, a condition that causes a miserable rash and sores that may rot your feet. Only stupid guys let that happen when they don't change their socks and boots and keep their feet dry. That's what we trench rats call trench foot."

"Men," the French officer continued, "death is a constant companion to those serving on the front line and I give you this advice because you must defend and protect yourselves. During battle there are constant shell fragments bursting around us from explosions that can kill or wound us badly, so stay low in the trenches to avoid them. There is one more thing you must know, there are rats, lots of real rats that insist on sharing the trenches with you. You will hate the sight of the little varmints and will want to club them, which we do, but they will still grow in numbers in spite of how many we kill. Keep in mind, however, they are not all bad, they can also save your life. They seem to have an instinctive awareness of danger and disappear when a barrage of shelling is about to happen. So if you don't see them, and it seems they have disappeared, get ready for a heavy barrage from the Bosch, the rats have warned you."

Ted felt overwhelmed by all he was hearing. The troops were quiet and tense as they listened to the gloom and doom from the French officer, but they knew they had to learn what war was all about and how to protect themselves. They had to know the realities of the situation or it could mean their death or destruction, so they listened as the Frenchman continued.

"I hate to tell you, my friends, but there are more things you must know. There are insects, lice, and nits that cause infection and fever when they bite you, and they are all around us. Some men shave their heads to prevent the lice from making their home in their hair, and the nits, when they bite it can cause infection and gangrenous legs, and you don't want an amputation. So keep yourselves clean and dry at all time as much as possible."

Ted felt sick at his stomach as he listened, especially when the officer told them about the stench from the latrine and from the rotting corpses that had not yet been picked up from the battlefield and hauled off. He finished his instructions by saying.

"Just remember, the Germans are undergoing and experiencing the same miserable trench life conditions that we do, but we are preventing the enemies' advancement right here in the heart of France. We thank you and your country for coming to help us.

"Viva la France, and God Bless America."

The troops all cheered and repeated in unison, "God Bless America." Sergeant Hicks called the men to attention, and they saluted the French troops as they marched away. Ted noticed how weary and exhausted the troops looked, some like death walking, but many took the time to express their gratitude to them saying.

"Glad you could make it, Yanks," with some stopping to shake the hands of the American troops. It was very emotional for Ted, he could see their distress and could feel their relief with the Americans there to help. He had heard some had been in the trenches for seventy days or more.

Captain David Cravy welcomed the troops as they arrived at the field headquarters and his speech was very much the same as the French officer gave them, but it was more lively and uplifting to encourage the men who were there to make a difference in this war. When he finished he wished them well and dismissed them to Sergeant Hicks.

Ted was well aware that their living quarters for the next several days, or perhaps weeks, would be the trenches. Their eating and sleeping area was virtually a cave dug out in the side of the trench and lined with sand bags, with a sand bag roof supported by wood rafters. Each cave, or bunker, held up to sixteen men, and some of the caves were actually large enough to have wooden plank beds for the men to sleep on. A few of the bunkers even had a rustic old wooden table in the center where the men ate when they were relieved of their duties for the day, and their only source of light in the bunker was a candle or a kerosene lantern. Ted thought as he looked around him, *This is my home now*, and he knew he had to make the best of it.

The time had come, he and his fellow soldiers were at war with the Germans. The sergeant ordered them to take their positions in the trenches with full equipment, gas mask, rifle, bayonet, canteen and fifty extra rounds of ammunition. They practiced looking through a trench glass, a long L-shaped box that stuck up over the trench lip, which was similar to a telescope that had a reflecting glass. It gave them the ability to see the areas in front of them. It was designed so they didn't have to stick their head up to see what activities may be going on in the battlefield, and Ted remembered the French officer telling them how to protect themselves, and the trench glass gave them the ability to stay aware of all activities.

They could see the German trenches several hundred yards away, and the barb wire which was strung between the two positions. The land between the French and German trenches is known as 'no-man's land,' and it is weary looking, nothing but broken trees, bomb craters in the ground, debris and barbed wire all over the battle field. It looked like death waiting for them when Ted saw it, he shuddered and his whole body shook with fear.

When he looked through the trench glass, he could see the dreary, desolate, lifeless area with rats moving about, eating on what looked like a corpse of a fallen soldier. The wind suddenly changed and blew across the trenches, bringing in the stench of death from the battlefield and the smell of burnt flesh. It was so overwhelming to Ted as the acrid smell of explosive cordite was brought into the mixture, causing his stomach to heave. He wanted to run and hide, but there was no place to go. It was at that moment he remembered the phrase "man's inhumanity to man," and knew exactly what it meant. War could never be an exciting adventure as he had once heard it called.

The Sergeant explained to them that after each battle, a temporary truce was usually called so both sides could remove the bodies of their fallen and wounded from the battlefield for treatment or to take them to the temporary morgue. At times, some of the bodies were missed if they were badly torn apart or just overlooked in the haste of clearing the field. Before Ted turned over the trench glass to the next soldier, he saw a body on the battlefield and lying beside it was a helmet that had a sharp point on the top, and he knew it was a German soldier who had lost his life. He tried to put some rationale into everything, but there didn't seem to be any sense to it all. He quickly handed the trench glass over to the next soldier, feeling very ill and nauseous, and he tried desperately to regain his composure. He knew he had to if he was going to get through this whole ordeal; he was at war with an enemy who was trying to destroy him.

Chapter 79

THE TRENCHES

The shelling began just as the Sergeant predicted it would, and the troops were ready, watching and waiting to return fire. Their first battle with the Germans had begun and the explosive sounds and gunfire was deafening. The shelling stopped momentarily, and Ted watched as the German troops climbed out of their trenches to rush across "no man's land" toward the Americans, opening fire once again.

The battle increased in intensity; the firing was continuous from both sides, but the German advancement didn't work and they soon withdrew back to the security of their trenches. The captain blew his whistle and ordered the troops to follow him over the top to advance against the retreating Germans with Sergeant Hicks leading the squad. The Germans began to increase their gunfire, and the Sergeant shouted, "Take cover!" just as a bullet whistled by Ted's head. He fell into a shell hole and began to shiver and shake with fear and his stomach heaved. For the first time in his life he felt absolute fear, the kind that makes you feel paralyzed.

As he lay in the shell hole, he began to think of his childhood and the thoughts quickly ran through his mind as he remembered how he felt afraid while he waited for his daddy to come home when he had been ornery, and how he was afraid of what his daddy might do. Would he grab me and lay me across his lap and spank me? And how he would scream and cry even before the spanking started. "No, no, Daddy, no, please don't spank me." He remembered going to the dentist or to the doctor for a shot with a needle, and the waiting and expectation of it all made him afraid. It was the fear of the unknown waiting for something to happen.

He recalled an old family friend of his dad who fought in the Spanish–American war, and this wise old soldier told them about two battles a man fights while in combat: the battle inside himself and the battle with the enemy. If he wins the first battle, chances are he will win the second, but if he loses the first, he usually doesn't have a prayer. That old proverb came alive in Ted's mind as he lay there in the shell hole, and the full understanding of what it meant became very clear to him. His heart was pounding, his hands and his legs were trembling, and he felt nauseated as the sweat rolled from his face; he was desperately trying to win the battle within himself.

He could smell the pungent odor of the smoke from the exploding ammunition and it actually stung his nostrils. He was suddenly startled back into reality when he heard the retreat whistle blow; he crawled out of his cover and there on the ground next to him was a fellow soldier, wounded and bleeding. He stopped and bent over him, and the soldier tried desperately to speak just as a shell burst nearby. Ted couldn't hear his words, he just saw his lips moving as he labored to speak. The loud burst deafened him temporarily and robbed him of hearing his fellow soldier's last words. He reached out to comfort him, and it was then that he realized he was gone. He took his friend's rifle and stuck it into the dirt and placed his helmet on it as a memorial to his bravery, and Ted saluted him before he moved on.

Another bombardment hit, and Ted jumped into a cover for safety; he wasn't anxious to get killed or wounded. He was going to be a father, and how he wished he was with Viola this very moment, and he began to question why he was fighting this crazy war. *Why am I here*, he asked himself? Ted couldn't rationalize in his mind just why he was in this situation, not knowing if he would be killed or badly wounded, and he knew the rest of the men must feel the same way and had the same questions in their minds.

He remembered how naive and clueless he was concerning war and his desire to be a good soldier, and he dreamed about coming home as a hero. Deep down that was what he still wanted, and as these thoughts penetrated his mind he suddenly realized the shelling had stopped. The battle had finally ended as the Sergeant ordered them back to the trenches. He took a deep breath as he sat in the trench, thanking God he was still alive, he had survived his first real battle in war and also the first real battle within himself.

Ted was assigned the 4:00 to 7:00 a.m. watch duty. He used the trench glass to keep tabs on any activity, if any, out in no man's land, and it was quiet most of the time with the exception of a few rocketlike bursts in the sky that lit up the field. There didn't seem to be any human activity or movement, but the rats were out in full force, darting from spot to spot, cleaning up the battlefield.

The dawn came in slowly and the sun began to peek over the horizon. In the eastern sky, the smoke sediments of the previous days' battle formed a thin membranous cloud, partially hiding the sun as it rose to wake the day. It showed through the cloud, giving it a beautiful color of indigo which soon changed into cerulean, and finally into a crimson rose color. Ted sighed as he looked upward, he was grateful there was still beauty in the world. God has a way of showing such beauty when he needed it the most. It reminded him that God was still in the heavens looking down on His great creation.

"Thank you, God," Ted muttered to himself.

The troops began to stir and wake up to face another day. A fellow soldier, Pvt. Jay Erdman, walked out of the bunker to go to the latrine. Ted observed him as he returned and for some reason the private stopped and stepped up on the ladder to look out over the battlefield, his head higher than the trench lip. A loud gunshot broke the silence of the morning and Pvt. Erdman fell backward into the trench wounded, with half of his skull missing. Ted watched in horror as he lay in the muddy trench dying from a direct shot from a sniper who was just waiting for someone to make that fatal mistake, the one that the French officer had told them about. That fatal error happened much too often and that is why the officer had pressed the point and warned them, and Pvt. Erdman was dead because of his curiosity.

Sergeant Hicks came out of his bunker when he heard all the commotion.

"What's going on, are the Germans on the move again?"

"No, sir, a sniper got Pvt. Erdman," he said as he pointed to him on the muddy floor of the trench.

"How in the world did that happen?" the Sergeant acted shocked at what he saw.

Ted related the incident to him and emphasized how it all happened; he had made that fatal mistake and his curiosity got the best of him. The Sergeant shook his head in utter distress.

"After all the warnings, it just shows how weak we are when we allow our human instinctive nature to take over."

"Yes, sir, guess he was just trying to make everything seem normal around here. He was just a happy-go-lucky guy and I liked him a lot," Ted said. "I saw him recently at the soldiers club and watched him play the piano for hours, he was a great musician, what a shame and loss to the world."

"Well, things are not normal, we are at war, and he lost his life at nineteen years old, his life was just beginning. He won't have the chance for a happy-go-lucky life now," the Sergeant said with great distress in his voice.

The news of Pvt. Erdman quickly ran through the entire battalion and each man renewed their interest in safety and self-protection. It suddenly seemed more intense and real to them now. "Keep your head down" had a new meaning to every one of them.

On the following night the quietness was interrupted by a German bomb blast as they began shelling the trenches. The Sergeant quickly ordered his men to prepare for action, and they opened up with counter artillery firing. A good night's sleep they had hoped for would be denied them. The Germans seemed to enjoy unnerving them and keeping them on edge; it was obviously part of their plan for the new residents of the trenches.

A German raiding party of about two dozen soldiers suddenly dropped into the American trenches with bayonets drawn, ready for a surprise raid. A German soldier moved toward Ted, but he acted quickly and turned his rifle butt into the German's face and knocked him to the floor of the trench and into the muddy water. When he tried to get up an over-anxious soldier stabbed him with his bayonet, killing him, Ted had hoped to take him prisoner and turn him over to the captain for questioning.

The hand-to-hand combat raged on for about twenty minutes with the Americans taking the upper hand and Ted right in the middle of the battle. A few of the Germans escaped and returned to the safety of their trenches, leaving several of their own men dead in the muddy waters. But it also took its toll on the American troops; they lost three men with two wounded. The men were muddy and totally unnerved by what had happened, but it gave them the incentive and motivated them to focus more on the reality of war, and it literally made them mad and eager to fight these mad men who wanted to destroy them; they vowed they would never let this happen again.

After the battle the captain commended the troops for their bravery, and Ted received a promotion to corporal and a written commendation for his bravery and actions. His brave actions had saved the lives of many of the troops.

"Thank you, sir," Ted responded.

A few days later the Sergeant gave Ted an assignment.

"I'm placing you in charge of a project, I want you to take three men with you and go to headquarters to get a permit from Lt. O'Malley for a truck to go to the warehouse to obtain some wooden planks to put on the trench floors so we don't have walk in the mud all the time. Let's clean up our house. Do you have any questions?"

"No, sir," Ted replied.

"Then let's get it done."

On their way to the warehouse, they saw a German fighter plane in the air, a Hun LVG two seater, as it began diving toward a French observation balloon with machine guns blazing. They pulled over to the side of the road and sat on the front seat of the old army truck watching the action in the sky. *It looked like it was about 1500 feet in the air*, Ted thought.

"What is that crazy fool trying to do?" Pvt. Eldon Field shouted.

"It's headed for the French balloon, they're trying to take it out," Pvt. Mosher said.

Aircraft guns from miles around began to fire on the plane leaving puffs of smoke exploding in the air near the plane, but the pilot seemed oblivious to the shelling around him and kept flying his mission straight toward the balloon. Then Ted and his men saw a British fighter plane, a Sop with two wings, come flying behind and above the German plane at a high rate of speed. *This spectacle in the sky was almost magical*, Ted thought. The German plane looked like a giant buzzard closing in on its prey, but the British pilot wasn't about to let him win this one.

A small specklike figure fell from the balloon, and seconds later the parachute opened and the French balloon pilot began floating down to earth. A great flash erupted and the balloon burst into flames, and a trail of black smoke soon followed. Ted's only hope was that the French pilot had enough distance between him and the balloon that he would land safely.

The German fighter spotted the British plane and angled back across the sky to engage him in a dog-fight. The machine guns rattled from both fighters and continued for a short while until the British plane fled the scene, evidently running out of ammunition. The German pilot then spotted the American truck on the road where Ted and his fellow soldiers sat watching all the action in the sky. The pilot began to turn to make a fly over, circling back and dipping lower above the truck with its machine guns blazing. The bullets hit the road in front of them, and Ted and his men woke up to the seriousness of the situation. They had become a part of the incident, and the Germans wanted meat.

They jumped from the truck as the plane circled once again, dipping lower over them. They lay in the ditch and watched their truck blow up and scatter into pieces all over the road. Just then two more German fighter planes joined the pilot and they proceeded to take out a nearby railroad station. Ted watched all the aftermath of the bombings in horror, wagons and equipment flying through the air, and frantic horses running helter-skelter down the road. The planes made one last fly over, probably to get a good view of their triumphant victory, before they disappeared out of sight.

Ted and his fellow soldiers walked the six miles back to headquarters to file a report of the battle and the loss of their truck. Sergeant Hicks thanked them for their report and for their actions.

"I'm glad none of you were injured. Men, you are dismissed."

Ted was exhausted from the days' events, both physically and mentally, and he fell on his bunk to rest. He heard the mail-call announced, the announcement that all the men wanted to hear, hoping to get a letter from home. He pulled himself out of the bunker to listen as they called out the names, and finally his name was called. He received three letters, two from Viola, and one from his parents. They were like valuable treasures to him. He returned to his bunk to read and cherish them, and he read them over and over again enjoying every word, especially those written by Viola. It was a touch of home.

Chapter 80

LETTERS AND HEADLINE

After reading his letters from home, Ted sat down and penned a letter to his folks back in Oklahoma.

Dear Folks,

I just received three letters from home, one from you and two from my lovely wife. I thought I would write to you first because, I wrote Viola yesterday and I haven't written you in several days. I am writing this letter by candle light, that's the only light we have in our bunker. It rained three out of the last four days so we slop around in the mud a lot, but I stay dry with my rain slicker. Even though it rains a lot it's not actually too cold here except at night, so I sleep under several blankets, but we're okay.

I heard a rumor that the 1st infantry get's first choice when it comes to rations and we get the leftovers, but I really doubt if that's true, we probably get the same. We are getting plenty to eat so don' t worry, we even get fresh meat on occasions. The food is really okay and everything is fine, we haven't done too much these last few days, not much activity so we're just taking it easy.

Well, Dad, how's the farm doing? Have you been getting enough rain this year? I'm anxious to hear how the crops are doing, I hope they are looking okay. Is old Bessie the cow still producing as much milk as she was, she sure has been a great supplier of milk for the family for a long time now, I would love to be there to milk her for you.

I miss not being able to help with the plowing and helping out on the farm, but most of all, Mom, I miss your cooking. But it's not too bad over here, we get all the pork and beans you'd ever want to have or eat, but seriously the food is okay.

I'm with a great bunch of guy's, our sergeant is really an okay guy and he doesn't rail on us too much, and that's good. But he is strict and makes us do things the army way, that's the way it has to be during war.

That's going to be all for now, don't worry about me, I'm okay, so please just continue to help my precious wife. I am so grateful that she came to live with you all while I'm over here. It saves me a lot of worry, especially now that she is in a family way and almost due, isn't it next month? Gosh, time has sneaked up on me, I'm so looking forward to hearing what it is, I think I want a girl but we're open for whatever we get.

We just got a new replacement the other day, a fellow from Claremore, Oklahoma, His name is Jim Davis, seems like a nice guy. He said he was born in OoLogha, Oklahoma, and has never heard of Deer Creek, but he is still a nice guy anyhow, just not well traveled I guess (ha). Claremore is where Will Rogers, the famous vaudevillian cowboy comedian lived and worked, in case you didn't know that, which I didn't until he told me. Well, that's it for tonight.

All my love, Ted

The next morning Ted sat on the latrine box, or the facility as some called it, reading the very first edition of the US Army newspaper, the *Stars and Stripes* that was delivered to their bunker. It was dated February 1918.

The main headline story read:

"General John J. Pershing, the newly selected commander of the American force arrived in France this month with great fanfare. When greeted by the French Government on his arrival he was given a medal, the Cross of Lorraine, and it was pinned to his uniform during a formal ceremony."

The editor wrote an introductory note:

"Our newspaper's mission is to provide the scattered troops of American forces, which are often mixed with British, French, and Italian forces, with a sense of unity and understanding of the role they play in the overall war. This eight-page monthly will also feature news from home, sports news, poetry, and cartoons. The newspaper will be delivered by truck and motorcycles throughout the entire Western Front. The Editor."

Ted continued to read the war news headlines with great interest.

"Germany's Kaiser Wilhelm II exhorts his soldiers to fight 'Like the Huns of old did under King Attila!"

"President Woodrow Wilson sends greetings to all his troops fighting in the Great War overseas, to stand fast and victory will be ours."

"Germany announced last month they are beginning their final offensive in the war."

"American combat forces are arriving in England daily."

"Victory at the Chateau Chavigny: The first all independent operation of American troops was an overwhelming victory."

"U.S. Soldier Alvin York displays heroics at Argonne: Corporal Alvin C. York reportedly killed over 20 German soldiers and captured an additional 132 in the ongoing battles in the Argonne forest, which will undoubtedly earn him the Congressional Medal of Honor."

Ted continued reading all the news as he sat on the latrine box. He read a poem penned by a soldier, the author's name is unknown. He laughed as he read it. It seemed to put a bit of light-hearted humor in his day, which is very scarce in the trenches.

"Beneath My Helmet"
In winter I get up at night
And have to scratch by candle light
In summer quite the other way
I have to scratch the live long day
A soldier boy should never swear
When cooties are in his underwear
Or underneath his helmet label
Or as far as they are able
The trench is full of these little cootie
But I'm growing quite fond of the brutie

The Sports news headlines was all about baseball:

"Babe Ruth, who broke the MLB single-season home run record for the Boston Red socks as an outfielder is nicknamed the Sultan of Swat, or the Bambino. Big controversy is swirling in the baseball world which is the talk of the town, and now there is talk afoot that the Manager of the Red Socks, Harry Freeze, will trade him next year to the Yankees. Ruth began his career as a stellar left handed pitcher for the Boston Red Socks, but he achieved his greatest fame as a slugger, and also had many achievements as a pitcher."

Ted began to read home news of the day. "Henry Ford's new Model T will cost $850, this is nearly 1/3 of the price of any other cars on the market, but still not cheap enough for the masses. Over the next few years Ford plans to perfect the assembly line production which will bring the cost down to $368. 00, making it much more affordable and consequently will sell hundreds of thousands more cars than any other company."

Ted was very surprised to read the feature article from the home news page. It was entitled, "Ten Days That Shook The World," and it was a report from the Associated Press which read:

"The trial against the International Workers of the World Union, the I.W.W., ended today. It was the biggest and longest court trial in American history and sixty-one of the hundred men indicted took the stand, including 'Big Bill Haywood' who testified for three days.

"Another I.W.W. worker testified before the court and told the judge: 'You ask me why the I.W.W. is not patriotic to the United States but I tell you, if you were a bum without a blanket, if you had left your wife and kids when you went out west looking for a job and had never been able to located them since; if your job had never kept you long enough in a place to qualify you to vote; if you slept in a lousy, sour smelling bunkhouse and ate food just as rotten as they could possibly give to you and get by with it; if deputy sheriffs shot your cooking cans full of holes and spilled your grub on the ground; if your wages were lowered on you when the bosses thought they had you down; if there was one law for the rich like Ford and Mooney and another for Harry Thaw; if every person who represented law and order in the nation beat you up and railroaded you to jail, and the good Christian people cheered and told them to go to it. How in hell do you expect a man to be patriotic? This war is a business and we don't see why we should go out and get shot in order to save the lovely state of affairs that you now enjoy.

"The jury found them all guilty and the judge sentenced Haywood and fourteen others to twenty years in prison. Thirty-three were given ten years, and the rest were given shorter sentences. The I.W.W. Union was fined $2,500,000 which shattered and dissolved it, and Haywood jumped bail and fled to revolutionary Russia, where he now resides.'

"As a result of the trial the Socialist Party membership slipped to 80,000, but Eugene V. Debs who is their candidate for President still managed to garner 919,800 votes, the most a socialist had ever received in America. This vote was representative of the American disillusionment with the country and World War I, and Debs himself spoke passionately against the country's involvement in the war."

As Ted read the paper about what happened to his onetime good friend, Big Bill, a loud deafening explosion from an artillery shell exploded right above the trench latrine throwing him to the ground and scattering dirt all over him. He dropped the paper into the mud and dived for cover, but a moment later he got up and moved quickly, pulling up his pants as he ran with several other shells hitting the ground all around him.

When he got to the bunker, he was shocked to discover it had taken a direct hit, and he immediately jumped in to help out and to see if anybody was trapped inside. The complete roof of the bunker had collapsed and he tried to move some of the trench logs, but it was useless. Most of it was completely buried from the hit and he knew the soldiers that were inside were trapped and probably all dead. He was shocked to see a severed leg sticking straight up out of the dirt.

His entire squad was inside except those on watch duty and himself. He just happened to be in the latrine taking his time reading the newspaper. One of his squadmates, however, was walking and stumbling around in a daze, crying and talking incoherent, and Ted reached out to help him.

Major Vernon Drake came running to the sight and took the dazed soldier's arm, and Ted started digging in the rubble hoping to find someone alive.

"It's too late, son, those who were in there have to be gone," he said as he took Ted's arm and pulled him away.

"Come with me," he ordered. Just as they were walking away someone shouted "Gas!" They immediately put on their masks and helped the dazed soldier with his, and hit the ground. Ted curled up in a fetal position, but the Major grabbed his arm and ordered them to get up.

"Get your rifle, and let's get out of here, we'll be under attack shortly. Keep your mask on and get yourselves together, now."

Everyone hated to hear the word gas; they knew it was lethal. Ted saw one young man on a stretcher, the medics rushing him to the first-aid station, and he knew that the poor fellow didn't get his mask on in time. A person only has about five seconds before a sniff of that gas gets in your lungs.

"That's too bad," the Major said.

"He is a nice young man, a new recruit, only been here three days. Hope he makes it, but if it is in his lungs he will have a difficult time surviving. It looks like he's not breathing very well, he is gasping for air. If he does survive, he probably will be disabled for the rest of his life."

The Major ordered the troops back to the trench, and when the warning was lifted, the Major told them.

"Let this be a lesson for us all, when we hear the word 'gas,' don't dilly-dally, get that mask on! Did you know that before we had gas masks, the practice to protect yourself was to urinate in your handkerchief and hold it to your nose, for some it worked, but for others it didn't. So let's be thankful that we now have gas masks. Now, let's get to our assigned stations, Walters, did you hear?"

"Yes, sir."

As Ted walked to his station he thought about the war. He had thought that after time passed and the war went on he would become accustomed to combat, but the opposite was true. After doing the same thing day after day, constant bombardment with gas and bombs makes you sick and scared all the time. The truth of the situation was he lived in a state of high anxiety, and it doesn't get any better, but worse. He had to be constantly vigilant, especially when they walked in the dark areas encompassed by the woods, they never knew if German troops or snipers were hiding behind the trees. The one thing that they did know was the Germans were seasoned fighters and crack shots.

He remembered when he first entered the army, he was a true believer. But now, he didn't know what the war was all about and he didn't want to be here, he should be home with his wife. The reality of war gave him second thoughts and he was tired of being continually scared and on edge. The night before they were bombarded most of the night and they weren't getting enough sleep. He was tired and he wondered why he had travelled half way around the world to possibly get himself killed.

He had began carrying his New Testament with him and reading it when he had the opportunity. He had also heard the story about a young soldier who carried his Bible in his breast pocket close to his heart, and a bullet fragment hit his pocket and the Bible deflected the bullet, it saved his life. He was saved by the Word of God. That story impressed Ted; he knew he could use all the help he could get. He liked to read the New Testament and believed that his personal Savior would guide his path between the bombs, shells, and bullets.

He reported back to his station and from the trench he could see north and south along the ridge where his fellow soldiers were fighting, and it gave him a new sense of himself, a sense of manhood knowing that everyone of them could be facing death, they had to be vigilant. The Major assigned them to man the trenches for the next several hours.

"Open fire and give cover," the Major suddenly cried out. Through the trench glass, he saw a medic bringing in a wounded soldier from "no man's land." They were both running as quickly as possible, dodging rifle and machine gunfire from the German snipers. While on patrol the soldier got hit in the leg and fell, and the medic turned back to help him get up on his feet, virtually having to half-carry the wounded dough-boy.

Just as they neared the safety of the trench, a German machine gun opened fire and shot them both, and the wounded soldier slipped off the shoulder of the medic and fell dead into the trench. The medic fell about an arm's length out with his arms extended reaching for help. From the trench a soldier raised up to help him by grabbing the medic's hand to pull him in, and he was struck by a bullet through his head. The soldier fell backward into the trench unknowingly pulling the medic with him. It seemed as if it was a last heroic act before he died. The brave soldiers lay at the bottom of the trench, all three lying arm in arm virtually holding on to each other. It appeared as if they were walking arm in arm to enter heaven's gate together.

Ted gazed down at them stunned and in disbelief, he was the young soldier who had told him about the Bible that deflected the bullet and saved a soldier, and this brave soldier still had his Bible in his breast pocket. Ted renewed his vow to always carry his from this day on and gratefully read it.

The remaining squad was still involved in open gunfire against the snipers until the fighting eventually died down and the Major ordered seize fire. Later when they were relieved on the front line, they were advised by Major Drake that their remaining squad would be reassigned to a new company under Sergeant Mark Alley.

The next morning after breakfast in the trenches, Sergeant Alley ordered the squad to report to headquarters for final reorganization, Ted was now assigned to Squadron No.307.

"Since you lost most of your gear and equipment when the bunker blew up, you will need to go to supply headquarters for replacements. I have ordered the supply officer to go with you when the travel permit and replacement chit arrives."

"Yes, sir," he replied. In a few minutes a horse drawn supply wagon arrived with the permit, and Ted thought it resembled an old black British-style box police paddy wagon. Later when they arrived at the supply depot and were issued all the equipment and supplies, they loaded up the wagon to go back to their base. On the road they spotted a German fighter plane in the air, and the pilot had apparently spotted them and began dipping down with their guns firing. They immediately stopped and jumped into the ditch to take cover, and the air and ground shelling went on for several minutes with shells exploding around them on both sides.

The horse was struck by a bullet and reared up in panic, and the driver ran out and grabbed the reins to calm him, but the wounded horse's flailing hoofs struck the driver in the face crushing his skull. The horse took off running, dragging him for several yards before the reins broke, and he was almost buried in the muddy road. Ted chased after the run-away horse and wagon, but when he caught up with them the horse had busted the harness and was running wildly down the road bleeding profusely leaving a blood trail behind.

The driver lay face down in the mud with the broken rein still in his hand. Ted reached down and pushed the mud away from the driver's face and virtually dug him out of the mud. He tried to find a pulse, but there was none, so he pulled him over to the side of the road. He felt devastated and began to walk, crying in despair at what he had just witnessed.

He headed back toward the trenches to report to the Sergeant and rejoin his new squad and his mind began to wonder as to why he was here in this place, and he felt like he hadn't been diligent enough to get out of all this insanity. The army is a crazy place, he thought, and he needed to see the Chaplain again, everywhere he went someone was getting killed.

He thought about Viola and the baby and knew that she needed him, and he also knew he desperately needed her. He felt dazed as he rambled along, he didn't belong here and he had to get out. He was a telegraph operator and the army had never used him in that capacity, and why wasn't he home doing telegraphy? As he stumbled along talking to himself he heard a voice, he paused for a moment to shake himself out of his stupor, but he heard the voice again.

"Hey, soldier, can we give you a lift?" The voice came from an army sedan that was driving slowly down the road next to him. His mind had been so isolated in his own thoughts he wasn't aware of anyone in his presence. He was surprised to see a car filled with three Army officers and a driver.

"If you are offering me a ride, sir, yes I would like that."

"We don't have any room inside, but step up on the running board and hold on soldier," the Lieutenant said.

"Yes, sir, thank you," Ted said as he jumped on.

"I just got my ride shot out from under me, I sure hope that doesn't happen again," he told the officer.

"We know, we saw the whole thing go down, and you and your fellow soldier performed admirably," the officer said from the back seat.

An officer stuck his head out the window and said,

"Corporal, my name is Captain Harry S. Truman, and these other men are Lt. Mark Collins and Captain Robert Prendergast. We are pleased to meet you, what you did back there was a very brave thing. We're from the National Guard, Unit 905, battery D, out of Independence, Missouri, and we just landed in La Havre on the troop ship, the *U.S.S. George Washington*. We're on our way to join up with our unit at Camp Coctquidon near Ruins. Where are you from, son?"

"I'm from Wichita, Kansas. I came in on the *U.S.S. George Washington* several months ago. We're almost neighbors, Kansas and Missouri are close together, sir."

Captain Truman smiled.

"Well, it's good to meet a neighbor so far away from home."

Lt. Collins chimed in the conversation.

"Yes, you were in a tight spot back there, we're sure glad you're all right, you performed well, and we saw you crawl out of the ditch to help your fellow soldier. We had stopped to avoid the air strike from the German plane but were not close enough to give you a hand. Sorry, for the loss of your fellow soldier, but glad you made it through."

Captain Truman told Ted.

"We're headed up the road to the artillery battalion, we're 'newbie's' reporting for duty hoping to help out on the front lines. Have you been on the front long, son?"

"About five months now, sir. You can let me off right up the road at Division 307, I really thank you for the ride, sir."

Ted stepped off the running board when the car stopped and stepped back to salute the officers just as a strange sight appeared in the sky. It was several hundred feet long and looked about the size of a football field, and it came straight out of the clouds. As it passed overhead it hid the sun for several seconds, it was like a large cloud passing over them.

"Oh, my God, look, what in the world is that. It looks like a giant silverfish?" Ted blurted out.

Captain Truman jumped out of the car.

"That's a German dirigible, some call them airships, and according to what I've read about them, it is 446 feet long and has six engines, two at the front, two in the middle, and two at the back. The Germans use it to carry large amounts of bombs and equipment to the front lines. It's probably headed for England. It flies too high for rifle fire to hit it, but one has been shot down just recently when it was coming in for a landing. Our country is in the process of developing aircraft guns that will soon be available that can hit the dirigibles in the air, and when that happens, they will explode and the crew will be helpless to escape. It will be a flying death trap."

The Captain continued.

"The Germans have also developed a bomber that can fly high enough to avoid being hit from the ground, and can drop bombs from high altitudes. Actually, London is under very heavy siege at the present time because of these bombers. There are a lot of new planes, tanks, and other war equipment being developed that we could never imagine or even visualize, it's really hard to believe."

"Another strange thing we saw that was even harder to believe," he continued to tell Ted.

"Just fifteen miles out of Paris along the banks of the Seine River, the French have constructed a decoy city which represents Paris, hoping to fool the German bomber pilots as they look from the air. The decoy city even has a false Eiffel Tower and roads leading to a false Arc De Triumph, and even a fake Opera house. When it's all lit up at night it looks like the real city of Paris while the real Paris is under total black-out after dark. There are lots of strange things going on in the world that are hard to believe, war brings out the best and worst in us."

"We must be on our way, Corporal, good luck, it was good to meet you, keep up the good work soldier," the captain said as they saluted.

Back at headquarters Ted reported the event and the driver's death to Major Drake. He also told them about the dirigible he saw, and he couldn't believe how big and massive it was.

"This really is your lucky day, Corporal, it might not seem like it right now, but you got out of that situation alive and we're sorry for the loss of our fellow soldier."

"Thank you, sir," Ted saluted with tears flowing down his cheeks.

"Take heart, young man, you're alive, you were spared and just think, you saw your first dirigible, something I have yet to see," the Major said to him sympathetically.

Mail call came later that evening and Ted's day ended on a positive note, he had letters from home. The letters from Viola were post-marked six weeks ago, that's how long it takes for their mail to catch up to them.

Dearest Ted,

I think about you constantly, of course I worry, but I have found I can get through most days without being overly anxious and I'm trusting in the Lord to keep you safe. I am doing fine, you will be a father shortly and your mother and I are trying to decide what we will name it.

If it's a girl, what do you think about Maxine or Greta, and I like Jack or Richard for a boy, but you might have another suggestion.

Everything is fine here and your mother and I are canning from the garden right now and putting up for the winter, it's lots of work being a farmer, isn't it? But we are having a great time getting acquainted, and I just love your folks.

Well, my darling husband, I will close for now, stay well and safe for me and our future family. All my love always.

Your loving wife, Viola E. Walters+

Dear son,

Well, we're having a great time here getting acquainted with Viola and loving every minute of it. She is a hard worker and a great help, we are in the midst of canning, the garden is giving us an abundance this year. Practically everything grew this year, we had several nice rains, and the corn is especially good this year, and I know how you love your corn. We were laughing how many ears of corn you could eat in one setting.

All the news here is about the war, oh, yes, Dad said to tell you the old mule died, had to get ourselves another one just the other day, the new one we're calling Blackie, I think because he is black. h He said he was going to miss old Buck, he was a good old jug head mule for all the many years we had him, which was a good long time. He hardly ever had to tell him twice to stop or go, seldom had to lay the whip on him.

You're not to worry, son, your wife is fine and she is cute as a bug, even with her big belly walking around the place, and she doesn't let it slow her down one bit. I'm not sure your dad will let her go when you guy's decide to go off and live separate from us after you return home.

Dad is really enjoying her presence and he thinks she is the cutest thing. It's a wonderful time in our lives, but everything will be better when we're all together once again. Don't you worry about anything, everything is fine here.

We got your last letter, sorry that the Chaplain hasn't had any luck yet getting you home, but don't be too disappointed, I understand the war is going well and it shouldn't be too much longer before it's all over, hopefully, and you'll be back home again soon. Stay safe, son, we're all right here and your wife is doing great, so don't let anything worry you. Oh yes, we have a new doctor in town now, and he has already examined Viola and declared she is as healthy as a horse, and everything looks fine. So don't you worry son, we are taking good care of her.

Dad is fine, the work on the farm is going well and we are getting close to harvest time. The wheat is looking good and soon we will be busy as all get out. Not a lot of help around since the army has so many of our boys, but we will get by.

Love, Mom and Dad

Chapter 81

THE ARGONNE FOREST

Ted's squadron had been on the front line for weeks, and they were tired and stressed out. Word came from headquarters they were to go to a rest camp for a few days to recuperate and get some much needed relaxation and time away from the front lines. A fellow soldier, Pvt. Robert Phillips, who had become a good friend of Ted's, were given liberty to go into the city on a three-day pass. He was one of the few soldiers that was with Ted in their original squad before they were re-assigned, and he was a crack-shot; he could shoot a fly off a leaf at hundred yards, they would tease him.

They toured the city on a bright red open-sided tour bus that chugged along the street with a tour guide pointing out the famous and interesting sights. They were fascinated by the Eiffel Tower, the famous structure they had heard about which opened in 1889 to celebrate the one hundredth anniversary of the French Revolution at the World's Fair. Ted thought about the telegraph poles he had climbed that made him rather nervous, and he couldn't imagine climbing up that tower that stood 984 feet into the air, as the tour guide told them.

They ate some strange foods that the French people seemed crazy about. One was called escargot that were snails especially prepared in a butter sauce. Ted had never heard of it before, and he really wasn't very impressed, but they had to try them. What he loved most about French food were the breads they baked and the freshly baked aroma that filled the streets. Seeing the sights of Paris with his buddy was quite enjoyable, but what he enjoyed most of all was the soft feather bed he slept in at night, quite a difference from the cold bunker.

Their leave ended much too quickly and it was time to go back to the front lines. They reluctantly climbed back on the truck to return; it was time to go back to the war. As they rode along, Ted was struck by the beautifully manicured countryside, and although the scenery was beautiful, the people he saw were mostly old men and women. He noticed that most of the women were dressed in black as if they were all in mourning, and he thought that perhaps they didn't have much to hope for lately, since most of their young men were in the army and many were being killed.

They came upon a small bombed-out village and most of the houses were destroyed with the household goods strewn all over the lawns and streets. They stopped to look around, Ted was hoping to find a souvenir like a German helmet to take back home with him, but he was out of luck. Someone had already cleaned out everything worth having. He remembered they had been warned by headquarters not to scavenger through the war-torn areas looking for memorabilia, that the paper leaflets being dropped by the German planes could be a trap to lure the soldiers into an area to become targets for sniper fire. They also dropped the leaflets to spread proproganda asking the Americans to go home. It was not their war and the Germans were good honest people. But the American and French soldiers knew the message was garbage and they might as well save the paper. It was no better than toilet paper, they would say.

Liberty was over and the men from Squadron 307 settled back into the trenches on the front line. Ted took some time to catch up on his letter writing and wrote to his folks back in Oklahoma.

Somewhere in France, November 1918

Dear Folks,

It has been ten days or so since I wrote you last, but I could not help it. We have been on the move a lot since then. I am with several other fellows writing letters home and it is now 2:30 in the morning and most of the men are asleep. But it's my turn to be on watch duty so I thought it would be a good time to write. Fritz, that's what we call the German soldier's, are quiet just now and I hope they stay that way while I finish this letter.

I came here on my birthday, so if you were wondering back home what I was doing on that day, I am telling you now it was anything but enjoying the celebration that Fritz and Uncle Sam took pains to give me. Fritz gets such a funny notion some times and he delights in seeing how close he can come to our humble abode with all his different caliber guns he has over here, so we do not lack for amusement.

We arc all well and feeling fine and we get plenty to eat, we eat a lot with the French and you can't beat French cooking. The French soldiers are our best pals, I think they are the finest kind of fellows, but I can't comprehend a lot of their lingo yet. Boy do I wish I had some good old American candy right now, it sure would taste good. Well, it looks like I am going to have to light another candle, this one is about at the end of the stick. What is going on in the good old U. S. A. anyway, where are my brothers and what are they doing?

This is a great life as one fellow said, if I ever get out of this, I'll sign a contract never to leave the U. S. A. again. But you really don't mind it when you get use to it. It's all a matter of course.

A fellow could write a history about the war while working his watch, perhaps someday I'll write a book about all my experiences, Well I must close now, I hope you're all well and happy. Say hello to every one for me, especially to viola my lovely wife.

Write often, Your Son Theodore

During a briefing to the troops Major Drake informed them that the generals were planning a large coordinated counter offensive to take place soon, hoping it would be the last and put the war to rest. They would join forces with the French who would be on the left flank, and the American divisions on the right. They also learned the Germans had an entire maze of trenches built on higher ground on the hillside, which meant they could look down on the American and French troops. The generals were changing their tactics to meet the challenges ahead of them.

After the briefing, the men hashed it over and speculated on the days ahead, hoping this would be the final offensive so they could go home and get away from having to hunker down in the trenches for days at a time. They would be glad to get away from the constant artillery barrages, the rat-infested bunkers, the unsanitary living conditions, and the constant risk of death. All these things they shared in common, and they were anxious to put it all behind them.

Suddenly the shelling began to explode all around them, the barrage of enemy gunfire began again, and they were back at war. They returned fire from their guns and canons which blew large holes in the ground and formed a canopy of red-hot steel and mud raining upon them. They could hear the enemies bullets whistle by their heads as they flew by, and the sergeant signaled for them to climb out of the trenches and move forward. The major fired his .45 pistol in the air as he waved the squadron forward, and the troops, several hundred of them, hit the ground running and firing their weapons as they advanced. The German shells exploded all around them, digging holes in the ground and hitting some of the American soldiers. It was devastating for Ted to see his fellow soldiers falling around him, but he kept up the fight and the battle lasted for about an hour before the Germans retreated.

Ted saw a soldier lying at the edge of the trench with his legs drawn up beneath him, he was holding his gun in both hands and crying aloud as he listened to the unholy explosive sounds around him; he was paralyzed with fear. The sergeant ordered the soldier to get up after he realized he wasn't wounded, he was just scared into a panic and wouldn't move. The flares lit up the sky and they were warned not to look directly at them, it could cause night-blindness and interfere with their vision to see the movement of the Germans, especially the snipers hiding and firing upon them from the forest.

But it was almost impossible not to look. The sky was lit up with constant red and yellow colors moving across the sky. Ted heard the Sergeant yell out, "Four o'clock, left of the tree stump." Ted's eyes darted back and forth looking for movement, but all he could see were tree stumps. He questioned himself, which tree stump does he mean, there are stumps all around the landscape. He could hear the zing of bullets hitting the dirt and puddles of water, splashing mud all over him skewing his vision of the battlefield. Suddenly a soldier next to him fell, he was mowed down by the intense machine gunfire. Ted kneeled down to assist him and saw it was his good friend, Robert Phillips, and he was gasping for air with blood gushing from his mouth and nose.

He whispered, "I think I'm dead," and he reached out for Ted as he took his last breath.

"Move on, there's nothing more you can do for him," the sergeant told Ted.

He moved on with his rifle in hand and his mind muddled in disbelief and fear. He stumbled over a body which caused him to lose his balance and fall into a deep shell hole. As he struggled to get up, he saw two German soldiers hunkered down in the hole who had already taken ownership of it. Ted immediately engaged one of the soldiers by throwing his shoulder into him, knocking him over, and he quickly drove his bayonet through his chest. While he tried to maneuver his bayonet loose Ted noticed the other German soldier was so frightened all he could do was stare and he appeared petrified. Then suddenly he moved and thrust himself at Ted, but Ted had already unsheathed his dagger and pointed it toward the breast of the German soldier.

"Nein, nein," he said as he grabbed Ted's hand to hold off the thrust, but Ted's weight and strength overcame him.

"O, mien Gott, nein," the young soldier cried out as his hand weakened and the knife entered his chest. He cried out once more.

"Nein, nein," he sighed and softly muttered. "Mater, mater," as he took his dying breath.

Ted rolled him away and felt a dire sense of remorse having to take a life, but he knew he had to act to save himself. He had to do it. It was either him or the Germans. Ted couldn't shake away the guilt and pain he felt, both German soldiers were so young. He lifted his tear-filled eyes upward to the sky and started saying the Lord's prayer, that was all that would come to his mind. The sky had gotten dark and it started to rain but Ted really hadn't noticed. He saw the sergeant looking down at him, he knew what had taken place. In fact, the sergeant had arrived just as Ted thrust the dagger into the young German soldier.

"Ok, Corporal, let me help you out of there. You are one lucky guy, glad you came out of that skirmish alive."

Ted wiped his eyes, picked up his rifle and reached up for the sergeant to help him.

"Get a hold of yourself, soldier, we have to go on."

He climbed out of the hole and noticed the shelling was much less than it had been. The Germans were retreating and the firing had fallen off to just scattered shots ringing out here and there. The French and Americans troops had succeeded in pushing the Germans back out of no-man's land and into the woods. The Germans were rapidly abandoning the field, and the troops quickly followed them into the woods chasing them until all became quiet. The enemy retreated deeper into the forest. Major Drake ordered a halt to the gunfire and to hold the line; he ordered his men to dig in and wait for further orders.

Ted noticed a soldier with a bird cage strapped to his back. The major wrote a note and gave it to the bird handler who placed it in a capsule and clipped it onto the birds' leg. Then he raised his arm into the air and the bird took off flying toward the front lines.

The major motioned to Ted.

"I have lost my runner in the battle, Corporal, he got his legs shot out from under him. He is at the first aid station right now probably flirting with some pretty nurse. I need a new runner, and you're it."

"Yes, sir," Ted responded.

Shots rang out again directed at the pigeon in flight. Apparently, a German sniper was trying to shoot it out of the air to interrupt the message delivery.

"I want you to take this message to Marine Captain Mills, the commander of the machine gun battalion on the right flank. Tell him we are sending a message to the French commander that our battalion in the center is stopping for resupply of arms, water, and food. We can't go any farther so we're digging in right here until we are resupplied. You got all that?"

"Yes, sir, I got it," Ted said as he took off running and sloshing into the muddy woods, hoping he wouldn't be seen.

He knew there would be snipers in the woods, and as he ran he spotted a German machine gun bunker and stopped in his tracks knowing he couldn't safely go any farther, but he knew he had to deliver the message. His only alternative was to take out the machine gun nest, so he unclipped a grenade and crawled closer to the bunker until he was close enough to toss it. The rain was coming down heavy enough that he had trouble seeing, and as he threw the grenade, he missed the target and it landed in a mud puddle in front of the bunker splattering mud all over the area as it exploded.

The German machine guns rattled away, firing across the woods and field that Ted needed to get across, so he unclipped his last grenade and threw it, but this time it was a direct hit into the bunker and the machine gun nest was silenced. He got up and ran, zigzagging across the open field until he came upon the right flank of the American line. He crawled up to the entrenched line as close as he could and called out.

"I am an American soldier and I have a message for your commander from the American 307 battalion commander."

He was told to stand up, raise his arms into the air and walk forward, which he was glad to do. As he approached the line he was surrounded by several US marines with rifles pointed directly at him.

"Corporal Walters here, sir, with a message for Marine Captain Mills." Ted walked into the trench area with his marine escorts and a soldier who was hunkered down in his foxhole yelled out.

"Hey, soldier, how's the war going?"

"I haven't heard lately, but I sure hope the Germans have surrendered," and he heard several soldiers laugh.

"I have a message for your captain," Ted said.

"He's up ahead, I'll take you to him." They proceeded to the captain's quarters. Ted saluted and the captain returned the salute and accepted the message, opened it, and quickly read it.

Ted watched as Captain Mills wrote a note back to Captain Drake, and as he wrote, he read it aloud, "I have less than half my men left, started out with three-hundred and now down to half our strength that are still able to fight. They have been doing a great job, but we also need help. We will resupply your unit as soon as we can."

He handed the note to Ted and said, "Corporal, you look familiar, don't I know you?"

"I don't think so, sir."

"Where are you from, Corporal, it seems to me that I know you from somewhere."

Ted replied, "I'm from Deer Creek, Oklahoma. My name is Ted Walters, sir."

"Well, Ted, it's good to see you again. You're talking to one of your neighbors who grew up on the farm next to your folks. I'm Billie Mills."

"I would have never recognized you in a million years. I heard you were in the army," Ted replied as he reached out to shake hands.

"I was when I first enlisted, but then I joined up with the Marines and was lucky enough to get into the officers' school. I was in the same grade with your older sister, Edith, and I had a few dates with her. I do hope she is well. That's my story, what's yours?"

"My family is doing well back on the farm. Edith was four years older than me, and I didn't know you dated her. She was married, but her husband died after four years of marriage. He died of pneumonia, leaving her with a son and a daughter. So she moved back home to Deer Creek and is working as the town's post-mistress.

"I was stupid enough to get myself drafted, so that's why I'm here. I had recently gotten married and was expecting a baby and thought I could avoid going into the army, but it didn't work and so here I am," Ted told him.

"It's really good to see you again, Ted. Imagine us meeting here in France under these circumstances, crazy, isn't it!"

"Where's your brother John?" Ted asked.

"He got himself killed three years ago in Kansas City in an accident, of all things."

"I'm really sorry to hear that," Ted said.

"I wish we could spend more time together, but the war must go on. We'll have to get together later so we can rekindle our friendship, but now, as you know we have a job to do. I need you to take this message back to your commander, Ted, and tell him we will try to supply him with all he needs at the front as soon as we can."

Ted took the message and prepared to leave.

"Good to see you, Captain Mills," he said as they saluted.

"Tell your folks hello for me in your next letter. I sure loved them and I hope to get back to Deer Creek some day to see everyone. Good luck, Ted, and have a safe trip back to your battalion."

Ted took off running and when he arrived back with his battalion they were all hunkered down. He handed the message to the major.

"We're here for the night, Corporal, so relax and get something to eat. We're glad you're back safe and sound, good job."

He went to a foxhole and settled in with a fellow soldier and was glad to be safely back with his battalion. The young soldier was eating his canned rations, "You don't happen to have any candy do you? I sure would love to have a big bite of chocolate, wouldn't you?" Ted asked him.

"Candy!" the soldier laughed. "You've got to be kidding, where would I get any candy?"

"I don't know why I said that, for some dumb reason that just popped out of my mouth. Guess it's on my mind, my sweet tooth wants to be fed." Ted laughed.

"Well, please just shut up about candy. If I had some I'd eat it myself, just drop the subject, would you!"

"Sure, I'm sorry, I'm not thinking straight, I guess. I'm Ted Walters, what's your name?"

"Ray Hastings, I'm from Oklahoma."

They shook hands.

"Really, I'm from Deer Creek, Oklahoma, myself."

Ray handed him a can of rations.

"This isn't candy, but it's food and all I have, and here's the latest copy of the Stars and Stripes newspaper if you don't have one." They both had a good laugh and Ted thanked him.

Ted wolfed down his rations as he read an article about a carrier pigeon named Cher Ani that was given credit for saving 198 soldiers trapped behind enemy lines. The trapped soldiers had sent a number of pigeons with messages telling headquarters of their location, but all the birds were shot down except one, and that was Cher Ani. Although the pigeon had been hit by a small piece of shrapnel, it persevered and flew high enough to avoid any more bullets and delivered the message safely. As a result, the trapped soldiers were rescued. The pigeon had become an immediate hero. Ted thought the story was great; strange how things work out sometimes, and it stayed on his mind until he drifted off to sleep.

Ted heard a voice saying, "Wake up, wake up," so he aroused himself and asked, "What's happening?"

"I think I saw movement down in that gulley below us." Ted stared at the gulley, and pretty quickly, he saw what looked like movement: somebody was crawling up the canyon very slowly. They both watched the movement of the potential danger as it slowly crawled up the gulley and shortly the subject was close to their foxhole, but they could only see something from time to time, the subject stayed low as he proceeded. They both prepared to fire, Ted set off a flare when he got close, and Ray spotted him, and shot him in the chest. The soldier stood up and proceeded to step towards them. Ray fired a second shot and the soldier fell backwards, his helmet fell off and revealed a young handsome golden blond angel-looking young man, with the most surprised expression on his face. He looked like he was no more than eighteen years old.

Ray said to Ted, "I wondered what he thought he was doing. He had to know he was being watched, but maybe not."

"Well whatever his mission was, it's over now," Ted said. "I don't know if I will ever forget that look on his face, it may haunt me for a long time."

Ray said, "Yes I feel the same way. It's a shame he was a nice-looking young man. The perfect image I've seen on one German Army-recruiting poster one time—blond, blue eyed, Nordic looking."

Ted said, "I suppose so, we'll, I'm going to try and get some sleep, if I can."

As Ted tried to close his eyes and get some rest, he was soon interrupted by a summon from the major; he had another mission for Ted to deliver a message requesting badly needed supplies. He wasn't sure he liked this runner's job, but he got up and made the trek for the good of the troops, remembering the importance of the messages and how they could save lives.

On his return the troops had been put on alert by orders of the general to prepare for a counter attack. While he was gone they were under direct fire and his foxhole had been blown up, but he was glad to hear Hastings had survived. He was on guard duty as luck would have it. Ted tried to settle in and get some sleep, but his mind wouldn't settle down; he kept thinking about his fellow soldiers in the battalion that didn't make it, and when he did drift off to sleep he dreamed that he was surrounded by Germans and tossed and turned all night.

The Major received a message from the general at headquarters that the French troops who were on their left flank had to retreat; they were stopped cold by the German forces. Of course, this brought about the need to send another message, so he summoned Ted once again to deliver the message to the French commander concerning their location and that they were on hold waiting for supplies and reinforcements to arrive. When Ted arrived at the designated location, the French troops were nowhere to be found. So he returned to the Major with that information only to find out that while he was gone another message had arrived telling them the French had been forced to retreat even farther.

The Major knew this was a vital time in the war. The Germans were advancing and the French and American forces were at a crossroads, the enemy had gotten behind the French and cut them off. But the American generals at headquarters were aware of the situation and were taking action to turn it around.

Headquarters ordered the American troops to hold their position in the center flank and sent in the marines of the 23rd Battalion for reinforcements to conduct a forced march over a ten-mile area to plug the gap and to support the French troops. However, they were met with heavy resistance from the Germans, but were still able to slowly advance and move forward. This left the American troops in the center flank, more exposed and in a weaker position, and the Germans began to increase their counter fire on them with their howitzers. The only thing the Americans could do was to hunker down and eat dirt as the shells exploded over their heads, hitting the ground in front of them.

Ted's foxhole was located next to the machine gun post, and the noise made his teeth chatter, along with the coldness of the air. The shelling increased and the sky filled with flares. The ground shook from the explosions and it seemed to last for the longest time. Ted thought it would never end. They lost about ten of their fellow soldiers and many others were wounded, but soon darkness fell upon the battlefield and nightfall was welcome; it brought the battle to a halt for the night.

In the Bella Woods' section of the Argonne forest, the fog moved in along with the morning hours and it was difficult to see through the mist. The troops knew the Germans were very close by; in fact, they were like ghosts in the fog, they could hear them talking, but couldn't see them. The Major was aware of the Germans' tactics and was able to determine their position and what would be coming. They would no doubt use flame throwers to advance toward the Americans.

"Fix bayonets and prepare to advance," the Major told the troops. When the bombardment began, the shells whistled over and above their heads, and they stumbled over the barbed wire on the battlefield as they advanced forward. They could smell the heavy stench of war as they ran through the maze and fog, but the fog lifted and the American troops were able to clearly see the Germans position. They were coming at them with their flame throwers ablaze, but the American sharp shooters were ready and took aim at the canisters, causing them to explode on the backs of the German soldiers. They stumbled and fell hitting their fellow soldiers causing them to fall in the blaze of flames and the entire battlefield was ablaze. It was the most awful and terrible thing Ted had ever seen. He winced at the sight of it and wanted to throw up; it was horribly shocking to watch, but the Germans had to be stopped.

The Americans had stymied the German soldiers and many of them were killed by their own flame throwers, and they were driven back deeper into the forest.

The American generals sent in fresh troops along with ammunition and supplies just in time to maintain their momentum and hold their position, and fortunately they were met by much lighter and scattered gunfire. The Germans had retreated and only left a rear guard to protect their retreat.

About an hour later, several hundred uniformed people arrived at the battle front, waving white flags and causing a great deal of confusion. They were unarmed and were arriving in droves, forced by the Germans into the American lines. It was confusing to the Americans, but what happened was that the Germans had emptied their prison camps and released all the prisoners, herding them onto the battlefield to hamper and confuse the advancing Americans. The Americans stopped their artillery so they could deal with the prisoners as they came onto their front lines, but through the confusion of it all it actually became an exciting time as the troops welcomed the prisoners back. Even the Germans seized their fire and bombardments during the entire event, but it gave them time to retreat and that's what they wanted to accomplish.

After the bulk of the prisoners made it safely through the American lines and moved off the battlefield, the Americans slowly continued their advancement and their momentum against the Germans. They came upon an area that resembled an immense grape-arbor and down the dirt road they could see a large warehouse building. The Sergeant ordered them to take cover when they began taking fire from the building, but after returning fire for a few rounds, they could see a white flag waving back and forth from one of the windows. The Major ordered ceasefire and sent in Sergeant Tom Hardin carrying a white flag in his hand, and who happened to speak the German language. Within a few minutes he returned with a German officer who wanted to surrender his troops to the Americans.

The Major was very pleased with the results of their battles and sent a message back to headquarters. In a short while, the general and his entourage arrived bringing several hundred fresh troops for relief. He thanked the troops for breaking the backs of the Germans and dismissed the entire battalion to return to Division headquarters for relief and rest, and encouraged them with the news that the war would soon be over. That was good news for them to hear. Ted couldn't wait to hunker down in front of a nice warm fire and rest.

A light snow began to fall and Ted felt unusually cold and tired, but he kept marching with the troops until they arrived safely back to the relief area. He began to feel sick and immediately went to his assigned bunk and hit the sack; he was so cold he had three blankets and his heavy overcoat over him and he was still shivering and coughing. He tossed and turned the entire night, only sleeping on and off.

In the morning, his clothing was completely wet from sweat and his skin color looked pale, and although he was shivering his whole body felt hot. He was sure he was going to die. He missed roll call, he couldn't get out of bed—he was just too weak. The Sergeant woke him up out of a delirious nightmare and instructed him to get up out of the sack and report to sick bay immediately, but then he realized Ted was too sick to obey his order.

"No, no, on second thought, we'll have you taken to sick bay, you're burning up, soldier." They placed him in an ambulance to be taken to the military hospital in Paris.

Several days later he woke up in a large hospital room with rows after rows of beds, his head was much clearer and he felt like he just might live.

"Glad to see you open your eyes, soldier, you were very sick. You're in the flu ward in Paris and have been here for several days. You're one of the lucky ones, many didn't make it through," the nurse told him.

"Here, eat some of this hot soup and try to keep it down, you haven't eaten for days," she continued.

"We need to get you strong again. Oh, by the way, the General came through yesterday and gave you a medal. It's lying on the stand by your bed. Some Major in your battalion recommended you for it. Congratulations, soldier. I think you'll be going home soon."

He picked up the medal beside him and asked.

"What's this for?" he read the commendation, "Medal of Bravery." Tears came to his eyes, he didn't feel brave at all. The ones who lost their lives in the battlefield were the brave men—they gave everything, even their lives. He felt very humbled.

"Come on now, eat your soup, you will need to recuperate for a long time, you are still very weak. This flu epidemic is very severe and we are losing many of our soldiers and civilians here and at home, it seems to be worldwide. Like I said, you are one of the lucky ones to be sure. Now, eat your soup, you need it to get stronger."

Ted watched the nurse walk down the aisle between the beds. She paused for a moment at one and pulled the sheet up over a soldier's head. He turned away; he didn't want to watch them take the soldier away. Tears welled up in his eyes every time they took another flu victim to the morgue. He felt so fortunate and kept thinking to himself why had the Lord spared him and not them. He knew he would be going home in a few days, and he felt very confused, but grateful. He had a lot to live for, but the burden of those who wouldn't be going home to their families and would miss such a reunion, lay heavy on his heart. He vowed at that moment to live a good life in honor of them, and he would represent them the best he could throughout his life. Every night, while he was at the hospital he wept until he finally fell asleep.

Chapter 82

GOING HOME

The final offensive of the war stretched across the entire western front, and the battles in the Argonne forest was the major area of the fighting. Ted had fought many long and hard battles side by side with his fellow Americans, along with the French, British, and some Belgian troops. When fresh troops arrived from America, their hopes were renewed that the war would soon be over. There was news that the German arms and supplies were becoming depleted, and their men were growing demoralized by the increasing setbacks in the battles. There were also rumors that the German soldiers were deserting, and the civilians were forcing strikes that drastically reduced their needed war supplies and equipment. All this news brought renewed hope that the war would soon be over.

Ted lay in his hospital bed, his mind constantly on his fellow soldiers who were still on the front lines. But when he heard the good news from the front, it gave him hope and spiritual strength; however, his body was still very weak, and he could hardly walk, but he was determined to get strong.

"Good news, Corporal, you're going home," General John J. Pershing said to Ted on a surprise visit to the hospital. Ted managed to lift his arm and salute the general, he knew he couldn't stand at attention.

"You're a good soldier, and you did a great service for our country. Get strong and enjoy your life, young man," the general said as he left his bedside.

Ted was so surprised he couldn't speak. He had looked forward to this day for months and now he heard the words, "You're going home," and he heard them from General Pershing himself. He was very torn; however, he kept having the crazy thought that he needed to be out there helping in the war effort, yet he knew Viola needed him at home to be with her and the baby. He worried about his fellow soldiers who were still on the front lines and thought if he were with them, he could help them end the war sooner. But the overpowering joy of going home took over his thoughts and it gave him the will to get well.

A few days later he sat on the deck of the troop ship, his army coat pulled tightly around him and his legs covered with a blanket, but he was still very weak. He was surrounded by other soldiers, many were wounded, going home without a leg or an arm, and he suddenly felt truly blessed. He wasn't wounded as many of them were, and he closed his eyes and gave thanks to the Lord and he also asked to "Keep my brothers on the battlefield safe."

As he was enjoying the sound of the ocean water splashing its waves on the side of the ship, a shipmate brought his mail to him. Headquarters had sent the mail to the ship for all the men who were going home. He was overjoyed, he had letters from home, both from Viola and from his mom and dad, and did it ever make him feel good.

The first letter he opened was from Viola, and her first words were, "Congratulations, you're a father, now!" His heart skipped a beat as he read further. "It's a girl. She weighs seven pounds, has beautiful dark hair, and is twenty inches long. Her name is Maxine, the name we talked about, and your Mother and Dad like it very much too. Remember, she helped pick it out.'

The letter continued, "I haven't heard from you lately, and I can't help but worry, but we are praying day after day for you. We have a terrible flu epidemic striking the country and many people are dying, but so far we are all right. We hear it's really bad over where you are too, so please come home safe to us. I need you, our baby needs you, and so do your folks. Love you with all my heart, Viola."

Ted's eyes filled with tears, tears of gratitude that his family was safe, and tears of happiness over his baby girl. Oh, how he wished he were home right now to hold them. He couldn't believe he was a father, it really hadn't soaked in yet, but he knew it was real—he was a father. As he mulled over in his mind the last few weeks he had experienced, he was glad he didn't tell them he had the flu. It would have only worried them even more. He felt so fortunate because at times he presumed he would be killed or wounded, or even die from the flu, but now he was on his way home. Again, he wondered why the Lord spared him but was very grateful that He did.

He sat next to a young soldier wrapped in a blanket and he looked pale and white as a sheet.

"Are you all right?" Ted asked him.

"I've been seasick from day one on this ship," he whispered.

"I almost wish I was back in the trenches. I think I would rather die there than here on my way home."

"Hope you feel better soon. Just think, you're on your way home and that will make you feel better. That's all I can think about. I don't ever want to see a trench again."

The New York harbor never looked so good. The soldiers cheered and shouted through their tears and couldn't wait to step back on American soil. Ted and all the other soldiers were placed on stretchers, and their shipmates carried them down the gangway to the awaiting military ambulances. The crowds had gathered at the harbor to greet their heroes. The heroes they had read about in the newspapers. They read about the Argonne battles which started in September and lasted into November until the Armistice was signed on November 11, 1918. The war was officially over, but with heavy loss. About 1.2 million soldiers were involved in the battles with 95,000 wounded and over 26,000 killed. The final battle in the Argonne ended the war while they were on the ship going home. He was truly overjoyed with the news, and he couldn't believe it was really over. They carried Ted and the rest of the war heroes through the cheering crowd, and he felt grateful to be alive, but he didn't necessarily feel like a hero. In his mind, it was the wounded men who were the real heroes.

They shipped the men by train to different military hospitals in the country, with Ted going to Fort Riley, Kansas. He felt lucky to be alive. The doctors at Fort Riley told him that most people didn't survive the Spanish flu, that's what the epidemic was called. A few weeks later Ted, sat on the sun-porch of the hospital when a nurse came with the good news: he was being discharged to go home. The doctors had declared him no longer contagious and well enough to go. He was so excited he could hardly contain his emotions. He was finally going home to see his family; it had been such a long time.

Chapter 83

HOME

*T*his is unreal. I'm alive and on my way home. I'm going to have a life with my family after all; the bloody war is over. This is the day I've been waiting for. That thought kept running through Ted's mind as the train made its way to Wichita. He leaned back and tapped his finger with the rhythmic timing of the clickity-clack of the wheels on the rails, and listened to the whistle blowing at the crossings, announcing the good news that the war was over. At least that's what it meant to him.

The sounds of the train brought back so many memories of the times he rode the rails in his earlier days. It made him feel completely at home, so relaxed and at peace. Perhaps this was the first time he felt so completely at peace; he had no fear of a sniper bullet or a surprise grenade coming at him, and he realized the depth of what real peace was really like. Home was where he wanted to be, the true place to find peace.

The train began to slow down, and from the window he could see he was almost home; he would see the Wichita Depot sign very soon. When the train came to a full stop, he saw them standing at the station—Viola holding the baby in a pink blanket with his parents standing next to her. They were so excited, almost to the point of jumping up and down for joy. He was surprised to see his mom and dad there too. They had obviously made the trip from Deer Creek for the grand homecoming, and they wouldn't miss it for the world as his mother would say.

The tears flowed freely from all of them as he stepped off the train. They all ran to him and words could hardly come through the tears, but the hugs and kisses were almost endless.

"Here, do you want to hold her?" Viola said as she handed him the pink bundle. He almost held back; she seemed so small and delicate, but he desperately wanted to touch her and hold her close. He reached out and

479

took her, and held on to Viola's hand also, not wanting to let them go ever again.

Ted couldn't believe how tiny she was, so soft and so beautiful. He wondered for a moment if it was real or just the dream that had run through his mind over and over again while he was on the battlefield. She was like a little doll, and he couldn't take his eyes from his little girl, his daughter, and it was hard for him to believe.

They spent the next few weeks of his homecoming in Deer Creek, getting re-acquainted with family. They talked incessantly, catching up on all the family news. Edith's kids were almost grown, both in high school, and Everett was still living in California. They heard all the war stories Ted had to tell and were even more grateful he was home and the war was over after they heard all about it. They really hadn't realized the danger he was in. Viola listened intently as the tears flowed down her cheeks. Ted really didn't want to talk about it, he was anxious to get back to family life and work and leave the war behind.

He contacted the Missouri-Pacific Railroad Division Supervisor and was told they were in need of an operator in Benton, Kansas, just a few miles out of Wichita. He readily accepted it; it sounded perfect for them. He was ready to get back to work and his life again, but it meant they would leave Deer Creek. Mom fixed the last home-cooked meal for them, Teds' favorite of fried chicken, mashed potatoes, and gravy, and he helped his Dad do the chores one last time, including milking old Bessie the cow.

The next morning, Dad took them into town to catch the train for Benton and to look for a place to live. Viola was excited thinking about having their own place and to use all their wedding gifts they had received from their friends when they got married. She was going to be a real housewife and mother, and settle down into a place of their own to raise their little girl. When they got into town, she insisted they go to the bank; she had a surprise to tell Ted about. She had saved most of the money he had sent home to her from his work and from the army, and to add to the surprise, his mom and dad had done the same. They had used what they needed during hard times and saved the rest for him when he came home.

He truly was surprised. He couldn't believe they had accumulated such a nice savings, enough to buy a house with some left over. They met with the only real estate agent for miles around to look at a three-bedroom cottage that was available for sale. It had a nice front porch, perfect for sitting out front in the evenings to watch little Maxine play in the nice yard, and it had a separate garage and a stone fireplace with a place to stack the wood. They fell in love with it; it was so beautiful and it would be their very first real home.

Now that they had their home, Ted came up with his own surprise for Viola, and that surprise just happened to be a brand new Model-T Ford, black in color, and he paid cash for it, all three hundred dollars. When he drove it up into the yard he was proud as a peacock, and she couldn't contain herself. He took her for a ride, and any of the neighbors who wanted to go. They were having the time of their lives as they drove around the town square, and they sparked the interest of everyone in town, especially the women as they watched Viola proudly riding beside Ted in her new wide-brimmed hat. She brought a new style into town that gave them something to talk about.

Viola busied herself making curtains for the windows, but in the meantime sheets would do. They bought a nice living room suite at the only furniture store in town and a baby bed for Maxine; they were ready to move in.

Ted reported to work at the depot Monday morning. He was relieving Mr. Bob Beck, an operator who had been retired, but was called back during the war to help out because of the shortage of operators in the country. Mr. Beck gladly showed Ted around the station, making him aware of all the procedures and responsibilities so he could get back to his retirement life. Ted was anxious to re-acquaint his ear to the telegraph key, and it all came back to him quickly, receiving and sending coded messages, handling the ticket sales, posting shipping rates, and routing passengers to anywhere and everywhere in the country.

He studied hard in the evenings, catching up on all the changes since he had last worked as a railroad telegraph operator agent. Viola kept busy making the house cozy and comfortable, making curtains and crocheting lacy doilies for the shelves to display her pretty vases and knick-knacks. They quickly developed new friends, one included a car mechanic who couldn't wait to get his hands on Ted's new car, to see all the parts and how it worked. They played cards in the evening and went to worship every Sunday morning.

Viola quickly got acquainted with the women in town, joining the right clubs, the sewing circle and cooking club, and they continually tried out new recipes to prepare for those special get-togethers. She quickly got the reputation as being one of the finest cooks in town, and of course, she gained the praise of her sewing circle friends as she sewed little dresses for Maxine so she could dress her as cute as could be.

Life was good, although times were difficult for many people in the country. The economy was not as good as people had hoped for after the war years, but Ted and Viola were one of the few families that maintained a steady income from the railroad. Most of their neighbors were merchants and farmers, wholly dependent on the weather, the rainfall, and the economy. Ted loved the farm, having grown up in that environment, so when he could he helped the neighboring farmers out during harvest with thrashing, stacking, and shocking wheat. He also remembered the plight of the farmers and wanted to help them whenever he could. There were some days the heat from the sun sent them to look for a shade tree or climb underneath a wagon for relief.

Ted spent most of his adult life as a telegraph operator, and for a while invested in a barber shop, but railroading was his life. As the years went by, Ted and Viola had three more children, their son Jack was born ten years after Maxine, and later another sister, Elsclidean, and a brother, Richard, came along making their family complete. He taught telegraphy to his son Jack during his teenage years, and his family and his job became his entire life.

Over the next twenty years, Ted worked as a telegraph operator in eastern Kansas, working his last years at the Durand railroad station which was located five miles east of Yates Center. He bought a little twenty-acre farm just outside of Yates Center, had a milk cow named Bessie, and other livestock such as pigs and chickens, and grew a garden to supply the needed food for the family. The world he built around him was a model of his childhood, just like home.

Ted believed in hard work and always carried out his responsibility to his family. He loved to read the Bible and his favorite passage in the New Testament was Ephesians, chapter 4, verse 28.

"Let him that stole steal no more, but rather let him labor, working with his hands the thing which is good, that he may have to give to him that needeth."

He took that verse to heart, not that he stole from others, but he was capable of working hard and provided for his family, and teaching his children the responsibilities of life, not leaving that responsibility for someone else to do.

The depression years came along, which affected many people, and since their little farm was located on the main highway leading out of town, Ted and Viola watched many people pass by, seemingly going nowhere. They were desperate families looking for jobs and hope, but where could they go? They were the result of our country's Great Depression. The people were walking or driving old cars and trucks which were loaded down with their worldly belongings, and many ran out of gasoline without any money to buy more. Ted would give them enough money to get them down the road.

To add to the dilemma, across the highway about a quarter of a mile, ran the railroad tracks leading East and West, and many of the freight trains that came through town were loaded with people, mostly traveling west to find a new life. Men, women, and children rode on top of the freight cars while others filled the empty boxcars, all seeking hope for a new life, and all looking very desperate.

Many of the people would stop at the Walters farm house asking for help, and Viola and Ted never refused anyone. It broke their hearts to see such desperation. In fact, they invited many of them in to eat at their table, and the stories of the peoples' ruined lives never seemed to end, but they did what they could for them and sent them on their way; at least their stomachs were full and they had clothes on their backs.

This was Ted's life—he regarded it as a good life. He was a hard worker, never a slough, and was always known for his good deeds. He worked the midnight shift the last years of his life at Durand, Kansas, and as his children always remembered, he ate oatmeal every morning for breakfast except on Sunday, that was family day. He made pancakes for them every Sunday morning, that was always their special day.

His family regarded him a good soldier just as General Mosby had written on his discharge document from the Rebel Army of the Baja, but more importantly to him, he was a good soldier as General Pershing told him on that very special visit at the military hospital in Paris, that was what he wanted to be in life, just a good soldier to his country and to his family, and they indeed thought of him that way.

ACKNOWLEDGMENTS

Theodore Edmund Walters was born March 5, 1890, and lived a somewhat exciting life that seemed to come his way, but very often he reached out and sought the excitement.

He worked as a telegraph operator, mostly on the night shift. He worked through World War II, the telegraph system had not yet been modernized, and he was looking forward to retirement at the age of sixty-two.

Viola worked at Beech Aircraft in Wichita, Kansas, during World War II while Ted stayed back home on the farm, working for the Missouri-Pacific R.R. doing his very important part for the war effort.

After the war was over, they settled back on their little farm and had many blessed times with family and friends, but on July 17, 1950, Ted suffered a massive heart attack and passed away at the age of sixty, but he left the legacy he desired. He was a good man and a good soldier to all his family and friends.

ALL ABOUT HOBOS

The history of the American hobo has always been fascinating to me since my father, Theodore E. Walters, took up that lifestyle at one time in his life. The hobo may be a thing of the past as history recorded it for us, but at one time a group of traveling strangers hopped the rails and criss-crossed the country with just the clothes on their backs.

They were different from the thrill-seeking vagabonds of today who may try their hand at becoming modern day hobos with cell phones in hand to communicate with their friends, and go from place to place depending on community services for their existence.

History is not clear when the hobo first appeared on the American scene but it was probably after the Civil War in the 1860's when many veterans returned home and hopped on freight trains to look for work on the American frontier, travelling west hoping for new opportunities.

The hobo was defined as a migratory or itinerant worker who was homeless and penniless and they saw themselves quite differently from those who were considered tramps or bums. Tramps avoided work, traveled and begged for their food while 'bums' didn't work or travel at all, unless the police directed them to move on.

The number of hobos greatly increased during the great depression era of the 1920s and 1930's. With no money or prospect of work at home many decided to travel by freight train to try their luck elsewhere, but the hobo life could be very dangerous. In addition to their existing problems of being itinerant and poor, they faced the hostility of railroad life and uncertainness of the world around them. The railroad security forces were sometimes brutal in their treatment, and some hobos told of incidents they faced jumping aboard a moving train, some would fall under the wheels causing them to be killed or lose a foot or leg. It was also common for the hobo to become trapped between cars, seriously injuring them or freeze to death in the very cold weather.

Statistics show more than twenty thousand people were living a hobo life in the 1930's, but many believe the number was much higher. According to history, notables who were once hobos before they became famous are as follows:

Louis L'amour, western novelist; Jack London, writer, author, and newspaper reporter; Robert Mitchum, famous movie actor; Carl Sandburg, world famous poet; George Orwell, author and writer; Woody Guthrie, songwriter, singer, and poet; and Jack Dempsey, famous world champion boxer. As most societies do, they develop a code to live by, even the unorganized society of hobos. They developed ways to communicate and help each other out, and they developed their own language using symbols. Listed are a few of their symbols which they posted on railroad water towers, on signs, mail boxes, and walls in many towns.

1. Circle with arrow combinations. This symbol contains information about which direction a hobo should go from the rails. If the arrow and circle are side by side, it means "go the direction of the arrow." If the arrow goes through the circle, it tells the hobo to avoid the area; the people were not friendly.
2. Triangle or a series of triangle in descending order indicate a woman with children who lives there who will gladly help them if they have a good story to tell.
3. Crucifix shape symbol usually means that if they speak about religion they are treated in a positive way.
4. U-shape usually means it is safe to camp in the area.
5. Animal image symbol was used to describe the people in the area, such as a cat meant a kind woman and a duck meant free telephone usage.
6. Two connected circles meant police don't like hobos and would probably chase you out of town.

Many poems and writings by hobos and about hobos have been published. These romanticize the image of the hobo in some cases. Some that I found interesting are written below. Enjoy them as I did.

Hobo Poem

All around the water tank
Waitin' for a train
I'm a thousand miles away from home
Just a'standin in the rain.

—Author unknown

Hobo

There's a race of men that don't fit in
They roam the fields and roam the sea
There's a race of men that can't stay still
And they climb the mountain crest
So they break the heart of kith and kin
For theirs is the curse of the gypsy blood
And roam the world at will
And they don't know to rest

—Robert Service, Poet

The Hobo

I will long remember when the hoboes came around
They walked along the railroad tracks and slept upon the ground
They'd stop at certain houses 'tis said they marked the gate,
to beg a bite. If you were lucky, they would work for what they ate.
If Dad was home, they'd sit awhile. Now many tales I've heard
about the many journeys, believing every word
'Twas usually a tale of woe; no family to care
if they wore ragged clothing and never cut their hair.

—Lillian Arnold Lopez "Pineylore"

Untitled

I'm sittin'
Drinkin'
Waitin'
Thinkin'
Hopin' for a train
—This is a poem **written by unknown traveler, it was
left written on the water tank at the Black Butte siding**

Hobo Lullaby

Go to sleep you weary Hobo
Let the towns drift slowly by
Can't you hear the steel rails hummin'
That's the hobo's lullaby
I know your clothes are torn and ragged
And your hair is turning grey
Lift your head and smile at trouble
You'll find peace and rest someday . . .

Copyright ? Sanga Music, Inc,

Nothing To Do But Go

I'm wandering son with the nervous feet,
That never were meant for a steady beat.
I've had many a job for a little while,
I've been on the bum and I've lived it in style,
And there was the road stretchin mile after mile,
And nothing to do but go.

—Author unknown

The End

Edwards Brothers Malloy
Oxnard, CA USA
December 31, 2015